Jacqueli

The Love Machine
Once is Not Enough

Also by Jacqueline Susann

VALLEY OF THE DOLLS
EVERY NIGHT, JOSEPHINE!
DOLORES
YARGO

Jacqueline Susann Omnibus

The Love Machine
Once is Not Enough

JACQUELINE SUSANN

A *Time Warner* Paperback

This omnibus edition first published in Great Britain by Time Warner Paperbacks in 2004

Previously published separately:
The Love Machine first published by Simon and Schuster in 1969
Published in the United States of America by Grove Press in 1997.
A Grove/Atlantic Book.
Published by Warner Books in 1998

Once is Not Enough first published in the United States of America in 1973
Republished in the United States of America by Grove Press.
A Grove/Atlantic Book.
Published in Great Britain by Warner Books in 1998

Permission to quote from the following songs is gratefully acknowledged;
'A Wonderful Guy' from *South Pacific*. Words by Oscar Hammerstein 2nd. Music by Richard Rodgers. Copyright © 1949 by Richard Rodgers and Oscar Hammerstein 2nd, Williamson Music Inc., New York, NY.
'The Gentleman Is a Dope' from *Allegro*. Words by Oscar Hammerstein 2nd. Music by Richard Rodgers. Copyright © 1947 by Richard Rodgers and Oscar Hammerstein 2nd, Williamson Music Inc., New York, NY.

A CIP catalogue record for this book is available from the British Library

ISBN 0 7515 3653 9

Printed and bound in Great Britain by
Mackays of Chatham Ltd, Chatham

Time Warner Paperbacks
An imprint of
Time Warner Books UK
Brettenham House
Lancaster Place
London WC2E 7EN

www.TimeWarnerBooks.co.uk

The Love Machine

To Carol Bjorkman

PROLOGUE:

THE LOVE MACHINE

MAN CREATED THE MACHINE.

A Machine does not feel love, hate or fear; it does not suffer from ulcers, heart attacks or emotional disturbances.

Perhaps man's only chance of survival is to *become* a machine.

Some men have succeeded.

A machine who passes for a man often rules societies—a dictator is a power machine in his country. A dedicated artist can turn into a talent machine.

Sometimes this evolution occurs without the man realizing it.

Perhaps it happens the first time he says, "I am hurt," and his subconscious replies, "If I cut all feeling from my life—*I cannot be hurt!*"

Amanda would have laughed if you had told her this about Robin Stone—because Amanda was in love with him.

Robin Stone was a handsome man.

He could smile with his lips.

He could think without emotion.

He could make love to her with his body.

Robin Stone was The Love Machine.

I

AMANDA

ONE

Monday, March 1960

AT NINE IN THE MORNING, she was standing on the steps in front of the Plaza Hotel, shivering in a linen dress. One of the clothespins that held the back of the dress together clattered to the ground. A dresser hurried to replace it, and the photographer used the time to reload his camera. The hairdresser quickly retouched a few stray hairs with a can of hair spray and the session resumed. The curious crowd that had gathered was delighted with this glimpse of one of the Beautiful People—a top fashion model, facing the blasting cold winds of March, in a lightweight summer dress. To add to the strangeness of the scene, there were cold-looking snowbanks on the hills of Central Park, reminders of a recent snowstorm. The crowd, comfortably bundled in winter coats, suddenly felt no envy for the shimmering creature they were watching who earned more money in a morning than they earned in a week.

Amanda was freezing, but she was impervious to the crowd. She was thinking of Robin Stone. Sometimes thinking of Robin Stone helped, especially when they had spent a wonderful night together.

This morning her thoughts were not comforting. She had not spent a wonderful night with Robin. She had not even heard from him. He had two lecture dates, one in Baltimore on Saturday, and one at some dinner in Philadelphia on Sunday. "I'll shoot my speech to them at seven and be back at New York by ten," he had promised. "Then we'll go to the Lancer Bar and grab a hamburger." She had sat around in full makeup until two in the morning. Not even a phone call.

The photographer finished. The fashion coordinator rushed to her with a coat and a container of coffee. She went into the hotel and sank into a massive armchair in the lobby and sipped the coffee. The icicles in her veins began to thaw. She would survive. Thank God the rest of the shots were indoors.

She finished the coffee and went up to the suite that had been engaged for the session. The clothes were hanging in a neat row. With the help of the dresser, she slipped out of the linen dress and changed into a pair of summer "at home" slacks. She adjusted the falsies in her bra, then checked her makeup. The electricity crackled as her comb went through the thickness of the soft honey-colored hair. She had washed it herself yesterday and set it the way Robin liked it, long and loose. This afternoon she had a three-hour session scheduled with Alwayso Cosmetics—they would probably reset it. Jerry Moss liked her in an upsweep; he claimed it gave the product more class.

At eleven o'clock she was closeted in the bathroom, changing into her own clothes. She opened her large bag and took out the container with toothbrush and tooth paste. She brushed her teeth in up and down strokes. She was doing the summer shades of lipstick for Alwayso today. Thank God for her teeth, thank God for her hair. And her face. Her legs were good, her hips were slim, she was tall. God had been very good; He had only been forgetful in one spot. She stared ruefully at the falsies in her bra. She thought of all the women who had watched her pose: working girls, housewives, heavy women, thick-ankled women—they all had bosoms. Bosoms which they took for granted. And she was flat as a boy.

Oddly enough this was an asset for the perfect model. But it certainly was no asset in one's personal life. She recalled the dismay she had felt when she was twelve and most of the girls at school began to sprout small "bumps" on top. She had run to Aunt Rose, Aunt Rose who had laughed: "They'll come, honey, only let's hope they don't get too big like your Aunt Rose's!"

But they *hadn't* come. When she was fourteen Aunt Rose had

said, "Now, honey, the good Lord gave you a beautiful face and a good mind. Besides, it's more important for a man to love you for yourself, not your face or your body."

This simple logic was all very fine when she sat in the kitchen listening to Aunt Rose, when neither of them thought she would ever go to New York and meet the kind of people she knew now.

Like the singer–she never thought of Billy in any other way. She had been eighteen, just starting to model, when they met. She had played his records in high school. When she was twelve, she had stood in line for two hours when he was making a personal appearance at a local movie house. Seeing him in person at a party was like a dream. And it was even more unbelievable when he singled her out. As Billy put it to some of the columnists, "It was instant romance!" From that night on, she was part of his entourage. She had never seen this way of life–the nightclub openings, the round-the-clock chauffeur, the large groups he took everywhere, songwriters, agents, song pluggers, press agents. And although they had never laid eyes on her before, they just accepted her as part of the family. She was amazed at the whirlwind courtship and all the attending newspaper publicity. He held her hand and kissed her cheek as the camera snapped, and on the fifth night they finally wound up alone–in his hotel suite.

She had never been in a suite at the Waldorf Towers–at the time she was still living at the Barbizon Hotel for Women. She stood in the center of the room staring at all the flowers and the bottles of liquor. He kissed her, loosened his tie and beckoned her toward the bedroom. She meekly followed him. He took off his shirt and casually unzipped his pants. "Okay, angel, unwrap," he said.

She had felt panic as she slowly undressed down to her pants and bra. He walked over and kissed her lips, her neck, her shoulders, while his fingers fumbled with the bra. It fell to the floor. He stood back, his disappointment evident.

"Jesus, baby, put the bra back." He looked down at himself and laughed. "Charlie here has already folded from shock."

She put the bra back on. She put on all her clothes and rushed out of the hotel. The following day he sent her flowers, besieged her with calls, pursued her. She relented and they had three wonderful weeks together. She went to bed with him, but she kept her bra on.

The singer returned to the Coast after three weeks. He never called her again. He salved his conscience by giving her a mink coat as a going-away present. She could still recall the amazement on his face when he found he had taken a virgin.

The newspaper publicity brought a call from the Nick Longworth agency. She signed with them and her career as a model was launched. He started her at twenty-five dollars an hour, and now, five years later, she was one of the top ten models in the country, booked solid at sixty dollars an hour. Nick Longworth made her study the fashion magazines, learn how to dress, practice her walk. She had moved from the Barbizon to a nice apartment on the East Side where she spent most of her evenings alone. She bought a television set and a Siamese cat. She concentrated on her work and studied the magazines. . . .

Robin Stone had exploded into her life at a charity ball. She had been chosen along with five other top models to appear in a fashion show for a charity ball at the Waldorf. Seats cost one hundred dollars. There was the usual dancing and entertainment in the Grand Ballroom; all the best people came. But there was one factor that set this ball apart from all the other similar glittering charity events: Mrs. Gregory Austin was head of the committee. Mrs. Gregory Austin's ball not only made all the newspapers, it also received television coverage on the local IBC station. And why not? Mr. Austin owned the IBC network.

The Grand Ballroom at the Waldorf was packed. Amanda and the other models were accorded the courtesy of "paying guests," since they were donating their time. Along with the five other girls, she sat at a table and nibbled at the dinner. IBC had placed six minor executives at the table as escorts for the girls. The men were attractive and bland. In the beginning, they made stabs at small talk, but gradually they fell into discussions of ratings and cancelations among themselves. Amanda barely listened. She covertly studied the table where Mrs. Gregory Austin sat with her friends. She recognized Judith Austin from her newspaper pictures and was secretly elated that Mrs. Austin's hair was tinted the exact color as her own. Amanda judged Judith Austin to be about forty, but she was very beautiful–small, elegant and perfectly understated. It was women like Mrs. Austin whom Amanda had tried to emulate in the early stages of learning how to dress–of course she still couldn't afford clothes like Mrs. Austin's, but she could get the copies.

After dinner she went to the dressing room to prepare for the fashion show. The IBC cameras were set up. The show would go on live for the local eleven o'clock news. She was sitting with the other models when there was a light knock on the door. Robin Stone came in.

The girls gave him their names. When she simply said, "Amanda," he wrote it down and waited. She smiled. "Just Amanda–that's all there is," she said. Their eyes met and he smiled. She stared at him as he went around the room, writing down the names of the other girls. He was very tall, and she liked the way he moved. She had caught him a few times on the local news before switching over to CBS and the late movie. Somewhere in the recesses of her mind she recalled he had once won a Pulitzer Prize as a newspaper reporter. Television certainly didn't do him justice. His hair was dark and thick, just beginning to tinge with gray. But it was his eyes. They suddenly caught her own, held them–almost as if he was appraising her. Then he flashed an easy grin and left the room.

She decided he was probably married to someone who looked like Mrs. Austin. By the time the show was over, Amanda had even pictured two small children who looked exactly like him.

She was completely dressed when he knocked on the door. "Hello, Miss One Name," he said with a grin. "Is there a Mr. One Name waiting for you at home or are you free to have a beer with me?"

She went to P.J.'s with Robin, toyed with a Coke and watched him in amazement as he drank five vodkas and remained absolutely sober. And she followed him back to his apartment without a spoken word or suggestion on his part. The pressure of his hand carried the message, as if it was mutually understood.

It was almost as if she had been under hypnosis. She entered his apartment without any sense of apprehension, stood before him and undressed without giving a thought to her bosom. And when she hesitated with her bra, he walked over and removed it himself.

"Are you disappointed?" she asked.

He tossed the padded bra across the room. "Only cows need boobs!" Then he took her in his arms and gently leaned down and kissed her breasts. He was the only man who had ever done this. She held his head and trembled. . . .

That first night he had taken her gently and wordlessly, then when both their bodies were moist with exhaustion, he had held her close. "Want to be my girl?" he asked. Her answer came in the darkness as she clung to him with more fervor. He broke the embrace, and those clear blue eyes searched her face. His lips smiled, but the eyes were serious. "No strings, no promises, no questions–on *both* sides. Okay?"

She nodded mutely. Then he reached out and made love to her again, with a peculiar combination of violence and tenderness. At last they lay back, exhausted and fulfilled. She caught a glance at the clock on his night table. Three o'clock! She slid out of bed. He reached out and grabbed her wrist. "Where are you going!"

"Home. . . ."

He twisted her wrist and she cried out in pain. He said, "When you sleep with me, you *stay!* You don't leave!"

"But I have to. I'm wearing an evening dress!"

Without a word, he released her and got up and began to dress. "Then I'll spend the night at your place."

She smiled. "Afraid to sleep alone?"

His eyes went dark. "Don't ever say that! I sleep alone. But when I go to bed with a girl, I *sleep* with her!"

They went to her apartment, and he made love to her again. And as she fell asleep in his arms she was filled with a happiness so acute that she felt sympathy for every woman in the world because they would never know Robin Stone.

Now, after three months, even her Siamese cat, Slugger, had accepted Robin and snuggled against his feet at night.

Robin didn't make very much money, and he was away many

weekends, doing lectures to augment his income. Amanda didn't mind not going to the Colony or "21." She liked P.J.'s, the Lancer Bar, the Piccolo Italia, Robin's hangouts. She loved double features, and she was trying desperately to learn the difference between a Democrat and a Republican. Sometimes she would sit in the Lancer Bar for hours, while Robin discussed politics with Jerry Moss. Jerry lived in Greenwich and his agency handled the Alwayso cosmetics account. It was Robin's friendship with Jerry that had landed her the color layouts for Alwayso.

She stood before the mirror in the bathroom of the Plaza, slipped into her woolen dress and walked into the living room of the suite.

The makeshift dining table had been removed. The photographer was packing his equipment. His name was Ivan Greenberg, and he was a good friend. She waved to him and the people repacking the dresses and left the suite, a golden image, her long hair flying, the singer's burnished mink rippling as she ran down the hall.

She went to the phone in the lobby and checked with her exchange. No word from Robin. She dialed his number–it rang tonelessly, the kind of a ring that tells you no one is home. She hung up.

It was almost noon. Where on earth was he?

TWO

HE WAS IN A SUITE at the Bellevue Stratford Hotel in Philadelphia.

He awoke slowly with the knowledge that the morning was all but gone. He heard pigeons murmuring on the ledge of the window. He opened his eyes and knew exactly where he was. Sometimes when he awoke in a motel he wasn't sure. Every motel room looked the same and he had to stop and recall the city, or even the name of the girl who slept beside him. But he was alone this morning, and this was not a motel. Good old Philadelphia and their Man of the Year dinner. They had sprung for a real suite.

He reached for his cigarettes on the night table. The pack was empty. There wasn't even a decent-sized butt in the ashtray. Then he saw the ashtray on the other side of the bed–long butts with orange lipstick on the tips.

He reached for the phone and ordered a double orange juice, coffee and two packs of cigarettes. He scrounged for the least damaged butt, scraped off the dead ash and lit it. There were longer butts in the other ashtray, with orange lipstick. He didn't take one. He got up and spilled the contents of that tray into the toilet. He watched them disappear, feeling he was also exorcising the girl. Damn it, he would have sworn she was single. He usually could spot them right away, the married women out for a secret thrill. This one had really fooled him, maybe because she was a cut above the average. Well, they were all one-night stands. Let their husbands worry. He grinned and looked at his watch–almost noon. He'd catch the two o'clock train back to New York.

Tonight he and Amanda would celebrate and drink a toast to Gregory Austin, the man who was taking him away from all this. It still seemed unreal, as hard to believe as the personal phone call from Austin himself at nine o'clock on Saturday morning. At first Robin had thought it was a gag–the chairman of the board of IBC calling a local newsman! Gregory laughed and told him to call him back on the IBC number to verify it. Robin did exactly that and Austin picked up the telephone on the first ring. Could Robin Stone come directly to his office? He was in Gregory Austin's office ten minutes later, his suitcase with him. He had to catch the noon train to Baltimore.

Austin was alone in his massive office. He came to the point immediately. How would Robin like to be the Head of Network News? He would also want Robin to bring in ideas for expanding the news department, and form his own team to cover the conventions in the summer. Robin liked the idea very much. But "Head of Network News"? The title was enigmatic. Morgan White was *President* of Network News. Randolph Lester was Vice-President. What, Robin asked, did "Head of Network News" *mean?* Well, it meant fifty thousand a year, more than double his present salary. And, as Austin put it, in answer to his question about the title, "Let's leave it this way for starters, shall we?"

It was one hell of a start. And when Austin learned Robin still had another year to go with his lecture contract, he simply made two phone calls, one to the lecture agency, the other to his lawyer, instructing him to buy out Robin's lecture contract. It had been as simple as that–simple and secretive. Robin was to stay away from IBC for a week. He was also to keep his mouth shut about the assignment. On the following Monday he was to come in and take over in the new job. Gregory Austin himself would handle the announcement his own way. . . .

He poured his coffee and lit a fresh cigarette. The weak wintry sun streamed through the hotel windows. A week from today he would be reporting at IBC for the new job. He took a long drag of his cigarette. Some of his good mood filtered away with the smoke. He ground out the cigarette. It conjured up the image of the girl with the orange lipstick. What was her name? Peggy? Betsy? Neither name hit a spark of recognition. But her name ended like that: Billie? Mollie? Lillie? The hell with it! It wasn't important. He sat back and pushed the coffee away. Once when he had come to New York for a weekend while he was still at Harvard, he had seen a show, *Lady in the Dark*. There was something about a girl hearing part of a tune–she could never get past the first few bars. The same thing occasionally happened to him. Only it wasn't a tune, it was a memory, a vision . . . He could never quite see it, but he sensed it. It was like being on the verge of an important recollection, and it left him with a sense of musky warmth, of happiness ending in panic. It didn't happen often, but it had happened last night, in one fast flash–no, *twice!* The first time had been when the girl had slipped into bed with him. The feel of her body, vibrant and soft–her breasts were magnificent. He didn't usually pay much attention to breasts–there was something childish to him about sucking a full breast. Why did men think of it as a sex act? It was a longing for Mama. There was something *weak* about a man who wanted to lay his head against a woman with big breasts. Robin dug blondes, clean and bright, slim and hard. There was a symmetry to their bodies that he found exciting.

But the girl last night had been a brunette, with beautiful full breasts. Oddly enough he had found himself excited. It was coming back to him now. He had shouted something when he hit the climax. But what was it? He never shouted ordinarily, not with Amanda, or any girl he stayed with. Yet he *knew* he had shouted something, just as he knew there had been other times when he had shouted and could not remember his words afterwards.

He lit a fresh cigarette and intentionally turned his thoughts to the new future that awaited him. This was a time for celebration. He had an entire week off.

He picked up the Philadelphia paper that had arrived with his breakfast. On page three he saw his picture with the man who had been honored, a balding corpulent judge. The caption read: ROBIN STONE, PULITZER PRIZE-WINNING NEWSMAN, TELEVISION

PERSONALITY AND LECTURER, CAME TO PHILADELPHIA TO SPEAK AND HONOR JUDGE GARRISON B. OAKES, 1960 MAN OF THE YEAR.

He poured himself some fresh coffee and grinned. Sure he had come to honor the judge, a man he had never heard of. He had come because they paid Universal Lecture Agency five hundred bucks.

He sipped his coffee, cheerful in the knowledge that he would never have to lecture again. It had sounded so easy in the beginning. He had been doing the local IBC news for about a year when Clyde Watson, head of the Universal Lecture Agency, sent for him. The agency occupied an entire floor in a new building on Lexington Avenue. And Clyde Watson, sitting behind the massive walnut desk, looked like a trusted stockbroker. Everything was designed to put the victim at ease, even the paternal smile. "Mr. Stone, why should a Pulitzer Prize-winning columnist wind up doing a local news show?"

"Because I quit the Northern Press Association."

"Why did you quit? Because you had no New York outlet?"

"No. Not being in a New York paper didn't bother me. That's just good for free tickets to theaters and free tabs at restaurants. That's not my scene. I'm a writer. At least I think I am. But NPA allowed every editor in every small town to hack my column to bits. Sometimes they only ran three lines. Three lines of a column that had taken me six hours to write. Writing doesn't come easy to me. I sweat over it. And for some guy to toss six hours of my life into a wastebasket–" Robin shook his head as if he felt actual pain. "At least at IBC I'm able to be a news analyst and there's no editing. I've got complete freedom–just the usual station disclaimer at the end."

This time Watson's smile was accompanied by an approving nod. Then a sympathetic sigh. "But it doesn't pay well."

"Enough to live on. My needs are simple. A hotel room. Enough paper for my typewriter," this time Robin grinned like a small boy, "and I steal all the paper and carbon from IBC."

"Writing the great book?"

"Isn't everyone?"

"When do you get the time?"

"Weekends, sometimes at night."

Now there wasn't any smile on Watson's face. He was going in for the kill. "Isn't it difficult doing it piecemeal? How can you keep the flow going? Shouldn't a writer be able to take a year off and give his book total concentration?"

Robin lit a cigarette. His eyes met Clyde Watson's with merely a slight show of curiosity. Watson leaned closer. "Universal Lectures could book you on weekends. I'm sure we could ask for five hundred–maybe even work it up to seven fifty."

"Doing what?"

"You pick a subject. I've read your columns." Watson held up a file to prove his point. "You could talk about amusing incidents that occurred when you were a correspondent. Mix it with anything timely. Play it serious. Play it light. I can *promise* you a lot of work."

"Why would anyone come to see me?"

"Look in the mirror, Mr. Stone. Women's clubs book the guest artists. They've had it with the bald-headed professors or comedians without sex appeal. You'd bring some glamour into their lives. A war correspondent, a Pulitzer Prize-winner–you'd be in big demand at dinners and colleges."

"And when would this leave me time to write my book?"

"Shelve it for now. Forget it. At the rate you're going it will take years. But two years of lectures and you can save enough to take a year off. Go away somewhere. Then, who knows–maybe another Pulitzer Prize, for the book? You don't want to be a local newscaster all your life, do you?"

It had sounded great. Even with the thirty-five percent the agency would take out of his fee for booking the lectures. He signed eagerly. His first lecture was in Houston. Five hundred dollars. One seventy-five back to the agency. That left three twenty-five. Then he read the small print: he had to pay his fare and hotel room. On that first lecture he had cleared thirty-three dollars. When he tried to break his contract, Watson merely smiled blandly. Sure he could break it–if he paid it off. That had been a year ago: a year of traveling tourist in planes, sandwiching his six-foot-three-inch frame into a narrow little seat, all-night flights with fat women and crying babies as seat companions. And the terrible motels, except for a rare case like Philadelphia, when a good hotel suite was included in the deal.

Robin stared at the suite. It was a proper setting for his farewell performance. Thank God it was over: no more tourist planes, no more mingling with the guests . . . He could forget about the speech–the speech that had gotten so pat he could deliver it stoned. The laughs always came in the same place, the applause was always the same. In the end, even the towns looked the same. There was always the good-looking, toothy Junior League girl on the welcoming committee to greet him, eager to discuss Bellow and Mailer and the state of the arts. And after the first martini he knew she was going to wind up in the kip with him.

Well, he had humped his way across forty-six states. Now he was "Head of Network News."

With the first lecture money he had taken an apartment. Nothing fancy but it was better than his hotel room. But he never had a chance to spend any time in it. There was the new desk, the big stack of yellow paper, carbons, even a new electric typewriter to replace his tinny portable. But the job at IBC took up his days, booze and broads took care of the nights, the weekends were spent traveling. Well, that was over now. He'd do a hell of a job at IBC, save every damn cent. And he'd write that book.

Sometimes Robin wondered about his writing. Did he really have it? The Pulitzer Prize didn't prove anything. Journalism didn't mean you had a book in you. And it was a book he wanted to do. He'd show the effect of war on men in politics–the resurgence of Churchill, the emergence of generals as politicians, Eisenhower–de Gaulle. . . . After that, he wanted to write a political novel. But most of all he wanted to see his book become a reality, see the yellow paper transformed into text.

Material things meant little to him. When he saw Amanda purr as she showed him a new pair of shoes, he sometimes wondered about his own lack of interest in possessions. Perhaps it was because he had always had them, at any rate until his father had died, leaving the interest on a four-million estate to Kitty. Upon her death the principal of the estate would be divided between his sister Lisa and himself. Meanwhile on $12,000 a month, the glorious Kitty was having a ball. Funny how he always thought of his mother that way: "the glorious Kitty." She was beautiful, small and blond–hell, she might have red hair by now. Two years ago, when she left for Rome, she was what he called a "plaid" blonde. Kitty said it was frosted. He grinned at the memory. For a fifty-nine-year-old broad she looked pretty good.

His life had been good as a kid–it had even been good through college. The old man had lived long enough to give Lisa the biggest wedding in Boston history and now she was living in San Francisco, married to a crew-cut idiot who was one of the richest real estate men on the West Coast. She had two wonderful kids–God, he hadn't seen them in five years. Lisa was . . . let's see he had been seven when she was born–she must be thirty now, a mother, all settled. And he was still on the loose. Well, he liked it that way. Maybe it came from a crack his father had made. He had been about twelve and his father had taken him out on his first round of golf.

"Approach the game as if it was a subject at school, like algebra–something you must master. You've got to be good in the game, son. Many a business deal is consummated on a golf course."

"Does everything you learn have to help toward making money?" Robin had asked.

"It sure does, if you want a wife and family," his father answered. "When I was a kid I dreamed of being Clarence Darrow. But then I fell in love with your mother and settled for corporate law. I can't kick. I've become a very rich man."

"But you loved criminal law, Dad."

"Once you have a family you can't do just what *you* want. They become your primary responsibility."

Robin learned to play golf. He had a seven handicap when he graduated from Harvard. He had wanted to take a liberal arts course, then major in journalism. His father had been against it, just as he had been furious when he caught Robin reading Tolstoy and Nietzsche.

"That's not going to help you with law," he said.

"I don't want to be a lawyer."

Robin's father stared at him and left the room. The next day Kitty gently explained how he owed it to his father to make him proud. Jesus, it sometimes seemed the only word he heard was "owe." He *owed* it to his father to play football–it was a good image for a lawyer. So he broke every bone in his body to become the best quarterback Harvard had that season. When he graduated in 1944, he might have gone into corporate law but he was twenty-one and there was a war on, so he enlisted in the Air Corps, promising to return and complete law school. But it hadn't happened that way. He saw a lot of action, got his captain's bars and landed on page two of the Boston papers when he was hit in the shoulder–at least *that* made the old man proud of him! It was a minor wound but it aggravated an old football injury and Robin had to remain in a hospital overseas. To ease the monotony he wrote about life in the hospital and the experiences of the other soldiers. He sent his copy to a friend who was with the Northern Press Association. They ran it, and his career as a journalist began.

When the war was over, he joined NPA as a full-time correspondent. Of course he got the usual arguments from both Kitty and his father. He *owed* it to his father to study law. Fortunately, Lisa had met Crew Cut and the entire household was spinning with the preparations for her wedding. Five days later, the old man dropped dead while playing squash. Well, that's the way he would have liked it, Robin thought. Dying with all his muscles intact and all his obligations to his family paid off.

Robin stood up and pushed the room-service table away. He was on his own, and he didn't owe anyone in the world a goddam thing. And he was determined to keep it that way.

He went into the bathroom and turned on the shower. The water sprayed hard and cold, knocking the last vestige of vodka from his brain. God, he had missed his Monday workout at the gym. And he had forgotten to call Jerry in New York and cancel the date. He grinned. Poor Jerry–he had probably gone to the gym alone. And Jerry hated the gym; he only went because

Robin forced him to go. Oddly enough, Jerry didn't seem to mind being flabby at thirty-six.

Robin began to hum. He would call Jerry and Amanda as soon as he got into New York. They'd meet at the Lancer Bar and celebrate. But he wouldn't tell them what they were celebrating–Gregory Austin had said he wanted to handle the announcement himself.

He began lathering the shaving cream on his face. God, he thought, I'd give anything to know just what's happening at IBC this morning.

THREE

TO EVERYONE AT IBC it began as an ordinary Monday morning. The "numbers" (as the weekly Nielsen ratings were called) were placed on every executive's desk. The first sign of disturbance came at ten o'clock. It was triggered by a simple message: "Gregory Austin would like to see Danton Miller in his office at ten thirty."

The message was transmitted from Mr. Austin's private secretary to Susie Morgan, Danton Miller's private secretary. Susie scribbled it on a pad and placed it on Mr. Miller's desk alongside of the Nielsen ratings. Then she headed for the Powder Room. She passed the secretaries in the "bullpen." They were immersed in their work; their typewriters had been clacking away since nine thirty. But the "Upper Echelon" (the VIPs' personal secretaries) arrived at ten, with dark glasses and no makeup. They checked in, letting their bosses know they had arrived, then dashed to the Powder Room. Twenty minutes later they emerged, looking like fashion models. One of the more progressive secretaries had even installed a large magnifying mirror.

The Powder Room was crowded when Susie arrived. As she spat into her mascara, she casually dropped her contribution to the gossip session. Gregory Austin had sent for Danton Miller! The first girl who left the Powder Room passed Susie's tidbit to a friend who worked in the legal department. In less than six minutes the news had traveled all through the building.

Ethel Evans was typing a release when the news hit the publicity department. She was so anxious to see Susie and get all the details that she didn't wait for the elevator. She ran down four flights and was breathless when she burst into the sixteenth-floor Powder Room. Susie was alone, adding a final dab of lip gloss, when Ethel found her.

"I hear your boss is getting his walking papers," she said.

Susie finished her lips. She picked up a comb and teased her bangs, conscious that Ethel was waiting for an answer. She hoped her voice contained the proper tone of boredom when she finally said, "Isn't that the usual Monday morning rumor?"

Ethel's eyes narrowed. "This time I hear it's on the level. Gregory has his weekly meeting with the heads of departments on Thursdays. To send for Dan on a Monday morning–well, everyone knows that has to mean the ax."

Susie suddenly felt concern. "Is that what they say upstairs?"

Ethel felt happier. She had gotten a reaction. She leaned against the wall and lit a cigarette. "It certainly figures. Have you gotten a load of the numbers?"

Susie back-combed her hair. Her hair didn't need it and she hated Ethel Evans. But if Danton Miller went, then *her* job went! She *had* to know if there was anything in the air. She knew Danton's job depended on the rise and fall of the numbers. It had never occurred to her that Gregory Austin's summons could be ominous. In the Powder Room she had imparted the news as further proof of Dan's importance. Now suddenly she felt panic. But she had to regain her poise–Ethel Evans was just a girl who worked in public relations. *She* was Danton Miller's private secretary! Her voice was calm when she answered. "Yes, Ethel, I've seen the numbers. But the ratings of network News are hardest hit. Morgan White is President of News. *He* should be the man to worry. Not Danton Miller."

Ethel laughed. "Morgan White is related to the Austins. Nothing can hurt *him*. Your boyfriend is the one who's in trouble."

Susie colored slightly. It was true she dated Dan, but their relationship was confined to an occasional dinner at "21" or the opening of a Broadway show. Secretly she hoped something would come of it, but so far all he had done was give her a light kiss on the brow when he left her at her door. But she knew she was assumed to be "his girl." They had even been coupled together in a Broadway column. She loved the prestige it gave her among the other secretaries.

Ethel shrugged. "Well, I'm just tipping you off. You'd better gird yourself for a tough evening with the Great Danton. If he gets the sack, it'll be awfully drunk out."

Susie knew Dan had a reputation as a heavy drinker, but he never took more than two martinis with her, and she had never seen anything ruffle his calm. She looked at Ethel and smiled. "I don't think you have to worry about Dan. If he did lose this job, I'm sure he'd have plenty of offers."

"You weren't here when Colin Chase quote, retired, unquote. When they asked him about his plans, he said, 'when you're captain of a dirigible and the dirigible blows up, that's it. After all, how many other dirigibles are there to go to?'" Ethel waited for this line to make an impact, then added, "It can get very lonely and cold sitting out there at Lakehurst, waiting for another dirigible to come along."

Susie smiled. "I don't think Dan will go to Lakehurst."

"Honey, *every* place is Lakehurst when you have no dirigible. Colin Chase still sits in '21' or the Colony every day, having three-hour lunches, stalling until it's time to go to Louis and Armand's for cocktails."

Susie studied her hair in the mirror. Ethel gave up. "Okay, play it cool if you like, but I'll bet you a lunch that Dan will go. He's in real trouble."

Susie stood alone in the Powder Room. She was concerned for Dan. But she was even more concerned for herself. If a new man came in, he'd bring his own secretary. She couldn't go back to the "bullpen"! She'd have to job-hunt. . . .

Oh Lord, she had spent a whole week's salary buying a dress to wear with Dan at the Emmy Awards dinner next month. She was feeling panic now. She *had* seen the ratings. Everything was down. Network News was hardest hit, but Ethel was right–Morgan White was related to the Austins. Danton would be the fall guy. True, he had looked calm enough this morning when she placed the message on his desk, but you could never tell when Dan was worried. His Madison Avenue training and his ubiquitous catlike smile made him seem in total command.

In fact Dan *was* worried. He sensed disaster the moment he saw the ratings. And when Susie put the phone message before him he felt the blood drain from his stomach. He loved the job. It was stimulating and exciting. And as he reveled in his power, his fear of failure grew. You couldn't take chances when you put your job on the line. Presidents of other networks could take chances. They didn't work for a maniac like Gregory Austin, who fancied himself a combination of Bernard Baruch and David Merrick. What was he trying to prove? You couldn't be any bigger than Gregory, unless you were Robert Sarnoff or William Paley.

At ten twenty-seven he left his office and walked to the elevator. He looked down the hall at the impressive walnut door with the gold lettering: MORGAN WHITE. Everything seemed serene in there. Sure, Morgan was safe. Gregory Austin had chosen Danton Miller, Jr., as the sacrificial lamb.

He nodded briskly to the elevator boy as the car took him swiftly to the penthouse floor. He smiled evenly at Gregory Austin's secretary as she announced him. She returned his smile and motioned him to go inside. He envied her, serene and secure in her paneled and broadloomed cubicle.

He entered the spacious reception room, where Gregory usually came out to greet VIPs—big sponsors or presidents of advertising agencies who were making multimillion-dollar buys of IBC air time. Beyond it was the conference room and Gregory's luxurious inner office.

If Gregory wanted to fire him, he'd probably be standing here, waiting to get it over with quickly. But Gregory wasn't here, so maybe it was a good sign. But what if Gregory wanted to make him wait and sweat? It could be a bad sign.

He sat on one of the leather couches and stared morosely at the handsome early American furniture. He glanced at the neat creases in the trousers of his Dunhill suit. God—right now, he was Danton Miller, Jr., President of Network Television. Five minutes from now he might be unemployed.

He took out his cigarette case. The slow burn of his ulcer warned him, but he took out a cigarette and tapped it against the case. He should have taken a tranquilizer before he left his office. He should have stayed on the wagon last night. Hell, he should have done a *lot* of things! He studied the cigarette case. He had selected it with great care. Three hundred dollars. Black baby alligator, trimmed with eighteen-karat gold. He could have gotten a solid gold one for the same price, but that wasn't the image of understated elegance he had styled for himself—the black suit, the black tie, the white shirt. He had twelve black suits, fifty black ties, all the same. Each tie had a small number in the lining so he could rotate them each day. A black suit simplified life: fine for the office, but equally presentable if an important dinner date came up. The cigarette case was a great prop. If he was asked to make a snap decision, he could reach for the cigarette case, select a cigarette, tap it against the case—it gave him time to think, to stall. It was also a substitute for cuticle picking, nail biting and other manifestations of nerves.

His hands felt damp. He didn't want to lose this job! This was power! There was no place to go after this, no place other than the Valhalla of ex-network presidents, the martini-laden four-hour daily lunch at "21."

He stared out the window. A watery sun was trying to shine. Spring would soon be here. This couch would be here in spring. Gregory's secretary would be here. But *he* would be gone. Suddenly he knew how a condemned man must feel as he walks to the electric chair and stares at the witnesses who must watch him die. He breathed deeply, as if savoring every last second of life; as if in a few seconds his life could be shot from under him. The large office, the trips to the Coast, the bungalow at the Beverly Hills Hotel, the broads. . . . He walked back to the couch. He didn't consciously believe in God, yet he sent up a small prayer—a promise. If he got through today without getting canned, things would be different. He'd make those numbers rise. He'd do it if he had to steal shows from other networks. He'd make it a twenty-four-hour-a-day job. He'd cut down on the booze, on the broads. This was a pledge—and he'd keep it. Hadn't he kept the rule he had set for himself against drinking at lunch? He had made that decision when he saw the disintegration of Lester Mark. Lester had headed a big advertising agency. Dan had watched him go from two to four to five martinis at lunch. Martinis bolster a man's confidence and loosen his tongue. He had watched Lester go from president of an advertising agency to vice-president of a lesser agency, from vice-president to unemployment, from there to full-time alcoholic.

Dan was convinced that the lunchtime martini was one of the worst occupational hazards of television. For this reason, he was strict in his abstinence during the day. What he did after hours he always considered his own business. But in this past year he had been doing it too much. Maybe that was why he had latched on to Susie Morgan, breaking another of his rules. (Keep your social life apart from your business.) Susie was too young for him, so he made no passes and stayed reasonably sober when he took her out. Besides, he couldn't really cope with a twenty-three-year-old: a girl that age has marriage spelled across her forehead. It was safer to get a hooker for sex or even jerk off. Girls like Susie were good for window dressing. He'd even give up the hookers if he held the job. He'd stay home several nights a week, just watch that goddam box, watch the competition, find out *why* IBC was lagging. Find out what the public really wanted. Oh, who the hell knew? Even the public didn't know.

The heavy door swung open and Gregory Austin walked in. Dan jumped up. Gregory was holding the ratings. He handed Dan the paper and motioned him to sit down. Dan studied the ratings as if seeing them for the first time. From the corner of his eye he watched Gregory pace up and down the room. Where did the man get the energy? Dan was ten years younger, yet he didn't walk with the same spring. Austin was not a tall man. Dan was five foot ten and he stood several inches higher than Gregory. Even Judith in her high heels sometimes appeared taller than Gregory. Yet there was a virility and a feeling of strength that emanated from him. His whole being crackled with excitement: the red hair, the freckles on the strong sun-tanned hands, his flat stomach, the quick movements, and the sudden disarming smile. The rumor was that he had led an active love life among the Hollywood starlets until he met Judith. After that, to Gregory, no other woman seemed to exist.

"What do you think of the numbers?" Gregory said suddenly.

Dan made a wry face.

"Notice anything particular?"

Dan took out the cigarette case. He tapped a cigarette.

Gregory reached over and took one, but ignored Dan's offer

of a light. "Been off them for a week," he announced. "I just hold one in my mouth. It works. You should try it, Dan."

Dan lit his own cigarette and exhaled slowly. He made another vow to the God who watched over network presidents. If he walked out of this room with his job intact, he would never smoke again.

Gregory leaned over. The strong hand with the red-gold hairs pointed to the news ratings.

"We're in the cellar," Dan said, as if making a sudden discovery.

"Notice something else?"

Dan's ulcer stabbed him. His eyes kept riveting to the two variety shows that were in the bottom ten. Shows that he had recommended. But he forced himself to look at Gregory with a bland innocent stare.

Gregory Austin's finger impatiently tapped the page. "Look at our *local* news. Not only does it hold its own, but some nights it even outrates CBS, ABC and NBC. Know why? A man named Robin Stone!"

"I've caught him many times, he's excellent," Dan lied. He had never seen the man or watched the eleven o'clock IBC news. Either he was loaded and fell asleep, or he turned to NBC and waited for the *Tonight* show.

"I've watched him every night for a month," Gregory stated. "Mrs. Austin thinks he's great. And it's the *women* who determine what channel their husbands pick for news. The man may win in the choice of any other show, but when it comes to the news, it's *her* choice. Because the news is the same on each network–it just depends on which newscaster you prefer to watch. That's why I've taken Robin Stone off local news. I intend to put him on our seven o'clock network show with Jim Bolt."

"Why keep Jim on at all?"

"He's got a contract to play out. Besides, I don't want Robin Stone stuck with just that spot. I have other plans for him. This man can be another Murrow, Cronkite, Huntley or Brinkley. We build him. And in turn he'll build the seven o'clock spot. By the end of this summer, his face will be known nationally. He'll be our anchor man at the conventions. We've got to build our news department. The only way to do it is with a personality. And Robin Stone is our man."

"Could be," Dan said slowly. He wondered what was coming next. This should be Morgan White's territory.

As if reading his thoughts, Gregory said, "Morgan White has to go." He said it quietly, without emotion.

Dan remained silent. This was a startling turn of events and he wondered why Gregory was confiding in him. Gregory kept everyone at a distance.

"Who would replace Morgan?"

Gregory stared at him. "What in hell have I been telling you? Do I have to lay it out? I don't want Robin Stone just as a performing newscaster. I want him to *head* the department."

"I think it's a marvelous idea." Dan was so relieved at his own stay of execution he could afford to be expansive.

"But I can't fire Morgan, he has to quit."

Dan nodded, still afraid to offer any comment.

"Morgan has no talent. But he has plenty of pride. It runs in the family. His mother and Mrs. Austin's mother were sisters. Great family–no business sense–but *great* pride. But that's what I'm counting on. When you leave here, I want you to send a memo to Morgan, announcing that you have hired Robin Stone as Head of Network News."

"Head of Network News?"

"There's no such job or title. I'm just creating it temporarily. Morgan will wonder what the hell it is, too. He'll come to you. You'll say that you created this job for Robin Stone in order to bolster the ratings. That Robin Stone will have a free hand in changing things in the news department–and will report directly to you. Get it?"

Dan nodded slowly. "Morgan will claim I'm butting into his department."

"Not butting in. As President of Network Television, you have the right to suggest changes in any department."

Dan smiled. "Suggest, but not *act*."

"Let's not fool with semantics. Morgan will come running to

me. I'll pretend it's a surprise, but I'll say that your job gives you the power to hire new personnel."

"Suppose Morgan doesn't quit?"

"He will," Gregory said. "I'm betting on it."

Then Gregory tossed aside his unlit cigarette and Dan stood up. The interview had ended. His life had been spared. He left the office with a new sense of security. His job was not in peril, and wouldn't be for some time. Gregory wanted him to be hatchet man on Morgan. He was dizzy at the thought of the new prestige this would give him in the business. Everyone knew Morgan's relationship with Gregory Austin. And now he, Danton Miller, Jr., would make the announcement that he had appointed Robin Stone as Head of Network News. They would actually believe that he was big enough to fire Morgan White and that Gregory Austin would sit back and accept it! The word would be out all over town: "Danton Miller, Jr., has autonomous power."

His hand shook as he wrote and rewrote the memo to Morgan White. After rephrasing it several times, he dictated it to Susie. He wondered how fast she'd get the news around the building. He sat back and reached for a cigarette, then, recalling his pledge, he tossed it unlit into the wastebasket.

He stood up and stared from his window. The sun was shining, the sky was almost a Wedgwood blue. Spring was coming and he'd be alive to greet it.

He turned around calmly as Morgan White burst into his office.

"What is all this about?" Morgan demanded.

"Sit down, Morgan. . . ." Dan reached for his cigarette case, hesitated, then snapped it open. Hell, if there was a God, He knew a man *had* to have a cigarette at a moment like this!

FOUR

THE DAY AFTER the big announcement was made, business went on as usual at IBC. Robin Stone's picture appeared in *The New York Times* with a brief statement announcing his appointment as President of News replacing Morgan White, who had resigned. There was a sense of suspended apprehension in the news department as everyone waited for Robin Stone to appear. Robin had always been a loner, so there was one speculation that took all precedence—"What was Robin Stone really like?" The only person who had come near to socializing with him was Bill Kettner, a cameraman. On two occasions he had gone to a bar with Robin after the eleven o'clock news. On both occasions it was to watch a night ball game. Robin Stone liked baseball. He could also polish off three vodka martinis as if they were orange juice. This was the sum total of information that had been dredged together.

A few of the girls had seen him at P.J.'s, always with a pretty girl. Sometimes Jerry Moss was with them. Jerry Moss seemed to be his only male friend. They met every day at the Lancer Bar for a drink.

"Where in hell is the Lancer Bar?"

Jim Bolt said he thought it was on West Forty-eighth Street. Sam Jackson was sure it was on First Avenue.

They looked it up in the phone book.

It was on East Fifty-fourth Street.

No one had ever been there.

On Wednesday afternoon, half the news department went to the Lancer Bar.

Robin Stone never showed.

On Thursday one of the researchers went there because he had liked the Lancer Bar.

Robin Stone was there.

With Jerry Moss and the most beautiful girl in the world.

There was nothing to do but wait for Robin Stone to make a move. It came late Friday afternoon. A message was placed on the desks of all news personnel:

THERE WILL BE A MEETING IN THE CONFERENCE ROOM ON THE EIGHTEENTH FLOOR, MONDAY AT TEN THIRTY.

ROBIN STONE

They began filing into the conference room at ten twenty. At ten twenty-five Ethel Evans entered. Jim Bolt glanced at her curiously. She had no business being here. But he was too concerned with his own problems to give her much thought. A new president meant a big shake-up. Yet he had to hand it to Ethel—barging in like this. He admired her guts and her easy confidence.

But Ethel wasn't as confident as she appeared. She noticed that most of the staff automatically took seats as if they had been assigned to them. It was a long room, the long table was the only furniture. Some extra chairs were against the wall. The door they had all come in by led to the outside hall. She stared at another door. A door that was ominously closed. Soon every seat was taken except the empty seat at the head of the table. Ethel hesitated, then she took a chair from against the wall, dragged it to the table and wedged it in between a researcher and a sportscaster.

At ten thirty Randolph Lester, Morgan's vice-president of News, entered the room. Ethel noticed that he looked fairly confident. Maybe Robin had given him some hint that his job was not in jeopardy. Randolph was wearing a black suit and black tie. The IBC image that Danton Miller had inspired. He smiled at them paternally. "Good morning, ladies and gentlemen," he said. "I know you've all shared IBC's excitement at the appointment of Mr. Stone to the presidency of News. Some of you have worked with him. Some of you will be meeting him for the first time. Both Mr. Gregory Austin and Mr. Danton Miller are proud to place all future news programming in Mr. Stone's hands. There will be some changes made–in fact, there will be *many* changes made. But I'm sure everyone will understand they reflect in no way on anyone's personal talent or accomplishment. The changes will be to extend our news coverage. To make for higher achievement."

"Why doesn't he just say higher ratings?" whispered someone near Ethel.

Someone else muttered, "See you in the unemployment-insurance line."

Randolph Lester continued, "IBC's policy has always been–" He stopped as the door opened and Robin Stone swung into the room.

There was a small spatter of applause, but something in Robin's eyes made it die before it began. Then he grinned and they all felt like ridiculous children who had done something foolish but were forgiven.

Robin Stone glanced down the table quickly, his eyes resting on no one. It was as if he was summing up the number of people, the room, the setting. Then he flashed an easy grin. Ethel noticed that everyone's resistance seemed to liquefy. The charisma of that grin was like a voltage of paralyzing electricity. To Ethel he was suddenly more desirable than any movie star. God, to break through that steel façade . . . to make this man tremble in her arms . . . to control him . . . even for a second! From her distance at the end of the table she could stare at him without catching his attention. She noticed suddenly that he smiled only with his mouth. His eyes were cold.

"I've studied the news operation," he said quietly. "Each and every one of you is good. But IBC is dragging in the ratings. We've got to add some juice to the operations. I'm a newsman –remember that. First, last and always. This is my first shot as an executive. But I will also function as a newsman. In the Air

Force, when they finally stuck a couple of bars on my shoulder, I still flew a plane as a fighter pilot."

Ethel watched him intently as he spoke. He was handsome, cold-looking but handsome. He had to be almost six three, and not an inch of flesh to spare. She *had* to diet. He was grinning again. He could win the war with that smile alone.

"I intend to stay with the action here. This summer I want to build a top team to cover the conventions," Robin continued. "By then Andy Parino, from our Miami station, will be established on the network—he'll also be part of our convention team. I want to *add* to the combination—not eliminate." He turned to Randolph Lester. "But first of all, suppose we go round the table and you introduce everyone to me."

The two men walked around the table and Robin shook hands with each person. His friendly grin was intact, but his eyes were remote and his greeting impersonal. It was almost as if he had never seen any of them before.

When Lester's eyes rested on Ethel, he seemed surprised, hesitated a second, then quickly passed by her. The entire procedure went so quickly that Ethel was unaware of the deliberate slight. She watched them return to the head to the table. But Robin didn't sit down. His eyes scanned the table and rested on Ethel.

He pointed to her. "I don't believe we were introduced."

She stood up. "I'm Ethel Evans."

"What is your function?"

She felt her face grow warm. "I'm with the public relations office . . ."

"Then what are you doing here?" He was still smiling and his voice was gentle, but the eyes chilled her.

"Well . . . I thought . . . I mean, someone has to be assigned to News. To publicize any new ventures. I figured you'd need someone." She sat down quickly.

"When I want someone, I'll notify the publicity department," he said with the same half-smile. "Now suppose you return to wherever you came from." Every eye watched her as she walked out of the room.

Outside in the hall, Ethel leaned against the door. She felt physically sick. She wanted to run away from that conference room–she could hear him talking inside–but she stood there. She couldn't move . . . she was in a state of shock.

Then she heard Lester ask Robin whether he wanted Mondays set aside for the weekly meetings.

"There will be no weekly meetings," Robin answered. "I call them as I see them. But I want one thing changed–"

There was a second of silence. She knew everyone was leaning forward intently. Then Robin's voice: "Get rid of this table, I want a round one."

"A round one?" This was Lester.

"Yep. A great big round one. I don't like to sit or stand at the head of a table. I don't want seats assigned. If we work as a team, we sit as a team. Get me a big round table." There was a moment of silence, then everyone began to talk at once and she knew Robin had left the room. She heard them chattering with nervous relief. They'd begin to file out in a second! She dashed down the hall. She couldn't wait for the elevator–she didn't want to face them. She ran to the stairway and ducked into the Ladies' Room on another floor. Thank God, it was empty. She gripped the sink until her knuckles were white. Tears of humiliation ran down her face. "You son of a bitch, I hate you!" She started to sob. "I hate you!" She wiped her eyes and stared into the mirror. A fresh flow of tears spilled over. "Oh God," she begged, "why didn't you make me beautiful?"

FIVE

AFTER HER DISASTROUS EVICTION from Robin's meeting, Ethel holed away in her office for the rest of the day. She didn't want to run into anyone in the halls—she was positive they were joking about her unceremonious departure.

She put the time to good use and typed out all the releases that had piled on her desk. At six thirty, the offices on the entire floor were empty. In her concentration on her work most of her humiliation had evaporated. Now she just felt drained—wrung out.

She took her mirror and tried to fix her makeup. She stared at herself disconsolately. Her face looked lousy. She put the cover on her typewriter and stood up. Her skirt was a mass of rolled wrinkles. It was too tight. Ethel sighed. Everything she ate went straight to her hips. She really had to go on a strict diet.

She took the elevator to the lobby. It was deserted but the coffee shop was still open. It was too late to go to Louis and Armand's on the pretense of looking for someone and maybe having a few laughs at the bar. Everyone she knew would be gone by now. The dinner crowd would be coming in. She went into the coffee shop and ordered black coffee. Usually she took cream and two sugars. The diet was officially on! She watched the waitress pour it into a cup. The girl's hands were red and cracked from washing dishes. She wondered about her. Didn't she have dreams? Didn't she hope to get somewhere? She had much more on the ball than Ethel, as far as looks went. She was slim and had a pretty face. Yet that girl was content to stand on her feet, slop up a wet counter, take crap from customers, smile at a dime tip—and Ethel Evans was making a hundred and fifty dollars a week!

She got out her compact and retouched her lipstick. She was no beauty, but she got by. More than got by—but it would be nice to have a little something going in the looks department. Damn that separation in her teeth. And damn that lousy dentist who wanted three hundred dollars for a cap job. She had offered to sleep with him if he'd do it for free and he had thought she was joking. When she let him know she was serious, he pretended not to believe her. Then she realized he didn't *want* her! Dr. Irving Stein, a lousy little dentist, didn't want her! Ethel Evans who only fucked the big boys—who was known at IBC as the "celebrity-fucker"!

She walked out of the coffee shop and hesitated in the lobby. She didn't want to go home. This was the night her roommate bleached her hair and the whole place would be a mess. But it was a good arrangement, sharing an apartment with Lillian, who worked at the Benson-Ryan agency. Their hours were alike and they dug the same scene. They had met at Fire Island. That had been a great summer. Six girls had anted up to share a cottage. They called it the House of the Six Swingers. They had a blackboard and kept score. Every time one of them banged a guy, the others had to put a dollar in the kitty. And at the end of the summer the girl who had banged the most men won the pot. Lillian had beaten Ethel out by more than a dozen men. But then Lillian wasn't choosy. She was a good girl, a fun girl, but a slob. She'd even bang an assistant director. In Ethel's book, an A.D. couldn't qualify for anything but a few laughs at Louis and Armand's bar, if she was desperate.

She was suddenly conscious that the doorman was staring at her. She left the building and started to walk. Maybe she'd stop at P. J. Clarke's.

They were three deep at the bar and she connected with some agency men. She stood there for over an hour, exchanging dirty jokes, toying with one beer, her eyes watchful for some good prospect at the door. Someone who might buy her dinner. . . .

At seven thirty she saw Danton Miller walk in alone. She wondered where in hell was Susie. He looked straight through her without even nodding and joined some men at the other end of the bar.

Another hour passed and then as if a timer went off, the agency men suddenly gulped down their drinks and raced to catch the last decent commuter train. And not one of the bastards picked up her check. She was hungry now. If she went inside and had a hamburger, Lillian would be through with the peroxide and jazz by the time she got home.

She sat alone at a small table and ate the hamburger. She was starving but she left half the roll. Damn, why had she had the beer? She weighed a hundred and forty now. Well, she had a small waistline and her boobs were sensational. Size thirty-eight–upright and firm. Her problem was her ass and thighs. If she didn't get it off now, she'd never lose it and next month she was going to be thirty. And still not married!

She could have been married, if she had wanted to settle for a civilian–the cameraman at CBS or the bartender in the Village. But Ethel wouldn't settle for anything less than a top celebrity. A one-night stand with a celebrity was preferable to a mediocre existence with a nobody. After all, when she held a movie star in her arms and he murmured, "Baby . . . baby," as his climax came, that moment made up for everything in the world. During that one moment she was beautiful–she was *someone*. She could forget who she was. . . .

She had always wanted to be beautiful, even as a child. Fat little Ethel Evanski from Hamtramck in Detroit. Eating mashed potatoes and fried onions, listening to everyone on the block talk Polish, playing potsy, double Dutch, double Irish, reading movie magazines, sending for genuine autographed pictures of Hedy Lamarr, Joan Crawford, Clark Gable. Sitting on the front steps and playing "The Game"–talking dreams and pretending they were real–with Helga Selanski, a stringy-haired little Polish kid the same age. The whole world was Polish on that block in Hamtramck. And the second-generation Poles seemed locked in, destined to marry their own kind. They went to movies and saw that there *was* another world, but it never occurred to them to try and enter it. But to Ethel, movies and the places she saw on the screen weren't merely two hours of silver escape. Hollywood was a real place. New York and Broadway actually existed. At night she would stay awake and listen to the radio, and when the voice announced that the music was emanating from the Cocoanut Grove in Hollywood, she would hug herself with excitement —at that very second, the beautiful music she listened to was being listened to by the famous stars who were there. For that one moment, there almost seemed to be physical contact, like she was *there*.

Ethel had always known she would leave Hamtramck. Getting to New York was Phase One in her dreams. One night when she and little Helga were listening to a band coming from the Paradise Restaurant in New York, Ethel began "The Game." Planning what she would wear when she grew up and went to such a place—what movie actor would escort her. Usually Helga played along with The Game. But on this night, Helga suddenly protruded her bony jaw and stated, "I'm not playing anymore. I'm too big." Ethel had been surprised. Usually she could make Helga do anything, but this time Helga was stubborn. "My mother says we shouldn't talk and play like this, it's time for us to be practical and not play make-believe games."

Ethel had answered, "It's *not* make-believe. I'm going there someday, and I'll know movie stars and they'll take me out—and kiss me." Helga had laughed. "Like fish! Kiss you! Oh Ethel, I dee-double-dare you to say that to anyone else on the block. You're not going anywhere. You're going to stay right here like all the rest of us and marry a nice Polish fella and have babies." Ethel's eyes had narrowed. "I'm going to meet stars . . . go out with them . . . maybe even marry one." Helga laughed. "See, my mother's right. She says it's all right to talk about Hollywood if we know we're just dreaming, but not to believe that it's true. You're crazy. And you won't go out with movie stars. You're Ethel Evanski and you're fat and ugly and live in Hamtramck, and what movie star would want to go out with you!"

Ethel had slapped Helga—hard. But she was frightened because she was afraid Helga might be telling the truth. But she *wouldn't* stay on the block and marry a nice Polish boy, raise kids and make mashed potatoes and onions! Why *had* her mother and father come from Poland if it was to live in a little Poland in Detroit?

The incident that triggered "The Game" into determined action was Peter Cinocek, a boy with protruding ears and large red hands who had "come to call" when she was sixteen. Peter was the son of a friend of Aunt Lotte's. He was a "real catch," half Polish, half Czech. Her mother and father had looked idiotic with delight at the prospect. She recalled how diligently her mother had cleaned the house. Everything had to be spotless the night Peter Cinocek came to call. She could still see them. Her mother nervously waiting, in a freshly ironed housedress. Her father skinny and bald, so old. God, he had only been thirty-eight. He had seemed worn and bloodless in her eyes, but her mother had appeared massive and strong.

She would never forget the night Peter Cinocek arrived. First she saw the big ears, then the pimples on his neck surrounding a great red boil that had not quite matured. But he could have been Clark Gable the way her mother had beamed as she placed a pitcher of lemonade on the porch and discreetly disappeared into the kitchen to wait.

Everyone on the block waited. Everyone in the small row of houses knew a "suitor" had come to call. She sat on the swing with Peter Cinocek. They sat in silence, listening to the creak of the swing, to the whispers of the neighbors on the porch that adjoined theirs. She could still see that house. A small cubicle, sandwiched in a long block of identical small frame houses. Every house had the same broken-down porch, the same small dinky dining room, the tiny living room, and the kitchen where everyone spent most of their time. And, oh God, the endless garbage pails and the cats that frequented the back alley. Even now she could still hear their mating sounds, and some disgruntled neighbor tossing out a pail of water to shut them up. Either their aim was bad or the cats were extremely passionate, because after a brief lull the mating yowls commenced again.

She thought back to that night when she sat on the creaking swing and listened to Peter Cinocek. He told her about his job at the A&P, then he took her hand in his. It felt moist and limp.

And he told her how he hoped to have a home just like this and many many children. That's when she had bolted off the swing and run! Of course she came back, when she was sure the big-eared Peter had gone. Her folks had laughed. In Polish they kidded, "Little Ethel, she was scared of a boy. Ah, but she was born to have children–nice broad hips, she would have an easy time."

Ethel was silent, but she doubled her efforts at school and that summer she got a job in an office in downtown Detroit and became fairly efficient as a secretary. She never dated. But she was not unhappy. She was waiting. Saving all her money–and waiting.

When she was twenty she had saved five hundred dollars and she came to New York. Her final job in Detroit had been in the publicity department of a small advertising agency. In New York she landed in the secretarial pool at a large advertising agency. Ethel's big chance came the day a drunken movie idol who was appearing on one of the agency's shows wandered into the office. She had been thrilled to follow him back to his hotel. He had sobered instantly when he found he had taken a virgin. But he had been too drunk to remember that the virgin had practically raped him. He was frightened there might be repercussions. He offered her money. Ethel haughtily refused. It had been love, she insisted. His panic mounted. He was married and loved his wife. Was there anything he could do for her? Well, she explained she wasn't exactly thrilled being in the secretarial pool . . . He had acted immediately. With quick finesse and help from his agent he arranged for Ethel's transfer to the New York publicity office of his movie company.

This was smorgasbord for Ethel. She met a lot of drunken actors, even some sober actors. And she did it all for love. The word spread, and Ethel's career had begun. When an opening came in the publicity department at IBC, Ethel took it. After all, she had practically gone through the movie company's talent list. IBC offered more money and a whole new arena with its ever-changing shows. She was good at her work and superb at her hobby–her job was secure at IBC.

She was well aware that her reputation had traveled from coast to coast. She enjoyed the notoriety, even her title. One of the Six Swingers from Fire Island had gone to work in Los Angeles in the publicity department of Century Pictures. She and Ethel exchanged voluminous letters. Ethel described every detail of each current affair, gave the man a rating, and even included the size of his equipment. Ethel had a funny style and Yvonne, her correspondent, had Ethel's letters mimeoed and they passed freely around the office. When Ethel learned this, she took even greater pains to be more descriptive. It worked almost like a paid ad for her. Many big names called her when they came to New York. Famous men . . . beautiful men. . . .

Often she wished Helga could see her on some of her dates with the handsome stars. Helga must be faded and loaded with kids by now. Helga had married Peter Cinocek!

She looked up suddenly. Danton Miller was standing at her table. He was very drunk.

"Hello, baby," he said with his Cheshire smile.

She smiled casually. "Well, well, if it isn't City Lights."

"Meaning what?" he asked.

"Like the picture of the same name. You only recognize me when you're drunk."

Dan pulled up a chair. He laughed. "You're a funny girl." He waved for another drink. Then he looked at her with a grin. "They say you're the greatest. Do you think I should lay you?"

"*I* choose who I lay, Mr. President. But don't feel sad–I've got you on my list, if there's a slow night."

"Is tonight slow?"

"It started that way . . ."

He threw his arm around her. "You're an ugly broad. In fact, you're really a beast. But I hear you're the greatest. Want to come home with me?"

"You make it sound so romantic."

His eyes narrowed. "I hear you also have a big mouth. That you spread the word, give a Nielsen rating on every guy you lay."

She shrugged. "Why not? My ratings save some of my girl friends from shacking up with a blintz."

Dan's smile was ugly. "Who the hell are you to give a guy a rating?"

"Let's say I have an excellent basis for comparison."

"Want a drink?" he asked, as the waiter placed his Scotch before him.

She shook her head and watched him drain the glass. He stared at her. "You're getting prettier by the minute, Gargantua. And I'm getting curiouser and curiouser."

"You're also getting very drunk," she said.

"Yeah, time to go home. Maybe I'll take you home with me."

"You forget, Mr. President. *I* make the decision."

He was almost humble as he stared at her. "Well, wanna come?"

She thrilled at the glorious surge of power. He was begging now. "If I do, you have to send me home in a Carey car."

"I'll send you home in a Rolls-Royce if you're half as good as they say." He lumbered to his feet and signaled for his check. She was relieved to see he automatically picked up hers.

"Are you sure you're sober enough to enjoy it?" she asked.

"You *make* me enjoy it," he challenged. "I think it's about time someone gives a rating on *you*."

She stood staring at him on the street. "Forget it. I'm too great to waste on a drunk."

He grabbed her arm. "Scared? Maybe your reputation is phony. Probably is. How could you be any different from any other dame—unless at the finish your cunt plays 'The Star Spangled Banner'?"

"I think I'll show you, little man." She hailed a cab and helped him in.

He had a nice apartment in the East Seventies. Typically bachelor and typically executive. He led her directly into the bedroom and fumbled out of his clothes. She saw the surprise on his face as she undressed. Her perfect breasts always caused this reaction.

"Hey, baby, you're stacked." He held out his arms.

She came to him. "A little better than Susie Morgan, huh?"

"Wouldn't know," he mumbled. He threw her on the bed. His kiss was sloppy. He tried to mount her but he was limp. She slid out from under him and rolled him over.

"Take it easy, sonny," she said. "You may be president of the network, but you're just a boy to me. Now lie back. Ethel will show you what love is about."

She started making love to him. And as his excitement mounted, as he responded and whispered, "Baby, baby . . . you're the greatest," she forgot that tomorrow he would pass her in the hall without a nod. Right now she was making love to the president of IBC. And right now she *felt* beautiful. . . .

SIX

DANTON MILLER tossed the trade papers aside. He couldn't concentrate on a damn thing. He spun his chair around and faced the window. In one hour he was to have lunch with Gregory Austin. He had no inkling what it was about. No warning, just the goddam phone call and the impersonal voice of Gregory's secretary.

So far the ratings were about the same. News was still in the cellar, but the new guy, Andy Parino, had just started cutting in from Miami a week ago. He had to admit it gave the show an extra dimension. Well, that was their problem. He had his own. The variety show was canceled. He was positive the Western Gregory had handpicked to replace it would bomb. And he was determined to come in with a mid-season saver. That's why he had spent every night of the past week with two writers and a half-baked singer named Christie Lane.

Last week he had stumbled into the Copa to catch a well-known comic—Christie was merely the supporting act. At first Dan had paid no attention to this forty-year-old second-rater who looked like an old-time Coney Island singing waiter. Dan had never heard of the bum. But as he watched him, an idea began to form. Suddenly Dan turned to Sig Hyman and Howie Harris, the two writers who had accompanied him, and said, "He's just right for what I want!" He knew they thought it was the whiskey talking. But the next morning he sent for them and told them he wanted to do a pilot with Christie Lane. They had stared at him with disbelief.

"Christie Lane! He's a stumblebum, he's over the hill," Sig Hyman stated.

Then Howie jumped in: "He can't even get a Saturday night at the Concord or Grossinger's off-season. Did you read the Copa show notices in *Variety?* Christie didn't even get a mention. The Copa girls' costumes did better than he did. He only plays New York as a filler-in when they've got a jumbo name. And those Irish ballads–" Howie rolled his eyes.

And Sig added the clincher: "Besides, he looks like my Uncle Charlie who lives in Astoria."

"That's just what I want!" Dan insisted. "Everyone has an Uncle Charlie they love."

Sig shook his head. "I hate my Uncle Charlie."

"Save the jokes for the script," Dan answered. Sig was right about Christie's looks. He looked like Mr. Average Man. He'd be perfect for a homey-type variety show. Sig and Howie gradually got the idea. They were top writers who had worked only for established stars. Three months ago Dan had given them each a year's contract to help him develop new shows.

"We make Christie the host," Dan had explained. "Form a stock company–girl singer, announcer, do sketches–and we make use of Christie's singing voice. If you close your eyes the bum sounds like Perry Como."

"I think he sounds more like Kate Smith," Sig said.

Dan smiled. "I tell you the timing is right. Television runs in cycles. With all the violence of *The Untouchables* and its imitators, the time is ripe for a show the entire family can watch. Christie Lane is a second-rater. But no one in TV knows him, so he'll be a new face. And we'll use a big guest star each week to attract ratings. I tell you it can work!"

Like many performers, Christie Lane had started in burlesque. He could dance, sing, tell jokes, do sketches. He worked with Dan and the writers with hysterical eagerness. Dan guessed him to be about forty. He had sparse blond hair, a large homely face, and a medium frame that was beginning to show the hint of a potbelly. His ties were too loud, his lapels were too wide, the diamond ring on his pinky too big, the cuff links were the size of half-dollars, yet Dan sensed he could create a likable character out of this oddly assorted but talented man. He was an indefatigable worker. Whatever town he played, he quickly scurried about and managed to pick up extra club dates on the side. He lived out of two wardrobe trunks and when he was in New York, he stayed at the Astor Hotel.

By the end of the first week, Dan's conception of the show had begun to take form. Even the writers got "with it." They wouldn't change the awful ties, the wide lapels. Christie actually thought he dressed well. He liked the goddam ties. This was the key to his character, Dan told them. They'd pick some good songs for him to sing, but at the same time allow him to do something corny of his own choosing.

Dan had sent a brief synopsis of the show to Gregory last week. Perhaps the lunch was about the show. But Gregory wouldn't waste a lunch just to okay a pilot. He'd send down word to go ahead . . . or to kill it. He hoped Gregory gave him the green light. It would be grim to have put in all this time and work for nothing. He got a headache at just the thought of all those nights in the smoke-filled suite at the Astor. Christie and those cheap cigars. And always the ever-present show girl from the Copa or the Latin Quarter sitting patiently and wordlessly; reading the morning papers; waiting for Christie to be finished. And the stooges–the two alleged "writers" Christie carried with him. Eddie Flynn and Kenny Ditto. They were supposed to supply Christie with jokes. As far as Dan could see they were "gofors." "Hey, Eddie, go for some coffee." "Kenny, didya go for my cleaning?" Christie came from a world where a man proved his importance by the stooges he carried. Sometimes he paid Eddie and Kenny as little as fifty dollars a week. When things went well he paid them more. But they were "with him." He took them to nightclub openings, the racetrack, on tour, and now, as Christie had stated, "My boys must be put on the show as writers. They should each get two C's a week."

Dan had hidden his amusement and relief. Four hundred dollars a week tacked on to a budget was minuscule in a major television production. And it would make Christie indebted. Sig and Howie would get the major credit on the screen, and it was always easy to list additional dialogue in small letters in the crawl at the end of the show. Of course they were still far away from the pilot. But if Gregory gave him the Go signal, he could have a pilot on tape by August. He hoped to do the show live–tape it at the same time, so they could use it for delayed markets. They could save a lot of money doing it live and Dan would be a hero if he brought it off.

For a brief moment he felt good. Then he thought of the lunch and the ulcer pain began. What in hell was the lunch all about?

At twelve twenty-five he entered the elevator. The operator punched the button to Penthouse. Dan had once said P.H. also stood for Power House. The name had stuck among the executives. A man could be made or broken up there. Well, he was prepared for anything. He had taken two tranquilizers right after the phone call.

He walked directly to Gregory's private dining room. He noticed the table was set for three. He was just taking out a cigarette when Robin Stone entered. Gregory walked into the room and motioned them both to the table.

It was a sparse lunch. Gregory was on one of his health kicks. You never knew what to expect. Gregory had a chef who had worked at Maxim's in Paris. You could come there one day and enjoy a cheese soufflé and flaming French pancakes, sauce that stabbed an ulcer and delighted the taste. This usually happened when Gregory read that a contemporary had died in a plane crash, or was stricken with cancer or some similar inexorable disaster. Then Gregory would smoke, eat all the rich food and say, "Hell, a flowerpot could fall on my head tomorrow." This state of gastronomic luxury would continue until another contemporary had a heart attack. Then the Spartan regime commenced again. Gregory had been dedicated to this present health kick ever since his last bout of indigestion.

In the beginning the talk was general. They discussed the chances of any team against the Yankees, and the effect of the weather on their golf scores. This was a lousy April. Hot as hell one day, then wham, down in the forties.

Dan silently made his way through the grapefruit, the two lamb chops, the string beans, the sliced tomato. He passed up the fruit Jello. He wondered what Robin Stone was thinking. But most of all his sympathy went to the chef whose talent was being stifled with Gregory's present regime.

With the coffee, Gregory went into his life story. He told Robin about IBC. How he had created it. His early struggles building a new network. Robin listened attentively, asking an intelligent question now and then. And when Gregory complimented Robin on the Pulitzer Prize and even quoted from some of his past columns, Dan was properly impressed. The old man must think a lot of Robin Stone to do all this homework.

When Gregory put the unlit cigarette between his teeth, Dan sensed the real purpose of the lunch was about to begin.

"Robin has some pretty exciting ideas," Gregory said expansively. "It would come under network programming–that's why I invited you here today, Dan." Then he looked at Robin almost paternally.

Robin leaned across the table. His eyes met Dan's. His voice was direct. "I want to do a show called *In Depth.*"

Dan reached for his cigarette case. The tone of Robin's voice had held no request. It was an announcement. He tapped the cigarette. So that was it. Gregory had already given Robin the go-ahead. This was just protocol, pretending to allow him to make the decision. He was supposed to nod and say fine! Well, fuck them–he wasn't going to make it that easy. He lit his cigarette and took a deep draw. As he exhaled, his smile was intact. "Good title," he said easily. "What would it be? A fifteen-minute news show?"

"A half-hour. Slated for Monday night at ten," Robin answered.

(The sons of bitches even had the time picked out!) Dan kept his voice even. "I think we have the new Western scheduled for that spot." He looked at Gregory.

Robin cut in like a knife. "Mr. Austin feels the *In Depth* show should go in there. It would prove IBC had integrity–expanding the news media to prime time, plus doing a new kind of news show. The Western can always go to another slot."

"Do you realize the money we'd lose? We have a chance to sell a cheap game show right after the Western. We'd have to give away the time following your kind of show." Dan was addressing Robin, but he was talking for Gregory's benefit.

"If the *In Depth* show comes off, you'll still get your prime time rate," Robin answered.

"Not on your life," Dan said coldly. "We also won't be able to get a sponsor interested in a half-hour news show." (He wondered why Gregory was just sitting there, letting him battle out this cockeyed idea with this egghead!)

Robin looked bored. "I know nothing about network sales. You can take that up with the sales department. My function at IBC is to bring some excitement and expansion into News programming, and I think this will be an exciting show. I intend to travel, to bring *In Depth* interviews to IBC about current world news. I might do some live shows out of New York or Los Angeles. I promise you this—I'll deliver a damn good news show that will be entertaining as well."

Dan couldn't believe what was happening. He looked at Gregory for support. Gregory smiled evasively.

"When would you put this show on?" Dan asked. It was too incredible to be true.

"October," Robin answered.

"Then you don't intend to go on camera before then?" Dan asked. "No seven o'clock news? No special coverage?"

"I intend to cover the conventions this summer."

"I assume you'll take Jim Bolt along. His face is well known, and he did a great job in fifty-six."

"He did a lousy job," Robin answered, with no change of emotion. "Jim is good with the seven o'clock news. But he shoots no juice or excitement at convention coverage. I'm forming my own team."

"Any ideas, or is this going to be another surprise?" Dan asked.

"I've got it fairly well planned in my own mind." Robin turned to Gregory Austin. "I'll take a team of four. The team will consist of Scott Henderson, Andy Parino, John Stevens from Washington and myself."

This time Gregory spoke up. "Why Andy Parino? He's not

politically oriented. I like him coming in from Miami, but for a convention–?"

"Especially for the convention," Robin answered. "Andy went to college with Bob Kennedy."

"What's that got to do with it?" Dan asked.

"I think Jack Kennedy will be the Democratic candidate. Andy's friendship with the Kennedys might enable him to get us some back-door muscle."

Dan laughed. "I don't think Kennedy has a chance. He made his bid for Vice-President in fifty-six and lost. Stevenson will be the candidate."

Robin stared at him. "Stick to time costs and ratings, Dan. You know that scene. Politics and news are my bag. Stevenson is a good man, but he's going to be the bridesmaid at this convention."

Gregory cut in. "Dan–I'm for giving him a shot with this *In Depth* show. Ratings may be the name of the game, but we need some prestige. If Robin makes a name for himself with the convention coverage, the *In Depth* show might turn out to be a commercial hit as well."

"You think you can buck Cronkite, Huntley and Brinkley, men like that, at a convention?" Dan couldn't keep the sneer from his voice.

"I'll do my damnedest. With Andy Parino along, I might get to tape an interview with Jack Kennedy. If he is nominated, it will make an excellent *In Depth* opening show. Then you can bet that Mr. Nixon will be delighted to give me an interview, for equal time."

"Okay," Dan growled. "So you land yourself the candidates–that's two shows. What else do you plan to do? As I see it, so far it's just a platform for political candidates."

Robin's smile was easy. "I plan to go to London and do an interview with some of the top British stars–like Paul Scofield, Laurence Olivier. Then do one with an American star of equal stature and compare the different attitudes. In May, Princess Margaret will wed Tony Armstrong-Jones. I have a friend with UPI who's a close friend of Tony's. I'll shoot for an interview with him. I'm planning on leaving next week for San Quentin to try and tape an interview with Caryl Chessman. His latest execution date is scheduled for May second."

"He'll be granted another stay," Dan snapped.

"I don't think so," Robin answered. "And there's such a mounting feeling against capital punishment that it's important to do a show on the subject."

"I think it's a little too controversial," Dan argued. "I think all the subjects you've picked are too far out. The public won't go for this egghead crap!"

Robin grinned, but Dan noticed the coldness in his eyes. "I think you underestimate the public."

Dan smothered his anger. He went for the cigarette case again. By the time he lit one he was able to get the right note of condescension in his voice. "I think these ideas of yours are gallant and crusading. But while you're off knocking down windmills, I have to fight sponsors, juggle programs and worry about ratings. Before you take off on this safari, I think we should feel out some sponsors–after all, a network is team play. You can't grab the ball and run off like a steamroller and expect me to hold the line without knowing the signals. I like your spirit, your enthusiasm, but have you seen the schedule of NBC, CBS and ABC? We need variety shows to compete with them."

Robin's voice cut in like an icicle. "I'm not going to pump sunshine up your ass. I'm here to create excitement for the News end of IBC. Maybe your job is to sit around and see what hits on other networks–then try and come out with carbon copies of their hit shows. Okay, that's your route. Not *mine!*"

Gregory Austin's eyes were shining. He jumped up and clapped Robin on the shoulder. "I talked like that when I was your age. I had the same enthusiasm when I said I was going to start the fourth network. I broke rules, I hustled, I didn't listen to the doubters. Go ahead, Robin! I'll send word to Business Administration to okay all expenses. You bring back those shows. Dan and I will work things out from this end."

Robin grinned and started for the door. "I'll start things rolling right away. I'll be in touch with you, Mr. Austin, from all points." Then he left the room.

Dan was still sitting at the table. He stumbled awkwardly to his feet. Gregory Austin was staring after the closed door with unmasked admiration.

"He's quite a man," Gregory said.

"If things work out," Dan answered.

"They will! And even if they don't, at least he's in there pitching. Know something, Dan? I think I've just bought myself the greatest piece of manpower in the industry."

Dan left the office. He went back to his desk. The outline for the Chris Lane show was on his desk. Suddenly the whole idea seemed limp. The steely arrogance of Robin Stone deflated him. But he picked it up and put in a call for Sig and Howie. He set a meeting for four o'clock. God damn it–he had to make the Christie Lane show work. The *In Depth* show would fall flat on its ass, he was confident of that. But Gregory liked action. Okay, he'd give him a show too. Maybe it wouldn't have Tony Armstrong-Jones or a Kennedy, and maybe the *Times* would murder it, but he'd deliver a hot commercial show and a rating. And in the end, when the stockholders met, ratings were all that counted. Prestige didn't pay dividends. Only ratings paid dividends.

He kept Sig and Howie in his office until seven o'clock. When he let them go, he demanded that they bring him more than an outline–he wanted a rough draft of a script and format within ten days.

When the writers left, Dan suddenly decided to go out and get drunk. He sure as hell rated it. He walked over to "21" and stood against the bar. The regulars were there. He nodded and ordered a double Scotch. Something was bothering him, beyond and above the set-to with Robin. He searched his mind. It wasn't Gregory's admiration for the man, Gregory blew hot and cold with equal force. A few weeks of low ratings and he'd be very disenchanted with Robin Stone . . . no, something that had happened in that dining room had unsettled him. Yet he couldn't put his finger on it. He retraced all the conversation, but he couldn't find the cause. He ordered another double Scotch. Then he relived the luncheon again—every word, even Gregory's life story. He felt that if he only remembered, he would have the key and know where to fight and what to fight against. The battle with Robin was out in the open. Time would prove him the winner and he would emerge stronger than ever. It was as if he had stumbled across a key to a bigger danger and lost it.

He thought about Ethel. Maybe he'd really tie one on and let her come to his apartment and do the cold-cream job. With Ethel, you didn't have to bother about satisfying her—in fact he got the feeling that she liked it better when she didn't even have to undress. He almost began to feel good. But the nagging feeling persisted of something wrong in his universe—something to do with Robin Stone. Again, he went over the luncheon from the top, all the way to Robin's exit: "I'll start things going right away." Dan slammed the glass down with such force it broke against the bar. A polite waiter immediately wiped it up. The bartender poured another double and handed it to him. Dan took it. Christ, that was it! Robin's exit line: "I'll be in touch with you, Mr. Austin, from all points."

In touch with *you*, Mr. Austin!

Robin Stone was supposed to report to *him*, Danton Miller. And Danton Miller should report to Mr. Austin. The son of a bitch was sidestepping him, going over his head—right to Gregory himself. And Gregory had allowed it. Well that settled it—he'd *have* to make The Christie Lane show a smash. Now he had to come up with a winner.

He walked outside to the phone booth and called Ethel Evans.

"Want to meet me at my apartment?" he asked.

"I'm no call girl."

"Meaning what?"

"I haven't eaten."

"Okay, meet me at P.J.'s."

"Is that the only restaurant in town?"

"Honey"—he softened his voice—"it's eight thirty. I can't make it a late night. Next week, I'll take you anywhere you want to go."

"Is that a promise?"

"I swear on my Nielsens."

Ethel laughed. "Okay, I'll change to slacks."
"Why change?"
"Because whenever I see a girl walk into P.J.'s at nine, all caked up, it looks like she was disappointed. You know, had her hopes geared for Voisin or the Colony. But when she walks in wearing slacks, it looks like it's her decision."
"You've got everything figured out, haven't you?"
"Yes—even you, great man."
He laughed. He didn't want to argue with her. "Okay, Ethel, see you in half an hour."
He returned to the bar and finished his drink. He looked at his watch. It was bad enough to be seen with Ethel; he was not about to be seen waiting for her. He signaled for another double.
Someone tapped him on the shoulder. It was Susie Morgan. God, she looked so fresh and pretty.
"Dan, you know Tom Mathews?"
Dan found himself shaking hands with a sandy-haired giant. The name rang a bell. Yeah, he had just been appointed to the CBS legal department. Or was it NBC?
The giant almost broke his hand pumping it. Jesus, how young and hearty did he have to be!
"Dan, look!" Susie held out her hand. A microscopic diamond in a Tiffany setting was on the proper finger.
"Well, well, when did all this happen?"
"Tonight!" she said. "That is, I got the ring tonight. We've dated occasionally for a year and just started going steady the last three weeks. Isn't it wonderful, Dan!"
"Just great. Lemme buy you both a drink."
"No, we're having dinner upstairs with Tom's folks. But I heard you were in here and I wanted you to be the first to know."
"When do I lose you?" Dan asked.
"You don't. Unless you want to. We're getting married in June, we'll have our honeymoon during our vacation. We both have two weeks coming. And, Dan, I'd love to continue to work for you until the lucky day when baby comes." She blushed and looked at the giant adoringly.
"You bet!" Dan nodded. "Let me know what you want for a wedding present."

He watched them as they left the room. It wasn't proper to be that happy. He had never been that happy in his life. . . .

But he had *power*. That was his kind of happiness. And he'd come up with a winner with the Christie Lane Show if it was the last thing he did. By then Robin Stone would have fallen on his ass with the *In Depth* show and there'd be a new president of News.

He looked at his watch. Holy God, ten o'clock. He signed his check and suddenly was aware that he was very drunk. He got into a cab and went home. So Ethel was waiting. So what? All he wanted to do was fall into bed. Let her wait. He didn't need to offer that cunt any explanations. She was a bum—and he was a big man!

SEVEN

ETHEL WAS WAITING. At ten thirty she called Dan. He answered after a few rings. "Who'sh this?"

"It's me, you drunken son of a bitch! I'm sitting at P.J.'s waiting for you!"

The receiver clicked in her ear. She stared at it for a moment, then slammed it down in fury. Christ! How had she ever allowed herself to get involved with him? Danton wasn't a movie star passing through on a one-night stand. And she didn't take any crap even from a movie star if he got out of line. She walked back to her table, paid her bill, and gave the place a final survey. She noticed everyone staring at a beautiful girl who had just entered the room, followed by two men. God, she was incredible-looking. They took the front table near the door. The girl looked familiar. Of course–she was on the cover of this month's *Vogue*. Ethel looked at the men. She had been so busy staring at the girl that she hadn't noticed them. One was Robin Stone, the other was Jerry Moss. She had met Jerry at a few agency parties.

She walked over to their table. "Hi, Jerry," she said with a smile.

He looked up and didn't rise. "Oh, hello there!" he said offhandedly.

She smiled at Robin. "I'm Ethel Evans. . . . We've met before. I'm with the publicity department of IBC."

Robin looked at her. He grinned slowly. "Sit down, Ethel, we can use another girl. This is Amanda."

Ethel smiled at her. The girl didn't return the smile. Her face was a mask but Ethel could feel the wave of resentment pour across the table. How can she be jealous of me? she thought. If I looked like that, I'd own the world.

Ethel took out a cigarette. Robin leaned across and lit it. She stared at him as the smoke curled toward his face. But he had switched his attention to his drink.

The silence at the table unnerved her. She felt Amanda's discontent, Jerry's uneasiness, and Robin's absorption with his drink.

"I just finished an assignment," Ethel said. Her voice sounded unnatural. She paused and almost whispered. "And then I stopped by to get a bite."

"No explanations," Robin said with the same easy grin. "You're here, relax." He caught the attention of the waiter. "What do you want, Ethel?"

She looked at his empty glass. She always made it a point to drink what the man drank. It started them off with at least one thing in common. "I'll have a beer," she said.

"Give the lady a beer," Robin said. "And bring me my glass of ice water."

The waiter brought the beer and a large glass of ice water. Robin took a long swallow. Amanda reached over and sipped it. She made a face and put it down vehemently. "Robin–" Her eyes were angry.

He grinned. "Don't you like ice water, baby?"

"That's straight vodka," she said.

Ethel felt a surge of excitement as she watched them curiously.

Robin took another long swallow. "So it is. I guess Mike made a mistake."

"You've got Mike trained," she said coldly. "Robin"–she leaned closer–"you said we'd be together tonight."

He threw his arm around her again. "We *are* together baby!"

"I mean . . ." Her voice was low and pleading. *"Together.* Not with Jerry and another girl. I don't consider that being with you."

He rumpled her hair. "I got Ethel for Jerry. Now we're a foursome."

Amanda's face remained impassive. "Robin, I have an early booking for a color layout tomorrow. I should have stayed home and washed my hair and gone to bed early. But I came out to be with you. And now you're drinking."

"Aren't you having a good time?" he asked.

"I'd be better off home. You don't need me just to sit here and watch you drink."

Robin stared at her for a moment. Then the slow grin appeared. He turned to Ethel. "What time do you have to be up in the morning?"

"I don't need any beauty sleep," Ethel answered, "it wouldn't help."

Robin grinned. "Jerry–we've just switched girls."

Amanda grabbed her bag and stood up. "Robin, I want to go home."

"Sure, baby."

"Well?" Her eyes were too misty to be angry.

"Sit down," he said gently. "I like it here. I want to stay awhile." Amanda sat down reluctantly, her eyes challenging, awaiting his next move.

Jerry Moss stirred uneasily. "Ethel, maybe you and I should cut out. There's a swinging party a friend of mine is giving, just a few blocks from here–"

"I want you both to stay." Robin spoke quietly but it was a command. Then he drained his glass of vodka and ordered another. He turned and looked at Amanda with a tender smile. "She is beautiful, isn't she? And she should have sleep. I'm a thoughtless son of a bitch. Really want to pack it in, baby?"

She nodded, as if not trusting her voice.

He leaned over and kissed her on the head. Then he turned to Jerry. "Put Amanda in a cab, Jerry, then come back. After all, we can't let New York's top model lose her sleep while we do some serious drinking."

Amanda got up and walked out of the room. Jerry followed her helplessly. Every man at the bar stared as she walked to the door. When she got outside she crumpled. "Jerry, what did I do wrong? I love him, I love him so much. What did I do wrong?"

"Nothing, honey. He's just turned off for this evening. When he turns off no one can get through to him. He'll forget it by tomorrow." He whistled and tried to flag a cab.

"Make him realize I love him, Jerry. Don't let that ugly cow move in. She's trying to–isn't she?"

"Honey, Ethel Evans is a one-night stand for everyone. Robin knows the score. Now get a good night's sleep."

A cab pulled up. He opened the door.

"Jerry, I'm going back there. I can't let him–"

He pushed her into the cab. "Amanda, you've only known Robin a few months. I've known him for years. No one ever tells him what he can or can't do. You want to know what you did wrong? And I'm only guessing, but you made noises like a wife. You told him not to drink. Don't crowd him, Amanda. This man needs space. He was always that way. Even at college. Now go home, get your sleep, I'm sure it will be all over by tomorrow."

"Jerry, call me when you leave him. No matter how late it is–how can I sleep when we've parted like this! Please, I've got to know, even if he tells you he's had it with me–or if he winds up with that girl . . ."

"He won't tell me anything. You should know that."

Jerry was suddenly aware that the taxi driver was enjoying the scene while his meter was clicking. He gave him Amanda's address.

She rolled down the window. "Call me, Jerry"–she reached out and grabbed his arm–*"please."*

He promised. Then he watched the cab disappear. He felt for Amanda. Robin hadn't been intentionally sadistic tonight. He had just turned off. Jerry had learned to recognize this trait in him. Maybe it was part of his charm. You could always count on Robin to do the unexpected. Like inviting Ethel Evans to join them.

"How about some hamburgers?" Jerry asked, as he returned to the table.

"You can afford to skip a meal," Robin said easily. "You missed gym twice last week."

"I live near here," Ethel said. "Why not come back to my place? I scramble crazy eggs." She looked at Jerry and added, "And I've got a very nice blond roommate. She might have a towel around her head but if we give her five minutes' warning, she can have the coffee going."

Robin stood up. "I'm not hungry. Jerry and I will walk you home. Then Jerry can walk me home." He picked up the bill and handed it to Jerry. "You sign it, junior. It's a write-off for you: entertaining a client."

Ethel lived at Fifty-seventh and First Avenue. She walked

quickly trying to keep up with Robin's long strides. "You live near here?" she asked.

"I live on the river," he answered.

"Maybe we're neighbors–"

"It's a long river," he said.

They walked silently the rest of the way. For once Ethel found it hard going. He had a way of answering that seemed to curtail any added conversation. They stopped in front of her building. "Are you sure you don't want a nightcap?" she asked. "I have some hundred-proof vodka."

"No. I'm packing it in for now."

"Well, I guess I'll see you. I'm sure you're going to be very happy at IBC, and if there's anything I can do–"

His smile was slow. "I'm happy everywhere, baby. See you around." Then he walked off with Jerry stumbling after him.

Ethel stared at them as they rounded the corner. She wanted Robin so bad she physically ached. Why couldn't she look like Amanda? Why did she have to always kid and come on strong to get a man? What did it feel like to have a man actually call you and want you and look at you as if you were the most desirable woman in the world? She walked down to the river and knew the tears were running down her face. Oh God, it wasn't fair! It wasn't fair to put the heart and emotions of a beautiful woman into the body of a peasant. Why hadn't her emotions been as commonplace as her body? Then she could have settled for Peter Cinocek, maybe even been happy with him.

"Oh, God"–she said it aloud–"I just want to be someone, to have a man who *is* someone care about me. Is that too much to ask?" Suddenly she felt an unbearable loneliness. All the dreams, the one-night stands–but she had *nothing!* Sure, a nice apartment, beautiful compared to Hamtramck, but just a three-room modern place, shared with another lonely girl who also went after one-night stands. Sure it was great to hold a star in your arms, but the next night he was gone.

She walked back to her building. She was positive that Robin Stone was in Amanda's arms by now. She pushed this thought from her mind. No use making herself more miserable. There would be another night.

When Robin and Jerry left Ethel, they walked a few blocks in silence. They passed a bar and Robin said, "Let's cut in here and grab one for the road."

Jerry followed silently.

"Where do you put it?" he asked.

Instead of the usual silent grin, Robin stared at the glass seriously. "Christ, I went so long without drinking, I've got a lot of making up to do. I came from a health-oriented family. My father never touched it."

Jerry laughed. "And I used to think you were a swinger at college."

Robin stared at him as if seeing him for the first time. "Were you around Harvard at the same time?"

"Class before you," Jerry said meekly. He was glad no one else was around. Everyone knew he and Robin had gone to school together and thought their friendship dated back to that time. That was one of the disturbing things about Robin. He always seemed attentive, but you never knew whether anything you said registered. Suddenly Jerry was angry at his own submissiveness. He turned to Robin with a rare show of spirit. "Where in hell did you think we met?"

Robin rubbed his chin thoughtfully. "I never thought about it, Jerr. I meet so many people. Seems I just looked up one day at the Lancer Bar and there you were." Robin signaled for the check. They walked out in silence. Jerry walked Robin to the large apartment house on the river. It suddenly occurred to him he had never been to Robin's apartment. Either he walked him home, or they met at a bar.

When Robin casually said, "Come on up for a nightcap," Jerry felt embarrassed. It was as if those clear blue eyes had read his thoughts.

"It's pretty late," he mumbled.

Robin's smile was almost a sneer. "Wife waiting to give you hell?"

"No. It's just that I have a long drive ahead, and I have an early appointment in the morning."

"Suit yourself," Robin said.

"All right. One fast beer," Jerry conceded. He followed Robin into the elevator. He would put in a good word for Amanda, he told himself.

It was an attractive apartment. Surprisingly neat and well furnished.

"A girl I knew—before Amanda," Robin said, as he waved his hand around the room.

"Why did you treat Amanda so badly tonight? She loves you. Don't you feel anything for her?"

"No."

Jerry stared. "Tell me, Robin—do you ever feel *anything?* Have any emotions?"

"Maybe I feel a lot of things, but I'm not able to show it." Robin smiled. "I guess life would be a lot easier for me if I could. I'm like an Indian. If I get sick, I just turn and face the wall and stay there until I get better."

Jerry stood up. "Robin, you don't need anyone. But for what it's worth, I'm your friend. I don't know why, but I am."

"Bullshit—you're with me because you want to be. You just said it yourself. I don't need anyone."

"Didn't you ever feel any obligations toward anyone?" Jerry knew he was probing, but he was helpless to stop.

"Yep. In the war. A guy saved my life and he didn't even know me. He was in another plane. Suddenly he pointed to my right. A Messerschmitt was coming at me. I dived and got away. Two minutes later he got hit. I owe him a hell of an obligation. I owe him my life. I tried to find out who he was, but seven of our planes were knocked out that day. I would have done anything for that guy—even marry his widow if she'd have me. But I never knew who he was."

"Then you'd feel the same way about a surgeon?"

"Nope. That's his job to save me. I'd be paying him. But this guy in the plane, he didn't know me. He didn't have to save my life."

Jerry was silent. "What kind of an obligation do you expect from a friend?"

Robin's smile was tight. "I don't know. I never had one."

Jerry started for the door. "Robin, I'm not going to give you my scout knife, or wait until you cross the street against signals and save your life. But I am your friend and I'll toss you some free advice. Don't write Amanda off as just another broad. I don't know her well, but there's something about her–I can't say what it is, but I sense it. She's quite a girl."

Robin put down his glass and came across the room. "Good God, I forgot about the bird." He went into the kitchen and switched on the light. Jerry followed him. There was a large ornate birdcage on the floor. And at the bottom a miserable little baby sparrow sat, staring at them.

"I forgot to feed Sam," Robin said, as he dug out some bread.

"That's a sparrow, isn't it?" Jerry asked.

Robin came over with a piece of bread, a cup of water and an eyedropper. He reached into the cage and gently took out the bird. It nestled in his hand with confidence. "The little jerk tried to fly too soon. It fell out of its nest and landed on my terrace and broke a wing or something. Amanda saw it happen. Naturally she rushed out and bought a cage, and I'm its new mother. She can't take it home: she's got a Siamese cat. The damn thing can walk up walls."

He held the little bird gently and it opened its beak expectantly. Robin broke off some bread crumbs and fed the bird. Jerry's amazement increased when Robin took the eyedropper and dropped some water down its little beak. Robin smiled sheepishly. "This is the only way it can drink." He placed it back in the cage and closed the door. It sat there and stared at Robin gratefully, its bright little eyes fastened on the tall man.

"O.K., Sam, it's nighttime now," Robin said. He switched off the light and walked back to the bar. "I don't think it's in pain," he said. "It eats like a son of a bitch–if something's in pain it doesn't eat, does it?"

"I'm not familiar with birds," Jerry answered. "But I do know that a wild bird can't live in captivity."

"Listen, as soon as the little jerk mends, I send him on his way. He's a smart little bird with a mind of his own. Did you notice how he closed his bill after he had some crumbs, and demanded water?"

Jerry was tired. It seemed incongruous that a man like Robin would be so gentle with a sparrow and so callous to a woman. "Why not call Amanda and tell her the bird is okay?" he suggested.

"She's probably been sleeping for two hours," Robin answered. "Her career comes first. Look—don't worry about Amanda. She's been around the turf, she knows the score."

Robin was pouring himself another drink when Jerry left. It was late, but he decided to walk to the garage. It would clear his head. On impulse he stopped at a drugstore and called Amanda.

"Jerry—I'm so glad you called. Oh, Jerry, he wound up with that cow, didn't he?"

"For your edification, we left that cow at her door maybe twenty minutes after you left."

"But it's so late—what have you been doing? Why didn't you at least call and tell me? I would have been able to sleep."

"Well, we walked, then we stopped at a bar, then we walked to his place, then we drank and talked. And then we fed the goddam bird. When I left him he was extolling its virtues—how brilliant it is: it knows when it wants water."

She laughed in relief. "Oh, Jerry. Shall I call him?"

"No. Amanda, play it cool. Give it time."

"I know. I'm doing my best. You do all the right things automatically when your heart isn't involved. You play it cool without even trying. It's different when you care. I've never cared before. I'm in love with him, Jerry."

"Don't let him know."

Her laugh was forced. "It's crazy, isn't it? To love someone, and have to hide it. You're a man, Jerry. Did your wife play it cool? Is that how she got you?"

He laughed. "Mary wasn't a top model and I'm not Robin Stone. And if I don't get home, I may not have a wife. Good night, honey."

EIGHT

THE FOLLOWING MORNING Robin awoke at seven. He felt good. No matter how much vodka he consumed, he had yet to experience his first hangover. He was properly grateful to whatever mysterious force in his metabolism created this phenomenon and decided to enjoy it while it lasted. He realized that one day he would wake up feeling like any other guy who drank too much. He went to the refrigerator and poured himself a large glass of orange juice. Then he got a crust of bread and lifted the cover off the birdcage. The sparrow was lying on its side, its eyes wide open, its body stiff with death. He picked it up and held it in the palm of his hand. Poor little fellow must have been busted up inside. "You never complained either, you little bastard," he said. "I like your style."

He threw on a pair of slacks and a sport shirt. Then he put the small body into a cellophane bag. He left the apartment and walked to the river. "A burial at sea, Sam. I can't offer you anything better than that." A battered gray barge was inching its way along. He tossed the little bag into the black water and watched it spin into the ripples created by the boat. "I'm sorry you didn't make it, fellow," he said. "But at least you have one true mourner, which is a lot more than most people can claim." He waited until the bag disappeared, then he walked back to the apartment.

He stood under a cold shower and when he turned off the water the phone was ringing. He quickly tied a towel around his waist and dripping water across the room, he grabbed the receiver.

"Did I wake you, Robin?" It was Amanda. "I have an early booking. I wanted to get you before I left."

He fished around for a cigarette.

"Robin—are you there?"

"Yep." He was searching the night table for matches. He found them on the floor.

"I'm sorry about last night."

"What about last night?"

"My walking out, but I just hated that girl and I guess I was tired and—"

"That was last night. Forget it."

"How about tonight?" she asked.

"Fine. Want to cook for me?"

"I'd love it," she said.

"Then it's a deal. Make it steak and that crazy salad."

"Robin, how's the bird?"

"It's dead."

"But it was alive last night!"

"It was?"

"Well—" She thought quickly. "I figure it had to be, or you would have told me.

"You're right. It kicked off sometime between two and five this morning. It was already stiff when I saw it."

"What did you do with it?"

"I tossed it in the river."

"You didn't!"

"What did you expect? Did you want it laid out at Campbell's?"

"No, but it sounds so callous. Oh, Robin, don't you ever feel anything?"

"Yep. Right now I feel wet."

"You know what you are? You're a cold son of a bitch." She said it as a statement of fact rather than in anger.

He laughed. She heard him drag on his cigarette.

There was a pause. "Robin—what do you want out of life?"

"Well, right now I want some eggs."

"You're impossible!" She laughed to break the mood. "Then you'll be here at seven. Steak and salad. Is there anything else you want?"

"You."

She laughed and some of her confidence returned. "Oh, Robin,

I forgot to tell you. Next week, I've been invited to the April in Paris Ball. They sent me two free tickets, and they cost a hundred dollars each. Will you take me?"

"Not on your life."

"But I *should* go . . ."

"Baby, I may not even be in town next week."

"Where are you going?"

"Maybe Miami, I want to start shaping up a team for the convention coverage with Andy Parino. He's with our O&O station down there."

"What's O&O?"

"Owned and operated. Each network is allowed to own and operate five stations. Want to come? Ever been to Miami?"

"Robin, I don't have vacations. I work all winter and summer."

"Which reminds me, I've got to work too. See you at dinner, baby. And for God's sake, keep that damn cat in the bathroom. He sat on my lap all through dinner last time."

She laughed. "He adores you. And, Robin–I love you." But he had already hung up.

Amanda grabbed a cab and headed for the Lancer Bar. That last job had run thirty-five minutes overtime. It meant a lot of money, but it also meant she didn't have time to go home and change. And she had wanted to wear the new pale blue raw silk. Robin was back from Miami and it was their last night together before he left for Los Angeles and the Democratic Convention.

Damn Nick Longworth! She had wanted to take ten days off and go to Los Angeles with Robin. It would have been so marvelous. Of course during the five days of convention she wouldn't see much of him. But after that he and Andy Parino were taking a few days off to play golf at Palm Springs. Robin's invitation had been casual, but he *had* invited her!

Nick had been adamant. She was getting to be one of the hottest models in town. In the fall he was going to raise her fee again. He had too many important bookings for her in July. When she had explained this to Robin, she had longed for him to say, "To hell with the bookings–I'm your future." But he had only said, "Sure, baby, I keep forgetting how much money there is in the rag business." And he had meant it.

But Nick was right. She had worked hard to get into this bracket. She needed the money and if she missed out on a few important jobs, it was more than just losing the money—it was giving another girl a chance to hit! She was on her way to the top.

She looked at her watch. She was ten minutes late and the cab was inching along. She sat back and lit a cigarette. No use worrying. Andy Parino was probably with Robin anyway. He had been with them every night since he arrived from Miami. She liked Andy. He was very attractive, actually he was probably better-looking than Robin. But she accepted his looks with the same apathy she felt toward the handsome male models she occasionally posed with. Beautiful, but so what? Yet just thinking about Robin made her feel light-headed. She wanted to get out of the creeping cab and run. But it was hot and humid outside and her hair would be ruined.

Their last night together. No, she mustn't even think that way. He'd only be gone ten days. But ever since he'd become president of News he was always going off somewhere. He had been to Europe twice. She wondered if Andy would stick with them all evening. The last three nights they had met at the Lancer Bar, then gone to the Italian place and she didn't have Robin alone until midnight. And the last three nights he had done an awful lot of drinking. Yet no matter how much he drank, it never seemed to affect his lovemaking. But she liked it better when he was sober—then she knew it was the man whispering the endearments, not the vodka.

The dim light of the bar made her blink. "Over here, baby!" She heard Robin's voice and headed toward the booth in the back of the room. Both men stood up. Andy smiled in his open friendly way. But Robin's grin and the fleeting second when their eyes met and held obliterated Andy, the bar, the noise—even her heartbeat seemed suspended in that one wonderful moment of intimacy no one else could share. Then she was sitting beside him, and he was back to talking politics with Andy. And the room and noise came into focus. She watched him as he talked. She wanted to touch him but she sat back, her face composed in the "Nick Longworth Look": slight smile–no movement of features–no lines.

The waiter placed a martini in front of her.

"I ordered it," Robin said, "I'm sure you can use it. It must be hell to stand under lights on a day like this."

She didn't like the taste of alcohol. In the old days (before Robin) she would order a Coke and blandly say, "I don't drink." But somehow her instincts had warned her that Robin would never stay with a girl who didn't drink. Most of the time she toyed with a drink. Sometimes she poured half of it into his glass. But today the martini felt cold and smooth. Maybe she was finally developing a taste for them.

Robin and Andy went back to the subject of the coming nomination. As the conversation continued, he unconsciously reached out and held her hand, which was his way of including her in a discussion that was over her head.

"Eleanor Roosevelt is coming as a last-ditch effort to help Stevenson, but he hasn't a chance," Robin commented. "It's a shame, he's a great man."

"Don't you like Kennedy?" Amanda asked. Actually she didn't care one way or another, but she felt she had to show some interest.

"I've met him. He has great magnetism. I intend to vote for him. I'm just saying it's too bad Stevenson is going to lose. It's very rare to have two good men on the scene at the same time. It happened with Willkie, but he was running against Roosevelt. Who knows what might have happened if Willkie had been born ten years later?"

Then they fell to discussing the Vice-presidential nominee. She heard the names, Symington, Humphrey, Meyner. . . . She sipped her drink and watched Robin's profile.

They went to the Italian place at nine. And when dinner was over and Andy suggested going to P.J.'s for a nightcap, to Amanda's delight Robin shook his head: "I'll have ten days of you, junior. This is my last night with my girl."

He was unusually tender that night. He ran his hand through her light hair and looked at her gently. "My lovely Amanda, you're so clean and sleek and beautiful." He held her close and stroked her neck. And he made love to her until they both broke away exhausted and fulfilled. Then he leaped up and pulled her out of bed. "Let's take a shower together."

They stood under the warm water. She didn't worry that her hair was soaked, that she had a job at ten in the morning. She hugged his wet body because now, this moment, was all that mattered. And when he reached out and turned on the cold water, she shrieked, but he laughed and held her close. After a moment her body grew used to it and it was wonderful. He kissed her with the water pouring on their faces. Then they got out of the shower and he grabbed a towel and wrapped it around them. She stood and stared into his eyes. "I love you, Robin."

He leaned across and kissed her. Then he kissed her neck, and her small flat breasts. He looked up. "I love your body, Amanda. It's clean and strong and wonderful."

He carried her back to the bedroom and made love to her again. Then they both fell asleep locked in an embrace.

Amanda awoke because Robin was lying on her arm. It was dark and her arm was numb. She eased it from under him. He moved slightly but did not wake. She saw the bright eyes of the Siamese cat glowing in the dark. Dear Lord, he had managed to push open the door. He inched forward and sprang on the bed. She held him quietly and nuzzled him. He purred in contentment. "I've got to put you back in the living room, Slugs," she whispered. "Robin doesn't like to wake up and find you around his neck."

She slipped out of bed carrying the cat. Robin stirred and his hand hit her empty pillow. "Don't leave me!" he shouted. "Please –don't leave me!"

She dropped the startled cat and rushed to his side. "I'm here, Robin." She held him in her arms. He was shaking, staring into the darkness.

"Robin"–her fingers touched the cold dampness of his brow– "I'm here. I love you."

He shook his head like a man coming out of water. Then he

looked at her and blinked as if he had just awakened. He grinned and pulled her to him. "What happened?"

She stared at him.

"I mean what in the hell are we doing sitting up like this in the middle of the night?"

"I was just putting the cat out and I was thirsty and then you yelled."

"I yelled?"

"You said, 'Don't leave me!' "

For a brief moment there was something close to fear in his eyes. Suddenly he smiled. "Well, don't go sneaking off again."

She clung to him. It was the first time she had ever seen him vulnerable. "I'll never leave you, Robin, never. I love you."

He held her away and laughed. He was in complete command again. "Leave me any time you want, baby. But not in the middle of the night."

She looked at him oddly. "But why?"

He stared into the darkness. "I don't know. I really don't know." Then he flashed his easy grin. "But you put an idea into my head. I'm thirsty too." He slapped her on the buttocks. "Come on, let's go into the kitchen and have a beer."

They drank the beer and he made love to her again.

The seasons melted into one another for Amanda. The early spring had brought Robin into her life. By summer their relationship had turned into a permanent blaze of excitement. He had been to Los Angeles and Chicago for the conventions. And each time he returned, she seemed to want him more than ever. Her love for Robin refused to find a level. It soared on and on to a peak of feverish infinity. And she was frightened of it because she knew Robin could not even begin to feel this kind of emotion. And the acclaim he received for his convention coverage did not add to her inner security. His new stature merely loomed as a threat—anything that took him away from her was a threat. If she ever lost him, she wouldn't want to go on. She fervently wished he was back doing local news.

In October they sat in his apartment and watched his first *In*

Depth show together. Gregory Austin called to congratulate him. Andy Parino called from Miami to congratulate him. Andy had just met a young divorcee and was in love!

Robin laughed. "Sure, it figures. With all the girls in Miami, a nice Catholic boy like you has to fall for a divorcee."

"Maggie Stewart is different!" Andy had insisted. Of course, he admitted, his religion did create a few barriers, but it seemed that the main obstacle was the lady herself. She didn't want to get married. Andy had hired her to do a five-minute spot on their local news, and as he put it, at least they worked together.

Amanda listened quietly. Perhaps it was then that the first vague pattern of her plan began to form. It crystallized into action a few nights later when she giggled at the deadpan delivery of a girl doing a commercial on *The Late Show*.

"Don't knock it," Robin said. "It's not easy to be natural when the red eye of the camera is on you."

"What do you think I do?" she asked.

He pulled her to him and said, "You, my lovely one, pose for one shot fifty times until they finally catch you looking like the angel that you are. And if that doesn't work, there's always the airbrush and retouching."

Amanda thought about it. If she did a good commercial on television, perhaps Robin would really respect her. She talked to Nick Longworth about it. He laughed. "Dear girl, it's a brilliant idea. Except: one, you can't talk. That's a talent in itself. Two, you can't be one of many girls in a party scene. We only use neophyte models in that area. I have three booked for a beer commercial. The only thing you could do would be a big glamour product, and those kinds of commercials don't just drop in your lap. Usually they go after a Hollywood-type spokeswoman–one who can be glamorous and also sell the product."

On Christmas Eve they trimmed a tree in her apartment. Robin gave her a wristwatch. It was very tiny and very beautiful but without a hint of a diamond on it. She masked her disappointment. She had given him a cigarette case, a slim gold envelope with a facsimile of his handwriting. Jerry dropped by for a pre-Christmas drink before he hurried home to Greenwich. He brought champagne and a rubber squeak toy for Slugger.

That night as they were going to bed, Slugger leaped on the bed with his new toy. Amanda moved to collect the cat and put him in the living room. "Let him stay, it's Christmas Eve," Robin said. Then he added, "Oh, I forgot something." He went to his jacket which was sprawled on a chair and took out a flat box. "Merry Christmas, Slugger." He tossed the box on the bed. Amanda opened it. Tears came to her eyes as she looked at the soft black leather collar. It had silver bells and a little silver tag with his name engraved on it.

She threw her arms around Robin and hugged him. "You *do* like Slugger–"

He laughed. "Sure I do. I just don't like him sneaking up on me. This way those goddam bells will warn me of his approach." Then he took her in his arms and kissed her and they didn't even hear the silver bells as Slugger disdainfully leaped off the bed and left the room.

NINE

IN JANUARY, the February replacements were announced in the television column of *The New York Times.* Dan smiled complacently when he saw that *The Christie Lane Show* was the lead story. He had sweated out the summer and literally wrung a good pilot out of Christie. And when Gregory viewed it and gave him the green light, Dan threw away the tranquilizers.

Tonight he would really celebrate. Unconsciously his thoughts went to Ethel. Maybe it had been a mistake assigning her to *The Christie Lane Show*. But hell, he had to pay her off some way. There was no one, but no one, who could compete with that dame in the feathers. She had flipped at the assignment. He knew it wasn't just the extra twenty-five bucks, the big attraction was the Hollywood guest star she would meet each week. Well, she was a good-natured nympho—and he sure as hell couldn't hump her more than twice a week. So if she wanted to slip in a Hollywood name on her free time, well, that was the least he could do for the bitch. And this way, maybe she'd lay off the "Take me to '21' " bit. Oddly enough, Ethel had no amorous inclinations toward Christie Lane. She said he gave her the creeps. "His skin is so pasty white, reminds me of a chicken's belly." From then on she referred to Christie behind his back as C.B.

Dan leaned back in his chair and his smile radiated contentment. All he had to do was wait until February. Then he'd bring in a big winner. He already had Alwayso as a sponsor. To go along with Christie as "Mr. Average Man," Dan had lined up a plain-looking girl singer, a homespun announcer, and each week a big-name guest star would add some glamour. He had hired

Artie Rylander, a top producer who had made his name in the fifties, doing live variety shows. Alwayso was going along, and doing their commercials "live." Once again, Dan reveled in his luck. A beautiful girl doing the commercials was the perfect contrast to the homey family format of *The Christie Lane Show*.

Right now Jerry's office was probably loaded with every beautiful model in town. Jerry intended to use a male "voice over," and have the model demonstrate the product. But as Jerry had said, they had to settle on one girl and stick with her. It was quite a problem.

Dan smiled. For months he had been closeted with Christie Lane, the "gofors," Sig and Howie, and Artie Rylander. And Jerry had an office stacked with beautiful models. He shook his head. He should have such problems.

But Jerry did have a problem. Amanda. Amanda with her cool Nordic features, her high cheekbones, the heavy blond hair, was perfect for the product; she had also done the Alwayso magazine layouts last year. Jerry wanted her for the show–but how would Robin take it if he hired her?

Would he say, "What the hell are you doing? Trying to suck up to me?" or, "That was damn nice of you Jerry. I sure appreciate it."

Suddenly he hated himself. Dammit, the issue should be who was best for the job and not how Robin would feel! He sat and stared at the picture on his desk of Mary and the kids. Was he abnormal in his feelings about Robin? That was ridiculous! He had no sexual desire for Robin Stone! He just liked him, liked to be with him. But *why* did he like to be with him? Sometimes Robin treated him with the same offhand conviviality he tossed at Carmen, the bartender at the Lancer Bar. Then there were days when Robin hardly spoke to Jerry at all. Or then again, Robin could be gregarious, almost glad to see him: "Your drink is waiting, Jerr." Yet secretly, he had the suspicion that if he suddenly stopped calling Robin, stopped dropping in at the Lancer Bar at five, he would never be missed.

He pressed the buzzer and told his secretary to send Amanda

in. A few seconds later she strolled through the door. God, she even walked like her damn cat. She was wearing a leopard coat, her blond hair streaming to her shoulders. Leopard! She also had a mink. All his wife had was an otter.

She sat down in the chair across from him, undaunted by the daylight that shot at her face. He had noticed that some of the older models always cautiously turned away from it. But Amanda's face was flawless and she knew it.

"You really want the job?" Jerry asked.

"Very much."

He stared at her. Jesus, she was even getting to talk like Robin. Short and to the point.

He saw her steal a glance at her watch. Sure, her time was valuable. Then he noticed the watch. Holy Christ–it was the Vacheron job, the tiniest watch he had ever seen. Mary had admired it in the window at Cartier's. But it cost over two thousand with the tax.

"That's a beautiful watch," he said.

She smiled. "Thank you. . . . Robin gave it to me for Christmas."

He was silent. He had sent Robin a case of a hundred-proof vodka. Robin hadn't even sent him a Christmas card.

Suddenly she leaned across the desk. Her eyes were urgent. "I want this job, Jerry. I want Robin to be proud of me." She gave him an imploring look. "Oh, Jerry, I love him. I can't live without him. You're his best friend. What do you think my chances are with Robin? It's been almost a year that we've been going together. And sometimes I think I'm no closer to him now than the first day we met. He's so unpredictable–what do you think, Jerry? Men confide in one another."

His entire mood changed. Suddenly he felt an odd sense of empathy with her. God, it must be hell for a girl to be in love with a man like Robin. He was glad he was a man. Glad he was just a friend to Robin.

"Jerry, I want to marry him," she said. "I want to have his children." Her face went tense. "You know what I've done with my evenings during the weeks he's away? I've taken a reading course at the New School. I've finished *Pickwick Papers,* and I've started on Chaucer. And when I tried to discuss them with Robin, he laughed and said he had no desire to be Professor Higgins. But I'll keep at it. Oh, Jerry–sometimes I wish I didn't love him this much. Even after he's spent the night with me, when he leaves the following morning, I snuggle against the towel he's used. Sometimes I fold it up and put it in my tote bag and carry it with me all day. And I reach for that towel and touch it. And it almost smells of him . . . and I get weak. I know it sounds silly, but I do this even when I know I'm going to meet him at the Lancer Bar that very day. And each time I walk in there I die because I think maybe he won't be there, yet he always is. And sometimes when I sit with him and he grins at me, I think, Oh God, can I just hold this moment, make it last forever. And that scares me because it means maybe I expect to lose him someday." She put her hands over her eyes as if to block out the thought.

Jerry felt his own eyes become moist in sympathy. "You won't lose him, Amanda, you're doing fine. You've held him almost a year. That's a record in itself." Then he handed her a contract. "I think you'll be just wonderful for our product. And it's our pleasure to have you on the show."

Tears threatened to spill down her face. She reached for the pen and quickly scratched her name on the contract. When she held out her hand she was once more in complete control.

He watched her as she left the office. Who would ever dream that this supergirl, this perfect creature, was going through a torturous love affair? It must be torture, loving Robin Stone. Because any woman would know she never really had him and sense that one day she must lose him. He knew the Amandas would come and go, while he would always be able to join Robin Stone at the Lancer Bar.

Two weeks later Jerry paid his first visit to a psychiatrist. He had been making love to Mary with startling infrequency. When she first brought it up, she had tried to make light of it: "Hey, you with your work and your golf on weekends–have you forgotten the woman you love?"

He had looked properly startled. As if it had been an oversight.

"Not once all summer," she said good-naturedly. "And now it's the middle of September. Do I have to wait until it's too cold for golf?"

He had made excuses, mumbling about how hectic the start of a new season always was. September was pressure time.

In November he blamed it on commuting. The weather was too hazardous to drive, and it was rough taking the train each morning, rushing for the train home. No, it wasn't because he was at the Lancer Bar with Robin Stone. He *worked* late!

During the Christmas season he had more excuses. Everything was hectic. In January he had Alwayso to contend with. The commercials had to be written, the product selected for the first commercial–hair spray, or the new iridescent nail polish? If these excuses appeased Mary, they did not satisfy the nagging doubt that was beginning to form in his own mind. Well, he *was* tired, the weather *was* lousy, and he had a cold that hung on. There were even times he blamed Mary's fat pink hair rollers. How was a guy supposed to be filled with desire when his wife slid into bed with fat pink rollers and a face loaded with night cream! To avoid arguments he kept silent. The atmosphere began to feel like a pressure cooker. And one night it exploded.

It happened on a Tuesday, a week after he had hired Amanda. He had spent the day checking the commercial copy. Everything went according to schedule. He had felt good. It had been one of those rare days, a day that had passed without any crisis. Even the weather was clear. He had taken the five-ten train and when he walked up the path to his house he suddenly felt a sense of well-being. It had snowed the day before. In New York it was already mashed into small banks of dull gray slush. But in Greenwich it looked like a Christmas card, clean and untouched. The lights that glowed in the windows beckoned warmth and hospitality. He entered and felt enveloped with contentment. The kids had yelled "Daddy! Daddy!" with pealing enthusiasm. He had played with them, enjoyed them, and felt relief when the maid took them off to bed. He had mixed martinis and had Mary's waiting when she came into the living room. He complimented her on her hair. She accepted the drink without smiling. "It's the same way I've been wearing it for a year." He refused to allow her lack of enthusiasm to penetrate his sense of tranquillity. "Well, it looks particularly good tonight," he said, as he raised his glass.

She stared at him suspiciously. "You're home on time. What happened? Did Robin Stone stand you up today?"

He was so angry he choked on his martini. Mary accused him of being flustered and he stormed out of the room. A tight knot of guilt began to form in his throat. Robin *had* stood him up. Well, not exactly, but when Amanda was in his office, she had begged off at four thirty, claiming she had a five o'clock modeling session. Secretly he had been pleased: Robin would be alone at the Lancer Bar. He called Robin the moment she left the office. "Lancer Bar at five?" he had asked.

Robin had laughed. "For Christ's sake, Jerry, it's my first day back in town. Amanda is cooking for me. I'm skipping the bar today, see you tomorrow."

His face had burned with anger. But after a few minutes he cooled off. Big deal! So he'd see Robin tomorrow. And it was high time he surprised Mary for once and got home early.

Of course he had made up with Mary. She had come up to the bedroom waving a fresh martini as an overture of truce. That night Mary didn't cream her face or use the fat pink rollers, but when they went to bed together he couldn't get it up. This had never happened before! Sporadic as their sex life had been during the past year, the few times they had been together, it had always been fully consummated. She had turned away from him and he knew she was crying. He buried his own fears and apologized to Mary–blamed it on himself, on the martinis, on the pressures of the new Christie Lane Show. Then he even went for a checkup and asked for a B-12 shot. Dr. Anderson said he didn't need B-12. When he finally stammered his real problem, Dr. Anderson recommended Dr. Archie Gold.

He stormed out of the office. He didn't need a psychiatrist! God–if Robin ever dreamed he even considered such a thing he'd–well, he sure as hell wouldn't waste time on him. Robin would look at him in disgust, he'd be a weakling.

He didn't care what Dr. Anderson said. He didn't care how many healthy normal men went to psychiatrists when they stumbled on some kind of "block." He would never go to a shrink!

But it was Mary who broke down his resistance. She greeted him with a smile each night. She never wore the pink rollers anymore. He noticed she had new eye makeup. She took to snuggling against him in bed, and twice he had tried—but it hadn't worked. Now he was afraid to try. Each night he pretended to be exhausted. The moment he hit the bed he'd fake the even breathing of a man who has fallen asleep. Then he would lie awake and stare into the darkness as Mary crept into the bathroom and removed her diaphragm. He could hear her muffled sobs.

Dr. Archie Gold was surprisingly young. Subconsciously he had expected a guy with thick glasses, a beard, and a German accent. But Dr. Gold was clean-shaven and nice-looking in a subdued way. He accomplished very little in the first session. Jerry had come right to the point: "I can't make it with my wife in bed, yet I love her and there is no other girl. Now, where do we go from there?" Before he knew it the fifty minutes were over. He was stunned when Dr. Gold suggested three visits a week. Jerry had been positive that whatever was bugging him could be straightened out in an hour. It was ridiculous! But he thought of Mary—the muffled sobs in the bathroom. . . . O.K. Mondays, Wednesdays, Fridays.

On his third visit, he did the entire session on Robin Stone. Gradually Amanda crept into the sessions.

At the end of two weeks he felt better. After some intensive Freudian soul-searching and probing back to his childhood, he had come to some disturbing revelations. He had personality problems but he was not a fag! At least that subconscious gnawing doubt had been removed. They discussed his father, an enormous virile-looking man who had ignored him during his childhood. Then he suddenly began going with him to the football games, and his father had cheered for Robin Stone until he was hoarse. "Now, that boy's magnificent!" his father would shout. "That's what I call a man!" He recalled one specific incident when Robin had whipped through an impossible wall of players to score a touchdown. His father had leaped to his feet. "What a boy—that's it, son!"

Through Dr. Gold's gentle probings he recalled other fragments of ego-damaging evidence. When it was finally conceded that Jerry was not going to grow any taller than five feet nine, his father had snorted, "How could I have spawned such a shrimp? I'm six foot one. Christ, you take after your mother's family. The Baldwins are all puny."

O.K. At least he understood some things now. In trying to gain Robin's friendship, he was still seeking his father's approval. He was jubilant with this discovery. "I'm right in my diagnosis, aren't I?" he asked Dr. Gold. The cool gray eyes merely smiled. "You must answer your own questions" was the reply.

"What the hell do I pay you for if you don't give me the answers?" Jerry demanded.

"I'm not supposed to give answers," Dr. Gold said quietly. "I'm here to prod you into working things out and coming up with your own answers."

The week before the show opened he stepped up his visits to daily sessions. He gave up his lunch hour. Dr. Gold preferred to see him between five and six, but Jerry refused to give up the Lancer Bar. He insisted it was his only way of escaping tension—sitting with Robin, having a few drinks. But when he missed the train, he was torn with guilt for Mary and the dinner that was ruined.

On such occasions Jerry would be abrasive with Dr. Gold, demanding to know why he suffered such guilt. Why did he *have* to go to the Lancer Bar each day and sit with Robin, knowing he would suffer guilt toward Mary?

"I can't go on like this—wanting to please Mary, wanting to please myself. Why can't I be like Robin? Have no conscience, be free."

"From what you say about Robin Stone, I'd hardly say he was free."

"At least he's his own man. Even Amanda feels she has no real hold on him."

Then Jerry told Dr. Gold Amanda's searing confession about carrying Robin's towel; Dr. Gold lost his usually bland expression and shook his head. "She really needs help."

"Oh come on! She's just a highly sentimental girl in love!"

Dr. Gold frowned. "That's not love, that's an addiction.

If a girl seemingly has all the attributes you give her, her relationship with Robin Stone should give her a sense of fulfillment. Not this kind of fantasizing. If he ever turned her against him . . ." Dr. Gold shook his head.

"You can't just sum up people this way. You don't know them!"

"When will Robin Stone be back?" Dr. Gold asked.

"Tomorrow. Why?"

"Suppose I meet you at your Lancer Bar. Then you can introduce me to Robin and Amanda."

Jerry stared at the ceiling. "But how would I explain you? I can't very well say, 'Hey, Robin, my shrink wants to case you.' "

Dr. Gold laughed. "It's conceivable we could be friends. We *are* about the same age."

"Could I say you're just a doctor, not a shrink?"

"Some of my best friends are people," Dr. Gold answered. "Couldn't you have one friend who is a psychiatrist?"

Jerry was nervous when he saw Dr. Gold walk into the Lancer Bar. Robin was on his third martini and today of all days Amanda was working and meeting Robin later at the Italian place for dinner.

"Oh, I forgot to tell you," Jerry said as Dr. Gold approached. "An old school buddy of mine is dropping by."

Jerry threw his arm around the doctor. "Archie"–the unfamiliar name almost stuck in his throat–"this is Robin Stone. Robin, Dr. Archie Gold."

Robin looked at the man with little interest. Robin was in one of his silent moods. He concentrated on his drink. Dr. Gold wasn't exactly loquacious either. His cool gray eyes calmly appraised Robin. Jerry began to babble nervously. Someone had to talk!

At one point Robin leaned across and said, "Are you a surgeon, Archie?"

"In a way," Dr. Gold answered.

"He cuts out ids." Jerry tried to make his voice light. "Would you believe it, Robin–Archie's a shrink. We ran into one another at a party and renewed old acquaintance and he told me–"

"Freudian?" Robin cut in, ignoring Jerry.

Dr. Gold nodded.

"Are you a psychiatrist or a psychoanalyst?"

"Both."

"You went through a hell of a long training–then you had to go through two years of personal analysis yourself, didn't you?"

Dr. Gold nodded.

"You're a good man," Robin said. "It must have taken a lot of guts to go through school with a moniker like Archibald. You must be very secure."

Dr. Gold laughed. "Insecure enough to shorten it to Archie."

"Were you always interested in this gaff?" Robin asked.

"Originally I wanted to be a neurosurgeon. But a neurologist often comes face to face with incurable illnesses. He can only prescribe medicine to ease the symptoms. But with analysis"–Dr. Gold's eyes suddenly became expressive–"he *can* cure the ill. The most gratifying thing in the world is to see a patient recover and begin to function, take his place in society and use his full potential. In analysis, there is always hope for a better tomorrow."

Robin grinned. "I know your bag, Doctor."

"My bag?"

Robin nodded. "You like people." He slapped a bill on the bar. "Hey, Carmen." The bartender came to him immediately. "This takes care of my tab. Give my friends another round and keep the rest for yourself." Then he held out his hand to Dr. Gold. "Sorry I have to shove off, but I have a date with my girl." He walked out of the bar.

Jerry stared after him. The bartender placed fresh drinks before them. "Compliments of Mr. Stone. Quite a guy, isn't he!"

Jerry turned to Dr. Gold. "Well?"

Dr. Gold smiled. "Like the bartender said, he's quite a guy."

Jerry couldn't conceal his pride. "What did I tell you? He got to you too, huh?"

"Of course. I wanted him to. I was more than receptive."

"You think he has any hangups–or bags?"

"I can't tell. On the surface, he's in complete control, and he seems to genuinely care for Amanda."

"How did you get that? He never even talked about her."

"When he left he said, 'I have a date with *my* girl'—possessive. He didn't say, 'I have a date with a girl,' which would be negating her importance, making her one of many."

"Do you think he likes me?" Jerry asked.

"No."

"No?" Jerry's voice held panic. "You mean he dislikes me?"

Dr. Gold shook his head. "He doesn't know you exist."

The control room was crowded. Jerry found a seat in the corner. In fifteen minutes *The Christie Lane Show* would go on the air—live! The entire day had been bedlam. Even Amanda had caught some of the tension. At the last rehearsal she had held the hairspray in the wrong hand and hidden the Alwayso label.

Christie Lane and his "gofors" seemed to be the only people unaffected with pre-show hysteria. They joked together, Christie mugged for the crew, the "gofors" went for sandwiches. They actually seemed to be enjoying the frenetic rehearsals.

The audience had already filed in. Amanda had said Robin was going to watch the show at home. Funny, Robin had never said a word, one way or another, about Amanda doing the commercial. Several times he had been tempted to ask her about Robin's reaction, but he couldn't without losing face.

Danton Miller entered, impeccable as ever in a black suit. Harvey Phillips, the agency director, rushed in. "Everything is shipshape, Mr. Moss. Amanda is upstairs having her makeup retouched. I told her to stick with the blue dress for the hair spray, and change to the green for the lipstick."

Jerry nodded. There was nothing to do but wait.

Dan told the director to click on the audio switch. The announcer had come onstage to do the usual corny warm-up. "Anyone here from New Jersey?" he asked. Several hands went up. "Well, the bus is waiting outside." The audience laughed good-naturedly. Jerry looked at his watch. Five minutes to air time.

Jerry suddenly began to wonder if the show would make it. It would be hard to tell even with the audience reaction. A studio audience loved every show. Why not—it was free. Tomorrow the reviews would come out, but reviews didn't matter in television.

Nothing mattered but those damn numbers. They'd have to sweat it out for two weeks. Of course he would get an overnight rating, but it was the second week that counted.

Three minutes to air time. The door opened and Ethel Evans slipped in. Dan nodded coolly. Sig was the only one who stood up and offered her his seat, but Ethel waved it off. "I've got a photographer with me. Right now he's taking some candids of Christie so I can service them to the papers." She turned to Jerry. "After the show I'll have him take some shots with Amanda and Christie." She flounced out of the booth and headed backstage.

One minute to air time.

Suddenly there was complete silence in the control room. Artie Rylander was standing, holding a stopwatch. He threw his hand down, the orchestra went into a theme, the announcer shouted, *"The Christie Lane Show!"* The show was on.

Jerry decided to go backstage. There was nothing he could do by remaining in the booth. His place was with Amanda, in case she developed any last-minute jitters.

She was sitting in a small dressing room fidgeting with her hair. Her cool smile gave him renewed confidence. "Don't worry, Jerry, I'll hold the hairspray so you can see the label. Sit down and relax, you look like a nervous mother."

"I'm not worried about you, honey. It's the whole show. Don't forget–*I'm* the one who made the recommendation to the sponsor. Did you watch any of the rehearsals?"

She wrinkled her nose. "For about ten minutes–until Christie Lane started making idiotic mating calls." She shuddered. Then seeing his face, she added, "But don't go by me. As a man he's repulsive, but the audience will probably love him."

The door opened and Ethel barged in. Amanda looked at her. It was obvious she didn't place her. Ethel's glance covered the room. She seemed surprised at finding just Amanda and Jerry. Then she quickly smiled and held out her hand. "Good luck, Amanda."

Amanda's expression was polite but curious. She knew she had seen the girl somewhere.

"I'm Ethel Evans–we met at P.J.'s last year. I met you with Jerry and Robin Stone."

"Oh yes." Amanda turned away and began spraying her hair.

Ethel sat on the edge of the dressing table, her large hips crowding Amanda. "It seems we're destined to be thrown together."

Amanda backed away, and Jerry tapped Ethel's shoulder. "Off, Ethel–you're blocking Amanda's light. Besides, this is not exactly the moment to renew old friendships."

Ethel's smile was friendly as she got off the makeup table. "You'll be great, Amanda. They'll go hoarse whistling when you come on." She took off her coat and, without asking, hung it on the wall. "I've got to park this somewhere. Listen, I came by for two reasons: one, to wish you luck; two, I'd like you to take some pictures with Christie Lane after the show."

Amanda looked at Jerry who nodded slightly. Then she said, "All right, but it won't take long, will it?"

"Just three or four pops of the bulbs." Ethel started for the door. "I'll sit out front and watch the show. And look, Amanda, you've got to be a sensation. God, if I had your looks I'd own the world!"

Amanda felt herself thawing. There was an urgent honesty in Ethel's voice and she saw envy in her eyes. She said, "My aunt always taught me it takes more than looks to bring happiness."

"So did my mother," Ethel answered. "But that's a lot of shit. I've got an IQ of one thirty-six, and I'd trade it in for half a brain and a pretty face. And I'll bet anything that your fellow with *his* big brain would agree. By the way, is he coming to catch the show?"

"Robin, come *here?*" The idea of Robin sitting in a studio audience was so preposterous that Amanda laughed. "No, he's watching at home."

Amanda's cool detachment vanished the moment Ethel left the room. She reached out and grabbed Jerry's hand. "Oh, I hope he'll be proud of me. Has he said anything?"

"What has he said to you?" Jerry asked.

"He just laughed and said if I wanted to get into this rat race, it was my headache." Her eyes went to the large clock on the wall. "I'd better go down, the show's been on for ten minutes."

"You've got five minutes, maybe more."

"I know, but I want to phone Robin and remind him to watch.

You know him—he might have made himself a few martinis, stretched out and fallen asleep."

The only phone in the theater was near the stage door. Jerry fidgeted as she stood and dialed in the drafty hall. The music was blasting, the applause was strong, the show seemed to be going well. Amanda hung up as the dime fell into the coin-return box. "It's busy, Jerry. And I go on in a few minutes."

"Get going now, you've got to cross behind the curtain to your set."

"Wait—I'll try him once again."

"Beat it," he said almost gruffly. "You've got to be in place when the camera swings to you. Go check your props. I'll call him for you."

He waited until she disappeared behind the backdrop and appeared on the small set designed for Alwayso. Then he dialed Robin's number. The droning busy signal continued. He kept dialing until the actual moment of the commercial. "Damn Robin," he swore to himself. "He knows the girl is going on, why does he have to do this?"

He walked to the wings in time to give Amanda a smile of assurance. Her face lit up and he knew she interpreted it as a signal that he had reached Robin. She was poised and at ease when the camera came to her.

He watched her on the monitor. She photographed like an angel. No wonder she made so much money. She was breathless from nerves when it was over. "Was I all right?"

"Better than all right. Just great. Now you can relax for five minutes—then change, do the lipstick spot, and you're home."

"What did Robin say?"

"I didn't get him. The line was still busy."

Her eyes brightened ominously.

He grabbed her by the shoulder and steered her to the staircase. "Go up and change. And don't you dare cry and ruin your makeup."

"But, Jerry—"

"But what? He's home, at least you know that. And he was probably watching while he was on the goddam phone. It might have been an emergency, even an overseas call. War could be declared for all we know. Maybe an atom bomb dropped somewhere. Believe it or not, *The Christie Lane Show* is not the biggest happening in the universe. We only *act* as if we're discovering a cure for cancer in here."

Christie Lane ambled over. Bob Dixon was on stage doing his medley. "Didja hear that applause! And all for me! I'm the greatest!" He put his hand on Amanda's arm. "And you're the beautifulest. If you play your cards right, Uncle Christie just might take you out for a sandwich after the show."

"Take it easy," Jerry said, easing Christie's hand off Amanda's arm. "You haven't put Berle or Gleason out of business yet. And what's with the uncle bit?"

"Haven't you heard what Dan-the-man has been saying all these months? I'm the family image. I remind everyone of their uncle or husband." He turned his watery blue eyes on Amanda. "Doll, do I remind you of any relative? I hope not, because it would be incest with the thoughts I'm thinking." Before Amanda could answer, he said, "Well, the movie star has finished his off key number. Now watch the *real* pro go out and kill them." Then he dashed onstage. Amanda stood very still, as if she couldn't believe what had occurred. Then she turned and started for the phone.

Jerry stopped her. "Oh no, you don't. You've got exactly six minutes to change your dress and touch up your makeup. *After* the show, you can call him. And I'll bet you a late supper at '21' that he's watched you. As a matter of fact, I'll take you both there to celebrate."

"No, Jerry–I want to be alone with him tonight. I'll bring him some hamburgers." She looked toward the stage at Christie Lane and shrugged. "Maybe I'm crazy, but they do seem to like him." Then she ran up the stairs to her dressing room.

Amanda did the second commercial with equal ease. When the show ended, the small backstage area turned into a mob scene. Everyone was shoulder-punching one another. The sponsors, Danton Miller and the writers were clustered around Christie, shaking his hand. The cameraman was flashing pictures. Ethel came over and grabbed Amanda. "I want to get a picture of you with Christie."

Amanda broke away and raced to the telephone. Ethel followed her. "Can't it wait? This is important."

Amanda ignored her as she dialed. She was conscious of Ethel standing and glowering. Jerry came and stood close at hand, protectively. This time there was no busy signal. It rang once, twice, three times. After the tenth ring, she hung up. Her dime returned. She dialed again. The same monotonous ring, and Jerry and Ethel were watching her. She could see the beginning of a smirk come to Ethel's lips. She straightened up. She was Robin Stone's girl! She wasn't going to let them see Robin Stone's girl crumple. He wouldn't like that. When he held her in his arms last night, their bodies close, he had stroked her head and said, "You're just like me, baby–resilient. No matter what anyone does to either of us, if we hurt, we hurt inside and no one will know. We don't cry on anyone's shoulders, or even to ourselves. That's why we belong together." She forced herself to think of this now, as the phone kept ringing to emptiness. She hung up and casually took the dime from the coin box. She faced Ethel and Jerry with a smile. "You know I'm an idiot, I guess I was so nervous about the show that I completely forgot–" She stopped, groping for some alibi.

"Was it still busy?" Jerry asked sympathetically.

"Yes! And you know why? He told me he was going to take the receiver off the hook so that no one would disturb him. And I forgot!" She turned to Ethel. "So let's take the pictures, then I'll dash to his place as we planned. And Jerry, would you be an angel and call Cadi-Cars? Tell them to send a limo for me."

Then she walked toward Christie Lane and stood between him and Bob Dixon, flashed her brightest smile and quickly squirmed out of Christie's arms as soon as the picture was taken. Fortunately he was so mobbed with the agency men he didn't see her slip away.

Jerry called for the car. He wondered about the phone story and thought it odd that she would forget. But her smile was too genuine. She was absolutely sparkling.

Ethel had also noticed Amanda's assurance. God, to be going home to Robin Stone–!

But once Amanda was in the protective darkness of the limousine, her smile dissolved. She gave the driver her home address. Well–eight dollars shot down the drain for the limo. And there were plenty of cabs around. But this had been the only thing to do. She had gone off with her head held high–she was Robin's girl, and this was the way he would want it.

Robin phoned bright and early the following morning. "Hello, star," he said lightly.

She had been awake half the night, vacillating between hating him, renouncing him, alibiing for him, and, through it all, wanting him. And she had promised herself to play it cool when and if he did call. But the early morning call caught her off guard.

"Where were you last night?" she demanded. (Oh Lord, this wasn't the way she had intended to act.)

"Watching you," he said, in his same bantering tone.

"You were not!" She was breaking every resolve, yet was powerless to stop. "Robin, I called you right before the commercial and the line was busy. I called you after the show and there was no answer."

"You're absolutely right. The damn phone started to ring just as the show went on the air. Not that I minded–it was Andy Parino, and I'd rather talk to him than listen to Christie Lane. But after I got off with Andy, someone else called. And I wanted to catch your great performance without any distractions, so the moment you came on, I turned off my phone."

"But you knew I'd call right after the show."

"As a matter of fact, I forgot I had turned the damned thing off."

"Well," she spluttered, "then why didn't you try me? I mean, even if you forgot you turned it off you could have called me. Didn't you figure I'd want to be with you after the show?"

"I know what it's like after a new show goes on. It's insanity backstage. I was positive that you'd be the center of attention with your sponsors. I thought you'd probably go off and celebrate with them."

"Robin!" she moaned in absolute helplessness. "I wanted to be with *you*. You're my guy, aren't you?"

"You bet I am." His voice was still light. "But that doesn't mean total commitment on either side. I don't own you, or your time."

"Don't you want to?" she asked. It was a wrong move, but she had to make a stab.

"No. Because I could never fulfill my end of the deal."

"Robin, I want to belong to you–totally. I want to give you all my time. You're all that matters to me. I love you. I know you don't want to get married," she rushed on, "but that doesn't mean I can't belong to you in every sense of the word!"

"I want you to be my girl, but I don't want to own you."

"But if I'm your girl, then you must know I want you to share everything with me. I want to be with you through everything–and when you can't be with me, I want to be home waiting until you come to me. I *want* to belong to you."

"I don't want you to get hurt." His voice was tight.

"I won't get hurt. And I won't nag–I swear."

"Then let's put it this way: *I* don't want to be hurt."

After a pause she said, "Who has hurt you, Robin?"

"What do you mean?"

"You can't be afraid of being hurt unless you've been hurt. That's why you've erected a steel door to put between us every now and then."

"I've never been hurt," he said. "Honestly, Amanda, I'd like to be able to tell you that some siren broke my heart when I was a boy in the war. But nothing like that ever happened. I've had girls –lots of them. I love girls, and I think I care for you more than I've cared for anyone."

"Then why do you hold back a part of yourself–and force me to do the same?"

"I don't know, I really don't know. Maybe I've got some crazy sense of self-preservation. Some instinct that tells me that if I didn't have that door, as you call it, I might get my head blown off." Then he laughed. "Oh hell, it's too early in the morning for soul-probing. Or maybe I haven't got a soul. Maybe if I opened that steel door, I'd find there was no one home."

"Robin, I'll never hurt you. I'll love you forever."

"Baby, nothing is forever."

"You mean you'll leave me?"

"I could go in a plane crash, a sniper's bullet could hit me–"

She laughed. "A bullet would bend if it hit you."

"Amanda." His voice was light, but she knew he was serious.

"Love me, baby, but don't make me your life. You can't hold on to people. Even if they love you, they have to leave you."

"What are you trying to tell me?" She was dangerously close to tears.

"I'm just trying to explain how I feel. There are certain facts we all know: one, you can't hold on to people; two, one day you have to die. We all have to die—we know it, but we ignore it. Maybe we feel that if we don't think about it, it may not happen. But deep down we know it will. I feel much the same about that steel door. As long as it's there to clang shut, I can't get hurt."

"Have you ever tried to open it?"

"I'm trying right now, with you." His voice was quiet. "I've unhinged it because I care enough about you to want you to understand. But I'm slamming it shut right now."

"Robin, please don't! Love me all the way. I know what the door is—it slams on *feeling*. You've closed that part of your brain. You *feel* love . . . but you refuse to think about it."

"Perhaps. Just as I refuse to think about death. No matter when I go, even if I'm ninety, it will be a hell of a disappointment to have to check out. But maybe if I don't care about anything too much, I won't be too sorry to leave."

She was quiet. He had never opened up this much to her. She knew he was trying to say something else.

"Amanda, I do care about you. And I admire you, because I think you also have your own steel door. You're beautiful, you're ambitious, and you're independent. I couldn't love or respect a girl if I was her sole reason for existing. I think in a curious way, the rocks in your head fit the holes in mine. Now: are we squared away?"

She forced herself to laugh lightly. "Everything's fine. Unless you stand me up for dinner tonight. Then I'll bash those rocks in your head into little pebbles."

His laugh matched her own. "Well, I can't risk that. I hear you Southern belles swing a mean right."

"Southern? I never said I was from the South."

"You never tell me anything, my beautiful Amanda. Maybe that's part of your charm. But when you talk, every once in a while some Georgia or Alabama comes through."

"Wrong states." Then after a pause she said, "I never told you anything about myself, because you never asked. But I want you to know about me, I want you to know everything."

"Baby, nothing is as dull as a woman without a past. And once you know all the details there is no past. Just a long dreary confessional."

"But actually you don't know anything about me–aren't you curious?"

"Well, I knew you had been around the turf when we met–"

"Robin!"

"I mean it in the nicest way. I'm too old to start up with a virgin."

"There haven't been so many men, Robin."

"Careful. Don't disillusion me. I've always been hung up on broads like Marie Antoinette, Madame Pompadour–even Lucrezia Borgia. Now if you tell me there was just that nice boy you met at college, you'll ruin the whole thing."

"All right, then I won't tell you about the South American dictator who tried to kill himself over me, or the king who offered to give up his throne for me. Meanwhile, shall I do the steak and salad bit for tonight?"

He laughed. The mood was broken and she knew she had put him at ease.

"Okay, baby. Steak and salad, and I'll bring some wine. See you at seven."

She fell back into bed and cradled the phone. Oh God, she just couldn't go on playing games like this. But she knew she would, she had to, until she had gained his complete trust. Then his guard would relax, and. . . . She jumped out of bed and turned on her bath. She felt wonderful. Even though she had two rough sittings, this was a marvelous day. The greatest day in her life. Because she knew she had the key to Robin Stone. Play it cool, demand nothing. The less she demanded the more he would give. And soon he would find that he did belong to her–it would happen so gradually he wouldn't even be aware of it.

For the first time, she felt confident. She knew everything was going to be just fine.

TEN

AMANDA'S NEW BURST OF HAPPY CONFIDENCE remained with her throughout the day. When a pose grew tiring, she relived her telephone conversation with Robin and forgot the lights, the kink in her neck and the pain in her back. Dimly she could hear the photographer say, "Yeah, baby, oh yeah, hold that look!"

Her final session ended at four. She checked with Nick Longworth's office.

"You'll like tomorrow's bookings," Nick sang out. "Eleven tomorrow at *Vogue*—and your old buddy Ivan Greenberg is doing the layout." She was delighted. The first job wasn't until eleven. That meant she could sleep until nine. She could make Robin breakfast. . . .

It was an unnaturally warm day for February. A haze hung in the sky and the air seemed thick enough to cut. It wasn't supposed to be healthy weather, but it was fifty-five degrees and she could walk without freezing and she was happy, and to her it was the most beautiful day in the world.

She went home, fed Slugger, set the table, made the salad and got the steaks ready.

She was never able to eat when she was with him, she just picked at everything. She had lost ten pounds during this year with Robin. Five foot seven and only weighed one hundred and eight. But it was great for photography and so far it hadn't affected her face.

She turned on the television set to IBC. Robin liked to watch Andy on the seven o'clock news. She usually sat snuggled in his arms while he watched, or sometimes she sat across the room and studied his profile. But tonight she'd watch it–she wanted to be interested in everything that concerned him.

Gregory Austin was also waiting for the seven o'clock news. Once again he had to hand it to Robin Stone. He had been right about using Andy Parino. Funny–he had actually brought Robin in to do news, and he was turning out to be one hell of an executive. Robin was a good man but he was a phantom–he rarely saw him. You'd think someone who traveled so much on IBC's money would at least check in and say hello when he returned. *In Depth* received excellent notices–the ratings were rising all the time–you'd think he'd want to take his bows.

Danton Miller always came fawning for *his* praise. The son of a bitch was on the phone the moment *The Christie Lane Show* went off the air. Well, it just proved you couldn't overrate the intelligence of the television audience. They were a bunch of slobs. *The Christie Lane Show* was a piece of tripe–Judith hadn't even been able to watch it! And the reviews in the morning papers were brutal. But the overnight Nielsen rating was sensational. Of course the two-week national Nielsen would tell the story.

He thought about this as he sat in the paneled den of his town house and switched on the built-in color set. To him, the best thing on television was the old technicolor movies on *The Late Show*. They didn't make girls like Rita, Alice Faye and Betty Grable anymore. Sometimes when he couldn't sleep, he'd raid the refrigerator and sit and watch the movie glamour girls he had been secretly in love with. He had Judith to thank for the color set. In fact, the entire den had been a surprise. She had it done last year while they were at Palm Beach. He had wondered about all those surreptitious calls–those quick trips she had to take to New York to see her dentist. And when they had returned from Palm Beach she had presented him with the den. Even had a big ribbon tacked on the door. He had been touched. Judith had great taste. The room was completely masculine. He knew that each piece of furniture had been carefully selected and had a history. The big world globe was supposed to have belonged to President Wilson. The desk was an antique. He didn't know the period, he didn't care about those things. He could tell you the exact date

Amos and Andy went on radio, and proudly show you the set of earphones he had built as a kid. But antiques, Oriental rugs, Ming vases–that was Judith's world and she understood his taste and didn't foist her own on him. She got him antiques, but by God, they were strong ones, none of those faggy thin-legged French jobs. "Your domain," Judith had said. "I'll only come when I'm invited."

A frown crossed his forehead. He felt a vague feeling of disharmony. He couldn't put his finger on it but he had felt the same way when they had moved here from the Park Avenue penthouse seven years ago. When Judith had pointed out the two master bedrooms separated by a small wall of closets: "Isn't this divine, Greg? Now you'll have your own bedroom and I'll have mine. And we each have our own bathroom."

He had liked the idea of "his" and "her" bathrooms, but had suggested turning one of the bedrooms into a sitting room. "I like sleeping in the same room with you, Judith."

She had laughed. "Don't worry, my love–I'll snuggle with you each night as you read the *Wall Street Journal*. But when I go to sleep, at least I'll sleep. I won't have to poke you eight times during the night to tell you to stop snoring."

She was right and it *was* practical. In the beginning he hadn't really believed he snored–until the night he had purposely set the tape recorder by his bed. The following morning he was in a state of shock–he couldn't believe those unearthly snorts had come from him. He had even gone for medical advice. The doctor had laughed. "Nothing wrong, Greg–everyone snores after they hit forty. You're lucky you can afford two bedrooms. It's the only civilized way to keep romance going in a middle-aged marriage."

After she had given him his den, she had gradually taken over the large library. Fancied it up, changed the color scheme, the drapes and some of the furniture. He hated the room now. It looked like one of those VIP suites at the Waldorf Towers. His autographed pictures of Eisenhower and Bernard Baruch had been transferred to his den. Silver-framed pictures of her relatives had replaced them on the fancy desk of the library. Oh what the hell, why shouldn't she have her relatives on display? She had the classy ones. Why shouldn't her twin sister who was a bona fide princess have her mug in a silver frame? And the two little princesses she had begot. And it was right to have that oil painting of Judith's father over the fireplace. God, the old man looked like an ad for some vintage wine. Gregory had no pictures of his father. They didn't take pictures to put in silver frames in the North of Ireland. Besides, Judith needed a library. She and her social secretary worked there every morning. He smiled at the thought of the word "work" applied to Judith. But then, maybe it was work planning all the parties, heading the charities, staying on the best-dressed list. He had to hand it to Judith–her personal publicity had been so great that people actually believed she had a personal fortune of her own when she married the two-fisted self-made Irishman named Gregory Austin. He smiled. Sure, she was social, went to all the right schools and studied abroad, but the family didn't have a dime. The rush of publicity when her sister married that prince had elevated the two girls to sudden fame. And now he felt Judith actually believed she *had* been wealthy in her own right before her marriage. So what–it must have been tough for her, watching her friends make their debuts and scrounging to keep up with them. She had been dropped from the Social Register when she married him, but he had brought her a new kind of society–the society that broke through every social barrier. Celebrity society. Talent was the greatest equalizer in the world. A Danny Kaye could be presented at court. A top politician could dine with a king. And the chairman of the board of IBC was welcome everywhere. Judith was a great girl and he was damn glad he had been able to supply the one missing ingredient in her perfect life. Judith Austin *was* society today. She was more than society–she *created* society. She made fashions, she was on the front page of that newspaper all the dames liked–*Women's Wear*. Whatever she wore became a trend. He still couldn't believe she belonged to him. She still seemed unattainable. He had felt that way the first moment they met, and he still felt the same way.

It was two minutes to seven. He went to the bar and mixed a light Scotch-and-soda for himself, a vermouth on the rocks for Judith. He wondered how she could drink the stuff. It tasted like varnish. But Judith claimed that all the great beauties in Europe only drank wine or vermouth. Of course, Judith meant the great beauties over forty. Funny how a beautiful woman like Judith could have an age complex. She entered the den after knocking lightly. This tapping was a joke—asking permission to come into "his" den. But he went along with it. He realized in some way it nullified any guilt she felt for taking over the library.

She took her place on the twin leather chair across from him. And he thought as he did every night when he saw her sitting there, "God, she's a beautiful woman." She was forty-six and looked barely thirty-five. He felt a sudden swell of pride and sense of well-being. He loved the goddam den—it had become a part of their lives. Even if they were going to the theater or giving a dinner party, they had their drink together in his den while they watched the seven o'clock news. To Gregory Austin, nothing got going until *after* the seven o'clock news. And Judith had dutifully built their social life around this order.

The news began: "Good evening and welcome to *News at Seven*. We are saving the last five minutes of our program for an unscheduled appearance of the president of IBC News, the star of *In Depth,* Mr. Robin Stone."

"What the hell!" Gregory sat on the edge of his chair.

"Since when has Robin Stone appeared on the seven o'clock news?" Judith asked.

"Since one second ago when I heard the announcement."

"He's a very handsome man," Judith commented. "But when I watch him on *In Depth* I get the feeling that he takes extreme care to let nothing of himself ever leak out before the camera. How do you find him?"

"Exactly like he is on television. You hit it right on the head. He's an enigma. Great surface charm, but everything else locked in."

Judith's eyes glinted with a touch of interest. "Let's invite him to dinner one night. I'd like to meet him."

Gregory laughed. "You can't be serious."

"Why not? Several of my girl friends are dying to meet him. He's never seen in public. And he's really catching on."

"Judith, you know my rule. I don't mix with hired help."

"When we go to the Coast we attend their parties."

"I do that because I figure you get a bang out of it. Besides, that's different. They're throwing the parties for us. We're not inviting them to our home. The New Year's Day bash we give takes care of them. And it's great that way. Makes them feel they're being presented at court."

She reached over and patted his hand. "For a man who was raised on Tenth Avenue, you're the biggest snob in the world."

"No, it's just business sense. Hell–I couldn't care less about dinner parties or social status. But anything that's hard to get is sought after."

She laughed. "Gregory, you're a wheeling-dealing bastard."

"I sure am. Even our New Year's Day party is no open house. Very few people from IBC make it."

She smiled. "The eggnog party is so square that it's *in.* And it was my idea. Do you know *Women's Wear Daily* said it was becoming an annual event? It even made Ernestine Carter's column in the London *Times.*"

"I think we had too many show-business names this year."

"We need them, darling. A few of them add dash to the party. And it isn't easy, Greg, getting the right people together at that time of the year."

He waved his hand, and listened to a news item that interested him. She was silent until the commercial came on.

"Greg, when can we leave for Palm Beach? We're usually there by the end of January. But you insisted on staying in town for the premiere of that dreadful *Christie Lane Show.*"

"I want to stay here for a few more weeks. I think we can build that show into a real winner. But you can go. I'll get there by the beginning of March at the latest."

"Then I'll leave Thursday–I'll have the house all set when you get there."

He nodded absently. The news had returned to the air.

Judith stared at the screen without really watching. "Well, I guess Robin Stone will have to keep until next New Year's Day . . ."

"Not even then." Gregory handed her his glass for a refill.

"Why not?"

"Because I'd have to invite all the presidents of the other departments. Christ, Danton Miller only made it for the first time this year." He leaned over and turned up the volume.

She handed him his drink. Then she hung over his shoulders. "Greg darling, my girl friends don't want to meet Danton Miller. But they *do* want to meet Robin Stone."

He patted her hand. "We'll see, that's a year away. Anything can happen by then."

Suddenly he sat forward. The camera came in for a tight close-up of Robin. Gregory could see why Judith's friends were interested. He was a hell of a good-looking guy.

"Good evening"– The clipped voice filled the room. "We've all been fascinated by the news story of a genuine adventure of modern-day piracy. I'm speaking of the Portuguese cruise ship *Santa Maria* that was seized at gunpoint in the Caribbean by twenty-four Portuguese and Spanish political exiles and six crew members. This raid was led by Henrique Galvão, a former Portuguese army captain. Three days ago, January thirty-first, Admiral Smith went aboard the *Santa Maria* thirty miles off Recife, Brazil, and held a mid-ocean conference with Galvão. Word has just reached me that Galvão has agreed to allow the passengers to leave the ship today. Galvão has been promised, along with his twenty-nine followers, asylum in Brazil by President Janio Quadros. There were also American tourists on board. But most of all, this reporter is interested in obtaining a filmed interview with Henrique Galvão. I am leaving tonight. I hope to bring back an *In Depth* interview with Galvão and perhaps some of the American passengers who were on the pirated ship. Good night, and thank you."

Gregory Austin clicked off the set in rage. "How dare he just take off like that without reporting to anyone! Why wasn't I told? He just returned from London a few weeks ago. I want *live* shows, not tape–that's our main selling point against the competition."

"Robin can't do all his *In Depth* shows live, Greg. It's the world-famous people who give it stature. I, for one, would be fascinated to see an *In Depth* on this Galvão. I'd like to see the man who at sixty-five has the courage to pirate a luxury liner with six hundred passengers."

But Gregory was on the phone, demanding that the IBC operator track down Danton Miller. Five minutes later the call came through.

"Dan!" Gregory's face was red with anger. "I'm sure you have no idea what's going on. *You're* sitting at '21' relaxing–"

Danton's voice was cool. "Yes, I was relaxing on a nice sofa in the lobby, watching our IBC seven o'clock news."

"Well, did you know about Robin's trip to Brazil?"

"Why should I? He doesn't have to report to anyone but you."

Gregory's face went a shade darker. "Well, damn it, then why didn't he tell me?"

"Perhaps he tried. You weren't in the office today. I tried to reach you several times during the afternoon with some further reports on *The Christie Lane Show*. The out-of-town notices were great. I had them put on your desk."

Gregory's face went rigid with anger. "Yes, I *was* out this afternoon," he shouted. "And I have a right to be out one afternoon in a month!" (He had purchased two new horses and had driven to Westbury to see them.) "Goddammit," he went on, "you mean, if I'm not there one day the whole network falls apart?"

"I don't think the network is going to fall apart because one guy takes off for Brazil. Still I don't like the idea of Robin Stone using the seven o'clock news as a publicity bulletin for himself. Gregory, I don't like the president of *any* department having this kind of authority. But, unfortunately, Robin does not have to check with me. Since you were unavailable, the announcement might have been his way of telling you. It's faster than Western Union."

Gregory slammed down the receiver. Danton Miller's obvious pleasure over the situation spiked his anger into a helpless rage. He stood staring into space, his fists clenched. Judith walked over and handed him a fresh drink. Then she smiled at him. "Aren't you being childish? The man has pulled a big coup, for *your* network. Everyone who heard the seven o'clock news will be looking forward to the interview. Now relax and have your drink. We're due at the Colony at eight fifteen for dinner."

"I'm dressed."

She patted his face gently. "I think you might have one tiny run-over with the electric razor. We're having dinner with Ambassador Ragil tonight. And he's got three Arabian horses you're keen on. So come on. Smile! Let me see the Austin charm."

His frown disappeared. "I guess I like to be Big Daddy all the way," he said grudgingly. "And you're right. Making that announcement was a superb piece of showmanship. It's just that it's *my* network–I created it, built it. I don't like anyone making decisions without my approval."

"You also don't like your trainer to buy horses unless you personally inspect them. Darling, you can't be everywhere."

He grinned. "You're always right, Judith."

She smiled. "And I think by next New Year's Day Robin Stone will be big enough to rate an invitation. . . ."

When Amanda heard the news, she stood staring at the set. It couldn't be true. Any second the buzzer would ring and Robin would be standing at the door. He was probably on his way now, and she'd drive to the airport with him.

She waited ten minutes. By eight fifteen she had smoked six cigarettes. She called his apartment. It rang monotonously. She dialed IBC. They had no idea of what flight Mr. Stone was using, but suggested she try Pan Am.

At eight thirty the phone rang. She banged her ankle against the table, rushing to it.

"This is Ivan the Terrible."

Her face fell. She loved Ivan Greenberg, but tears ran down her face from disappointment.

"You there, Mandy?"

"Yes." Her voice was low.

"Oh–did I interrupt anything?"

"No, I was just watching television."

He laughed. "That's right, now that you're a big TV star you've got to keep up with the competition."

"Ivan, I adore you, but I want to keep my line open. I'm expecting an important call."

"Okay, pussycat, I know–I heard the seven o'clock news–the Great Stone Man is off, so I thought you might grab a hamburger with me."

"I've got to get off the phone, Ivan."

"All right, get a good night's sleep–we have an eleven o'clock sitting tomorrow."

She sat and stared at the phone. At nine fifteen she checked with Pan Am. Yes, there was a Mr. Robin Stone booked on the nine o'clock flight. The flight had gone on schedule—it had been airborne for fifteen minutes. She flopped into a chair while the tears ran down her face in black rivulets. Her mascara was all but gone and her false lashes were coming loose. She pulled them off and put them on the coffee table.

She got up slowly and walked into the living room. She had to talk to someone. Ivan had always been her confidant.

She dialed nervously and gasped in relief when he picked it up on the second ring.

"Ivan, I want that hamburger."

"Great, I was just leaving. Meet me at the Tiger Inn: it's a new joint on First Avenue, at Fifty-third. Right near you."

"No, you get the hamburgers and bring them here."

"Oh, I dig. Torture time."

"Please, Ivan, I've got steaks if you like, and a salad—"

"No, baby, if you stay home it'll be like real hysterics—and that means swollen eyelids tomorrow. Not when you're sitting for me, pussycat. I had to work an hour on the lights when the Stone Man took off for London a few weeks back. You want a hamburger, meet me at the Tiger Inn. At least there you'll have to keep your composure."

"I look awful. It would take me an hour to redo my eyes."

"Since when have you run out of dark glasses?"

"Okay." She felt too weary to resist. "I'll be there in fifteen minutes."

The Tiger Inn was enjoying a flash of popularity. It was almost filled. Amanda recognized some models and some advertising men. She toyed with a hamburger and stared at Ivan, mutely demanding an answer.

He scratched his beard. "There's no answer. He loves you this morning—and disappears this evening. With all the great cats in this town, you have to pick a character like Robin Stone. I mean, it's not even your *scene*. After all, who is he, what is he? Just a newscaster."

"He's not just a newscaster. He's president of IBC News!"

He shrugged. "Big deal! I bet if I mentioned both your names at every table here, they'd all know you and say 'Robin *who?'* When you walk into a restaurant, everyone knows you. But Robin Stone?"

Her smile was weak. "Robin doesn't care about things like that. We don't even go to the right restaurants! He has an Italian place he adores and the Lancer Bar. Sometimes I cook."

"God, what a thrilling life you have."

"I love it, Ivan! Look, I've been in this town *five* years. I've seen every place and nothing matters but being with the man you care about. I love him."

"Why?"

She scratched Robin's initials on the wet paper napkin. "I wish I knew."

"Is he better than anyone else in the feathers? Like, does he have a new scene?"

She turned her head away and the tears slid down under the rims of her dark glasses.

"Cool it, Mandy," he said. "Those cats across the room are staring."

"I don't care. I don't know them."

"But they know you! Christ, baby, you're on two covers this month. You're really hot. Enjoy it–make it pay!"

"Who cares?"

"You'd better care. It's a cinch that Robin Stone isn't about to pay your rent or buy you any fur coats. Maybe making money doesn't mean anything to you? Or maybe you have rich relatives or something like that going for you."

"No, I have to work. My mother's dead. I was raised by an aunt. I have to support her now."

"Then you'd better get with it! Make this year pay off. Because next year there could be a new girl. If you make it to the very top –play it smart and establish a top salary–you'll be a top model for maybe ten years."

The tears slipped down her cheeks again. "But it's not going to get me Robin."

He stared at her. "What's your scene, baby? Self-destruction? You enjoy sitting around and crying for him? Is that going to turn him on?"

"You don't think I've already lost him?"

"I only wish you had. Because he's bad news. A guy who walks through life without getting turned on destroys everything he touches."

"No, I ruined it. I know I did, this morning on the phone. I smothered him."

"Mandy, you're sick. Look, nothing is ruined. Maybe he's not so bad. Maybe *you're* just some kind of nut."

"Why? Because I'm hurt? I have a *right* to be. Look what he did to me!"

"Okay, what did he do? He left on a job without calling to say goodbye. Big deal! How many times have I done the same thing? And you've understood, because we're friends."

"That's different than love," she argued.

"You mean love fucks up everything."

She managed a weak laugh.

"Look, maybe Robin is a nice cat. I'm only reading him from you. But you should work your pretty little ass off to be a big smash. Make him proud of you—that's the way to hold a guy!"

"Oh, Ivan, you make it sound so simple. In a few minutes you'll have me waiting for his cable to arrive."

"Could happen. But you'll be a loser if you just sit around crying. Let word get to him that you're having a ball."

"Then he'd have a real excuse for dropping me."

"The way it sounds, this cat doesn't need an excuse for anything. He does what he wants to do. Try playing it cool. Go out with other guys while he's away."

"With whom?" she demanded.

"I'm not running an escort service, pussycat. You must know plenty of guys."

She shook her head. "I've been seeing no one but Robin for a year."

"You mean no one else has ever made a pass?"

She smiled slightly. "No one that I've paid any attention to, including that horrible Christie Lane. But that wasn't a real pass. He just asked me out."

"You could do worse."

She looked at him to see if he meant it. When she realized he was serious, she made a wry face.

"What's so bad about Christie Lane?"

"You saw the show. He hasn't an ounce of sex appeal. He's a slob."

"Well, I wouldn't exactly rush and ask him to pose for *Esquire*. He's a nice average guy who happens to be a big star."

"He's not a star. I mean he's star of *The Christie Lane Show*. But did you see the notice in the *Times?* He has to be canceled after thirteen weeks."

"In thirteen weeks you could get a hell of a lot of publicity going out with him."

"But I can't stand him."

"I'm not telling you to go to bed with him. Just let some of his publicity wash off on you."

"But it wouldn't be right to go out with him just for publicity."

He took her chin in his hand. "You're a nice girl. A nice, *stupid* girl with an unlined face. A nice, stupid girl who thinks that face will stay intact forever. Honey, I'm thirty-eight and I can still get all the eighteen-year-old chicks I want. And when I'm forty-eight or fifty-eight with gray in my beard, I'll still get them. But when *you're* thirty-eight, you'll only get high-fashion jobs–full length, that is. If you've taken care of yourself! But no more face ads, or hands–the ugly brown age freckles will have started. And even a slob like Christie Lane won't look at you. But right now, and maybe for the next ten years, you can have anything and anyone."

"Except the only man I want."

He sighed. "Look, I know you're a sweet, regular girl or I wouldn't be sitting here wasting all this time when I've got a lot of work piled up and three chicks I could score with at the drop of a dime. Face it–Robin doesn't function like other people. He's like a great big beautiful machine. Fight back, baby, it's your only chance."

She nodded absently and scribbled the initials R.S. on the table with the swizzle stick.

ELEVEN

JERRY MOSS ALSO WAS OUTRAGED at Robin's departure. He had checked with Robin at lunch and Robin had said, "Lancer's at five."

Jerry had waited until seven and only found out what had happened from Mary, who had accidentally heard Robin on the seven o'clock news.

He had a long session with Dr. Gold the following day. No, Dr. Gold did not think Robin was intentionally sadistic—he felt most of Robin's actions were based on an unconscious effort to avoid close ties with anyone. He demanded nothing of his friends and in turn wanted no demands made on him.

Amanda's talk with Ivan had helped her. When she arrived to do the second *Christie Lane Show* she had worked herself from deep depression into a state of self-righteous anger. The rehearsals had the same frantic excitement but the tension was gone. There was a sense of fun and goodwill, a certain confidence that permeates the atmosphere when there is the smell of a hit.

This time, when Christie Lane asked her to go out after the show, she accepted. They went to Danny's Hideaway with his "gofors" and Agnes, a show girl from the Latin Quarter who obviously belonged to one of them. Amanda sat beside Christie, but aside from asking her, "What do you want to eat, doll?" no other conversation passed between them. Jack E. Leonard, Milton Berle and several other comedians came by to congratulate Christie. He was thrilled with the attention and tried to trade jokes with them.

Then, as he watched Milton Berle walk down the room to the front table, he said to Eddie Flynn, "I think we're sitting in left field."

The show girl said in a tinny voice, "No, Chris, honest. As long as you make this room, you're in good shape. It's known as the Cub Room. The squares with the brown-and-white shoes sit in the other rooms. This is the *in* room."

"How would you know?" Christie snarled.

"I know," she said calmly, loading butter on a breadstick. "I once came here with a square–oh, long before I met you, lover," she said as she gave Eddie's arm a reassuring pat. "And we were led right into another room. I dug right away where all the action went on when I saw all the celebrities being shown in here. But the square, he was from Minnesota, he had no idea. He collected matches to take home and was happy as a clam."

"Yeah, but Berle has the front table. And look, the McGuire sisters are at the other."

"Marty Allen is sitting along the side." This was Kenny Ditto.

"Yeah–but up *front* on the side. Someday I'm gonna sit at the front table. And someday I'll go to the '21' Club."

Amanda was surprised. "Haven't you ever been there?"

"Once," Christie said. "I had a date and all she wanted was dinner at the '21' Club. I called and made a reservation. Then, wham–upstairs left field, in a corner. And like Agnes said, the girl I was with didn't know the difference. She collected matches, too. But I *knew.*" He seemed thoughtful. "I got to get my name in the columns. That Ethel Evans isn't any good–Eddie, tomorrow we start with our own press agent. Smell around, find out who'll work for a C-note a week. All he has to do is get me three column mentions a week. Nothing else."

It continued on throughout dinner. Christie Lane and his "gofors" plotting his career. The show girl ate everything in sight. Amanda learned that Kenny Ditto's name was really Kenneth Kenneth–Christie had tacked the Ditto on, and Kenny was thinking of legalizing it. Kenny Ditto was a better name for a writer, it stood out on the crawl on the show.

Amanda sat with them feeling strangely isolated, yet relieved at being left to herself. When they drove up to her apartment building,

Christie remained in the cab and let Eddie take her to the door. He shouted out, "How about tomorrow night, doll? There's an opening at the Copa."

"Call me," and she dashed into the building.

He called the following morning and she accepted the date. It was better than sitting home moping about Robin. That night Christie exuded confidence. The Copa was his "home ground." They had a ringside table. She was crammed in among Christie, the "gofors," and the new press agent–a skinny boy who worked for one of the major publicity firms. He explained that no decent press agent would take on an account for that money, but if Christie paid in cash he would "moonlight" and deliver the three column mentions a week.

After the Copa, Christie wanted to go to the Brasserie, but Amanda begged off, pleading an early call. The following morning, Ivan called to congratulate her on an item in Ronnie Wolfe's column which stated she and Christie were the new big romance in town. "Now you're making sense," he said. She was frightened at first, but when three more days passed with no word from Robin, she decided to see Christie again. It was another nightclub opening, another table filled with the "gofors," the press agent and a second-rate dance team who had latched on, hoping for a guest shot on Christie's show.

The night of the third Christie Lane telecast was charged with excitement. The two-week Nielsens had come out–Christie Lane was in the top twenty! The sponsors appeared, Danton Miller was shaking everyone's hand, everyone was congratulating everyone. Alwayso gave Dan an immediate renewal for the following season. Thirty-nine weeks firm. That night Danton Miller threw a little victory party at "21" after the show. Christie unloaded his "gofors" and took Amanda. Jerry Moss came with his wife. They had a table downstairs in the middle section and although none of the captains knew Christie Lane, everyone knew Danton Miller and some of them even knew Jerry Moss. At one point in the evening, Danton Miller tried to make the proper small talk with Amanda. He complimented her and said she was excellent on the commercials.

"I'm used to a camera," she said modestly. "My real feat was learning to hold the lipstick without letting my hand shake."

"Have you ever acted? Pictures? The stage?"

"No, just modeled."

He looked thoughtful. "But it seems to me I've heard of you–"

"Perhaps in magazines," she said.

Suddenly he snapped his fingers. "Robin Stone! Didn't I see your name coupled with his?"

"I've gone out with him," she said carefully.

"Where the hell is he? And when is he coming back?" Dan asked.

"He went to Brazil." She was conscious that Jerry had stopped talking and had turned his attention to them.

Dan waved his hand. "That tape from Brazil came in over a week ago. Then he sent us one from France. He actually saw de Gaulle." He shook his head in amazement. "But now I hear he's in London."

She sipped her Coke and kept her expression bland. "I imagine he's getting wonderful tapes over there."

Danton smiled. "The ratings are pretty good, and for a news show it's solid. But your new boyfriend is our jumbo!" Dan looked at Christie and smiled.

Her new boyfriend! She suddenly felt she was going to be sick –physically sick. She was grateful that it was an early evening. Dan had a limousine and they dropped her off first. But Ivan was right. Two days later one of the afternoon papers carried a feature story on Christie Lane. The caption was THE MAN WHO LIVES NEXT DOOR. Amanda's picture was featured in a three-column cut: "The man who lives next door doesn't date the girl next door –he dates the top cover girl!" Christie was quoted as saying, "We've just been dating a few weeks, but man, I'm really hung on her." She threw the papers down in disgust. And she slammed down the phone on Ivan when he said, "Now you're getting smart, baby."

She reread the story. It was horrible–horrible! She stared at the open, vacant face of Christie Lane and felt nausea. So far they had been surrounded with stooges and comics and backslappers. But what would happen if there ever came a time when they were alone?

A few minutes later the phone rang and a jubilant Christie bellowed, "Doll–did you see the jazz in the papers? Well, this is only the beginning. Christie is going up, up, and up. And tonight we celebrate. Alone. I got Danton to get us a good table at '21' for cocktails and then we're going to dinner at El Morocco. Danton is fixing it–so we sit in the right place and not in Squaresville."

"I'm sorry, Christie," she answered. "I have a late booking, and a very early appointment tomorrow morning."

"Break it. You're going out with the new King–"

"I can't cancel my bookings. I earn too much money."

"Doll, whatever you lose, I'll pay you! What's the total?"

She thought quickly. She had no early bookings and her last appointment was at five. "Well, three hours tonight, and two tomorrow morning."

"Okay–what's the tab?"

She could hear him chewing on one of those foul cigars. She started calculating. "Between three hundred and seventy-five and four hundred dollars."

He whistled. "You make that kind of loot?"

"I get seventy-five dollars an hour."

"You're fulla shit!"

She clicked the receiver in his ear.

Two minutes later he rang back. "Doll, forgive me. It's just an expression. I mean, you knocked me on my ass. Eddie's girl, Aggie, well, she models for those confession magazines–and she gets ten bucks an hour. Fifteen if she wears a bathing suit, and twenty if she shows her tits."

"I don't do that kind of modeling."

"Maybe I better wise Aggie up. If there's this kind of cash in modeling, what the hell is she doing posing for that crummy kind of dough?"

"Christie, I have to leave, I'm late as it is–"

"You're right. Listen, doll, for that kind of money, you need your sleep. We'll make the big leagues another night. But I have to keep the '21' bit–a lady from *Life* magazine is coming to have a drink with me. It's a shame you can't make it, you could cash in on the publicity if *Life* decides to do me."

"I'm sorry, Christie."

She hung up and resolved never to go out with him again. Never!

Then Ivan called. "I guess by now you've read *all* the papers," he said. "Well, at least the Christie Lane story saves your face, pussycat."

"What do you mean?"

"I thought America's top model would automatically go to the society columns first—you mean you haven't seen them?"

"No." She began rustling through the papers.

"Page twenty-seven. I'll hang on while you cut your wrists."

Robin's familiar grin hit her immediately. He had his arm around someone called Baroness Ericka von Gratz.

"Are you still there, pussycat?"

"Do you enjoy being sadistic, Ivan?"

"No, Amanda." His voice was low and serious. "I just want you to face facts. I'll be home if you need me."

She hung up slowly and stared at the paper. Baroness Ericka von Gratz was attractive. Robin was relaxed, from the look of it. She read the story:

> Baroness Ericka von Gratz has not been around London since the death of her husband, Baron Kurt von Gratz. Those of us who have missed the fashionable pair are delighted to know she has come out of her mourning since the arrival of Robin Stone, American television journalist. The baron was killed in the Monte Carlo races, and for some time it was feared the lovely baroness would not recover from her mental depression. But for the past ten days she has gone to the theater and several intimate dinner parties with Mr. Stone. And now the pair have gone off to Switzerland to stay with the Ramey Blacktons in their Swiss chalet. Skiing or romancing—it's hard to tell —but everyone is delighted that our lovely Ericka is smiling again.

She thumbed through the other paper. There was another picture of Robin and the baroness. She threw herself on the bed and sobbed. She pounded the pillow as if she were slashing at Robin's smiling face. Then, with a sudden change of mood, she sat up. Good Lord, she had a three o'clock sitting for Halston and his new summer hats! She rushed and got ice cubes, wrapped them in a towel and put them on her eyes. Then she ran the hot water for compresses: if she alternated with the hot and cold on her eyes for half an hour, she would look all right. She had to keep the appointment–she wasn't going to lose a job because of Robin. He certainly wasn't pining away for her!

Then, with another swift change of mood, she dialed Christie Lane. He answered immediately. "Doll, I was just half out of the door on my way to the Friars. You just caught me."

"I've canceled my late bookings," she said.

"Look, I was only kidding when I said I'd make it up–I can't afford that kind of scratch." He sounded frightened.

"I'm not asking you to pay me. I just suddenly decided I was working too hard."

His voice changed immediately. "Oh, great! So everything's still on. Meet me at '21' at six-thirty. That's when the broad from *Life* will be there."

The evening went off easier than she had expected. The waiters had obviously been primed by Danton Miller. The table at "21" was in the center section downstairs. She forced herself to drink a Scotch–it might make the evening more palatable. The girl from *Life* was extremely nice. She explained that she had been sent over to "talk" to Christie about an interview. Then she was to write her impressions and the senior editors would decide whether they wanted to follow it up and assign someone to do a story.

Christie managed a weak laugh. "This is a new slant–being interviewed for an interview! How classy can a magazine be!" The unexpected humiliation deflated his ego. Amanda suddenly realized that most of his bravado was merely a pretense to cover his terrible insecurity. Her heart went out to him. She reached over and took his hand.

The girl from *Life* was also sensitive to his mood. She forced an easy laugh. "They do this with everyone, Mr. Lane. Why, just last week I did research on an important senator and the editors turned the story down."

Some of Christie's self-assurance returned. He insisted that she accompany them to El Morocco. Amanda realized that he was desperate for the story. He told the reporter about his humble beginnings, the early poverty, the honky-tonk nightclubs he had played. To Amanda's surprise, the girl was actually interested. As she began to take notes, Christie's enthusiasm soared. He threw his arm around Amanda and winked at the reporter: "Imagine a bum like me winding up with a fancy society-type cover girl!"

At the end of the evening, Amanda asked to be dropped off first. She closed the door wearily as she entered her apartment. She was bone-tired. It was an effort to take off her clothes. She wanted to flop on the bed and go right to sleep. She took off her makeup and automatically began the hundred strokes on her heavy blond hair. She stared at the brush. Good Lord, it was filled with hair. She'd have to stop using the Alwayso spray. No matter how much Jerry praised it, the stuff was murdering her hair. She dropped the can into the wastebasket. She finally fell into bed and was gratified that she was so tired—at least she wouldn't lie awake and think of Robin and the baroness.

She spent the next four evenings with Christie, followed by a reporter from *Life* and his photographer. But she couldn't forget Robin Stone. At the end of the week, the *Life* story was finished. It looked fairly certain that they would use it. But as the reporter had said, you couldn't be positive until it was "locked in." The final shots were taken while she was doing her commercial on the show.

Christie stood backstage with her and watched them leave. "It's in the bag!" he said, throwing his arm around her. "Tonight we're really going to celebrate. And we've got something even more important to celebrate—the new ratings just came out. Now I'm in the top ten! Do you hear that, doll? Two weeks ago I was number nineteen. This week I'm number eight! Only seven shows to beat! We gotta celebrate. And there's something else: we never really been alone. Tonight, you and me, we're gonna go to Danny's Hideaway together—alone."

When they were ushered to the front table, Christie was like a child in his happiness. To Amanda it seemed as if the ratings had been posted on the front page of *The New York Times*. The entire restaurant seemed to know. Everyone, including Cliff, the public relations man, stopped by to congratulate him. Christie basked in his new glory. He called out to other performers, left her alone several times while he "table-hopped." Then he ordered steaks for both of them. She sat stiffly and picked at her food, while he ate with enthusiasm, his elbow on the table, his head lowered to the food. When he had finished, he used two fingers to dig for a fragment of food lodged between his back teeth.

He stared at her half-eaten steak. "Something wrong with the meat?"

"No, I've had enough. I'll get a doggy bag."

"You got a dog?"

"A cat."

"I hate cats." Then he smiled. "Does it jump on your bed at night?"

"Yes, it snuggles with me."

"Then tonight we go to my place." He looked at her dress. It was a beaded sheath she had worn on the show. "We'll stop at your place and you can feed the cat and change your dress."

"Why do I change my dress?"

He grinned awkwardly. "Well, look, doll, tomorrow morning how's it gonna look, you traipsing through the Astor lobby in that getup?"

"I have no intention of traipsing through the Astor lobby. Tomorrow morning I will be in my own bed."

"Oh, you mean you want to do it–and go home?"

"I want to go home. Now."

"What about the fucking?"

She colored visibly. "Chris, I don't want to get up and walk out on you. But if you ever use that language again, that is exactly what I will do."

"Come on, doll, you know it don't mean anything when I say things like that. But I'll be careful. Shit, I was raised backstage, I learned those words when most kids were reciting nursery rhymes. Tell you what–every time I say one of them words, I'll give you a buck. No, better make it a quarter. With a buck a throw and my vocabulary–you could retire."

She managed a smile. He was trying to be nice. It wasn't his fault that she felt such physical revulsion for him, but she longed to get away from him. "Chris, I want to go home, alone. I have a headache, it's been a long day."

"Oh sure, you stood around holding up that heavy lipstick. I only sing and dance and do sketches."

"But you're talented. You've been doing it all your life. I panic every time I see those three cameras coming at me. And facing that audience–it takes a lot out of me. You're born to it."

"Maybe. All right, we'll let the fuck–the lovemaking–go till tomorrow night. No, I got a benefit tomorrow, maybe the following night. Is that a date?"

"I don't know–"

"Whadya mean?"

"I just don't leap into things like this."

"We been going together a long time–"

"Three weeks and four days." (It had been four weeks and four days since Robin left.)

"Hey, you must care to number the days like that. Well then, when? Or are you still carrying a torch for Robin Stone?"

She knew she had reacted visibly. The question had caught her off guard.

He seemed pleased. "Oh, I been doing my own investigating."

"It's no secret that I've gone out with Robin Stone. He's a very good friend. An old friend. I've known him over a year."

"Then you're not carrying the torch?"

"Who ever told you that?"

"Ethel Evans."

She was silent. She had no idea that Ethel was so perceptive. Only this evening, while Ethel was backstage, she had acted as if she hadn't a thought in the world for anyone but Christie Lane.

Christie mistook her silence for bewilderment. "You remember Ethel Evans–the big-assed publicity dame with the loud mouth. She's laid every guy from coast to coast and brags about it. God, did you see her tonight? Falling all over the guest star. She's living up to her title: the Celebrity Fucker."

"Maybe it's men like you who make her bad news," she answered.

"Meaning what?"

"Hanging such a title on her and spreading gossip. After all, have you ever had an affair with her?"

"No, but everyone I know has had her–every big shot, I mean."

"Then you're giving lip service to something you've only heard."

"Why the big defense for that big-assed dame? You should hear her knock you."

"Take me home," she said tightly.

"Oh, Jesus. Doll, I'm sorry." He took her hand and looked at her intently. He placed her hand on his chest. "I go for you, Mandy–this is the first time I've ever said it and meant it. I really go for you. And it could be for keeps."

She saw the large blue eyes pleading. The open, homely face was vulnerable and she knew he was telling the truth. Tonight on the air he had intentionally sung "Mandy"–the song Al Jolson made famous. When he got to the line "Mandy, there's a minister handy," he had turned and looked right at her in the wings. The camera crew had gone crazy trying to change shots. She didn't want to hurt him, she *knew* what hurt was–she had been living with it for so long. She patted his hand. "Look, Chris, you're going to be a big star, you've got everything good ahead for you. You'll have millions of girls, nice girls, beautiful girls–"

"I don't want *them*. I want *you*."

"Chris, we've only been out together a few times. You couldn't love me, you don't *know* me."

"Doll, I've knocked around plenty. I've seen the dregs–low-down nightclubs, low-down girls. All my life I wanted something better. That's why I stayed single-o this long. I'd grab off a hooker when I needed it, but I never made no emotional attachment. See what I mean? Then, wham! Along comes this show–and you! All in one package. For the first time I'm in the big leagues, with a hit show and a lady at my side. Oh, I've seen ladies before–classy broads at benefits I've played–so I can tell the real McCoy. Only all the ones I've seen have been buck-toothed and flat-chested. But you're the whole package–and I want you."

She blanched, thinking of her small breasts. But what difference did it make? He'd never know. She looked at him with candor. "I like you, Chris. But I'm not in love with you."

"That's enough for me," he said. "I'm willing to wait. But just promise me one thing: give me a chance. Go out with me, date me, and eventually you'll want to go to bed with me. And if it works out–it'll be for keeps. Maybe it'll even be marriage." He stopped her objections. "Wait. Just wait–that's all I ask."

She knew what he was feeling. And if letting him hope made him happy, what harm would it do? At least tonight he would go to bed with a dream. Eventually he would be a big star—and the bigger he got, the less she would matter.

She kissed him good night outside her apartment. When she let herself in, she found a telegram had been slipped under the door. She picked it up and opened it lethargically—probably an invitation to a new discothèque:

> ARRIVING AT IDLEWILD AT 2 A.M. YOUR TIME, TWA FLIGHT 3. NOW IF YOU ARE REALLY MY GIRL, YOU'LL HIRE A CAR AND BE IN IT. ROBIN.

She looked at her watch. Eleven forty-five. Oh, thank God, she could make it! She rushed to the phone and ordered a car. She'd never be able to figure Robin. He wouldn't waste a dime to call and say goodbye, yet he'd send a wire to announce his arrival. She would have time to change her makeup, her dress—she had to look her best when she met him. She was singing as she rubbed the cream on her face. And for the first time in four weeks and four days she wasn't the least bit tired.

She stood at Gate 7. The plane had just arrived. Passengers began to disembark. She saw Robin immediately. He was different from other men. Other men walked. Robin sort of sailed through people. He dropped his attaché case and threw his arms around her. "How's the new television star?" he asked.

"Thrilled to see the world's greatest newsman." She matched his tone and vowed not to mention the baroness.

He put his arm around her and walked to the car.

"I don't understand," she said. "I thought you were in London. But your wire came from Los Angeles."

"I took the polar route and stopped off in Los Angeles for a few days." He reached into his pocket and handed her a small package. "A gift for you—I forgot to declare it. I'm a smuggler."

In the car, she snuggled against him and opened the package. It was a beautiful antique Wedgwood cigarette box. She knew it was expensive, but she would have preferred something half the price and more personal.

"I hope you still smoke." He laughed, reached for a crumpled pack of English cigarettes and offered her one.

She inhaled and almost choked on the strong tobacco. He took it away from her and kissed her lips lightly. "Miss me?"

"Well—you took off leaving me with two steaks. I didn't know whether to miss you or kill you."

He stared at her absently, as if trying to recall.

"I mean, you could have called me and said, 'Hey, baby, take the steaks out of the oven, I can't make it.' "

"Didn't I?" He seemed genuinely surprised.

"Forget it. The cat had a marvelous meal."

"But you knew I had gone." He seemed vaguely troubled.

"Well, I heard you announce it on the air. But, Robin, you were gone for so long."

He put his arm around her and drew her closer. "Well, now I'm back. Tired?"

She clung to him. "Never for you."

His kiss was long and deep. His eyes were gentle and he touched her face with his hands almost like a blind man trying to see. "My lovely Amanda. You are beautiful."

"Robin, while you were away I went out with Christie Lane." He appeared to be trying to place the name. She added, "The star of the show."

"Oh. Yes, I hear he's catching on big. I've kept up with the ratings."

"My name was coupled with his in the columns."

"Did it raise your modeling fee?" His grin was friendly.

She shrugged. "It's quite high."

"Good."

She looked at him. "People—well, some people—think I'm his girl. I wanted you to know it's just talk. I didn't want it to bother you."

"Why should it bother me?"

"I thought it might. . . ."

He lit another cigarette.

"I guess I was foolish to worry," she said.

He laughed. "You're a celebrity. Celebrities get their names in columns."

"And you don't mind that I went out with Chris?"

"Why should I? I wasn't exactly a hermit in London."

She pulled away from him and turned toward the window. She stared at the darkness of the night and the cars flashing by in the opposite lane. He reached out and took her hand. She pulled it away.

"Robin, are you trying to hurt me?"

"No." He was looking at her honestly. "Nor are you trying to hurt me."

"But I'm your girl–aren't I?"

"You bet you are." (That damned grin of his.) "But, Amanda, I never said I wanted you on a leash."

"You mean you don't mind that I went out with him, or you wouldn't mind if I continued to see him?"

"Of course I wouldn't mind."

"What if I slept with him?"

"That's up to you."

"Would you care?"

"If you told me–yes, I would care."

"You mean you'd want me to hide it."

"All right, Amanda: are you sleeping with him?"

"No. But he wants me to. He even talks about marriage."

"Suit yourself. . . ."

"Robin, tell the driver to stop at my place first."

"Why?"

"I want to go home–alone."

He pulled her back into his arms. "Baby–you came all the way out to Idlewild to meet me. Why the switch?"

"Robin, don't you see that–" Suddenly he kissed her and she stopped trying to explain.

They spent the night together, locked in one another's arms. There was no more talk about Christie Lane. It was as if Robin had never been away–it was like it had been in the beginning.

Like it was every time they were alone, in bed. Urgent, exciting and tender.

Later as they lay together smoking and relaxed in a peaceful closeness, she said, "Who is the baroness?" It had just slipped out. She regretted it instantly.

His expression didn't change. "A broad."

"Now, Robin, I read about her, she's a baroness."

"Oh, the title is real, but she's a broad. One of those kids spawned during the war. At twelve she was doing it with GIs for candy bars. Then she married the baron–he was a fag, also a voyeur. Ericka knew all the tricks. She's not a bad girl, she's got a bona fide title, money for the first time and she likes to swing. I met her at an orgy."

She sat up in the darkness. "An orgy!"

"They're very large in London. I hear they're catching on in Los Angeles, too."

"And you like that sort of thing?"

He grinned. "What's not to like about it? It's better than television over there. They only have two channels, you know."

"Robin, be serious."

"I am. Did you ever meet Ike Ryan?"

The name was familiar. Suddenly she recalled. He was an American film producer who was based in Italy and France, and was making quite a name for himself.

"You'll like him. We met in London. I was feeling rotten. The weather was getting me down and he invited me to one of his parties. There were three Italian movie actresses, the baroness, Ike and me. It was ladies' night in a Turkish bath."

"And you participated?"

"Sure, why not? First I watched the girls with each other, then Ike and I lay back and the harem took care of us. Ericka was the best–trust the Germans to perfect any art–so I carted her off for myself. But Ike's a real good guy. He's going to L.A. to set up his own company. He'll give that town a shot in the arm."

"With orgies?"

"No, with pictures. He's a gambler, and he has great style. He's also good-looking. Women like him."

"I think he's disgusting."

"Why?"

"Because, I mean, to do things like that!"

He laughed. "Am I disgusting?"

"No. I think you're like a bad little boy who feels he's being very daring. But this Ike Ryan, he originated it–"

"Baby, it started way back with the Greeks."

"And you'd want me to meet a man like that? Be seen out in public with him? If I were seen with him and you, everyone would think I was that kind of a girl. Would you want that?"

He turned and looked at her very seriously. "No, Amanda, I promise you: I'll never take you out with Ike Ryan."

Then he had gotten up and taken a sleeping pill along with a beer. "I'm still on European time. I'm overtired. Want one?"

"No, I have to be up at ten."

He got back into bed and took her in his arms. "My beautiful Amanda, it's good to be with you. Don't wake me when you leave in the morning. I have a busy afternoon ahead–mail piled up, appointments–I need some sleep."

In the morning she dressed and left his apartment quickly. She was tired that day and not very good in her work. And her hair was coming out again. She called Nick and asked him for a dermatologist. He laughed. "You're molting, darling. It's just nerves."

"It probably is," she said. "Robin's back."

"Call your doctor and get a B-12 shot or something–and for God's sake, don't spend every night making love."

"I don't have a doctor." She laughed. "I've never needed one. Do you know someone good?"

"Amanda my love, you are so young and healthy it's disgusting. I have six doctors. One for throat and ears, one for my prostate, one for my slipped disc. Want my advice, stay away from them all. Get a good night's sleep, and once that *Life* story comes out all your worries will be over."

He was probably right. She was finished with her work by three. She went home to take a nap. Slugger jumped into bed and curled up in her arms. She kissed his tawny head. "It's not night, darling. We're just resting." He purred gravelly in contentment. "You're the only male who's reliable, darling, but Robin's back and when he comes tonight, don't hate me for exiling you into the living room."

She knew she had slept. She sat up with a jolt. It was dark—she tried to orient herself. What day was it? Suddenly she remembered. She turned on the light. Nine o'clock. Slugger jumped off of the bed and growled, demanding dinner.

Nine o'clock! And Robin hadn't called! She checked with her service. No calls. She dialed Robin. After ten empty rings she clicked the receiver. She didn't sleep the rest of the night. Slugger, sensing something was wrong, nestled close to her.

The following day she waited until six, then she called him. After all, he might be ill. He answered, and he was fine. It was just all the desk work that had piled up. He said he would call tomorrow.

The following morning she caught his name as she scanned one of the columns:

> **Ike Ryan and Robin Stone were at El Morocco with two beautiful Italian actresses. Their names were too long for this reporter to remember, but he'll never forget their faces and their—wow!**

She threw the paper on the floor. He had been feeling her out, knowing Ike Ryan was coming to town. Oh Lord, why had she said she wouldn't be seen with him?

That night she went out with Christie. They went to Danny's. She was very quiet and Christie was disgruntled: they had been seated at a small table along the wall. One of the front tables was occupied by a group of Hollywood celebrities. The other was empty, with a RESERVED sign prominently displayed.

"Probably some other Hollywood joker," he said, eyeing the table enviously. "Why is everyone so impressed with movie people? I bet more people know me than most of the stars in Hollywood."

She tried to cheer him; no use both of them being miserable. "Christie, this is a marvelous table. I like being in the center of the room, you can see everyone."

"I belong at the best table everywhere!"

"Wherever you sit is automatically the best table," she said.

He stared at her. "You believe that?"

"It's more important if *you* do."

He grinned and ordered their dinner. After a short time his good humor returned. "The *Life* story is locked in," he said. He looked at her longingly. "Mandy, right now there's something I want more than *Life*. How do I have to prove myself? I love you. I feel like a jerky high-school boy, sitting just holding your hand. I been doing a lot of thinking. How *can* you get to love me if you don't sleep with me? I know there's no one else. Eddie was trying to tell me that the word around was that you were dead-stuck on Robin Stone. But I read the column today. . . ."

"Chris, since you brought it up, I think I ought to tell you–" She stopped, her attention suddenly riveted to the four people who were being shown to the front table. Danny himself was ushering them in. Two beautiful girls, two men. And one of the men was Robin!

She felt that strange light-headedness that often comes with shock. Robin was lighting the girl's cigarette and giving her that very private grin. The other man was probably Ike Ryan.

"Tell me what, doll?"

Chris was staring at her. She knew she had to say something, but she was powerless to remove her eyes from Robin. She saw him lean over and kiss the girl on the tip of her nose. Then he laughed.

"Oh, look who has my table," Chris said. "I watched him one night–wanted to take a gander at my competition. I tell you, I couldn't watch more than ten minutes. He was yelling about Cuba and all that kind of shit, and some jerk was agreeing with him. Big deal. Did you get a load of his ratings against mine?"

"He's in the top twenty-five, that's excellent for a news show." She wondered why she was defending him.

"I'm gonna be number one, you watch. And everyone treats me like I'm number one–except you."

"I–I like you very much."

"Then put up or shut up."

"I want to go home." She really felt ill. Robin was listening to the girl with his head bent close.

"Oh, doll, let's not fight. I love you, but we've got to make it together."

"Take me home. . . ."

He looked at her oddly. "If I take you home, that's it. I know when I'm licked."

She watched him sign the check. They would have to pass Robin's table. Chris stopped at almost every table on the way out, greeting people loudly. She knew Robin had to notice her. When they passed his table, he stood up. He wasn't the least embarrassed. In fact, he seemed actually glad to see her. He congratulated Chris on his show, and introduced everyone at the table. The two girls were both Francesca something–Italian starlets–and the man was Ike Ryan. She was surprised when Ike stood up. He was six feet tall, with black hair and blue eyes. He was tanned, strong-looking, good-looking; nothing like she had envisioned.

"So this is *the* Amanda?" He turned to the two girls and spoke Italian. The girls nodded and smiled at her. Then Ike said, "I just told them what a big shot you are, Amanda."

"Tell 'em about me," Christie said.

Ike laughed. "I don't have to. They know who you are. They've been glued to the television set since they got here."

It seemed an eternity, but they finally left. Amanda shot one last glance at Robin, hoping to find some message in his eyes, but he was talking and the girl was smiling. Obviously she understood *some* English.

Christie was glum as he hailed a cab. Suddenly she took his arm. "I'll go back to your place, Christie."

He was pathetically exuberant. "Oh, doll–but hey, what about the fancy dress? Want to stop off at your place and change?"

"No, I'll leave you after–after we do it."

"No, I'll even go along with the cat. We'll go to your place. I got no place to go tomorrow. Then I can stay there and you can get up whenever you want."

Her flesh began to crawl. "No, there's a cameraman coming up tomorrow, early. It's only ten-thirty now, so if I go to your place, and leave in a few hours, it will work out."

"But I want to be with you all night–hold you in my arms."

She fought back her feeling of nausea. She had deliberately chosen the Astor as the lesser of the evils. At least she could get up and leave when it was over.

"It has to be this way," she said quietly.

"Doll, I'll take it any way I can get it. Oh boy, are you gonna be happy! I'm the greatest–wait till you see."

She was positive that everyone in the Astor lobby knew her plans as she walked to the elevator. She felt that even the taxi driver had looked at her in contempt when she got out of the cab. But how many times she had sailed through Robin's lobby, even greeted his doorman with a cheery good morning–it had all seemed so natural and wonderful. . . . No. She musn't think of Robin, not now.

She walked into the bathroom of Christie's suite and took off all of her clothes. She stared at her flat breasts, then walked into the bedroom defiantly. He was lying on the bed in his shorts, looking at the racing form. His jaw dropped in disappointment. "No tits!" Her eyes were cold–challenging him. He laughed and held out his arms. "Well! I guess it proves that all the classy ladies are skinny. At least you haven't got buck teeth. But come on over–you won't be disappointed at the size of my joint. Look what good old Chris has just for you. . . ."

She submitted to his embrace in the darkness. She lay back while he panted and gyrated through her. She knew he was trying to please her. Oh God, if he went on for hours, nothing would happen. He could never rouse her–ever. She prayed for him to get it over. He suddenly leaped off her and fell to his side, groaning. After a few minutes he said, "Don't worry, doll, I pulled out in time. I won't knock you up."

She lay there quietly. He took her in his arms. His body was clammy with perspiration. "I didn't make you come, did I?" he said.

"Chris, I–" She stopped.

"Don't worry, let me catch my breath and I'll go down on you."

"No, Chris. It was wonderful! I was just nervous, that's all. Next time I'll wear something, don't worry."

"Listen, I've decided. We're gonna get married. At the end of the season. I've got six weeks booked in Vegas this summer for big money. We'll get married there. You'll have a ball, it'll be our honeymoon. So don't wear anything: if you get pregnant, great—we'll get married even sooner."

"No, I don't want to have a baby until after we're married. I wouldn't want people to think that was the reason."

"Listen, doll, I'm forty-seven. I'm leveling with you. Everyone thinks I'm forty. Even Eddie and Kenny don't know. But since you're gonna be my wife, I want you to know the real scene. I been careful with money all my life. I always made my forty or fifty thousand for the last fifteen years. And no matter what I made, I put half of it away. By the time I'm sixty, I'll have a million in annuities. Twenty years ago I met this guy in Chicago, he's a big tax expert. I got his kid out of some trouble, nothing serious, a slight car accident. But I had connections and I squared the rap and the kid's father, this Lou Goldberg, was so grateful that he became my father, mother, lawyer, tax man, everything. He said to me right then that I was a second-class talent, but if I listened to him, I'd wind up a first-class citizen. And he started taking half my money—I was maybe only earning a couple C-notes a week then—but Lou invested it. By now I got quite a portfolio—stuff like IBM that does nothing but double. Now that I've made it big, Lou still takes half. And if this keeps up—my new success, I mean—well, in a few years I'll have not one but two million. And the way he's investing it, I'll have over six thousand a month tax-free, without even touching the principal. We can leave that to our kid. Now that I've got you, everything will be perfect. And I want us to start having a kid right away, so when I'm sixty, at least I'll still be able to go to ball games with him and see him go to college like I never did. Don't ever tell anyone, but I never got past sixth grade—I was hawking candy in burlesque when I was twelve. But our kid will have everything!"

She lay very still. What had she done! This poor idiot. . . .

She suddenly got out of bed and went into the bathroom and dressed. Chris was dressing when she came out.

"Don't bother," she begged. "I can get a cab." She was anxious to get away. She couldn't bear his lovesick eyes.

"Nah, it's still early. I'll take you home and then drop by the Stage Deli. Eddie and Kenny will probably be there. I'll have a cup of coffee with them and kibitz. I'm so happy I can't sleep—I want to tell it to the world."

She let him hold her hand on the ride home. He kissed her good night at the elevator. Then she went into her apartment—ran to the bathroom and threw up.

Robin called the following day. He never mentioned the Italian girls. He was leaving that afternoon for Los Angeles with Ike Ryan. He wanted to do an *In Depth* on Ike. He felt it would be more exciting if it were filmed on location. In Ike's office, on the set. From there he was flying back to London on the polar route, and he had no idea when he'd return. She never mentioned the baroness or the Italian starlet, and he never mentioned Christie Lane.

TWELVE

ON MAY FIRST, Amanda awoke fifteen minutes before her "wake-up" call. Tomorrow *Life* magazine would be on every newsstand, but the Plaza Hotel always got *Time* and *Life* a day earlier. She dressed quickly. For the past six weeks she had vacillated between eagerness and apprehension. Everyone was waiting for the *Life* story. Christie felt it would make him an international celebrity. Nick Longworth was all set to raise her fee to a hundred an hour.

She took a cab to the Plaza and dashed into the lobby. The bright red cover caught her eye as she approached the newsstand. She dropped the money on the counter and walked quickly to a large easy chair in the lobby near the Palm Court.

It was a ten-page spread with a big headline: THE CHRISTIE LANE PHENOMENON. She was featured with Christie in four pictures and there was one of her alone, posing for Ivan in a chiffon dress in Central Park. And it was no wind machine swirling that dress–she would never forget how cold it had been that day. As she read, she was pleased that the reporter had been unusually perceptive. There was a graphic description of the way she had stood facing the March wind without flinching. It took a peculiar kind of strength to be a model, he noted. It was all very complimentary to her. And although it painted Christie as a man of the people, it slyly revealed his bad grammar, his flamboyancy, his total absorption with his new fame. (So far–so good, she thought.) She read on:

> To go along with his new prominence, Christie Lane has taken himself a girl fit to be the consort of the new top minstrel man of television. A beautiful cover girl–Amanda. She is not just the girl he loves. She is a symbol. Proof that

> the world of second-rate nightclubs is a thing of the past. Because Amanda is definitely first-rate. And after seeing them together, they are not the incongruous pair one might think. Christie Lane worships the elegance of this beautiful girl. And perhaps the lovely Amanda finds reality with Christie Lane. When a girl stands outdoors in thirty-degree temperatures, wearing a chiffon dress and a Palm Beach smile, she probably welcomes the honesty of a man like Christie Lane. Perhaps she is anxious to toss away the June-in-January world of a fashion model to find a real world with this very real man.

She shut the magazine. That last line! How would Robin take it? She walked out into the bright sunlight. Although she dated Christie and occasionally went to bed with him, she felt she barely knew him. They were never alone, except for the torturous few hours together at the Astor. Christie spent at least two nights a week with his writers; there were benefits, interviews—all time-consuming, all part of being a star. Yet he was planning to marry her in Vegas! She had let him talk—the summer had seemed so far away. But now it was May!

She had to break with Christie Lane! She had only continued seeing him because of her loneliness and longing for Robin. She could never really care about anyone else. But at least she was making Christie happy. . . .

The story in *Life* caused a great deal of excitement. She actually felt famous, especially on the nights after the show, when she came out of the stage door and all the autograph kids called her by name. But she didn't hear a word from Robin, until the Sunday before Decoration Day. She had just hung up on Christie. He was playing Decoration Day at Grossinger's for a fabulous fee. He had wanted her to go along with him—but she refused.

"Ah, come on," he pleaded. "We'll have a ball. Even Aggie is taking off from the Latin Quarter—"

"I can't afford to lose the money. Besides, I'm not Aggie—I'm not a camp follower."

"What's with the camp-follower crap? We're getting married this summer."

"*If* and *when* we're married, I'll go to places where you play. Right now I'm staying in New York and keeping my modeling appointments. I'm not going anywhere as part of the Christie Lane caravan."

"Ah, shit, you and your highfalutin ideas. I hadda go fall in love with a lady!" He hung up, disgruntled but not angry.

After she had hung up, she thought about it. Why hadn't she just said, "I'm never going to marry you"? Because she was frightened! She was frightened of what would happen if Robin ever disappeared for good. She would go to pieces. She had tried breaking with Christie once, told him she was never going to see him again. The break lasted only five days. . . . At least with Christie she was able to keep her sanity. There was always a nightclub opening or a benefit, and being with Christie was better than being alone.

The phone rang. She picked it up lethargically, thinking it was Christie calling back to make one last plea. The crisp voice caught her off balance: "Hello, Celebrity."

"Robin! Oh, Robin! Where are you?"

"I just came in. I've been away, covering the Eichmann trial. I just read all about you on the plane–caught up with all the back issues of *Life*–and, by God, there you were!"

"What did you think of it?" She forced herself to sound casual.

"Just great," he said with enthusiasm. "It makes you sound almost as exciting as you really are."

Her throat was tight–but she kept her voice light. "You almost sound like you missed me."

"I did."

She barely listened. She was planning their evening. It was five o'clock–too late to wash her hair, but she could put on a fall. She hoped they would stay in. Thank God it was Sunday–Jerry was in the country and couldn't tag along. She had steaks in the freezer, but she was out of vodka.

"Are you still as beautiful as ever?" he was asking.

"Come see for yourself."

"Fine. Meet me at the Lancer Bar tomorrow at seven."

She was so disappointed she couldn't speak.

He took her silence for indecision. His voice was light. "Or has

Christie Lane cut me out of the picture?"

"No—but he's asked me to marry him."

"He might be a good bet at that. His show will go on forever."

"Would you care, Robin, if I married Christie Lane?"

"Sure I'd care. I'd hate like hell to lose you. But I can't compete against marriage."

"Why not?"

"Look, baby, there's only one reason for marriage, and that's to have kids. I don't want any kids."

"Why?"

"They're one hell of a responsibility."

"In what way?"

"Look, Amanda—I have to be loose, be able to pick up and go. You can do that with a girl, even a wife. But you can't do it to a kid. What kind of a father would I make?"

She was trembling. Marriage had always been a subject he had refused to discuss. But now they were actually discussing it.

"Oh, Robin, I think you'd make a marvelous father."

"A father should be with his kid."

"Did your father leave you?"

"No, he had nine-to-five hours. And Kitty was a good mother: we had nurses and cooks, but she was always there. And that's the way it *should* be."

"Then I don't understand—what makes you feel you would run out?"

"My work, baby," he said tightly. "And although it's never happened to me, I know that if I was a kid and my father wasn't there it would kill me—I know it. Don't ask me why, I just feel it."

"Robin, we don't have to have children now. . . ."

"Then why get married?" he asked.

"To be together."

"We're together, except when I need to be alone. Like tonight—I've got a desk piled with mail. I feel like tossing it all in the basket. I may do just that." There was a pause. "I just did. The bills will arrive again, and I don't think they'll turn off the electricity if I'm one month late."

"All right, the mail is gone. Now we can be together tonight," she said.

"Amanda, that's why I'm against marriage. I *want* to be alone tonight." His voice suddenly became gentle. "Do you understand now, Amanda? I'm not geared for marriage. I like things the way they are."

"And the little setups Ike Ryan arranges!"

"Ike Ryan–now where did you drag that name from? I haven't seen or thought of him in ages."

"And what about the baroness? Or is that a name you haven't thought of in months?" She knew she was destroying herself, but she couldn't help it.

"Amanda darling, another awful thing about marriage is explanations. I don't owe you any, nor do you owe me any. Now, how about tomorrow? Are you free?"

"I'll *make* myself free." Her voice was sullen.

"Good girl."

"Are you here for some time? Or are you flying off somewhere?"

"Baby, I'm so tired of traveling, I never want to leave again. I'm going to stay put until fall."

"That's good." Her gloom evaporated. "We go off the air in two weeks."

"Oh, that reminds me, Jerry Moss invited me up to Greenwich for the July Fourth weekend. They have a great house and a pool. Would you like to come?"

"I'd love it, Robin."

"Great! See you tomorrow night."

She sat very quietly for a long time. She lay awake half the night. The following morning, she called Jerry Moss at nine o'clock.

"Jerry, I've got to see you. It's urgent."

"I'll probably see you at the Lancer Bar. I'm meeting Robin there at five."

"I'm not getting there until seven. But I've got to see you *alone*. It's very important!"

"Lunch?"

"No, I have a twelve o'clock session. Can I come to your office? Say, ten o'clock?"

"It's a date. I'll even have coffee waiting for you."

She sat across the desk from Jerry and sipped the coffee. She told him about Chris, implying that there had been no intimacy between them. In a way it wasn't a lie—there was no intimacy. She merely lay back, gritted her teeth and submitted to him.

Then she said, "That's why I had to come to you, Jerry. You're the only one who can help me."

He looked startled. "Me?"

"If I go to Vegas with Chris, I'll have to marry him. If I *don't* go to Vegas, I'll lose him."

Jerry nodded. "It's a simple decision. A sure bet against a long shot."

"I want a chance at that long shot," she said. "Robin will be in town all summer. He's invited me to your place for July Fourth."

Jerry was silent. Then he said, "Go to Vegas, honey—marry Chris. Don't waste any more time on Robin."

"Why? Has he told you something I don't know?"

"No, but look—did you ever hear of Ike Ryan?"

"I know all about Ike Ryan. But he doesn't see him—or do those things anymore."

Jerry smiled. "I have a friend who's a psychiatrist. When Robin told me about the action he got with Ike, I happened to bring it up with him and he said that Robin probably hates women."

"That's ridiculous!" she snapped. "This friend of yours doesn't even *know* Robin. How can he come up with a statement like that!"

"He's *met* Robin—"

"Are you trying to hint that Robin's queer?" Now she was actually angry.

"No. I'm saying that as people—as friends—he likes men. He digs women, but only for sex—he doesn't really like them. He's actually hostile to them."

"And you think that's true?"

"Yes. But I think Robin likes *you*—as much as he can like a woman. He'll force your hand eventually; *you'll* be the one to break this up."

"Jerry. . . ." Her eyes were soft. "Help me. . . ."

"How can I help you?"

"Keep me from going to Vegas with Christie. You can tell Christie I've signed a contract for the commercials on the summer replacement show and I have to stay here and do them live."

He looked at her. "Go to Vegas, Amanda. Christie Lane is offering you a future, a real life, kids—the works."

"Jerry," she was pleading. "I want one last chance with Robin."

"I thought you had more class, Amanda. Where's your gambling spirit? If I cared that much for someone, I'd toss the dice and go for broke. Give up Christie Lane. Shoot for Robin! So you lose a chance for a good marriage and security. If you were thirty-five, I'd say you couldn't risk it. But you're young, and you must have plenty of money saved."

"I don't save any. I can't."

Jerry shrugged. "Then stop buying all those 'name' clothes. God, Mary buys things in Greenwich for forty-five dollars."

"Mary doesn't make a hundred dollars an hour. And don't forget, I use my clothes on the show. Being well dressed is part of my business. And I'm *scared* of not having money, Jerry, scared of being without it."

"In my book, a girl with two men in love with her shouldn't worry about being alone. And a girl who makes a hundred dollars an hour shouldn't worry about not having money."

She clenched her hands. "Jerry, have you ever been poor? I mean *dirt*-poor. I was. I was white trash. It kills me when Chris talks about Miami, and how he played small clubs, and how he vowed to play the big time in the big hotels. I was born in Miami—in a charity ward. My mother was a Finnish chambermaid in one of those fancy hotels. I suppose she must have been pretty. I only remember her as being skinny and tired. But one of those rich men who stayed at that hotel must have thought she was pretty. I don't even know who my father was. I just know he was some rich man who could afford to spend the winter in Miami and knock up some little chambermaid. After I was born we lived in what they called Niggertown, because the only woman who was decent to my mother was a colored girl who worked in the hotel. It was a shanty, a tar flat–you pass them when you drive to the airport. This woman–her name was Rose–she got my mother to the charity hospital when I was born. And then we lived with her. I called her Aunt Rose, she's the finest woman I've ever known. Later on, when my mother worked at night, Aunt Rose would come home and make supper and see that I studied and hear my prayers. My mother died when I was six. Aunt Rose paid for the funeral and kept me with her just like I was her child. She made me finish high school–she worked for me, she clothed me–then she sent me to New York on a bus with fifty dollars she had saved." Amanda stopped and the tears overflowed.

"I'm sure you've repaid the fifty," he said.

"I sent her fifty dollars a *week* in the beginning. But it would take me a lifetime to repay her for her love. A year and a half ago, Aunt Rose had a stroke. I rushed down to Florida–it was right before I met Robin–and I got her into a hospital. It wasn't easy, they weren't exactly thrilled about having a sick old colored woman. But I met a sympathetic doctor, and he helped me get her in a private room. Naturally she had no hospital insurance, nothing. She was there for six weeks–that cost four thousand dollars with nurses and therapy. You try explaining that to the Bureau of Internal Revenue. 'Is she a relation, a dependent?' they ask. 'No: just someone I love.' But they figure she has Social Security, like one hundred and fifteen a month or something, and she can go in a charity ward. But according to law she's not my kin–I wasn't adopted. And those heartless guys down there, they see someone like me come in and they think, 'A model, one hundred an hour–she makes more in a day than I make in a week.' "

"Where is she now?" Jerry asked.

"That's just it. I couldn't leave her alone, even when she was discharged from the hospital. I tried to get someone to care for her, but it didn't work. So I brought her up here to a nursing home on Long Island. That cost a hundred a week. Okay, it was fine, and I visited her every week. Then about eight months ago she had a massive stroke. I had to move her to another nursing home where she gets round-the-clock care. And now I'm paying two hundred and fifty dollars a week."

"Do you still visit her every week?"

She shook her head. "It hurts me too much, and she doesn't even know I'm there. I go about once a month and on New Year's Day. I always used to call her on New Year's Eve when I first came to New York–and once I couldn't get through because the circuits were tied up, and I was frantic. And she said, 'Child, you call me on New Year's Day from now on. I don't want to ruin your night having you worry about getting to a phone.' "

Amanda sat up straight. "I grew up knowing the power of money, Jerry. Money enabled my unknown father to get out of town and go through life without even knowing me. *Lack* of money made my mother afraid to fight. And the only thing that is giving Aunt Rose some comfort now is *money*. So you see, Jerry, I can't gamble. I have to go for the sure thing. But I've earned the right to have a chance at the one man in the world I love! I can't settle for Christie without trying for Robin first."

He went over to the small bar he kept in the office and poured two shots of Scotch. He handed her one. "Amanda, I think Alwayso should do their commercials live this summer. I order you to stay here in town." He clicked his glass against hers. "I'll do my part, honey," he said. "Here's to the Fourth of July and a long, wonderful summer. We'll have a ball."

She managed a faint smile. "I hope so–because in the fall I'll have to make a decision."

The summer was over. She had been with Robin every night. Sometimes they went to the Hamptons for weekends. On Labor Day weekend they remained in New York. They went to Greenwich Village, walked down the narrow streets, sat for hours in a coffee bar on Cornelia Street.

Now it was October–the new season had begun. *The Christie Lane Show* was back on the air. *In Depth* had started its second season. Christie was demanding that she set a date for the marriage and Robin was off again on his sporadic trips. It was as if the summer had never happened. In spite of her vow, she knew she would go on–putting off Christie, waiting and hoping for Robin. She lost the few pounds she had gained during the summer–yet whenever Robin returned she felt fine. She couldn't make a decision–she waited.

Oddly enough, it was the sponsor who forced her to decide: On the fifteenth of January Alwayso was moving the show to California for the rest of the season.

"We go out as man and wife!" Christie insisted. "We stop off in Chicago and get married!"

"I won't get married on the way to anywhere. If I go to California, we'll get married out there," she replied.

The decision to move the show had been made the week before Christmas. And Robin was in London.

On Christmas Eve she met Jerry at the Lancer Bar for a drink. Jerry wasn't happy about California either. It meant spending a great deal of time out there. . . .

They both stared morosely at the bar with its cheerful little Christmas tree, and the false snow and the holly that was strung across the mirror. Their eyes met. She raised her glass. "Merry Christmas, Jerry."

"You look drawn, Amanda."

"I feel drawn and quartered," she said.

He reached out and took her hand. "Look, honey, you can't play a waiting game any longer. Put it to Robin on New Year's Day."

"Why then? How do I know I'll see him?"

"Hasn't Chris been invited to Mrs. Austin's New Year's Day party?"

She managed a smile. "Has he ever! That's all he talks about. He acts as if it's a command performance at Buckingham Palace."

"In a way, it is. Judith Austin rarely extends invitations to people at IBC. This year seems to be an exception. Danton Miller was kind of surprised that Robin was also invited. And I happen to know Robin is flying back New Year's Eve. He kidded me about celebrating it twice due to the time change. Robin will be at Mrs. Austin's. He won't dare turn it down."

"And what do I do?" she asked. "Walk up to him and say, 'It's now or never, Robin'?"

"Something like that."

"I can't–I'm not going to that party."

"Why, hasn't Chris asked you?"

"Of course he has. But I always spend New Year's Day with Aunt Rose. Of course I haven't told that to Chris. He knows nothing about it. I just plan to have a headache that day."

"But you said she doesn't recognize you, Amanda."

"I know, but I sit with her, and feed her–and New Year's Day, well, that's our day together."

"Will she know whether it's January first or January second?" Jerry asked.

"I'll know, Jerry."

"Look: go to the party, Amanda. And put it on the line to Robin. Get a clear-cut yes or no out of him. If it's no, then write him off. Two years is long enough to wait for anyone, even Robin. And you can visit your aunt the following day."

She seemed thoughtful. Then she nodded. "Okay, this is it!" She crossed her fingers. "Here's to nineteen sixty-two–either I make it, or I'm through! God, I'm a poet. Let's have a vodka martini, Jerry, the kind Robin drinks–and let's wish that bastard a Merry Christmas wherever he is!"

THIRTEEN

THE INVITATION to the Austin New Year's Day party read "Eggnog, Four to Seven." Chris wanted to pick Amanda up at three thirty. She insisted on making it four thirty.

"But, doll, we're supposed to be there at four."

"Which means no one comes until five. And anyone who is really anyone arrives at six."

He grudgingly agreed. "Who knows from all this classy protocol? I guess I really need a wife like you."

By three o'clock she had tried on six different outfits. The black dress was flattering–she could wear it with a string of pearls and Robin's gold watch. Funny about the watch–everyone seemed to admire it, maybe because it was so tiny. Nick Longworth said it was very expensive.

Chris had given her a gold charm bracelet for Christmas. She hated it, but she knew she had to wear it. She stared at the disc that said *Mandy and Chris*–it was so heavy and it clanked on everything. It definitely wouldn't go with the black dress.

She took out the Chanel suit. It was one of Ohrbach's line-for-line copies. Even the real Chanel cloth. But Judith Austin would be able to tell the difference. She probably had the original. Well, she wasn't out to impress Mrs. Austin. And Jerry had been right. She had watched IBC's *News at Noon*. They had a shot of Robin arriving at Idlewild at six that morning.

She had it all planned. It would be easy to slip away from Christie at a cocktail party. She'd go directly to Robin and say, "I want to talk to you tonight. It's urgent." She'd arrange to meet him later, after she unloaded Chris. And tonight it would be settled–one way or another. Chris thought she was all set for the Coast, but Jerry had given her a contract that she did not have to sign until the end of the week. Oh God, it had to work! In the last few weeks she had reversed many of her ideas about Christie. He was not just a simple good-natured slob. In some ways, especially concerning money, he could be absolutely cold-blooded. The other night, his fishy eyes had gone to a steely gray when he said, "You're playing it real cute, doll. Lou Goldberg tipped me off about you. Lou says you've been stalling our marriage date waiting for a shot like this."

"I don't understand," she said.

"You want to marry me in California–they got community property out there. If we divorce you'd get half of everything."

Since the thought had never occurred to her, the amazement on her face was real. "If I marry you, it's for keeps," she said.

"You bet it's for keeps." He had grinned. "And what's mine is yours–as soon as we have our kid."

Lou Goldberg had come to New York over Christmas. He was a nice man in his early sixties. She had tried to be pleasant, but she wasn't a very good actress and Lou's sharp eyes had taken in everything–the way she "allowed" Chris to hold her hand, her lack of spontaneous affection.

Today she *should* be with Aunt Rose–New Year's Day was a big visiting day at the nursing home. Maybe they wouldn't feed Aunt Rose her dinner, thinking she would be there to do it. Well, she'd call from the party just to make sure.

About twenty people had arrived when they entered the Austin town house. Its dark quiet luxury was impressive. The butler took their coats and directed them to the large living room. Amanda recognized a senator, several socialites, several movie stars, and a top comedy star from CBS (she had read that IBC was after him). She also saw Danton Miller, and in the corner, chatting earnestly with Mrs. Austin, was Ike Ryan. Amanda recognized him immediately. In the past few months Ike Ryan had exploded on the Hollywood scene. His flamboyant style made good copy. His first major picture was in the final stages of editing. The publicity began when he signed one of Hollywood's top glamour girls to star in it. She had immediately left her husband and embarked on a wild romance with Ike Ryan. The moment the picture was finished, he had dumped her, and taken up with a new little starlet whom he promised to feature in his next film. The rejected star tried sleeping pills but was saved when she phoned her estranged husband. A few weeks later the young starlet also tried sleeping pills and was saved by Ike whom she called at the zero hour. Ike had made the front pages–swearing he had come to Hollywood to be a producer, not a lover. He had tried all that once before, he stated. He had married the girl he went to school with in Newark. They had been divorced five years ago. Now he was immersed only in his work. Sure he fell in love–every day. But not for keeps.

He was good-looking in a rugged way. His mother had been Jewish, his father a second-rate Irish prizefighter. Ike talked about this in his interviews, claiming he had the best from both sides. Amanda guessed him to be forty. He was tanned, with some gray beginning to show at the temples in his black hair. His nose was short and puggish, giving a boyish quality to his square-jawed face. Judith Austin seemed captivated with him.

This surprised Amanda. Judith Austin was everything that Amanda wanted to be. She was slim and elegant, her ash-blond hair twisted into a French knot, and she wore a velvet "at home" gown. Amanda had seen it in *Vogue* and knew it cost twelve hundred dollars. She noticed that Mrs. Austin wore very little jewelry–small pearl earrings, nothing else. Then her eye was caught by the enormous pear-shaped diamond that hung loosely on her finger. It had to be at least thirty carats.

She and Christie stood alone, oddly isolated in the crowded room. Danton Miller saw them and came over and graciously made some small talk. Chris clung eagerly to Danton and the two men launched into a discussion of ratings.

Amanda looked around the room. It was a wonderful house. Aunt Rose would be thrilled if she could see her here now! She suddenly thought of the nursing home. She excused herself and asked the butler for a telephone. He led her to the library and closed the door. She looked around her, awed by the dignity of the beautiful room. She went to the desk and ran her fingers over it gently. It looked French. She saw all the buttons on the phone and the blank cardboard where the number should be. Unlisted–naturally. She stared at the picture of Judith in the silver frame, then leaned closer. It was signed "Consuelo," in that funny back-hand style all society women had. Of course, this was her twin sister–the princess! She dialed the nursing home. It was busy. She sat down and opened the silver box on the table and lit a cigarette. She studied the other silver frame that showed the two little princesses taken when they were about ten and twelve. Maybe they were debutantes by now, beautiful debutantes in Europe without a care in the world. She tried the nursing home again. It was still busy.

The door opened. It was Ike Ryan. He grinned. "I saw you slip out. As soon as I could break away I came looking for you. I'm Ike Ryan. We met at Danny's Hideaway last year."

She hoped her blank stare told him she had no recollection of the incident. Then in a detached voice she said, "I came in here to make a phone call, but the number I'm trying to get is busy."

He waved his hand. "That's what I'm after too. Mind if I use it?" Before she could answer, he reached over and took the phone and began to dial. He stopped midway and turned to her. "Hey, are you free after this party?"

She shook her head.

He went back to his dialing. "Then I'll put through this call. I guess you're serious about that joker you came with. You were with him at Danny's when we met."

"I do the commercials on *The Christie Lane Show*." She wondered if Robin had ever mentioned her to Ike Ryan.

His number answered. "Joy, hi, sweetheart, want to make it for dinner at nine? I'll send my car for you. We got three parties we can go to, or we might wind up at the Sixth Avenue Delicatessen. Depends how I feel. What? Sure I do–would I stop in the middle of a business deal to call if I didn't? Okay, toots." He clicked the phone and turned to Amanda. "See what you've missed?"

She smiled wryly.

He stared at her. "I like you. Most broads fall all over me."

"I'm not a broad. I have a contract to go to California for some TV commercials, and the 'joker' who brought me here happens to be very much in love with me."

He smiled. "Where you staying on the Coast?"

"At the Beverly Hills, if I go–"

"If you go? I thought you had a contract."

"I do. I haven't signed it yet."

"What's the *efsher?"*

"Efsher?"

He smiled. "It's a Yid word. My old lady used to use it. It loses in the translation but I'll try and give you an example of *efsher*. Let's see. Oh yes! My sister was a beast before I sprung for the nose job which finally landed her a husband. But before that she never got dates. And so one weekend she was going to Grossinger's with several girls she knew, all pigs like herself–you know the type. No, you wouldn't. Virgin Jewish girls past twenty-five. Hysterical! Real losers. The kind that's stopped hoping. My sister was one of them. So this weekend I remember my sister was packing slacks, a tennis racket, a bathing suit, and my mom said, 'What, no pretty dresses?' My sister said, 'Look, Mom, I've been to these places. There are never any unattached men. So this time I'm going to relax. I'll play tennis. I'm going for a rest, not to look.' Then my mom walked over with my sister's best dress, plunked it in the suitcase and said, 'Take it, *efsher*.' "

Amanda laughed. She found herself warming up to Ike Ryan.

"Get it?" he asked. *"Efsher* means 'maybe'–a possibility, a dim hope. What's your *efsher,* toots?" Then, as if sensing her change of attitude, he said, "Listen, want to change your mind about tonight? I can always cancel that date I just made."

"I don't break dates," she said.

"Neither do I when I *care* about them." He stared at her intently. Then he smiled. "Come to the Coast, toots. I think we got a future together."

The room suddenly seemed so empty after he left. She realized it was after six. Robin might have arrived. She quickly dialed the nursing home. Still busy! She checked her makeup and returned to the party. She'd try later.

The large room had filled and spilled over to the drawing room and the dining room. She wandered into each room, scanning every face, but Robin wasn't there. She found Chris, rooted to the same spot, still talking to Danton Miller. Danton seemed relieved to see her and immediately broke away.

"Where the hell you been?" Chris asked, as soon as they were alone.

"Combing my hair," she said coldly.

"You been gone twenty minutes. Dan Miller was stuck standing with me."

"Well, if you're such a big star, where are all your fans?"

Chris stared at all the famous people in the room. "It's funny," he sighed. "I know everyone I see, but I see no one I know. Doll, let's go. I don't belong here."

"Oh, Chris, at least try and look like you're enjoying yourself."

"Why? Where's there a rule that says we gotta enjoy it? So we were invited–Eddie Flynn *also* invited us to a party. He's giving it in his suite at the Edison. Some of the kids from the Copa are coming–it's for Aggie because she quit the line at the Latin Quarter to go to the Coast with Eddie. Now, that's a party that'll have some laughs."

She looked toward the door. Her heart quickened. But no, it was just another tall man. . . .

At eight fifteen Amanda finally gave in and allowed Chris to drag her to Eddie's party at the Edison. The Copa girls and the Latin Quarter girls had gone to do their dinner shows. Amanda sat on the couch and started to drink Scotch. Chris was relaxed –this was his kind of party. He brought over some pastrami sandwiches.

"Here, doll, this is better than that fancy food at the Austins'."

She refused and poured another Scotch. "Better eat," Chris warned her, cramming the sandwich into his mouth. "I've had three of these, so I don't feel like dinner."

"I'm not hungry," Amanda said.

Agnes joined her on the couch. "Is that how you models keep your figures?" she asked. "You're making a big mistake. The corned beef is to die over."

"I'm just not hungry," Amanda said. The Scotch suddenly made her feel drowsy and she yawned.

Agnes looked at her sympathetically. "Too much New Year's Eve, last night?"

"No, not really. Chris played a club date. It was very quiet really–that is, if you can call the Grand Ballroom at the Waldorf quiet."

"Last year me and Eddie were with Chris at the Fontainebleau. Oh, none of us lived there. Chris was playing a club date. That was before the show started on the air. You know something? Me and Eddie, we had more fun before we made it big on television. I mean–there were laughs. That's the way it should be on holidays."

"I don't like New Year's Eve or any holiday," Amanda said.

By eleven o'clock she was quite drunk. Chris wanted to go someplace for coffee but he finally agreed to take her home.

He held the cab while he walked her to the door. This was a courtesy she had finally drummed into him but he still thought it was ridiculous. "Maybe you get your kicks hearing that meter running," he said.

"Ike Ryan has a car and chauffeur," she said.

"Just a rented job," he snapped.

"But he doesn't use cabs–"

"That'll be the day, when I pay eight bucks an hour while a chauffeur sits around and listens to the radio." He kissed her quickly, conscious that the taxi meter was clicking. "Remember, doll–when I'm sixty, we'll have it made. A guy like Ike Ryan might go down the drain."

She stumbled as she let herself into the apartment. She felt a queasy feeling in her stomach and the beginning of a monumental headache. She checked with her answering service. One message, from the nursing home. Sure you can bet they had called –those nurses were waiting for the twenty-dollar bills she passed around on New Year's Day.

But no call from Robin! Well, this was it. No more–what was that word?–*efsher*. Yes, no more *efsher*. She'd go to California! She'd *marry* Chris! Suddenly she went rigid as a new thought came into focus. Then she went limp with shock. California! Who would visit Aunt Rose? She always went once a month–always on a different day, at a different hour, to check on her. If she went away, they'd leave her neglected. Why hadn't she thought of this until now? Because until this minute she had never actually believed she would go. She hadn't even bothered to sublet her apartment. She had still hoped for Robin.

She thought for a moment, then on impulse she dialed Jerry at home. His wife answered. Amanda apologized for the late call but explained it was urgent.

"Jerry–I can't go to California."

He sounded elated. "It worked, huh? I told you to put it on the line with him!"

"He never showed," she said slowly.

"Then why don't you go to California?"

"It has nothing to do with Robin," she said wearily. "Jerry–it just hit me. I've been so busy thinking of myself, of Robin, of Chris. I forgot about Aunt Rose. I can't just take off. Who will visit her?"

"I'm sure there must be good nursing homes on the Coast."

"But, Jerry–how could I move her?"

"Get Chris to charter a private plane. Get a nurse to go along with you."

"He doesn't know about Aunt Rose and I don't know how he'd take it."

"Listen, Amanda–Chris has come up the hard way. If anything he'll respect you twice as much. And it will make him happy to be able to help you."

"Oh, Jerry, if Chris does that, I'll try to love him. And I'll be good to him. I really will. I'll make him happy. I'm going to call him right now."

Christie's phone didn't answer. That meant he was at the Copa bar, the Stage, Lindy's or Toots Shor. She tried them all and finally located him at Toots Shor.

"Chris, can you come here? I want to talk to you."

"Doll, I'm sitting with Toots, and Ronnie Wolfe just joined us. I want to get a plug in his column."

"I have to talk to you."

"Jesus, everyone is here. It's jumping. Come on, doll, grab a cab."

"Chris, I can't talk with all those people. This is important. It's about us, our future."

"Jesus–all night we were together. At the Austins' you just

stood there like a lump. Why didn't you talk to me then? We had plenty of privacy. People stayed away from us in droves."

"Are you coming, Chris?"

"Doll, I'll be there in, say, half an hour."

"No." The Scotch was hitting her. She felt groggy. "Now, while I'm still awake. This is important. Come right away."

"Okay, I'll be there."

"Hurry."

"Is it all right with you if I stop and take a leak first?"

She clicked the phone. Then she undressed. He probably would want to go to bed with her. Well, if he would arrange to bring Aunt Rose to Los Angeles, to a good nursing home, he could sleep with her every night. She'd even try and respond.

She put on a robe, combed her hair, fixed her makeup and put in her diaphragm.

Chris finally arrived. He took off his coat and took her in his arms and began to kiss her.

"Chris, later. I want to talk to you."

"We'll talk, but after–" He pulled the string of her robe and it fell open. He stopped suddenly. "Okay, you win. I don't want to make love to a statue. For all the action I'm getting, I could look at *Playboy* and jerk off."

She closed her robe and crossed the room. "Sit down, Chris, I've got quite a bit to say."

He sat very still while she spoke. She told him everything, omitting nothing. His eyes widened as he listened, then he shook his head in sympathy.

"You poor kid, you had it as rough as me."

Tears came to her eyes. "Then you'll help me, Chris?"

"Doll, how can I help?"

"Move Aunt Rose to the Coast!"

"You must be kidding!" he said. "You know what that will cost? We can't take a sick dinge on the plane!"

"Don't you dare call Aunt Rose that."

"All right! Even if she was snow-white, you still can't take a person with a stroke on a plane."

"You can *charter* a plane."

"Sure, for thousands of bucks!"

"Well . . . you certainly have enough money."

He stared at her. Then he stood up and paced the room. He whirled around, his finger shooting out at her. "Are you crazy! I got a cousin, a first cousin, a flesh-and-blood cousin, and he wanted to borrow two thousand to buy into a business and I turned him down. Know why? Because I'm like you. No one ever did anything for little Chris. My folks were poor too. My old man was in burlesque. He cheated on my old lady. She cheated on him, they both split, remarried–neither of them wanted me. I made it on my own from the time I was twelve. I got a half brother. I don't give him a dime! Because if it was all reversed, I know damn well he wouldn't give me the right time."

"Then you won't do it?" she asked.

"Kee-rist! Next thing I know, you'll want Aunt Rose to move in after we're married, stretcher and all."

"If she got better, why not?"

"Because I won't let my family poach on me–and I'm not about to lay out my money for an old——lady I never met. This could cost maybe ten thousand!"

"It might," she said coldly.

"Do you know how hard I work to make ten thou?"

"I heard you got that every week as a raise."

His eyes narrowed. "You been doing a Dun and Bradstreet on me?"

"Everyone knows the sponsor gave you a ten-thousand-dollar raise. You made sure that it got into every column."

"Well, the government gets seventy percent. See, that's what I mean. For me to lay out ten thou, I have to make a fortune."

"All right, Chris, please go."

He crossed the room and grabbed her. "Amanda, doll, I love you. I'm not cheap. Look, let's say we have a kid and it wasn't feeling right, I'd toss out ten thou in a second to the right specialist. Everything I got will be for you and the kid. But no relatives. Especially someone who's not even a blood relative," he added.

"She's like my mother!"

"Holy shit!" he exploded. "Only to me could this happen! I think I've found me the classiest broad in the world. And suddenly as a little dividend you spring a black relative on me–not even a healthy one we could pass off as the maid! Doll, when you say you want to talk, you sure don't fuck around!"

"Get out, Chris."

"I'll go, but you sleep on it. And don't get sullen and think I don't love you. I love you plenty—and I'm a liberal too! I figured maybe you came from some fancy family. Here I was, always apologizing about my background—and you coolly tell me you're illegitimate, you were raised by a black chambermaid, and does it matter to me. Not a bit! I still love you and I want to marry you. But I ain't forcing my crummy family down your throat, and you can't force yours on me. When we're married, the money we spend will be on *our* kid. But one thing, Mandy—" He stopped. "Jesus—even that name sounds lousy now. The next thing I know you'll want to name our kid Rastus. From now on no one calls you Mandy. It's *Amanda*. Did your aunt tag that on you?"

"No," she said quietly. "My real name is Rose. Nick Longworth changed it when I started to model. Rose Jones wasn't glamorous. He thought Amanda sounded English—Noel Coward and all that."

"Well, it did until I learned about dear old Aunt Rose. Look, doll, I shared dressing rooms with colored acts. They're my friends. Eventually things will change. I hope they do. But I'm not big enough to go on a one-man crusade. Let someone else do it, and I'll join. But all my life I've been an almost-was. I played every crummy joint in the world. Loads of guys have done the same and never risen above it. But I've made it. And I'm offering it to you! But just you! Not your aunt, my cousin, my half-brother—it's us all the way."

He grabbed his coat and started for the door. "We forget tonight, understand? It never happened. I don't know no Aunt Rose. You're Amanda, the top model—we've got it made together." He slammed the door.

She sat very still for a few minutes. Then she got up and poured herself a drink. Oddly enough she understood how Chris felt. Well, it proved one thing—she couldn't afford the luxury of love. Because no one really cared. Everyone was out for number one! She'd never see Christie Lane again or Robin Stone! She'd quit the show, tell Nick to concentrate on getting her bookings, even if she had to cut her price. She felt no guilt about Christie now. She'd work, take care of Aunt Rose, and marry the first decent man who came along so that she could have a child and give it a decent start in life. She took a sleeping pill, set the alarm and turned off her phone.

The alarm went off at nine. Her head ached. She reached for the phone to check with her service, then changed her mind. If there were any calls, they would only be trouble.

She took a cab to Queens. The small lobby of the nursing home was half empty. A few old women sat and watched television in wheelchairs. One woman was doing a child's jigsaw puzzle. Another just sat and stared into space. An attendant was taking down a moth-eaten Christmas tree.

She went to the elevator and pushed the button to the third floor. She never announced herself. It was best not to give them any warning.

She opened the door of the room. The bed was stripped.

Miss Stevenson, the supervisor, came rushing in. She looked upset.

"We called you last night," Miss Stevenson said.

"I tried to call in," Amanda said. "The line was busy. Why have you moved Aunt Rose?" She suddenly panicked. "Is she worse?"

"She's dead," Miss Stevenson said.

Amanda screamed. Then she flew at the woman and grabbed her. "What happened? How?" Amanda shouted.

"At six o'clock when we brought her dinner, she suddenly sat up. Her eyes were bright. She said, 'Where's little Rosie?' We told her you were coming. She lay back and smiled. She said, 'I'll eat with little Rosie. I don't like to eat alone. When she gets home from school we'll eat–' "

Amanda began to sob. "She thought she was in the past. But she might have recognized me."

Miss Stevenson shrugged. "When it seemed you weren't coming, we tried to get her to eat. But she kept saying, 'I'm waiting for my child.' Then at eight we came back, and she was sitting up just as we had left her. She was dead. We called you–"

"Where is she?" Amanda asked.

"In the morgue."

"The morgue!"

"We couldn't keep her here."

Amanda dashed to the elevator. Miss Stevenson followed. "I'll give you the address. You can make your funeral arrangements from there."

She made arrangements for the cremation and services. Then she went home, turned off the phone and slept.

When Jerry called the following day, she told him what had happened.

Jerry tried to hide the relief in his voice, but he said it was for the best. "Now you can go to California with a clear conscience," he said.

"Yes, Jerry, I can go to California."

She finished an entire bottle of Scotch that night. Then she stared at herself in the mirror. "Well, that's it. Now you belong to no one! No one gives a good goddam about you. It's a rotten world!"

Then she fell into bed and sobbed. "Oh, Robin, Robin, where were you? What kind of a man are you? I stayed at that party waiting for you, while Aunt Rose was waiting for me. I could have been with her–she *would* have recognized me, died in my arms, knowing someone cared."

She buried her face in the pillow. "I hate you, Robin Stone! I was waiting for you while Aunt Rose died, and where were you? Oh God–where were you!"

He had been watching the Rose Bowl game. He had reached the apartment at seven in the morning, fallen into bed and slept until noon. When he awoke he went to the refrigerator, took two hard-boiled eggs and a can of beer into the living room, turned on the television set and stretched out on the couch. He took the remote control and clicked through the stations. He stopped at IBC. They were covering the pre-football-game pageantry. There was the usual fanfare, the floats, the interview with Miss

Orange Blossom or whatever she was. They were always the same type: long-limbed sunny-looking girls who might have been weaned on double orange juice. In fact this one looked like her mother's milk had been orange juice. The nice white teeth, the clean hair, the nervous smile. Well, she'd have one day of glory, a week of local popularity and three pages in a scrapbook to show her children.

He stared at the girl with little interest. She was saying she wanted lots and lots of children. God, wouldn't it be wonderful if just once one of them said, "Oh, I just want to fuck!" He pitied the poor girl who was interviewing her. He could only see the back of her neck but she had a good voice. He caught a quick glance of her profile as she signed off: "This is Maggie Stewart with Dodie Castle, Miss Orange Blossom of 1962–and now back to Andy Parino."

Andy came on to interview an old-time football player. Robin switched to CBS to catch the game, then he switched to NBC. He was restless. He turned to Channel 11, watched an old movie and dozed off. When he awoke he clicked off the set and dialed Amanda, stopped midway and hung up. She was probably out, and besides, he wanted to cool it with her anyway. He was tired . . . the weather in London had been very bad, but that English girl had been a real swinger, and when he got her with the baroness she had gone right along with the scene. Ike Ryan had introduced him to the orgy game. Hell, they weren't orgies–they were just group sex. Ike Ryan had a theory about making a girl become part of an orgy. You make her do it with you, then with a friend while you watch, then with another girl–and by then you've cut her down to size. Once she's gone along with that scene, she can't play games–none of that "send me flowers" jazz. You've reduced her to what every woman is, once you've stripped off the fancy manners: a broad.

Maybe he should try it with Amanda. That would sure as hell cut off the marriage talk. But something in him went against the idea. Because somehow he knew she *would* go along with it–she would do anything to hold him. But she wouldn't forget it like the baroness or the English girl. And he didn't want to hurt Amanda. God, in the beginning he had felt so safe with her. But lately she seemed always on the brink of bursting at the seams. Well, it was time to cut out. He had given her plenty of reason—he always liked the girl to be the one to walk; at least it left her pride intact. Maybe this thing with Christie Lane would really work out.

He picked up the phone and asked for the IBC tie line. He got Andy in the control room and wished him a Happy New Year.

"How's Miss Orange Blossom?" he asked.

"Chicken-chested and knock-kneed," Andy answered.

"She sure as hell looked good on camera."

"Maggie made her look good."

"Maggie?"

"Maggie Stewart—you probably only caught the back of her head. She's just great!"

Robin smiled. "Sounds like there's something really going with the two of you."

"There is. I'd like you to meet her. Why not come down for a few days? You could use a vacation. The golf is great here."

"I never need a vacation. I enjoy every day as it comes. I've just come back from Europe with some great tapes. Now I want to do some live shows. Listen, chum, don't go marrying this girl until I case her!"

"I'd marry her tomorrow if she agreed."

"Andy, I'll bet you anything she's just another broad."

Andy's voice was hard. "Don't kid about Maggie!"

"Happy New Year, sucker," Robin said, and hung up.

He lit a cigarette. He thought of all the nights he and Andy had roamed up and down the Seventy-ninth Street Causeway together, stopping off at each bar, winding up with girls, swapping the girls in the middle of the evening. . . .

He threw on his coat and went out into the night. It was cold and clear. He walked down Third Avenue, all the way to Forty-second Street. He cut across town and hit Broadway. He stared at the glaring row of movie houses and pizza joints.

He passed a movie house, bought a ticket and walked in. A man from the next aisle came and sat beside him. After a few minutes Robin felt an overcoat tossed casually on his leg. Then a timid hand groped along his thigh. He got up and changed his seat. Five minutes later a stout Negro girl with a blond wig nestled close to him. "Want a good time, honey? Right here? I put my coat over you and do the greatest hand job you ever had. Five bucks."

He changed seats again. He sat next to two teen-aged girls. Suddenly one of them whispered, "Give me ten dollars." He stared at her as if she was insane. She couldn't be more than fifteen. Her friend was the same age. He ignored her. "Give me ten dollars or I'll scream out in the theater that you tried to feel me up. I'm a minor–you'll get into trouble."

He got up and dashed out of the theater. He walked a few blocks and stopped at an all-night cafeteria for some coffee. He reached into his pocket–Christ! His wallet was gone. Who had it been? The fag with the overcoat? The hooker? The delinquent teenagers? He turned up his collar and walked home.

FOURTEEN

THE CROWD AT THE POLO BAR at the Beverly Hills Hotel was thinning out. But it was still too noisy to try and make a long-distance call. Jerry decided to make it from his room. God, he hated this town, but the show had climbed to the number-two spot. It had been a good move switching the show to the Coast for the second half of the season. But there'd be three more months in the land of eternal sunshine, palm trees and loneliness.

He went to his room and placed a call to Mary. Thank God for the summer replacement show–he'd have to go back and help make the decision. That meant an entire week in New York. He wouldn't even mind the commuter train.

The operator rang him back–the line in Greenwich was busy. He canceled the call. He was meeting Christie and Amanda at Chasen's at eight thirty. It was one of the rare nights that Amanda had agreed to go out. She was always tired lately. Her room was down the hall, and like clockwork the DO NOT DISTURB sign went on her door every night at eight thirty. Of course she did have long hours–she had picked up most of the top modeling assignments in California. Christie Lane was vehement about California. He insisted the whole town closed down at ten thirty. Night after night he sat in a large rented house playing gin with Eddie Flynn and Kenny Ditto. Christie wasn't comfortable at any of the Hollywood places. He claimed he never got a decent table. He had sulked for weeks when Amanda refused to go through with the Valentine's Day wedding. She insisted she didn't want to get married and rush back to work–she wanted a real honeymoon. Christie had finally agreed. Now they planned to get married the day after the show went off for the summer.

Jerry wondered about Amanda. She was with Christie the night of the show, and perhaps a couple of nights during the week. She refused to make the Hollywood scene, wouldn't go to the Cocoanut Grove or any of the openings that Christie adored. So Chris roamed Hollywood with Kenny, Eddie and the show girl. Each night they wound up at the drugstore at the Beverly Wilshire Hotel, hoping to run into some comics or other displaced New Yorkers who missed the midnight coffee klatches of the East. According to Chris, this was his first shot at California, and his last! He'd finish out the season, but he had served notice on the sponsors that he would do all the shows from New York the following season. Jerry was all for it–he was as lonely as Chris.

But Amanda didn't seem to miss New York at all. She had never looked better, and she was getting some interest from picture producers. Her entire attitude seemed to have changed–as if the California climate had effected some change of chemistry in her personality. Her easy smile was always there, but Jerry felt there was something missing in their relationship. It was almost as if they had never known one another. He had given up asking her to dinner. She always made the same plea: "I'd love it, Jerry, but I'm tired and I'm doing a big layout tomorrow." Well, maybe he had been exorcised along with Robin. She never mentioned his name or asked about him.

Jerry looked at his watch–eight forty-five. Christie and Amanda must be furious. He put in a call to Chasen's. Christie came on right away. "Where in hell are you?"

"I'm waiting for a call from New York. I'll be a little late."

"Then we'll cancel. I'll wander over to Schwab's." Christie sounded glum.

"Why, it's not as if you're waiting alone. You've got Amanda."

"She conked out."

"What happened?"

"She called me an hour ago. She has a sore throat–must be from the smog. So she took a sleeping pill and went to bed. I'm sitting here all alone. Jesus, this is a real hick town–no one goes out except on weekends. And if you're not in pictures you don't mean a damn thing out here. Hey, Alfie and his pack just came in–"

"Alfie?"

"Jerry, you're not with it. Alfred Knight."

"Oh, the English actor."

"Christ! You'd think he was *Sir* Alfred the way everyone's jumping around here. You should see what's going on. I had a reservation. Know where they put me? In left field. But Alfie boy, who just happens to waltz in, gets the big front table, the number-one spot. I think he's a switch-hitter. I not only hate the town–I also hate the people."

"Cheer up," Jerry laughed. "June will be here before you know it."

"I can't wait."

Jerry hung up and sat on the bed and lit another cigarette. Maybe Amanda would have something from Room Service with him. He called her.

She was polite, but she refused his invitation.

"I couldn't eat, Jerry, my throat is sore and I have a swollen gland in my neck. I'm coming down with something, and the show is in two days. I want to look all right–it would be terrible if I missed it."

He hung up and felt vaguely let down.

He suddenly felt hemmed in, and lonely. He opened the French doors onto the lanai garden outside his room. Amanda raved about her garden. She said it was wonderful to lie out there at night and look at the stars. He stepped into the patio of the garden. The night sounds of the crickets seemed intensified by the silent darkness. Amanda's garden was three doors down. Suddenly his loneliness engulfed him. He had to talk to someone. Maybe she wasn't asleep. He didn't want to ring and disturb her, but a pill didn't always work–he knew from experience. He went out to his garden hoping to see if her lights were on. No luck! Each patio was enclosed by a high wooden wall. He tried his gate–it was stiff, but he got it open. He walked down the path toward her patio.

Suddenly he heard another gate being opened. He ducked behind one of the giant palm trees. It was Amanda. She came out and looked around cautiously. She was wearing slacks and a loose sweater. She was heading toward the bungalows. On impulse, he followed her. She stopped in front of one of the bungalows and looked around. Jerry knew he was hidden by the darkness and the massive foliage. She tapped on the door. Ike Ryan opened it.

"Jesus, babe, where in hell have you been?"

"I wanted to wait a reasonable time in case Christie called back. I just turned off my phone."

"When are you going to unload the bum?"

"As soon as the show goes off. I might as well finish the season with no hard feelings."

The door closed. In the shadow of the window he saw them embrace.

He called Room Service and tried to watch television. But his thoughts were on the bungalow across the way. It was two o'clock when he heard the scraping sound of her patio gate. No wonder she was always too tired to go out—a swollen gland!

Actually she did have a swollen gland. Ike had noticed it too. When she returned to her room she stared at herself in the mirror. Her makeup was messed up. Ike was not the most gentle lover in the world, but she was sure he cared about her. He kept at her to break up with Christie. When she explained that the show was her main source of income, he said, "Listen, toots, you'll never have to worry about a buck as long as you're with me." But that wasn't exactly a marriage proposal. Well, she'd stall till June, then ask him right out. And if he didn't want to marry her, she'd marry Chris. It wouldn't matter too much, one way or another. Suddenly she was tired; all the blood seemed to drain from her. She had been taking amphetamines. They pepped her up—of course they killed her appetite, but she forced herself to eat. But tonight she had hardly been able to pick at her food. There were little cold sores on her gums and on the roof of her mouth. Maybe a penicillin shot would help, or a good night's sleep. She fell into bed.

The following morning she felt worse. When she brushed her teeth, her gums bled. She was alarmed—this was some kind of infection. She called Jerry. Yes, he knew a doctor, but from her symptoms it sounded like a general run-down condition. "Maybe it's trench mouth," he said.

"Oh God, Jerry, where would I have gotten that?"

"I can't imagine," he said coldly. "After all, you stay home every night."

She noticed the tinge of sarcasm in his voice. "Well, I guess I better see a doctor."

"Wait until after the show tomorrow. Meanwhile, gargle with peroxide-and-water. I had it once, it's not such a big deal." Then he hung up.

She took two amphetamines before she left for her modeling job. They gave her some energy but her heart was racing. The photographer drove her to Malibu. She stood in the bathing suit while the shots were set up. The sun was beating down on her, but she got on the water skis and managed to hang on. They completed the shot on the first take. The photographer wanted one more to play it safe. She felt wobbly as she got back on the skis. The boat began to move, the photographer followed in his boat, she bent her knees and held the rope, then pulled herself straight as the boat gathered speed. Suddenly everything seemed to sway–the sun was falling into the sea, and she felt the cool softness of the ocean close over her.

When she opened her eyes, she was on the beach–wrapped in a blanket. Everyone was staring at her with concern.

"I guess I just blacked out," she said.

She spent the rest of the day and night in bed. When she woke the following day her face was fine and her mouth seemed better, but her legs were black-and-blue. She must have bruised them when she fell–probably banged them against the skis in the water. Thank goodness she could wear a long dress on the show!

The following day she felt worse. The sores had returned to her mouth, but it was the bruises that frightened her. They had fused into one alarming pattern of purple covering her entire legs from the ankles to the thighs. When Christie called, she told him about it.

"Well, you're the one who wants to go out on those crazy jobs. According to the law of averages you shoulda died of pneumonia two years ago. Standing in summer clothes in zero weather! You're run-down. And anyone would be bruised if they fell with water skis."

"Chris, find me a doctor . . ."

"Look, doll, I'm meeting with the writers in ten minutes. Then

I got a UP interview. There must be a croaker connected with that fancy hotel."

The doctor in the hotel was out on call. She was desperate now. She canceled her afternoon booking. She was supposed to pose in tennis shorts but makeup couldn't cover her legs. She was dozing off when Ike Ryan called. At first she was evasive, then she told him the truth.

"Don't move, toots. I'll be right over with the best doctor in L.A."

In less than twenty minutes Ike appeared accompanied by a middle-aged man carrying the usual satchel. "This is Dr. Aronson. I'll leave you two alone. But I'll be right out in the hall, so just holler if he gets fresh." His wink at the doctor proved they were friends of long standing.

Dr. Aronson examined her with impersonal casualness. He checked her heart and her pulse and nodded approvingly. She began to relax. His easy attitude told her nothing was radically wrong. He looked into her mouth with a light. "How long have you had these blisters?"

"Just for a few days. But it's my legs that worry me."

He felt her neck, and nodded. There was no change of expression on his face when he examined her purple-blotched legs.

She explained about the water-skiing accident. "Do you think that's what it is?"

"It's hard for me to tell. These things are probably all unrelated, but I'd like to put you into the hospital for a few days. When was the last time you had a blood test?"

"Never." She was suddenly frightened. "Doctor–is something really wrong?"

He smiled. "I doubt it. Probably just a case of old-fashioned anemia–all you fashionable girls lack blood. But I want to rule out a few things."

"Like what?"

"Well, mononucleosis for one thing–there's a lot of it around. You have some of the symptoms–fatigue, the bruises, headaches."

"Couldn't I have the tests in your office? I'm afraid of hospitals."

"If you like. I'll give Ike the address and we'll arrange for them tomorrow."

She watched him as he left the room. She felt better. She went into the bathroom and combed her hair. She really looked awful, and Ike would be back any second. She put on some lipstick, added some mascara, then settled into bed.

Ike came into her room with a big smile. "Pack your bag, put in your prettiest nightgowns, and be all set when I get back. I'm going down to the bookstore and buy you all the top novels."

"Where am I going?"

"To the hospital–and no back talk. Listen, toots, the doc thinks you may have mononucleosis. If you have, you'll infect the whole damn hotel–you won't even be able to get room service. Besides, he feels you should have complete bed rest, maybe even some transfusions to build you up."

"But a hospital–Ike, I've never been sick!"

"You aren't sick now, but this is Hollywood, toots. Everything is done larger than life. And if you're Ike Ryan's girl you don't schlepp to a doctor's office for tests. You lie in state like a duchess. I've ordered the biggest corner room. Listen, for a few days live it up. I'm footing the bills–it's a cinch a broad like you has no hospital insurance."

"No, I've always been healthy."

"Okay. You be ready when I get back. And just leave word you've gone to Frisco for a job. And that you'll be back in time to do the show."

Jerry was waiting at the Lancer Bar. At this moment he should have been in Los Angeles attending the Christie Lane rehearsal, but he had decided to stretch his week in New York to ten days. It was two o'clock in Los Angeles now, the bedlam was just beginning. He sipped his martini and waved as Robin approached the bar.

After his second martini, he knew he was going to miss the last decent train home. Robin was telling him about a new idea he had for a news show when the bartender signaled Jerry to the phone. He was surprised. "For me? I never leave word that I'm here."

Robin smiled. "Your wife is probably tracking you down."

It was Christie Lane. "Listen, Jerry, I called your office and you were gone for the day. I called your home and your wife said to try you here. Jesus, am I glad I got you. Amanda ain't doing the show tonight. We put in a rush call and got a model. She'll get by, but I think you should do something about it."

"Where is she?"

"It's all a mystery to me. The other day she disappeared. Just left word she was going to Frisco on a job. Then today she calls and calmly announces she can't do the show. This was at nine in the morning yet! And where is she? In the hospital."

"Hospital!"

"Relax, nothing is wrong. I threw a raincoat over my p.j.'s and tore over. And there she was, in a big sunny room, the place filled with flowers, all made up, looking gorgeous. She claims she's anemic and isn't leaving until she gets all built up."

"Well, she must need it if she's there, Christie. A hospital doesn't let someone check in for no reason."

"In Hollywood? Are you kidding! Half the broads in this town check in for what they call nervous exhaustion. It's really to catch up on their beauty sleep. Look, I saw Mandy–she never looked better."

"I'll be out the end of the week, Christie. And look, don't worry about Amanda. I'm sure it's not serious."

"I'm not worried–I'm goddam mad. Even if she's just doing a commercial, she's part of a show. And you don't just skip a show for a rest cure. I know it sounds corny, but I played joints when I had flu. I sang when my throat was killing me. I don't go along with anyone who goofs on a show. This is a business I love. It's given me everything I've got. And she's got to respect that. What kind of a marriage will we have if she thinks she can just casually cancel a show like she used to with some of her modeling bookings? You know what I mean?"

"I'll talk to her when I get back."

He hung up and went back to the bar. Robin listened carefully as Jerry told the story.

"She's not the type to just check into a hospital," Robin said.

"Ike Ryan is behind this," Jerry muttered.

"What has Ike to do with it?"

Before he realized it, he was telling about Amanda's secret visits to Ike's cottage. "If you ask me," Jerry went on, "I think the sore throat was just a buildup–I'll bet you anything Ike knocked her up and she's there for an abortion. What do you think?"

Robin frowned. "I think you're a goddam pussyfooted sneak!" Then he slammed down a bill on the bar and walked out.

Amanda was still in the hospital when Jerry arrived on the Coast. She was propped up in bed, looking beautiful, in full makeup. But he was startled when he saw the large bottle of blood and the needle attached to her arm. She noticed his surprise and smiled. "Don't let it bother you. I'm just taking my bag of tomato juice."

"Why the blood transfusion?" He asked as he sat on the edge of a chair.

"So I can get back to your show faster."

Suddenly the door opened and Ike Ryan burst in. "Hi, toots, I got you all the trades and a new book." He looked at Jerry curiously when Amanda introduced them. Then he held out his hand. "I've heard a lot about you. Amanda says you've been a hell of a good friend."

"We go back together," Jerry said weakly. The man's energy overwhelmed him. In an effort to reinforce his authority he said, "This is all very nice, and I know Amanda is enjoying the attention, but she *does* have an obligation to me–and above all, to the show." He turned to Amanda. "When do you plan to leave?"

"The doctor thinks at the end of the week . . ."

"She'll go when she's completely rested," Ike snapped.

Jerry stood up. "Then perhaps we ought to find a permanent replacement for the rest of the season." (God, he hated himself for acting this way!)

"No," Amanda begged. "Oh, Jerry, no, please–I'll be back next week. Maybe even this week." She looked pleadingly at Ike.

He shrugged. "Whatever you want, toots. Listen, I've got some calls to make. I'll use the booth down the hall. Goodbye, friend." He looked at Jerry coldly.

The moment they were alone, Jerry's manner changed. His voice was sincere and earnest. "Look, Amanda, maybe you *should* quit the show. This guy seems crazy about you."

"He hasn't asked me to marry him . . ."

He groaned. "We're back to that game again?"

Her face went taut. "Look, Jerry, right now Ike wants me because he knows Chris wants me. But if I'm without a job, without Chris, Ike might suddenly get disenchanted with me."

"Where did you get all that faith and trust?"

"I was born with it," she said coldly. Then her eyes went soft. "Jerry, I'll be back. I feel wonderful already. I guess I needed this rest. I've been going at such a pace for six years. Do you realize I've never had a vacation?"

He patted her on the head. "Relax, honey, the job is yours for life. I'll call you tomorrow."

He left the room and walked down the hall. Ike Ryan was waiting for him. "In here, buddy," he said, motioning to the small waiting room.

"I have to get to my office," Jerry said.

"Not until we have a little talk. You're some fine friend. She hasn't got enough trouble--you have to threaten her, yet."

"Anemia isn't that serious," Jerry said.

"She only *thinks* she has anemia." Ike stared at him. "I'm gonna trust you. No one knows this. Just Doc Aronson and me. And nobody is *gonna* know it--especially Amanda. She's got leukemia!"

Jerry sank on the couch. His hands were shaking as he reached for a cigarette. Then he looked up, his eyes straining for hope. "I've heard of people who live a long time with leukemia."

"Not the kind she has."

"How long has she got?"

"It might be minutes. It might be six months."

Jerry turned away but his composure broke. He hated himself, but he sobbed openly. Ike sat beside him and clasped his shoulder. "Look, they're trying a new drug. I've had it flown here. It costs a thousand a shot. She started on it two days ago and her blood count has gone up. It's too early to hope, but if things go right . . ."

"You mean she has a chance?"

"She has a chance to *walk* out instead of going out in a box. She has a chance for a remission, maybe six months–and who knows, by then they might find the cure, or another miracle drug."

"What can I do?" Jerry asked.

"Just keep your mouth shut. Make Christie Lane stop heckling her with this show-must-go-on jazz! And you tell her the job is waiting."

"I already have."

Ike shook his head. "The damnedest thing is, if the drug works the doc says it will be dramatic. She'll be fine in like a week. For how long, no one knows. Why in hell does she want to work? She's got so little time."

"Because she thinks you might ask her to marry you–but only if she's working and is independent."

"Oh, for Christ's sake." Ike Ryan got up and walked to the window.

Jerry started for the door. "But as you say, she won't last more than six months. You don't have to worry about that. And it's better if she *does* work. She'll believe the anemia story then."

Ike turned and held out his hand. They shook solemnly. "If anyone knows about this, I'll break your head in," he said.

Jerry promised but he knew he was going to break his word. He was going to tell Robin. Amanda had so little time–and Robin was the only man who mattered to her. He could tell she liked Ike, *liked* him, but she never looked at him the way she had looked at Robin. But he would sit on it for a few days and see how she reacted to the new drug.

Ike Ryan watched him leave, then he walked slowly down the hall to Amanda's room. He stood very straight and forced a smile on his face, then he opened the door and sailed in. A nurse was removing the needle from Amanda's arm.

"Tonight I'll bring champagne and some new books, but now I got to get to work." He started for the door, then turned. "By the way, toots, there's something I meant to ask you and it always slipped my mind. Will you marry me? You don't have to give me your answer for at least ten minutes. I'll call you when I get to the studio."

Amanda responded to the new drug. Within a week her blood count was normal–she was in a state of remission. Ike was jubilant, but Dr. Aronson warned him–a remission was not a cure.

"But for the time, she can live a normal life, right?" Ike asked.

"Let her do anything she wants. God knows how long she'll feel this well," the doctor replied. "But I want her to come to the office every week for a blood test. We've got to watch her red-corpuscle count."

"Every week? She's going to get suspicious."

"No, she's in excellent spirits and she has no idea anything is seriously wrong."

Ike came to bring her home from the hospital. "I just rented a palace on Canyon Drive. Wait till you see the joint–I moved in yesterday. It's got everything–even a cook and butler. When do you want to get married, toots?"

"When I finish the show."

"You kidding? That's six weeks away."

"It would be rough working with Christie if he knew."

"Who says you have to work with him? Quit the damn show."

"That wouldn't be fair to Jerry–he gave me the show when I wanted it. The girls they tried while I was gone weren't right. They're all so thrilled that I'm making it back for tomorrow's show."

"I still think you should wait a week or so."

"Ike, I've had almost three weeks' rest. I feel marvelous." The happiness suddenly faded from her eyes. "But Dr. Aronson said I have to have blood tests every week. Why?"

Ike shrugged. "Probably to make sure you don't lose all this health."

"Well, I'm going to eat liver every day. And I've been reading about blood–all the things that are good for you."

"Now don't start practicing medicine," he said.

She tucked her arm in his and the chauffeur took her bag.

"Ike, I'm so relieved. I'll admit it now: I was scared when I came in. I've never been sick before, and when I was lying there that first day, I thought, 'Wouldn't it be awful to have to check out now . . . to die without ever having a child.' I'm so grateful that I'm well. And I know what it is to be unhappy, to be hurt. That's why I want to finish out the show."

Ike dropped her at her hotel. The moment he reached his office he called Jerry. "You've got to make her quit the show–she thinks she owes it to you to finish the season. She's got so little time, I don't want her to throw away an hour–let alone six weeks. Yet if *I* force it, she may get suspicious. Think of something!"

Jerry stared at the smog-laden sky, at the pale sun trying to burn its way through. It wasn't like the summer sun in Greenwich –or the sparkling orange sun they had in the fall. Amanda would never see that sun again or know the clear cold of the winter. Tears came to his eyes.

He reached for the phone. Robin's secretary announced that Mr. Stone was in conference. "Tell her to get Mr. Stone *out* of conference," Jerry shouted to the long-distance operator. "This is an emergency!" After a few minutes Robin came on.

"Yes, Jerry."

"Are you sitting down, Robin?"

"Come to the point. I have ten people waiting in the conference room."

"Amanda has leukemia."

There was a terrible silence. Then Robin said, "Does she know?"

"Only three people know–the doctor, Ike Ryan and me. You make the fourth. She's been given some drug and it's worked wonders. She's even doing the show tomorrow. But they give her six months top. I thought you'd like to know."

"Thanks, Jerry." He hung up.

Amanda enjoyed her first day back at the hotel. The suite was filled with flowers. Dozens of roses from Ike, gladiolas from the hotel, a plant from the cast, and some cheap spring flowers from Christie. His note said, "Am taking publicity pictures–call you at six. Love, Christie." At four o'clock a waiter arrived with a baked potato loaded with Iranian caviar and sour cream. The note read, "To hold you till I get there for dinner. Love, Ike."

She reveled in the luxury and ate the potato, but she knew she would have to start watching her weight. She had gained five pounds in the hospital. The phone rang at six and she picked it up lethargically. It had to be Christie.

"Hello, star–how are you?" The voice crackled across the line.

For a moment she couldn't speak. It was Robin, just like that, with no explanation for not ever calling. . . .

"I've just come home from the hospital." She finally found her voice.

"What was the matter?"

"Anemia. I'm fine now. Didn't Jerry tell you?"

"I've been away, I haven't talked to Jerry. Listen, baby, I have some business in L.A. and I'm flying out Sunday. I should get there around five your time. Think you can spare an evening for an old friend?"

"I'd be delighted, Robin."

"Good. Dinner on Sunday–that's a date."

She hung up and lay back against the pillow. No need to get excited. He probably only had a few days and figured there was good old Amanda, just waiting. So he had called. Why not? She was a sure thing–it was easier than calling around and finding someone.

After all, Hollywood wasn't his territory. He didn't know too many people and he didn't want to waste an evening. Well, she'd see him–you *bet* she'd see him–and she'd show him how it felt when someone else called the shots! But how? Stand him up? Keep him waiting at Chasen's all alone?

She thought about it for an hour. Suddenly she knew what she was going to do–it would be wonderful! She couldn't wait until Sunday.

FIFTEEN

ROBIN CHECKED INTO THE BEVERLY HILLS HOTEL at five o'clock. The desk clerk handed him an envelope. Inside was a hastily scrawled note from Amanda:

> *Dear Robin, It's my birthday and Ike Ryan is having a few people drop by. I have to get there early because I'm guest of honor. I can't wait to see you.*

When he got settled in his suite he reread Amanda's note. There was a phone number and an address on North Canyon Drive. His first inclination was to call and leave word that he'd wait for her at the hotel. He hated cocktail parties. Then he abruptly changed his mind. From now on it was going to be whatever Amanda wanted. He reached in his pocket to check the small gold circlet—if they could break away from this party early enough, they'd fly to Tijuana and get married. He called the doorman and ordered a cab.

North Canyon Drive was a maze of parked cars. He paid the driver and walked up the driveway. Hollywood homes were deceiving in appearance: the front was always modest. But when you entered, there was an explosion of unbelievable splendor in the back. Ike's home was no exception. The marble entrance hall was crowded, the enormous living room had the usual enormous bar and people were clustered around it three deep. Glass doors opened onto a patio with an Olympic-size swimming pool—there was even a tennis court. He felt slightly disoriented, unprepared for the mob scene he had stumbled upon. Then he grinned: he should have known better. This was Ike's idea of a little gathering. He saw familiar faces, faces he had seen on the wide screen. There was enough earning power in this room to support a small country–actors, producers, heads of studios and directors, even the top screenwriters, and the usual assortment of beautiful girls.

Suddenly Amanda crossed the room to greet him. He had forgotten how lovely she was. Death couldn't be lodged in that slim wonderful body!

"Robin!" She threw her arms around him. He was surprised at her open display of affection. "Robin, you're here! It's wonderful to see you. Oh, but you don't know many people." She broke the embrace, took his hand and shouted, "Hey, everybody–*quiet!*"

The room grew still.

"I want you to meet Robin Stone. He came all the way from New York. You all know who Robin Stone is." Her voice was derisive. "You must know–he's the star of *In Depth!*" Her gaze was innocent. "None of you seem impressed, but he's a very big man in New York."

A few people pretended to recognize him with feeble nods, then turned back to their own conversations. Robin's lack of expression hid his surprise at her odd behavior. But Amanda merely shrugged.

"That's Hollywood for you," she said lightly. "They still refuse to recognize that television is here to stay. And as for news programs–darling, news is something they only hear on radio when they drive to the studio, and only if it butts into a music program. So forgive them, angel, if they don't recognize and fawn over you. Paul Newman, Gregory Peck, Elizabeth Taylor–that's the name of the game in this town."

She led him to the bar for a drink. Ike Ryan greeted him warmly, then crossed the room to greet a director who had just entered. Amanda handed Robin a glass. "Filled with your favorite brand of ice water–only this is one-hundred proof, imported."

Suddenly there was silence. Then a swelling murmur grew as everyone stared at the handsome young man who had entered.

"Oh, look!" Amanda cried. "Ike even got the Big Dipper to

come." Her eyes shone as Ike led the handsome, bronzed man to the bar.

"You know this good-looking bum?" Ike asked with a grin.

Amanda's smile went coy. "Oh, Ike, everyone knows Dip Nelson. I'm honored that you came, Mr. Nelson. Ike ran your new picture for me when I was in the hospital."

Dip looked slightly embarrassed. Robin was embarrassed too. He wondered what in hell had gotten into Amanda. Then she said, "Oh, Dip, this is Robin Stone, an old, old friend. He's like family, aren't you, Robin?"

Dip shook hands with Robin, then several women crowded around him and he was literally carried across the room.

"Poor Dip, he hasn't a chance with those women," Amanda said.

Ike smiled. "The Big Dipper can take care of himself. No talent–just brawn, dimples, and looks. But he's hot box office now, and that's all that counts."

Amanda nudged Ike. "Darling, speaking of box office . . . look who just came in!"

Robin watched as Ike and Amanda went to greet a slim good-looking man–Alfred Knight, the English actor who had made such an impact on Hollywood. He searched the crowd for Chris Lane and spotted him across the room in a corner. Poor Chris–he not only looked like an outsider, but he'd soon need a program to be able to tell the players. He still thought he was engaged to Amanda. Robin finished off the vodka, got a refill and remained at the bar. It promised to be a very entertaining night.

The caterers began setting up tables around the pool. And suddenly it hit Robin that Amanda's birthday was in February. Or was it January? It had to be one of those months–he remembered celebrating it during a snowstorm.

He was just starting on his fourth vodka when there was a loud roll of drums. Amanda was standing in the center of the room. "Everyone! I–we–have an announcement!"

Amanda held up her hand. There was a large diamond on her finger. "Ike gave this to me today–but it's not a birthday present. In fact it's not my birthday at all, it's just our way of announcing our engagement!"

Everyone began to talk at once. Christie Lane looked like an animal that had been impaled. He stood there, mute and glassy-eyed. One of the guests ran to the piano and began to play *Lohengrin.* Gradually the crowd returned to their original groups and resumed their conversation and drinking. From across the room, for one instant Amanda's eyes met Robin's. Their glance held; her eyes were dark with triumph. He raised his glance in a silent toast. Then she turned and let Alfie Knight waft her to another part of the room. Robin saw Ike crossing to the den. He put down his drink and went after him.

Ike smiled as Robin approached. "Well, you gotta admit I'm a barrel full of surprises."

"I want a few words with you, chum."

"What? No congratulations?"

"Where can we go? This won't take long."

Ike signaled a waiter for drinks, then he led Robin to the pool area which was deserted.

"Okay, shoot. What's on your mind?" Ike said.

"Amanda."

"That's right, you had a swing around with her once." Ike swallowed his shot of bourbon neat. Then he stared at Robin's untouched drink. "Aren't you going to toast the groom?"

"I know about Amanda," Robin said quietly.

Ike's eyes narrowed. "What do you know?"

"Jerry Moss is a friend of mine."

"I'll kill that little punk. I told him to keep his mouth shut."

"Stop playing the tough guy. Jerry did what he thought was best. I came out here to ask Amanda to marry me."

"She doesn't need your charity," Ike snapped.

"Is that what you're giving her?"

"You said it–I didn't."

"Ike, we've shared the same scene, and I'm not knocking it. I like it too. But Amanda won't go that route. She can't, and especially not now."

Ike's smile was cold. "If I didn't like you so much I'd knock the shit out of you. Just what kind of a bastard do you think I am?"

"No special kind, just a bastard. I don't want Amanda to get hurt."

Ike looked at him curiously. "Are you in love with her?"

"I care about her—I care about making the rest of her life happy."

Ike nodded. "Then we're both coming in on the same beam."

"You mean that?"

Ike leaned across the table. "Look, this is no time for fun and games. This is the truth game. Are you in love with her? Just tell me that, tell me you love her and I'll send for Amanda right now and give you your shot. Let the best man win. But if you're here to make some grandstand gesture, forget it. She doesn't need any favors from you—when the time comes, I think I have a better setup to give her what she needs."

"All right, chum, since we're playing the truth game"—Robin's face was grim—"are *you* in love with her? Seems to me you haven't answered that question."

Ike stood up and stared at the dark pool. "Of course I'm not in love with her," he said quietly. "But then, neither are you."

"That's the way I figured it from the start," Robin said. "Then why the marriage bit?"

"Why not?" Ike asked.

"As I see it, she'll tie you down. Stop some of your action."

Ike smiled. "She can help my image."

"I don't get you."

"Maybe you didn't read the newspapers. Last month my wife —my ex-wife, we've been divorced for five years—did the Dutch act: pills. Thank God she did it in Wisconsin. She was there visiting my son over the Easter holidays. He goes to school there. She took pills—a whole fucking bottle—and left a note saying she couldn't live without me. Thank God for Joey, that's my kid. He grabbed the note and sent for me. I schmeared around some money and we made it look accidental." Ike sighed. "Five years I haven't seen that broad. I never loved her—we went to school together, and she gave me her all in our senior year. We got married, only she never grew with me—always chewing my ass off, wanting me to sell ties for her uncle. I stuck it out till Joey was twelve—then I walked. I've been sending her all the money a dame could use. Christ, I even agreed that her alimony would continue if she remarried. So she spends all this time living in the past, then decides to get back at me by taking her life.

"You should have seen that note—made me the biggest shit

ever. Joey and I burned it, but there have been snide rumors around this town that she committed suicide. Then there were two crazy broads who also tried it–I don't get it, what's with these dames and sleeping pills? I'm not that big a lover. Then a scandal magazine tagged me: 'For Ike Ryan–dames are dyin'.' It's just this crazy business: there are no men out here. They'll latch on to a doorknob if it wears pants. Half the big stars in there, the women, are here with their fag hairdressers. Anyway, my reputation isn't exactly sympathetic. I can use a little good press. When Amanda goes, people will look at me in a different light. They'll realize I made the last months of a doomed girl happy ones–great ones. I'm gonna give her the biggest razzle-dazzle whirl any girl ever had. And when they close the lid on her pretty puss, at least she'll have gone out in style."

Robin sat in a stunned silence. Then he said hoarsely, "You're using her. You son of a bitch–you're using her."

"Let's say I need her, but not half as much as she needs me." Ike came close, his face hard. "Listen, I've seen *you* operate. You have ice water for blood, so don't sit in judgment on me. She digs me, and I'm going to make her goddam happy. I'll charter planes, fly her all over the world. I'm gonna load her with diamonds. What can you do for her? Fuck her? So can I. Although God knows how long she'll have the strength for that. But can you let her go out in the style I'm offering? I know about her past–and I think she rates Roman candles right now. Can you top it, newsman?"

Robin stood up. His eyes were as hard as Ike's. The two men faced one another. "No, I can't. But you better live up to it. Make damn sure it's not just talk. Otherwise, I'll find you, Ike–no matter where you are–and I'll break every bone in your body."

For a moment their eyes locked in tense silence. Ike smiled and held out his hand. "It's a deal." He turned and went back to the house. Robin hadn't taken his hand. He sank into a deck chair and sipped his drink. He felt wrung out and empty. Ike didn't care for Amanda; Ike cared for his own image. Yet what difference did "caring" make? Results were all that counted. He looked at his watch. It was still early; he could get the midnight plane out.

"Too late for a tan." He looked up. It was Dip Nelson.

Robin grinned. "I guess I could use some sun."

Dip lit a cigarette. "Boy, is that a grind in there! You from New York?"

Robin nodded.

"I thought so. Are you in this racket?"

"No, thank God."

He stared at Robin speculatively. "Let me guess–a relative of the bride?"

"Distant." Then he added, "Incidentally, count me as one of your fans. I've seen some of your pictures. You handle a horse very well."

Dip looked at him oddly. "You putting me on?"

"Not at all."

"Then what kind of a line is that? What about my acting?"

"That's pretty lousy." Robin smiled.

For a split second Dip wavered between anger and action. Then he laughed and held out his hand. "Well, at least you're an honest man."

"I don't think acting really counts," Robin said. "It's star quality that makes it in pictures, and from the reception you got in that room, you obviously have it."

Dip shrugged. "Like you said, I did the horse routine for years. One crappy Western after another, then suddenly they came into vogue, and I'm a star. But it's my new picture that's causing all the excitement. It opens in New York next week. I play a Madison Avenue anti-hero type. The works: skinny tie, gray suit, like you. Hey, is that your racket?"

"In a way."

"Oh-oh, here comes Bebe. Let's duck out of here."

"Who's Bebe?"

"Her husband's a top producer. Come on, want to blow this party?"

"You must be reading my mind," said Robin.

"Follow me!" Dip headed for the cabanas. They slipped into the dark dressing room. "Now stay very quiet. She's too loaded to come this far."

They stood quietly in the silent darkness while the producer's wife wobbled around the pool calling for Dip. Finally she gave up and went inside.

Dip loosened his collar. "Boy, there's nothing worse then a menopause broad in heat. Listen: between you and I, don't let the movie-star bit put you off base. I'm a one-woman man. Oh, I may have to fuck a little to get certain parts, but I don't go after a broad like Bebe like some of these male whores out here."

He shivered. "There's nothing worse: a forty-year-old with the figure of a twenty-year-old until you get them in the sack–then it's like Jello. Everywhere you touch, you sink in–soft thighs, flabby belly, flopping tits."

"Sounds like you've had experience."

"It was either 'ride a horse' forever or ride Claire Hall for one picture. So I rode Claire and became a star. Come on, the coast is clear. We can duck out through the hedge."

He led Robin to the longest Cadillac he had ever seen.

"Like it?" Dip asked proudly.

"It sure as hell is impressive," Robin answered.

"Custom-made: the only gold convertible in town. I mean real gold–this is twenty-two-karat paint, and the leather is gold kid. It's part of the image I'm building. The golden man–gold hair, gold car. The leather alone cost me two G's."

The car eased down the lane. Dip headed down Sunset Boulevard. "You got any special plans?"

Robin smiled. "Just the midnight plane back to New York."

"A guy like you must feel out of place in this town."

"A guy like me certainly does."

"It's just a matter of being a winner, then you're secure even in Bombay. My old lady taught me that. She died in the motion-picture relief home."

"I'm sorry."

Dip waved his hand. "Look, she never had it so good. I hadn't made it yet, so we had no choice. But it's a great setup. They have their own cottages, they sit around and talk shop. She was an extra; my old man was a stunt man for Fred Thompson and Tom Mix. One of the best. That was before I was born. He taught me to ride. He got killed on a stunt and my mother was stuck supporting me. And she wasn't young. I was a change-of-life kid. They say they're always brighter. Would you believe it–I never went to high school?"

"It hasn't seemed to hurt you," Robin said.

"Sometimes I miss it, like when I'm not sure about my English. Scripts are fine, they're all written . . . but those interviews—I know I murder the English because sometimes the interviewers think I'm putting them on and they tell me to stop with the cowboy twang."

"You can cut off at the next turn and drop me at the Beverly Hills Hotel, if it's not out of your way," Robin said.

"What's your rush? It's only seven o'clock. Or have you something lined up?"

"No, but I'm sure you have."

Dip grinned. "You bet I have! We're going to catch my girl—she sings in a place on the Strip. Wait till you see her, she's only nineteen and all woman."

"Won't I be butting in?"

"Nah. Besides, I want you to remember your one night in Hollywood. I know how you felt at that party. I once was on the outside looking in. And no one helped me. It was so bad I just stood and talked to the piano player. I stood there so long that someone asked me to sing. They thought I was part of the combo. When I saw you tonight I thought, There's a guy who's lost, and I, Dip Nelson, I'm Mr. Big—I am the action. And I figured I wasn't going to be like all the crumbs who were part of the action when I was nobody. I was damned if I'd dress up that bitch Amanda's party. I had to put in an appearance for Ike Ryan. So I showed, and blowed. But at least I'll show you a little fun."

"Well, you've more than done your bit," Robin said. "There's no reason to entertain me the rest of the evening. That's going beyond the call of duty."

"Nah, what the hell. I'd be sitting alone while Pauli sang anyway. She's in this lousy joint, but she belts out a song better than Garland or anyone you ever heard. She'll make it, you'll see. Only I got to give her some class first. She's real basic. She was a virgin when I met her, there's no one in her life but me. But we can't get married until I have three hot pictures under my belt. See, I'm today's sensation, but only with one picture. The next two will tell the story. And when they click, I can marry Pauli. No studio will be able to tell me what to do. And meanwhile I can smooth out some of her rough edges. I'm not apologizing for her–she's all talent and heart. Wait till you see her, you'll dig."

He slid the car up to a small restaurant. "She only makes seventy-five clams a week, but at least they let her sing what she wants to, and she doesn't have to mix with the customers."

The owner greeted Dip effusively and led him to a banquet table along the wall. The place was half filled. Men sat in sport shirts, most of the girls wore slacks. There were about twenty people at the bar, mostly beer customers.

"She goes on in about ten minutes, then she'll join us." He saw Robin glance at his watch. "You sure you haven't got a date tonight?"

"No, it's just that I have to check out of my hotel."

"I'll drive you to the airport."

"Oh, that's not necessary."

Dip flashed a big grin. "When I go, pal, I go all the way. Say, what's your racket in New York–advertising agency you said, huh?"

"No. I'm with International Broadcasting."

"The only thing I watch on TV is the movies. I figure I can learn from them. What do you do at IBC?"

"News."

"You a researcher or something? You write?"

"At times."

"I bet you went to college, huh?"

Robin smiled. "Does it show?"

"Yeah, you carry yourself pretty good. But college–that's a time waster, unless you want to be a lawyer or a doctor. I want to be a superstar! God, I can taste it, I want it so bad. I want to be able to tell everyone to go fuck themselves!"

"What about Pauli?"

"She's with me all the way, old buddy. And when we get married, if she just wants to be a wife and no career, hell, I won't push her. She's loaded with talent. But all she wants is to marry me and have a lot of babies. What about you–I guess you have a wife and a couple of kids?"

"No."

"Just a girl you're hung on to?"

"No, not even that."

Dip looked at him suddenly. "How come? Hey, you're straight, aren't you?"

Robin laughed outright. "I think women are wonderful."

"Then what's your hangup? I mean, at your age you should be married and have kids. Now me, I'm only twenty-six."

Robin's grin disconcerted him.

"Okay–so I'm thirty-one. But I can get by for twenty-six, can't I?"

"In the Hollywood light."

"Say, that's good. How old are you?"

"Forty in August."

"And no marriage ever?"

"Nope."

"And no serious girl?"

"I had one, but she got engaged."

Dip shook his head sympathetically. "Hit you hard, I bet. It's rough to find a real girl–especially out here. Every dame is out for number one."

"And you're not?" Robin asked.

Dip looked hurt. "You're goddam right, I am. But have I crapped you on *one* thing? I only pull the act when it's for my career. But when I'm with people I like, I level."

"And you like me?"

"Yeah, I guess I do. Say, I don't even know your name."

"Robin Stone."

Dip looked at him suspiciously. "You're sure you're not light on your feet? Look, if you are, Pauli will spot it in a second. She can spot a fag a mile away." Suddenly he punched Robin's arm. "She's coming on now. Wait till you see this explosion of talent!"

Robin leaned forward as the slim young girl came into the spotlight. She had red curly hair and he guessed by the freckles on her shoulders that it was natural. Her nose was short and almost comically upturned. Her mouth was large, her eyes saucer-wide and innocently blue. But when she sang, he was disappointed. Her voice was true, but she was ordinary. A garbled imitation of Garland and Lena. He had heard a hundred girls like Pauli, only they were better-looking. The only time she held his attention was with her takeoff on Carol Channing. Then she came to life–she had a definite comic flair. Her set ended to scattered applause and wild whistling from Dip. He thumped Robin on the back. "Now I ask you–is she beautiful? Has she got class? Turns the whole joint into the Waldorf the minute she steps onstage!"

Both men stood up as the girl came to the table. "This is my fiancée, Pauli. Pauli, say hello to Robin."

She smiled slightly and sat down. Then she looked at Robin curiously.

"He's from New York," Dip said quickly.

"Oh, listen, Dip, your press agent wants you to call him as soon as you come in," Pauli said, without listening.

Dip got up. "You two talk. Robin's at IBC."

Pauli watched him as he left the table. Then she turned to Robin. "What are you doing with Dip?"

"We met at a party."

Her eyes narrowed. "What's a guy in mechanics got in common with Dip?"

"Mechanics?"

"Didn't he say you worked with IBM?"

"IBC: International Broadcasting."

"Oh. Say, have you any pull to get me a guest shot on the Chris Lane show?" He decided he didn't like her, but he owed it to Dip. "Yes, I might be able to swing it."

Her eyes lit up. "Honest–could you really?" Then she looked suspicious. "What do you do at IBC?"

"The news."

"Like Huntley and Brinkley?"

"In a way."

"Then how come I never heard of you? I watch the seven o'clock news a lot. I know who Walter Cronkite is, but not you."

He smiled. "You've ruined my whole evening."

"How can you get me on *The Christie Lane Show?*"

"I can ask him."

Her stare was calculative. Then on the wild chance that he might be leveling, the saucer eyes went soft. "If you'd ask him, I mean, if you'd swing it, I'd–well, I'd do anything to get on that show."

"Anything?" Robin smiled and held her eyes.

Her stare was level. "Yes, if that's what you want."

"And what do you want?"

"To blow this crumb joint."

"Dip will arrange that eventually."

She shrugged. "Look, you just met him. I mean, you and him aren't buddy-buddy, because I never heard him mention you before."

"You're batting a thousand."

"Well, look, just between the two of us"–her voice lowered–"Laurence Olivier he's not. So he's handsome, but he has no talent. So far he's been lucky."

"I gathered from Dip that you had no ambitions–just wanted to get married and make babies."

She waved her hand in disgust. "Would any girl in her right mind stand up here and sing to these crumbs three times a night if she didn't know she was going to make it big? I *know* I've got it."

"Where does Dip fit in?"

"I dig him. I really do. I gave him my virginity. Honest to God. I was pure when we met. But I know Dip. He lives and breathes his career. He wouldn't last two minutes with a girl who had her own interest at heart. He wants to be the big shot all the way. So I pretend I'm nothing. Most of the time I sit and listen to how great things are going for him. And I'm burning inside me because I know *I'm* the one who's great. And there he is, going to the top because of his looks. That's all he has. Not a brain in his head."

"He wants to help you. He told me so," Robin said.

"Yeah, he talks. But words are cheap. Look–about the Chris Lane show, can you arrange it?"

"If I do, will you be grateful?"

"Mister–I take it you got a wife?"

"Maybe."

"Well, you get me on the Chris Lane show and anytime, anyplace, you just snap your fingers and I'll be there. I pay off–I got a big sense of honor." He reached for a cigarette. She picked up the matches and lit it for him. She leaned across and said, "Well, is it a deal?"

He smiled. "You know, you little bitch," he said softly, "it would almost be worth it–for Dip's sake."

"I don't get it."

Robin's grin was easy. He kept his voice even. "You're right about one thing: Dip hasn't a brain in his head, or else he would have seen through you. He thinks you're an angel. But you're a broad. No, not even a broad–you're a rough, no-talent cunt."

He stood up and smiled. His quiet calm seemed to infuriate her. "If you think I'm scared you'll tell Dip all these things, forget it. You open your stinking mouth and I'll tell him you made a pass at me."

"Tell Dip I got a phone call." He put down a ten-dollar bill.

"What's that for?" she asked.

"I think the going rate for a call girl is a hundred. Take this as a down payment. I think you're on your way." He walked out of the club.

SIXTEEN

CHRISTIE LANE FINISHED THE SHOW the first week in June. He left for New York the following day.

On July fourth Amanda and Ike were married in Las Vegas. The front pages of all the tabloids featured pictures of the wedding–Amanda and Ike surrounded by several stars who were playing Vegas. They were flying to Europe for a honeymoon.

Chris held a wake in his suite at the Astor Hotel. Eddie, Kenny, and Agnes sat with him. He paced up and down. He cried. He talked: "God, if only I could get drunk. But I don't like booze."

"Let's go out on the town," Eddie suggested.

"I played it so straight with her," Chris kept repeating; "I even helped her find a place here to board her goddam cat."

"I wonder what'll happen to the cat," Agnes asked.

"I hope it croaks–it was the only thing she really cared about."

"I bet she sends for the cat when she comes back from Europe," Agnes said.

"Who gives a shit!" Christie roared.

"Well, you brought it up," she answered.

"I played it so straight with her," Chris repeated. "Why did she do it? Look at me . . . I'm better-looking than Ike Ryan."

"Whaaat?" This was Agnes.

Chris whirled on her. "You think he's good-looking?"

"He's sexy-looking," she said sullenly.

Eddie shot her a murderous look. "Hey, Aggie, you looking to be replaced? This is no time for funnies."

"I still think he's sexy-looking," she said stubbornly.

"Look, Chris," Kenny cut in, "how's about us getting a table at the Copa? I know some of the kids in the line. They got three new dancers. One is gorgeous, only nineteen. I bet she'd like you. She's a nice girl."

Chris kicked the coffee table so hard the leg came off and it collapsed. "Nice girl! I *had* a nice girl–a gorgeous girl! Christ, she'd give me a dirty look if I said a bad word in front of her. And she turns out to be the worst double-crossing cooze around. No dame in burlesque would act like that. I'm through being a nice guy and I want no part of *nice* girls. I want a bum! I'll treat her like a bum and no one will get hurt. Just find me the biggest bum in town–the best joint-copper!"

"Call for Ethel Evans–" Eddie chanted, mimicking a pageboy.

Chris snapped his fingers. "That's it!"

Eddie laughed. "Oh, come on–I was kidding. Listen, Chris, if you want a bum at least get a pretty one. There's a dame in town from Frisco–"

"I don't want a pretty bum, or a dame from Frisco. I want Ethel!"

"But she's a beast," Kenny said.

"I don't want a beauty queen. I want a fucker! Get me Ethel!" His eyes narrowed. "If I'm seen with a cunt like her, *that* will show them. They'll figure Amanda couldn't mean much to me if I could wind up enjoying a broad like Ethel. Get her!"

Eddie called Jerry Moss in Greenwich. Jerry sighed and promised to do his best. He located Ethel in Fire Island.

"What is this, a gag?" she demanded.

"No, Christie Lane *personally* asked to see you."

"That's a quaint way of putting it!"

"Ethel, you've boffed every guest star on Christie's show."

"I missed a few. Don't forget they did the last half of the season from the Coast."

"They're not going to the Coast next season."

"Great. I'll get a new diaphragm."

"Ethel, our star is unhappy. He wants *you*."

"But I don't want him."

"I'm asking you to go into town."

Her voice was icy. "Is that an order?"

"Let's say it's a *request.*"

"The answer is no."

"Then perhaps I'll have to call Danton Miller and ask him to take you off the show." Jerry hated himself, but he had to make one last-ditch effort.

Her laugh was nasty. "I can always handle Danton."

"Not against a sponsor. And whether you like it or not, Ethel, that's what I am."

"Really? I thought you were Robin Stone's personal maid."

He kept his voice even. "I am not dealing in personalities with you."

"Oh, excuse me. I guess this is all impersonal—you calling me and telling me to come in town to fuck Chris Lane."

"Put whatever connotation on it you wish. You earned your reputation. And it's not my job to be on the phone with you on July Fourth either. I'm doing it because I'm part of the Christie Lane show. Obviously you have no idea of teamwork."

"Oh, cut the agency shit," she snapped. "I want you to get this straight. I'm not a call girl. When I hump a guy, it's because I dig him. For a year and a half Chris Lane never looked at me twice—thank God! And now all of a sudden I'm Elizabeth Taylor. What's the big deal?"

"Amanda married Ike Ryan today."

There was a pause. Then she laughed. "Hey, your friend Robin Stone must be upset too! Now why don't I go console *him?* I'd even swim back for that."

"Are you coming in?"

She sighed. "Okay. Where do I find lover boy?"

"At the Astor."

She laughed. "Wouldn't you know? All my life I've waited to meet someone who actually lived at the Astor!"

Christie was alone when she arrived. "Hey. What's the big idea?" he asked. "You're in slacks."

"You didn't expect me to walk in nude, did you?"

He didn't smile. "No, but the gang is at the Copa. I was waiting to take you over and join them."

She stared at him. "The Copa?"

"Come on!" he ordered. "We'll grab a cab and go to your place. I want you to change into a dress so we can go to the Copa."

He sat in her living room thumbing through a magazine while she dressed.

In the cab, he sat huddled on the other side of the seat, morose and uncommunicative, but once they entered the Copa, his entire personality changed. He flashed a broad smile, held her arm and introduced her to everyone they met with a proprietary air. He held her hand through the show; he even lit her cigarette. She sat through it all grimly. She had seen the show, she was tired and she wanted to get the evening over with.

It was close to three when they returned to the Astor. She had never had such a grueling time. The Copa, then the Copa bar, the Brasserie and a stop at the Stage Delicatessen. Now they were alone. She undressed silently. He was already naked, lying expectantly on the bed. She looked at him and felt a crawling revulsion. There was something so repulsive about a man without a hard on. How had Amanda done it? To go from a man like Robin Stone to this slob!

She walked to the side of the bed, completely naked. He couldn't mask his amazement as he stared at her enormous, well-shaped breasts.

"Hey, doll, for an ugly dame you sure got a build." He grabbed her rear. "Now if you'd just lose some of that ass, you'd almost have a great figure."

She pulled away from him. His hands were clammy. She didn't want him to touch her.

"You have any shaving cream?" she asked.

"Sure, why?"

She went to the bathroom and returned with the container. She spread the shaving cream all over her hands. "Now lie back, you big television star."

In less than five minutes he lay spent and groaning. She slipped into the bathroom and dressed quickly. When she returned to the bedroom he was lying motionless, his eyes closed.

"So long, Chris." She couldn't get out fast enough.

He reached out and grabbed her hand. "Doll, I never had it like that. But it's not fair, I mean, nothing happened for you. Christ, I never even got to touch you."

"That's all right," she said softly. "I know you felt blue tonight. I just wanted to make you forget, make you happy."

He pulled her down to the bed. Then he stared at her. "You know, that's the nicest thing anyone ever said to me. Look, I appreciate it. I know you came all the way in from Fire Island tonight. Is there anything I can do?"

She longed to say, "Just forget about me and leave me alone." But she merely smiled.

He pulled her down. "Give us a kiss."

His lips were soft and blubbery. She managed to pull away without showing her repugnance. Then she leaned down and kissed his sweaty brow and dashed from the apartment without even asking for cab fare.

He called her the next morning and invited her to dinner. She had nothing better to do, so she accepted. He took her out every night for two weeks. The columns began coupling their names together. He invited her to accompany them to Atlantic City when he went to play the Five Hundred Club. She was beginning to enjoy the sudden personal publicity she was getting as Christie Lane's girl. She had never been anyone's "girl." So she went along. Her picture appeared with Chris in one of the morning papers, showing them in a rolling chair on the boardwalk, hinting of an "engagement."

Jerry Moss grew slightly apprehensive. He called Christie in Atlantic City.

"Christie, you're not serious about this girl?"

"Of course not. Listen, Jerry, Dan's got the first two shows for the new season fairly set. Who are you getting to replace—" He stopped.

"We'll use a different girl each week," Jerry said. "But I want to talk to you about Ethel."

"Yeah?"

"You know her reputation."

"So?"

"Do you think it's smart bringing her to Atlantic City? The columns are writing about you and Ethel. She's not good for your image. The public wants to see you coupled with a nice girl, a beautiful girl."

"Listen, buster, I went with a *nice* girl, a beautiful girl. Maybe the public was happy, but I got my brains kicked in. The public wasn't around to hold my cock the night Amanda got married. But Ethel Evans was!"

"Everyone in the business knows about Ethel," Jerry argued. "So far the public knows nothing. But after this engagement rumor in the newspapers, the public will want to know more. And how will it look to the public to know their family man goes with a whore!"

"Don't you say that!" Chris said roughly. "She never took a dime from a guy!"

"Chris, are you taking her seriously? I mean, you're leaving for Vegas in a few weeks. You're not taking her there, are you?"

"Too much plane fare involved. It ain't exactly Atlantic City where we hire a car and all pile in."

"Then you're not serious about her."

"Of course not. But I know one thing. She's there when I want her. She's nice to me. She doesn't cheat. And she hasn't been with another guy since I started dating her. And anything I want to do is okay with her. I'm relaxed with Ethel. He paused as if recalling something. Then he laughed. "Take Ethel to Vegas! That's like bringing a tuna-fish sandwich to Danny's Hideaway."

It had been a dull summer for Ethel. She worked on a variety show that featured new talent. She didn't dig guitar-playing groups. Even the guest stars were youth-oriented. She was relieved when Labor Day arrived. When Christie Lane returned to New York she was almost glad to see him.

She was with him constantly during the month of September. The show didn't start till October and he had most of his evenings free. She was bored to death with Kenny and Eddie and Agnes. She hated the Copa bar, the Chinese restaurants (always the cheapest ones), but most of all she hated the racetrack. He never offered to place a bet for her, so out of boredom she placed two-dollar show bets of her own and occasionally won sixty cents. She loathed any physical contact with him, but to her relief she soon realized he wasn't a highly sexed man. Twice a week more than satisfied him, then he would lie back and read the racing form.

She was really marking time until the show would begin and new guest stars would arrive. Then she would give Christie and his stooges the brush.

A week before the opening show, two television magazines came out with stories on Christie, featuring Ethel Evans.

Jerry sat in his office and stared at the pictures of the smiling couple—God, they really looked like a pair of bookends! But now he really had to take some action. This thing was getting out of hand. He made an appointment to meet Danton Miller for lunch.

At first Dan was amused. "Come on, Jerry, you're borrowing trouble. The hicks in the sticks never heard of Ethel."

Jerry snapped his knuckles. "Dan, this is serious. Tom Carruthers is a Baptist as well as a sponsor. He didn't even approve of some of the rock singers we had on the summer replacement show. So far he thinks Ethel is a nice homespun girl. He's even had her to dinner with *Mrs.* Carruthers. If one of those scandal magazines ever decides to do some real research on Ethel, we're dead! She's got a girl friend on the Coast who saved all her letters with ratings of the stars in the kip. She's had them mimeoed and passes them around. If those letters ever got into print! Incidentally, Dan, I hear your 'rating' is listed, too."

Dan's smile disappeared.

"Look, Dan, I'm not a prude. That kind of publicity might help a swinging singer, but not our little old minstrel man. He appeals to a family-type audience. Carruthers even wants to try for an earlier time spot next season so that more kids can watch. He wants to stay with Christie Lane for life. You've got a gold mine with this show—and we can't let Ethel stand in the way. It's too big a risk."

Dan poured himself a second cup of coffee. Jerry Moss was making sense. One shot of notoriety and the Christie Lane-type sponsorship would pull out. They had gone along with the

Amanda "romance" because it represented the Walter Mitty dream of every average Joe. A plain guy winding up with the most beautiful girl in the world. If Christie could do it, anything was possible. He gave people hope. They had fantasized with him even more when Amanda jilted him for the flamboyant Ike Ryan. And now they were latching on to Ethel Evans because she looked like the average girl. Jerry was right! It really was a mess!

The luncheon ended with his ulcer burning and his promise to step in and end the Ethel Evans-Christie Lane relationship immediately.

Dan thought about the situation for several days. He knew he'd have to take her off the show. Jesus, what had she said in her letter about him? He called the publicity department. He was informed that she could be reached at the beauty parlor. Beauty parlor! It would take a plastic surgeon to help her. He took the phone number and placed the call.

"Hi!" She sounded very cheerful.

"Is today some kind of holiday I don't know about? Why the unsolicited afternoon off?"

She laughed. "I go steady now and have to look nice. And tonight's the big night."

"Tonight?" He suddenly remembered. The TV Golden Personality Award. IBC had taken a table. Next to the Emmy, this was the biggest TV event.

"Are you going?" he asked. He knew it was a stupid question –of course she was going.

"Are you?" she countered.

"I have to. Chris is up for an award, so is Robin Stone, and Gregory Austin is on the dais."

"I guess I'll see you then–we'll probably be sitting at the same table. Oh, by the way, Dan, what was it you called me about?"

"Maybe I wanted to ask you to go with me," he said. This was not the moment to give her the ultimatum. It had to be done in person.

Her laugh was not nice. "Let's stop playing games. My hair is wet and I want to get back under the dryer. What's the reason for the call?"

"I'll talk about it tomorrow."

"We do the show tomorrow. I'll be busy, and Carruthers is giving a little party after the show."

"Only you won't be going," he said. He knew his timing was bad, but this was too much.

"Come again?"

"Tonight will be your last public or private appearance with Chris."

She was silent for a moment. Then she said, "Are you jealous?"

"This is an official order."

"By whom?"

"Me! *The Christie Lane Show* belongs to IBC. It's my duty to protect a property. Let's just say your image is not right for a family-type show. So after tonight I want you to give Chris the air."

"And suppose I don't?"

"Then you're fired from IBC."

She was silent.

"Do you hear me, Ethel?"

Her voice was hard. "Okay, sonny boy. Sure you can get me fired. But maybe I don't care. IBC isn't the only game in town. There's always CBS, NBC and ABC."

"Not if I spread the word about why you were fired."

"You mean it's illegal to boff Christie Lane–or presidents of networks?"

"No. But sending pornographic writing through the mail is. I happen to have some copies of letters you wrote to a girl friend in Los Angeles giving graphic and clinical reports on your sex life."

She tried to brazen it out. "Okay–so I won't work. It'll give me more time for Christie."

He laughed. "From what I understand, generosity is not one of Christie Lane's virtues. But maybe you know another side of him. After all, I forget how close you are. Maybe he'll set you up in an apartment, give you an allowance."

"You son of a bitch!" Her voice stabbed through the phone.

"Look. Dump Christie. Your job stays and I'll see that you get assigned to another show."

"I'll make a deal," she said. "Get me the Robin Stone show and Christie Lane won't be able to get me on the phone."

Dan was thoughtful. "We offered to assign someone to him way back, but he refused. Let me see what I can do. I promise I'll try and swing it. If not, there are other shows."

"I said the Robin Stone show."

"I'm afraid you're not in a position to call the shots. I'll *try* and get you Robin Stone. But remember, tonight is the last time you see Christie Lane. You make an appearance at his show tomorrow, and you're through!"

That night she dressed with care. Her hair had grown longer and she had added an auburn tint. The green dress was good—low-cut and showed her breasts to full advantage. Her hips were still too large, but the full skirt hid them. She appraised herself in the mirror and she was pleased. She was no Amanda, but if she remembered not to smile and show that damn separation between her teeth, she didn't look bad. Not bad at all. . . .

The Grand Ballroom of the Waldorf was jammed. Chris led her in and shouted greetings to every table he passed. The dais was impressive: stacked with heads of all the networks, some Broadway stars, the mayor, and a motion-picture executive. Ethel spotted Gregory Austin and his beautiful wife in the center of the dais. A columnist was talking to her. Her head was bent almost as if she was giving audience, rather than listening. Ethel followed Chris to the IBC table, directly in front of the dais. Dan Miller was already seated. He was with a thirtyish-looking brunette. Trust Dan to dig up the right type for tonight. Almost like he called an agent and said, "Send me a society type—black dress, pearls, not too big on the boobs." There were two empty seats beside her. Could they be for Robin Stone? They had to be—all the others were taken. That meant he'd be sitting right next to her. She hadn't counted on such a windfall.

He arrived late with an exquisite girl, Inger Gustar, a new German actress. Ethel took out a cigarette. Christie made no move, but to her amazement, Robin held out his lighter.

"I admire your taste," she said quietly. "I saw her picture last week. She can't act, but it doesn't matter." When he didn't answer, Ethel pressed on. "Is this serious or just something new?" She tried to make her voice bantering.

He smiled and said, "Eat your grapefruit."

"I don't like grapefruit."

"It's good for you." He didn't look up.

"I *don't* always like the things that are good for me."

The music began. Robin suddenly stood up. "Okay, Ethel, let's try it."

She flushed with delight. Could that mean she had finally gotten through to him? Maybe the green dress and the red tint to her hair had helped more than she thought. He danced for a few minutes in silence. She pressed closer to him. He pulled away and looked at her. His face was void of any expression and his lips barely seemed to move. But the words came out cold and clear.

"Listen, you silly broad, don't you know that maybe for the first time in your life you have a chance at the brass ring? I gave you credit for some brains–now use them, and try and come up a winner."

"Maybe I'm not interested in brass rings."

"Meaning what?"

"Meaning Christie Lane doesn't appeal to me."

He threw back his head and laughed. "You really are choosy. I like your guts anyway."

"And I like everything about you." Her voice was insinuating and soft.

She felt his body stiffen. Without looking at her he said, "Sorry, no dice."

"Why?"

He pulled away and looked at her. "Because I'm choosy too."

She stared at him. "Why do you hate me?"

"I don't hate you. Let's say that until now the only thing I felt about you was that you had a fair amount of brainpower and nerve. But now I'm beginning to wonder. You've got Christie Lane, don't sell him short. He may not be Sinatra, but his show is hot. He'll last a long long time."

"Robin, tell me something. Why did you ask me to dance?"

"Because it's going to be a long night and I'm not up to ten or twelve veiled propositions from you. I thought I'd set the record straight right off. The answer is no."

She looked at the German girl dancing near them. "No for tonight." She smiled.

"No for any night."

"Why?" She looked into his eyes.

"Want me to be frank?"

"Yes." She smiled without showing her teeth.

"I couldn't get it up for you, baby–it's as simple as that."

Her face went tense. "I didn't know you had problems. So that's your hangup."

He smiled. "It would be with you."

"Maybe that's why Amanda blew you off for Ike Ryan. The great Robin Stone–all charm, all talk, no action. She even cheated on you with Chris."

He stopped dancing and took her arm. "I think we'd better go back to the table."

Her smile was evil. She refused to move. "Oh, did I hit you where it hurts, Mr. Stone?"

"I feel no pain, baby. I just don't think you're entitled to gossip about Amanda." Once again he tried to lead her off the floor, but she forced him into a dancing position.

"Robin, give me a chance. Try it with me just once! No strings! You can have me whenever you snap your fingers. And I'm good insurance. I'll satisfy you–you'll never lose your head over a girl like Amanda again."

He looked at her with a strange smile. "And I'll bet you're healthy as a horse."

"I've never been sick in my life."

He nodded. "It figures."

She looked at him evenly. "Well?"

"Ethel"–he almost sighed–"send in your first team with Chris Lane!"

"I can't." She shook her head. "It's not up to me–I've been given orders to cut out."

He was genuinely interested. "By whom?"

"Danton Miller. Sure, it's great for him to bang me whenever he wants, but this afternoon he informed me I am to give up Chris–seems we are getting too much publicity. I'm not good for the family image and if I don't follow his orders he's going to fire me."

"What are you going to do?"

Well, at least she had his interest. Maybe this was the tactic —don't come on strong, play it for sympathy. Why not? She had tried everything else. She tried to work some tears to her eyes but nothing happened. She said, "What can I do?" and looked at him helplessly.

"You're losing me with the Shirley Temple bit. If you're a broad, act like one, don't suddenly turn girlish and beg for sympathy." He grinned at her. "You've been playing a man's game, with a man's rules. I'd put you up against Danton Miller any day."

She stared at him curiously. "You mean I should fight Dan Miller?" She shook her head. "I haven't a chance—unless you give me a job working on your show. You said I have a brain—let's forget sex for now. Give me a chance, Robin. I can do a lot for your show. I can get you important publicity."

"Forget it." He cut her short. "I'm not a performer—"

"But let me be assigned to your show. I'll type, do anything you want."

"Nope."

"Why not?" She was pleading.

"Because I give nothing out of charity, pity or sympathy."

"What about friendship?"

"We are not friends."

"I'll be your friend. I'll do anything for you—just name it."

"Well, right now there's nothing I want more out of life than to end this dance."

She broke away from him and stared with hate. "Robin Stone —I hope you rot in hell!"

His grin was easy. He took her arm and led her off the floor. "That's it, baby, get some spirit. I like you better this way." They had reached the table. He thanked her for the dance with a pleasant smile.

It was a long dull evening. Chris was chosen as the outstanding personality in a new show. Robin's *In Depth* show won the news category. When the speeches were over the curtains on the opposite side of the room parted, the band played a fanfare and everyone groaned inwardly as they turned their chairs to watch the entertainment.

Robin grabbed the German girl and they ducked out the moment the lights dimmed. But Chris remained at the table along with the other IBC personnel and watched the show.

Ethel stared at the two empty chairs. Who the hell was *he* to have the independence to walk out? Even Danton Miller sat and watched the tedious show. Chris wouldn't have dared to leave and Chris was twice as important as Robin Stone. Come to think of it, Chris was even more important than Dan Miller. Dan could get fired any time—and right now he was in favor *because* of Chris! How dare he threaten her! As long as she had Chris she was bigger than Danton Miller. And bigger than Robin Stone. Suddenly she realized that Chris was the only thing she had going for her. She was thirty-one. She couldn't just keep going on humping any celebrity that came along. In a few years they wouldn't want her.

She sat in the darkness oblivious to the polite laughter of the audience, as the new idea took hold and grew. Why should she give Chris the air? Sleeping with him was one thing—but to be Mrs. Christie Lane! The enormity of the idea was overwhelming. Of course it would be a long hard pull. She'd have to plant the idea gradually. Then she could tell them all to fuck off. Dan—Robin—the whole world. *Mrs.* Christie Lane! Mrs. TV Star! Mrs. *Power!*

It was three in the morning when they reached the Astor. Chris had offered to drop her at her own apartment. "I have to be at rehearsal at eleven tomorrow, doll."

"Let me come and just sleep with you. We don't have to have sex, I want to be with you, Chris."

His homely face broke into a smile. "Sure, doll. I just thought you'd be more comfortable in your own place, changing and all. because you got to be at rehearsal tomorrow too."

"That's just it—I don't."

He turned to her in the darkened cab. "Come again?"

"I'll tell you when we're upstairs."

She undressed silently and slipped into bed with him. He was looking at the racing form. His stomach was billowing over his shorts, a cigar was clamped between his teeth. He motioned to the twin bed. "Sleep in there, doll. No humping tonight."

"I just want to cling to you, Chris." She put her arms around his flabby body.

He looked at her. "Say, you're acting funny. What's up?"

She burst into tears. She was surprised how easily they came. She was thinking of the humiliation Robin Stone had caused her, and the tears grew into full-fledged sobs.

"Doll–for Chrissakes what's the matter? Did I do something? Tell me."

"Oh no, Chris, it's just that this is our last night together." She sobbed in earnest now. She was sobbing for all the rejections, all the men she had loved for just one night, all the love she had never had.

"What in hell are you talking about?" He put his arms around her and clumsily tried to pat her head. God, she even hated the smell of him, cheap shaving cologne and sweat, but she managed to think of Robin on the dance floor. She thought of the German girl who was probably in his arms, and her sobs increased in volume.

"Doll, tell me, I can't stand to see you like this. You're the strongest girl in the world. I was telling that to Kenny the other day. I said, 'That Ethel–she'd kill for me.' What's this shit about this being our last night together?"

She looked at him with the tears running down her face. "Chris, how do you feel about me?"

He rubbed her hair and gazed into space thoughtfully. "I dunno, doll, I never give it much thought. I like you. We have a ball together. You're a good sport–"

She started to sob again. This pig–he was rejecting her too!

"Now, doll, I mean look–I wouldn't let myself fall in love. Once is enough. But there's no other girl. You're with me as long as you want to be. Like Kenny and Eddie. So what's all this talk about our last night?"

She turned away and stared straight ahead of her. "Chris, you know about my past."

The color came to his face.

"That's just it," she sobbed. "But that's not the real me. What you know *now* is the real me. You're afraid of getting hurt because of Amanda–well, it happened to me. A boy in college, we were engaged. I was a virgin, and he walked out on me. I was so hurt, I decided to screw every man in the world, just to get even with him. I hated him, I hated life, I hated myself. Until you came along–then it was as if I was purged. I met a fine human being, I really cared. I began to like myself, and the real Ethel Evans emerged. All the past was a put-on. What I've been to you is really what I am."

"I understand, doll, and I'm even beginning to forget about your past. So what's the big deal? Am I asking questions?"

"No, but, Chris–before you came along, I–I went with Danton Miller."

He sat up straight. "Oh shit, him too! Didn't you miss anyone?"

"Chris, Dan really dug me. He got jealous of everyone I went with. He put me on your show so he could keep an eye on me. He was livid when Jerry arranged for us to date. But he figured it would be a one-night stand. He had no idea I'd really fall in love with you. Now he's jealous."

"Fuck him!"

"That's just what he wants."

"You're kidding!"

"No, he called me today, and told me he didn't want me to see you anymore. That he wants me to hold myself free just for him. I told him to go fuck himself and he said I'm to give you the air tonight. I'm not to go near your show–if I do, he'll have me fired from IBC. If I give you the air, I can stay. He'll even get me other shows with more money. But I can't do it, Chris–I can't live without you."

"I'll talk to Dan tomorrow."

"He'll deny it, and you'll have an enemy. He says he made you and he can break you."

Christie's jaw tightened. Ethel realized she had made a wrong move. Chris was still insecure. Dammit, he was afraid of Dan Miller.

"He can't touch you, Chris–you're the greatest. But he can get rid of me. It seems I wrote a lot of silly letters to a girl I thought was my friend–about some of my romances. Dan has copies of the letters."

"You know, some dames have a big mouth, but you got a big typewriter. Why in fuck did you ever write letters? You can hurt the guys too."

"I know, and maybe God is punishing me. But how did I know Yvonne would have copies made? Why doesn't God pay *her* back? I wrote them on the spur of the moment, as a joke. But that's all past. My problem is now."

"Okay, so you quit the show," Chris said.

"Then what?"

"You could get another job—CBS, NBC, any of the networks."

"No, Dan would blackball me. I'm finished."

"I'll get you a job, and right now."

"Chris, it's three thirty."

"Who gives a shit!" He picked up the phone and asked for a number. After a few rings, Ethel heard a sleep-filled voice answer. "Herbie? Chris Lane. I know it's late, but look, sweetheart, I'm a man who acts on impulse. It seems to me the other day at the track you said you'd give anything just for the prestige of having your office handle my public relations. Well, I just might give you the chance. Starting tomorrow."

Herbie's staccato voice rattled through the phone. He was elated. He'd do a hell of a job. He'd be at rehearsal at eleven.

"Hold it, Herbie. There's a few stipulations that go with the deal. I'll pay three bills a week—I don't care what the going rate is. You got a crummy office on Broadway with some borscht comics and a few dance teams. But if you got Christie Lane, you're in the big leagues. And I may be able to throw some work to your cockamamie clients. Only there's a deal goes with it: you got to hire Ethel Evans. Sure she's with IBC, but I want her to quit and just work for me. Only *you* pay her. How much—a C a week? He looked at Ethel. She shook her head frantically. "That's chickenshit, Herbie, one twenty-five?" She shook her head again. "Wait a minute, Herbie." He turned to Ethel. "What do you want—opera?"

"I get a base pay of one fifty at IBC, twenty-five extra for doing your show—that's one seventy-five."

"Herbie, one seventy-five and it's a deal. So it only leaves you one and a quarter, but look at the prestige, baby. Well, I see your point, okay, one fifty." He ignored the elbow Ethel jabbed into him. "Sure, Herbie, she'll be at your office at ten tomorrow."

"You mean with all your big pull, I'm taking a cut?" she asked.

"The man is right, you can't make more than he makes out of the deal. Now relax. At IBC you have to work on a lot of shows. With Herbie it's just me, and you can live on one fifty."

Ethel was furious. She knew Herbie . . . he'd make her punch a time clock and the hours would be murder. Her job at IBC had prestige. Herbie ran a shlock outfit. Everything was all botched up, but she was stuck now.

"Chris, I've signed my death notice, you know that."

"Why? I just got you a new job."

"At IBC I had fringe benefits–hospitalization, nice clean air-conditioned offices."

"So you got me. Isn't that what you wanted?"

She snuggled close to him. "You know that. I gave up IBC for you–I could have stayed, done other shows. But I gave it up to work for Herbie Shine. But what are you doing for me?"

"Are you crazy? Didn't I just get you a job?"

"I want to be your girl."

"Christ, everyone knows it."

"I mean officially–can't we at least say we're engaged?"

He put down the racing form. "Forget it! I'm not marrying you, Ethel. If and when I get married, I want a decent girl. I want kids. Your cooze is like the Lincoln Tunnel, everyone's been through it.

"And I suppose Amanda was a decent girl . . ."

"She was a bum, but I thought she was decent. At least I know about you."

"And you don't think a girl can change?"

"Maybe. We'll see." He picked up the racing form.

"Chris, just give me a chance–please!"

"Am I throwing you outa bed? You're with me–wherever we go–aren't you?"

She threw her arms around him. "Oh, Chris, I don't just love you, I worship you. You're my God, my Lord, my king. You're my life!"

She crawled down to the bottom of the bed and began running her tongue along his toes. It nauseated her, but she tried to pretend he was one of the movie stars she had adored.

He started to laugh. "Hey, that feels good. I never had nothing like that."

"Lie down. I want to make love to every part of you. To show you how I worship and adore you. I always will—no matter what you do. I'll always love you. I love you so much. . . ." She began moaning and making love to him. Later when he lay back panting and wet with perspiration he said, "But, doll, that's not right. I came like crazy. Jesus—right down to my toes. But nothing happened with you."

"Are you mad?" she said. "I came twice, just making love to you."

"You're kidding!"

"Chris, don't you understand? I love you. You excite me, I come just when I touch you."

He put his arm around her and rubbed her hair. "Well, how about that! You're sure a crazy dame, but I like it." He belched loudly and he picked up the racing form.

"Hey, it's after four and I got to do my homework. You better get in the other bed and go to sleep. You got to get up early and give Dan your notice and go to Herbie's office. Go to sleep, doll."

She went into the other bed and turned her back on him. She gritted her teeth and said, "I love you, Chris."

He got out of the bed and headed for the bathroom. On the way he patted her buttocks. "I love you too, doll. Only don't forget, I'm—I'm forty-two, and I got a big career that got started late in life. And that's all that counts to me." Then leaving the door open, he sat on the toilet and had an explosive bowel movement. She threw the covers over her head. The pig! And she had to crawl to him! But she'd get even. She'd marry him! If it was the last thing she did—then she'd tell everyone to fuck off. Especially him!

Ethel ripped the copy from the typewriter and flung it on Herbie Shine's desk. She stood there, her eyes narrowed, as the small compact balding little man read it carefully.

"It's okay," he said slowly. "But you don't give the address of the restaurant."

"Herbie, it's a general release for the columns. Either the name 'Lario's' catches, or forget it. No column prints the address."

"But this joint is off the beaten track. We got to make people aware of it."

"If they'd spring for an opening party and have some celebrities and all the columnists, they'd make every paper. But they're like all your accounts–too cheap to do things right."

"On that you're right, especially my jumbo account, Mr. Christie Lane. He's the cheapest of them all. Lario's is a small place. They can't afford to go for all that free booze and food for a party. But better make some of those IBC people go there, also Christie Lane."

"Look. Chris is paying you on his own. He hated that last restaurant you handled, the one on Twelfth Street you made me drag him to–cost him three bucks in cab fare each way. I didn't hear the end of it for days."

"He also stiffed the waiters," Herbie said.

"Chris figures when he's on the cuff it's all the way."

"Anyone knows you still take care of a captain and a waiter."

"Not Chris."

"Well, why don't you tell him!"

"I'm not running an Emily Post course." She put her coat on.

"It's only four o'clock. What kind of banker's hours do you think you're keeping around here? You didn't come in till ten fifteen this morning."

"When I was at IBC I often came in at ten thirty, and I left when I wanted to. Sometimes I was in at nine and left at six. Look, Herbie, I'm good at my job. I get my work done and make my own hours. Next thing I know, you'll want me to punch a time clock."

"I'm not IBC. I have three people working for me. We handle twelve accounts. You make more than the other two and you work half the hours I do."

"Then fire me."

He stared at her with an ugly smile. "I'd love to. And you

know it! But we both need Chris Lane—and you're not walking out of here at four o'clock."

"Watch me."

"Okay—then I'll dock you."

"Then I won't walk out. But when I arrive at Ike Ryan's big opening tonight, with my hair not done, Chris is going to ask some questions. And I'll tell him about the classy job he got me."

"Go get your hair done, you bitch."

She smiled and walked out of the room. He watched her broad hips wiggle, and like everyone else he wondered what Chris Lane saw in her.

Ethel knew a lot of people were wondering what Chris Lane saw in her. She sat in the Copa bar, trying to smile as Eddie and Kenny cracked jokes. She hated Chris more than ever tonight. Every important person was at the opening-night party Ike Ryan had thrown. Okay, so there was bad blood between Chris and Amanda, then at least they could have gone to Sardi's where the other first-nighters would be. But Chris didn't feel comfortable in Sardi's. He got a back table. He was a selfish tight bastard! She glanced at her dress. It was two years old. When she had hinted for a new dress for the opening, his eyes had narrowed: "What kind of crap is that? I buy all your meals, your rent isn't high. With one fifty a week you should dress like a fashion plate. Besides, Lou Goldberg just made me take another annuity."

Lou Goldberg was the key. He was coming in next week. She had to charm him and convince him that she was good for Chris. She opened her compact and added some lipstick. She simply *had* to get her teeth capped. She had hinted in every way about a mink coat for Christmas, but of course it fell on deaf ears with Chris. Well, she'd just wait till Lou Goldberg came to town—then she'd really send in the first team.

She sat tense as the dentist put the Novocain needle into her gum, even though she knew it really wouldn't hurt. She relaxed and soon the stonelike feeling crept into her lip, her mouth and even up to her nose. It was happening! She was going to have the teeth capped. And she had Lou Goldberg to thank for it. She lay back and shut her eyes as the dentist approached with the drill. She heard the buzz against her teeth. She felt nothing. She tried not to think that two healthy teeth were in the process of being ground into stumps. But it had to be done to close that goddam separation.

She thought about Lou Goldberg. Their evening together had been successful beyond her wildest expectations. She had planned it perfectly. She stayed late at the office intentionally and dashed into Dinty Moore's in the oppossum coat and blue wool dress. "I'm so sorry I didn't get home to change," she apologized, "but Mr. Shine is a slave driver. And I wanted to look my best for you, Mr. Goldberg. Chris talks about you so much–I almost feel as if I know you."

He was a nice-looking man. Tall, gray-haired, older than Chris. But he was slim and walked like a younger man. It hadn't been easy. In the beginning Lou Goldberg was suspicious and guarded. She played it guileless and warm. Her entire conversation centered on Chris–his career, his talent, how she admired the way he took his success, how lucky he was to have the advice of Lou Goldberg, how he didn't splurge to put up a false front like some performers. "Everyone loves Chris now," she said. "They'd love him even if he wasn't big, because he's *nice*. And I guess he could always get work. But it's later that a man needs security. If he's ill, no one cares then but his family. And he's lucky to have *you* for family, Mr. Goldberg."

She had watched Lou Goldberg melt before her eyes. His guard dissolved and he looked at her with warm interest. Soon he was asking questions–personal questions. That meant he was interested. She played it direct and simple. Her parents were Polish, good God-fearing people who went to church every Sunday. Yes, they were still alive. They lived in Hamtramck. She almost choked as she explained she sent them fifty dollars every week. And Lou had swallowed it. God, if she sent them fifty a month, her father would retire!

Lou Goldberg beamed approvingly. "I like that, most girls don't think of their families. They just use their money to put things on their backs."

"That's because they want to impress people," she said. "I was afraid to come here in this dress, but then I realized you wouldn't care. Not from the things Chris has told me about you. You size people up as soon as you meet them. He said you could always spot a phony a mile away."

"I usually can," he said happily. "And you're a real girl."

"Thank you," she said modestly. "My whole life has changed, just knowing Chris. I wasn't always this way. I did some rather stupid things. But I was young, and wanted to feel beautiful." She laughed. "I know I can never be, but it doesn't matter now. If Chris loves me, that's all I want."

Lou reached out and patted her hand. "You're quite nice-looking, my dear."

Ethel pointed to her front teeth. "Not with this . . ."

"But that could be fixed," Lou said. "Dentists do marvelous jobs today."

She nodded. "But it costs at least three hundred dollars."

Lou looked at Chris meaningfully. Chris evaded the glance. Ethel pretended the subject was over and returned to her hamburger.

"Chris, I want you to have Ethel's teeth done," Lou said.

"Oh, she looks fine to me this way."

"It's for *her* sake. If she doesn't feel she looks well–"

And so it had been arranged. Lou had written the check himself.

"I'll take this out of your money, Chris," he said, as he handed Ethel the check. Then he laughed. "You know, I taught this boy to be thrifty, but sometimes he overdoes it. Chris, you really should get some new suits."

"I got three new ones–I use them on TV. And I'm working on a deal. A tailor downtown told me he'll furnish me all the suits free if I give him a credit. Dan Miller said no plugs, but when I renegotiate my contract next year I'm gonna insist."

"You can take it off income tax," Lou insisted.

"Sure, but if I can get them free, why not?"

Chris wanted everything free. Ethel lay back, her face numb, the dentist's drill humming away. She had swung it! When she had won Lou Goldberg's confidence, Chris's whole attitude had changed. He actually believed she *was* reborn. As he had put it, "I feel like God. I recreated you from a bum into a lady!" And she smiled and held his hand. . . . God, she had wanted to slap his smug idiotic face—but she was getting the teeth, and they'd be ready in time for the dinner at the Waldorf. Of course she was a long way from getting *him*. Some of the columns hinted they were engaged, but marriage was still the last thing on his mind. She had toyed with the idea of getting pregnant, but he was one step ahead of her. He wouldn't let her use a diaphragm. The few times he actually made the effort to do anything, he used a condom. Mostly he just lay back and let her make love to him! He actually believed she came from just touching him. . . . Well, at least she had the teeth and Lou Goldberg's approval. That was a good start. And she would buy a new dress for the dinner.

The dinner at the Waldorf was exactly like all the other dinners at the Waldorf. Dan Miller arrived, escorting an exact replica of his other conservative "date." Only this one had frosted hair. There were two empty seats at their table . . . Robin Stone never appeared. Ethel was sorry she had sprung for the dress. The only eventful moment had been her introduction to Mrs. Gregory Austin. This had occurred as they waited for their coats at the checkroom. Ethel had been properly humble, Mrs. Austin properly gracious as she complimented Chris on his show.

Chris reveled in it as he undressed that night. "Didja hear Gregory Austin himself come over and tell me I'm the greatest? And he didn't have to. He went out of his way to tell me. You know he coulda just nodded. He's known for that, you know—staying apart from his stars. Jesus, I'll never forget his New Year's Day party. I think he nodded to me once and wondered who the hell I was." Chris flopped on the bed stark-naked. "Come on, baby, make my lob come to life. After all, it's an honor for you to be able to please the King."

She ignored him and undressed slowly. Chris gazed into space complacently. "Know something? That name isn't good enough. The King. There are a lot of kings—there's a King of England, of Greece, of Sweden, of—well, there's plenty of Kings. But there's only one Chris Lane. I got to get a tag."

"You could always try God for size."

"Nah, that's sacrilegious." He thought about it. "Hey, how about 'fantastic'! Yeah–that's it: Mr. Fantastic. Start getting that tag put after my name in the columns, baby. I *am* fantastic. Didja notice even Mrs. Austin told me how much she enjoyed me? That's because I'm the greatest–"

"She'd think you were the cheapest, if she knew how I worked for Herbie Shine and the hours I put in."

"She'd be more shocked if you were a kept woman," he growled. "There's nothing unrespectable about working."

"Ha! Everyone knows you're banging me. They think you're too cheap to keep anyone."

"No one says I'm cheap."

"I'm the living proof. I've been your girl for almost five months. They laugh at my clothes but they're not laughing at *me*–they're laughing at you!" Then as she saw the color come to his face, she felt perhaps she had gone too far. She softened her voice. "Look, I don't care whether you give me anything or not. It's just that Herbie Shine. He's been needling me, hinting that you're cheap, that if you weren't, you wouldn't have me working in an office like his. And it's such a crummy office, Chris. I don't think he should handle you. Eventually you should have Cully and Hayes."

"At a G a week?"

"You can afford it."

"That's pissing money away. They get you invited to all the fancy parties but not a line in a column. At least Herbie gets me a few column plugs."

"But Herbie can't get you lined up with any magazine stories."

"The IBC publicity office takes care of that. I only want column mentions from Herbie."

"You're paying Herbie three hundred a week for column mentions."

"Actually one fifty. The other one fifty goes for your salary."

"That's what *you* think–I work on ten other accounts for him. And you're paying for that!"

"The son of a bitch," he said softly.

"Chris. Hire me and unload Herbie!"

His smile was nasty. "You mean I should pay you three hundred a week? It doesn't add up. This way I got both you and Herbie working for me."

"Herbie doesn't lift a finger for you. He just makes you go to his crappy restaurants and gets your name in a column that way. And the restaurant is paying him. Look, Chris, pay me two hundred–that's a hundred less than you pay Herbie. And I'd do the same job. I know all the columnists–I can place all the items for you. And I'd be free to be with you whenever you wanted and keep your hours. Like last week I had to leave you at two at the Copa because Herbie had an early assignment for me on one of *his* accounts. This way I could stay up all hours, and Herbie won't be taking your money and laughing behind your back."

His eyes narrowed. "That lousy little punk." He was silent. Suddenly he smiled. "Okay, doll, you got yourself a deal. I paid Herbie until the end of the week. Get your paycheck on Friday, then tell Herbie to go fuck himself. Tell him Chris said so."

She leaped on him and covered his face with kisses. "Oh, Chris, I love you, you are my master, my life!"

"Okay, now dive. Make Mr. Fantastic happy."

After Chris was satisfied he settled with his racing form, and she browsed through the morning papers. She leafed through the *Daily News* and stopped at page three. There was a big picture of Amanda being carried on a stretcher to the hospital. Ike was holding her hand. Even on the stretcher Amanda looked beautiful. She read the story carefully. Amanda had collapsed at a party. The diagnosis was internal hemorrhaging from an ulcer. Her condition was listed as "satisfactory." Ethel carefully hid the paper. Chris hadn't mentioned Amanda in a long time; she was sure he was over her. She wondered how Robin had felt when she married Ike. Then she thought of the two empty chairs at the table tonight. She had to admire his nerve. How did he have the guts not to show–?

SEVENTEEN

ROBIN HAD INTENDED TO SHOW. He had told Tina, the new pride of Century Pictures, to be ready at eight. He had even ordered a car. He was glad he had gone to that movie opening last week. Usually he ducked those things, but he had started back on his book and had worked every night for several weeks. He was in the mood for some relaxation. And God had created Tina St. Claire for just that purpose. She was a beautiful brainless idiot who had come to New York to promote a picture. She only had a small part but the stars had been unavailable, so Tina St. Claire, Georgia hopeful turned starlet, had agreed to go on the junket. And *go* she had—San Francisco, Houston, Dallas, St. Louis, Philadelphia, and finally New York. This film company had staffed her with a press agent, a studio-loaned wardrobe, and a suite at the St. Regis which she barely had time to see. In three days she had done seven television appearances, ten radio shows, four newspaper interviews and had appeared at a department store to autograph the sound-track album. (That had hurt her ego more than her feet: she had stood for two hours and no one had come.) Then the whole thing had culminated in the premiere and an opening-night party at which the press agent handed her a return ticket (tourist) to Los Angeles along with instructions to check out of the hotel the following day.

She had been heartbroken. After two bourbon-and-Cokes at the party, she had met Robin and told him her tale of misery. "Heah I've worked my li'l ole butt off, and I have to go right back. Foah what! To jes sit and wait till another small part comes up! My first trip to New Yoak and I declare I haven't seen a thing!"

"Stay on," Robin offered. "I'll show you around."

"How? I can't afford that hotel. I just have ten dollahs hard cash and my plane ticket back. I only make one twenty-five a week! Would you believe it? My sister is a waitress in Chicago and she makes moah!"

Two bourbon-and-Cokes later she checked out of the St. Regis and into his apartment. For a week Robin lived amidst mascara, eye shadow and pancake litter. He couldn't believe a girl who wound up looking fresh and natural could use so much gook on her face. She had more paintbrushes than an artist. He had been forced to move his manuscript to the office. According to Tina, his desk had the best light for putting on her eyelashes. Actually he found he liked working in the office. From five until seven he could turn off the phones and accomplish a great deal.

He took the page from the typewriter and looked at his watch. Quarter to seven. Time to pack it in. Tina was leaving in four days and he could go back to working nights in his apartment. She was a hell of a girl, but he was not sorry that her stay was drawing to a close. She was his equal in every way. Insatiable in bed, asked no questions, made no demands.

He put the manuscript away and lit a cigarette. He didn't want to go to the Waldorf. But it was Mrs. Austin's charity and he had to show. Well, he'd grab Tina and duck out after the speeches. He had promised to take her to El Morocco. It wasn't his scene, but he owed it to the little nympho! He used the electric shaver in his office because Tina had also established a beachhead in the bathroom. She kept her night creams and douche bag there. He plugged in his razor and turned on the television for the seven o'clock news.

He had just finished shaving when Andy Parino came on. He was talking heatedly about another saucer sighting. Robin listened without too much interest until the saucer pictures flashed on. They were blurred, but by God, it looked like the real thing. He walked over to the set–he could swear he saw portholes on the damn thing.

"The Pentagon claims it was a weather balloon." Andy's voice was derisive. "If that is the truth, then why have they sent a man from Project Bluebook down here to investigate? Do we dare presume that in the vast universe ours is the *only* planet to breed life? Why, even our sun is not as good as some of the other suns. It's a Cepheid, an inferior star in the galaxy. Why shouldn't a planet in another solar system harbor human life perhaps twenty million years more advanced than ours? It is time we had a real investigation–and threw the findings open to the public."

Robin was fascinated. He had to talk to Andy.

It was getting late, but what the hell, they'd get to the Waldorf at eight thirty. He got Andy on the tie line and complimented him on the saucer picture, then asked for more details.

"It's exactly as I told it on the air," Andy said.

"You told it good, baby. Who wrote it?"

There was a moment of silence. Then Andy said, "Maggie Stewart." When Robin failed to respond, he added, "You know, I've told you about her."

"She sounds like a smart girl."

"I still can't get her to marry me–"

"Well, like I said, she sounds smart. How's the weather down there?"

"Seventy degrees, clear as a bell."

"It's thirty here and looks like rain."

"Know something, Robin? If I was president of News, I'd make it my business to find news in nice warm places in winter and cool places in summer."

"I wish I could."

"Well, I got to run. Maggie's probably sitting at the bar at the Gold Coast. It's right on the bay. You can see all the yachts pull up. Man, it's great. You sit at the window and stare at the moon and water."

"You've got it made." Robin's voice was filled with envy. "I've got to climb into black tie and make it to the Waldorf."

"You're crazy, you only live once. Why not come down here for a few days and unwind?"

"I wish I could."

"Well, I've got to run. This guy who sighted the saucer is joining us for dinner. He's no crackpot. Teaches high-school math, so he was even able to approximate its speed. I figure it might make a good show–maybe on a Sunday afternoon."

"Wait a minute!" Robin said. "It might make a hell of an *In*

Depth. Let's say we got your math teacher and a few other creditable sighters from different parts of the country, with pictures. And we got some of those guys from the Pentagon on, and really shot the questions to them–"

"Want me to send you all the stuff?" Andy asked.

"No, I'll come down. I want to talk to this teacher."

"When will you be down?"

"Tonight."

There was a pause. Then Andy said, "Tonight?"

Robin laughed. "I'm taking your advice. I need a few days of sun."

"Okay, I'll get you a suite at the Diplomat. It's near my apartment, and it has a great golf course. I'll have a limo meet you."

"See you at twelve thirty then."

"No, Robin–you'll see a big black empty limousine. I told you, I have a date with Maggie."

Robin laughed. "You son of a bitch! You shacking up together?"

"When you see Maggie, you'll know better than to ask anything like that. We don't even live in the same building."

"Okay, Andy. See you tomorrow morning."

It was eight fifteen when Robin let himself into his apartment. Tina was standing in an evening dress, her long red hair done up in Grecian style. "Honey"–she danced around him–"yoah'll nevah guess what. The studio tole me I have an extra week before I have to report–isn't that divine? But, lovah, it's late, I have youah tux all laid out. The car is waitin'–"

He went into the bedroom and pulled out a suitcase. Tina followed him.

"I've got to go to Miami," he said.

"When?"

"Tonight. Want to come?"

Her face wrinkled into a pout. "Honey, ah live in Los Angeles. Los Angeles is just Miami with smog."

She stared in amazement as he went to the phone and made his plane reservations.

"Robin, you just cain't flip off lak this. What about this big dinnah for your boss?"

"I'll send a wire tomorrow with a proper apology." He picked up his bag, grabbed his overcoat and started for the door. He tossed some bills on the table. "There's about a hundred there!"

"When will you be back?"

"In about four or five days."

She smiled. "Oh–then I'll still be heah."

He looked at her. "Don't be."

She stared at him in bewilderment. "I thought you *liked* me."

"Baby, let's put it this way: we met on a pleasure cruise on the Caribbean. This is the first port of call, and you're getting off."

"What would you do if I decided to stay on the boat?"

"Toss you overboard."

"You wouldn't!"

He grinned. "Sure I would. It's *my* boat." He kissed her forehead. "Four days–then out!" She was still staring when he left the apartment.

The limousine was waiting at the airport in Florida. The suite at the hotel was in order; there was even ice and a bottle of vodka. The note said: "Call you in the morning. Have a good night's sleep. Andy."

He sent down for the Miami papers. He undressed, poured himself a light drink and settled comfortably in bed. The picture of the smiling girl on page two looked familiar–Amanda! It was one of her fashion shots, her head thrown back, a wind machine tossing the hair. The caption said HOMETOWN BEAUTY ILL. He read the story quickly and placed a call to Ike Ryan in Los Angeles.

"Is it serious?" Robin asked, when Ike came on the line.

"With her every fucking second is serious. She's been living on borrowed time since last May."

"But I mean–" Robin stopped.

"No, it's not curtains. Look, I've learned to live with death, I've been dying a little every day. You know what it's like, Robin, to see a girl looking gorgeous–the goddam illness makes her even more beautiful. Makes her skin like china. I watch her, I can see when she's tired and pretends not to be. I can also see something like the beginning of fear in her eyes. She knows it's not natural to be this tired. I kid her and pretend I'm tired too. I blame it on California, the change of air, the smog, everything. Oh, what the hell. Thank God she's rallied. They've given her two pints of blood. Tomorrow they're starting a new drug. The doctor thinks it will work, and with luck she'll have another few months of remission."

"Ike, she's made it since April–that's eight months more than they predicted in the beginning."

"I know, and I tell myself she'll have another remission. But the damn leukemia cells build up a resistance to the drug. Comes a day when you've gone through all the drugs–and that's it."

"Ike, she has no idea, has she?"

"Yes, and no. She's suspicious. She'd be an idiot if she wasn't, what with a blood test every week. And a bone-marrow test every month. Christ, I saw her get it once and I almost fainted–they stuck a needle right into her bone. And she never bats an eye. Later I asked her if it hurt and would you believe it, this girl just smiles and nods yes. When she asks me why the test has to be *every* week, I just toss it off and say I want a strong broad and a rush job done on it. But she asks funny little questions. And I catch her reading all the medical columns in the newspapers. Deep down, she knows something's dead wrong, but she doesn't want to believe it. And she's always smiling, always worrying about me. I tell you, Robin, I've learned a lot from this girl. She's got more gallantry than anyone I've ever met. I never really knew what that word meant until Amanda came along. She's scared to death and never shows it. Know what she said tonight? She looked at me and said, 'Oh, my poor Ike, what a drag I am. You wanted to go to Palm Springs.' "

Ike's voice broke. "I love her, Robin. I didn't go into this thing loving her. I did it for lousy stinking selfish reasons. I thought she'd have six months and then quietly lie down and die. I planned to give her a ball while she lasted–then a big send-off, and I'd take bows. I looked at it like I was booking a show, for a limited run. Does that make you want to puke? Boy, all those little broads that I've pushed around can sure have the last laugh now. For the first time in my stinking life, I'm really in love.

Robin, I'd give every cent I got if they could cure her." Ike was sobbing openly.

"Is there anything I can do?" Robin felt helpless, hearing a man cry, a man like Ike. Yet there was nothing he could say.

"Christ," Ike said. "I haven't cried since my old lady died. I'm sorry I let it out on you. It's just that this is the first time I've been able to talk about it. No one knows but just you and me, Jerry and the doctor. And I have to keep playing it light for Amanda. It's been all locked up inside me. I'm sorry."

"Ike, I'm at the Diplomat Hotel in Miami Beach. Call me every night if you like. We'll talk."

"Nope. Tonight helped–but that's it. I can take everything except when she asks me to give her a baby. She wants a kid so much. You should see her with that cat. She talks to it, babies it."

"That cat has a lot of class," Robin said.

There was a pause. Ike's voice was low. "Robin, tell me something. You and me–we've met broads–loads of them, real bitches. Wanna bet they'll live to a hundred? But this kid who never had a break, never did a wrong thing to anyone? . . . why? What's the answer?"

"It's like rolling dice, I guess," Robin said slowly. "The hungry guy with his life's savings on the line comes up with snake eyes. If Paul Getty ever picked up the dice, he'd probably make ten straight passes."

"No, there's got to be more to it than that. I'm not a religious guy, but I tell you these last eight months have made me stop and think. I don't mean I'm gonna rush into a church or a synagogue, but there has to be a reason for things. She's only twenty-five, Robin, just twenty-five. I got twenty years on her. What in hell have I ever done to get double her span? I can't believe that maybe a year from now she'll be gone, leaving nothing but some eight-by-ten glossies to prove that she was around. Why should she go when there's so much beauty in her, so much life to be lived, so much love that she has to give?"

"Maybe just what she's done for you in these past months is reason enough for her existence. A lot of people pass through this world and leave no mark."

"I know one thing," Ike said. "I'm going to make this the

greatest Christmas she's ever had. Robin—I want you to come. You've got to! I want to make it a slam-bang Christmas."

Robin was silent. He hated illness—and seeing Amanda and knowing . . .

Ike felt his hesitation. "Maybe I'm being selfish," he said. "You probably have your own family to be with. It's just that I want to give her every possible kick, make every second count."

"I'll be there," Robin said.

II

MAGGIE

EIGHTEEN

At two a.m. Maggie Stewart was still awake. She had smoked an entire pack of cigarettes. For three hours she had paced back and forth–from the living room to the small terrace overlooking the bay. She liked facing the bay–the ocean was enormous and empty, but the bay sparkled with life. It was dotted with large yachts–their flickering lights sent shimmering reflections in the dark water. She envied the contentment of the people sleeping on them: it must be like a large cradle with waves lapping against the side–the easy lilt of the boat. She clenched the railing of the terrace until her knuckles went white.

Robin Stone was here! In the same city. They would come face to face tomorrow. What would she say? What would he say? Oddly enough her mind raced back to Hudson. For the first time in almost a year and a half she allowed herself to think about him. Long ago, or rather, right after her marriage to Hudson, she had learned it was best to ignore unhappiness. Thinking about it nourished it and kept it alive. Tonight, for the first time, she allowed the image of Hudson Stewart to come into focus. She saw his face, his smile that had gradually turned bitter–and then that ugly final frightening smile. That was the last she had seen of him–that terrible smile before she blacked out. It seemed so long ago, when she had lived in that big house as Mrs. Hudson Stewart III. Why was it that men were forgiven for anything–but a woman had to go by the rules?

She had married Hudson when she was twenty-one. Officially it had lasted three years. It was hard to recall just what she had felt in the beginning. She had wanted to be an actress. It was a dream that began when she was a child, the first time she had seen Rita Hayworth on the screen. It had crystallized when she saw her first legitimate show at the Forrest Theater. The living actors on the stage made everything in pictures pallid and unreal. This was what she would become. She made this decision when she was twelve and announced it at dinner. Her parents smiled and dismissed it as another adolescent phase. But she joined an amateur theater group while she attended high school and instead of going to dances, she spent her weekends studying Chekhov. The real explosion came when she announced she had no intention of going to college–she intended to go to New York and try for the theater. Her mother went into convulsive sobs. "Oh, Maggie," she sobbed, "you've been accepted at Vassar. You know how I've stinted and saved to send you to college!"

"I don't want to go to college. I want to act!"

"It costs money to live in New York–it could take a year or more before you got a job. What would you live on?"

"The money you've put away for Vassar. Just give me half of it."

"Oh, no! I won't give you money to go to New York and sleep around with actors and dirty old men who produce shows. Maggie–no nice girl goes to New York."

"Grace Kelly went to New York–she was a nice girl."

Her mother was adamant: "She was one in a million. And she was rich. Oh, Maggie, I never had a chance to go to college. Your father had to work his way through. It was our dream to send our daughter to the best school. Please–go to Vassar, then when you graduate, if you still want to go to New York–well, you'll still only be twenty-one."

And so she had gone to Vassar. She met Hudson when she was in her senior year. She thought him fairly attractive but her mother had gone wild with excitement. "Oh, Maggie, this is everything I've ever dreamed of! One of the best families in Philadelphia, and so much money. If only the Stewarts will accept us. After all, we're respected, and your father is a doctor."

"I've only had two dates with him, Mother, and I *still* want to go to New York."

"New York!" Her mother's voice became shrill. "Listen, young lady, get those ideas out of your head. I saved to send you to Vassar. I knew as soon as you told me you were rooming with Lucy Fenton that things were going to work out–you *had* to meet the right boys through Lucy!"

"I'm going to New York."

"On what?"

"Well–I'll get a job to support myself, and then try for the theater."

"And just what kind of a job do you think you could get, my fine lady? You can't type. You aren't trained for a thing. I should never have let you join that acting group in high school, but I thought you would get it out of your system. And don't think I didn't notice the moonstruck way you looked at that foreign-looking boy."

"Adam was born right here in Philadelphia!"

"Then he needed a bath and a haircut!"

She was amazed that her mother remembered Adam. She had never mentioned him. He had been a member of the Theater Arts group she had belonged to in high school. He had gone to New York and just this season he had come to Philadelphia with a real Broadway show. Of course it was a road company and he was only assistant stage manager. But he had made it. He was a real professional. The play had remained for a three-month run and she had seen him every weekend. Even Lucy thought he was divine. And then, the night before the play closed, Adam had asked her to come back to the hotel with him. She had hesitated–then tucked her arm into his: "I'll spend the night with you because I realize I want to spend my life with you. But we can't get married until I finish college. My mother will have a fit as it is. She never believed I'd go to New York and really try for a career. At least I've got to please her by graduating."

He had taken her face in his hands. "Maggie, I'm really dead stuck on you. But–look, honey, in New York I live in the Village with two other guys. Half the time I'm living on unemployment insurance. I can't even afford my own apartment, let alone a wife."

"You mean you intended to sleep with me and run?"

He laughed. "I run to Detroit, then Cleveland, then St. Louis, then back to New York, and hope my agent has lined up a job in summer stock. I want to get a crack at directing. It'll mean one of the lesser companies–and no money. Yes, Maggie, I'm running. An actor has to keep running all the time. But I'm not running out on you. That's the difference. You can always trace me through Equity."

"But what about *us?* What would we have together?"

"As much as any two people struggling in the theater can have. I'm hung on you, maybe I even love you. But you can't plan in this business. It's not a nine-to-five job, no steady salary coming in. No time for babies, a nice apartment. But if you want to come to New York after college–fine. I'll show you the ropes–get you to my agent. Maybe we can even shack up together."

"What about marriage?"

He had brushed her hair lightly with his hand. "Don't leave Philadelphia, Maggie. Not if you think that way. Either you're an actress or you're a wife."

"Can't I be both?"

"Not with a struggling director. It couldn't work. Actors and actresses are *dedicated*. They go hungry–they work–they dream–"

"Don't they fall in love?" she asked.

"All the time. And if they love, they go to bed together, but if a job comes along that separates them, well, that's the way it is. But an actress never feels alone because that burning thing inside called talent keeps her going."

"I want to go to bed with you, Adam," she said.

He paused. "Maggie . . . you have gone to bed with a guy before?"

Her eyes challenged him. "I'm not one of those burning actresses yet. I still have a nice clean bedroom all to myself."

"Then let's keep it that way. If and when you get to New York, look me up."

Hudson's entrance into her life, coupled with her graduation from Vassar, made their six months together so frenetic that she barely had time to analyze her emotions. She tried not to be influenced by her mother's pathetic eagerness but she was caught up and carried along by the excitement Hudson brought into her life. The country club; her first visit to the racetrack; the two-week vacation in Ocean City as house guest of Mr. and Mrs. Hudson Stewart II.

In September their engagement was announced and Hudson gave her a seven-carat emerald-cut diamond. Her picture appeared in the *Inquirer* and the *Bulletin*.

She found herself "going along" as if it was a production at the Theater Arts and Hudson was an actor playing opposite her and at the end of the third act the curtain would fall, she'd hear the applause and it would be over.

But as the date of the wedding grew closer, she suddenly realized that when the curtain came down, she would be Mrs. Hudson Stewart III. Oddly enough her mood became one of tranquil acceptance, until she had lunch with Lucy, a week before the wedding.

They were sitting at the Warwick, discussing the plans for the wedding, when Lucy casually said, "Have you ever heard from that actor–Adam? I saw him on a TV commercial the other day. He had no lines, he was shaving, but I'd never forget those eyes of his. He's rugged-looking. Jewish men are supposed to be exciting."

"Jewish?" It had never occurred to her.

"Adam Bergman," Lucy reminded her. "I remember one night he was talking–you were probably too starry-eyed to hear him–and he said an agent had suggested he change his name, because Bergman was too Jewish. And Adam said, 'I'll stick with it; Ingrid did all right.' " When Maggie didn't answer, Lucy added, "I guess that's life. We all fall in love with the wrong man. And it's all right, just so long as you *marry* the right one and settle down and have babies. Especially you–you'll get a million every time you have one. Hudson's father's already given Hudson's sister two million. That's why she's been pregnant two years in a row. Bud and I have to wait until my father dies."

"But you love Bud, don't you?"

"He's nice enough."

"Nice?" Maggie didn't hide her surprise.

Lucy smiled. "I don't have your looks, Maggie. I just have family name and lots of money."

"Oh, Lucy, you are–" Maggie stopped.

Lucy cut in with a smile. "Don't you dare say 'personable' or that I have brains. I do have brains, and there's nothing I can do about my looks because they're not bad enough. That's why I picked you as a roommate, Maggie. I thought, If I room with the most beautiful girl in school some of it has to rub off on me. And that was when I first began to get some attention. I met Harry that summer. He was a desk clerk at a hotel in Newport. Can you imagine *my* mother letting me marry Harry Reilly who lives in the Bronx and goes to NYU? Not that Harry was asking me to. But in the fall I met Bud, and my mother is happy as a clam. I guess I am too–we'll have a good life. But at least I had two glorious months with Harry."

"You mean you–" Maggie stopped.

"Of course we went all the way. Didn't you with Adam?"

Maggie shook her head.

"Oh Lord. Maggie, you're an idiot. Why not? A girl should go to bed with a man she's ape about at least once in her life."

"But how will you explain it to Bud? I mean not being–"

"That's archaic. You mean about the bleeding and all? I'm getting measured for a diaphragm; I'll just tell Bud the doctor deflowered me."

"But won't he be able to tell?"

"I can fake it. I'll just remember my first night with Harry. I'll lie back and play dumb, whimper a bit, tense myself, and it will work. Want to know something? I never even bled with Harry. But I was hard to get into–I guess that's the virgin bit. Poor Harry broke two rubbers before he made it. And I'll see to it that Bud has a hard time–the first night, anyway."

Maggie hadn't had to fake anything with Hudson. Even the pain was real. Hudson had been rough. He tried to enter her immediately. It had hurt–and she had hated the whole thing. And it was the same the second night, and the third. They were on the *Liberté* en route to Paris for their honeymoon. The cabin was luxurious, but she was taking Bonamine and felt drowsy. Perhaps things would be better once they left the boat. At the George V in Paris, it was even worse. Hudson drank a lot and fell on her each night, without even an attempt at tenderness or affection. He satisfied himself and immediately fell into a dead sleep.

When they returned to Philadelphia and settled in the beautiful home near Paoli, she had thought things would be different. Hudson returned to work, she hired a staff, gave dinner parties, went to the club for golf lessons, and joined committees of various charities. Her pictures made the society sections of all the newspapers. She was the new young leader of Philadelphia society. Hudson was like a stallion, methodically taking her in bed each night. He never bothered to kiss her or touch her breasts anymore. In the beginning, she had felt she was at fault for not reaching her climax, but as the months passed she lost hope. She only longed for some display of affection in their nightly ritual. When she tried to feel Lucy out, she was answered with a shrug. "Sometimes it works with me, sometimes it doesn't. But I moan and pretend it's wonderful anyway. How is it with you and Hudson?"

"Oh great," Maggie had said quickly. "But as you say, it doesn't happen with me all the time either."

"Look–it hasn't happened with us for three months. *My* climax, I mean. Yet I'm two months pregnant. So obviously it doesn't have anything to do with making babies. But you'd better make Hudson go easy on his drinking. That can make a man temporarily impotent."

Maggie felt that a baby would change things between them. On the surface everything was fine. He was polite in public, he held her close when they danced, but they had nothing between them when they were alone.

She learned about Sherry at the end of their first year of marriage. Hudson had been going to New York alone on business frequently the last two months. On this night she was in the bedroom, dressing for dinner. Hudson was waiting downstairs. The phone rang. She was late, and continued to fuss with her hair knowing that the maid would pick it up. It continued to ring. Then through one of the odd timings of fate, she picked it up just as Hudson picked up the extension downstairs. She was about to hang up when she heard a female voice whisper; "Huddie? I had to call you."

She felt oddly calm as she listened. Hudson's voice was also conspirational. "Dammit Sherry, I told you never to call me at home."

"Huddie–this is urgent."

"Can't it wait until tomorrow? Call me at the office."

"I can't, because I'll be at work then, and I can't call long distance–even if I reverse charges some of the girls would hear. Can anyone hear me? Is your wife around?"

"She will be soon. What do you want?"

"Huddie, the test came back, I'm definitely preg."

"Christ, again!"

"Well, I can't help it if the diaphragm slips. And you won't wear anything."

"Same doctor still in Jersey?"

"Yes, but he's upped his price to a thousand."

"Well–do it."

"Huddie, he wants cash. I made an appointment for next Monday."

"Okay. I'll get to New York on Sunday and give you the cash –no, I better make it during the week. Maggie might get suspicious if I go on Sunday. Make it Thursday. I'll be at your place at eight. God, I wish my wife was as fertile as you. Your baby is costing me a thousand to unload–hers would get me a million."

He clicked the receiver. Maggie stood and waited until the girl's phone clicked. Then she hung up slowly. She felt numb. Something like this had never occurred to her. She read about it happening to other people–but it couldn't happen to her. Yet if she confronted him, what good would it do? She was twenty-two, equipped to do nothing. A divorcée in Philadelphia, even with alimony, was a lonely woman. She was stuck. There was no place to go.

She remained silent about Sherry but she joined a little-theater group. Hudson didn't object. He was delighted with the avalanche of free evenings. The program director from the local IBC station came backstage after the second production and offered her a television job as a Weather Girl. Her first impulse was to turn it down, until he realized it would give her something to do every day.

She took her job seriously. She watched television, especially the network shows. She went to a diction teacher every day and her improvement was swift. After six months she was promoted to the news department and a daily half-hour show of her own. It was called *Maggie About Town*. She did interviews with celebrities–local and national–covering everything from fashion to politics. Within a short time she became a personality in her own right. Heads turned as she entered a restaurant or theater with Hudson. His attitude toward her success was one of scornful amusement.

He had replaced Sherry with a girl named Irma who worked in his office. He no longer bothered with elaborate excuses on his evenings out. Yet he methodically made love to her three times a week. She submitted with impassive silence. More than ever, she wanted a child.

So the marriage had stretched out–for almost three lifeless years. But she did not get pregnant even though all the tests proved she was thoroughly capable. She sometimes wondered if they could just go on drifting like this. Something had to end this aimless relationship.

It came about by accident. For months the Man of the Year dinner had been extensively planned. It was scheduled for the first Sunday in March. As a local celebrity, Maggie was on the committee and required to sit on the dais. The mayor would also be there, and Judge Oakes who was about to retire was to be honored. Robin Stone had been booked as guest speaker.

Maggie had read Robin Stone's columns. In her small experience in Philadelphia with interviews, she had learned that people rarely resembled the image projected in their work. But Robin Stone's picture fit the image of his column: strong, clipped, virile, hard-hitting. She wondered what the man himself would be like.

At six o'clock she was dressed and waiting. Hudson had not come home. He always spent Sunday at the country club. She called and found that he had not been there all day. She should have known–that was just another excuse to be with his girl of the moment.

Well, she was *not* going to miss the cocktail party. It might be her only chance to actually meet Robin Stone. After the dinner, the guests of honor usually dashed for a train. She looked at her watch. If she left immediately, she could make it. That meant Hudson would have to come in on his own.

When she got to the hotel, she went directly to the Gold Room. Robin Stone was surrounded. He was holding a martini and smiling politely.

Maggie accepted a lukewarm Scotch with soda from one of the trays. Judge Oakes came to her. "Come with me, I'll introduce you to our guest speaker. We've all lost our wives to him."

When Judge Oakes presented her, Robin smiled. "A newsgirl? Come now–you look too beautiful to be an egghead." Then with no warning, he inched her away from the group and took her arm. "There's no ice in your drink."

"It is pretty dreadful," she answered.

He swallowed the rest of the martini. "So was this." He put his glass in the Judge's hand. "Take care of this for me. Come on, newsgirl, we'll get you some ice." He led her across the room. "Don't look back," he muttered. "Are they following us?"

"I doubt it, just glaring in stunned surprise." She laughed.

He walked behind the bar and said to the surprised bartender, "Mind if I make my own?" Before the man could answer, Robin was pouring a large amount of vodka into the pitcher. He looked at Maggie. "Want me to reinforce your Scotch–or will you try a Stone special?"

"The Stone special." She knew she was being stupid. She hated martinis. She also knew she was staring at him like an idiot. *Enjoy this second, she thought. Tomorrow you'll be sitting with Hudson –back in your own dreary world, and Robin Stone will be in another hotel, in another city, mixing another martini.*

He handed her the glass. "Here's to you, newsgirl." He took her arm and they crossed the room and settled on a small couch.

She knew every woman in the room was staring at her. But once again she felt that odd new reckless freedom. Let them stare! But *she* couldn't just sit and stare at him. She had to say something.

"I read that you'd given up your column and gone on a lecture tour. But I miss the column." She felt it sounded forced and unnatural.

He shrugged. "They were probably chopped to mincemeat when they got here."

"No, sometimes they were quite long. But I suppose you like doing this better." He swallowed his drink and then reached over and took her untouched martini. "No, newsgirl–I don't like this better. I just do it for money."

He offered her a cigarette and lit it. "And what do you do on that little box?"

"News–women's angle mostly."

"And I'll bet they watch you and listen to you."

"Is that so incredible?" she asked.

"No, it's television. Wonderful thing, that little box," he said. "It's created a race of beautiful people."

"But don't you think *seeing* people makes it more personal–creates a better understanding?"

He shrugged. "Oh, it creates a love for certain people. The whole world loves Lucy, Ed Sullivan and Bob Hope. At the moment. But they're fickle–remember how they loved Uncle Miltie? Tell me, newsgirl, whom do *you* love on television?"

"I'd love you–" She stopped, horrified.

He grinned. "You're the first sensible girl I've ever met. You get right to the bottom line."

"I mean I'd love your thinking, your views."

He finished the drink. "Don't qualify it, newsgirl, or you'll ruin everything between us. The world is full of hedging broads. I like your style. Come on, let's get a refill."

She followed him as he carried the empty glasses back to the bar and marveled at the ease with which he had polished off both their drinks. He made two more and handed her one. She took a sip and tried not to make a face. It was almost straight vodka. People joined them and most of the women gradually drifted back; once again he was surrounded. He was polite, answered their questions, but he held her arm and never left her side. Her eyes kept drifting to the door. Suddenly she prayed that Hudson wouldn't appear.

There was a small tinkling chime. The chairman of the committee clapped his hands.

"Where do you sit, newsgirl?" Robin asked.

"I guess at the other end." She heard her name. "That's me." She broke away and got into line.

Robin tapped the chairman who stood beside him. "How would you like to change seats with my newsgirl? Both you and Judge Oakes are very attractive but I didn't travel ninety miles to sit between the two of you when I have a chance to have a lovely lady at my side."

As they entered the ballroom, Robin steered her to the seat next to his on the dais. Maggie felt the entire audience was staring. Robin ordered fresh martinis. His capacity seemed unlimited. Three martinis and Hudson would be clobbered. Robin appeared absolutely sober. But no one could consume so many martinis without feeling something.

She saw Hudson enter and take his seat at the far end of the dais. As he sat down, she knew the man next to him was explaining the unexpected change in the seating arrangements. And she couldn't help but be pleased at the surprise on his face.

She heard the chairman introduce Robin. Just as Robin was about to stand, he leaned over and whispered to her, "Listen, newsgirl, I'm going to pack this in as quickly as I can. I have a suite here if I want it. They've been more than generous, your Philadelphia organization. If you'll cut out and meet me there, I'll stay over. Otherwise, I'm going to run for the eleven-thirty train when all this is over."

He rose and waited for the applause to die down. Then he leaned over and said in her ear, "Come on, newsgirl, give me the bottom line."

"I'll be there."

"Good girl, Suite 17B. Wait a decent interval after I leave—and then come up."

He made his speech, and the award was finally presented to Judge Oakes. Guests from the ballroom congratulated the judge. Newspapermen asked him to pose with Robin and the women surrounded him. He signed a few menus for them, looked at his watch and said he was expecting an overseas call. He shook hands with Judge Oakes, waved at everyone and left.

It was eleven o'clock. Hudson walked down from his spot on the dais and sat in Robin's empty seat. "Was the cocktail party a big thrill?"

"I enjoyed it," she said.

"Let's go."

She was suddenly frantic. How could she have promised Robin Stone? What had gotten into her? She couldn't even blame it on the martini . . . she had just sipped it. She had no intention of going to his room!

"This is the last dinner I'll ever come to," Hudson said. "And you complain about Saturday night at the country club. At least I have a few laughs there. And we mingle with our own kind."

"It's part of my job," she said.

"Job?" he sneered. "Which reminds me—we're going to have to do something about that. Too many people are talking about it. Dad says some of his friends think it looks bad, you sitting across a mike interviewing all those types. That writer you talked with last week looked like a real Commie."

She didn't answer. Hudson talked this way every now and then and it passed. It was better to let him rant on. He drained the glass and deliberately refilled it.

"You really don't care about me, do you, Hudson?"

He poured himself another drink and sighed heavily. "Oh, it's not you. It's us. . . . Our families. . . . Sometimes I feel I've had it. . . . But don't worry, I won't leave you. Where can I go? Neither of us can have any real freedom until you get knocked up a few times. Christ, that's the least you could do."

She stood up. "Hudson, you make me feel sick."

"Come off it. I saw that mother of yours at the wedding, beaming. And your father, all handshakes and cigars. What were they so happy about? Hello, young lovers? Not on your life! It was the Stewart money. But you're not keeping your half of the bargain. You're supposed to have babies." He stared at her. "Maybe we should go home and try tonight."

"Maybe if you didn't drink so much," she said.

"Maybe I have to drink to get excited about you. I'm a man, I can't fake it." She walked out. He followed sullenly. At the checkroom they ran into Bud and Lucy. Lucy was pregnant again.

She was also slightly drunk.

"We're going to the Embassy. Want to come?"

Hudson stared enviously at Lucy's stomach. "Sure, why not!" He grabbed Maggie by the arm and they all crowded into the elevator.

Bud's chauffeur was waiting. "Leave your cars," Lucy suggested. "We'll come back for them."

The Embassy was crowded. They sat in the smoke-filled room, squeezed around a tiny table. Some members from the country club were at the next table. They decided to put the two tables together. There were some jokes among the men, a bottle of Scotch was put on the table and Maggie sat hemmed in thinking of the man in Suite 17B.

She *had* to call him. She would tell him the truth, that she had accepted in a moment of crazy impulse, that she was married. It wasn't fair to make Robin Stone sit and wait. He worked too hard.

She stood up suddenly. "I have to powder my nose." There had to be a phone in the Ladies' Room.

"I'll go with you," Lucy said as she lumbered to her feet. "I'm dying to hear what Robin Stone said. I saw him lean over and speak to you several times. Coming, Edna?" she called to one of the girls.

The group headed for the Powder Room. There was an open phone. An attendant was sitting near it. It was hopeless. She patched up her makeup and was noncommittal about Robin Stone. They had talked about television, she explained. She tried to hang back, but Lucy and Edna waited. When they returned to their table there was no sign of Hudson. Then she saw him across the room–sitting at a table with a group of people, his arm around a girl. She recognized the girl, a new member of the club, a recent bride. Hudson's arm was gently massaging her bare back. Her husband sat across from her and did not see it. Suddenly Maggie stood up.

"Sit down," Lucy hissed. "Maggie, you know it means nothing. Hud always has to prove his charm with every new member."

"I'm going . . ."

Bud grabbed her arm. "Maggie, you've got nothing to be concerned about. That's June Tolland. She's mad for her husband."

She broke away and ran. She didn't stop running until she reached the street. Then she walked to the corner, hailed a cab and told the driver to go to the Bellevue Stratford Hotel.

She rang the bell of Suite 17B. It was a loud ring, an empty ring. She glanced at her watch. Twelve fifteen. Maybe he had left, or gone to sleep. She rang again, then she turned and started down the hall. Suddenly the door swung open. He was holding a glass. "Come on in, newsgirl, I'm on the phone."

She entered the living room of the suite. He motioned to the bottle of vodka and went to the phone. It was obvious he was talking business, something to do with clauses in a contract. She went through the motions of mixing herself a drink. He had taken off his jacket. His shirt clung to him and she saw the small initials, *R.S.*, near his chest. His tie was loose and he talked earnestly and to the point. She noticed the bottle of vodka was half empty and once again she wondered at his capacity. He finally hung up. "Sorry to keep you waiting, but then, you didn't exactly break any track records getting here."

"Where do you go tomorrow?" She suddenly felt shy and nervous.

"New York. No more lectures ever again."

"Why do they call them lectures?" she asked. "I mean, tonight —you were wonderful, you talked about everything. Your adventures overseas, people—"

"I suppose it dates back to when some fink actually went out with slide pictures and—oh, who the hell cares." He put down his drink and held out his arms. "Come on, newsgirl, aren't you going to kiss me?"

She felt like a schoolgirl. "My name is Maggie Stewart," she said. Then she was in his arms.

He made love to her three times that night. He held her close and whispered endearments. He caressed her. He treated her like a virgin. And for the first time she realized what it was like when a man made love for the sole purpose of trying to make a woman happy. She reached a climax the very first time. And then it happened again. And the third time she fell back in gratified exhaustion. He held her close and kissed her gently. Then as he began to caress her again she pulled away.

He buried his face in her breasts. "It's been different tonight. I'm very drunk–tomorrow I may not remember any of this. . . . But I want you to know, this is different."

She lay very still. Somehow she knew he was telling the truth. She was afraid to move, afraid to break the spell. The cool crisp Robin Stone suddenly seemed so vulnerable. In the dim light she stared at his face against her breasts–she wanted to remember every second, she would always remember, especially the word he yelled each time at the climax.

He pulled away suddenly, kissed her, reached out and lit two cigarettes and handed one to her. "It's two thirty." He nodded toward the phone. "If you have to be up at any special time, leave a call. I've got nothing to do but catch a train to New York. What time do you have to be at work?"

"Eleven."

"How's nine thirty? I'll get up with you and we can have breakfast together."

"No, I–I have to leave now."

"No!" It was a command–but his eyes were almost pleading. "Don't leave me!" he said.

"I have to, Robin." She jumped out of bed and ran to the bathroom. She dressed quickly and when she returned to the bedroom he was lying back against the pillows. He seemed completely composed. He lit a cigarette, then looked at her oddly.

"Who are you running off to? Husband or lover?"

"Husband," she said, trying to meet his eyes. They were so amazingly blue and cold.

He inhaled deeply and blew the smoke to the ceiling. Then he said, "Did you risk anything coming here tonight?"

"Nothing, except my marriage."

"Newsgirl, come here." He held out his hand. She came to him and he looked at her as if trying to see into her brain. "I want you to know something. I didn't know you were married."

"Don't feel guilty," she said gently.

His laugh was odd. "Guilty, hell! I think it's funny. . . . So long, newsgirl."

"My name is Maggie Stewart."

"Baby, there's another name for girls like you." He leaned over and ground out the cigarette.

She stood at his bed for a moment. "Robin, tonight was different for me too, it meant something, it meant an awful lot. I want you to believe that."

Suddenly he threw his arms around her waist and buried his head in her dress. His voice was low and urgent. "Then don't leave me! You keep saying you love me, but you leave me!"

She had never said she loved him! She gently pried herself loose and looked at him in amazement. Their eyes met but he seemed to be looking somewhere far off as if he was in a self-induced trance. She decided the vodka had finally hit him. He couldn't know or mean what he was saying.

"Robin, I've got to leave you–but I'll never forget you."

He blinked and then stared as if seeing her for the first time. "I'm sleepy. Good night, newsgirl." Then he switched off the light, turned on his side and promptly fell asleep. She stood there unable to believe it. He was not faking. He *was* asleep.

She drove home with mixed feelings. The whole thing had been insane. He was two men and they never seemed to fuse except when he made love to her. Well, he had said it himself: tomorrow he would not even remember it, she would be just another girl on one of his whistle stops. But did he act this way with all girls? It didn't matter. The only thing that counted was tonight.

She let herself into the house quietly. It was four o'clock.

She crept into the bedroom. It was dark; in the shadows she saw Hudson's empty bed. Luck was with her. He hadn't gotten home yet. She undressed quickly. She had just turned off the lights when she heard the crunch of gravel in the garage path. She pretended sleep when he crept into the room. His cautiousness amused her. The way he lurched around the room, trying not to arouse her. Soon she heard him snoring in deep drunken sleep.

For the next two weeks she plunged into her work and pushed Robin Stone from her thoughts. She had almost succeeded until the day she opened her diary to check an appointment and saw "Curse due." She was four days late! And Hudson hadn't come near her in three weeks. Robin Stone! She had taken no precautions with him. Hudson had brainwashed her into actually thinking she couldn't get pregnant.

She buried her face in her hands. She didn't want to get rid of it! Robin's baby would be a baby conceived in love. . . . And Hudson wanted a baby. Oh, no! It was an outrageous thought! . . . But why not? What could be gained in telling Hudson the truth? It would hurt Hudson–and the baby. She stood up with sudden determination. She was going to have it!

When a week passed and her period did not come, she faced the real task of getting Hudson to make love to her. He had never stayed away this long. The model must be wearing him out, or perhaps he had found a new interest. When Hudson was in the flush of a new romance, he never came near her.

That night she snuggled against him in bed but he pushed her away.

She bit her lip in the darkness. "I want a baby, Hudson." She put her arms around him and tried to kiss him. He turned his head. "Okay, but cut the love crap, honey. We're playing for babies now–so let's fuck."

She went to the doctor when she had missed her second period. He called her the following day and congratulated her. She was six weeks pregnant. She decided to wait a few weeks before breaking the news to Hudson.

A few nights later they were having one of their rare evenings at home alone. He was quiet throughout dinner. But the surliness that had become part of his personality was not in evidence. He was calm, thoughtful. He was almost gentle when he suggested they go upstairs to the den and have an after-dinner drink. He sat on the couch and watched her as she poured the brandy. He took his glass, sipped it thoughtfully, then said, "Can you get away from your little television chores in about three months?"

"I could get a leave–but why?"

"I've told Dad you're pregnant."

She looked at him in amazement. Then she realized Dr. Blazer had probably told him. She had told the doctor she wanted to keep it a secret because of her work but he probably never thought she wanted to keep it from Hudson. This accounted for his new mood. Her smile was filled with relief. Her instinct had been right. A baby would change things.

"Hudson, there's no need to go away. I could work almost up to the date if the camera just gets head shots of me."

He looked at her curiously. "And how do we explain to Dad and to everyone your nice flat tummy?"

"But I'll–"

"We can't fake it. Everyone has to think it's the real thing. Even Bud and Lucy. One slipup, and Dad will find out. I've got it all worked out. We tell him we want a trip around the world as a pregnancy present. Because after the child is born, we won't feel free to leave it. Then we'll say it was premature and have it born in Paris."

"I don't understand, Hudson. I want my baby born here."

His old sneer returned. "Don't get carried away with the game. I merely *told* him you were pregnant. That doesn't make it so."

He got up and poured himself another glass of brandy. "I've made all the arrangements. We can get a baby in Paris. The doctor I talked to has a contact there. They even match the looks of both parents. There are three babies up for adoption that will be born in seven months. We just pay all the mother's hospitalization, first class. The mother turns the baby over immediately–she never even sees it or knows what sex it is, or who gets it. I've asked for a boy. Then we get a new birth certificate and it's made out as our baby. And the lucky little bastard not only nets us a million, but comes up with dual citizenship if he wants it. Then we return to America in triumph."

She laughed with relief. She got up from the couch and walked over to him. "Hudson, now it's my turn for a surprise. All these elaborate plans–you don't need them."

"What do you mean?"

"I really am pregnant."

"Say that again," he snapped.

"I'm *pregnant.*" She didn't like the way he was staring at her.

His hand lashed across her face. "Bitch! Whose is it?"

"It's mine, ours–" She felt her lip begin to swell, and the taste of blood in her mouth. He came closer and grabbed her shoulders and shook her. "Tell me, you whore–whose bastard are you trying to pass off on me?" His hand whipped across her face again. "Tell me, or I'll beat it out of you!"

She broke from him and ran out of the room. He dashed after her and caught her in the hall. "Tell me! Whose bastard are you carrying?"

"What difference does it make to you?" she sobbed. "You were willing to take someone else's in Paris; at least this is mine."

The anger suddenly drained from his face. A slow smile came to his lips. He pushed her back into the den. "You're right. You're absolutely right. You bet I'll let you have it. In fact you're going to have one every year, for the next ten years. Then if you're a good girl, I'll give you a divorce with a nice fat alimony."

"No." She sat on the couch and looked at him with a calm she didn't feel. "It's not going to work. I won't raise my baby in an atmosphere of hate between us. I want a divorce now."

"I won't give you a dime."

"You don't have to," she said wearily. "I'll live with my family. I'll make enough on television to provide for the baby."

"Not when I get through with you."

"What do you mean?"

"That baby means a million bucks to me. Either you have it, and give it to me, or you'll never work again. I'll smear you through every newspaper. You'll be through on TV and your family won't be able to face anyone in this town."

She put her head in her hands. "Oh, Hudson, why? Why did it have to be like this? I made a mistake–one night, one man. It never happened before. It will never happen again. I wanted it to work with us. But you've made me so miserable, I didn't even feel like a woman with you. Perhaps what I did was wrong. I'm not going to bring up the things I know about you." Her voice broke. "I thought we still had a chance. I guess I was crazy, but I thought it would make you happy having a baby. I thought it might bring us together. And that once the strain was off you, we'd have more babies–babies of our own–"

"You idiot! Can't I get it through to you? I'm sterile!" he yelled. "I took tests last week–I'm sterile, I can never make babies!"

"But what about those abortions you paid for?"

"How do you know?"

"I know."

He pulled her off the couch. "So you had detectives on me!" He slapped her face. "Well, I was taken! All those broads I paid off who said I knocked them up–they took me! Like you just tried to do. But now I know: I'm sterile."

She pulled away from him. Her tears streaked her face and she knew her lip was cut. But she felt sorry for him. She started to leave the room. He grabbed her roughly. "Where are you going?"

"To pack," she said quietly. "I can't stay in this house with you."

"Why?" he said nastily. "You stayed all along when you knew what I was up to–we're even now. Two of a kind. It might even work better this way. We'll each go our own way–as long as my father never hears about it."

"I don't want to live like that."

"Then how do you account for the little bastard in your belly?"

"I knew about you . . . and all your girls. Then I met someone. I don't know how it happened. I guess I needed someone who cared–even if it was just one night. To know he cared for me . . . was aware that I existed . . . even if it was just for a few hours."

He slapped her again. "This is what you need?" His hand shot across her face again. Her head rocked back in pain. Then with one quick dart she broke from him and ran out of the room. He ran after her. "I'll beat the hell out of you–is that what you were looking for? I used to beat Sherry with a strap, she liked it." He began to unstrap his belt.

She screamed and hoped the servants would hear. She ran down the hall. His belt was in his hand–the alligator belt she had given him for Christmas. He lashed out at her. It caught her in the neck. She saw the hate and perversion on his face and knew real terror. She backed away from him and screamed. Where were the servants? He was insane! The belt hit her face, just missing her eye. He could blind her! She backed away in panic and felt herself falling backwards down the stairs. She hoped in that split second she might break her neck and die instantly and never have to see his face again. And then she was lying there at the bottom of the stairs. Hudson was staring at her legs. She felt the first clutch of pain. She clung to her stomach. She felt the blood running down her legs. Then she felt the slap of his hand across her face. "You dirty bitch–you've just leaked away a million dollars."

It was suddenly cold on the terrace. She walked into the living room and poured herself a Scotch. It all seemed to have happened in another world, yet it was barely two years ago. She dimly recalled the jangling of the ambulance, the week in the hospital, the way no one had questioned the lacerations on her face and neck, the polite way the doctor pretended to believe it was a result of the accidental fall—and the fight everyone put up about her decision for an immediate divorce. Everyone but Hudson. Her mother thought she was having a nervous breakdown. Losing a baby often did that. Even Lucy had pleaded with her to reconsider.

She had decided on Florida for the divorce. It would take three months, and she wanted the sun and time to rest, time to heal the hurt she felt—help her plan a new start. She took a leave of absence from the station.

Although Hudson's attorneys had agreed to pay all the divorce costs, including her stay in Florida, she took a small apartment, and lived frugally. After two months, she felt no hurt—just emptiness: Hudson no longer existed; but she was young and her strength returned, and soon the idleness began to pall.

She applied at the local TV station. Andy Parino had put her on immediately. She liked Andy. She wanted to care. To care meant you were alive. They drifted into an easy comfortable love affair. Andy made her feel good—made her enjoy being a woman. But Hudson had killed or destroyed some part of her. The part that made her really care.

After a few months, she felt secure. Andy cared for her and she liked her job. It was time to throw off this self-induced lethargy. Time to *feel*—to dream and hope—and she had tried, but nothing happened. It was as if Hudson had paralyzed all her emotions. When Andy asked her to marry him, she refused.

And now tonight, for the first time, she had felt the stirring of life. She was going to see Robin Stone again. She couldn't wait to see the expression in his eyes when they met. . . .

NINETEEN

MAGGIE SAT at the Gold Coast bar and wondered if she looked as nervous as she felt. Andy had spent the day on the golf course with Robin. Robin had told him to assign his seven o'clock news to a staff announcer for the next few days. She looked at her watch–they should be here any second. She lit a cigarette and suddenly realized she had a fresh one going in the ashtray. She hastily stubbed it out. She felt like a schoolgirl–a schoolgirl waiting to come face to face with her first love. But she was nervous. Any second Andy would walk in with Robin Stone, and they would meet. She stubbed out the second cigarette.

She caught sight of herself in the mirror across the bar. The even tan of her skin blended into the beige silk dress. Her skin had been so white in Philadelphia. When Robin had let his hands run over her breasts, he had said, "White, white, mother-white skin." But the tan was more flattering. She knew she was beautiful. She had always known it. But she regarded it as merely a statistic: one was either tall or short, homely or beautiful. Until now, her beauty had not given her any pleasure. If anything, it had caused disaster. But tonight she was suddenly glad she was beautiful. She had dressed carefully–the dress matching the tone of her skin seemed to emphasize the green of her eyes. Cat's eyes. Andy called her his black panther. Tonight she felt like a panther–taut, crouched, ready to spring!

It had been her idea to meet here. She didn't want a jumbled meeting in the dark of a car. She wanted them both to walk in. She wanted to see Robin's look of surprise. . . . This time she would have command of the situation.

She was just finishing her drink when she saw Andy come through the door—alone. She kept her face impassive as he joined her at the bar and ordered a Scotch. She was damned if she'd ask. But where *was* he!

"Sorry I'm late, Maggie," Andy said.

"That's all right." Finally she couldn't stand it. "Where's your friend?"

"The big TV star?" Andy took a long swallow of his drink.

"Isn't he coming?" She wanted to kill Andy for making her draw it out of him.

"Maybe. You should see the commotion he caused at the Diplomat—you'd think he was Cary Grant. Seems like everyone watches that show of his, at least everyone we ran into on the golf course."

Maggie lit another cigarette. She had never allowed herself to watch Robin's show. That had been a part of the cure. Like not thinking about Hudson or the past. Of course he was famous now. That had never occurred to her before.

"On every hole he had to stop and sign an autograph," Andy was saying. (She could still recall how he had tried to hide his annoyance at the Bellevue when he was forced to sign those menus.)

"It was a big bore," Andy went on, "until the little blonde caught up with him on the seventeenth hole."

She snapped to attention. "Who?"

Andy shrugged. "A guest at the hotel. She couldn't have been more than nineteen or twenty. She left her own foursome to get Robin's autograph and never rejoined them. She walked the rest of the way with us, right down to the eighteenth hole." Andy laughed. "Betty Lou, yeah, that's her name." He raised his glass. "Here's to Betty Lou—she earned me twenty bucks." He took a long swallow of his drink and went on.

"She came on so strong for Robin that she made him forget the game. When he sees a good-looking broad it's like a radar beam, and dear little Betty Lou laid it right on the line. Robin dug her. He also dug a big divot, landed in a trap and wound up taking a seven on the hole. Until then he had been only four over par. That's how I won my twenty bucks. Let's go inside, I'm starving."

They were about to order when Andy was called to the phone. He returned with a grin. "The great lover is on his way."

It was almost nine o'clock when Maggie saw Robin stride into the restaurant. He looked clean and fresh. Then she saw the little blond girl. Maggie knew instantly that she had been to bed with Robin. Her hair had lost its shape and her makeup looked patched.

Andy stood up. "Hi, Betty Lou." He hugged her like a lifelong buddy. Then he turned. "This is Maggie Stewart. Maggie, Robin Stone."

He looked at her with an easy smile. "Andy tells me you also play golf. You'll have to come with us one afternoon."

"I have a twenty-five handicap," she said. "I'm afraid I'm not in your league."

"Oh, that's the same as me," Betty Lou pealed. "We can have a real foursome."

Robin ordered two vodka martinis. Betty Lou acted as if she not only owned Robin Stone but had known him all her life. Robin was casually attentive. He lit her cigarette, ignored her in conversation, yet intuitively let her know that he was glad she was with him. Maggie saw him reach for the girl's hand and occasionally flash her a grin, but his entire conversation was directed to Andy.

Suddenly Maggie wondered if Betty Lou had been an intentional ruse on Robin's part, to make the "confrontation" easier. Andy must have told him about their relationship.

In an effort to go along with Robin, Betty Lou joined him in a second martini. The first one had left its mark. The second was lethal. By the end of dinner, she was leaning on her elbow, her hair falling into the spaghetti. She looked at everyone with glazed eyes. Robin suddenly noticed her condition. "Too much sun and golf, sometimes that's a bad combination with alcohol."

Maggie liked his defense of the girl he had just met. They all helped her out of the restaurant and piled her into Robin's car. After they dropped Betty Lou off, Robin insisted they go to the Diplomat for a nightcap.

They sat at a small table. Robin toasted Andy. "To you, chum —thanks for the first vacation I've had in years. And to your lovely lady." He looked at Maggie. Their eyes met. Her stare was challenging but his blue eyes returned an innocent gaze. Then he said, "I've been hearing nothing but raves about you. You're every bit as lovely as Andy said. And your report on the UFOs fascinates me. I read it today. Where'd you get the information, and how do you know so much about the subject?"

"I've always been fascinated with it," she answered.

"Let's all meet at your office tomorrow at eleven, Andy. You and Miss–" He stopped and looked at Maggie. He seemed to draw a blank.

"Maggie," Andy said quietly. "Maggie Stewart."

Robin smiled. "I'm awful with names. Well, let's all meet and kick this thing around. See if there's a network show in it."

They finished their drink and said good night in the lobby. Maggie watched Robin stride to the elevator.

She was silent as they drove away. In the darkness of the car Andy said, "Look, don't be hurt because Robin forgot your name. That's the way he is. Unless he's banging a girl, he doesn't know she's alive."

"Take me home, Andy."

He drove silently down the drive. "Headache again?" His voice was cold.

"I'm tired."

He was sullen as he stopped in front of her apartment. She didn't even try to appease him. She jumped out of the car and ran into the building. She didn't wait for the elevator, just ran up the two flights of stairs to her apartment. Once inside, she slammed the door and leaned against it. Tears ran down her face. Then her sobs came in dry choking gasps. Not only didn't he remember her name–he didn't remember that they had ever met before!

Maggie made an effort to study the script. She hadn't looked at it since Robin's arrival. Of course the first performance at the Players' Club was still three weeks off–but she wanted to be good. After all, this was Eugene O'Neill, and Hy Mandel was coming from California to see her. Probably nothing would come of it. The director of an independent film company had seen her on television and asked her if she was interested in a screen test. She said she was interested in becoming an actress–but no screen test. She couldn't take time from her television show to fly to California. Perhaps it had been her lack of interest that had caused him to pursue it. He had called Hy Mandel, a top Hollywood agent, and put in a rave about her. And now he was actually coming to see her perform in a semiprofessional group.

Well, after tonight she'd have plenty of time to concentrate on O'Neill.

This was Robin Stone's final night in town. He hadn't seen Betty Lou again. The second night he had come up with a swimming teacher named Anna. Then there was a divorcée named Beatrice. Then he had chartered a boat for three days and gone off alone to fish. He had returned this afternoon and Andy told her they'd have dinner together. She wondered who'd be his date –Betty Lou? Anna? Or the divorcée?

Andy called just as she was finishing her makeup. He was in high spirits. "I've just had a long talk with Robin. Guess what! He doesn't want to do the saucer thing as an *In Depth*. He wants to make it a special on its own–and he wants us to work on it. That'll mean a trip to New York and all expenses paid!"

"I hope it doesn't happen while I'm doing the O'Neill play."

"Maggie, twenty-six is a little old for a girl to tackle Hollywood. You belong right here–with me."

"Andy, I–" She had to tell him it was all over between them. That there never had really been anything.

But he cut in. "Listen, Maggie, don't say anything to Robin about Amanda."

"Amanda?"

"The girl whose picture I showed you in the newspaper the day before yesterday."

"Oh, the one who died of leukemia?"

"Yes. She was a friend of Robin's. He was on the boat when it happened and probably doesn't know about it. There's nothing he can do: the funeral was today, so why ruin his vacation?"

"But she was married to Ike Ryan," Maggie said.

"Yes, but she and Robin were a big deal for a long time. He went with her for almost two years."

Maggie thought about it as she finished her makeup. Two years—that meant Amanda had been his girl the night they had been together at the Bellevue. Her eyes narrowed as she stared at herself in the mirror. "All right, you fool. You're acting like a twenty-six-year-old virgin! Did you secretly nurture the idea that you had really been something special to Robin Stone?"

She parked her car at the Diplomat. She was aware that several men turned to stare as she walked through the lobby. Had they been staring like this all along? Had she been living in such a vacuum that she had never noticed? Suddenly she felt a current of excitement as she walked into the bar. Robin stood up and smiled. "Andy will be right back. He's being a cruise director. I'm booked out on the noon flight tomorrow but he's trying to switch me to a later plane so we can get in one last round of golf." He signaled the waiter. "What's it going to be? The usual Scotch?"

She nodded. "And who is your date tonight? The usual divorcée?" The strange inner excitement gave her voice just the right tone of flippancy.

He grinned. "You're my date tonight. You and Andy. I just want to drink and relax with two good friends. Maybe even get smashed."

Andy's smile was victorious when he returned to the table. "You're all set. Six o'clock tomorrow. Personally, I think you're crazy going back. Ellie, my connection with National, says it's fifteen degrees in New York. And Santa Claus is coming to town. All that slush and those Santas standing in front of department stores with tinny little bells, and no taxis—" He shook his head and shuddered.

Robin stared at his empty glass and signaled for another drink. "I'd like to stay, but I have a very special date Christmas night in Los Angeles."

Robin had four martinis. Maggie toyed with her second Scotch and once again marveled at his capacity. But he had appeared perfectly sober that night in Philadelphia when he admitted he was very drunk. Drunk enough not even to remember her! They went to the Fontainebleau and caught Sammy Davis. She had a steak. Robin ignored food, and methodically drank vodka. Andy tried to keep up with him.

They wound up at a bar on the Seventy-ninth Street Causeway. The place was heavy with smoke. Robin had a bottle of vodka placed at the table. Maggie stuck to Scotch. It was too noisy to attempt conversation. Robin drank silently and Andy sloshed at his drink.

At one in the morning Andy passed out. Maggie and Robin struggled to help him into the car.

Robin said, "We'll dump him at his place, then I'll drop you."

"But my car's at the Diplomat," she said.

"No sweat, take a cab there tomorrow. Put it on expenses–tell Andy he okayed it before he passed out." She directed him to Andy's building. Robin tried to lift Andy out of the car. "He's a dead weight," he groaned. "Come on, Maggie, I need some help." Between them they half carried, half dragged Andy to his apartment. Robin dropped him on the bed and loosened his tie. Maggie stared at him with concern. She had never seen anyone pass out from drinking. Robin's smile was reassuring. "Not even one of your flying saucers could wake him now. He'll feel horrible in the morning–but he'll live."

They returned to the car. "I'm just a few blocks away, that long low building down there," she said.

"How about going somewhere for a nightcap first?"

She directed him to a small bar nearby. The owner recognized Robin, placed the bottle of vodka on the bar and immediately launched into a discussion on professional football. Maggie sat with a watery Scotch and listened. It was incredible–Robin seemed absolutely sober.

They closed the bar and he drove her to her apartment. For a moment they sat in the darkened car.

"Do you have any vodka up there?" he asked.

"No, just Scotch."

"Too bad. Good night, Maggie, it's been great."

"Good night, Robin." She turned toward the door, then impulsively turned back and kissed him. Then she dashed out of the car and rushed to her apartment.

She felt exhilarated. If a man wanted to kiss a girl, he just upped and did it. This time, she had taken the initiative. She felt as if she had struck out for female emancipation. She had broken one of the ironclad rules. From now on she was going to break a lot of rules. She sang as she undressed. She started to put on her nightgown, then tossed it aside. From now on she would sleep in the nude. She always wanted to, but it hadn't seemed proper. She went to the bureau drawer and took out all the filmy nightgowns and put them in a shopping bag. Tomorrow the maid would have a bonanza. She slid into bed and turned off the lights. The cold sheets felt wonderful–she felt a sense of freedom she had never known. She wasn't sleepy but she shut her eyes. . . .

Someone was banging on her door. She switched on the light and looked at the clock. Only four thirty. She must have just fallen asleep. The banging became more insistent. She threw on her robe and opened the door, leaving the safety chain intact. Robin Stone was standing there, brandishing a bottle of vodka.

"I've brought my own nightcap!" he said.

She let him in.

"It was in my room, gift of the management. But I didn't feel like drinking alone."

"Do you want some ice?"

"No, I'll drink it neat."

She handed him a glass and sat on the couch and watched him drink. Suddenly he turned to her. "I'm smashed."

She smiled slightly. A pulse began to beat in her throat.

"Want me, baby?" he asked.

She got up from the couch and walked across the room. "I want you," she said slowly. "But not tonight."

"It's got to be tonight–I'm leaving tomorrow."

"Put it off a day."

"What will make tomorrow any different than today?"

"I want you to remember me!"

"Be good, baby, then I'll never forget you."

She turned and faced him. "Sorry, but I've already auditioned."

His eyes were mildly curious. Suddenly he was at her side, and with a swift movement opened her robe. She grabbed at it, but he wrenched it off. He stood back, staring at her speculatively. She fought her embarrassment and met his gaze defiantly.

"Big beautiful tits," he said. "I hate big tits." With another quick unexpected move, he lifted her in his arms, carried her into the bedroom and flung her on the bed. "I hate brunettes, too." He took off his coat and loosened his tie. She was frightened suddenly. There was an odd expression in his eyes—as if he was looking at her without seeing her. She jumped up, but he pushed her down. "You're not leaving me. I'm a big boy now." He sounded strange, as if he was talking to himself. His eyes had the stare of a sightless man.

She watched him undress. She could make a dash for it, call for help—but she felt frozen with curiosity. Perhaps this was the way a victim of a murderer felt. Paralyzed—unable to resist. He stripped off his clothes and came to her. He sat on the bed and stared at her with strange expressionless eyes, and when he leaned over and kissed her gently, her fear evaporated and she responded eagerly. He stretched out beside her, their bodies close. She felt him sigh—his body relaxed. His mouth searched for her breasts. She clung to him—every resolve disappeared. She was fused with excitement and emotion, and when he took her, she reached a climax with him. And as he clung to her he shouted the same three words he had shouted in Philadelphia: *"Mutter!* Mother! *Mother!"*

Then he fell off her. In the darkness she saw the same glazed look in his eyes. He caressed her cheek and smiled slightly. "I'm smashed, baby—but this was different, this is not like the others."

"You said that to me once before in Philadelphia."

"Did I?" He showed no reaction.

She snuggled against him. "Robin, has it been different with many girls?"

"No . . . yes . . . I don't know." He sounded drowsy. "Just don't leave me." He held her close. "Promise me that—never leave me."

She clung to him in the darkness. All right, she told herself. This is your chance. Throw him out of bed. Say "Goodbye, newsman." But she couldn't.

"I'll never leave you, Robin, I swear."

He was half asleep. "You're just saying that."

"No, I've never said that to anyone in my life. I promise. I love you."

"No, you'll leave me . . . to go . . ."

"To go where?" She had to know.

But he was asleep.

She saw the sky lighten and she lay there wide-awake. She stared at his handsome head. His cheek was warm against her breast. It didn't seem possible. He was *here*–sleeping in her arms. He belonged to her! She was glad she had told him about Philadephia. He had asked her not to leave him then. And she had–perhaps he had been really hurt. That would explain tonight: in his drunken state he thought she was still married–of course! She felt she would explode with happiness.

She lay there half dozing, waking every few minutes to stare at the man in her arms to reassure herself that it had really happened. She saw the streaks of dawn–and marveled at the suddenness with which the sun claimed the sky, the sea gulls calling to one another, announcing a new day. It *was* a new day, a wonderful day! The sun filtered into the room; soon it would reach the man in her arms. She had forgotten to draw the drapes last night. She eased herself out of bed and tiptoed across the room. Soon the cool darkness covered the room. It was nine o'clock. She slipped into the bathroom. She wanted him to sleep off all the vodka. She wanted him to feel good when he awoke. She caught a glimpse of herself in the mirror. Good Lord–she must have been in a daze last night, she had never bothered to remove her makeup. She was glad she had wakened first. Her lipstick and mascara were smeared. She creamed her face, took a shower and put on light makeup. She pulled her hair back into a ponytail and put on a blouse and slacks and went into the kitchen. Did he like eggs? Bacon? Maybe the smell of it would make him ill after all that vodka. She put the coffee on and opened a jar of tomato juice. That was supposed to be good for a hangover. She left the frying pan out–if he wanted eggs she'd make them. God, she'd do anything for him.

It was almost noon when she heard him stir. She poured some tomato juice into a glass and brought it to him in the bedroom. He groped for it in the darkness. She watched him as he drained the glass. Then she drew the drapes. The sunlight flooded the room. He blinked several times and looked around the room.

"Good God. Maggie!" He looked at the bed, then back at her. "How did I get here?"

"You arrived on your own at four thirty in the morning."

Like a somnambulist he handed back the empty glass. "Did we –yes, I guess we did." He stared at the bed. Then he shook his head. "Sometimes when I get very drunk, I draw blanks. I'm sorry, Maggie." Suddenly his eyes went dark with anger. "Why did you let me in?"

She fought the panic that was choking her.

"Oh God!" He ran his hand through his hair. "I can't remember. I can't remember."

She felt the tears roll down her face, but her anger kept her from breaking down. "That's the oldest line in the world, Robin. But you can use it, if it makes you feel better! The shower is in there."

She stalked into the living room and poured herself some coffee. Some of her anger dissolved. The bewilderment in his eyes *had* been real. Suddenly she knew he was telling the truth. He didn't remember.

He walked into the living room, knotting his tie. His coat was on his arm. He dropped it on the couch and took the cup of coffee she handed him.

"If you want eggs, or toast–" she said.

He shook his head. "I'm sorry as hell about all this, Maggie. Sorry for what I did to Andy. And most of all sorry because of you. Look–I'm leaving. You don't have to tell Andy. I'll make it up to him–I'll find a way."

"What about me?"

He looked at her. "You knew what you were doing. Andy didn't. He's your guy."

"I'm not in love with Andy."

He grinned. "And I suppose you're madly in love with me."

"Yes, I am."

He laughed, almost as if it was a private joke. "I must be a whiz when I'm smashed."

"You mean this has happened often."

"Not often. But it *has* happened before, maybe two or three times. And each time, it scares the hell out of me. But this is the first time I've ever been confronted with the evidence. Usually I wake up and know something has happened, something I can't quite remember. It's usually after I've really been on a bender. But last night I thought I was safe, that I could tie on a load—there was just you and Andy. What the hell happened to him?"

"He passed out."

"Yes, I remember that. I think that's the last thing I do remember."

"You don't remember any of the things you said to me?"

His blue eyes were candid. "Was I awful?"

Tears came to her eyes. "No, you were nicer than anyone I've ever known."

He put down the coffee and stood up. "Maggie, I'm sorry. Really sorry."

She looked at him. "Robin, do I mean anything to you?"

"I like you. So I'm going to give it to you straight. You're a bright beautiful girl, but you're not my type."

"I'm not your—" She couldn't get it out.

"Maggie, I don't know what motivated me to come here. I don't know what I said, or what I did. . . . And, oh Jesus, I'm sorry I've hurt you." Then he came to her. He touched her hair softly but she pulled away. "Look, Maggie, you and Andy pretend this never happened."

"Please go! I told you—it's over with Andy. It was over before last night."

"It will be rough on him. He cares about you."

"I'm not right for him. I don't want him. Please, get out."

"I'm going to transfer him to New York," he said suddenly. "There's not enough news coming out of here anyway. What about you—do you want to work in New York?"

"Oh for heaven's sake, stop playing God!"

He looked into her eyes. "Maggie, I wish I could buy back last night. This hasn't happened to me in a long time. The last time was in Philadelphia."

She stared at him. "You remember that?"

He shook his head. "She was gone when I woke up. I just remember she wore orange lipstick."

"I wear orange lipstick."

His eyes widened with disbelief.

She nodded mutely. "It's insane. I was doing the news there."

"Jesus–are you following me?"

She felt outraged with anger and humiliation. Before she realized it her hand lashed out across his face.

His smile was sad. "I guess I deserved that. . . . You must really hate me, Maggie–all these days we've been together and I never remembered."

"I don't hate you," she said coldly. "I hate myself. I hate all women who act like sentimental idiots or lose control. I'm sorry I hit you. You're not worth it."

"Don't try to be hard, it's not your natural behavior."

"How do you know what my natural behavior is? How can you know anything about me! You've made love to me twice and don't remember. Who are you to tell anyone what I am? Who are *you? What* are you?"

"I don't know, I really don't know." Then he turned and left the apartment.

TWENTY

When Robin left Maggie's apartment he checked out of the hotel and went directly to the airport.

New York was clear and mild. The temperature was in the low forties. Idlewild Airport was crammed with good-humored holiday travelers. Robin hailed a cab and reached his apartment just before the heavy traffic jam began. He promised himself to go on the wagon until Christmas Eve in Los Angeles.

There was no important mail. The apartment was neat. He felt oddly depressed. He opened a can of tomato juice and placed a call to Ike Ryan. Amanda was probably out of the hospital by now.

"Where the hell have you been? *Now* you call!" Ike's voice was flat and oddly indifferent.

"How are things?" Robin asked cheerfully.

" 'Just call me if you need me, Ike!' " Ike mimicked. "Oh, brother . . . did I call! I called you for two days!"

"I was on a boat. Why didn't you leave a message?"

Ike sighed. "What good would it have done? You blew the funeral."

Robin hoped he hadn't heard correctly. "What funeral?"

"It was in all the papers. Don't tell me you didn't know."

"Ike–for Christ's sake. I just came back to New York. What happened?"

Ike's voice was leaden. "Amanda was buried day before yesterday."

"But just a week ago you said she was coming along fine."

"That's what we thought. The day she died . . . even that morning she looked great. I arrived at the hospital around eleven.

She was sitting in bed—all made up—in a beautiful dressing gown, addressing Christmas cards. The drug was working. I expected to take her home in a few days. Suddenly she dropped the pen and her eyes went blank. I ran to the door and yelled for nurses, doctors. Within seconds the room was filled with people. The doctor gave her an injection, and then she fell back asleep. I sat there for three hours before she opened her eyes. She saw me and smiled faintly. I held her in my arms and told her everything was gonna be fine. Then she looked at me, clear-eyed again, and said, 'Ike, I know, I know!' " Ike paused.

"Know what, Ike?" Robin asked.

"Oh Christ, who knows? I think she was telling me she knew that she was dying. I rang for the nurse. She came with the needle but Amanda pushed her away. She clung to me, like she knew there wasn't much time. She looked at me and said, 'Robin, take care of Slugger—please, Robin.' Then she lost consciousness. The nurse said to me, 'She didn't know what she was saying, she was talking in the past.'

"She woke again about an hour later with that sweet smile on her face. She reached for my hand. God, Robin, those eyes were so scared and big. She said, 'Ike, I love you. I love *you.*' Then she closed her eyes and never regained consciousness. She died an hour later."

"Ike, her last words were for you. That should give you some comfort."

"If she had said, 'Ike, I love you,' period, then it would have been fine. But she didn't. She said, 'I love you, I love *you.*' As if she had to try and convince me it was me she loved and not you. That was part of the sweetness and gallantry of Amanda. She knew it was the end, and she wanted to leave me with something positive to cling to."

"Ike—don't brood on it. She didn't know what she was saying."

"Yeah. Say, is it all right with you if I keep the cat?"

"The cat?"

"Well, by right it's yours. Because, conscious or not, she said for you to take care of Slugger. And I'd respect her wishes right down to the end. But I want the cat—it's like having a part of her."

"Oh, for God's sake," Robin said. "Of course the cat belongs to you."

"I've been sleeping with it every night," Ike said. "The cat senses something is wrong. We're both lost souls."

"Ike, give the cat a saucer of milk and sleep with a blonde."

"With my luck, I'm doing a war picture. Not a broad in it. Just twenty guys who all look like John Wayne. But what the hell –I guess I'll be okay. Merry Christmas, Robin."

"Sure. Same to you, Ike."

He hung up and sank back in the chair. Amanda was dead . . . it didn't seem possible. She couldn't have cared about him. Ike was just off balance with his misery. Poor guy, what a lousy Christmas he would have. The thought of Christmas wasn't exactly a cheerful idea to him either. Suddenly he had an urgent desire to spend Christmas with someone he cared about. Who was there? His mother? His sister? Well, Kitty was in Rome, and Lisa –God, he hadn't seen her in ages. He didn't even know what her kids looked like. He put in a call to San Francisco.

Lisa sounded genuinely surprised. "Robin! I can't believe it. *You* calling me. I know–you're getting married."

"Lisa dear, it's a week before Christmas–and odd as it may seem, I do occasionally think of my family. Especially around this time of the year. How are the kids? And good old Crew Cut?"

"Still crew-cut and still the most wonderful man in the world. Robin, I should be angry at you–all the times you've been to Los Angeles and never called. We're only an hour away by plane. Kate and Dickie would love to see you. You've just caught us. We leave in an hour for Palm Springs. We've become tennis nuts. Going to spend the holidays there with Dick's family. When are we going to see you?"

"Next time I'm in L.A., I promise." He paused. "How's the glorious Kitty?"

She didn't answer immediately. Then she said, "Robin, why do you always call her that?"

"I don't know. Maybe after the old man died."

"You mean my father."

"Come on, Lisa: how's Kitty?"

"Why *do* you call her Kitty?"

He laughed. "Okay, what is Mummy up to these days? Is that better?"

"She was a good mother to you, Robin."

"She sure was, and I'm glad that she's having a ball. How is she?"

"Not well. She has what they call walking coronaries–mild little heart attacks. She was hospitalized for a month. She's all right but the doctor warned her not to overdo things. She carries nitroglycerin tablets. And she moved into a big house in Rome. Of course there's someone else on the scene now–this one is twenty-two. I think he's a fag. She says he cooks for her, waits on her hand and foot and adores her. She gives him an allowance. Can you stand it?"

"I think it's great," Robin said. "What do you want her to do, have an arthritic old man creaking around? I'm like Kitty, I also like them young and attractive."

"Don't you ever want children and a home of your own?"

"Hell, no–and I'll tell you something. I don't think the glorious Kitty did either. I think she had us because it was the thing to do."

"Don't say that!" she said hotly.

"Oh come off it, Lisa. We always had a nurse, at least you did. I can still remember how frightened Kitty was when she had to hold you. And I can't remember her ever holding me when I was a baby. I think we were just part of the scheme–a boy and a girl to go with the house."

"She loved kids," Lisa snapped. "She wanted children so much, she had almost given up when I arrived."

"Shows you how much I mattered," he said lightly.

"No. It was different. After all, we are seven years apart. She wanted a house full of kids. She almost died having me, and she had three miscarriages after me."

"How come I never knew any of this?"

"I never knew about it either. But a year after Dad died, she came to visit us for a short time. I was three months pregnant with Kate. And she said, 'Don't just have one, Lisa–or even two.

Have a house full of children. I have so much money to leave to you and Robin. You both can afford many children. And life means nothing without them.' That's when she told me a lot of things. I wanted her to live with us but she was dead set against it. She said I had my own husband and life–and it was up to her to make her own. She was determined to live in Europe."

"I guess girls are closer to their mothers," he said quietly.

"I don't know, but I do know children are important. Mother knew that. I wish you felt the same way."

"Well–happy Palm Springs and Merry Christmas."

"Same to you. I guess you'll wind up surrounded by blondes. But have a nice holiday, Robin." She clicked the receiver.

He rubbed his head thoughtfully. The holiday season stretched ahead. The idea of the saucer special was beginning to take form in his mind, but he knew nothing could be accomplished until after the first of the year. Meanwhile there was Christmas to get through. He could go to Los Angeles and try to help Ike out of the doldrums, but the idea of sitting and rehashing Ike's frustration over Amanda was depressing.

He called a model he had dated. She had gone to West Virginia for the holidays. He tried an airline hostess. Her plane was two hours late, but her roommate was available. He arranged to meet her at the Lancer bar. She was a nice-looking clean-cut kid. They had a few drinks together. He stuck to beer. He bought her a steak. She was ready to go home with him, but he dropped her back at her own apartment. He took a long walk, then he watched *The Late Show* and fell asleep. He awoke at four in the morning. He was damp with sweat and although he couldn't remember, he was aware that he had had a nightmare. He lit a cigarette. Four in the morning; that meant it was ten o'clock in Rome. The more he thought about it, the more sense it made. He placed a call. The voice that answered was masculine and spoke in stilted English.

"Mrs. Stone, please," Robin said.

"Please, she is still asleep. May I take the message?"

"Who is this?"

"May I in turn ask the same question?"

"I'm her son. Robin Stone. Now who the hell are you?"

"Oh." The voice took on a tone of warmth. "I have heard

much about you. I am Sergio, an excellent friend of Mrs. Stone's."

"Well, look, excellent friend, I'm going to grab the first flight I can get for Rome. I want to spend Christmas with my mother. How is she feeling?"

"She is quite well, but she will feel even better when she hears this news."

Robin kept his voice cold. If this was a sample of the charm these gigolo types dished out, no wonder so many women were taken in. This one was getting to him right through the phone. "Look, excellent friend, you can save me a cable if you reserve a room for me at the Excelsior."

"I do not understand–"

"The Excelsior. It's a big hotel on the Via Veneto."

"I know the hotel well, but why should you stay there? Your mother has a very large *palazzo,* ten bedrooms. She would be most hurt if you did not stay with her."

"Ten bedrooms!"

"It is a nice villa. Very restful for her."

I'll bet, Robin thought; plenty of freedom for little Sergio to have his boyfriends as house guests. But he remained silent.

Sergio said, "If you will wire the time of your flight, I will meet you."

"That's not necessary."

"But it will be a pleasure."

"Okay, chum, you really earn your keep, don't you?"

"I am looking forward to our meeting."

The plane landed at eleven at night, Rome time. Robin was suddenly grateful for the time difference. He could greet Kitty and go directly to sleep. In a way he wished he could stay at a hotel. The role of house guest wasn't to his liking, even if it was his own mother's home. After all, a *palazzo* in Rome with Sergio was a far cry from the rambling brownstone he and Lisa had shared with Kitty in Boston. And he was sure Sergio in no way resembled his father.

He saw the handsome young man in the skinny pants the moment he got off the plane. As Robin came through the gates, he rushed to him and tried to take his hand luggage.

Robin waved him off. "I'm not decrepit, junior."

"My name is Sergio. May I call you Robin?"

"Why not?" They walked toward the baggage area. The boy was exceptionally handsome, better-looking than any movie star. Definitely light on his feet but he didn't swish. And he had more than just the looks and accent going for him. His manner was right—eager and enthusiastic, yet not subservient. The son of a bitch acted like he actually was glad to meet him. And he was a whiz with the baggage—whatever it was that he was rattling in Italian sure as hell worked. Immigration stamped his passport; and while everyone else fought and tried to find their luggage, Sergio merely peeled off some lire, and within seconds a bent old porter came up with Robin's bags and piled them into a long red Jaguar. Robin was silent as they sped along the modern highway that led into town.

"Nice car," he finally said.

"It belongs to your mother."

"I'm sure she speeds around in it every day," he said acidly.

"No—I drive. She had a large chauffeur-driven Rolls, but in Rome such a large car in our traffic is not good. And the chauffeur—" Sergio rolled his eyes toward heaven. "He had arrangements with gas stations. He was making much money off your mother. Now I do the driving."

"And you've found a cut-rate gas station, I'm sure."

"Cut-rate?"

"Forget it, Sergio—how is my mother?"

"I think she is more well than she has been for a long time. And your arriving has made her so very happy. We are planning a big Christmas party in your honor. Your mother likes parties, and I think it is good for her, makes her dress nice. And when a woman dresses up and looks beautiful, she feels well."

Robin sat back and watched Sergio navigate through the tiny squealing cars and jammed traffic in the center of the city. Gradually they eased their way into a less congested area and headed for the Appian Way. Sergio drove into an enormous tree-lined drive. Robin whistled. "Looks like Nero's summer palace. What's the rent on this place?"

"No rent," Sergio said. "Kitty bought it. Very nice—yes?"

Kitty was waiting in the large marble entrance hall. Robin embraced her gently. She seemed smaller than he remembered, but her face was smooth and unlined. At first glance, standing there in the red velvet hostess pajamas, she looked to be about thirty. She led him into an enormous drawing room. The floors were pink marble and frescoes lined the high walls. Sergio disappeared, and Kitty led him to the couch. "Oh, Robin–it's so good to see you." He stared at her tenderly. Suddenly he was so damn glad she was his mother. He saw the age spots on the hands that contrasted so incongruously with the young unlined face. And yet, sitting here with him, she suddenly seemed like a little old woman. Her body seemed to collapse–even the smooth face looked old.

Then Sergio entered and he witnessed an amazing transformation. Kitty sat up. Her body seemed vibrant–she grew two inches, her smile was young–she *was* young as she accepted the glass of champagne Sergio offered.

"I made for you vodka martini on the ice," Sergio said. "Kitty said this is what you drink. Is it made correct?"

Robin took a long swallow. It was incredible. The son of a bitch made a better martini than the bartender at Lancer's. Sergio disappeared again and Kitty took both of Robin's hands. "I'm a bit tired, but tomorrow we'll catch up on everything. Oh, Sergio, you are sweet." The boy had returned with a tray of cold lobster.

Robin dipped a piece into some sauce. He suddenly realized that he was hungry. Sergio had no end of talents. He stared at the young man, standing straight and erect near the fireplace, and wondered what made a boy who had everything going for him turn queer. If it was money he wanted, there had to be young Italian heiresses who would go for a guy with his looks. Why tie up with an older woman? Easy: an older woman was grateful for any small favors. Grateful enough to let him have an occasional boy on the side.

"You called just in time," Kitty was saying. "We already had our plane tickets for Switzerland. I had promised Sergio ten days of skiing."

Robin's face showed his concern. "Why didn't you tell me I was interrupting something?"

She waved her hand. "Oh, it didn't matter one way or the other to me. Heaven knows I don't ski. Poor Sergio was the one who had looked forward to the trip. But it was his decision not to go. When I woke up, he announced that you were coming and that he had already canceled our reservation at the lodge."

Robin looked at Sergio. The young man shrugged. "I think perhaps the air is too thin for Kitty anyhow. With her heart, maybe she should not go to the Alps."

"Nonsense! The doctor said it was all right!" Kitty said. "But this is much nicer. We're all together. And–has Sergio told you?–we're going to have a big party Christmas day. I'm making a list. Of course many people will be away on holiday, but all the strays who are stuck in Rome will be here. And, Robin, you are going to stay until after New Year's. After all, we gave up the Alps for you, so don't dare run off."

"But if I stay for a few days you could still go to Switzerland."

"No. We'd never get reservations now. As it was, we had to make them months in advance. So now you have to stay."

Kitty put down her glass. "Time for me to go to sleep." Robin stood up but she waved her hand. "Now you finish your drink. It's late for me, darling, but you're still on American time, so you can't be sleepy." She kissed him lightly. Sergio came and took her arm and she looked at him gently. "He's a nice boy, Robin. He's made me very happy. He could be my son." She turned to him suddenly. "How old are you, Robin?"

"I hit the big one last August."

"Forty." She smiled. "Suddenly that seems so young. But it isn't young when a man hasn't married." Her eyes were questioning.

"I guess I can't find anyone as attractive as you."

She shook her head. "Don't wait too long. Children are very important."

"Sure," he said hollowly. "That's why you need Sergio. We're a big comfort to you, Lisa and me."

"Robin, a mother really loves her children only if she loves them enough to let go. I didn't have children as annuities against loneliness in my old age. They were part of my youth–the wonderful thing I had with your father. Now they must have their youth and their children." She sighed. "Those years–they are the really happy ones of one's life. I see that now as I look back. Don't let it slip by you, Robin." Then she left the room with Sergio at her side. He watched them disappear at the top of the stairs.

He poured himself a shot of straight vodka. He was tired but he wasn't eager to go to bed. He had nothing to read . . . and this strange new sense of loneliness persisted. His glance went to the top of the winding stairs. Were Kitty and Sergio making love? He shivered. It was a mild night—but he was cold. He walked over to the fire. Maybe it was the goddam marble. He shivered again.

"I lit the fire in your room."

He turned—Sergio was standing at the foot of the stairs.

"I didn't hear you," Robin said. "You sure pussyfoot around."

"I intentionally wear rubber soles. Kitty often takes small unexpected naps. And I do not wish my footsteps to disturb her."

Robin walked back to the couch. Sergio sat beside him. Robin moved away and looked at the young man. "Look, Sergio, let's get this straight right from the start. Get your pleasure with my mother or with boys. Just don't get any ideas about me."

"Forty is late to be unmarried."

Robin laughed without mirth. "Good thinking. But you're off base. I dig girls, buddy—I dig them so much that I never intend to settle for just one." The dark-brown liquid gaze of the man unsettled him. "Look, why aren't you in bed with the glorious Kitty? That's what you're getting paid to do."

"I am with her because I like her."

"Yeah, I like her too. But I left her when I was your age, and she was a lot younger and prettier."

Sergio smiled. "But she is *not* my mother. There is love between us—but not the kind you think. Your mother does not want sex, she wants affection, someone to be with her. I care for her. I will always be very good to her."

"You do that, Sergy." Robin's voice was tight. He found himself reevaluating the boy. He no longer resented him. In a crazy kind of way he thought Kitty was lucky. He felt a surge of gratitude toward Sergio.

"Tell me about your work in the States," Sergio said.

"There's nothing to tell . . . I'm in news broadcasting."

"Don't you like it?"

Robin shrugged. "It will do–it's a job."

Robin poured himself some more vodka. The young man jumped up and brought him the ice bucket.

"Everyone has to have a job," Robin said slowly.

"We are a Catholic country and there is no divorce. Poor people have bambinos. So they must have a job and work hard–even at jobs they do not like. But the man of affluence, he does not have just a job. He works at a business of his choosing. He enjoys life. All businesses and shops close every day from noon until three. A man of means enjoys life over here. At lunch he goes to his mistress. He has a long lunch–wine–he makes love. Then at night he goes to his wife, and he relaxes again. But you Americans –you take jobs you do not care about. Tell me, do you ever take wine with lunch?"

Robin laughed. "The idea would never occur to me."

"But why? Your mother will leave you so much money–why should you work so hard at just a job?"

"I don't work that hard. Maybe we do rush a lot, but we also don't expect to be supported by women. Lovers or mothers."

Robin watched, but the implication missed its mark. Sergio's expression never changed.

"Will you work on this news job all your life?" The question was asked with sincere interest.

"Nope. One day I'll take off and write a book."

Sergio's eyes lit up. "I read all the time. Kitty is helping me much with education. I had so little. I am reading Wells's *Outline of History* now. Do you write like Mr. Wells?"

"I'm writing like me–which is the only way, good or bad. Trouble is, I sandwich it in during odd hours."

"I think you should give up this job and come and live with us. You could write here and we would all be very happy together. Please, Robin, it would make Kitty happy, and I would like it much."

Robin smiled. "I'm too big for a roommate, friend."

"Oh, you would have your own room. We would block off a suite for you. And on vacation you could go skiing with me. Please, Robin!"

"Sergio, the last time anyone looked at me like that we went to bed for three days. Only difference was, it was a girl. Now cut it."

"It shows?"

"You're damn right it shows."

"Does it bother you?"

"If you want me to stay–cut it."

Sergio sighed. "I understand. It's just that you are–everything that I would dream to find in a man. I cannot help it, any more than a girl could help it if she saw you. Yet if a girl stared at you this way, you would not hate her. I stare at you from the heart. I cannot help the way my emotions go. But do not worry." He held out his hand. "Shake, Robin. We'll be friends."

Robin was surprised at Sergio's firm grasp. "That's a deal." He put down his glass and started up the stairs. "Oh, by the way, where do you sleep, chum?"

"Down the hall. In an adjoining room to your mother."

Robin's grin was slow. Sergio's eyes were serious. "She has a heart condition. I think I should be within calling distance."

"Good night, Sergio–you've outdistanced me."

Sergio smiled and walked toward the fireplace. "I'll put out the fire. The servants arrive at seven. I left a thermos of hot coffee on your night table on the chance you might awake earlier."

Robin laughed as he started up the steps. "I'm glad there's only one of you, Sergio. If there were many more you might put girls out of business."

Kitty spent the next few days immersed in elaborate preparations for Christmas. Food had to be purchased, wines, Christmas ornaments, a tree. Each day she gave Robin and Sergio a list and sent them off like two children. Robin relaxed and entered into the spirit of it all. Sergio drove and knew all the right shops. Often they were forced to stop and have a long lunch while they waited for the shops to reopen. Robin found himself enjoying the leisurely pace. He even drank wine. He had fallen into an easy relationship with Sergio. The boy was gentle and kind. He began to feel a paternal affection toward him.

Sergio asked eager questions about the States. He was interested in New York, Chicago, but it was Hollywood that seemed to hypnotize him. He had devoured fan magazines. The beach houses and lavish estates amazed him. "In Rome, maybe three or four people live so magnificently. In Hollywood, *everyone* has their own swimming pool. That would be a wonderful life. Here I have no chance for the cinema, so many young men look like me—but in Hollywood I would be different."

"Can you act?" Robin asked.

"Do you have to act for pictures?" The eyes were innocent. "I hear it is made in little pieces, and the director tells you what to do."

"Well, there's a little more than that to it. Why not study drama? Kitty wouldn't mind."

Sergio shrugged. "It is just a dream. I am happy being with Kitty. And these last few days, Robin, they have been the happiest of my life."

The day before Christmas, Sergio dragged him to a jewelry shop on the Via Sistina. The owner of the shop, a fat balding man, quivered with excitement when he saw Sergio.

"Sergio, you have come back," the man said.

"I want to see the mirror," Sergio said coldly.

"Oh yes, you bad boy. I told you it was yours if you wanted it." He reached in a case and brought out a beautiful little Florentine gold mirror. Sergio stared at it with admiration.

"What in hell is it?" Robin asked. He was growing uncomfortable. The owner of the shop was staring at Sergio hungrily, yet Sergio seemed impervious to the man's attention.

"Kitty admired it," Sergio said. "She saw it a month ago. It's a mirror for her purse. I tried to save, but I only have half the money."

"Sergio"—the man's voice was oozing oil—"I told you, pay what you can. The rest will be a gift from me."

Sergio ignored him. He pulled out some crumpled lire. "Robin, I need—well, twenty American dollars more would do it. Can it be a present from both of us to Kitty?"

Robin nodded. He handed the owner the money, and with a shrug of disappointment the fat man disappeared to wrap the gift.

Robin walked around the store staring at the various cases of jewelry on display. Sergio followed. "He has very beautiful things –he is a collector."

"Seems like jewelry isn't the only thing he collects."

Sergio's eyes drooped mournfully. "He is famous for his presents to young boys."

Robin laughed. "Sergio, the way he looked at you–you've got it made. Hold out for marriage."

"I never met him until I came to find the price of the mirror. He offered it to me for nothing if I . . ."

"Why not, Sergy? He's not much older than Kitty."

"I would have to sleep with him."

"Well?"

"I only sleep with someone who attracts me."

Robin walked away. The boy was giving homosexuality a crazy kind of dignity. Sergio followed him. "That is true, Robin. I have had only a few friends. There has been no one since my last friend became ill."

"And how soon will you leave Kitty for another friend?"

"I will not leave her. It is not easy for me. The men that I could love, they love women. I will not take up with any man just because he is homosexual. I would rather be with Kitty."

"Stay with her, Sergio. I promise you, if and when Kitty goes, I'll see that you get an allowance for life."

Sergio shrugged. "Money is not everything to me." He paused. "But would you buy me a Christmas present so I can remember you?"

They were standing near a tray of diamond-studded men's wristwatches. A glint of suspicion came to Robin's eyes. "Okay, chum, what is it that catches those big brown eyes?"

"Over here." Sergio led Robin to a case that held some gold slave bracelets. "I have always wanted one of these."

Robin suppressed a smile. The bracelets were about eighteen dollars. He waved his hand. "Take your pick." The boy was childlike in his enthusiasm. He finally selected the least expensive one. Plain gold links with a nameplate.

"Can I have my name put on the front? There is extra cost for that."

Robin smiled. "Go the whole route. Put on whatever you like." Sergio actually clapped his hands. He lapsed into excited Italian with the owner of the shop. Robin browsed through the store. Suddenly his attention was caught by a black-enameled panther with green jeweled eyes staring up from the case.

He beckoned the salesman. "How much is that?"

"Four thousand."

"Lire?" Robin asked.

"Dollars."

"For that!"

The young salesman immediately placed it on a piece of white velvet. "It is the most beautiful pin in Rome. It comes from India. A maharaja had it made. It is three hundred years old. The emeralds in the eyes are priceless. You would not have to pay duty as it is an antique."

He stared at the panther. The jeweled eyes were the exact color of . . . He turned away. Then with a quick change of heart, he told the man to wrap it up. Hell–why not? He sure owed Maggie something after that night. As he wrote the traveler's check it occurred to him he had never spent this kind of money for anything. Yet oddly enough he felt exhilarated. He put the box in his pocket. Then he went to collect Sergio, who refused to go until he got a written guarantee that the engraving on the bracelet would be ready at closing time that day.

Robin couldn't remember a nicer Christmas Eve. The fireplace was crackling, the tree reached to the ceiling–they even popped corn to string on the tree. At midnight they opened the gifts. Kitty had given both Robin and Sergio diamond cuff links. Robin was embarrassed and touched at the small gold St. Christopher medal Sergio gave to him. "It has been blessed," Sergio explained, "you travel so much." Kitty was delighted with her gift. She toasted them both with champagne and throughout the evening Sergio kept staring at the shiny new bracelet on his wrist.

The following day the villa overflowed with guests. Robin drank a lot and wound up in an apartment facing the Borghese gardens with a beautiful Yugoslavian girl whose husband was in

Spain on business. They spent the following afternoon making love. He returned to Kitty's *palazzo* exhausted, but very content.

The week passed quickly.

Sergio drove him to the airport. "Call me if she doesn't feel right. And, Sergio, make her get checkups. She won't tell you when she's not feeling well–she doesn't want to act like an old woman–but call the doctor if there's the slightest suspicion."

"Trust me, Robin." They were walking to the gate. Robin's luggage had been checked, the flight had been announced. "And, Robin–perhaps you should see a doctor, too."

"Hell, I'm strong as a horse."

"I mean another kind."

Robin stopped suddenly. "What are you getting at?"

"Something is bothering you. Two nights in a row you shouted in your sleep. Last night I ran to your room–"

"What did I say?"

"You were thrashing about in the bed, asleep, but with a hurt sad expression on your face. You were hugging the pillow and shouting, 'Don't leave me! Please!' "

"Too much vodka," Robin said. Then he shook hands and boarded the plane. But he thought about it on the trip home. He thought about it when he showed the pin at customs and had to pay an enormous tax–if he ever saw that son of a bitch on the Via Sistina again who had said *no duty!* And he kept thinking about it on the taxi ride home. The whole thing didn't add up. At the height of his affair with Amanda he had never bought her such an expensive present. And here he was with a four-thousand-dollar trinket for a girl he couldn't even get it up for unless he was drunk. Maybe it was guilt, but four thousand bucks plus duty was a hell of a high price to pay for one night. A night he couldn't even remember.

TWENTY-ONE

He went into immediate action the moment he returned to New York. He notified the legal department to draw up a contract for Andy Parino. He mailed it to him with a short note stating his offer to join the network in New York. He also mailed the panther pin to Maggie with a note saying, "A belated Merry Christmas–Robin." Three days later Andy phoned and eagerly accepted the offer.

"Sure you won't miss anything down there?" Robin asked.

"Hell, no. It's all washed up with Maggie and me anyhow."

"I'm sorry."

"No, it just wasn't in the cards. She's–well, she's too complicated for me. Right now she's rehearsing like crazy–some Hollywood agent is coming to catch her in a play. I want a girl who puts me ahead of Eugene O'Neill."

"Fine. I'll assign you to Network News–you'll still work with Jim Bolt. And you can start sitting in on my *In Depth* taping sessions to get the feel of it. In a month or so, I'll let you try one. By next season I hope to turn it over to you and go on to something new."

"I've been running all your tapes and studying them. I don't know whether it's going to be that easy to step in your shoes."

"Do your own thing–and they'll buy it."

"Thanks for the vote of confidence. I'll sure try my damnedest!"

By the end of the week, Robin had caught up with all his back work, and scheduled a taping for *In Depth*. He looked at his appointment pad–the afternoon was free. He unlocked his desk drawer and took out his manuscript. It seemed years since he had looked at it. Well—tonight he'd take it home and work on it, and lay off the vodka. He hadn't been to the Lancer Bar since he returned.

His secretary came in with a package. He had to sign for it. He scribbled his signature and stared at the brown-paper wrapping. It was heavily stamped and insured. He opened it and found the Italian leather box with the black panther pin. There was a typewritten note: "I only accept gifts from friends."

He tore up the note and put the box in a small wall safe where he kept his contracts and private papers.

He put the book back in his desk drawer and left the office. When he arrived at the Lancer Bar, Carmen the bartender was effusive in his greeting. "Mr. Stone, it's been so long! The usual?"

"Make it a double to celebrate my return," Robin said.

He finished the drink quickly and ordered another. This was going to be one of those nights. He was beginning to hate the nights. He knew he had dreams . . . several times he had awakened in a sweat. But he couldn't remember them. He hadn't remembered his dreams in Rome, yet Sergio said he had shouted two nights in a row. He finished the second drink and ordered another. Maggie sending back the pin bugged him. But why should it? She didn't mean anything to him. Nothing seemed to add up lately. Maybe Sergio had something. He crossed the room and picked up the phone book. Why not? It was worth a visit to a shrink to stop the dreams. He leafed through the pages. There sure were a hell of a lot of Golds but there couldn't be more than one Archibald Gold. He found it listed on Park Avenue. He hesitated a moment, then quickly dialed the number. Dr. Archie Gold picked up on the second ring.

"This is Robin Stone."

"Yes."

"I'd like to see you."

"Professionally or personally?"

There was a pause. "I guess professionally."

"Could you ring me back at six? I have a patient."

Robin hung up and walked back to the bar. He finished his second drink; then exactly at six he rang Archie.

"Okay, Doc, when can I see you?"

He heard the ruffling pages and knew the doctor was going through his appointment book. "I have a few openings," he said. "Some of my patients have gone south for the winter. Would you like to come next Monday? I could put aside ten o'clock. We could start with three visits a week."

Robin's laugh was hollow. "I don't want a course. Just one shot will do. I want to talk to you about a specific problem. Why don't you come over to the Lancer Bar for a drink? I'll pay for the drink and your time–like it was an office visit."

"I'm afraid that's not the way I work."

"I talk better when I'm drinking," Robin said.

"I listen better in my office," the doctor replied.

"Then forget it."

"I'm sorry. But you know my number if you change your mind."

"What time is your last appointment tonight?"

"My last patient is due now."

"That means you're free at seven."

"I plan to go home at seven."

"Archie–I'll come to your office if you'll see me tonight."

Dr. Gold was not misled by Robin's casual tone. From a man like Robin, the phone call itself was a cry for help.

"All right, Robin, seven o'clock. You have my address?"

"Yep. And listen, Archie old boy, one word of this to your friend Jerry and I'll break your head in."

"I never discuss my patients. But if you have any doubts perhaps you should go to another doctor. There are several good men I could recommend."

"No, Archie baby, you're my man. See you at seven."

Robin sat across the desk from Dr. Gold. The whole idea struck him as ridiculous. He never opened up to anyone–how could he tell this placid-looking stranger what was bugging him?

Dr. Gold recognized the silence and smiled. "Sometimes it's easier to talk about intimate things with someone you don't know. That's why bartenders are the recipients of so many confidences. In a way the psychiatrist and the bartender have a great deal in common. We remain in our spot; you only have to see us when *you* want to. You don't run into us in your day-to-day living."

Robin laughed. "You've made your point. Okay–it's as simple as this. There's a girl." He paused. "I can't get her out of my mind –but I don't dig her. That's what's so crazy."

"When you say you don't dig her–do you mean you dislike her?"

"No, I do like her. I like her a lot. But I can't make it with her in bed."

"Have you ever tried?"

Robin shrugged. "Seems when I was pissy-eyed drunk I went after her on two separate occasions, and judging from her reactions, I was pretty good."

"Then what makes you say you can't make it with her?"

Robin lit a cigarette and exhaled thoughtfully. "Well, the first time it happened I woke up the following morning and she was gone. I couldn't even recall her face–or her name. I just knew that she was a brunette with big tits. And something disturbed me when I thought about it that morning. I couldn't remember a thing, yet I sensed I had done something or said something I shouldn't have. Then to compound the felony, I run into the lady two years later and have absolutely no recollection that we had ever met. She was making it with a buddy of mine. I thought she was beautiful, good company, and she was with him. Which was fine with me, because, like I said, she wasn't my type. We double-dated a few nights–then I went off for some fishing, alone. On my last night there, I went out with them. It started out as a great evening, only I got roaring drunk. My buddy passed out and I wound up with the lady. I have no recollection of being with her –except that I woke up the following morning in her bed. And I must have made it with her pretty good because there she was making breakfast and chirping little mating calls."

"What was your feeling about her?" Dr. Gold asked.

Robin shuddered. "Fright. It was almost like waking up and finding you were with a boy, or a child–someone you *shouldn't* have gone to bed with. And because I did like her, I leveled with her." He ground out the cigarette. "I was rough. I told her how I felt. She was so damn beautiful, yet when I thought of sex with her I felt this sudden revulsion, and I knew I couldn't make it."

"Revulsion for her?"

"No. Revulsion about sex–as if doing it with her would be dirty, incestuous. Yet I like her. Maybe I like her more than any girl I've met. But I can't feel a physical drive for her."

"And you want to go to bed with her, or–let me put it this way: you would like to have this hangup, as you put it, removed so that you can fulfill a relationship with her."

"Wrong again. I don't care if I never see her again. But I don't like dark areas in my brain. This girl is beautiful–why should I feel this way? And it's happened before, just in a few isolated cases, but always with a brunette. Only they were never quite the caliber of this girl and fortunately I never saw them again. This thing with Maggie–it was an accident. I just happened to get roaring drunk."

"Just happened? Were you drinking an unusual drink? Something you were unaccustomed to?"

"No, vodka. That's what I always stick with."

"Were you aware that you were ordering too many drinks?"

"I guess I was."

"Let's go back to the first time with this girl. Two years ago. Were you very drunk when you met her?"

"No, but I was drinking."

"And then you purposely proceeded to get drunk?"

"Purposely?"

Dr. Gold smiled. "It would seem that way. I wouldn't say you were the kind of a man who is caught off guard."

Robin looked thoughtful. "You mean that subconsciously I wanted this girl and intentionally got drunk so I could make it with her?" When Dr. Gold didn't answer, Robin shook his head. "Doesn't add up–because I don't dig this type of girl. Why would I want to make it with her? Drunk or sober, she's not my type."

"What is your type?"

"Slim, golden, clean hard-bodied girls. I like the smell of gold hair. Maggie is sultry–like a jungle cat."

"Have you ever been in love?"

He shrugged. "Hung on girls, sure. But I've always been able to walk away from it. Know something, Archie. Everyone is *not* heterosexual or homosexual. There are people who are just plain sexual. They dig the bed scene, but don't necessarily fall *in* love.

Take Amanda: she was great. I thought we had a marvelous relationship. Yet from what Jerry told me, I hurt her very badly. But I was never aware of it. I only cut out toward the end when she tried to swallow me. And even then I was only cooling it–but I had no idea that all along I'd been hurting her."

"You really never knew?"

"That's right. If I took off to tape a show in Europe and didn't write, I figured she knew the score–that I was coming back, and it would be to her. And when I did come back, I couldn't wait to get into the feathers with her. It was great."

"Yet you are conscious that you have hurt this other girl, Maggie."

Robin nodded. "Yes."

"Why would you be unaware that you were hurting Amanda, whom you really desired, yet be so painfully aware of this girl you don't care about?"

"That's why I'm here, Archie. *You* tell me."

"What did your mother look like?"

"Oh Christ, let's not go into the Freudian jazz. I had a healthy happy childhood. Kitty is blond, nice, clean–" He stopped.

"And your father?"

"He was a hell of an outgoing guy. Strong, all muscles. I have a nice kid sister. Everything was shipshape in my childhood. We're only wasting time there."

"All right . . . father, mother, sister. All healthy relationships. Let's locate the dark stranger. Was it a nurse? A schoolteacher?"

"My first teacher was a hunchback. That was kindergarten. My nurse–well, I must have had one, but I can't recall. There were servants–a chauffeur took me to school. There was a nurse when Lisa was born–a gray-haired job."

"Was there any rivalry between you and your sister?"

"Hell, no. I was her big brother. I was protective of her. She looked like a tiny Kitty: blond, white and clean."

"Do you resemble Kitty?"

Robin frowned. "I have her blue eyes, but my hair is dark like my father's, although now it's turning gray pretty fast."

"Let's go back to before Lisa was born. What is the first memory you have?"

"Kindergarten."

"Before that."

"None."

"You must be able to recall something. Everyone remembers one small incident in early childhood. A pet, a playmate, happiness, disaster."

Robin shook his head. Dr. Gold pursued: "A conversation, a prayer?"

Robin snapped his fingers. "Yes—one thing. Maybe it was a conversation, but it was just a line and I can't remember who said it: 'Men don't cry. If you cry you're not a man, you're a baby.' For some reason it stuck with me. I believed it. I believed that if I didn't cry I could have anything I wanted. Whoever said it must have made an impression on me because I never cried after that."

"You've never cried?"

"Not that I can recall." Robin smiled. "Oh, I'll go to a corny movie and get a lump in my throat. But in my own personal life" —he shook his head—"never."

Dr. Gold looked at his watch. "It's five to eight. Would you care to make an appointment for next Monday? My fee is thirty-five dollars an hour."

Robin's expression was one of disbelief. "You must be some kind of a nut. I've been here almost an hour, to discuss a girl that I have some hangup about. We've solved nothing—and you want me to come back."

"Robin, it's not natural to be unable to recall anything in your childhood."

"Five years old is not exactly middle-aged."

"No, but you should be able to recollect some incident that occurred before, unless—"

"Unless what?"

"Unless you are intentionally blocking it out."

Robin leaned across the desk. "Archie, I swear to God, I have not blocked out anything. Maybe I have a lousy memory—or did it ever occur to you that perhaps nothing ever happened that was worth recalling?"

Archie shook his head. "Very often when something traumatic happens, the brain automatically builds amnesia as scar tissue."

Robin walked toward the door. He turned to the doctor. "Look I lived in a nice big house, with two nice parents and a pretty little sister. No skeletons in my closet. Maybe that's the bit. Maybe things went too smooth, maybe kindergarten was the first jolt I got–the hunchback teacher–maybe that's why my memory starts there."

"Who told you a man doesn't cry?"

"I don't know."

"Was it before kindergarten?"

"It had to be, because I didn't cry in kindergarten when the other kids did. They were all scared of the teacher–the poor bitch."

"Then who said it?"

"Archie, I don't know. But whoever it was, I bless them. I don't like to see men cry. I don't even like to see women or babies cry."

"Robin, I'd like to try you on hypnosis."

"Are you crazy? Look, Doc, I was in the war and got shot up a bit. I can think of a hell of a lot of things I went through that could have loosened some screws, but I came through in one piece. I came here to get one specific question answered. You come up zero. Okay. Be a sport and admit it. Don't try to make good by digging back into my childhood to see if a nurse belted me when I was two or three for messing up my toys. Maybe she did and maybe she had black hair and green eyes and big tits–okay?"

"You know where to find me if you decide to try it my way," Dr. Gold said.

Robin grinned. "Thanks, but I think it's easier and less expensive to duck if I run into a green-eyed brunette." He closed the door and walked into the night. Dr. Gold stared at the notes he had made, and put them in a folder. He would not destroy them: Robin Stone would return.

Robin glanced at the February Nielsens. The news department was finally giving the other networks real competition. This week it was second in its time period. *In Depth* was still in the top twenty-five. He had given Andy a shot at it last week and it had gone well. He studied the presentation of the saucer project—the research staff had come up with some exciting new angles. It would make a hell of a show.

He met with Danton Miller the following day and explained his intention of easing out of *In Depth* and letting Andy take over permanently the following season. Oddly enough, Dan raised no objections.

"Giving up acting?" he said with a smile. "Your adoring public won't like that."

"I intend to do a news special once a month," Robin explained. "Take some subject that no one will touch. Dig into it, lay it bare. This could be the first." He handed Dan the saucer presentation. Dan read it carefully.

"Sounds like a Sunday afternoon project—it might grab the kids," Dan said. "But it's not a nighttime show."

"I think it is. Why not try one shot in May or June in prime time, when the big shows are having reruns? That should be an honest test."

"If you like, I'll slate it for a Sunday afternoon, April or May. But not at night."

"I don't want Sunday afternoon," Robin said. "You know damn well it would get no rating. The baseball games would kill it. I'm looking for sponsor interest for the fall."

Dan smiled. "If you want to line up a staff and put this science-fiction crap on tape, that's up to you. But it has no place in my network planning."

Robin reached over and picked up the phone. Dan's secretary came on. "Would you call Mr. Gregory Austin. Tell him Robin Stone and Danton Miller would like to see him at his earliest convenience."

Dan's face drained of color. He recovered quickly and forced a smile. "That was a bad move," he said easily. "You just went over my head."

"But not behind your back." For a moment their eyes locked in silence. When the phone rang it seemed unnaturally loud. Dan reached for it. The secretary announced that Mr. Austin could see them immediately.

Robin stood up. "Coming, chum?"

Dan's eyes narrowed. "Seems like I have no choice." Then he smiled. "I'm curious to see Gregory's reaction to your Buck Rogers drama. He'll realize I've vetoed it–and Gregory doesn't like having his time wasted to act as referee. That's why I'm president of Network Television. My decision on matters like this is final. But I think I'll let you dig your own grave."

Dan sat back as Robin outlined the saucer project to Gregory. When he had finished, Gregory turned to Dan. "I gather you're against it."

Dan smiled and held his fingers together pyramid style. "Robin would like to do a show like this next season. One a month–in prime time."

Gregory looked at Robin questioningly. "A saucer show every month?"

Robin laughed. "No, I want to do an hour of television comparable to a *Life* magazine spread on a subject that's in the news. Saucers, politics–anything that's timely or newsworthy. Instead of doing a personality–like our half hour on *In Depth*–we do a subject, for an hour. An important movie could be filming–we'd go on location, talk with the stars, the director, the author. We could go into the private life of a television personality–take Christie Lane. The public keeps asking what he's really like–"

The mention of Christie Lane brought a sudden look of concern to Gregory's eyes. He turned to Dan. "That reminds me, we only have Christie signed for another season. Has anyone done anything about getting him signed to a new long-term contract?"

"We've started the negotiations," Dan said. "He wants to start reruns the end of April so he can pick up all that Vegas money. He's also booked some fairs. He gets ten thousand a night for them. He's still doing the shows live, but we've been taping them for the rerun bank. And next season he wants to go to tape–he's secure enough now. There's no problem there. But Cliff Dorne says we're miles apart in money–in what he's asking and what we want to give. We've agreed to give him a big raise, but he wants to form his own company–split ownership of the show with us. And he wants ownership of his tapes after the first rerun to sell to the independents. Plus many other fringe benefits. It's not going to be easy–both NBC and CBS are hot on his tail."

The secretary crept in and announced that Mrs. Austin was calling. Gregory rose. "I'll take it in the other room." Both men watched him disappear into the inner office. Dan was the first to break the silence. He leaned across and tapped Robin on the knee. His voice was low. "Listen to me: I hope you've learned a lesson. You've had a chance to look behind the scenes of network planning. There's more to it than being an Ivy League reporter. You've bored Gregory with your piddling science-fiction show. You've taken up my time and his. You are president of News. I am president of Network Television. I work alone—I'm not looking for a partner."

Robin laughed. "This sounds like a Madison Avenue version of a Chicago gang war: You have the South Side and I take the North Side."

"I have *both* sides. You have News, period. And you don't mix into programming. I'm not a newsboy playing part-time actor, part-time executive. This is my life—not a hobby. And no one cuts into it."

"I have no desire to shoot for any of your marbles. But I am president of News and I have a show that I think should go on. You have to give me the time. If you say no, then I have to—"

"You have to pass! Get it? Pass! The next time I say I don't want a show—you pass. There are to be no more calls to Gregory Austin!"

Robin's grin was easy. "Well then, Mr. President, just don't pass too quickly."

Gregory Austin returned. "Sorry, gentlemen. I never let personal calls interfere with business, but then Mrs. Austin is my most important business." His face softened as his thoughts reverted to his wife. Then he cleared his throat, and his expression took on the matters at hand. "I was telling Mrs. Austin your idea about the saucer special. She was intrigued. I never realized that there is a romanticism to space that appeals to women. Go ahead with the saucer project, Dan. Slate it in May in place of one of Christie's reruns. If it gets a rating, then we'll talk about a monthly series." He looked at Dan. "I'll work with Cliff Dorne on the Christie Lane renewal. Anything else on the agenda?"

Dan stood up. "I guess that's about it."

Gregory waited until both men reached the door—then almost as an afterthought he said, "Oh, Robin, would you wait one moment. There's something I want to talk to you about."

Dan left and Robin eased himself into a chair. Gregory stared after the closed door and smiled. "Dan's a good man. An ambitious man. Hell, we all are. That's why he's good. I like the idea of you thinking of other projects. Only from here on, if they're outside the news department, come to me first—and I'll pass them on to Dan as my idea. It will keep peace in our little family."

Robin smiled. "I'm still new at network protocol." He made no move to leave, because he sensed this wasn't the real reason Gregory had detained him.

"Robin"—Gregory's manner was suddenly oddly shy—"I know this seems like trivia, and it has nothing to do with the line of duty—but what happened to you on January first?"

Robin's brow creased. January first. . . . So far as he could recollect, Sergio had driven him to the airport.

Gregory lit a cigarette. "Gained ten pounds," he said sheepishly, "so I'm back smoking—just until I knock off the weight." Then he said, "Our eggnog party."

Robin's expression was blank.

Gregory studied the ash on his cigarette. "You've been invited two years in a row. Not only haven't you shown, but you've never even sent a note of regret."

"Good God! How rude of me! I was in Rome this year, and the year before I think I was—" He frowned, trying to recall. "I was in Europe then, yes, I remember, I returned on New Year's Day. And there was all that mail. I'm ashamed to tell you what I did with it—on both occasions. I stared at it, and then dumped it all into the wastebasket. After all, no one expects you to answer Christmas cards, and I figured the bills would come again the following month. I guess Mrs. Austin's invitation was among them. I'll write to her immediately."

Gregory smiled. "I assumed it was a misunderstanding. But you know how women are. Mrs. Austin was wondering if it was a personal slight."

"That's the last thing I would want her to think. The hell with a note—may I call her?"

"Of course." Gregory scribbled down the number.

Robin returned to his office and placed the call to Mrs. Austin.

"Now, Robin Stone," she said, "you didn't have to call. I know this is Gregory's doing."

"It is–and I'm grateful that he told me. I've been out of the country on both occasions of your New Year's Day parties."

She laughed when he told her of the way he had disposed of his mail. "I think that's a marvelous idea," she said. "I wish I had the nerve to do it. I'd miss so many dull events."

"Mrs. Austin, I promise you–next year I shall go through every Christmas card, searching for your invitation."

"Oh come now, Robin." She paused. "Forgive my informality, but we do watch your show. I feel as if I know you."

"Mrs. Austin, I promise, no matter where I am, on January first, nineteen sixty-four, we have a definite date."

Her laugh filtered through the phone. "I certainly hope we're not going to have to wait that long to meet."

"I hope not. But I want you to know, I like eggnog. I really do."

"I'm sure Gregory has told you he hates it. Oh, Robin"–he heard the rustle of paper–"I'm having a small dinner party March first. We've just returned from Palm Beach–the weather has been so unreliable there that we've decided to stay in New York. Would you like to come?"

How had he gotten into this? But he had those two goddam New Year's Days to make up. "I'd be delighted, Mrs. Austin."

"Oh, my sister will be in town. The dinner is really in her honor. The prince couldn't get away. Shall I make you her dinner partner, or is there someone you would care to bring?"

"I'd like to bring a young lady," he said quickly.

Without pausing, she said, "That will be fine. Eight thirty, March first, black tie."

He hung up and stared at the phone. Well, so the princess was here solo. He was not about to step into the role of the "personable extra man"! If he passed inspection as her dinner partner there would be other invitations. This way he had nipped it at the start. But now he had to dig up a girl. Well, he had ten days . . . he'd think of someone.

He forgot about Mrs. Austin in the week that followed. He

spent two days in Washington for the saucer project. He had selected a director and a producer and had set March fifteenth as the tentative taping date. Everything was in order. Everything except the one call he had to make. Maggie Stewart. He didn't *have* to call her, but her story on the sighting in Florida had sparked the entire idea. Andy was set to do a segment and he *had* promised Maggie that she'd participate in the show. He put in the call. When she came on the line he wasted no time on amenities. He explained the setup and asked if she was interested.

She was equally impersonal. "Of course I'd be interested in doing the show. When do you want me there?"

"As soon as possible!"

"Today is the twenty-fifth. How is March first? That will give the station time to get someone to fill in for me."

"March first is fine." He turned to his appointment pad and saw the notation: "Dinner party at the Austins'." "Maggie, I know you don't owe me anything, but you could do me one hell of a favor."

"Yes?"

"Come in February twenty-eighth and bring an evening dress."

"For the show?"

"No, for a dinner party on March first. I want you to go with me."

"Sorry, I'm coming in to work."

"You're absolutely right. But, well, I'd wish you come. It's a black-tie dinner at the Austins'."

She hesitated. "You really want me to go with you?"

"Yes, I do."

She laughed and her voice lost some of its reserve. "Well, it just so happens that I have a smashing dress that I'm dying to wear."

"Thanks, Maggie. Wire the time of your arrival. I'll send a car to meet you at the airport. And I'll book a reservation for you at the Plaza."

He called the Plaza to reserve a room, and suddenly decided to change it to a suite. Business Affairs would probably chew his ass off, but she rated it. Everyone lived well on IBC's expense account–why not Maggie?

Her wire arrived on the morning of the twenty-eighth: ARRIV-

ING AT IDLEWILD AT 5. NORTHEAST AIRLINES FLIGHT 24. MAGGIE STEWART.

He ordered a car; then on a last-minute impulse he called Jerry Moss. "Can you be loose at four? I have to meet a girl at Idlewild. I have a car–"

"And?"

"And I don't want to meet her alone."

"Since when did you need a chaperone?"

"Jerr–I have my reasons."

"Okay, I'll meet you in front of the IBC building at four."

It was close to eleven o'clock and Robin was drinking slowly and steadily. Jerry finished his coffee. The whole evening had been crazy. This Maggie Stewart was the most incredibly beautiful girl he had ever seen. Yet she had greeted Robin as if she barely knew him. And when Jerry suggested they all have a drink at the Lancer Bar, both Robin and Maggie had refused simultaneously. They had dropped her at the Plaza and then Robin had dragged him to Louise's for dinner. The restaurant had almost emptied, yet Robin sat toying with his drink. Long John Nebel stopped by on his way to do his all-night show.

"I listen to him when I can't sleep," Robin said. "He's tied to another network or I'd use him on the saucer show. He knows all about that jazz."

Robin ordered another drink and lapsed into silence. Jerry sensed Robin's mood and didn't try to pry. But what was all this about listening to Long John Nebel? That meant he wasn't sleeping well–it also meant he wasn't bedding down with a chick. You listened to Long John when you were lonely, or afraid of sleep. Robin an insomniac? This was a new twist.

Suddenly Jerry said, "Look, Robin, I don't know what's bugging you, but this Maggie Stewart is really special. If you blow this, there's something wrong with you."

"There's not a God-damned thing wrong with me," Robin snarled. "And get this straight. There's nothing between Maggie Stewart and me. I just brought her here because she's good at her job."

Jerry got up. "If you want to stay and drink all night, do it alone. I sat with you because I thought you needed me."

"I don't need anyone," Robin answered. "Run home to your wife."

Jerry started from the table, then he turned back. "Look, Robin, I'm not going to blow off at you, because I realize there's something eating you. You haven't been the same since Florida. And whether you admit it or not, it's tied up with that girl." Then he walked out.

Robin sat and drank until the restaurant closed. Then he walked home and turned on the radio. It was easier to fall asleep with the radio, you didn't wake up with the light of television glaring at you. He poured himself another stiff vodka. This was the first night he had tied one on since his visit to Archie. He got into bed and listened to Long John. He drifted off to sleep just as Long John was talking about some water you had to drink. Water. . . . That was a nice thought. . . . Think of a boat, he told himself, a boat and water. . . . A nice bunk. . . . Sleep. . . . Sleep. . . . He was on a boat, in a bunk. The bunk turned into a large bed. Maggie was holding him, stroking him, telling him everything was going to be all right. He felt good. He believed her. Then she slipped out of bed and Jerry was waiting in the other room. She was balling with Jerry! He came running in—she led him back to bed and snuggled against him and told him it was just a bad dream. She kept stroking his head. . . . He relaxed. . . . She was warm. . . . Then he heard her leave the large bed again, heard her giggling in the other room. He walked in . . . Jerry was gone. She was sitting on the couch with Danton Miller. Dan was sucking at her breast . . . Danton looked up and laughed. "He's jealous," Dan said. Maggie didn't smile. Her face was serious. "Go back to bed and stay there." It was a command. And for some crazy reason he knew he had to obey her.

He woke up. Christ, it was four in the morning. Another one of those dreams—John Nebel was still talking. Robin switched to an album station and finally drifted off to sleep.

He picked up Maggie the following evening. She was right, the dress was a knockout and he felt guilty because the dinner party at the Austins' was stiff and formal and dull. Everyone was pleasant, but small talk always got him down. He sat at Judith Austin's left and struggled to keep his attention from straying. Somehow he managed to be attentive, ask the proper questions when she spoke of her charities or the weather at Palm Beach. His eyes roamed down the long table to Maggie. She was stashed between a neurosurgeon and a stock-market specialist. He envied her easy graciousness and wondered what the hell she was finding to talk about with them.

Later, when he stood in the lobby of her hotel and thanked her for "helping him out," he noticed that every man who passed turned to stare at her. Why not? She looked better than any movie star. Suddenly he said, "How about a drink? I think you deserve one."

"I take it you're on the wagon–I noticed how you toyed with the sauterne at the Austins'. Are you even afraid to have wine when you're with me?" The green eyes stared at him with a tinge of mockery.

He took her arm and led her to the Oak Room.

He signaled the waiter. "The lady will have Scotch. Bring me a double vodka."

"You don't have to prove anything," she said. "I'm aware of your weaknesses."

"Drinking is not one of them," he said tightly.

"Oh, I was beginning to think you had lost that talent, too."

He waited until the waiter put down the drinks. Then he reached out and took her hand. "I want us to be friends, Maggie."

She let her hand remain in his and their eyes met. "We can never be friends, Robin."

"You still hate me?"

"I wish I did. Oh God, I only wish I did. . . ."

He withdrew his hand abruptly and drank the vodka straight, in one long swallow. Then he signaled for the check.

"I have a lot of work piled up at home," he said as he signed the check.

"You don't have to lie," she said. "You haven't so far. Why start now?"

"No, it's true. I'm moonlighting–working on a book. I've set a goal to write five pages every night, no matter when I get home."

She looked at him with interest. "Is that your secret ambition?"

"I try and tell myself it is."

"Isn't it?"

He suddenly looked very tired. "Maggie, I don't know what the hell I want or don't want."

Her expression softened. "Are you unhappy, Robin?"

"Who said I was unhappy?"

"Anyone who doesn't know what he wants is afraid to find out. It's as simple as that. Unless he's frightened of his own secret thoughts."

"Thanks, Doctor, I'll call you when I need your couch again." He stood up and helped her with her coat.

Maggie went to her room and tossed her evening bag on the bed in anger. Just when everything had been going so great! Her eyes dimmed. Why kid herself? Everything was going nowhere. It was all in her mind. And she was going to put him right out of her thoughts. His invitation to the Austins' had stirred false hope. He had just needed a presentable date. It was as simple as that. Well, she had the whole weekend to herself and she was not going to sit in her room and hope he'd call! She'd get up early–see a matinée–see a double feature at night. She would not be here if he called. And when she walked into the office on Monday, she'd act as if she barely knew him. She took a sleeping pill, left a DO NOT DISTURB sign on the door, and a wake-up call for ten.

It seemed as if she had only slept a few minutes when she heard the wake-up call. She tried to reach for the receiver, but the sleeping pill made her arm as leaden as her head. It rang again. With a supreme effort she managed to pick up the receiver. The impersonal voice of the operator said, "I know you have a DO NOT DISTURB sign but a telegram has arrived marked 'Urgent, deliver at once.' "

She sat up and switched on the light. It was only seven fifteen. "Send it up," she mumbled. She got out of bed and put on a robe. She still slept in the nude–even the cold weather could not change that.

She signed for the telegram. As she walked back into the bedroom a sudden feeling of apprehension took hold of her. She had been too sleepy to think, but who would send her a telegram? Was her mother or father ill? She ripped it open. She read it quickly —she couldn't believe it!

> STELLA LEIGH PREGNANT. MUST BE REPLACED IMMEDIATELY. HAVE SOLD CENTURY PICTURES ON USING YOU. TRIED TO REACH YOU BY PHONE FOR THE LAST SIX HOURS. NO ANSWER. CALL COLLECT AS SOON AS YOU RECEIVE THIS. HY MANDEL.

She put in the call to Hy Mandel and did not reverse the charges. Let Mr. Robin Stone and IBC pay for that too! She heard Hy's voice as the operator informed him long distance was calling. Poor Hy—it was only five in the morning out there. Well, he said to call immediately.

"Maggie!" He had snapped awake immediately. "How fast can you get out here?"

"Hold on," she said easily. "What is the part? And how much does it pay?"

"What is the part? Does Stella Leigh play bit parts? It's the lead—opposite Alfie Knight. They've been shooting around Stella for a week. She thought she had a virus, throwing up all the time. The shmuck didn't even know she was pregnant. Now look, Century is way behind schedule as it is. I've gotten them to give you a straight twenty thousand for the part, plus an option for another picture at terms to be discussed. They'll also pay for a suite at the Beverly Hills Hotel."

"Oh, Hy, how did you ever swing it?"

"To tell the truth, I had almost given up. You and your attitude about no screen test. I raved about you in the O'Neill play, but no one would listen. And yesterday when we got the news about Stella, I tried again. Frankly I didn't think we had a chance, but the director got excited and said you were exactly what he wanted—a new face."

"Who is he? And how does he even know what I look like?"

"Haven't I got your pictures spread all over Hollywood?"

"Oh, Hy—I hope I don't let you down."

"You won't. Listen. In the O'Neill play you didn't exactly give Geraldine Page anything to worry about. A big dramatic stage star you're not. But you've got something: personality, a flash, and *that's* star quality. It doesn't always take talent to be a star, but it takes some intangible thing. I think you got it. I remember when Ava Gardner came out here–she was just a kid, but she had that same something you've got. The way she moved. You remind me of her. That's what I told the director."

"Oh Lord," she laughed. "That poor man–he's going to be disappointed."

"Nah, wait till he sees you. And he's about the hottest director in town right now. He just finished a smash picture and Century nabbed him for Alfie: Adam Bergman."

"Adam!"

"You know him?"

"I worked with him once, way back, in a little-theater group. Oh, Hy, I'm so thrilled."

"Listen, can you get here tonight? It would give you all day Sunday to read the script and get set. Monday they want you right away for wardrobe and makeup tests. I'll make the reservation at the hotel out here."

"Yes! Yes! I can leave today."

"Okay. As soon as you get the flight, wire me the number and the time of your arrival. I'll meet you."

She hung up and tried to assemble her thoughts. She felt exhilarated. She would see Adam again! She was delighted about that. But she was even more delighted to be walking out on Mr. Robin Stone.

Robin returned to his office after viewing the saucer tape. The more he thought about the show, the more he was convinced that it should go on in September and be the first of a series of a new type of show. He could make it a happening. That was it! He got up and paced his office. A *Happening*–that would be the title! If he could only sell Gregory on it–but he needed some other "Happening" ideas to throw at him at the same time. He thought about Christie Lane: What was the chemistry that had suddenly turned him into a national idol? Why hadn't he been an idol five years ago when he was doing the same songs in saloons?

It would make a great hour. *The Happening of Christie Lane.* He'd do interviews with nightclub owners who had played him when he was a second-rater, interview his "gofors," Christie's family—he had to have some kind of a family—even interview that awful Ethel Evans he was going with. And there had to be all kinds of interesting characters connected with his past.

He put his plan into action by making an unofficial visit to the penthouse floor the following morning.

"Robin—without realizing it, you've come up with just the bait we need!" Gregory's voice crackled with enthusiasm. "We're in the middle of a six-lawyer hassle trying to get Christie to sign a new contract. He's playing it cute, but if we tell him we'll do an hour special on him with you moderating it, Robin it's—" He stopped, at a loss for complimentary adjectives. "Don't say a word to anyone about this. Especially Dan. Let me talk to Christie myself. Of course you won't mind if I pretend this comes right from the top of my head. I'll throw it in at lunch tomorrow. I'm even going to have the slob and his lawyers meet with me and my lawyers in the private dining room. I'll tell him no network has ever done this for a star—and they haven't either! We'll make this the first Happening and let the saucer special follow."

Three days later the trades carried the news that Christie Lane had signed a new five-year deal with IBC. The following day Gregory sent for Robin and Danton Miller and outlined the idea of the special.

Dan listened carefully. Robin watched his reactions. He was positive Dan remembered that he had suggested a Christie Lane show for the series. But Gregory was acting as if the idea had suddenly struck him a few days ago. Dan wasn't fooled. Robin knew that. But Dan would have to play the game and go along; the Cheshire smile appeared, he nodded approvingly. Then a slight frown appeared, signaling that his thoughts had run into an obstacle.

"I think the conception is brilliant, Gregory, especially as it has locked Christie in for IBC. But I'm just wondering if Robin is the man to moderate the show. No offense, Robin. It's just that your image doesn't actually go with divulging the life of a man like Christie Lane. We need a top star to present Christie—a

Danny Thomas, or Red Skelton. Someone who'd have empathy with him."

Gregory was caught off guard. It made sense. Dan's smile was openly victorious. Robin leaned forward. His expression was bland and his voice even. "I disagree."

Dan's smile remained fixed. His voice was patronizing. "I'm sorry. But as President of Network Television, I know a little more of what appeals to the public than a newsman who spends half the year in Europe."

Robin didn't smile. "I agree that you know about programming. But I think you know absolutely nothing about human nature. You put on a star with Christie Lane and you rob him of the spotlight. It becomes the Danny Thomas or Red Skelton show featuring Christie Lane. It is to be *his* show, about *him*, with no one overshadowing him in any way."

Gregory stood up. "He's absolutely right, Dan! Put on another star as emcee and you have another variety show. This is the first show of a series I want Robin to do."

Dan nodded tightly, then turned to Robin. "Lay low on the romance angle," he warned.

"The public wants romance," Robin answered.

"His romance won't bear close scrutiny," Dan said.

"It'll only make him more colorful," Robin insisted.

"No romance!" Dan snapped. "Besides, the public isn't interested in Christie's love life."

Gregory interrupted. "You're wrong again, Dan. Christie has to have a girl. Personally I'm always suspicious of a man who is over forty and has never been married. With Christie it's understandable–he's always been a gypsy. But we need the girl angle now. Who is she and what's wrong with her?"

"Ethel Evans," Dan said. "She used to work in publicity for us. She's one step removed from a hooker."

"Can't we find some other girl?" Gregory asked. "Why not give him a lot of girls? Hire beautiful models, link him with several."

"Ethel would never stand for it," Dan said. "And if you're going to use girls, you have to use her too. The public has read too much about her."

"What's she doing now, besides laying him?" Gregory asked.

Dan laughed. "Believe it or not, she's his personal press agent!"

"Fine," Robin interrupted. "Let's make her just that in the special. Every star has a Girl Friday!"

Dan nodded slowly. "It's an angle -it sure as hell would whitewash everything. We can't dismiss her from his life; she's been in too many fan magazines with him as it is."

Robin smiled. "Fine. Now it's your problem to make Christie Lane buy it."

Dan's laugh was ugly. "Oh, he'll buy it—but will Ethel?"

TWENTY-TWO

THE PRESENCE OF DANTON MILLER at the Hotel Astor somehow seemed to emphasize the shoddiness of the room. Ethel stared at a stain on the carpet and wondered why Christie always wound up with one of the rattiest suites in the place. Probably because he always asked for the one that cost the least. And there was Dan, incongruously elegant, sitting in a faded club chair. And Christie, oblivious of the expression on Dan's face when he had seen the suite, sat puffing away at a cigar. Ethel was coiled tight as a spring. Her suspicions had been aroused when Dan casually phoned and said he'd drop by to talk over the mechanics of the special. Dan wasn't the type to just "drop by." And what was all this crap about "mechanics"? It was going to be Christie's life—his friends, the people he knew on the way up. His Happening! That's all she had been hearing for the past two weeks. Christie acted like he was being immortalized. But she could understand his excitement. As star of *The Christie Lane Show,* he appeared in a format. He sang songs, played in sketches, introduced guest stars. But the Happening was *him.* Everyone on it would be talking about *him,* no buildups for Hollywood guests—just *him!* The "gofors" were even springing for new suits. And Agnes kept dropping gentle hints. Oh, she didn't expect to *really* be on it, she claimed, "but when all my friends kid me about being a camp follower, I just tell them I'd rather be a tiny part of Christie's life than the star in anyone else's." Christie hadn't given her the nod yet, but Ethel sensed he'd give in. And gradually, Ethel had even been caught in the general excitement. She started a rigid diet and bought two dresses to wear on the show.

But the full impact of her own importance on the show never really occurred to her until Danton Miller "casually dropped by."

Ethel sat and listened silently as Dan spoke about the special. To Ethel's amazement, his enthusiasm matched Christie's. Everything he said whetted Christie's appetite, inflated his ego. As he talked, the event of Christie's Happening took on the proportions of an Academy Award feature. It had to win the Emmy. When he got to the "mechanics" her eyes narrowed. And as she listened, her worst suspicions were realized. All the fancy footwork was just a cover-up. Dan's prime objective was to de-emphasize her —throw a smoke screen around the real role she played in his life. She couldn't believe it! She listened as Dan casually explained about the models they would hire to act as Christie's dates. The debutante who had already agreed to attend the opening of Aqueduct with him. The great shots they'd get with Christie visiting her father's stables.

"It gives you another dimension," Dan was saying. "Christie Lane is not just everyone's Uncle Harry—beautiful girls are attracted to him, debutantes adore him. We've even dug up a poetess and we'll show the two of you browsing around Doubleday's. Christie Lane is erudite! Of course Ethel will play an important role on the show. We'll have shots of her handling your mail, on the phone making your appointments—"

Ethel fastened her eyes to a sun spot that was working its way across the faded rug. This was the final humiliation. Lumping her with the "gofors." But when you got down to it, what else was she? They serviced him by running errands, she serviced him in bed. They even earned the same kind of money. For the first time in her life she felt defeated. She even lost the will to fight. Maybe it was Dan's supercilious manner, maybe it was the suite, but suddenly she felt as shabby as the soot-stained drapes that hung limply on the grayish windows. She suddenly saw herself through Danton Miller's eyes, and she wanted to run! Oh God, what had happened to fat little Ethel Evanski who sat on a stoop in Hamtramck and had the dream? How had she turned into Ethel Evans who sat in a smoke-filled suite at the Astor listening to Danton Miller evasively and politely plotting to alibi her presence in Christie's life? How had it all happened? She had only wanted to be someone—was that so wrong? She wanted to burst into tears, lunge at Danton Miller, scratch that snobbish smile off his face. . . . How could he sit there and look so impeccable and spotless? Who the hell was he to intimate she wasn't good enough to be Christie's girl? Dan had slept with her. Why hadn't it soiled him and his goddam black suit? But she remained silent. Because everything Dan said made sense. With the models, the debutante and the poetess, it *would* make a better show. And to Christie the show was all that mattered. That was one argument she could never win. Oddly enough, she didn't care what anyone in the business thought. They would all know it was a cover-up. But for the first time she thought of her mother and father, and even Helga. In their eyes, she was "engaged" to Christie Lane. How would it look when they saw Christie with all the glamour girls, and fat little Ethel Evanski sitting on the sideline with the "hired help"? She fastened her eyes to the sun spot on the rug. She didn't dare look up. Her throat was tight and she was dangerously close to tears. Christie's lusterless eyes were objective and thoughtful. Dan was still going strong, coming on for a big flash finish. Then he leaned forward. "Well, Christie, what do you think?"

Christie bit off a piece of his cigar and spat it on the floor. "I think it stinks."

Ethel looked up. Dan was too surprised to answer.

"What is this shit with me and the debutante or a poet? Everyone knows Ethel is my girl."

Ethel's lips parted in amazement. The slob was actually sticking up for her!

Dan shrugged. "Of course you go with Ethel. I know it, and you know it. But we've all done a lot of thinking about this Happening and the conclusion is unanimous. They think it will make a more exciting show if you are seen with many girls instead of one."

"Are we doing a glamour show, or the Happening of Christie Lane?" he asked.

"It's better for the ratings if we can combine them both."

"My show is in the top five, right? And it's not because of models or debutantes—it's *me!*"

Dan nodded. "But, Christie, let's not forget you do have big-name guest stars on your show, pretty girls for the commercials, and an occasional girl singer to do a duet with you."

"What about Ethel?" Christie's voice was gravel-hard.

"Ethel is very attractive," Dan said quickly. "As a matter of fact, Ethel, I've never seen you look better." His smile was indulgent. She answered it with a baleful glance.

Christie ignored the byplay. "So?" he demanded.

"We're afraid of scandal magazines. So far we've been lucky —but just let one of them start with Ethel's love life, and they'll all leap on the wagon."

"I'd sue them," Christie said. "She's been with no one but me for almost a year. I can prove it."

"I'm afraid you'd only be proving their point. Yes, Ethel's been *with* you—living with you! That's why they figured the 'girl Friday' was such a good gimmick. It would explain *why* she is with you so much."

"Wait a minute!" Christie waved the cigar. "Who the fuck is *they?*"

Dan took out the cigarette case. "Let's put it this way, Christie. Robin Stone is *also* part of this show. If the scandal magazines hit at him on his first show because of Ethel, he could lose his blue-chip sponsor on the entire series. You've got to remember there is a large world outside of New York, Chicago and Los Angeles—a world where people go to church every Sunday, get married and celebrate golden anniversaries. Those people love you. You come into their living rooms. You can't blatantly state: 'This is the girl I live with—take it or else.' "

Dan took advantage of Christie's silence, and forged on with renewed emphasis. "No matter how you look at it, Christie, it adds up to this: you can't take the chance of acknowledging Ethel as your girl on the special."

"Okay. She won't be my girl," Christie said quietly. "She'll be my wife."

Dan's face lost its usual bland expression. His lips parted—but no words came. Ethel leaned forward—there had to be a catch!

Christie nodded, as if to affirm the decision to himself. "Yeah, you heard me. I'm gonna marry Ethel."

Dan had recovered from his initial shock and managed a weak attempt at his feline smile. Christie sat back as if the matter was settled, but Ethel sensed the battle had just begun. Dan was marshaling his forces, readying for another attack.

It came immediately. "Funny." Dan's tone was almost melancholy. "I had you down in my book as one of the great romantics."

"A what?" Christie asked.

"A man who would only love one woman all his life. I was positive that's the way it was with you and Amanda. The night she died I was even afraid you might cancel the show. But you're a pro. I knew how you felt, but you realized that life goes on. When a man loses the only thing that matters, he finds a substitute–a temporary replacement."

For the first time Ethel understood the temporary insanity of blind fury that caused murder. She wanted to leap at Dan's throat. But this was no time for her to come on tough–not as long as Christie was carrying the ball. She clutched the arm of the sofa until her knuckles went white. And dredging her resources for a final gust of control, she managed a voice as cautious as his own: "You seem to forget, dear Danton, that Amanda had left Chris for Ike Ryan. She died as Mrs. Ike Ryan, not as Christie's girl."

Dan's tone was conciliatory. "Ah, but the greatest lovers of all are the lovers who lose and go on loving. To me Christie Lane is that kind of a man."

Christie jumped up. "What is this bullshit? Is that your idea of a great lover? To me it sounds like a number-one shmuck! A shmuck who sits around weeping for a broad that walked out on him! Oh no, Danny boy, I'm Christie Lane. I'm a big one, Buster! I came up the hard way–I've gotten real kicks in the gut. One little blond broad is no earth-shattering event in *my* life." He walked over to Ethel and took her hand. "Take a good look, Mr. Miller–this is a real broad. A great broad. Sure, Ethel and I started out as just two people on the town together. But after a few dates I forgot I ever knew Amanda."

Dan's smile was sad. "I reread the *Life* story just the other day, and it really got me. Especially when you said Amanda was the only girl you ever thought about marrying. The girl you wanted to have a child with." He sighed. "But it's really too bad, the Amanda thing was going to make a great part of your special."

"What has Amanda got to do with my special?" Christie asked.

Dan's voice was low and intense: "We were going to show blowups of the pictures you took together for *Life*. Get a clip of Amanda doing the commercial–and use the tape of that great moment when you sang 'Mandy' to her. Remember–when we cut to the wings and took a close-up of her face listening to you?" Dan shook his head sadly. "Can you see it? There wouldn't be a dry eye in the audience. Every newspaper in the country would write about it–the special with the love story of the century. Amanda–the only girl in Christie's life. And when she married someone else, he bore her no ill will. But when she died, a little bit of him died with her. The public will lap it up. That explains the models, the debutante–because after Amanda, there can't be any *one* girl in Christie Lane's life. Then, as you sing, the announcer's voice will say, 'Women love to listen to Christie sing –but Christie will always sing his love songs to a girl who can never hear them.' Then we show you on the town, proving that you're trying to forget. Christie, the public adores a lover; they'll dismiss the fact that she married Ike Ryan. They were only married for a short time. Tell me, how many girls do you recall being with Sinatra? There've been plenty–but the fans think he still sings only to Ava Gardner. The lyrics take on a stronger meaning–the world loves a lover, especially if he's lost someone. We can say that Ethel Evans is your most constant companion, that she cared for Amanda too–they were friends and worked on the show together, she understands the loss you've gone through. Christie, can't you see it?"

Christie's expression was bland. "You should be a movie writer, Dan." Then his voice went hard. "What kind of shit-kicking show do you expect me to do? Is *this* the Christie Lane Happening? The story of a man who came up the hard way, who was still just a second-rater when he hit his fortieth birthday? Everyone wrote him off–and two years later he made it big! *There's* your story–the heart of it–right there! That's the Christie Lane *Happening*. Get it? My Happening–about *me!* If the day ever comes when I need to rattle a dead girl's bones to have a show, then I'll sell shit! But right now I'm selling my talent, my life. And neither you nor Mr. Robin Stone is going to dictate to me what I am. I am me! Get it? *Me!* And I'm marrying the only broad I care about–Ethel Evans."

Dan walked to the door. "I'm sorry. Perhaps I just took the *Life* story too seriously–all that talk about how much you wanted a baby with Amanda, so it would look like her, be like her. . . ."

"Bullshit!" Christie yelled. "You bet your ass I want a kid. I want a son. I want to give him everything I didn't have. And Ethel and I will have one hell of a kid together!"

Dan bowed slightly. "May I wish you both happiness. I think it's wonderful. Christie, after listening to you, I've changed my mind. You and Ethel–well, one might almost say it's a marriage made in heaven." Then he left the room.

Christie stared after the closed door for a moment. Then he turned and started toward the bedroom. Without glancing at Ethel, he said, "Call Lou Goldberg. Tell him to come to town. Call Kenny and Eddie. Tell them to find out about blood tests and all that jazz. Call the mayor. See if we can get him to marry us." He disappeared into the bedroom.

Ethel sat on the couch. She couldn't believe it. He really meant it! She was going to be *Mrs.* Christie Lane. She looked up as Christie came from the bedroom, carrying his topcoat.

"Well, what are you sitting there for?" he asked. "Don't you want to get married?" Then as she nodded mutely, he snapped his fingers. "Well, move it–start making the arrangements."

She leaped from the couch and with one convulsive dash landed in his arms. "Oh, Christie." Her tears were genuine. "You really mean it?"

He seemed embarrassed as he gently broke her embrace. "Sure, sure. Now make the calls, doll." He started for the door.

"But where are you going?"

He paused. Then with a weak smile he said, "I'm gonna buy us wedding rings."

When Christie left the Astor he walked uptown. He reached Forty-seventh Street, and headed toward the block known as jewelers' row. Several guys he knew had booths—the Edelmans always gave him good bargains when he sprung for gold cuff links for the writers and crew at Christmas. He saw them through the window as he passed their store. He waved and wondered why he hadn't stopped. But he continued to walk east. He found himself heading toward Fifth Avenue. His pace quickened as he slowly became aware of his subconscious destination. He broke into a run. By the time he reached Fiftieth Street he was short of breath. He hesitated for a moment, then slowly walked up the stone steps of St. Patrick's Cathedral.

Christie had been born a Catholic. He accepted this fact the way a person accepts the color of his skin. He didn't practice the religion, he couldn't even remember his catechism though he had known it by heart when he took his first communion. But with his parents' divorce his formal religious training had come to an abrupt end. His mother had remarried—the guy was a Baptist and his half brother was raised as a Baptist. Or was it Methodist? He hadn't gotten along with his stepfather and had left home at fourteen. Now, as he stood in the soft darkness of St. Patrick's Cathedral, all the forgotten rituals slowly came back from his memory. Unconsciously he dipped his fingers in the holy water and made the sign of the cross. He walked past tiers and tiers of burning candles and gazed at the Stations of the Cross. He saw a woman enter one of the small confessionals. Suddenly he had an overwhelming urge to make a confession. He approached a confessional nervously. Then he stopped. It had been so long. The last time he had gone was when he was fourteen, after the first time he got laid. He had hoped that the act of confession might prevent him from getting the clap. He had been so eager to get into the girl, he hadn't realized what a beast she was until it was over. But what could you expect in a doorway for fifty cents? A woman came out of a confessional and crossed to a pew. He watched her kneel and take out her rosary. Her eyes closed, her lips moved as she fingered each bead. All he had to do was go in, kneel: "Forgive me, Father, for I have sinned." He walked into the confessional, knelt and mumbled, "Forgive me, Father, for I have sinned."

"Yes, my son?"

Dimly he saw the shadowy outline of the priest behind the screen.

"I have committed many mortal sins," Christie began. "I have lived with a woman who is not my wife. I have taken the Lord's name in vain."

"Do you intend to make amends?"

"Yes, Father. I am going to marry this woman and have a child and I will–" He stopped. He wanted to say, "I will love and cherish her," but the words stuck in his throat. He jumped up and rushed out of the confessional. He walked to the front of the church. He knew there must be a side exit somewhere. His gaze wandered along the wall where the rows and rows of lighted candles wavered in the dim light. Several people were kneeling before the Virgin Mary. He wandered down the side of the church toward the back. Under each statue was a blaze of lighted candles. It looked like a sea of light–each flame representing a personal prayer. Suddenly he passed an altar that was dark. It took him a moment to realize that only one solitary flame flickered–*one* candle among two trays of unlit candles. It glowed, defiant and proud in its pathetic loneliness. It didn't seem fair–the only saint in the whole place who wasn't doing any business. He looked at the plaque. St. Andrew.

He looked around to make sure no one was watching, then he slipped to his knees. The stone steps were hard. He put his head in his hands, then he looked up. "Okay, Andy, old pal, I'm gonna give you my business. From the look of things you got nothing much to do but listen to me. This one lone candle you've got going for you is almost burned out, so you probably already attended to it." He stood up. Was he nutty or something? Talking like it was real, talking to plaster. . . . Besides, there were no saints. They were just radical nuts who got killed for a cause. And what did it all matter in the end? They were dust and gone, and people were still sinning and fighting and dying. Like Amanda. Amanda. . . . He stopped and the tears came to his eyes. He put his face in his hands and sobbed quietly. "Oh, Mandy," he whispered, "I didn't mean a thing I said in that room. Oh, dear God, if there is a heaven and You are listening, tell her I didn't mean it. Mandy, can you hear me, doll? I love you. I never loved no one else. I never will. And it doesn't matter that you didn't love me. I loved you and that's all that counts. Maybe that's why I'm marrying Ethel. I loved you and you went off with someone and it hurt. I guess I kind of remembered it today and suddenly I thought—why should I hurt Ethel? I don't love her, but she loves me. So why not make her happy? So you see, doll, indirectly, you're the reason Ethel is gonna be happy. And when I have my kid, then I'll be happy. Why is it like this, Mandy? Why does Ethel love me and I loved you, and oh shit—excuse me doll—but why can't people love together? But I'm gonna give my kid everything. . . . And look, Mandy, maybe when I walk outa here I'll think I'm crazy, but right now, this very second, I believe you can hear me. And I believe this St. Andrew is with you, and maybe there is something after we kick off. I can't start being a knee bender and going to Mass, but I'll tell you this—I'll raise my kid as a Catholic, and I'll never say a wrong word in front of him. And, doll, I'll never stop loving you. I think you know it, don't you; Mandy? You're not down in the earth in a box. You're up there somewhere—and you're happy. I can feel it. Jesus—I *can* feel it!" He paused and for a moment her lovely face seemed so close and she was smiling. He smiled too.

"Okay, doll, take care of yourself up there. And who knows? If there *is* a second time around, maybe we'll make it together." He shut his eyes. "St. Andrew, help me be a good father. And give me a good healthy son." He stood up, then suddenly he knelt again. "And by the way, thank the Head Man up there for all the luck He's thrown my way. And pray for my intentions."

He stood up and dropped a quarter in the box, took a taper and lit a candle. Now two candles flickered together. But oddly enough the one extra light seemed to make the tiers of gray unlit candles more prominent. He gazed at the statue of St. Andrew. "I know how you feel—like I did when I played to empty nightclubs with maybe two tables taken. I used to look at those white cloths on all the empty tables and go snow-blind." He reached into his pocket and took out a dollar, jammed it into the box and lit four more candles. It still looked meager compared to the other saints. Christie shrugged. "What the hell, I'm not gonna be chintzy." He took out a twenty-dollar bill and stuffed it in the box. Then he studiously lit every candle. He stood back and proudly surveyed the effect. "Andy, old boy–when them priests come around to check the house tonight, are they gonna be surprised–you're gonna have the biggest Nielsen of them all!" Then he walked back to the wholesale district and bought two gold wedding bands.

The wedding received enormous press and television coverage. Even the events leading up to the nuptials made news. Lou Goldberg took over the second floor of Danny's and threw a tremendous "bachelor" party for Christie. Every male star who was in New York attended. The columnists printed some of the jokes told at the dinner. Television comics pulled good-natured gags about it. But there was not one joke pulled about Ethel. They all sensed that the slightest stab could blow the lid off the pressure cooker, which held Ethel's past.

But Ethel had several bad moments. The first hurdle was the arrival of her mother and father a week before the wedding. Christie sprung for a double room at the Astor. Ethel didn't argue on the "room" bit. Her parents had never been to a hotel, they probably wouldn't know what to do with a suite anyway. As it was, she had to warn her mother *not* to make the beds. She had been stunned when she met them at Penn Station. (Of course they wouldn't fly! The idea of New York was traumatic enough!) But she couldn't believe that these two tiny people were her folks. Had they shrunk?

They were awed with the Astor, speechless at meeting Christie, and viewed the city itself in terrified fascination. They insisted she take them to the top of the Empire State Building. (She had never been there herself.) And then there was the boat ride around New York. They *had* to see the Statue of Liberty. Next on the list–sure they had a list; half of Hamtramck had worked on it–was Radio City. The picture was okay, but to sit through that stage show! They adored it. She was relieved when the "gofors" took over with Grant's Tomb, the hansom ride in Central Park and the trip across the George Washington Bridge. At first she was volubly grateful to them until it suddenly hit her as the future Mrs. Christie Lane: they were *her* "gofors" too. Meanwhile, she used this respite to cover the stores in search of a suitable wedding dress. It had to be on the conservative side. It was wild—Christie's sudden decision that they get married by a priest. But it was a good sign—he really meant it to stick. As far as she was concerned, she would have been married by a witch doctor as long as it was legal. She had talked to Father Kelly—no, she didn't have to convert, just promise to raise the children as Catholics. *Children!* He'd get one child. *One!* But not until she was ready. She was thirty-two and had spent too many years hunting bargain clothes and watching the right side of the menu. For the first time she was going to have a wonderful wardrobe, take massages, go to the best beauty parlors. She wasn't about to spend six months in maternity clothes. Not right now. Not when she was finally getting everything she ever wanted.

They were married the first week in May in a double ring ceremony at St. Patrick's Cathedral, with her folks, Lou Goldberg, the "gofors" and Aggie in attendance. Christie wanted it that way, and until the final "I do" was said, she wasn't going to argue a single point. When the ceremony was over, everyone kissed everyone. Suddenly she noticed that Christie had slipped away. She saw him crossing to the other side of the church. She followed him curiously, stood at a distance and saw him kneel at an altar. The nut was lighting *every* candle! And he put twenty dollars in the box! She returned to the wedding group without his seeing her. She hadn't realized how much he cared for her. For Christie to part with twenty bucks—it had to be love. But then, a lot of men who were penurious changed after marriage. This was a good omen.

Christie took everyone to dinner, and then they all went to the station to see her folks off. That night when she went to Christie's suite at the Astor, she was registered at the front desk for the first time.

She made no comment about spending her honeymoon at the Astor. Christie was immersed in the special and then they were going to Vegas for six weeks. That was the time to make all the future plans. She'd tell him to deposit five thousand in her checking account every month—maybe ten. After all, he had a great new deal at IBC for next season. And she would call a renting agent before she left and have them line up a duplex on Park Avenue.

She spent the first week of her married life sitting in the darkened theater watching Christie tape the Happening. Her part with Christie would be location shots: restaurants, theaters. Right now they were re-creating the atmosphere of his TV show so he could sing a few songs. Ethel had quickly contacted a renting agent, an elegant woman named Mrs. Rudin, who arrived at rehearsal one day with floor plans for several excellent apartments. Christie ambled over during a break. Ethel introduced him to Mrs. Rudin. He listened quietly while Ethel explained. Then he clamped his teeth on his cigar. "Listen, lady, roll all them blue prints up and forget it. Ethel and I are plenty comfortable at the Astor."

Ethel's face burned with silent rage. She waited until the woman left. Then she cornered him backstage. "How dare you do that?" she demanded.

"Do what?"

"Embarrass me in front of a renting agent."

"Then don't bring them around and you won't be embarrassed."

"But we have to get an apartment."

"What for?"

"Christie, do you expect me to always live at the Astor with your two wardrobe trunks in the living room, one dinky closet for both of us, one bathroom–"

"Listen, I seen the joint you and Lillian shared. That wasn't exactly the Ritz."

"I wasn't Mrs. Christie Lane then."

"Well *Mr.* Christie Lane is happy at the Astor."

She decided this was not the place to fight it out. She had the whole summer to wear him down. "I'm going to Saks to buy a bathing suit for Vegas. Oh, by the way, I want a checking account."

"So open one."

"I need something to put in it."

"You've been earning two hundred a week before we were

married. I was talking it over with Lou. He'll still send you the same check each week. You can keep doing my publicity–you got nothing else to do anyhow."

"But what about my spending money?"

"Two hundred bucks isn't exactly chicken feed. Besides, now that you don't have to kick in your half of the rent to Lillian you'll have more money. Two hundred a week is plenty of spending money. Some families of eight live on that."

She sank into a seat in the empty theater. Suddenly she felt as if she had been tricked–like hitting an oil well and waking up the next morning to find it had run dry. And when the special was finished and they left for Vegas, the feeling persisted. Bellboys and motel managers called her Mrs. Lane. Other than that her life hadn't changed. Actually her life had been better *before* the marriage. There had always been a few nights a week that belonged to her–nights where she could sleep in the privacy of her apartment with Lillian. Now she spent every second with Christie, the "gofors" and Agnes. And in the fall, back in New York, it would still be the Copa bar, Jilly's and dinners with the "gofors." But she was damned if she'd go back to the Astor.

She brought it up to Christie one night after the show. "What's wrong with the Astor?" he demanded.

"I don't want to live there."

"Where do you want to live?"

"In a nice apartment, with a dining room, a terrace and *two* bathrooms!"

"All those rooms for just the two of us? I took a house in Hollywood once, but Eddie, Kenny and Aggie lived with me. And even then we had too much space. Look, once we have a kid, then we'll talk about apartments. Sure, with my kid I'll want a dining room. I want him to learn right, but as long as there's just you and me, it'll be a hotel suite."

The following night she didn't wear her diaphragm.

TWENTY-THREE

ROBIN SAW THE PICTURE OF MAGGIE in the morning paper while he was having his coffee. He read the caption: MAGGIE STEWART, CENTURY'S NEWEST YOUNG STAR, IN NEW YORK TODAY TO DO LOCATION SHOTS FOR "THE TARGET."

Her makeup was a little more pronounced, her hair was longer, but she looked great. Suddenly he had an insatiable urge to see her. He placed a call to the Plaza. She was registered, but her room didn't answer. He left word that he had called.

He was in the middle of a meeting when his secretary quietly entered the room and placed a note before him: "Miss Stewart on the phone." He waved her off and went on with the meeting. It was five o'clock before he had the chance to return her call.

"Hi!" She sounded impersonal and cheerful.

"How's the big movie star?"

"Beat. I'm playing a high-fashion model whose life is in jeopardy. In the opening scene an attempt is made on my life while I'm shooting fashions in Central Park. Naturally, in true Hollywood form, we're shooting it last. That's why I'm here."

"It sounds exciting."

"I hope it is. As soon as this scene is finished they'll start to edit and score the picture."

"Have you another lined up?"

"I've had several offers but my agent wants me to wait until this one comes out. It's a gamble. If I'm good I'll get much more money and offers of better parts. But if I flop, I'll lose the things that I could grab now."

"It sounds like a rough decision," Robin said.

"I'm a gambler," she said. "I'm going to wait."

"Good girl. By the way, how long will you be in town?"

"Just three days."

"Want to have a hamburger with me at P.J.'s?" It had slipped out before he realized it.

"Why not? Room service takes forever. Just give me time to get out of eight layers of pancake and into a shower."

"Seven o'clock all right?"

"Fine. I'll meet you there." She hung up.

Robin stared at the phone thoughtfully. She hadn't even given him the chance to offer to pick her up. Was she intentionally playing it cool? Then that meant she still had ideas. . . . He quickly put in a call to Jerry Moss.

At seven thirty they were still waiting for her at P.J's. "Maybe she's standing me up," Robin said with a smile.

Jerry looked at him curiously. "What's with you and this girl?"

"Absolutely nothing. We're just friends–almost old acquaintances, you might say."

"Then why are you afraid to be alone with her?"

"Afraid?"

"Last time she was in, you made damn sure I was with you when you met her plane."

Robin sipped his beer. "Look, chum, she was once Andy Parino's girl. They had just broken up when she came here that time. I didn't want him to think I was horning in on him. That's probably why I asked you along. I don't recall."

"Oh, that explains everything. And tonight I'm here to protect you from Adam Bergman?"

Robin's glance was direct and curious. "Adam Bergman?"

"This season's bright young director," Jerry explained. "He did that show that won all the awards on Broadway last year. I forget the name–about a lesbian and a fag. Mary and I walked out after the first act, but he's the new sensation." Robin didn't answer. "Funny," Jerry went on, "maybe I'm old-fashioned but I like plays that have a plot–you know, beginning, middle and end. But today–" He stopped, as he heard the buzz that went through the room. Everyone's attention was focused on Maggie, who was walking toward them. Robin stood up. She pretended to remember Jerry, but he was positive she did not. She did not apologize for being late. She ordered a bowl of chili and rummaged through her bag for a cigarette.

"I'd offer you one of mine, but I've given them up," Robin said.

"Then you'll have to get me a pack, I forgot mine."

For some reason it pleased Jerry to see Robin jump up and go to the cigarette machine. He returned with the cigarettes, opened the pack and held a match for her.

"When did you give them up?" she asked.

"Two days ago."

"Why?"

"Just wanted to prove I could kick them."

She nodded as if she completely understood. When she finished the chili she said, "I'd like a beer, then I'm afraid I'll have to leave. Early call tomorrow."

Robin ordered the beer. A mob was queuing up at the door. Suddenly Robin jumped up. "Excuse me–I see a friend of mine."

They watched him go to the door and greet a couple who were standing in line. In a few minutes he returned, bringing them with him.

"Maggie Stewart, Jerry Moss; this is Dip Nelson and Pauli–" He turned to the girl. "I'm sorry, Pauli. I don't remember your last name."

"It's Nelson now."

"Congratulations." Robin signaled for some chairs. "I think we can all squeeze in here."

"I just want to eat and run," Pauli said as she sank into a chair. "Man, am I tired. We've been rehearsing all day–we've got only three weeks before our break-in date."

"We're doing a nightclub act," Dip explained. "We're breaking it in at a country club in Baltimore. No money, just to iron out the kinks. Then our first big date is July Fourth weekend at the Concord. We get five big ones for the one night."

"That's big money, isn't it?" Robin asked.

"Yeah, but the act is costing us over twenty-five thousand."

"Twenty-five thousand!" Robin's amazement was real.

"Why do you think we rehearse eight hours a day at Nola

Studios?" Pauli demanded. "Hey, waiter, two chilis, two cheeseburgers and two Cokes."

"See, we have special material," Dip explained. "Choreography, all the jazz. Pauli's a good dancer and it breaks up the singing bit. We've got two weeks booked in Vegas at fifteen thousand a week. That'll get us more than even. Then Reno, and in September the Persian Room at the Plaza. That's what really counts—the New York reviews."

"Why the big interest in a nightclub act?" Robin asked.

"Did you see my last two pictures?" Dip asked.

"I certainly did."

"Well, then you must know they were bombs."

Robin grinned. "No, I can pretty much tell what will go on TV, but I go to movies to unwind."

"Well, you musta seen the grosses in *Variety,*" Pauli cut in.

"I don't read the picture news."

"Look, I know the picture business," Dip said. "I may not know much about anything else, but when my agent comes to me with an offer for an independent at only one hundred thou, I said, 'Dip—now's the time to go!' "

"Well, with that kind of money you have no worries." Robin wanted to turn the conversation into more general areas to include Maggie and Jerry.

"Are you kidding!" Dip said. "I bought her old man and old lady a house."

"A dumperino," Pauli said. "A small place in Los Angeles. Don't act like maybe you set them up in Truesdale. . . ."

"But I bought it outright, didn't I? Forty-nine thousand isn't chopped liver. So no matter what ever happens to us, they'll be fine. And I bought us a house—you should see it. The furniture and decorator set me back a hundred G's. Right in Bel Air. I hated to leave it. But you got to leave before you cool off. We'll be a smash with our act and Hollywood will be on its knees, and the Big Dipper will be right back on top."

"With Pauli right beside you," she said.

"Right with me. Like I said when we got married. We're a team—for keeps."

"See, I won't take a screen test," Pauli confided to the table at large.

"I agree." It was the first word Maggie had said.

Pauli looked at her curiously. "Oh, you in the business?"

"She's playing the lead in Alfred Knight's new movie," Robin explained.

"Oh." Pauli looked at Maggie as if seeing her for the first time. "Yeah, that's right, you're the girl who's having the big affair with Adam Bergman."

Maggie's expression never changed. It was Dip who looked horrified.

For a few moments there was an uncomfortable silence, but Pauli was completely occupied with her hamburger. When she popped the final morsel into her mouth, she said, "Get the check, Dip, I got to get some sleep. We got another eight-hour rehearsal session tomorrow."

Robin smiled. "It's my pleasure to buy the hamburgers. Just think, I'll be able to say I knew *the* Pauli Nelson before she became a star."

She turned and faced him squarely. "Know something? I don't have to take this shit from you. Who in hell are you anyway? Dip made me watch the *In Depth* show. Big deal! I noticed they kicked you off it–another guy's doing it now."

"Pauli!" Dip grabbed her arm. "Robin, I'm sorry. And listen –I *am* sorry you lost *In Depth*. Got anything in the works?"

Robin smiled. "A new show in the fall, called a Happening."

Dip looked genuinely relieved. "I'm glad, buddy boy. You're like the Big Dipper. They can't keep us down, right? Same network?" When Robin nodded, Dip said, "Well, listen, how well do you know Andy Parino?"

"Quite well."

"That's where you can help me, old pal of mine!" Dip flashed his bright smile. "Before we open at the Plaza, if you could swing it so we get interviewed on the *In Depth* show–Pauli and me?"

"If you want it, you've got it."

"No kidding?"

"My word."

Dip stood up. "I'll call you when we get back to town."

When they left the restaurant, Robin took Maggie's arm. "Come on, Jerry and I will walk you home."

"I don't want to walk."

"Jerry, hail a cab for the lady," Robin said.

"Jerry, *don't* hail a cab for the lady," she said, imitating his tone; "the lady has her own car." They suddenly noticed the large limousine that was waiting.

"Thanks for the hamburger and fascinating table talk. I'll try and return the hospitality if you're ever in California."

Jerry watched the car disappear down Third Avenue.

"She really digs you," he said quietly.

"Sure, she's mad about me." Robin's voice was hard.

"No–I mean it. She's an actress, don't forget. And probably a good one, because tonight she was playing one hell of a role."

"What do you mean?"

"She sure wasn't the same girl I met at the airport last February. And no girl changes that much in three months."

"Maybe this Adam what's-his-name has made the difference."

"Maybe."

"Let's cut over to the Lancer Bar and have a drink." Robin said.

"No, I'm cutting down to the station; I can still catch the last train home. If I were you, I'd call Maggie Stewart and ask to buy her a nightcap at the Plaza alone."

"No, thanks."

Jerry stopped. "Tell me, Robin, is she like the cigarettes?"

"I don't get you."

"What in hell are you trying to prove by giving up Maggie Stewart?"

Maggie left town and Robin threw himself into his work. He did four pages on his book every night. Tina St. Claire arrived for a week to promote another picture. He let her move in, enjoyed having her in bed each night, but when she left he felt the same relief at reclaiming his apartment. He worked hard on the Happening series and lost all sense of time or days. And suddenly he stared at his desk calendar and realized that July Fourth was coming up. It fell on a Thursday–that meant a long empty weekend. There wasn't even anyone he particularly wanted to shack up with. Jerry Moss was elated when Robin lethargically agreed to come out to Greenwich. Robin realized it meant an endless round of parties, but they had a swimming pool and he might be able to get in a few rounds of golf.

Maggie's wire arrived July second:

> ARRIVING JULY THIRD TO DO SOME TELEVISION PROMOTION FOR THE PICTURE. DO YOU REALLY THINK ELIZABETH TAYLOR STARTED THIS WAY? WILL BE IN TOWN FOR A FEW DAYS. MAYBE YOU CAN CUE ME ON MY AD LIBS. MAGGIE.

He called Jerry and canceled the weekend. On Wednesday he left his office at five. When he got home he called the Plaza. He learned she had checked in two hours earlier but had left to tape *The Johnny Carson Show*. Well, it was a muggy night, and the weekend stretched ahead. No sweat.

He called her on Thursday. She was out. He left a message and went out and shagged some golf balls.

On Friday he left two messages.

On Saturday he didn't bother to call.

His phone rang Sunday morning at nine. The hell with her! Let *her* spend the day alone. He waited until the exchange picked it up on the third ring. He took a shower, then dialed back his exchange for the message.

A Mr. Jerry Moss had called from Greenwich.

He felt oddly let down. Now, what would Jerry want at nine o'clock on a Sunday morning? He returned the call.

"Are you enjoying yourself in hot sunny New York?" Jerry asked.

"I'm getting a lot of work done."

"You missed a lot of great parties. Rick Russell threw a big one last night. You know who he is—a big wheeler-dealer who puts corporations together. Even has his own airline."

"I can see it all," Robin said. "Outdoors, tents, Japanese lanterns, drunks, mosquitoes."

Jerry laughed. "All of that, plus a friend of yours who was guest of honor: Maggie Stewart."

"What was she doing there?"

"Drinking, dancing, slapping mosquitoes like all of us. Rick Russell is celebrating his fifth divorce. He's not bad-looking, especially when you think of all those millions. Seems they met on the plane coming in from Los Angeles and he's stuck to her ever since. He's sending her to Chicago today in his private plane."

"I like to see a lady travel in style. By the way, Jerry, what did you call me about?"

There was a pause. "Why, I–I thought you'd want to know about Maggie."

"Why?"

"I, well–" Jerry sounded uncomfortable.

"If you thought I cared about her, this would be a rotten play on your part. Trying to give me some lumps, Jerry?"

"Oh no, I know you don't care about the girl," Jerry said quickly.

"Then why waste my time with this call?" And Robin clicked the phone.

He went to a double feature in the afternoon. When he came out it was dark. The streets were empty. Tomorrow the noise of traffic would shriek through the air. But right now the city belonged to him. He stopped at a Nedick's on Third Avenue and had a hot dog. Then he walked aimlessly crosstown. He reached Fifth Avenue and found himself in front of the Plaza.

"Want some fun, mister?" The remark came from a short plump overbleached woman in her forties. She was holding the arm of a skinny red-haired girl who couldn't have been more than nineteen. The young girl was obviously a novice. The older woman shoved her toward Robin. "Fifty bucks, and she has a room."

The girl was wearing a sleazy dress. Her skin was acne-scarred under the heavy makeup. Robin started past them. The blond madam grabbed his arm. "Forty–how's that? Come on, you look like a fellow who needs a little relaxation."

"I'm too relaxed," Robin said and walked away. He hadn't gotten halfway up the block before he was approached by another girl. Not bad-looking either.

"Fifty bucks for a trip to heaven, mister?"

He laughed and continued to walk. Obviously fifty bucks was the going rate. And Central Park South was now their beat. He passed the Hampshire House. Another girl sidled up but he quickened his pace. He suddenly remembered a bookstore on Seventh Avenue that was open at night. He'd buy something light, grab a sandwich and go home and read.

"Want a good time, mister?" He was standing face to face with an Amazon.

She was a mean-looking broad–she had to be over six feet tall. Her dyed jet-black hair was teased into a massive beehive. It was a warm night but she carried a mink stole. Her black eyes were beady, her nose was long and narrow. A big woman . . . big tits. . . . Suddenly a thousand lights seemed to explode in his head. His smile went slack.

She smiled too. "Fifty bucks and I got a room."

"I got a better offer down the street."

She shrugged. "Elsie's breaking in a new one. She's only turned three tricks since she got here. And from what I hear, she still belongs back with the coal miners in Scranton. I can really give you a good time."

"Maybe I should make you pay me," he said. "I'm supposed to be a pretty good stud."

"With me it's women for pleasure, men for business," she said.

"A dike, huh? Well you're an honest cunt, at that."

"And you're a good-looking bastard. Okay, I'll make it forty bucks."

"No favors. I'll pay the full rate. Where's your room?"

"Come with me, lover." She tucked her arm through his and they walked toward Seventh Avenue. She had a room in a dark building on Fifty-eighth Street. It was obvious she didn't live there. From the darkness of the building, it was also obvious that most of the rooms were rented for a similar purpose. The lobby was deserted and a self-service elevator wheezed its way to the third floor. There was a dampness in the hall and the paint was peeling off the small door she opened. "It's not a palace–I call it my work room."

He stepped into the narrow bedroom. A black shade covered a

curtainless window. There was a bed, a sink and a small bathroom with a stall shower and a toilet. The overhead light seemed unnaturally bright. She smiled and methodically began to undress. Everything she wore was designed for her trade. The black lace brassiere with holes that bared the large brown nipples. She wore no pants, just a tight black lacy garter belt that left an ugly red mark against her large white stomach.

"Like it with the black stockings on or off?" she asked.

"Everything off." He hardly recognized the voice as his own as he began undressing quickly.

She took a dirty towel and wiped the bright lipstick off her mouth. Her massive body was amazingly well proportioned. "Hand over the fifty, lover, that's ground rules."

He went through his pants and handed her two twenties and a ten. She tucked it into her purse. "Okay, lover, do anything you like. Just try not to muss the hair or the eyelashes. The evening's young and I'm hoping to turn a few more tricks tonight."

He grabbed her and threw her on the bed. His movements were strong and direct. She whimpered slightly. "Hey, lover–take it easy. What are you trying to prove?"

Just as he reached his climax, he withdrew.

"You didn't have to do that. I'm wearing something," she said.

"I wouldn't chance letting a little bastard get born like this," he muttered.

She looked at her watch. "You did that in three minutes flat. You're entitled to another shot." She leaned over and began to run her tongue along his body. He pushed her away, turned her on her stomach and stabbed into her again.

He kept ramming into her, driven by a fury he did not understand. When he finally rolled off her, she jumped off the bed and went to the sink. She grumbled as she washed her stomach. "Jesus, for a classy-looking guy, you play rough."

He lay on the bed staring vacantly into space. She stood before the sink, a mass of white nudity, and applied her lipstick. "Okay, mister–start moving it. Time to go home to your wife. I bet you don't dare try any of this stuff with her, huh? Just nice ordinary fucking."

"I have no wife," he said tonelessly.

"Well, go home to your mother then–I'll bet you live with her. Guys like you always do."

He leaped up and grabbed her by the hair.

"Hey, take it easy lover–be careful of the hair. I told you, I still got work to do. Now go home to Mommy."

His fist cracked at her jaw. For a fleeting moment, before the pain telegraphed itself, her eyes stared at him in almost childish bewilderment. Then as the pain stabbed through her consciousness her mouth parted with a moan and she dashed toward the bathroom. He caught her by the arm.

"Please," she whimpered. "You know I can't make any noise, it'd bring the cops. Please–let me go."

He grabbed her huge breasts in his hands and put his mouth to them.

"You're biting me," she moaned, struggling to get away. "You've had your fifty bucks' worth!" With a final burst of strength she pushed her knee in his groin and broke away. He came after her. For the first time there was fear in her eyes. "Look, mister," she shouted, "I'll give you back your money! Go home to your mother! Suck *her* breasts!"

"What did you say?"

Sensing she had found his weakness, she lost her fright. She pulled her naked body to its full height. "I know about you mama's boys–you're closet queens, but you want Mama! Do I look like Mama, sonny boy? Well, go home to her. This mama has to work now."

Once again his fist crashed at her jaw. Only this time he did not stop. He kept slamming at her. Blood was streaming from her nose and mouth. A broken bridgework fell to the floor. He felt her jaw crack, and he kept hitting her until he felt pain in his knuckles. He stopped to look at them curiously and she slumped to the floor. He stared at his hand as if it didn't belong to him. It was covered with her blood. He looked at the limp form on the floor. He walked to the bed, lay down, and passed out.

When he opened his eyes, he saw the light on the ceiling and the shadowy bodies of three dead moths who had been lured under the glass. Then he saw the bloody sheets. He sat up and stared curiously at his raw knuckles. Suddenly he saw the massive inert girl on the floor. Oh God–this time it hadn't been just a nightmare. It had actually happened. He got off the bed and approached the enormous limp body. Her lips were grotesquely swollen, a trickle of blood was running out of her mouth, blood from her nose was crusted on her upper lip. He leaned over her. She was still breathing. Good God–what had he done! He dressed quickly. Then he reached in his pocket–he only had thirty dollars. That wasn't enough. This girl had to go to the hospital. And he couldn't just leave her. He looked around the room. No phone. He peered out into the hall–nothing there. He had to get her a doctor. There had to be a phone booth down the street.

The lobby was still deserted. He walked out of the building and the darkness of Fifty-eighth Street folded around him. He headed toward the drugstore at the corner. He had to phone for help.

"Hey, buddy boy, what are you doing around here?" It was Dip Nelson in an open convertible.

Robin walked over to the car. "I'm in trouble," he said tonelessly.

"Aren't we all?" Dip laughed. "We played at the Concord last night and we bombed."

"Dip . . . do you have any cash on you?"

"Have I ever–ten C's and a check. Why?"

"Dip–give me the thousand in cash, I'll give you a check."

"Get in the car and tell me about it." They drove through the park and Dip listened silently. When Robin finished, Dip said, "Let's take first things first. One, do you think she'll recognize you? I mean, suppose she's seen you on TV, then what?"

Robin shrugged. "Then the shit hits the fan."

Dip shook his head in wonderment. "Buddy, I don't know how they let you cross the street alone. If you want to make it to the top, you got to see to it that the shit *never* hits the fan! Look–it would be your word against hers. Would anyone take the word of a prostitute against a solid citizen?" He looked at the clock in the car. "It's ten thirty. What time would you say all this happened?"

Robin shrugged. "I went to a movie; I'm not wearing a watch, but it was dark when I came out."

"Then it had to be about eight thirty, maybe nine. We'll get our alibi set for eight just to play it safe."

"Alibi?"

"Me, sweetheart. The Big Dipper is your alibi. *If* you need one. We say I went to your apartment at seven thirty. We sat around and talked shop, then we took a drive. When I check the car in at the garage, I'll make sure someone there notices us."

"But what about the girl?" Robin asked. "She's out cold."

"Whores never die. She'll be out on the street tomorrow as good as new."

Robin shook his head. "I hurt her pretty bad. I just can't let her lie there."

"What ever made you pick her up? Christ, I saw you with the most beautiful broad in the world at P.J.'s."

"I don't know, I can remember seeing her—then something like a rocket went off in my head and the rest is as if I dreamed it."

"Look—want some advice? Leave her be. What's one whore more or less?"

Robin suddenly gripped the door. Dip looked at him oddly. "Anything wrong, pal?"

"Dip—did you ever have a crazy feeling as if you had gone through something before, heard the same words, even though it's just happened?"

"Sure, there's some kind of name for it. Has to do with the mind—getting something a beat late. It happens to everyone. There's even a song about it called 'Where or When.' "

"Maybe," Robin said slowly.

"So cut her from your mind. Make like it never happened," Dip said.

"No—I can't. She's a human being . . . she might even have a kid."

"I thought you said she was a self-admitted lesbo?"

"Yes, of course. You're right."

Dip drove the car down Fifty-sixth Street and pulled into the brightly lit garage. The attendant leaped to greet him. "How did she drive, Mr. Nelson?"

"Like an angel," Dip said. "As a matter of fact my friend and I have been driving around in her since seven thirty. You recognize him, don't you? Robin Stone—remember the *In Depth* show?"

The attendant nodded as a concession to Dip. Then he said, "Mr. Nelson, did you remember to bring that autographed picture you promised–for my daughter Betty?"

"Would I forget?" Dip opened the glove compartment and handed him a manila envelope. "All signed with love and kisses."

They left the garage and Robin started back toward Fifty-eighth Street. Dip hurried after him and tried to talk him out of it. "Look–she could be up there turning another trick by now."

"I only pray to God she is," Robin muttered. They stopped before the dark building. Dip looked around cautiously. "Well, maybe I'm as nutty as you, because I'm gonna go up there with you. Come on, let's go."

Once again the self-service elevator creaked its way to the third floor. The door was slightly ajar just as Robin had left it. They both stared at the unconscious woman on the floor. Dip let out a low whistle. "She's a big one."

"Give me the thousand," Robin said. "I'll put it in her purse. Then we'll call the doctor from the outside."

"Sure, and the doctor puts her in the hospital and she comes to and rats on you."

"But she didn't recognize me."

"Buddy–when a whore has a thousand bucks on her, they're gonna ask a lot of questions. So she describes you, and that's how trouble could start."

"What else can we do?" Robin asked.

"You stay here, buddy boy, the Big Dipper has an idea. Lock that door. When I come back I'll give it two short knocks. Don't open for anything else." Before Robin could answer, he was gone.

Robin sat on the bed and stared at the massive white body on the floor. He cradled his head in his arms. The poor bitch. What had gotten into him? This was the first time he had ever tried it with a brunette sober. And the last! Good God, suppose it had been Maggie.

She stirred and moaned. He got off the bed and put a pillow under her head. Then he took his handkerchief, held it under the cold-water tap and tried to wipe the crusted blood off her lip. He stroked the hair from her face. "I'm sorry," he whispered. She half opened her eyes, moaned, and once again lapsed into unconsciousness. "I'm sorry, you dumb whore, I'm sorry. Oh Jesus, I'm sorry."

He opened the door when he heard the two quick taps. Dip brandished a bottle of gleaming red capsules. "Did I ever come up with an idea."

"Seconals?" Robin asked.

Dip nodded. "Now, we just have to get them down Brünnhilde."

"It will kill her."

"I only got eight. She can't die from eight. A human being, maybe–but it would take dynamite to put that whale away."

"But why the pills?"

"We get her on the bed, the empty pill bottle beside her–it's got no label so it can't be traced. Then we go out and put in a call to the police. I'll fake the voice, say I had a date to get laid, and found her this way. I'll say she always threatened the Dutch act. That's the way most whores end up anyhow, unless a guy like you does it for them. Then the ambulance will come and cart her to Bellevue, pump her stomach, and by the time she comes to they'll never believe anything she tells them nor will they care. And while she's there they'll patch up whatever damage you've done. Now all we gotta do is get Primo Carnera on the bed."

She was a dead weight. They were both out of breath when they finally propped her up. Dip forced the pills into her mouth and slugged the water down her throat. She gurgled and the pills and water came sliding down her face. Dip pushed them back, shoved more water into her mouth. Robin held her head up so she wouldn't choke. His shirt was damp and he watched in agony until Dip finally got the pills down her.

"Okay, let's scram," Dip said. "Wait–" He took out a handkerchief and started wiping the place for fingerprints. He flashed Robin a wink. "All those B detective pictures I did are finally paying off. I know all the shticks. Did you touch anything, buddy boy?" Dip took a small leather case from his pocket. In it were a slim gold comb, a nail file and a nail clipper. Robin stared in horrified fascination as Dip cut her long red claws. Then he methodically cleaned the rest of her nails with a file.

"That's in case any of your hair was in it." He stared around the room. "I think that covers it." Then, using a handkerchief, Dip went into her bag and took out her wallet. "Her name is Anna-Marie Woods. She lives on Bleecker Street."

"Give me that address." Robin took the driver's license and jotted down the name and address. Then he handed it back to Dipper who replaced it in her bag. "She's got close to a hundred bucks on her–here, take it."

"Are you crazy!" Robin pushed it away.

"You didn't write down her address so you can take her dancing, did you? You want to send her some money, right? Well, you can also add this to it. Otherwise it's a cinch some orderly or patient will steal it from her at Bellevue."

Robin took the money and nodded dumbly. He understood why Dip had made it in pictures. He was constantly trying to outthink the next person. Maybe you had to when you came up the hard way.

They left the room cautiously. Their luck held and they reached the street without meeting anyone. Dip made the call, but Robin refused to leave until he was certain help arrived. Dip was against it, but they stood in a doorway across the street. Within ten minutes they heard the sirens. Three police cars pulled up before the house. Two minutes later an ambulance arrived. From nowhere a large crowd gathered–it seemed to Robin as if they emerged from the ground. "I've got to go over and see if she's alive," he whispered.

Dip started with him, but Robin pushed him back. "Now who's not thinking? With that blond hair and Hollywood tan, you'd have the crowd forgetting the ambulance and mobbing you for autographs. No one will recognize me."

"Don't be too sure," Dip hissed.

"From the look of them, I can be sure. And I'm also sure they saw *all* your B detective pictures." Robin crossed the street and mingled with the curious onlookers. A few minutes later the ambulance attendants came down with the stretcher. He breathed easier. Her head wasn't covered–that meant she was still alive.

He returned to Dip after the ambulance clanged its way through the red light and the crowd dispersed. Dip took his arm.

"Okay, buddy boy, I think you've had a big night. You better go to bed now, alone."

Robin stared at him. "Dip, what can I do for you? Name it."

"Forget it." Dip jabbed him on the arm. "Pauli and I have it made. In September you can get us on *In Depth* before we open at the Persian Room. Now—let's hail separate cabs a few blocks from here. We follow the B pictures to the very end."

Robin got home and took a sleeping pill. An hour later he took another and washed it down with vodka. Within moments he fell into a hard sleep. When he awoke the following morning, he called Dr. Archie Gold. "This is Robin Stone. I think I'm ready for the full course."

TWENTY-FOUR

ROBIN looked relaxed and in complete command of himself as he sat across from Dr. Gold.

"Have you ever picked up a prostitute before?"

"Never."

"Have you ever thought about it?"

"Never."

"And you say you passed up one that was fairly attractive. What made you go for this one?"

Robin squashed his cigarette. "That's why I'm here. She was a brunette."

Archie's gray eyes held a faint show of interest. "Could you have been testing yourself for Maggie?"

"What do you mean?"

"You'd have nothing to lose but your fifty dollars if you didn't get an erection with the prostitute."

Robin shook his head. "No, I don't think it was that at all. Something funny exploded in my head when she approached me. From the moment I went with her, I felt as if I was dreaming."

Dr. Gold studied his notes. "You know, the last time you were here, I told you I wanted to put you under hypnosis. I still do."

"That's ridiculous–we can certainly talk things out. . . ."

"I don't want to waste my time and your money. I'd like to put you under and use a tape recorder. Then you can hear your answers, and perhaps we can go from there." He noticed the frown appear on Robin's face. "When we talked last January, we hit a block. You can't go back to your early childhood. It's not that you refuse to remember–you *can't* remember. And until now, you have separated sex from love. You have no ability to put them together. What you feel for Maggie is the desire to love. Yet love *with* sex seems incestuous to you. We've got to find out the reason. There's not a clue in anything that you've told me in the last visit. And I assume you held nothing back." He paused. "Robin, how old are you?"

"I'll be forty-one next month."

"Have you ever thought of marriage?"

"No. Why should I?"

"Every man naturally assumes that one day he will marry. When did you first become aware that you wanted to be a loner?" Dr. Gold asked.

"I don't know. It was something I always felt."

"There we go again," Archie said triumphantly. "Something you *felt*—when? How? Don't you see, we have to go back." He stood up. "Robin, we're only going in circles. I think you've had enough for today. Come in tomorrow. Do you think you can give me three hours?"

"Three hours?"

"I want to put you under and use a tape recorder. After we both listen to the tape, I have a feeling we'll cut right through to the core of the problem."

"We'll have to make it in the evening," Robin said. "Would six be all right?"

"I'll see you here at six."

The following day Robin scanned the newspapers to see if there was anything about Anna-Marie. He finally found a brief mention on the fifth page of the *News:*

> A woman was found brutally beaten in a furnished room on West 58th Street. Police arrived after receiving an anonymous phone call. She did not live in the room and offered no explanation for being there. She was taken to Bellevue where it was discovered she had a long record for prostitution. No charges are brought against her, and she has been unable to name her unknown assailant. Her condition is not serious and she will be discharged from Bellevue tomorrow.

Robin went to the bank, withdrew two thousand dollars in small bills and sent it to her home address in a plain manila envelope. He still had reservations about the hypnotism deal, but he arrived at Dr. Gold's office at six. When his eyes rested on the tape recorder he felt a small chill of apprehension. "You actually think this is going to work?"

"I hope so," Archie answered. "Take off your coat and loosen your tie."

Robin took out his cigarettes. "Might as well get comfortable. Do I use the couch? I'll even try that if it will help."

"No, sit there, in the straight chair. And forget the cigarettes. Robin, you're not going to fight it, are you?"

"Listen, neither of us has time to play games."

"Fine! Now I want you to clear your mind. Fasten your attention to that seascape on the wall. All you see is the water . . . your feet are relaxing . . . all sense of feeling is leaving them . . . your legs are also floating . . . the feeling is creeping up through your body . . . you are weightless . . . your hands will drop at your side . . . your head and neck are relaxed . . . your eyes will close. Close your eyes, Robin. Now . . . you see nothing but darkness . . . it is velvet darkness . . . you are falling asleep. . . ."

Robin was aware that Dr. Gold had dimmed the lights. He was positive it was not going to work, but he followed Dr. Gold's instructions. He stared at the damned seascape. He told himself all feeling was leaving him. He pushed every thought from his mind but the quiet voice of Dr. Gold. . . . He could hear Archie's voice. It wasn't going to work. He could still hear Archie's voice. The darkness behind his eyes was heavy . . . but it wasn't going to work. . . .

He opened his eyes. He was on the couch. He sat up and stared aimlessly around the room and reached for his cigarettes. "How did I get over here? A few seconds ago I was on that chair."

"That was two and a half hours ago."

Robin jumped up. "What time is it?"

"Quarter of nine. You arrived here at six."

Robin picked up the telephone and dialed for the correct time. The singsong voice said, "At the tone, it will be eight forty-seven." He hung up and looked at Dr. Gold in total disbelief. The doctor smiled at him.

Robin looked at the tape recorder questioningly. Dr. Gold nodded.

"Well, for God's sake–play it for me!"

"You've had enough for one night. I want to listen to it myself alone tonight. Then tomorrow I'll play it for you."

"Did I make sense?" Robin asked.

"You made some startling revelations."

"For Christ's sake, play it for me. How can I sleep tonight wondering about this?"

Dr. Gold placed two green pills in an envelope. "Take these when you get home. Can you be in my office at six tomorrow?"

The pills worked. He had a good night's sleep, but he was tense and impatient the following day. He chained-smoked and found it impossible to concentrate on the work at hand. By the time he reached Dr. Gold's office, he was taut with nerves.

"Robin," said Dr. Gold, "before we start, I want you to bear this in mind. People tell the truth under deep hypnosis. Every word you hear on that tape will be your voice. At times it may even sound strange because I took you back to your childhood and you even spoke as a child. But I want you to listen with an open mind and not fight anything you hear."

Dr. Gold walked to the machine. "Ready?"

Robin nodded and sat down. The hum of the tape began. The first voice was Dr. Gold's:

DR. GOLD: Robin, you are under . . . you will hear my voice and react to everything I tell you to do. Now get up from that chair and walk to the couch. Good. Now lie down, Robin. We are going back . . . way back . . . you are a little boy. You are five years old . . . you are in bed. . . .

ROBIN: Yes, I am in bed.

Robin sat on the edge of the chair and stabbed his cigarette out. Jesus, the voice was younger and lighter–but it was *his* voice!

DR. GOLD: You are in bed. What kind of a bed is it?

ROBIN: A nice bed. Kitty is kissing me good night.

DR. GOLD: Robin, you are four years old. You are in bed. . . . (*Silence on the tape*)

DR. GOLD: Robin, you are four years old . . . four years old. . . .

ROBIN: Why do you call me Robin? My name is Conrad.

DR. GOLD: All right, Conrad. You are in bed . . . what do you see?

ROBIN: Mama is in bed with me, but . . .

DR. GOLD: But what?

ROBIN: She only pretends to stay, until I am asleep. Then she leaves me. She leaves me every night.

DR. GOLD: How do you know she leaves you?

ROBIN: Because I always wake up and hear her in the other room . . . when she's with them.

DR. GOLD: Who is "them"?

ROBIN: I don't know.

DR. GOLD: Where is your father?

ROBIN: We haven't got a father.

DR. GOLD: We?

ROBIN: My mother and me . . . we have no one. Just us . . . and them.

DR. GOLD: Who is "them"?

ROBIN: Lots of times it's Charlie. Sometimes it's others.

DR. GOLD: They come to visit your mother?

ROBIN: Yes . . . but they wait until I'm asleep.

DR. GOLD: What do you do when you hear them out there?

ROBIN: Nothing anymore. Not after Charlie slapped me.

DR. GOLD: When did Charlie slap you?

ROBIN: A while back . . . when I came in and found him on top of Mama on the couch.

DR. GOLD: Does she still go into the living room after you're asleep?

ROBIN: Yes, but not with Charlie. She never let him come back again. On account of him hitting me. And I'm the only man she loves . . . we only have each other . . . no one in the world cares about us . . . we just have each other. . . .

DR. GOLD: How old are you?

ROBIN: I'll be four tomorrow, August twentieth. And my mother is going to take me to Boston to see the pigeons on the Commons. . . .

DR. GOLD: Where do you live?

ROBIN: In Providence, Rhode Island.

DR. GOLD: Aren't you going to have a birthday party with your little friends?

ROBIN: We have no friends. There's just us.

DR. GOLD: Rob–Conrad, it is a week after your birthday. What are you doing?

ROBIN: I'm still mad at my mother.

DR. GOLD: Why?

ROBIN: A man came on my birthday. He knocked on the door just as we were leaving for Boston. Mama said we were going out . . . for him to come back later that night. He gave her some money and said someone had sent him. Mama gave me a nickel and told me to go to the corner for ice cream and to sit on the stoop and not come in till she sent for me. I was sitting there eating my ice-cream cone and a big boy came by and took it from me. I ran inside . . . Mama was in our bed . . . the man was with her. I'm mad at her. No one sleeps during the day. It was my birthday. She yelled at me . . . told me to go out. . . . (*Silence on the tape*)

DR. GOLD: Conrad, it is Thanksgiving. You are four . . . what are you doing?

ROBIN: Mama made a goose. People with large families have turkeys. But we're a little family, just us . . . so we have a goose. But we have cranberry sauce with real berries in it . . . and she's making the goose just like she had it when she was a little girl in Hamburg.

DR. GOLD: Conrad, were you ever in Hamburg?

ROBIN: No. My mother was born there. Lots of sailors were there, and that's when she met *him*. And he brought her to America and married her.

DR. GOLD: And then you were born? He was your father?

ROBIN: No. He got killed. He wasn't my father. He was just the man my mother married. He wasn't any good. She told me. He worked and drove a truck selling whiskey and that wasn't allowed. And one night everyone in his truck got shot. And Mama was all alone. See, there wasn't even me . . . or anyone. She was alone. But the man who owned all the trucks told my mother not to worry. And he sent lots of men to visit her and cheer her up and give her money and a year later God sent me to her.

DR. GOLD: Did your mother know which man was your father?

ROBIN: I told you . . . we had no father. Just mother and me. And we moved a lot because policemen don't like a little boy living alone with his mother without a father, and if they catch us they'll put me in a home away from Mother and send her back to Hamburg. But she's saving her money and then one day we will *both* go back to Hamburg and live with my *Grossmutter* . . . and I will have children to play with and not be alone. See, right now, that is why I am not allowed to get friendly with children in the neighborhood, because they would ask questions about my father . . . and then they would tell the police I had no father. . . .

DR. GOLD: Conrad, it is a week after Thanksgiving, at night. What are you doing?

ROBIN: I am in bed, but Mother is in the other room with George. He's been here every night. He says he will get us passports and he gives Mother money every night.

DR. GOLD: Who is George?

ROBIN: One of them. . . .

DR. GOLD: Conrad, it is two weeks after Thanksgiving, at night. Is your mother with George?

ROBIN: No . . . *He* was there.

DR. GOLD: Who is he?

ROBIN: Another man.

DR. GOLD: Who was the other man?

ROBIN: I don't know. I woke up and felt the bed empty and knew Mother was in the next room. I was hungry and wanted the coconut cookies she kept in the icebox. I had to go through the living room to get to the kitchen. So I tiptoed in because I remember when Charlie slapped me . . . and Mother gets mad if I don't stay in bed. . . .

DR. GOLD: Who was with your mother?

ROBIN: I never saw him before. He was on his knees on the couch . . . bending over Mother.

DR. GOLD: What was he doing?

ROBIN: His hands were on her neck. I stood very quiet and watched. Then he got up and left. He didn't even say goodbye to Mama. I walked over to the couch and she was asleep . . . only she wasn't really asleep, her eyes were open and she pretended to be asleep. And when I shook her she rolled off the couch and she was lying on the floor with her tongue hanging funny and falling to the side and her hair all dark and messed up. I loved to sleep against her breasts . . . they were so soft and warm under her nightgown. I didn't know what they looked like before, and they look so ugly now without the nightgown. I hate them! And her hair is black and looks too black against her face, and her eyes look funny, they look right at me as if they don't see me. I'm scared. *"Mutter*. Mother . . . *Mother!"* (*Silence on the tape*)

DR. GOLD: It is the next day. Where are you?

ROBIN: In a big room . . . everyone is asking me questions. I keep asking for Mama. They want to know what the man looked like. I want Mama. I want my mother. Then a big lady in white comes and takes me into a room where there are a lot of children. And she tells me this is where I will live. And that all the other little boys in the room are like me . . . they have no mothers. I ask did my mother go to Hamburg and she says no. And one boy says, "Your mother is dead." And I ask, "Did Mother go to the angels?" And the big lady in the white dress laughs and says, "Not your mother, sonny. Bad people don't go with the angels, and she deserves what she got, bringing a kid like you into this world with the life she led!"

And I . . . I hit her . . . I hit her. . . . (the voice screams. Then after a pause the voice continues.) Everything is going dark . . . but people are coming around me. But I'm not crying . . . Mama said I was a man and men don't cry. I won't cry . . . I won't say anything . . . I won't eat . . . I won't listen to them. Then they'll have to bring me back to my mother. This is what she meant. . . . They found we had no father . . . they've taken me to this big home . . . away from her. But I won't think about it . . . I won't listen to them. . . . (*There is silence on the tape*)

DR. GOLD: Conrad, it is Christmas. Where are you?

ROBIN: (*in a faint voice*) It is dark . . . I'm asleep . . . dark . . . dark. . . . There is a tube like a little straw in my arm . . . but it doesn't hurt . . . nothing hurts . . . I sleep . . . sleep. . . . Ever since that bad dark lady left me to go to Hamburg . . . she never loved me . . . I will sleep and not think of her . . . she was bad. . . .

DR. GOLD: It is two weeks later. Conrad. Where are you?

ROBIN: I am sitting up in a big bed with sides around it. Two ladies in white are with me and one is very glad that I am sitting up. She asks me my name. I have no name. I don't know where I am. A man in a white coat comes and looks in my eyes with a light. He is nice . . . they bring me ice cream. . . .

DR. GOLD: It is your fifth birthday, Conrad. Where are you?

ROBIN: Why do you call me Conrad? My name is Robin Stone, and I'm having a birthday party. And Mommy and Daddy and all my friends are watching me blow out the candles.

DR. GOLD: Do you like Mommy?

ROBIN: Of course. I was sick, did you know that? When Mommy and Daddy came and took me from the hospital I didn't even know them. But I do now.

DR. GOLD: What does Mommy look like?

ROBIN: She's pretty and nice and has yellow hair and her name is Kitty.

Dr. Gold clicked off the set. "The rest goes exactly as you stated–Lisa being born, all the rest of it."

Robin sat back. His shirt was drenched, his face was drained of color. He looked at Dr. Gold. "What does it mean?"

Dr. Gold's gaze was direct. "It's pretty obvious, isn't it?"

Robin stood up. "It's a pack of lies!"

The doctor's expression was sympathetic. "I knew how you'd feel. At nine o'clock this morning, I phoned the Providence *Journal*. They went through the back issues for Thanksgiving 1928. They finally found this item: "Police broke into an apartment, after receiving an anonymous phone call. A woman was found strangled and her four-year-old child was sleeping on her breast. The woman had been dead seven hours. She had been charged with prostitution several times, but never convicted. Police believe it was the killer who called, but there are no clues, as the child is the only one who saw the murderer and cannot describe the killer."

"And that's it?" Robin asked.

"One more item. Three days later." Archie continued: "Police tried to show pictures of various sex offenders to the child, but he seems to be in a comatose state. He is at the Good Shelter Home in Providence, Rhode Island."

Robin walked to the window. "So I'm not me. I'm a little bastard named Conrad." He turned and stared at Archie. "Why did you do this to me? Why? Wasn't I better off not knowing?"

"Better off picking up strange prostitutes and almost killing them? Better off not being able to have a decent relationship with a woman?"

"I could have stayed away from whores. I was happy as I was."

"Were you? I also doubt if you could have stayed away from whores. Maggie's rejection of you caused something to stir which set off a chain reaction. And when you saw the prostitute, you unconsciously felt the old anger at your mother for leaving you—for being a 'bad woman.' There was, as you put it, an explosion in your brain. You acted out a dream fantasy, of hate and love."

"Why would I hate? That kid on the tape loved his mother!"

"Of course he loved her. Too much. There was no one else in his life but her. Yet young as he was, his subconscious knew he had to hate to survive. But even hate can be painful, so he chose to forget—with self-induced amnesia. When you saw the prostitute, something from your subconscious came through—hate. When you met Maggie, the subconscious also stirred—love. The love you felt for your mother. You also saw Maggie as a beautiful girl *you* desired. But the subconscious rebelled. That's why you had to get drunk to be able to have sex with her. Sober, your subconscious ties her up with Mama."

"And now because you tell me this I'll walk out of here and be able to lay Maggie?"

"It's not that simple. Eventually yes. After you've learned to understand your drives, your desires, and what motivates them. When that happens, you won't need a clean antiseptic-looking girl to rouse you and a girl like Maggie to love from a distance. You will be able to give love and accept love in a total fulfillment."

"Archie, I'm going to be forty-one. It's a little late for a personality change. I think I'd rather have gone on grabbing a nice blond dish when I felt the urge." He sank into a chair. "Jesus, I'm not me—Kitty's not my mother. I don't know who my father was. I don't even know who my mother was." His laugh was forced. "And I pitied Amanda! Me! The lowest kind of bastard there is. I'm Conrad who?"

"You *are* Robin Stone. A name does not make a man. But you've been living with some of Conrad's scarred emotions. Get them out, air them. Keep the good ones, discard the wrong ones."

"What would be the wrong ones?"

"The hate for his real mother."

"Oh, she was a charmer," Robin said. "At least Amanda's mother did it with one guy. Mine was a bum."

"She was a poor little German girl alone in a strange country. Obviously the man she married worked for a bootlegger. When he was killed the boss probably set her up as a prostitute. And don't forget, when you were born she could have gotten rid of you. Dumped you into an orphanage in the very beginning. But she loved you—tried to give you a home, tried to save money to take you back to the only world she knew. She loved you, Robin."

He clenched his fists. "Why in hell didn't Kitty tell me? Why did she raise me to believe I was her own child?"

"It's obvious you went into shock. When you came out of it, you had complete loss of memory. To tell you that you were adopted might have reactivated the bad memories, which—young as you were—you wanted to blot out. She probably was advised *not* to tell you." He saw a hard gleam come into Robin's eyes.

"Look here, Robin, I don't want you to feel one second of self-pity. You're a very lucky man. You had a mother who loved you. And Kitty who loved you enough to adopt you and keep the secret from you. A man who has been given that much love has no right to skim through life giving nothing of himself."

Robin stood up. "As I see it, I've no right to skim through life *making* nothing of myself."

"What do you mean?"

"Lisa knows the truth–something she said makes me realize that. And of course Kitty knows. She probably is worried about me–that I might revert to type or collapse. She feels I need protection. That I'm weak. They think I need a wife and children as an anchor. God, I've gone through the last thirty-five years on a pass. Kitty and Lisa secretly pity me. Well, I don't need pity. And I don't need a wife. I don't need a child–I don't need anyone. Including you! Get it! I don't need *anyone!* And from here on in, no one gives me one goddam thing–I'm going to get it for myself." He grabbed his jacket and tore out of the office.

TWENTY-FIVE

MAGGIE stretched out in the large bed. She smiled as she heard Adam's loud baritone reverberating from the bathroom. She wanted to get a good night's sleep. Tomorrow was Sunday and Adam had promised to work with her on the new script. Just thinking about it brought on the fear. The fear she had been living with ever since Karl Heinz Brandt had selected her to star in his new picture. It was all very well for Adam to tell her not to be frightened about working with Karl Heinz but she was terrified. Karl Heinz was known for his sadistic attitude toward actors. He would humiliate the biggest stars to get a performance from them. She pushed the thought from her mind and picked up a copy of weekly *Variety*. Somehow there never seemed time to read anything other than the daily trades. You read them while they were doing your hair or makeup. How long had it been since she had read a newspaper? The gossip columnists attacked her for living openly with Adam Bergman at his beach house. They unearthed the fact that she had once been Mrs. Hudson Stewart. They condemned a "nice" girl for flagrantly ignoring matrimony. Oddly enough, the publicity enhanced her value. She was becoming a "personality." And when Karl Heinz selected her to star in his new picture, the new avalanche of publicity turned her into a "hot" property.

One national magazine called her the "Lady of the Dunes," and ran a photograph of her, walking barefoot with Adam in the moonlight along the beach in Malibu. Her constant refusal of invitations to all the "right" parties had also caused her to become a bit of a legend. Actually, she didn't go because she was scared to death. She enjoyed living with Adam, she enjoyed working with him, she enjoyed him in bed. And neither of them ever thought about marriage. The subject was never even discussed.

She thought about this as she leafed through *Variety*. When she came to the television section, she lit a cigarette and scanned every item carefully. She checked the ratings. Christie Lane was number one! Robin's Happening show was in the top twenty.

She had heard from him last February–he was planning a Happening on the world of fashion. The communication was merely a typed letter offering her expenses, first-class accommodations at the Plaza and a fee of five thousand dollars if she wanted to guest-star as the commentator. She had typed a letter on a piece of Century's stationery, explaining that Miss Stewart's television fee was twenty-five thousand, but unfortunately her picture commitments would prevent any negotiations for a television appearance. Then she had signed it "Jane Biando, secretary to Miss Stewart."

Adam came out of the shower with a towel around his waist. She watched him as he combed his hair. She told herself she was very lucky. She adored Adam. Then why did she always subconsciously think of Robin? Did she still want him? Yes, dammit, she did! Maybe Alfie Knight had explained it best. He was in love with Gavin Moore, the designer, yet he had gone wildly on the make for her during the picture. And when it was over he continued to call her. One day he said, "Luv, you may *just* have to have an affair with me and get me back to being a happy well-adjusted homosexual."

"Now, Alfie, you're not in love with me," she had answered.

"Of course not. I adore Gavin. He's the love of my life–this season. But, luv, when I'm in a picture I have to mesmerize myself into being in love with my leading lady so I'll come across butch. Unfortunately, it sometimes works too well, and when the picture is over, I have to rush to Palm Springs to get the lady off my back. But you've been so distant that you've become an obsession with me."

She had told this to Adam and he had laughed. "You owe it to him, he made you look great in the picture. And an obsession is the worst type of sickness. With an obsession, you've got to come to grips with it–not let it smolder and take hold of you."

"You mean you'd let me sleep with Alfie?" She was teasing.

"Sure, if you let me watch." He meant it.

To her amazement, she had called Alfie and told him Adam's offer. Alfie accepted eagerly. He came to the beach house and made love to her while Adam lay beside them on the bed. The crazy part of it was that she felt no shame. And when it was over, she watched while Alfie made love to Adam. And it all seemed perfectly normal and relaxed. Afterwards, they all went into the kitchen and made scrambled eggs. And they remained the best of friends.

Perhaps Adam had a point. Alfie was back with Gavin but her obsession about Robin Stone was still festering. She was positive that one day they would get together. He would be tanked up on vodka–that was the only way it could happen. And when he yelled *"Mutter,* Mother, *Mother,"* she'd leap out of bed and throw a pitcher of cold water on him. Let him try and say he'd had a blackout after that!

Adam cut into her thoughts by dropping the towel and coming to her. When it was over they raced into the ocean, and when they went back to the house she curled into Adam's arms and fell asleep and dreamed of Robin.

They flew to San Francisco to catch the sneak preview of the picture. She sat clutching Adam's arm while he nibbled the buttered popcorn. Karl Heinz sat in front of them with a young ingenue. A few other members of the cast sat across the aisle.

She watched the film intently and wished she could be objective enough to analyze her performance. She knew that she had never looked as exciting–the cinematography was fantastic. She was all eyes, cheekbones and windswept hair. The clothes were fantastic. Adam had complained that she was too thin, but it certainly paid off on the screen. She shifted nervously in her seat. The big scene was coming. When it began she peered cautiously at the audience. She couldn't believe it–people were actually affected by her performance.

And then the music swelled and the picture was over. Adam grabbed her hand, whispering as they ran up the aisle of the theater, "Baby, you've turned into one hell of an actress. That last scene really had it." They got out of the theater just as the audience was beginning to spill into the aisles. They stood across the street and waited for Karl Heinz and the others. Maggie was still apprehensive until Karl Heinz approached. His face was beaming. He held out his arms and kissed her.

A week after the sneak preview, Hy Mandel, her agent, met her in the Polo Lounge at the Beverly Hills Hotel. He waited until they had ordered a drink, then he tossed the new contract to her with a flourish. "We did it, honey! When the heads of Century lamped the screening of the new epic, they realized it was stupid to try and force you to stay with the old deal at seventy-five thousand a picture. Like I said, 'Gentlemen–she'll do these pictures for you as an unhappy actress. And what will happen? She'll be unhappy and she'll be lousy. And you'll destroy a potential star. What will the stockholders say to that? Especially since it's now a road-show picture–three and a half hours with an intermission yet. *Starring* Maggie Stewart.' I hammered it home. How will it look, I asked them, if they didn't know how to take a star another director created, and continue to build her. And it worked! Look at the new terms–two hundred and fifty thousand apiece for the next two pictures, and three hundred thousand for the third, plus twenty percent of the net profits!"

She nodded and sipped her Bloody Mary. Hy rushed on. "Now look, principal photography on the new picture won't start until February. They want you back January fifteenth for wardrobe."

"January fifteenth! How wonderful! It's only December tenth!"

"That's right. We've arranged a nice little vacation for you."

She looked at him suspiciously. He laughed. "So maybe it isn't exactly a vacation, but we had to give a little to get. Now, there's going to be a tremendous opening of *The Torn Lady* in New York, and–"

"The Torn Lady?" She wrinkled her nose. "Is that the title they've settled on?"

"Don't knock it, honey. When it was called *Henderson,* that automatically geared it toward the male star. This way, it's your picture."

She smiled. "All right. Now what's the hitch? What do I have to do?"

"Well, it's not really anything rough–a trip to New York to attend the opening isn't exactly factory work."

"It also means interviews, television shows, and not a minute to myself."

"Wrong again. The picture opens December twenty-sixth. You don't have to be in New York until the twenty-second."

"And I work from the twenty-second straight through the big gala opening night."

"Yes, but meanwhile you're free from now until the twenty-second. And if you want to go to New York earlier and see some shows, they'll spring for that. Or if you want to stay on a week after . . . it means a vacation either way. As long as you're back here the fifteenth. Why not go now? It's all on Century."

She shook her head. "I think I'll stay at the beach and just rest. The good weather is still holding out."

"Maggie"– he paused–"I don't want you to stay at the beach–with Adam."

She looked at him curiously. "Everyone knows I live with Adam."

"Why don't you two kids get married?"

"I don't want to."

"Then why live with him?"

"I'm lonely. I'll stay with him until I–" She stopped.

"Till you find the right man? Maggie, did it ever occur to you that you won't find anyone else as long as you stay with Adam?"

"I've found him."

Hy stared at her with unmasked surprise.

"I found him four years ago," she went on, "but–"

"He's married?"

She shook her head. "Hy, let's forget it. I'm happy with my work, happy with Adam."

"I'm sixty years old," he said slowly. "I've been married to Rhoda for thirty-two years. Rhoda is fifty-nine. At the time I married her I had a small office on West Forty-sixth Street and Rhoda was teaching school. When we got married she was a twenty-seven-year-old virgin and I wasn't surprised. We expected girls to be virgins in those days. Today a twenty-seven-year-old virgin would be a freak. Today a guy who is true to his wife is a freak. Well, I'm one of those freaks. So maybe Rhoda is twenty pounds overweight. And maybe I've slowed down–it's been two or three years since Rhoda and I slept together. But we have a good life. We got grown children and grandchildren and we still have a double bed and we enjoy lying in it together and sometimes even holding hands when we watch television. But we hold hands with a different kind of love now. Ever since I got to be a top agent out here–and now especially since you've become so hot–I suddenly find I'm being given the eye by twenty-one-year-old beautiful shiksas. These same little shiksas wouldn't have given me the right time when I was in my prime. There was one just the other day–I never saw such a body. She bent down and all but dropped the boobies on my desk. But you know something? I look in the mirror each morning when I shave. I see a guy with too little hair and too much belly. Maybe if I took on the little blonde I'd get it up pretty good. Maybe we'd roll together in bed. But who am I kidding? She's not rolling with me because of my profile. It's my connections she wants. So I say, Hy, is it worth it? And I say no. But I've seen other guys my age get tied up with girls younger than their married daughters. But I will say they don't flaunt it. They go to La Rue Saturday night with their wives. They go to Hillcrest every Sunday with their wives. See what I mean? If they want it on the side, okay–but they keep up some semblance of a front for the children and the wife. Maggie, you have no children–but you have a public, and there are a lot of people who still think like me and they won't pay three dollars to go see a beautiful girl crying over dying and leaving her child and husband when they know she's flagrantly living at a beach-house without a wedding ring."

"I've spent enough of my life living up to conventions and rules," she said sullenly.

His sigh was heavy. "Maggie, what is it with you kids today? Am I that out of touch? Look, all I ask is for you to marry Adam, or get your own place. Then sleep with him, run up and down the beach with him–but please get your own place."

She laughed. "All right, Hy, when I come back from New

York, I'll check into this hotel. Meanwhile, you can look for an apartment for me."

"It just so happens, I've already accidentally stumbled on just such a place. A furnished apartment at the Melton Towers–four hundred a month, switchboard service, right in Beverly Hills. Come. I'll drive you there."

She saw the apartment. It was perfect for her needs–a large living room, full kitchen, master bedroom, small den with a wet-bar. The manager who showed the apartment had the lease all drawn up. Maggie laughed when she realized Hy had chosen the apartment before their talk. The next day Adam helped her move. He stayed at the beach, as he was blocking out the script for a new picture.

After two days alone in the new apartment, she grew fidgety. Adam was leaving the following week for location shots in Arizona. She'd be alone in Los Angeles. She called Hy and told him that if the studio still wanted to pay her way, she'd go to New York and do the publicity.

Adam took her to the airport. She posed for the airlines publicity man. Then Adam took her to the TWA Ambassadors lounge for a drink. "I'll be away for three months with the picture," he said. "When I come back, I'll move in with you. It's a nice apartment. Besides, it gets too damn cold at the beach in March."

She stared at the planes being serviced on the airfield. "I told you what Hy said."

He smiled. "Well, tell him I'm a nice Jewish boy, too. We might as well get married, Maggie. I think it could work. You won't mind if I shack up once in a while with another dame."

"I don't think I want marriage to be that way," she said slowly.

"Oh, you want it all neat and orderly like the kind you had in Philadelphia?"

"No, but I don't want to be *part* of a marriage–like the apartment, the furniture. I want you to be jealous of me, Adam."

"You didn't exactly blindfold yourself when Alfie was in bed with us."

"But don't you understand–that wasn't the real me."

He looked at her with his intense direct stare. "Cut the shit, Maggie. No one goes back. The girl that slept with Alfie is you. Now suddenly you start getting dewy-eyed about what you want in a marriage. What we've had at the beach is what there is to marriage in our kind of life."

He took her silence as acceptance and reached for her hand. "We'll get married when I come back from Arizona. I'll release it to the press after I leave you today."

She pulled her hand away. "Don't you dare!" Her eyes flashed in anger. "I'm not about to throw my life down the drain living with you and pretending that acting is art. It's a business! But there's more to life than living this business every second, and making excuses for sexual deviations because we're artists. I want a husband, not a bright young director who smokes pot and makes it with a boy occasionally for kicks."

His expression was grim. "When you sound off, you don't try to sugar-coat it." He snapped his fingers. "Just like that–we're through."

"Maybe we really never got started, Adam."

"Well, good luck. But the beach house is always waiting."

A press agent named Sid Goff from Century Pictures was waiting when Maggie's plane landed at Kennedy Airport in New York. The photographers moved in and the bulbs went off. Sid took her hand luggage and escorted her to the long black limousine the studio had ordered. The press followed and bombarded her with questions while the luggage was stored in the trunk. There was one final flash of cameras, the car pulled away from the airport and she leaned back and relaxed.

"Don't let all that action fool you," Sid Goff said glumly. "We may not make a paper."

"What are you talking about?" she asked.

"Diana Williams is due in on the next flight. She'll probably grab all the newspaper space tomorrow."

"I thought she was doing a TV series," Maggie said.

"It's been canceled–so now she suddenly wants to do a Broadway show. Ike Ryan has signed her. It goes into rehearsal in February."

Maggie smiled. "Well, don't be concerned. All Century cares about is press coverage on the day of the premiere."

"That's what *you* think," Sid said mournfully. "If we don't make the papers with pictures of your arrival, I'll be able to hear the screams from California without a telephone. We have some TV shows lined up—also newspaper interviews." He fumbled in his pocket for an envelope and handed her the typed schedule. "Then as I understand it, you can stay on until January fourteenth if you like, and Century will pick up the tab. We've got you booked at the Plaza until the twenty-sixth. If you want to stay on, be sure to let the hotel know right away."

She scanned the schedule he handed her. "This is incredible," she said. "I don't even get Christmas off—you've got two parties I'm supposed to attend."

"John Maxwell is one of Century's biggest stockholders. He has a big duplex at River House. It'll be loaded with rich civilians, but he likes celebrities and he definitely put in a request for you. The one at The Forum you've got to make—all the press will be there. It's Ike Ryan's party for Diana Williams."

"I don't go to parties," she said.

Sid Goff stared at her unable to believe he had heard correctly.

They drove in silence for a few minutes. Then he said, "Miss Stewart, I was given to understand that your agent had told Century that you would be available to promote the picture and grab all the publicity you could. This is Karl Heinz Brandt's picture for Living Arts Productions. Century is springing for the trip to build you into a star for themselves."

"I realize that," she said quietly. "And I agree to all interviews and television appearances. But there is no stipulation that says I have to make appearances at parties for stockholders. If Mr. Maxwell wants me to come, my fee is twenty-five thousand for an appearance."

Sid Goff leaned forward and studied his shoes. "Okay, Miss Stewart, maybe you have a point about John Maxwell. They really can't force you to go there. But there will be a lot of news coverage at Diana Williams' party. Please—at least make an appearance there."

She looked at his worried frown and relented. He had a job to do, and if making an appearance at Diana Williams' party would help, why not? But she was damned if she'd appear at John Maxwell's.

Since she had four days free before the interviews began, she invited her parents to New York. She saw to it that they had theater tickets and took them to dinner. Sid Goff arranged for tables, limousines, and keeping the fans at bay. Her parents returned to Philadelphia the day before Christmas in a state of subdued shock about their daughter's newly acquired fame.

She felt unbearably lonely Christmas Day. She had a tiny tree her family had brought for her and a wilted poinsettia plant . . . compliments of the studio. The endless Christmas carols on radio only depressed her more. She almost welcomed the idea of the Christmas party for Diana Williams at The Forum—at least it would get her out of the hotel suite.

Sid Goff called for her at five. "We only have to stay an hour," he told her. "Then you can cut out and join your friends and do whatever you wish."

"What are you doing later, Sid?" she asked.

"The same as you—cutting back to be with people I really like. My wife and her family. They're holding dinner for me until I get there."

The Forum was mobbed. Several cameras went off in her face as she entered. Ike Ryan's press agent cornered her to pose with Ike and Diana Williams. Maggie was amazed at Diana's appearance. She couldn't be forty, yet she was so burned-out looking. Thin, too thin. And her charged exuberance seemed to teeter on the verge of hysteria. She was too happy, too friendly—and the glass of orange juice in her hand was spiked with gin. Maggie posed with her. They exchanged the usual compliments. Maggie felt so young and healthy beside the girl. She also felt compassion. Everyone was dancing attendance on Diana but when the haunted eyes looked back at people, they didn't really focus.

Maggie was just passing the bar and heading for the door when she came face to face with the tall bronzed man who was entering. He stared in disbelief, then the familiar smile came to his eyes. She couldn't believe it. Robin Stone at a Christmas party for Diana Williams!

He grabbed her hands as his own astonishment turned into delight. "Hello, star!"

"Hello, Robin." She managed a cool smile.

"Maggie, you look marvelous."

Sid Goff moved off discreetly, but Maggie knew he was dreaming of the turkey dinner and his family. "I've got to leave," she said. "I have some other appointments."

His grin was filled with understanding. "I'm here on business too. I'm trying to talk Diana Williams into doing a Happening show. It's a murderous project, even if she agrees, but Ike Ryan is a friend of mine. I'd film the first day of rehearsal on the bare stage with the work light, then catch Philadelphia and the dress rehearsal and the New York opening night, and cut to interviews with Diana and Ike and the cast–" He stopped. "I'm sorry, Maggie–this is a hell of a way to tell you I'm glad to see you."

Maggie laughed, then she turned and looked at Diana. "Do you think she still has it?"

Robin's expression was odd. "I thought you'd be the last person to judge talent by Hollywood standards. Diana Williams is one of a kind. Diana bad is better than most Hollywood stars good. She started on Broadway almost twenty years ago when she was seventeen. Diana wasn't created with camera angles, Klieg lights and press agents."

"I think I really must leave now," she said coldly.

He caught her arm. "I must say this is a great start. How did we get into all this?" He smiled. "Let's get to more important matters. When can I see you?"

"I don't know." Suddenly she smiled challengingly. "The premiere of my new movie is tomorrow night. Maybe you'd like to see what Klieg lights and press agents can do. Would you like to escort me?"

"I don't like wearing black tie to movies. I enjoy seeing my movies when I eat popcorn. How about the next night?"

She looked at him evenly. "I'm talking about tomorrow night. I never plan too far ahead."

Their eyes held for a moment. Then he flashed the familiar grin.

"Okay, baby, for you I'll give up the popcorn. What time shall I pick you up and where?"

"Eight o'clock at the Plaza. The movie starts at eight thirty, but there is television coverage first. Unfortunately I have to be there."

"No sweat. I'll be there at eight."

The press agent reappeared and escorted her to the door. Robin watched her leave, then he made his way across the room to Diana Williams.

At five to eight she began to get nervous. It was ridiculous to worry, she told herself. Above all, Robin was a gentleman. He wouldn't stand her up–and besides he wasn't supposed to arrive until eight. At three minutes to eight she wondered if she should put in a call to Sid Goff and have him stand by.

The phone rang sharply at eight. Robin was in the lobby. She took one last glance at herself in the mirror. He would probably loathe the way she looked: the white beaded dress (borrowed from the studio), the white mink coat (on loan to the studio from a Hollywood furrier), and the long black hair, lengthened by a "fall" (courtesy of the studio hairdresser who had arrived at her suite to recreate a hair style she wore in the film). It was crazy, she decided as she rode down the elevator. She had tons of hair–why did it have to hang down the middle of her back? And the large diamond-and-emerald earrings (also on loan and heavily insured) made her feel topheavy.

Robin smiled when she stepped out of the elevator. Oddly enough the slight nod that accompanied his smile seemed filled with approval. They didn't speak until they got through the autograph fans in front of the Plaza who braved the cold and snapped her picture and demanded autographs. When they were finally settled in the limousine, she leaned back, then sat forward quickly. "Good God, I'll lose my hair."

He laughed with her. "I thought it had grown since yesterday."

"Is it too much?" she asked hesitantly.

"It's marvelous," he said. "Look–regard the entire thing as a costume ball. That's what it is really. You're playing a movie star–give 'em their money's worth. If you're going to do it, go all the way."

The crush at the theater was frightening. Their limousine had to stand in line for fifteen minutes as bejeweled occupants of other cars alighted. When the mink-clad women who stepped out were unrecognized by the fans, there was a groan of disappointment. Maggie peered at them cautiously from the safety of the car. Wooden barricades and police forced back the crowd. Across the street a truck held a huge Klieg light. A red carpet was actually on the sidewalk. Newspaper cameramen were waiting anxiously, looking curiously disoriented in their tuxedos. As her car finally reached the entrance, the press swarmed forward. The crowd cheered and surged forward breaking through the police line. A few hands reached out to touch the white mink, voices yelled "Maggie, Maggie–" Sid Goff and another press agent surrounded her protectively. She looked for Robin. He had disappeared. She was frantic. She felt herself being swept toward the tall man who was handling the microphone. She was standing beside him. Bulbs were flashing. The television lights were being held by hand. The TV camera moved in. Oh God, where was Robin?

And then somehow, Sid Goff was helping her off the stand and she was ushered into the lobby and Robin was waiting with that wonderful grin that said he understood just how it was. He held her arm and they braved the well-dressed audience who were all congregated in the lobby staring at one another. She made her way to her seat, which seemed to be a cue for the audience to follow and begin the frantic search for their seats as the lights went low and the music and credits began to roll.

When the final scene came on, Sid Goff sneaked down the aisle and beckoned to them. In a half crawl they ducked out of their seats and rushed up the aisle. They reached their car just as the doors of the theater opened and disgorged the glittering audience.

Robin took her hand. "I think you handled it beautifully. And you were excellent in the picture. Now tell me–is there more to this awful night, or are you free?"

"There's a champagne supper at the Americana Hotel."

"Naturally."

Then they both laughed. Suddenly the idea of sitting in the brightly lit ballroom at a table with Karl Heinz and the leading man and his wife and posing for more pictures seemed unbearable.

"I'm not going," she said suddenly.

"Good girl. How about the Oak Room of your hotel?"

"No, I have a better idea. These earrings have to go into the vault anyhow, and if I don't take off some of this hair, I'm going to have a blinding headache. Suppose I change into slacks and we go to P.J.'s?"

"You are the most brilliant girl in the world. But you can't be the only one who gets out of these trappings. Tell you what–I'll drop you and leave the car. When you are ready, you can come and pick me up."

Twenty minutes later she was back in the car, bundled in slacks and a white lamb sport coat. She wore dark glasses and smoked nervously as they drove to his apartment building on the East River. He was waiting outside, and he walked briskly to the car. He was wearing a white sweater and gray pants and no overcoat. As he slid in beside her, he said, "Even P.J.'s isn't private enough. How about the Lancer Bar?"

She nodded and the driver headed toward Fifty-fourth Street. The place was empty except for a young couple who sat in the back booth drinking beer and holding hands. Robin ordered a Scotch for her, a martini for himself, and two large steaks.

Then he led her to a secluded table. He raised his glass: "This picture will do you a lot of good, Maggie."

"But did you think I was good?"

"Let's put it this way–you'll convince the critics that you can act."

"That means *you* don't think I can?"

"Does it matter?"

She smiled. "I'm curious."

He pursed his lips thoughtfully. "Baby, you can't act your way out of a barrel. But it doesn't matter–you photograph like a goddess. You'll have a big future."

"Don't you believe there is any such thing as star quality? That's all I hear out there."

"Yes, but she's got to be a genius or a nut."

"Maybe I still qualify."

He laughed. "I don't mean IQ genius–I mean emotional genius. Maybe there's a thin line between genius and madness, and thank God you don't fit into either category. Diana Williams is a genius and a nut. And a poor lost soul. Come to think of it, I don't think I've ever met a happy adjusted genius." He reached across the table and took her hands. "Thank God you're just a beautiful lady who through some crazy fluke has fallen into an incredible bit of luck. But you're not a nut–you're everything a man thinks of when he dreams of the ideal girl."

She held her breath and waited for the disclaimer, the veiled insult that would knock her down. But their eyes met and he did not smile.

It was one o'clock when they left the Lancer Bar. "Do you have many appointments for tomorrow?" he asked.

She shook her head. "I'm on my own from here on in."

His pleasure was real. "How long can you stay in town?"

"Until the fourteenth of January, if I wish."

The car had pulled up to the Plaza. He looked at her earnestly. "*I* wish it. Can we have dinner together tomorrow?"

"I'd love it, Robin."

He kissed her gently and led her to the elevator. "I'll call you before noon. Sleep well." And then the elevator door closed and he was gone.

She heard the phone ring at eleven. She let it ring a few times. It had to be Robin and she wanted to be fully awake. When she answered it, the even tones of the desk clerk asked her at what time she expected to check out.

"I'm not checking out," she said angrily. "I'm staying on for at least two weeks." Then she hung up and punched the pillow into place. She would go back to sleep–she didn't want to wake up until Robin called. But the phone jangled again. This time it was the assistant manager.

The smooth voice was apologetic. "Miss Stewart, your reservation ends today. We were told that you would notify us if you intended staying on. Unfortunately the hotel is one hundred percent booked. Had you told us–"

She was wide-awake now. Good Lord, she had forgotten. Well, she'd find another hotel. The assistant manager was eager to be helpful. He would personally try to relocate her. Fifteen minutes later he called back. "Miss Stewart, the situation is very tight. The Regency, Pierre, St. Regis, Navarro, Hampshire House–all of them are booked solid, not even a double room is available, let alone a suite. I haven't tried the commercial hotels, I didn't know how you would feel."

"Thank you very much. I'll see if Century can do something." She put in a call to Sid Goff. When she told him the situation, he seemed totally defeated. "Maggie, I warned you to let them know. Let me get on the phone and see what I can do."

She was packing when Robin called. She explained her predicament. "I'll probably wind up in Brooklyn, the way things look. Sid Goff hasn't called back yet, and if he can't come up with something, no one can."

"Tell Sid Goff to forget it," he said. "I'll take care of it."

Twenty minutes later he called from the lobby and told her to send down her bags.

The limousine was waiting. When they were settled in the car he gave the driver his home address. She looked at him curiously.

"It isn't the Regency," he said. "But a maid does come in every day and it's comfortable enough—even for a star like you. I'll stay at the club."

"Robin, I can't do this to you."

"You haven't. *I've* done it."

She liked the apartment. Unconsciously her eyes drifted toward the king-sized bed and she wondered how many occupants it had known. He handed her a key. "Feel free to come and go as you choose. I'll come by to take you to dinner." He pointed to the bar. "All I ask in lieu of rental is your services as a bartender. If you want to be my girl you've got to learn to make a vodka martini. Three ounces vodka, a drop of vermouth, and no lemon peel. I like olives."

She started obediently toward the bar. "Maggie!" He laughed. "It's just past noon. I'm talking about this evening."

She had the martinis ready at seven. She had also bought two steaks and some frozen asparagus. After dinner they watched television and he held her hand as they snuggled on the couch. When the eleven o'clock news came on, he went to the kitchen and brought back two cans of beer. Then he said, "This is *your* place. Tell me when you want me to leave."

"Whenever you want to go," she said.

He pulled her to him. "I don't want to go–"

He took her in his arms and kissed her. All right now, she told herself: tell him *you* don't feel in the mood and *he* doesn't rouse *you!* But she clung to him and returned his kiss and when they went to the king-sized bed they came together eagerly. But this time his tenderness was not caused by the vodka, and when the moment came and his body went tense he didn't shout *Mother*–and she didn't throw the pitcher of cold water on him.

The next five days with Robin were unbelievable. They went out to dinner each night. Sometimes they bundled up and took a long walk and once they went to a double feature at a local movie, but each night they made love and fell asleep in each other's arms.

She thought about it now as she watched him sleep. She slid out of bed, put the coffee on and stared out at the grayness of the East River. She had never been this happy and she had fourteen more days. But why only fourteen days–why not forever? Robin was in love with her, there was no doubt about it. They had never discussed that terrible morning in Miami; somehow she sensed it was a closed subject. But what they were having now was no one-night stand. He was comfortable with her, he enjoyed being with her–maybe it was up to her to make the first move. Of course it was! How could he ask her to give up her career? She'd have to make him understand that for the first time in her life she was happy.

"It is a terrible-looking river on a gray morning." He had come into the kitchen and was standing behind her. He leaned down and kissed her neck. "Come to think of it, it's a lousy-looking river even on a beautiful day. The sun seems to point out its failings. Those awful little islands, and the tugboats."

She turned around and hugged him. "It's a *beautiful* river. Robin, I want to marry you."

He held her off and smiled. "I must say this is an auspicious way to start a new year."

"It would work, Robin, really it would."

"Perhaps. But not right now–"

"If you're thinking about my career, I've thought it all out." He smiled and reached for the coffee. "I'll make eggs," she said quickly, "and there's orange juice."

"Stop making noises like a wife," he said easily. Then he took his coffee cup and disappeared into the bedroom. She didn't follow him. She sat at the small table and stared at the river and sipped her coffee. Well, he hadn't said no–but he certainly was far from enthused at the idea.

Ten minutes later he came into the kitchen. She looked up in surprise. He was wearing a turtleneck sweater and had his overcoat on his arm. "I'll be back in an hour, I have some work to do." He leaned over and kissed her head.

"On New Year's Day!"

"There's a tape at the office I have to edit. I work better when I'm alone, especially when the whole building is empty–it gives me a sense of privacy. And, Maggie, I hate to impose on you, but do you think you could face an eggnog party at five?"

"An eggnog party?"

"Mrs. Austin's New Year's Day party–I've blown it three times in a row. At least I remembered to send a wire last year. But I've got to make an appearance this time."

"Oh, Robin, I sent back most of the fancy wardrobe. It was all borrowed finery and I've been living in a beach house–all I own is slacks and a few black dresses. What is in that closet is *it!*"

"I like a girl who travels light. The black dress will be fine."

"But it's a wool dress–"

"Maggie"–he came to her and stroked her face–"you'd pass anywhere in anything. Now, go do the dishes and help earn your keep."

Then he left the apartment.

It was cold but he walked. Archie Gold hadn't wanted to come out, but Robin had been insistent. He was sure Maggie hadn't heard him on the phone, the kitchen was at the other end of the apartment and he had kept his voice low.

He reached the office just as Archie arrived. "Robin, I don't come out like this for my regular patients. You walked out on me a year and a half ago, and now you suddenly call and tell me an emergency has come up."

Robin eased into a chair. "I need your advice. Maggie Stewart is in town. We made it together. It was great–she's living with me."

Archie lit his pipe. "Then there is no problem."

"The hell there isn't! She wants to get married."

"Most girls do."

"It wouldn't work. Look, there's more to marriage than shacking up with a girl. That is, for a girl like Maggie. In the past five days she's told me everything about her life–her first marriage, her past relationship with Parino, the guy in California, and the beach house. She's leveled all the way."

"And what have you done?"

"I've listened, chum. And I'm not about to talk. Let's see, how would I start? Oh by the way–my name isn't really Robin Stone."

"It is legally your name."

"Sure–but somewhere inside of me there's a little bastard named Conrad. *That's* me, too. And Maggie wants kids . . . the whole works," Suddenly Robin slammed his fist on the desk. "Dammit, Archie! I was going great until I met you–I enjoyed sex, I operated just fine!"

"You operated as a machine. Now Conrad is fighting to merge with Robin. The man that kept Conrad locked away wasn't alive –he felt nothing. You admitted that yourself. And now for the first time you're at odds with yourself. But it's a healthy sign: You're feeling emotions, conflict, worry. And that's normal."

"I liked it better the other way. I told you when I walked out of here last time that I'd make the name Robin Stone count for something. And I will. But I don't need Conrad! I want to forget about him."

"Robin, why don't you go to Hamburg?"

"What the hell would I do there?"

"You know your mother's name. Look up her family–maybe your origins would surprise you."

"Conrad's mother was a whore!" He spat it out.

"She *became* a whore. To support Conrad. You may discover that you're proud to be Conrad!"

Robin stood up. "God damn you, can't you understand–I don't *want* to know Conrad. I don't want to worry about hurting

Maggie Stewart! I don't want to miss her when she goes to the Coast. I don't want to miss or need *anyone!* I never have before . . . and I never will."

Dr. Gold stood up. "Robin, don't run out on yourself! Can't you see what's happening? You've started the process of giving—of combining love with sex. The experience has upset you. That's normal. But don't run from it. Of course there will be problems—but the day you can turn to someone and say *I need you* will be the day you become a complete person. And Maggie is that someone. Robin—don't shut her out."

But Robin had already slammed the door.

It was cold, but Robin walked back to his apartment. His mind was blank and he felt a strange calm. Maggie was in the living room, wearing the black dress. He looked at her curiously. "What time is it?" he asked.

"Four thirty."

He smiled, but his eyes were cold. "Well, take off the dress. We've got a good hour before we have to show at that party." Then he took her into the bedroom and made love to her. When it was over he looked at her with a detached smile. He seemed oddly pleased with himself. "You don't know it, my girl," he said evenly, "but Robin Stone just made love to you, and it worked."

"It's always worked," she said softly.

"This time it was different." Then he slapped her bare bottom. "Move it, baby, we're due at an eggnog party."

Maggie answered. I don't want to miss her when she goes to the Coast. I don't want to miss a [illegible] anyone? I [illegible] there before [illegible] and I [illegible]."

Dr. Gold [illegible]. "Ralph, don't [illegible] on yourself. [illegible] what's happening? You've started the process of [illegible] of good faith [illegible]. The [illegible] [illegible] [illegible] [illegible] [illegible] there will be [illegible] the day [illegible] [illegible] [illegible] [illegible] [illegible] [illegible] [illegible] [illegible]."

Ralph turned and [illegible] the door.

It was cold, but [illegible] [illegible]. [illegible] [illegible] and he felt a strange calm. Maggie was in the living room, waiting [illegible] [illegible]. [illegible]

[illegible]

He [illegible] [illegible]. [illegible]

[illegible]

[illegible] [illegible] [illegible].

III
JUDITH

TWENTY-SIX

JUDITH AUSTIN STEPPED OUT OF THE TUB. She caught sight of her body in the mirrored walls . . . she studied every angle. She was reed-thin, but dieted constantly. At fifty, one didn't dare chance the risk of spreading. Connie was lucky—she skied, on the Alps and on the water, and she was firm as a rock. It had been nice having Connie around, but thank God she had gone back to Italy to spend Christmas with the prince and the children. It had been an endless round of parties. Everyone was so damned impressed with a title. She shook her leg before the mirror. Yes, the flesh on her thigh was getting soft. Connie's thighs were like a rock. Maybe she should take up some sport. But the sun and wind had caused fine wrinkles in Connie's skin. Judith leaned closer to the mirror: just a few tiny lines around the eyes. In a good light she could pass for thirty-eight, maybe even thirty-six. She headed the best-dressed list and was still known as one of the most beautiful women in New York. And Connie's last visit had unleashed a new burst of national publicity—"the most beautiful twin sisters in the world."

Judith wondered if Connie was still in love with Vittorio. She sat down on the stool and toweled herself slowly as the realization hit her. Three years had passed without a breath of romance in her life. Three years ago she had broken off the thing with Chuck.

They had met during the summer at Quogue. Chuck was a golf pro, twenty-eight, blond. It had started when she took some lessons on her short irons. He put his arms around her waist to keep her from pivoting. "It's all in the hands with a wedge, Mrs.

Austin." Their eyes met, and that's how it began. During the summer, Gregory came out for long weekends and she had planned on getting Chuck transferred to the club at Palm Beach. Everything was divine until he made that remark: "Judith, wouldn't I be great doing the golf commentary on TV, like Jimmy Demaret or Cary Middlecoff?" It had disturbed her, but she had forced herself to dismiss it.

He had taken the job in Palm Beach. She arrived on January second, and for three weeks it had been wonderful. Gregory was still in New York, and each night Chuck crept into her mansion through the side entrance. Then he mentioned the television idea again. She had been intentionally vague. He shrugged. "Well then, maybe I'll try for tournament golf and go out on tour."

On tour? That offered all kinds of interesting possibilities. She might pop off and join him occasionally. He described the tournaments he wanted to enter—of course he'd have to practice every day for about a month or he'd never make the cut: "I'd need about ten or fifteen thousand," he said.

She stared at him. "Ten or fifteen thousand what?"

"Dollars. It costs money to hit the tournament trail. If I won any big purse I'd pay you back."

That had been the end of Chuck. She had refused to take his calls after that night.

It was the first time a man had ever gone after her with any ulterior motive. That had been three years ago—three years with nothing exciting in her life. Nothing but Gregory. She really loved Gregory, but she wasn't *in* love with him. And being in love was the only thing that made life worth living. She would never have married Gregory if it hadn't been for Connie.

The beautiful Logan twins: Judith and Consuelo. Daughters of Elizabeth and Cornelius Logan. A beautiful couple, beautiful twin daughters, a magnificent heritage. They had everything—except money. She would never forget their "poverty." Somehow the Logans always managed to live in the "right" apartment; she and Connie went to the "right" schools, and although it was whispered that Cornelius Logan had lost everything in the crash, everyone knew that Grandmother Logan still had enormous wealth. Grandmother Logan had paid for the big coming-out ball.

She had also paid for the girls' first trip to Europe on their twenty-first birthday. Connie had met Vittorio. Judith had come back empty-handed.

Judith was twenty-six when she met Gregory Austin. She had seen his picture in the newspapers and knew he dated movie actresses, society women and debutantes. He was thirty-six, unmarried, and owned a radio network. He bragged about his lack of formal education: "I never finished high school, but I can read the stock-market pages better than Bernard Baruch." His first job had been a runner on Wall Street. When the market crashed, he made his first million selling short. With the profits he bought a small radio station in upstate New York, continued to buy stock when it hit the all-time low, sold when it climbed, and with each big financial gain purchased a new radio station. When he was thirty he formed the IBC network. His cocky manner and flamboyant behavior made him a colorful personality. His quotes made good newspaper copy. He enjoyed women, but marriage was the last thing on his mind, until he met Judith Logan. Perhaps it was her lack of interest that challenged him. Gregory always sought the unattainable.

Judith went out with him a few times because of his persistence and was amazed to find herself suddenly in the "news." She was even more amazed when her closest friends wanted to throw small dinner parties for "that fascinating red-headed spitfire." And when Consuelo wrote and said she had met him in London and found him sexy and exciting, Judith suddenly looked at Gregory Austin in a new light. She also realized that he *was* offering her a kingdom–there was no coat of arms, but in some circles the IBC crest was even more impressive. He opened the door to a world of opulent spending. Vittorio had money, but Connie's jewelry was "family" jewelry that had to be passed on to her children and their children. Gregory presented Judith with a twenty-five-carat diamond engagement ring, a diamond necklace as a wedding present, and fifty thousand dollars to open her checking account. The wedding itself made both the society pages and theatrical columns.

Gregory was stunned to find he had married a virgin. He bought her the Palm Beach estate to celebrate their first year of marriage. He presented her with a diamond bracelet at the end of the second year. By the end of the third year, there was nothing else he could give her. And by then, the only thing she really wanted was romance. Sex with Gregory had been a complete disappointment. She had no basis for comparison, yet somehow she sensed she would discover romance when the proper moment presented itself. It happened when she was thirty-two. She decided to go to Paris to visit Connie. The war was over, everyone was in a festive mood, and Judith was anxious to show off her jewels and furs to Connie. Gregory couldn't get away but he sent her off with his best wishes and an enormous letter of credit. She met the opera star on the boat trip over. She skipped Paris and they stayed in London together. She never saw Connie and it never occurred to Gregory to ask why her letters bore English postage stamps.

After that it had been easy. There had been the Italian movie star, then for two years there had been the English playwright, then the French diplomat. . . . Dear Connie had proved valuable in the long run–one could always dash to Europe to visit one's sister: twins were supposed to be close. Of course Connie had been extracting her pound of flesh lately–all these visits to the States. . . . But in the last three years she had not gone to "visit Connie" at all. She sat and thought about it now–three years of *nothing.*

She finished her makeup and stood up and surveyed her naked body. In the beginning she had been unhappy because she hadn't been able to get pregnant. She had tried desperately until she was thirty, even considered adopting a baby, but Gregory was forty and didn't really care. "The network is our baby," he would say. And a child was a responsibility. . . . Now, as she stared at her flat stomach, she was suddenly glad there were no stretch marks. But her breasts *were* sagging and her thighs were getting loose. She held her arms over head. There, that looked fine–and in bed when she lay down they went into place. But her stomach was soft, even though it was flat. . . .

She went to her closet and reached for the purple velvet dress, then with a sudden change of mind decided on the red lamé hostess gown. And she'd wear the gold-and-ruby necklace. For the first time in ages, she felt a sense of anticipation in choosing a dress. An inner excitement had been building subconsciously for three days, ever since Robin Stone's note of acceptance arrived.

Until this moment Judith had refused to acknowledge it even to herself: she was dressing for Robin Stone. Suddenly she realized that she had wanted him since she first set eyes on him. Yes, she wanted Robin Stone! This would be her last and most exciting romance. But she knew she would have to make the first move, let him know in a terribly subtle way that she was interested. A man like Robin would take it from there. It was an ideal situation. It offered unlimited possibilities. He traveled so much. She could easily meet him abroad.

At four thirty she went downstairs to check the bar and hors d'oeuvres. At four forty-five Gregory appeared in his smoking jacket. He looked tired—well, Palm Beach would straighten him out. At five o'clock the first guests arrived. Naturally it was the senator and his wife. Why did the dull ones always arrive first? You were trapped talking to them until other guests arrived. But when the butler ushered the middle-aged couple into the living room, Judith's smile was brilliant.

"Hello, Senator. No, my dear, you are *not* early. You are just divinely punctual and I'm so glad. It will give us time for some chitchat."

Danton Miller arrived ten minutes later. He was alone. For once, Judith was glad to see him. It gave her an excuse to escape from the senator. Soon the door chimes grew constant. Within twenty minutes the crowd filled the living room and began to spill into the library and dining room. The party was on.

Robin Stone arrived at six. She floated across the room and held out her hands.

"You kept your promise." Her smile was radiant and she accepted the introduction to Maggie as if she had never seen her before. Then she eased away to greet new guests. That damn girl! She was so tall and beautiful! Judith held herself erect. She had felt small and dumpy beside Maggie Stewart. She moved effortlessly through the room greeting people, talking with them. . . . And through it all she kept one eye on Robin Stone and Maggie Stewart. Oh Lord, there was Christie Lane with his dreadful wife. Gregory had insisted she invite them. The girl–Ethel, yes, that was her name–was talking to Maggie Stewart. Chris was standing like a wooden Indian. Oh marvelous–Robin had moved off to talk to the senator.

This was her chance. She eased her way to his side. Then with casual deliberation, she took his arm and said, "This is your first time here. Would you like the tour?"

"Tour?"

"Yes." She led him from the room to the outer hall. "Most guests like to see houses. And they rarely get beyond the living room, library and dining room." She stopped at a heavy oak door. "This is off limits to guests but I'd like you to see it. It's Gregory's den, his pride and joy."

"The house is deceptive," Robin said. "It's quite large, isn't it?"

Her laugh was easy and light. "Don't you know? It's really two brownstones–we broke the entire wall that separated the houses and wound up with fifteen large rooms instead of thirty small ones."

Robin looked around the den with obvious approval. "Good room for a man."

Her face was wistful. "Unfortunately he spends too much time here."

He nodded. "I imagine he thinks his problems out."

"Do you hole away like that too?"

He smiled. "My problems are on a smaller scale. I have just one department to worry about. Gregory has the entire network."

She threw her hands up in mock despair. "Is business the only kind of problems men have? I envy you."

His grin was noncommittal.

"A woman's problems can't be obliterated by a drink and an hour of deep thought in a den," she said.

"Maybe she hasn't tried," Robin answered.

"How do you erase loneliness, Robin?"

He looked at her curiously. For one second their eyes met. Her stare was challenging, with a hint of intimacy. Her voice was low when she spoke. "Robin, I love Gregory. In the beginning of our marriage we had something very wonderful. But now he's married to IBC. He's much older than I . . . the excitement of the network is enough for him. He brings his problems home—sometimes I feel I don't exist for him. I see him in crowds, at parties, at dinners. I know he loves me, but I'm just part of his empire. I feel so lonely and isolated. I'm not the type of woman who plays cards or enjoys meeting other women for lunch."

"Everyone has their own kind of loneliness," Robin said.

"But why should they? Life is so short. We're young for such a short time. I always believe if you don't hurt anyone, that's all that counts." She shrugged helplessly. "Gregory played the market when he was young, and he once said, 'It's the biggest and best crap game in the world,' but he doesn't play the market anymore—now the 'numbers,' as he puts it, are his big excitement. But a woman *can't* exist that way. She needs affection." She looked down at her hands and twisted the large ring. "I've found it perhaps once or twice." She looked at him. "It never took anything away from Gregory. It never touched my love for him. It was a different kind of love. I just gave someone something that Gregory didn't have the time or sensitivity to accept." Then in a small voice she said, "I don't know why I'm telling you all this. I hardly know you." Her smile was suddenly shy. "But friendship is not just a matter of time, it's a matter of understanding."

He took her by the shoulders and grinned. "Judith, you are a lovely woman, but I'd advise you to be careful whom you open up to like this."

Her eyes looked up to him appealingly. "I don't open up like this. I never have before—I don't know what's the matter with me, Robin."

He turned her around and steered her toward the door. "Too much eggnog," he said with a smile. "Now, let's get back to your guests. That's one way of not being lonely."

Her stare was direct. "Is that the only solution?"

He took her arm and led her back to the living room. "I'm with a young lady who might get very lonely in this crowd. Happy New Year, Judith. And stay away from the eggnog." He left her and went directly to Maggie Stewart.

Judith was in a state of shock, but she moved about greeting people, her smile intact.

Maggie's smile also remained intact. She had seen Robin leave the room with Judith Austin and was aware they had stayed away some time. Judith Austin was a very beautiful woman. But the sight of the tall handsome man crossing the room and coming to her side dispelled her uneasiness immediately.

He took her arm possessively and started to ease her away from Ethel and Christie Lane. Suddenly his attention switched to the door. Everyone in the room looked at the frail girl who entered. Then a murmur went through the sophisticated group. No matter how quietly she entered, Diana Williams *entered* a room. She stood there hesitant and alone, almost childlike. Gregory Austin rushed to greet her and protectively put his arm around her. In a split second everyone was surging around her. Diana accepted all the introductions with modesty.

"Boy, Ike Ryan sure doesn't know what he's doing this time," Ethel said, as she watched the commotion. "Diana's shot. She has to go up in smoke."

Diana finally broke through the crowd and came to Robin. Gregory Austin was still holding her arm possessively. "Robin," he chided, "why didn't you tell us you had invited Miss Williams to our party? We didn't know she was in town or we would have extended the invitation personally."

"You invited me on Christmas Day at Voisin," Diana said accusingly. "When you didn't call for me, I figured I had misunderstood and you expected me to meet you here."

"Allow me to make up for my rudeness by getting you a drink," Robin said. He and Gregory both led her toward the bar, leaving Maggie with Ethel and Christie.

Ethel was talking about her new suite at the Essex House: "We just moved in yesterday," she told Maggie.

"Big deal," Christie said. "Living room, two bedrooms, and it's three times as expensive as the Astor."

"Well, I can't exactly see myself pushing a baby carriage down Broadway," Ethel snorted. "At least the Essex House is across from the Park. It will be good for the baby."

"Oh, I didn't know. Congratulations," Maggie said, forcing herself to show an interest she didn't feel.

Christie beamed expansively. "The rabbit died last week. When the doc told me the news–well, I was so happy I was ready to do anything."

"Except move from the Astor," Ethel snapped. "But he finally gave in."

"Yeah, and she's got me sleeping in the other bedroom. Only until the baby comes, then we fix it up as a nursery. But I guess she's right, an expectant mother needs all her sleep. Hey, you two broads chat a minute. I see Dan the Man, and I want to talk to him." He crossed the room and grabbed Danton Miller's arm.

Maggie felt uneasy with Ethel. She didn't know her and she wasn't especially good at girl talk. "When do you expect the baby?" she asked.

"The end of August, or the beginning of September. I'm three weeks late, but the rabbit test was positive."

There was a moment of uncomfortable silence. Then Maggie said, "I think it was very wise of you to pick a hotel near the Park. It will be wonderful for the baby."

"You don't think I intend to stay there?" Ethel asked. "Christie doesn't know it yet, but next season he's doing the show from California."

"Oh, I see." Maggie didn't, but she had to say something.

"I'll swing it. With Christie the magic word is 'baby.' I'll tell him the Park is no good for the kid–muggings and all that. And once we get out there I'm determined it'll be a whole new life–a big house, and all the right people. I'm going to make him hire Cully and Hayes–we've got to get in with the right people so our kid will know the right kids. I tell you, Hollywood is just waiting for Ethel Evans Lane."

"You might be disappointed," Maggie said. She scanned the room quickly and wondered where Robin was.

"He's in the den with Diana," Ethel said.

"I beg your pardon?"

"Your boyfriend–Diana's latched on to him."

Maggie was too stunned to answer. For a moment there was an uncomfortable silence. Then Dan and Christie joined them.

"We been talking about a new time slot for year after next," Christie said. "Would you believe it–the sponsors are lined up, doll, waiting for me for two seasons after this?"

"May I get you a refill of this sticky stuff?" Dan asked, as hc smiled at Maggie.

There was a loud burst of laughter from the den. Obviously Diana was holding court. Dan smiled and lowered his voice conspiratorially. "I noticed you came here with Robin Stone. Does that mean you have to leave with him?"

"It's the normal procedure, isn't it?" she asked.

"Too bad. I was about to ask you to dinner. How long will you be in town?"

"About two more weeks."

"May I call you?"

"Well–" She thought quickly. She couldn't just say no, and it would never do to let him know where she was staying. "Let me call you," she said. "I plan on visiting my family in Philadelphia tomorrow. I don't know how long I'll be away."

"You know where to reach me?"

"IBC." She smiled. "And now I think I'd better join Robin." She left Dan and went into the library. Diana was holding everyone's attention with a funny story about her twin sons.

"God, they're getting so gigantic," she was saying, "I can't lie about their ages. And naturally the Beatles are their idols. *They* also have long hair. Oh, my dear, they are absolutely Carnaby Street. The other day I was about to introduce them as my babies and I stared at these two seventeen-year-old, six-foot hunks of children and I suddenly said, 'Meet the twin cantors.' "

Everyone laughed more uproariously than necessary. Robin didn't laugh. He watched her carefully and when she handed him her empty glass, he beckoned the waiter for a refill.

Maggie made her way to his side and slipped her arm through his. "It's seven o'clock," she whispered, "and I'm starving."

"There's a table full of hors d'oeuvres," he said, keeping his eyes riveted on Diana.

"I'd like to leave–"

"I'm working, baby." He patted his pocket. "I have a letter of agreement all ready. I've been carrying it around with me for two weeks. All she has to do is sign. And if you're a good girl you can be the witness."

"How long will it take?"

"I hope it happens tonight at dinner."

"She's coming to dinner with us?" she asked.

"She's coming to dinner with me. And if you like, you can come too."

She turned and left the room. She didn't look back but she sensed he never looked after her. She saw Dan Miller shaking hands with Mrs. Austin. His coat was on his arm. She crossed the room and joined him.

"Does that dinner invitation still hold?"

"It certainly does. Do you like Pavillon?"

"It's one of my favorite restaurants."

Pavillon was beginning to empty. As Maggie sat and toyed with a brandy, she wondered what Robin had thought when he discovered she had left. It was almost eleven o'clock. He was probably home, watching the news. Her anger evaporated and suddenly she felt guilty running out on him. What difference would it have made if Diana had gone to dinner with them? Robin needed Diana's signature for the Happening! She had been childish, and–worst of all–openly possessive! She had never acted that way with any man, not with Adam or Andy, because she never cared enough. Perhaps that was the secret of her success. Was that really true? Did you have to pretend to be disinterested in a man to hold him? She had sat through this dreary dinner with Dan just to play a game with Robin. But it was ridiculous–she *had* Robin, she loved him. Why was she sitting at Pavillon listening to this idiot's life story?

"I'm glad there is really nothing between you and Robin," he said suddenly.

She looked at him curiously. "Why do you say that?"

"Because I don't like him."

"He's a very good friend of mine." Her tone held a warning.

He smiled. "I still don't like him–and it's not personal."

Well, she didn't like anything about Danton Miller. Especially his smug smile. "Perhaps you're afraid of him," she said coldly.

"Afraid?"

"If your dislike isn't personal, then I assume it has something to do with business. I know you're both at IBC and I know a little bit about network policy. Robin has certainly expanded beyond just the news area, so there must be some rivalry between you."

He threw back his head and laughed. When he looked at her his brown eyes were almost slits. "I'm not afraid of the Great Stone Man, and you know why? Because he has too much pride —and that will be his destruction."

"I should think pride would be an *asset*."

"There's no place for it in this business. I'll tell you something, Maggie. When it comes to infighting, I have no pride. That's why I'll survive. There comes a time when you have to crawl a little, no matter how high and mighty you are. But Robin Stone will never crawl. That's why he won't survive. And that's the only word that counts in this business. Survival."

She picked up her pocketbook, hoping he would take it as a cue to end the evening. He noticed it and signaled for the check. "I'm boring you, talking about business. Shall we go someplace for a nightcap?"

"I'm very tired, Dan, and I have to be up early tomorrow."

When he hailed a cab, she told him she was staying at the Plaza. He dropped her and waited until she walked inside. Then she crossed the lobby, slipped out the Fifty-eighth Street side and took a cab to Robin's.

There was no light under the door when she put the key in the lock. Perhaps he had gone to sleep. She tiptoed through the darkened living room to the bedroom. The room was dark but she saw the dim outline of the bed, rumpled and unmade from their afternoon of lovemaking. It was empty. She walked back into the living room and was just about to turn on the light when she saw the sliver of light under the door of his den. She smiled —he was in there working on his book. She walked to the door and had her hand on the knob when she heard the voices. It was Diana and she sounded drunk.

"This carpet isn't very soft . . ."

Robin laughed. "Well, I told you to go make the bed."

"I don't fuck in another woman's sheets!"

Then there was silence.

She opened the door quietly. She couldn't believe it. Both of them were completely nude. Robin was stretched out in the club chair in the corner of the room, his eyes shut, his arms behind his head. Diana was on her knees making love to him. Neither of them was aware that she was standing there. She backed out of the room and closed the door quietly. Then she went back to the bedroom and switched on the lights. She dragged her suitcase from the closet, then with an abrupt change of mind left it on the floor. Why bother for a few pairs of slacks and one dress? She'd never want to wear anything she had worn with him again. She collected her makeup and her wallet and started from the room. She turned back and stared at the bed. The bed she had shared with Robin just a few hours ago. The bed she had expected to share with him tonight and every night. The bed she thought was part of her future–the bed that Diana wouldn't get into unless there were fresh sheets. How many girls had slept in it? How many more would sleep in it? She rushed to the bed and tore at the sheets, but she couldn't rip them into the shreds her fury demanded. No one was ever going to sleep on these sheets again, or on that bed! She remembered there was a can of lighter fluid in the medicine chest and raced into the bathroom to get it. She poured it over the sheets and the headboard, and then struck a match, held it to the book of matches until it all flared, and tossed it on the bed. With a hiss, a hot orange flame licked across the sheets.

She ran from the apartment. She walked through the lobby and stopped at the door. In a quiet voice she said to the doorman, "I just rang Mr. Stone's doorbell and there was no answer, but I thought I smelled smoke coming from inside." As the doorman dashed to the elevator, Maggie casually crossed the street and stood watching under the canopy of another apartment house. A slow smile crossed her face as she saw the blaze of light from Robin's bedroom window. In a few minutes there was the sound of sirens. Soon the blaze of fire went dark and gusts of heavy smoke poured out of the window. She saw Robin come out onto the street with the other tenants. He had thrown his trench coat over some pants. Diana was wrapped in his overcoat but she was barefoot, hopping up and down on one foot on the cold pavement. Maggie tossed back her head and laughed. "I hope she gets pneumonia," she said aloud. Then she walked down the street.

She walked five blocks before the reaction set in. She began to shiver, and damp sweat broke out on her forehead. Good God, what had she done! She could have killed him. She could have killed everyone in the building. She felt faint as she realized the horror of her actions. Suddenly she understood how people could kill in a moment of rage and plead temporary insanity. She hadn't even thought of the danger of the fire spreading. . . . Thank God it was all right! She saw a cruising cab, hailed it and mumbled, "Kennedy Airport." Then she leaned back against the seat. She'd have to wait hours to catch a plane to Los Angeles, but it didn't matter. The cab cut through a dark tree-lined street as it headed toward the East River Drive—it was the street where the Austins lived. She glanced at the solid brownstone. There was a light on the second floor. How she envied a woman like Judith Austin, secure in her beautiful brownstone fortress. . . .

At the moment, Judith Austin was standing before the mirror silently reappraising herself. She smiled at the mirror and studied her smile. It certainly looked forced. Well, that was the smile she had held until nine thirty, until the last guest had finally departed. Her head ached and she had longed to go to her room, but she had forced herself to have a quiet snack with Gregory in the privacy of his bedroom. She had nibbled at the cold turkey and listened to him gripe. The parties were becoming too goddam show-business-oriented. Next year he would personally check the list—if there *was* an eggnog party next year.

Ordinarily she would have argued, or soothed him, but tonight she was too immersed in her own thoughts. When she finally left him for the privacy of her own bedroom, she had flung herself across the bed fully clothed and tried to sort the events of the evening in her mind.

But now, as she stood in her nightgown, she had to face the unhappy realization that Robin Stone had *not* taken the bait. Suddenly her defenses crumbled and tears rolled down her face. She had held them back all night. She had not allowed herself to think of his rejection. She couldn't afford to—not before all those people, not with Gregory. But now she could give in to her emotions. Suddenly she blew her nose. She would not cry! Tears were a luxury she could not afford. Oh, a few nice diamondlike drops at a sad play, or at the news of the death of a friend; tears that could gently slide down the corners of her eyes without damaging the mascara on the bottom lashes. But no out-and-out tears, no sobbing: that meant puffy eyelids the next day and bags under the eyes. And she had a luncheon date at the Colony and a formal dinner party at night.

But Robin had rejected her. No, not actually rejected her—just ignored her veiled offer. Veiled! She had never come on so strong with anyone in her life. In the past it had never taken more than a look, a subtle smile, to bring on instant reaction. Oh God . . . she wanted him so! She needed someone to hold her and tell her she was lovely. She needed love. She wanted Robin! She wanted sex with someone who would make her feel young and desirable. It had been months since Gregory had tried. Oh God, to be young again, and have a man like Robin *want* you, to sit in dark bars and hold hands, to walk along the sand in the Hamptons and look at the moon. . . . Judith's love began in her heart and mind—the orgasm was only incidental. For her, as long as she was emotionally involved, the experience was gratifying. If she could have Robin's arms around her, feel his naked body close to her own, touch his face—nothing else would matter.

Gregory had never excited her as a man. Even when he was young, vigorous and hearty, he lacked the spark that ignited romance. Right from the start sex had never been important to him. He knew nothing about any variations in lovemaking. He said none of the right things at the proper moments—he had never gone down on her in his entire life. Perhaps it was her fault. Perhaps she had made him feel she was above it. But she had never been able to feel one tinge of the excitement for Gregory that she had felt for her "outside" lovers. He wouldn't believe the abandon she displayed in bed with them—the abandon that came from the thrill of romance. Yet there was so much she admired about Gregory. She loved him with the same devotion she had for her father and her mother. She would be lost without him. They had a marvelous life together. She was never bored with Gregory–only there was no romance and never had been. Perhaps a man who was a dynamo was incapable of expressing the sentimental little things that meant so much to a woman. But Robin Stone was just as forceful as Gregory, even more so. Yet you felt it was all pent up inside him. And tonight he had left with that washed-up actress, Diana Williams. How could a man who was so unattainable to her be available to starlets and broken-down has-beens? It wasn't fair! To have Robin would be the supreme conquest. He wouldn't be just an extracurricular lover. He had the same vitality she admired in Gregory, but Robin was beautiful, exciting–oh God, to be loved by a man like that!

But he had rejected her. Perhaps he thought it was too dangerous? Of course–that must be it! If they had an affair and it ended badly he might feel his career would be hurt. She had to make him understand that if they had a month together–a year together–no matter how they parted, it would in no way affect his job at IBC.

She walked to the mirror and gazed at her face. Good Lord, there was over an inch of slack loose skin. It had all happened so gradually. She pulled the skin tight. She looked marvelous! Well, that settled it: tomorrow she'd start searching for the right doctor. And she'd have to get some pills. She hadn't had the curse in five months and the night sweats were murder. You couldn't sleep with a man like Robin and wake up in the middle of the night bathed in perspiration.

She slipped into a robe. Odd that Gregory hadn't come in to say good night and hurl one final threat that this was positively the last eggnog party. She would go in and kiss his forehead and wish him a Happy New Year if he was awake. Now that she had made her decision about her face and the plan to get Robin, she felt exhilarated. She would have to tell Gregory about the face-lift and explain that it was just for her own vanity. There'd be no problem about her disappearing from the scene–she'd pretend to be visiting Connie in Rome.

Her smile vanished the moment she entered his bedroom.

He was lying across the bed, fully clothed. Alarm and conscience constricted her throat.

"Greg," she whispered softly.

"That eggnog has formed a rock in my gut," he groaned.

She breathed with relief. "You say that every year, but you drink more than anyone else. There's no rule that says you have to drink it. You could always have Scotch. Now come on, get undressed."

"I can't move, Judith. Whenever I try, the pain stabs at me."

"Shall I get you an Alkie?"

"I've had two."

"Gregory, you just can't stay like that, lying across the bed. Come on, now."

He made an attempt to sit, but doubled over. His face was white and he looked at her blankly. "Judith, this is something different."

She was at his side immediately. "Where does it hurt?"

"In my gut."

"Then it's just indigestion, Greg. Try getting undressed, then you can relax." He tried to move and cried out in agony. She rushed to the phone and called the doctor. She noticed that Gregory did not stop her. He sat on the bed, doubled over, rocking back and forth.

Dr. Spineck arrived in twenty minutes. Judith was downstairs, waiting to let him in. "David, I'm glad you could come."

"I'm glad I checked with my service. From what you tell me it doesn't sound like heart."

"I think it's plain old-fashioned indigestion. I hate to call you out, but he's never had it like this."

She waited outside the room while the doctor examined him. When he called her in, Gregory was sitting in a chair, fully dressed, quite calm.

"I gave him a shot of Demerol to ease the pain," Dr. Spineck said. "I think it's the gall bladder."

"That's not serious." It was more of a statement than a question.

"We'll have to take some tests," he answered. "But you're right. It's not serious. Just unpleasant."

They drove to the hospital in the doctor's car. Gregory was installed in a corner room. Nurses were summoned. Blood tests were taken. Judith was shunted to the lounge where she sat and chain-smoked. After half an hour. Dr. Spineck appeared. "It isn't going to be as simple as we thought. A stone is lodged in the duct and he needs an operation immediately. I've summoned Dr. Lesgarn. He'll be here any second."

At one o'clock Gregory was wheeled out of the room. The floor nurse brought Judith some coffee. She sat in Gregory's room and waited. She must have dozed off, because Dr. Spineck touched her cheek gently. She sat up and stared in startled surprise at her surroundings. In a flash she reoriented herself and glanced at her watch—it was four in the morning. Her eyes shot to the bed where Gregory should be. In alarm she looked at Dr. Spineck. He smiled. "Gregory's all right. He's in the postoperative room. He'll be there for hours. I've arranged for nurses around the clock."

"He'll be all right?" she asked.

He nodded. "He must have had gallstones for quite some time. It was a rougher operation than we counted on. He can't jump out of bed and be back at the office in two weeks—he's got to take the rest of the winter off and recuperate."

"He'll never do it," she said.

"He *has to,* Judith. He's not that young any more. None of us are. This operation has been a shock to his system. I doubt whether he'll feel up to any work for a few months."

"How soon will he come down?"

"Not before ten or eleven in the morning. I'll drive you home."

It was almost dawn when she got into bed. Poor Gregory—he'd hate having to take things easy. She'd have to stay in Palm Beach all winter and . . . She suddenly hated herself. How dared she think of Robin? Tears came to her eyes. "Oh, Gregory, I do love you," she whispered into the pillow. "I love you very much. Please get well." And she vowed that from now on she would never even think of Robin Stone, but even as she made the promise, she knew she would not keep it. She was filled with self-loathing because, as she lay alone in the dark room, she found herself wondering who Robin Stone was in bed with. . . .

Robin was in a narrow bed in a small room at the Harvard Club, alone.

He smiled for the first time that night. At least Maggie had seen fit to warn the doorman after she set the fire. He knew it was Maggie when he saw her suitcase on the floor and the charred matches from the Pavillon on the bed. He was beginning to find the situation amusing. He laughed aloud at the thought of her walking in and catching Diana copping his joint! And the worst thing had been that nothing was happening with him. In a way, thank God for the fire–he never would have been able to get it up for that crazy dame. She didn't even know how to go down on a guy–her teeth had been like razors. Yes, the fire had come just in time. Diana had been sobered by it too, and was delighted to be dropped at her hotel. But why had he brought her home in the first place? She had signed the contract at Jilly's. And if he felt he had to pay her off, he could have gone to her hotel. Archie would say that he *wanted* to be caught, wanted to get Maggie off his back. Well, it was all for the best, and all it had cost him was a bedroom. It had also cost him Maggie Stewart. A slight frown formed between his eyes, then he forced a smile. "No, Conrad, *you* lost Maggie. Not I. You're dead, you little bastard, *dead.*"

On an impulse he lifted the telephone and asked for Western Union. Where did she live? Well, he'd send it to Century Pictures. She'd get it.

The telegram was delivered to Maggie at the Melton Towers after it had kicked around the mailroom at the studio for three days. She read it, and then bought a small frame and hung it on her bathroom wall. It said:

> I TAKE IT ALL BACK. YOU WILL BE A STAR. YOU'RE A NUT!
> ROBIN.

Judith sat at Gregory's bedside every day. For the first time she realized he dyed his hair. It had never occurred to her that the red hair streaked with gray was not completely natural. But after a week in the hospital she noticed it was more white than red and on the back of his neck it was completely white. His unshaven face had a white stubble, and suddenly he looked like a tired old man. But she knew he was feeling better when he began taking an interest in the world around him. By the end of the second week he was checking the Nielsens. He also sent for his barber and told Judith to "go shopping or something." When she returned at five, his hair had its usual red tone, the hospital gown had been replaced with his own silk pajamas, he was reading *Time* magazine, and he looked every inch the chairman of IBC. But he had lost a great deal of weight and for the first time he looked his age. She shuddered and wondered how she would look if she had gone through a similar siege. André had been touching up her hair for fifteen years. Good Lord, she might be completely gray. And without makeup–!

Gregory put down the magazine, picked up the telephone and asked for IBC.

"Please, darling, both Dr. Lesgarn and Dr. Spineck say *no work*. In fact when you get out of here, they insist you take a long rest."

"I intend to," he said. "We're going to Palm Beach for the entire winter. It'll be the first vacation I've taken in years." He reached out and took her hand. "Judith, I'm so damn grateful that it was just gall bladder. I'd been having these awful pains for some time, but usually I could shake them. I don't mind telling you, I was afraid to get a checkup. I was positive it was cancer. If I'd had the strength, I'd have shouted for joy when they said it was only gall bladder. And this winter I'll enjoy playing golf and being with you. That's why I've got to get on the phone and set things in order."

His first call was to Cliff Dorne, head of the legal department. "Cliff, I want you here within the next half hour. Now switch me to Robin Stone."

At five thirty Robin Stone and Cliff Dorne arrived. Judith was sitting in the easy chair. "Would you like me to go out to the lounge while you talk?" she asked.

"No, stay, Judith," Gregory said. "This is an important decision. I want you to hear it. Robin, how would you like to be president of IBC?"

Robin didn't answer. It was Cliff Dorne who reacted.

"President of IBC?" Cliff repeated. "What is Danton Miller?"

Gregory shrugged. "Dan is president of Network Television."

"And what exactly is president of IBC?" Cliff asked.

"A new title I've just made up. It merely means a division of power while I'm away."

"But do you think Dan will sit still if Robin is placed up there with him?" Cliff asked.

"Yes, because Dan still has the same power. He's always had to report to me, only this time he'll do it through Robin. And Robin can check everything with me."

Cliff nodded. Then for the first time they both looked at Robin.

Robin stood up. "Sorry, but I pass."

"Are you insane?" Gregory sputtered.

"I'd be insane to take such a job. As I see it, I'd have two months of infighting with Dan, yet actually I'd be nothing more than a glorified watchdog and messenger boy. Then you return from Palm Beach with a nice tan and I go back to being president of News, with a brace of enemies and one of Dan's ulcers."

"Who said you go back to News?" Gregory asked.

"I assume the job is temporary. Any created title always is."

Gregory rubbed his chin thoughtfully. "Perhaps it *was* in its original inception, but the more I think of it, the more sense it makes to keep it as a permanent setup."

"But essentially I'm a newsman," Robin said.

"Balls!" Gregory shouted. "You've jazzed that Happening show into a real piece of entertainment. Without realizing it, Robin, you have unconsciously gone away from News. If I didn't know you better, I'd think you were also after power."

Robin's smile was easy, but his eyes were like steel. "Perhaps I am."

Gregory smiled. "I don't make snap judgments. I've done my homework on you." He reached for a sheaf of papers on his night table. "You doubt me? Okay: you're from Boston. You're going to come into money of your own someday. Your father was one of the biggest lawyers there. Your mother lives in Rome. She's not well—I'm sorry about that. You have a sister in San Francisco whose husband is wealthy in his own right. Now a man with this kind of background likes to do a job well. He has built-in security, so he does not hunger for power. You take me, Robin—I grew up on Tenth Avenue, one of the kids I played with went to the chair. I know it sounds like a Bogart movie, but it happened that way. Some of the kids on my block also made it big as lawyers, politicians, and doctors. Because the kids on that street *had* to have power. If they went into crime, they didn't fool around with robbery. They became killers. And if they went into business they became killers. I'm a killer. Dan's a killer. You aren't. I wouldn't trust you with running the financial end of a network for five minutes. You always went way over budget with *In Depth*. You built it into a prestige show. Now that Andy Parino is on it and Cliff, here, keeps an eye on things, the show's making money for the first time."

"It's also not as good," Robin said. "I was planning to have a meeting with Andy next Monday. We're doing too many shows based in New York. We need some European flavor."

"You'll have no such meeting," Gregory snapped. "That's what I mean about you and finances. The show has decent enough ratings. We can milk another season out of it. Fortunately we're getting a big enough price on the Happening show to make some money—even with you running it." Gregory smiled to take the bite out of his words. "But I didn't ask you here to lecture you on the economics of television. Dan knows them well enough. Cliff knows them even better. And one thing about Dan, he'll never recommend a show that won't make a profit."

"What about quality?" Robin asked.

"The public doesn't want quality. We have a few quality shows that we keep on. And they're losers. You know what the public wants. *Shit*—that's what it wants. The high ratings of the old movies prove it. I won't go that route yet. As long as I can, I'll try to create new shows for prime time. But we can still be commercial. And that's what Dan is. Now, if we combine your taste with Dan's commercialism—we've got a winning ticket."

Robin built his fingers into a pyramid. He studied them. Then he looked up. "Who moves to president of News?"

"I'll let you make that suggestion."

"Andy Parino."

"I don't think he has the ability," Gregory said.

"I'll keep an eye on him. He'll report directly to me."

Gregory nodded. "Okay, I'll go along."

"What about a contract?" Robin said.

"Dan has no contract."

"I want one."

"For how long?"

"One year." Robin did not miss the fleeting expression of relief on Gregory's face. "Gregory, this may not work out. But I want you to know something. I am not going to be just your telephone pal. I'm going to *be* president of IBC. I'm going to come up with ideas, throw them at you, fight for them if I think they're right. I need the assurance of one year. No one can tell anything in six weeks. But after a year, well, either it works or I walk away from the title and go back to News."

Gregory nodded. "That's fair enough. What do you think of sixty thousand a year plus expenses?"

"I think it's ridiculous."

"Dan started at fifty."

"What is Dan making now?"

"Seventy-five, plus expenses and stock options."

Robin nodded. "That sounds better."

Gregory was silent for a moment. Then he smiled. "I like your guts. I also like the idea that you want to carry the ball. Okay, Cliff will draw up the contract." Then he held out his hand to Robin. "Good luck to the president of IBC."

Robin smiled. "And may the chairman of the board have an excellent vacation." Then he looked at Judith with a hint of intimacy in his smile. "Take good care of him, Mrs. Austin."

The news ripped through Madison Avenue like a tornado.

Dan Miller was in a state of shock but he pretended that Robin's new title had been his idea. He faced the press with his usual smile and made a statement. "He's a good man, and I need someone to pitch in while Gregory is away."

But he spent hours staring at the skyline from his window, wondering what everyone in the business thought. He took tranquilizers and avoided "21" and restaurants where he might run into agency men. He holed in at night, and when he read that Robin was taping the Diana Williams Happening, he prayed that Diana would do one of her famous walkouts–then Robin would be stuck with egg on his tape.

But as January passed, Dan's fears began to diminish. The cancelations had been decided several months back. The new shows had been selected by Gregory in November: a few seemed to be making it, a few were bigger bombs than their predecessors. And now it was time to start viewing pilots for the fall season.

By February he had completely regained his confidence. Then he heard about Robin's new offices. A suite on the penthouse floor! Dan went storming into Cliff Dorne's office.

Cliff tried to dismiss it. "Where can we put him? You tell *me*. Andy Parino has inherited Robin's office. There just is no space. Gregory had a thousand feet of space closed off up there. He always intended to make it into a gym and sauna bath. Because of the shortage of space, he's turned it into offices for Robin."

"How does it make *me* look–Robin sharing the penthouse floor with Gregory!"

Cliff sighed. "Okay, tell me where to put him and I'll be glad to oblige."

"They should have put *me* there," Dan snapped. "And given Robin *my* office."

Cliff smiled. "Not very good thinking for a man who's telling everyone Robin has been kicked upstairs. Put him in your office, Dan, and he's replacing *you*. Then you're kicked upstairs for real."

Dan had no recourse but to remain grimly silent. The newspapers were going all out on Robin's new assignment. In the beginning Robin had refused to comment. But he finally capitulated and gave a mass interview the day he took possession of his new suite of offices.

He stook behind the large desk as the questions were fired at him. His answers were polite but evasive. The press sensed his reluctance to talk, and feeling they were covering an important story, they zeroed in on him. As an ex-newspaperman, Robin felt an empathy for them. Their job was to get a story.

"Let's talk about television itself, rather than my new title," he said with a smile.

"What about television?" a young man asked.

"It's an octopus. It's no longer just a little box, it's the Love Machine."

"Why the Love Machine?" a reporter asked.

"Because it *sells* love. It *creates* love. Presidents are chosen by their appeal on that little box. It's turned politicians into movie stars and movie stars into politicians. It can get you engaged if you use a certain mouthwash. It claims you'll have women hanging on your coattails if you use a certain hair cream. It tells the kids to eat their cereal if they want to be like their baseball idol. But like all great lovers, the Love Machine is a fickle bastard. It has great magnetism–but it has no heart. In place of a heart beats a Nielsen rating. And when the Nielsen falters, the program dies. It's the pulse and heart of the twentieth century–the Love Machine."

The newspapers all carried the story. Dan read it and glowered. Especially when columnists began to try to tag Robin as the Love Machine. "Perhaps Mr. Stone is comparing the box with himself," wrote Ronnie Wolfe. "His way of giving unlimited time to a beautiful girl is well known. And like the machine he speaks of, Mr. Stone can also turn off with equal ease."

Dan threw the paper across the room. Dammit, that was only adding to Robin's image: call a man a heel with women and suddenly he gets charisma. He reached for another tranquilizer, gulped it down and wondered what the son of a bitch was doing in that plush new office. What new scheme did he have going? Rehearsals for the Diana Williams show had been postponed for two weeks. The newspapers reported that Byron Withers, the leading man, had bowed out, claiming his part had been cut down from the original concept, in deference to Diana. Byron Withers! Where did these has-beens get their nerve–thinking they could come to Broadway after three pictures and share equal billing with Diana Williams? Although he was rooting for Robin's demise, Dan still respected Diana's talent. He put down the newspaper and hoped it was a phony item and that it was Diana herself who was being difficult.

Robin also wondered if Diana was being difficult. Was she on the pills and booze? Ike Ryan swore she was fine and eager to begin rehearsals. "As soon as we find the right leading man," Ike said. "He doesn't even have to sing great–just look the part."

He was just leaving for the viewing room when his secretary peeked in. "A Mr. Nelson is waiting outside to see you."

For a moment Robin looked blank. As he stared at her, the secretary added, "It's Dip Nelson, the movie actor."

Robin's smile was warm. "Of course, show him in."

Dip strode in giving the secretary a radiant smile. She fluttered with excitement and stumbled out of the room. Robin laughed. "She's a forty-year-old virgin, she'll never be the same."

Dip shrugged. "If that's the case, I may even grab her by the ass when I leave–let the poor woman die happy." He whistled as he took in the office. "Well, old buddy pal, this is quite a layout you got yourself."

"How's it been going, Dip?"

The handsome blond man sat on a chair and threw his long legs over the side. "Between you and I, it's been going lousy until today."

"What happened to your Persian Room engagement? I kept watching for the announcement."

Dip shrugged. "The act bombed. We kept it on the road for over a year and milked what we could out of it, but I didn't dare bring it into New York. See, I did some analyzing. Pauli and me–we don't mesh."

"You mean the marriage is over?"

"Over! It's never been more solid, pal. It's just that our personalities don't go to form a good act. Look, when she does comedy or straight singing on her own, she's great. And when I do my old song and dance, I'm great. I kill them with my imitations. I swear when I do Godfrey with the uke–buddy boy, you can't tell the difference. Ted Lewis *knows* he's listening to himself when I say, 'Is everybody happy?' But the thing is, I'm one style and she's another. But listen, buddy boy, my agent told me Ike Ryan is looking for a leading man to play opposite Diana Williams–and the

Big Dipper is a natural for the job. You once said you owed me something. Well, how about booking Pauli and me on *The Christie Lane Show?* It would serve as an audition for me for Ike Ryan, and also we could use the scratch. I hear they pay five G's for guests. And it will give Pauli some coverage too. She's gonna be mad enough if I get the lead opposite Diana Williams and split the act–but if it comes from the Chris Lane show, it won't look as if I went after it."

"I'll take care of it. How soon do you want to go on?"

"Like *yesterday!*"

Robin picked up the phone and called Jerry Moss. "Jerry, who is the guest star on the next week's Chris Lane show? Lon Rogers? Well, cancel him out. I don't give a damn if Artie Rylander picked him–IBC will pay him off. I want Pauli and Dip Nelson booked in his place. And if there are any repercussions just say the word came from me. . . . Sure, say I *hate* Lon Rogers, that *I* want him canceled. . . . Hell no, I think Lon is as good as any baritone around–but I want Dip and Pauli in that spot. Fine."

He hung up and smiled at Dip. "It's done."

Dip shook his head in awe. "Buddy boy, you've sure come a long way while we've been out on the road."

The following morning Robin's secretary announced that Danton Miller was waiting in the outside office. Robin was on the telephone talking to Gregory in Palm Beach. "Have him wait," Robin answered.

Dan's anger blistered as he sat in the outer office. When he was finally admitted, he spat the words out before he was in the door. "Not only do you butt into my shows, but you play it cute, and make me wait."

"What's so important to bring you here in person?" Robin asked with a cordial smile.

Dan stood in front of him, his fists clenched. "Now you're in the booking business. How dare you go over Artie Rylander's head and put a crummy team on my top show."

"IBC's top show," Robin answered.

"What's your excuse?" Dan demanded.

Robin's stare was cold. "I stopped making excuses when I was five years old."

"Why are they on the show?" Dan demanded, in tight-lipped fury.

"Because I happen to *like* them. They're a new team. They haven't been on television. That in itself is refreshing. I'm tired of seeing the same old Hollywood names, the ones we pay five thousand–and then see them with Johnny Carson, Merv Griffin or Mike Douglas a few days later for scale. From here on in, no plugs for pictures are allowed on any of our shows."

"Listen, you son of a bitch–"

The secretary buzzed. Robin snapped the box on. Her voice came through.

"Your reservation to Rome is confirmed, Mr. Stone."

"Rome!" Dan looked like he was going to have a stroke. "Why in hell are you going to Rome?"

Robin stood up. "Because my mother is dying." He walked past Dan, then he stopped at the door. "And I have Gregory's permission to stay as long as I'm needed. I hope you can manage to get along without me for a few days." When he left the office Dan was still standing in the center of the room staring after him.

TWENTY-SEVEN

SERGIO WAS WAITING at the airport when Robin arrived. "I did not cable you sooner," the boy explained. "We thought it was just another seizure. But yesterday the doctor said I should notify her family. Did I do right?"

"You did just fine, Sergio," Robin said. He was aware that the boy's eyes were shining with tears. He waited until they were in the car, then he asked, "How does she seem?"

Through the corner of his eye he saw the tears spill down Sergio's face. "She is in a coma," he said.

"Did you notify my sister?" Robin asked.

"Lisa and Richard are on their way. Their names were in Kitty's address book. I sent them the same cable I sent you."

It was ten in the morning when they reached the clinic. Robin was only allowed a brief glance at the waxen face under the oxygen tent. She died at eleven thirty that night without regaining consciousness. Lisa and Richard arrived an hour later. Lisa went into immediate hysterics and had to be given sedation. Richard stood by, stoic and helpless.

The following morning, Robin, Sergio and Richard met with Kitty's lawyer and discussed the funeral arrangements. Kitty's will would be probated in the States. The trust was to be divided evenly between Robin and Lisa, but Kitty had left the villa, the car and all of her jewelry to Sergio. Lisa stayed in bed all day. The following morning she appeared at breakfast, pale and silent, as Sergio and Robin were having their second cup of coffee.

"Kitty wanted to be cremated," Robin said. "We made all the arrangements yesterday. Richard sat in for you."

Lisa said nothing. Suddenly she turned to Sergio. "Do you mind having your coffee in the other room? I want to talk to my brother."

Robin's eyes narrowed. "This is *his* house," he said. But Sergio had already taken his coffee into the living room. "That was goddamned rude," Robin said tonelessly.

Lisa ignored him and turned to her husband. "Well, are you going to tell him?"

For a moment Richard looked embarrassed. Then he stiffened with an attempt at righteous courage. "We're contesting the will."

"Just what are you contesting?" Robin asked cautiously.

"Sergio getting the villa and the jewelry. We can't lose."

"What makes you so sure?"

Richard smiled. "Once we start legal action, the estate will be held up. Sergio will need money to live on. It's obvious he has none. After a few months he'll be delighted to settle for a few thousand dollars. Of course, we will also claim that Kitty was not sound of mind when she made the will—that the boy used pressure to make her draw it up."

"I'll fight you on it," Robin said evenly.

"You'd stick up for that little faggot?" Richard asked.

"I'll stick up for anyone who was good to Kitty."

"I'll have him investigated," Richard said. "I'll prove he played on the emotions of a sick old woman."

"Who the hell are you to prove anything? Were you ever here? Did you ever see them together? I did. And for that reason my word will carry more weight than yours."

"Oh no, it won't," Lisa said in an odd voice. "I happen to hold some trump cards that might lessen the power of *your* word. And the attending publicity might embarrass you at your network. To say nothing of your personal life."

Richard shot her a warning look. "Lisa, we can win legally. Let's not get personalities involved."

"I might have expected this from you," Lisa snapped at Robin. "After all, what are you really? Just a lucky bastard—"

"Lisa!" Richard's voice held a warning.

"No, why *shouldn't* I shock him? I'd *like* to see big brother lose his cool just once in his life! It only proves that in the end class will tell. He's about as much my real brother as that fairy in the other room." She turned to Robin. "You were adopted when you were five!"

She paused, waiting for Robin's reaction. Richard seemed to be the only one affected. He looked out toward the patio to hide his embarrassment and displeasure.

Robin's gaze was level. "Lisa, at this moment, nothing gives me greater satisfaction than the realization that we are in no way related."

"Your mother was a whore!"

"Lisa!" This was Richard.

"Let her go on," Robin said evenly.

"Oh, I kept it a secret these past few years. I didn't know until then. Kitty told me when she was ill. She said if I was ever in trouble to go to you. That you were a strong person. That she really loved you as if you were her own. She adopted you because she had given up on having a child of her own, and she wanted one. Dad had a friend in criminal law and he told him about a case he was handling–about the poor little orphan in a coma in an orphanage hospital in Providence. Mother insisted on adopting him. Your real mother was strangled! You *had* no father. But Mother, *my* mother, worshiped you, because two years later the impossible happened–she had me! I can't stop you from getting your end of the estate–that's all legal, Dad made that stupid will. But I can sure stop you from letting that fairy wind up with anything!"

"*Try* it. I enjoy a good fight."

She jumped up and tossed her coffee in his face. "You knew it all along, about being adopted! You cold-blooded bastard–*I hate you!*" Then she ran out of the room.

Richard sat stunned. Robin calmly mopped his face and shirt. "Thank goodness the coffee was lukewarm," he said with a smile.

Richard stood up. "I'm sorry, Robin. She doesn't mean any of it. She'll get over it." He started from the room. "Oh, and Robin –don't worry, I won't let her contest the will."

Robin smiled at him. "Crew Cut, maybe I've misjudged you."

Kitty's body was cremated. Lisa silently took possession of the urn and she and Richard took a flight out the following day. Obviously Richard exerted some control, because she made no further mention of fighting Sergio on the will. When they were gone, Robin poured himself a stiff drink. Sergio watched him silently.

"I want to thank you, Robin. I was sitting in the other room the day your sister reacted so violently. Unfortunately I could not help but overhearing. Is it the truth about you being adopted?"

Robin nodded. Then he turned with a quick grin and said, "But it's also true that you are now a man of means."

The boy nodded. "She left me much jewelry. Pearls, a twenty-carat emerald-cut diamond. Now I can go to America!"

Robin whistled through his teeth. "Sergio, you really struck it big."

"What I am trying to say is perhaps you want the ring or the necklace to give to a lady you care about?"

"Nope. You keep it all. You were there when she needed you."

Sergio stared at him. "What are you going to do, Robin?"

"Well, for one thing, I'm going to get pissy-eyed drunk. Tell you what, Sergio, let's really tie one on, find us some girls–" he stopped. "You really don't go for women? Not at all?"

The boy shook his head. "Even with Kitty. I was just her very good friend."

"Okay, you be *my* very good friend tonight. Let's go and get drunk."

"I will go with you, but I will not drink."

At two in the morning Robin was singing as they wandered down the cobbled streets. He was dimly aware that Sergio was holding him up. Several times he tripped and would have fallen if it had not been for Sergio. He had never gotten so roaring drunk. The last thing he recalled was falling across the bed before he passed out. He awoke the following morning with the first hangover he had ever known. He was under the covers, disrobed down to his shorts. Sergio came in with a pot of inky-black coffee. Robin took it and eyed him curiously.

"Sergio, how did I get my clothes off?"

"I undressed you."

"That figures. Did you enjoy yourself?"

Sergio looked properly insulted. "Robin, the trouble with people is that they think a homosexual will go for just any man. If you were with a girl and she passed out, would you take her just because she was a woman?"

Robin's grin was apologetic. "I had it coming. Sorry." Then, in an attempt to break the somber mood, he grinned and said, "Sergio, I should be insulted. I thought you dug me."

For a second there was a glimmer of hope in the dark eyes. Then he caught Robin's smile. "You joke. But I will always wear this bracelet." He held out his arm. "I know you like women, but one day I will find a man I care about who also will care for me."

Robin sipped the black coffee. It tasted awful but it cleared his head.

"You hate what I am, don't you, Robin?"

"No, Sergio. At least you know what you are, who you are and what you want out of life."

"Does it bother you not knowing your real mother?"

"Yes–it makes me feel in limbo," Robin said slowly.

"Then find out who she *really* was."

"You heard what Lisa said. Unfortunately it's the truth. I have an old newspaper clipping in my wallet to prove it."

"Germany is not far away."

"Meaning what?"

"You know the name of your mother, the city she came from. She might have relatives, friends–you could learn about her."

"Forget it."

"You mean you would take the word of Lisa and a newspaper clipping? I am what she calls a fairy. It is true. But I am also a person. Perhaps your mother was a good person. Find out what she was like."

"Hell, I don't speak German. I've never been to Hamburg."

"I speak German and I've been to Hamburg, I know it well."

Robin smiled. "Sergio, you are a man of many talents."

"We could be in Germany in a few hours. I would go with you."

Robin threw back the covers and leaped out of bed. "Know something, Sergio? I've never been to Germany and I'd like to have a look at it. *Especially* Hamburg. I dropped some bombs over it once, but I only saw it from the air. Also I'm very partial to German girls. You make the plane reservations. We may not find out anything about my mother, but it's a cinch we'll find *something!*"

They checked into the Four Seasons hotel. The suite was Old World in its charm and furnishings. Oriental-type rugs, thick comforters on the bed. Sergio went right to the phone and began to call all the Boesches listed in the directory. Robin ordered a bottle of vodka and sat at the window, sipping his drink and watching the darkness fall on the city. People were waiting for buses. Mothers were dragging children down the street as the stores began to close. The Alster River looked serene and dark. So this was the enemy he had bombed. The city the British had bombed. It looked like any city in America. He half listened to Sergio's faultless German as he made call after call. On the eighth call, Sergio called to him excitedly. He was writing a number, an address.

"We have luck," he said as he hung up. "These Boesches said they are distant cousins of a Herta. We can see them tomorrow."

"Keep trying," Robin said. "There might be more than one Herta."

At the end of an hour they had located five Herta Boesches who had gone to America. One was still living in Milwaukee–that ruled her out. The others had not been heard from.

Sergio looked crestfallen. "I have not been a success and it seemed like such a good plan. I am most sorry, Robin."

"Sorry! Are you going just to sit there and cry in your beer? At least show me Hamburg. Is there any night life in this town?"

Sergio laughed aloud. "Robin–no town in the world has the kind of night life Hamburg has."

"You've got to be kidding! Better than Paris?"

"Paris! They are prudes. Their clubs are for tourists. Come, I will show you night life. But we will take no more than one hundred dollars with us, and get it changed into small bills at the desk. Where I am going to take you, it is most easy to be robbed."

They took a cab and Sergio directed the driver to a given point then they got out and walked. "This is the St. Pauli district," Sergio explained.

They walked down the brightly lit street. "This is the Reeperbahn." It was more brightly lighted than Broadway. A skyscraper stood next to a bar called Wimpy's. Across the street was a bowling alley. But what struck Robin most was the people. Masses of people, all walking in a leisurely way. It reminded him of a shopping crowd on Fifth Avenue before Christmas, without the frantic pace. These people were strolling aimlessly. Robin and Sergio walked on silently passing a conglomeration of stores–auction houses, furniture shops–the entire street was a maze of neon lights. Men with goods, hawking like American auctioneers and everywhere the smell of sausage. On impulse Robin stopped at a stand. "Two *Weisswurst,* please."

Sergio stared at it. "What is it, Robin? It looks like a white hot dog."

Robin bit into it and speared the hot sauerkraut. *"Weisswurst.* I haven't had it since–" He stopped, suddenly speechless. "I just saw her, Sergio! I saw a crummy little round table and a beautiful lady with black hair place a dish of this before a little boy. It was hot and good." Robin pushed the plate away. "This is junk compared to the way she made it."

They left the stand and walked in silence. "I saw her face," Robin kept muttering. "I'm beginning to see everything. She was beautiful–dark with flashing black eyes, like a gypsy."

"I am glad," Sergio said.

"She was still a whore. But at least I remember now. God, she was beautiful. Let's celebrate, Sergio. We're not going to spend the whole night walking down a German midway, are we? This may be your idea of night life, but it isn't mine."

Sergio took his arm and led him across the street. They turned right and walked a block. "Ah, this is it," Sergio said, "the Silbersackstrasse."

Robin stared as if they had suddenly entered another world. Girls accosted them openly. *"Amerikaner–Spiel?"* One of the bolder ones chased after them. "Three-way good time, all of us?"

Robin smiled and they walked on. Every few steps a girl emerged from an alley or a doorway. The proposition never varied. They made the girls who paraded down Seventh Avenue and Central Park South look like debutantes. These were rough little Fräuleins, educated to cater to the sailors with their striped shirts and eager appetites. They cut through another street and

Sergio stopped before a dark, wooden planked gate. The white painted letters read: VERBOTEN! Sergio opened the door. Robin followed him in silent amazement.

"This is Herbertstrasse," Sergio whispered.

Robin couldn't believe it. The long cobbled street was narrow and lined on both sides with solid rows of tiny two-story houses. The windows of the downstairs rooms went from floor to ceiling. And in each lighted window sat a girl. A few windows were dark. Sergio pointed to the upper room: "That means she is working." People flowed up and down the street studying the girls. To Robin's amazement he saw women walking there with men. He spotted a well-known movie star with dark glasses and a bandanna —the German representative from her picture company was giving her a "tour." Robin felt as open-mouthed as the actress. He couldn't believe anything like this still existed. The girls behind the windows seemed oblivious of the people who walked along the street. They sat in tiny bras and G-strings, sipping glasses of wine. Their hard mascaraed eyes seemed to stare past the spectators. Occasionally one girl would turn to her companion in the next window and make a comment. The other would laugh. *Laugh?* How could there be laughter in a world like this? What did these girls feel and think? How could they laugh?

"Christmas Eve is the sad night," Sergio whispered. "They actually have little trees in the windows and they give each other gifts. Then at midnight they cry."

"How do you know all this?"

"My sister worked here," Sergio said quietly.

"Your sister!"

"I was born during the war. My father was killed in Tunisia. My mother did the best she could to support me and my three brothers. We were all under ten. My sister was fourteen. She began working the streets to bring us food from the Americans. Later she wound up here in the Herbertstrasse. She died last year at thirty-five. That is a long life for a girl in the Herbertstrasse. Come, I will show you where they go after they are thirty." He led Robin into an alleyway off the main section of the Herbertstrasse. Here the windows faced a blank wall. They were relegated to fat older women in their thirties. Robin looked at a blowsy hennaed woman with a gold tooth and muddy eyes. A beery-faced man with a red-veined nose knocked on her window. She opened it. He stood with three other men. A guttural argument ensued. Suddenly she slammed her window shut. The men shrugged and tapped the next window where a straw-haired woman sat with a kimono covering flattened breasts that hung to her waist. There was more conversation. She opened the door and the men entered. The lights went off as the group went upstairs.

"What was that all about?" Robin asked.

"It was a matter of price," Sergio explained. "They were willing to pay the proper amount of marks for the man who would have the affair, but the others wanted to be allowed to watch for a small bit of money."

Robin laughed. "A group plan."

Sergio nodded. "The second one agreed, but she made them promise that if they masturbated while watching she would make them pay to clean the rug."

They walked back to the main section of the Herbertstrasse. In one window, Robin saw a girl who reminded him of the prostitute he had beaten. She was standing wearing boots and held a whip.

"Advertising her talent," Sergio whispered.

They returned to the Reeperbahn and wandered into a discothèque where they were quickly shown to the door. Robin had a quick glimpse of women dancing together, holding hands at the bar. Here men were *verboten*. They stopped at a café where the barker at the door promised "wonderful nudes." Robin shrugged and Sergio followed him inside. The place was jammed with sailors and they were shown to a small table in the back. The nightclub floor was elevated and a girl had stripped down to complete nudity–no pasties or G-String. There was a scattering of applause and the girl went off. Now music began. Another girl came on–she looked about nineteen–fresh-eyed and eager in a pink chiffon dress, and her smile held the guilelessness of a girl going to her first prom. "This one probably sings," Robin decided.

She walked around the floor grinning at all the sailors and tossing greetings to them. They shouted back good-naturedly–she was obviously a favorite. Then the music began and she started to strip. Robin couldn't believe it. She was attractive and fresh—she would have looked more natural as a young junior secretary at the IBC network than strutting on that floor, chatting with the sailors. Suddenly she was completely nude. She stood there and pivoted with the same cheerful grin. The bitch enjoyed her work. Then she pulled a chair to the center of the floor and sat on it and spread her legs, grinning merrily all the while. She finally left the chair and walked around the club, leaning down to each table and allowing the men to suck at her breasts. She came to their table, looked at Robin and Sergio, then laughed and shook her head. She winked at them knowingly and went on her way.

Robin threw some money on the table and started out of the room. Sergio hurried after him. They walked down the street in silence.

"That girl," Robin said. "She couldn't have been more than twenty. Why? *How?*"

"Robin—these girls are the product of the war. They grew up struggling for food. And children like that grow up with a different set of values. To them sex is not love—sex is not even for pleasure. *It is a way to survive.*"

As they walked down the street, girls accosted them every five feet. "Look, I'm packing it in," Robin said.

"Come to one more place before we go back to the hotel."

They entered a cabaret on Grosse Freiheit Strasse. It was elegant and subdued. And attractive people were sitting quietly at tables, conversing with one another as a muted string trio played German love songs. It was a long room dimly lighted, paneled with Austrian drapes. There were groups of men, which aroused Robin's suspicions, until he saw several heterosexual couples, holding hands and listening to the music.

"The food is excellent here at the Maison Bleue," Sergio said.

"You eat. I want to get loaded."

Sergio ordered a steak which he attacked with such eagerness that Robin felt guilty—he had forgotten they had skipped dinner. Robin ordered a bottle of hundred-proof vodka to be left on the table. He sipped it straight. It felt like hot white velvet. . . .

The string ensemble stopped playing. A drummer joined the band, cymbals were crashed, a guttural announcement was made, and the show began. Robin watched without too much interest. It was obviously a high-class supper club. A French *chanteuse* named Véronique came out. She was good, a true contralto. She finished to polite applause. He poured himself another shot of vodka. He narrowed his eyes to place the next girl in focus. She was blond and vapidly pretty and she was singing something from *Gypsy*. Ethel Merman didn't have to worry. He looked up groggily as the orchestra went into a fanfare. Then the leader shouted, *"Brazillia!"* And a slim dark girl stepped into the spotlight.

Robin sat up. She was worth the fanfare. She wore a man's evening jacket over a leotard. Her black hair was tucked into a French knot under a black slouch hat worn at a rakish angle. Slowly she began an apache dance. It was amazingly good. The girl had a solid classical ballet background. She finished in a frenzy and whipped off her hat and let her black hair cascade down to her shoulders. The applause was strong, but she did not leave. She waited until it subsided, then the music began the familiar beat. She swayed suggestively and removed her coat. Slowly she fell to her knees, then like a snake shedding its skin, she writhed her way out of the leotard, revealing a smooth white body with tiny silver bikini pants and bra.

The music went faster, the lights began to flicker; he saw the silver-and-white body leaping into the air, falling into splits. The lights dimmed. She pulled off the bra and bikini pants, the lights came up to give the audience a fleeting flash of the nude slim body and the small compact breasts. Then the lights went off, and she disappeared to loud applause. The show was over and Robin was quite drunk.

"I want to meet Brazillia," he announced.

"We'll go to Liesel's down the street where they all go for breakfast. You'll see Brazillia there."

Robin looked at his watch. "Are you kidding? It's three A.M. This place is about to pack in. Nothing will be open."

"There are places in Hamburg open twenty-four hours."

Robin paid the bill, but insisted upon sending a note to Brazillia telling her to meet them at Liesel's. Sergio patiently wrote it in German and gave it to the waiter along with a handful of marks. The waiter returned and an exchange of German passed between him and Sergio. "She will be there," he told Robin. "Come—we will leave." Robin followed obediently.

Liesel's was obviously owned by the fat woman who greeted them and led them into a cellar with small tables and checked cloths. Sergio ordered beer. Robin's gaze wandered as he sipped vodka. A tall good-looking man entered and sat at a table across the room. Soon a few effeminate men joined him. The tall man stared at Sergio. Robin was drunk but he was able to detect the instant radar that went up between Sergio and the man. "You're sure this is where Brazillia comes, and not just a faggot hangout?"

"It's everything. It is also the only place on the block that serves breakfast." Sergio was staring at the good-looking boy across the way.

Robin patted him on the shoulder. "Okay. Sergy, go join the boys."

"I will stay with you. Perhaps Brazillia will not come. I do not want you to be alone."

"Listen, chum, I don't need a caretaker. And don't worry, she'll show."

"Robin, I don't like it. You know what kind of a girl Brazillia is, don't you?"

"Beat it, or the muscle man across the room will lose interest. He probably thinks I'm your date by now."

"But, Robin—"

"Do I have to toss you out?"

At that moment the door opened and she entered. She looked around the room hesitantly. Robin stood up and waved. She walked directly to his table. "Beat it, chum," he said under his breath.

Sergio shrugged and joined the table across the room. Brazillia sat down beside him. The woman who ran the place brought her a cognac.

"I speak English," she said in a low throaty voice.

"You don't have to talk, baby."

He glanced up in time to see Sergio leave with the handsome man. Sergio waved and Robin formed a victory sign with his fingers. The girl sat and silently drank her cognac. Robin ordered her another. He reached out and held her hand. She returned the pressure. A blond, effeminate young man entered the room and walked over to their table. He spoke a few words in French to Brazillia. She nodded and the man sat down. "This is Vernon. He does not speak English. He is waiting for a friend and does not like to stand at the bar alone."

Robin signaled for a drink for Vernon. To his surprise the fat woman brought him a glass of milk. "Vernon does not drink," Brazillia explained.

Just than a tall rugged man entered. Vernon gulped down the milk, and dashed to meet him. "Poor Vernon," Brazillia said. "He does not know what he wants to be."

"It's pretty obvious," Robin said.

Brazillia sighed. "During the day he tries to live like a man. At night he is a woman. It is sad." Then she turned to Robin. "Are you here for wild thrills?"

"I like any kind of thrills."

"If you expect something wild and crazy with me, go away." She sounded weary. "You are handsome. I would very much like to go to bed with you. But I would like a night of love, of beautiful sex–no sickness. You understand?"

"That's fine with me."

"It will be like that?" She was almost pleading.

"You call the shots, baby."

"Excuse me a moment." She walked to the bar and whispered something to Vernon. He nodded with a faint smile. Then she returned. "Let us go."

As he paid the check he wondered what her deal with Vernon was all about. But then, many girls had fags as confidants and close friends. Amanda even said a model friend of hers lived with a fag. And look at him with Sergio.

A cab was parked outside but she tossed her head in dismissal. "I live near here."

She led him through dark cobbled streets until they came to a large building. They went through a wooden door into a courtyard. Suddenly there was a look of Paris about the place. The geraniums in the window boxes, a stray cat prowling around, middle-class domesticity. They walked up to the second floor. She leaned down and picked up a loaf of bread and put the key in the door. "I always have bread delivered, in case I have had too much cognac. If I eat bread, I don't wake with a hangover."

The apartment was small, but totally feminine. Sparkling clean and almost virginal with the white ruffled bedspread and the dolls on the bed. There was a picture of Brazillia on the dressing table. And on the mantel above the fireplace was a picture of one of the girls in the show–the one named Véronique.

"She's too good to open the show," Robin commented. "She could make it in New York." Then he reached out and caught her around the waist. "And you're too damn good a dancer to strip. You're really good."

Brazillia shrugged. "It gives me extra money and makes me a headline act. Ah, but what is the difference? None of us will go anywhere no matter how badly we want to. Once you live and work on the Reeperbahn, it is too late. But I was in America once. I played Las Vegas."

"You did?" Robin was surprised.

"Yes, not doing what I am doing now. I was part of a chorus. There were six of us. We did a straight dance, to support an old has-been American singer. He could barely get out the notes and we came on behind him to drown him out. That was ten years ago. I was eighteen and I had hoped to study the ballet seriously. But when the act was finished, all I had left was a return ticket home. So I came back."

"Where is home?"

"It was Milano. I stayed there for a time." She poured him a cognac. "Then I realized that trying to wait on tables and live the bourgeois life that was expected of me was as dishonest as–" Again she strugged. "Come, are you like all the others–must the life story be part of the evening?"

"No. You don't have to tell me a damn thing, Brazillia. But you are young and attractive. Don't give up all your dreams."

She pushed him on the couch and sat on his lap. "Tonight I am having a dream come true." She ran her fingers along his profile and her tongue flicked his ear. "To have a handsome man like you want to make love to me."

"Eager to make love to you," he said. He kissed her gently, she clung to him. . . . Then she pulled him to his feet and led him to the bedroom.

The moment they were in bed she became the aggressor. Suddenly she seemed to be everywhere. Her tongue was like butterfly wings across his eyelids, her firm young breasts were against his chest, her long dark hair fell on his face. She made love to him and he lay back powerless to do more than accept her love. When it was over he lay limp with pleasure and exhaustion. In the dim light he reached out and stroked her head. "Brazillia, I'll never forget tonight. It's the only time in my life that a girl made love to me."

"I enjoyed it, Robin."

"Now it's my turn."

"You don't have to . . ."

"You crazy little idiot. I want to." He stroked her face and her body and when he entered her he moved rhythmically and held back. He wanted to please her. He moved deeper and faster. She was clinging to him, but he sensed she wasn't ready. He continued the steady rhythm for what seemed an eternity. A pulse was beating against his temple, he was using every bit of strength to hold back. And still he felt she wasn't ready. This had never happened to him before. And he had never held back this long without pleasing a woman. He gritted his teeth and kept moving. He *had* to please her! Then he felt the unbearable yet wonderful weakness flood through his groin as he reached his climax. He fell off her exhausted, with the knowledge that he had not satisfied her. She reached out and touched his cheek. Then she snuggled against him and kissed his brow, his nose, his neck, "Robin, you are a marvelous lover."

"Don't pretend, baby." He got up and went to the bathroom. It was frilly, like the rest of the apartment, and complete with bidet. He showered and returned in his shorts. She held a lighted cigarette out to him and patted the bed. He stared at her lovely body. The breasts stood upright under the sheer nightgown she had put on. She smiled. "Come, have a cigarette."

His smile was weary. "Brazillia, in my country they think I'm pretty good in the kip. But I'm not up to another session." He took the cigarette and began to dress.

She jumped out of bed and threw her arms around him. "Please, stay with me all night. I want to sleep in your arms. Tomorrow morning I will make you breakfast. And if the day is nice, we can take a walk. I will show you St. Pauli in the daylight, and then perhaps in the late afternoon we can make love again. Oh, Robin, it was so wonderful—please stay."

He began knotting his tie.

"Didn't you like me?" she asked.

"I liked you plenty, baby." Then he turned to her and reached in his pocket. "How much?"

She turned and sat on the bed. He walked over and touched her shoulder. His voice was gentle. "Come on, Brazillia, how much? You name it."

She lowered her head. "There is no charge."

He sat beside her and lifted her face. Tears were spilling down her face. "Honey, what's wrong?"

"You don't like me," she sobbed.

"I—?" He was bewildered. "Look, I'm not about to give you my fraternity pin, if that's what you mean. But I liked you plenty. I'm only sorry I didn't rate with you."

In a flash her arms were around his neck. "This was the most wonderful night of my life. Robin, you are completely straight."

"Straight?"

"When I saw you with the boy, I thought, well, you were the butch kind. But you are a man and it is wonderful."

"Sergio is a friend—a good friend. Nothing more."

She nodded. "I realize. And he took you slumming."

"Stop putting yourself down. He showed me the night life of Hamburg. Period."

"How did you feel, doing it with me?" she asked.

"It was great. I'm just sorry nothing happened at your end."

She looked at him and smiled. "Robin: it's all here with me." She touched her breast. "Holding you and loving you is my thrill."

He touched her hair softly. "You mean you never come?"

"I can't anymore."

"Why not?"

"Some things that are taken off cannot be replaced." His stare was blank. Suddenly she looked frightened. "Robin, you didn't know! Oh my God—" she jumped off the bed and ran into the other room. He followed her. She huddled against the wall and stared at him. She was genuinely frightened.

"Brazillia." He came to her. She backed away as if she expected him to strike her. "Brazillia, what is the matter?"

"Please, Robin–go." She dashed across the room and handed him his topcoat. He threw it on the couch and grabbed her. He was shaking with fear.

"Now tell me what this is all about. No one is going to hurt you."

Her dark eyes searched his face. She was trembling. "I thought you knew what kind of a place Maison Bleue was."

"No, I don't," but the first terrible suspicions were beginning to gnaw at him.

"Vernon–he is the one who opened the show, the one you admired. When he wears a wig he calls himself Véronique. He is my roommate."

He dropped her arm. "And you. What is *your* real name?"

"My name was Anthony Brannari–before I had the operation."

"You're a–"

She backed away from him. "I'm a girl now, I am a girl!" she screamed.

"But you had balls once," he said slowly.

She nodded and the tears streamed down her face. "I am a girl now. Don't hit me, don't be angry! Oh God, if you knew how I suffered to become a girl. Do you know what it is to *be* a girl and be trapped in a man's body? To *feel* like a girl, *think* like a girl, *love* like a girl? I was always a woman inside."

"But the breasts?"

"Silicone. And I took hormones. Look, feel my face–I never shave. And my arms and legs are smooth. I *am* a girl now."

He sank on the couch. A transvestite. He had banged a goddam transvestite. No wonder the poor bastard couldn't come. He looked at the cowering creature. "Come here, Brazillia. I'm not going to hit you. You're right–you are a girl."

She ran to the couch and started to snuggle against him. He unpried her arms gently. "Only now that I know what you *were*, let's have a man-to-man talk."

She moved to a respectful distance on the sofa. "All those broads in the show–they're men?" When she nodded, he said, "Did they all have the operation?"

"Except Vernon. He still holds out. He feels he won't be able to use his passport and get back to Paris if he has it. Although he wants to go–it is so sad for him. He is in love with Rick, the man he was meeting tonight. Vernon swallowed iodine three months ago over him. That is why he cannot drink. Rick is–how you say? –a switch hitter. Sometimes he goes for a real girl, sometimes he goes for a butch guy. Poor Vernon is neither."

"In Vegas, did you fool them too?"

"Oh no. Then I was a male dancer."

Robin stood up and reached into his pocket. He didn't have too many marks. But he had over a hundred dollars in American money. "Here, Brazillia–buy yourself a new dress."

"I don't want it."

He tossed the money on the couch and left the apartment. He heard her sob as he closed the door. His own throat tightened. He was not sorry for what had happened to him. He was sorry for the poor lost creature inside. He ran down the rickety steps. The first signs of dawn were beginning to streak through the sky. The night people of the Reeperbahn were going to bed. Couples walked arm in arm. Sailors with striptease girls, men with men, men with girls who suddenly looked suspiciously masculine to him. These people–all their dreams and hopes had turned to sawdust. The world was not made for losers. Brazillia was a loser.

Suddenly his own problems seemed very small and he was filled with anger. Gregory Austin was afraid of Dan. But he wasn't afraid of Robin Stone. Gregory thought he was a loser. Well, from now on, he'd call the shots. All at once he was eager to get back to New York. He was also eager to see that nut Maggie Stewart in California, but she could wait–she could wait until he became the biggest winner of them all!

TWENTY-EIGHT

ROBIN returned to New York in time to catch Dip and Pauli on *The Christie Lane Show*. Dip looked great, sang off key and moved woodenly. Pauli looked awful, sang great, and moved like a ballerina. He couldn't believe it. She had stopped imitating Lena, Garland and Streisand. Pauli had come into her own. She had a haunting style and unbelievable phrasing. Robin wondered when this metamorphosis had occurred. Perhaps in knocking around nightclubs with Dip she had given up the dream of making it and because she no longer had hope, she had unconsciously dropped the affected mannerisms—and Pauli herself had come through. Whatever it was, it was nothing short of a miracle. Even the ridiculous upturned nose and prominent teeth worked for her.

Dip came barging into his office at eleven o'clock the following morning. He sprawled into a chair and stared into space with bloodshot eyes. Then he leaned forward. "I'm going to kill her."

Robin was taken off guard. "What happened?"

"My agent called an hour ago. That fucking Ike Ryan. His taste is in his ass! He doesn't want me. He's settling for Lon Rogers—that broken-down baritone!"

"But you said you were going to kill *her*. Who is *her?"*

"Pauli!" Dip's eyes blazed. "Ike Ryan offered her a job as a standby for Diana Williams, and that stupid bitch is going to take it! After all I've taught her, all the class I tried to give her—she's going to be a standby!"

"Maybe it's for the best," Robin said. "At least you'll have some money coming in."

"She's getting three hundred dollars a week. I used to *tip* more than that around the Beverly Hills Hotel! Besides, where does it leave me? How do you like that cheap little cunt! Sashaying off and leaving me in the crapper." Anger gave him renewed vitality. He jumped up and began to pace. "Know something?" His eyes were black with rage. "I'm going home and pack. I won't be there when the *star* returns from signing her shitty little contract. Let her see how long she can get by without the Big Dipper. And I'll also throw her old lady right out of the house. But first I'll break every bone in Pauli's body!" He dashed out of the office.

Robin was still thinking about Dip and Pauli when his phone rang. It was Cliff Dorne. At the same moment, his secretary announced that Danton Miller was in the outer office. Before he had a chance to speak to either of them, Dan pushed his way in. "You're not keeping me cooling my heels out there. Did you see the notices on your act? The girl was okay, but Dip Nelson was the longest stage wait I've ever seen. The show never recovered after him. I hope from now on you'll keep your hands off my show!"

Robin ignored him and went back to the telephone. "Yes, Cliff, sorry for the interruption." Dan saw his expression change.

"When did it happen? Mount Sinai? I'll be right there." He hung up. Dan stood there, still glowering in rage.

Robin looked at him in surprise, as if suddenly remembering his presence. "Gregory's sick again." He started for the door.

"I thought he was in Palm Beach." Dan's anger had dissolved into shock.

"He flew back an hour ago and checked into Mount Sinai."

"Is it serious?"

"They don't know. Cliff says he's been feeling lousy for the past week. It seems he went to the hospital in Palm Beach for a checkup, but he doesn't trust them so he came here for observation."

"Want me to go along?"

Robin looked at him curiously. "Of course not."

And once again he left Dan standing in the middle of the room, staring after him.

Gregory was sitting in a chair in the hospital room, huddled in a robe and his silk pajamas. He was tan, but his face was drawn under the healthy color. Judith was also tanned but she looked tired. Cliff Dorne looked concerned. Robin forced a smile in an effort to dispel the heavy atmosphere of gloom.

"You don't look sick to me," he said cheerfully.

"It's the Big C," Gregory said morosely. "I know it."

"Greg, stop talking that way," Judith pleaded.

"No one takes this long to recover from a gall bladder operation. I know that. And I'm in constant pain."

"The same place?" Robin asked.

"Who knows? Everything hurts. I can't even take a leak without pain. It's all through me, I know it. And the hell of it is, no one will tell me. They tried to say it was prostate trouble in Palm Beach. But I know they told Judith the truth–it's cancer."

Her eyes went to Robin's beseechingly. "I've told him over and over–it's prostate. I'm not keeping anything from him."

"Sure," Gregory snapped. "They'll put me through tests here. Everyone will show me charts that say it's negative. Everyone will give me big smiles, and then sit around and watch me die inch by inch."

"You'll bury me first, and soon, if you keep this up." It was Dr. Lesgarn's crisp voice as he entered the room.

"Look, Gregory, I've studied your tests from Palm Beach. It's prostate, all right–and we'll have to operate."

"What did I tell you?" Gregory's tone was triumphant. "You don't operate on prostate unless it's malignant!"

"Now I don't want any more of that talk," Dr. Lesgarn said firmly. "I want everyone out of here. I'm going to give you some sedation, Gregory. You've had a tiring trip and I want you in good condition for the operation tomorrow."

"You're going to cut?" Gregory suddenly sounded frightened.

"Yes. And you'll be fine."

"If it's malignant, *then* what?"

"Then we'll talk. But, Gregory, cancer is not a death sentence. There are many men who live long healthy lives after a prostate malignancy if it is caught in time."

"I've heard about those cases. They lose their balls–eventually even their pecker. They go piece by piece."

Dr. Lesgarn motioned Judith to leave. She walked across the room to Robin and Cliff. Dr. Lesgarn took out some cotton and swabbed Gregory's arm. Gregory pushed him away. "Tell me, before you knock me out. *Is* it malignant?"

"No one can swear one hundred percent on anything until we go in and see. But I will tell you this: I've operated on prostate malignancies, and you have none of the symptoms. I'd say it was a ninety-nine and nine-tenths chance that it is not."

"But there is that one chance?"

Judith swept over to his side and kissed his cheek. "Come on, now–you're the biggest gambler in the world, and never in your life have you had such odds in your favor. Why be chicken now?"

He managed a slight smile and she kissed his brow. "I'll be here tomorrow morning before you go to the operating room. Now do as the doctor says–rest and relax. I love you, Greg."

Then she quickly left the room with Robin and Cliff. The three of them walked down the corridor silently. She didn't speak until they reached the elevator. "When I looked into his eyes, I saw death." She shuddered. "He really believes he's going to die."

They reached the street. The long Lincoln was waiting. The chauffeur stood at attention. "Want me to ride home with you?" Cliff asked.

"I need a drink," she said.

"I think we all could use one," Robin agreed.

"I'll have to pass on it," Cliff said. "I have a long drive out to Rye, and I want to be here first thing in the morning too."

"I'll take care of Mrs. Austin," Robin said.

They got into the car. "There's a bar I like–unless you want the St. Regis or Oak Room or something special."

She leaned back against the seat. "No, any quiet place will do."

As she entered the Lancer Bar, Judith glanced around curiously. So this was where he went. It was dimly lit; she was grateful for that. He led her to a back booth and ordered her a Scotch. She waited until he had taken a long swallow of his martini, then she said, "What do you think will happen, Robin?"

"I think he's going to be all right."

"You're not just saying that?"

"No. People who think they're going to die rarely do. He's too frightened to die."

"I don't understand."

"During the war, after I got hit, I was in the hospital. It was a long ward with rows and rows of beds. There was a guy to the right of me who was loaded with shrapnel. He had to go through five operations. Each time he went up, he was sure it was his last day on earth. But the guy on the other side of me read the papers. He smiled at lot and all the while he was quietly hemorrhaging to death. I'm of the opinion that when death is in you, it fills you with a curious calm. After all, everything builds up its own resistance and immunity. Death probably carries its own emotional anesthesia."

"You make me feel much better," she said.

"It's not going to be easy either way," he said quietly. "The real trouble will begin after the operation."

"You mean lack of sex." She shrugged. "Robin, there's never been any wild kind of thing between us, even in the beginning. IBC has always been Greg's consuming passion. It hasn't been easy for me for years."

"I wasn't thinking of you," he said cryptically. "I was thinking of Gregory–he won't believe it's not malignant."

"And what about me?" she demanded. "Gregory doesn't know how to accept any setbacks. Illness is foreign to him. What do you think the last few months have been like for me? I've lived with a whimpering invalid. He wouldn't play golf, he kept taking his own pulse . . ."

"Isn't marriage supposed to be for better or worse?"

"Is that what you believe?" she asked.

"If I was married, that's what I'd believe."

"Maybe you *would,*" she said slowly. "Only I haven't had much of a marriage."

"This is one hell of a time for you to find out."

"Don't look at me as if you hated me, Robin. I've given my share to this marriage."

"This marriage? Is that how a woman thinks of it? Not *our* marriage?"

"Now you're beginning to sound like a sentimentalist."

He ordered another round of drinks. "That's the last thing I am. But I thought women were."

"I was, once. When I married Greg I thought it would be wonderful. But he didn't want any of the things that go to *make* a marriage. He didn't particularly want children, he wanted a *wife*. To run his homes—Gregory always liked possessions—the town house, the house in Palm Beach, the house in Quogue. . . . It's been a full-time job."

"Well, running a network isn't exactly a hobby."

"I know that. I've respected his work, and I've accepted all his friends, made them my friends. But a woman needs more than a social life and playing the role of the perfect hostess. I've missed so much. When I look back it seems like a pretty empty life."

"Well, this is no time to dig up the past. Right now your main concern is to get this man well. He'll need you. So stop crying in your beer about being just a possession. From now on you'll be Florence Nightingale, Sigmund Freud and the best friend he ever had. I liked your speech at the bed—about being a gambler. Your instincts are right, Judith. You've got to know when to be tough and when to give in with a patient. An emotional crackup is harder to cure than physical illness. You've got to make sure he doesn't crack—because if he does, then you'll *really* know what trouble is. I've seen guys go that route. They're still lolling around in bathrobes, doing jigsaw puzzles at veterans' hospitals."

"But why? I mean with Gregory. Men with less strength sail through a gall-bladder operation. And even a prostate operation. He hasn't been himself since he first went to the hospital."

Robin lit a cigarette. "Sometimes illness hits a strong guy harder than the little guy. As you said, illness is foreign to Gregory. He doesn't know how to handle it. He's always been prepared for any emergency in business. It never occurred to him that his body was vulnerable. It's shot the pins from under him. And to a man like Gregory illness robs him of his dignity."

She looked at him pleadingly. "Robin—*help* me."

"I will."

She reached out and clutched at his hands. "Robin, I'll try. But I can't do it alone. I've been in an ivory tower for so long. I have no close friends. Women I lunch with—well, they tell me *their* troubles. I've never confided my problems to any of them. I felt above all that. Suddenly I have no one to turn to, and I don't want anyone to know about Gregory's operation. It sounds so castrating. Robin–can I feel free to call you, to cry on your shoulder?"

He smiled. "I have big shoulders, Judith."

She sat back and sipped her drink. Her eyes looked past him. "Greg's worried about the network too. Dan's been giving out too many interviews. Gregory gets ulcers every time he reads them. It's *his* network and he hates anyone else to take bows."

"Sometimes it's hard to avoid the press," he answered. "I duck them, so they go after Dan. After my one mass interview, I cut out."

She smiled. "It must kill Dan. You've outwitted him without realizing it. In refusing to give interviews, you've made yourself an enigma–they write and speculate about you all the time. I rather like the title they've given you: the Love Machine."

He frowned. "They'll get tired of it. Publicity is the last thing I'm after."

"Greg knows that, and he doesn't resent your publicity. It's natural for you to get it. Dan's been in this business all his life, but even though you've been seen on TV, you're still a mystery man to Madison Avenue. You intrigue them, they want to dig, to find out what makes you tick."

"I think you're overrating their interest." He swallowed his drink. "Want another?"

"No. I have to be up at dawn tomorrow. Will you be there?"

He shook his head. "Someone has to mind the store. But please call me as soon as you know the results."

"I will. Do you have a private line at IBC?"

He took out his notebook and scribbled it down.

"Put down your home number, too," she added.

"IBC can always get to me. I have a direct line at home."

"Robin–remember what you said about your shoulders? If I find myself alone in the small hours, if it all closes in on me, I may need to talk to someone . . ."

He wrote down his unlisted home number. "Anytime." He handed her the slip of paper.

She sat in bed and wrote both his numbers in her phone book. She listed them under L. No name, just the numbers. "L" meant

Love. That was how she always listed the man she cared about. She stretched out in bed. The night cream was heavy on her face and she wore a net to keep the oil from ruining her hair. She felt elated. Gregory did not have cancer. And once the operation was over, perhaps he'd snap back to his old self. And meanwhile during his recuperation she'd see Robin every day.

Gregory was on the table six hours. During this period, Judith called Robin twice for reassurance. He sounded concerned and told her he had two meetings, but would come if she needed him. It was finally agreed that he would drop by at the end of the day. He kept assuring her that everything would be all right.

Dr. Lesgarn appeared at three in the afternoon. Gregory was in the postoperative room. The news was excellent. There was no malignancy.

Gregory was wheeled down at five. He was conscious, but the tube in his nose and the needle in his arm made him seem like a vegetable. An hour later Dr. Lesgarn came in and told him the results. Gregory turned away from him with a sneer.

Judith ran to the bed and took his hand. "We're telling you the truth, Greg. I swear."

He pushed her away. "Lies! It all sounds so pat! You're a lousy actress, Judith!" She ran out of the room and leaned against the wall of the hospital corridor, trembling. Dr. Lesgarn came out and shook his head. "I gave him a shot, but it's going to be rough to rid him of this cancer obsession."

They both looked up as Robin came striding down the hall. His confident smile and healthy good looks only served to make Gregory seem like a shell of a man.

"I talked to the doctor an hour ago," he said, nodding at Dr. Lesgarn. "He gave me the good news."

"Gregory doesn't believe us," she said.

Robin looked properly sympathetic. "Cliff released a story to the newspapers. We said it was the same ailment–gall bladder. I think that will cover things."

"You've had a long day, Mrs. Austin," Dr. Lesgarn said. "I think you should go home."

Her smile was gaunt. "Right now, I just want to sit down and have a drink and some food. I haven't eaten all day."

Robin took her to the Lancer Bar. This time she dismissed the chauffeur. At least Robin would take her home without feeling self-conscious. She looked around the room as they sat in the same booth. Did he always come to this place?

Obviously he had read her expression because he said, "I would have taken you elsewhere, but unfortunately I had made a previous appointment to meet someone here. But the steaks are good and the drinks are even better."

She sipped her drink cautiously. On an empty stomach she would feel it, and she wanted complete control, tonight of all nights.

"Will I be intruding on your appointment?"

"Not at all." He suddenly stood up. Judith stared as a tall young girl headed toward the booth.

"Robin, I am late. Sorry."

"It's all right." He motioned the girl to slide in beside him. Then he said, "Mrs. Austin, this is Ingrid. She works for TWA, and we've flown together many times."

The girl turned to Robin with a warmly intimate smile. "We had to circle Kennedy for half an hour tonight, air traffic was so heavy. That's why I'm late."

Robin signaled for a drink for Ingrid. Judith noticed the waiter automatically brought her a vodka-and-tonic. That meant she had been here before with Robin. She had a slight accent–Swedish, or one of the other Scandinavian languages. She was tall and almost too thin, with long heavy straight blond hair and bangs hanging below her eyebrows. Her eyes were heavily made up but she wore no lipstick. And when her slim hand slipped possessively into Robin's, Judith wanted to reach out and stab her. Oh God, the vibrancy of youth! Ingrid in her white silk blouse and plain skirt suddenly made her feel squat and bulky in the Chanel suit. The girl could not be more than twenty-two–she was old enough to be her mother! The girl was also too young for Robin, yet she was staring at him with open adoration. Oh God, it *was* a man's world. Age didn't count with a man. Ten years from now, Robin would still have a twenty-two-year-old stewardess staring at him like this.

She opened her purse and took out a gold cigarette case. Robin immediately reached over with a light—at least he still remembered she was at the table. Well, she wasn't going to give up without a fight. Not to this snip of a girl—a girl who would serve her on a plane: a *waitress!*

Judith watched Robin carefully. How could he allow an airline stewardess to share even a part of his life? How many simple girls like this had he given his body to, while she had to sit there longing for him—planning, scheming?

Robin ordered another round of drinks. Judith wished she could eat something—she felt the first Scotch already. Robin held up his glass and toasted Gregory's health. Then he had to explain to Ingrid who Gregory Austin was.

"I am sorry." Ingrid was sincere, as she turned to Judith. "I wish him a very fast recovery. Was it serious?"

"Just a checkup, baby," Robin said. "He flew in from Florida because he likes New York doctors."

"Do you fly with us?" Ingrid asked.

"We have our own plane," Judith answered.

"Oh, how very nice." Ingrid did not seem overly impressed.

"Judith, you must get Gregory to take an interest in the network, even while he's at the hospital having his checkup." Robin's gaze was serious as he emphasized the word checkup. "I want you to force him into taking an interest. Do you understand?"

She nodded. Ingrid stared at both of them. "Well, I don't," she said. "Poor Mr. Adlen, he—"

"Austin," Robin said.

"All right, Mr. Austin. Well, my father had to go through a checkup once, and he said it was awful. Swallowing chalk, taking X-rays. Let him relax and forget business, I say."

Robin smiled. "Baby, do you tell the pilot what to do when the weather gets rough?"

"Of course not. Tower control and the navigator do that."

"Well, I'm tower control and Judith is navigator."

"I *still* think the poor man should be left to have his checkup in peace," she said.

Judith had to admire her. She wasn't cowed by Robin's dismissal. But then, she had been to bed with Robin and knew her power. And why? Just because she was young. Oh God, when she was young she had taken her youth for granted too.

"I'm hungry," Ingrid said suddenly.

Robin beckoned the waiter. "Get the lady a steak. And bring me a double vodka." Then he turned to Judith. "What would you like? I'd advise the steak and the tossed salad."

"What are you having?"

He pointed to his glass.

"I'll have another Scotch," she said quietly.

"No steak?"

"No steak."

A slow smile crept to his eyes. "Well, well. Judith, I like your style. It takes more than a few knockdowns to make you lose a fight–you're back there slugging at the sound of the bell. I guess that's why you're a winner."

"Am I?" she asked challengingly.

"You sure as hell are!" He raised his glass in salute. Ingrid looked on in bewilderment. Suddenly she stood up. "I think perhaps you should cancel my steak. Suddenly it seems I am not needed here."

Robin stared at his glass. "Suit yourself, baby."

She grabbed her coat and went to the door. Judith tried to look concerned. "Robin, perhaps I should go? You and this girl–"

He reached across the table and took her hand. "Don't play games, Judith. It's not your style. This is the way you wanted it, isn't it?"

From the corner of her eye, she saw Ingrid hesitate at the door, hoping Robin would come after her. Judith waited until she left. Then she said, "I don't want to hurt anyone."

"Ingrid won't bleed–at least not for long," he said. He canceled the steak and asked for a check. They finished their drinks in silence, then walked out of the restaurant. "I live down the street," he said.

She slipped her arm through his as they walked. This wasn't the way she had planned it, not so cut-and-dried. There wasn't any romance this way. She had to make him understand that he meant something to her. "Robin–I've cared about you for a long time."

He didn't answer, but he took her arm from his and held her hand. "You're a winner, Judith. Don't try to qualify things."

When they entered his apartment, she suddenly felt insecure, like a girl beginning her first affair. And suddenly she felt the perspiration between her breasts, on her brow—those God-damned flashes! Little reminders that she wasn't a carefree young airline stewardess!

Robin made her a light Scotch and poured a large shot of vodka for himself. He drank it standing in the middle of the living room. She sat on the oversized couch and longed for him to join her. There was a fireplace and some fresh wood. If only he would light it, and they could sit in the darkness in the glow of the fire and play some of the records she saw stacked near the hi-fi. She wanted him to hold her in his arms. . . .

He suddenly walked over to her, took the drink from her hand and led her into the bedroom. She felt panic. Would she have to undress in front of him? Ingrid probably let him undress her . . . reveling in her nakedness and firm young body. She was wearing a panty girdle. Nothing was less sexy—despite her slimness, it pushed up her loose flesh into unflattering ripples.

He pointed to the bathroom as he loosened his tie. "No dressing room, but take that."

She stumbled into the bathroom and undressed slowly. She saw a maroon silk robe hanging on the door. She put it on and tied the sash. When she opened the door, Robin was standing looking out the window. He was stripped to his shorts. The room was in darkness, but the light of the bathroom reflected on his broad shoulders. There wasn't an ounce of extra flesh on him. She hadn't realized how well he was built. She came up behind him. He turned when he saw her and took her hand. Almost gently he led her to the bed. He looked at her and smiled. "Well, they say an experienced woman is the greatest. Prove it, dear lady—get down there and make love to me."

She was stunned, but wanted him so much that she complied. After a few moments he tossed her on her back and ground into her. It was over in less than a minute. Then he lay back and reached for a cigarette.

"Sorry I didn't put on more of a show," he said with an apologetic smile. "But I'm never very good when I've been drinking."

"I loved it, Robin."

"You did?" He looked at her with amazement. "Why?"

"Because I was with you. That's what makes the difference."

He yawned. "If I wake up during the night, I'll try and please you more." Then he kissed her lightly and turned away from her. After a few minutes his even breathing told her he was actually asleep. She stared at him. So this was the Love Machine. Now what? He expected her to go to sleep. Ingrid would. His other girls probably did. Well, why not? Gregory was in the hospital. She had no one to report to. But suppose she got the sweats in the middle of the night, or snored? Gregory had made her sleep in the same room with him in Palm Beach, and he said she snored. He teased her about it but seemed secretly pleased—another reminder of old age.

She lay there and stared at the ceiling. Age changed everything. One couldn't spend a night locked in a man's arms because of night sweats and snoring. And if she fell asleep at a bad angle her breasts would hang. Suddenly she looked down at the maroon robe she still wore. He hadn't even bothered to take it off. He hadn't even seen her body or touched her—just entered her and pleased himself.

She slipped out of bed and went to the bathroom and dressed quietly. When she came back into the bedroom, Robin was sitting up. He seemed to have sobered completely.

"Judith, did I conk out that fast? What time is it?"

"Midnight." Back in the Chanel suit she felt poised and assured.

"Why are you all dressed?"

"I feel I should be home, in case the hospital calls."

He jumped out of bed and threw on his shorts. "Of course. I'll get dressed and take you home. It won't take a second."

"No, Robin." She went to him and put her arms around him. It was only midnight; if he was up and dressed he might still call Ingrid. Besides, he'd hate her if he had to dress and go out. "Robin, I can catch a cab. Please, go back to bed. You have a hard day ahead."

He put his arm around her waist and walked her to the door.

"Will I see you tomorrow?" she asked.

"No, I'm going to Philadelphia for a few days. I want to tape Diana Williams doing her show."

"When will you be back?"

"Two or three days—all depends."

She put her arms around him. "Robin, you've never kissed me."

He kissed the top of her head obediently.

"I mean *really* kiss me."

He smiled. "Not in a drafty doorway." He stared at her curiously, then he said, "Come here." He took her in his arms and kissed her deeply. "There," he said, as he released her. "I can't let you go home unfulfilled, not with the risk you took."

After he closed the door, she walked to the elevator wondering why she felt so let down. She had been with Robin, and she would be with him again. Only next time she wouldn't let him drink so much.

But in the two weeks that followed, the rapid deterioration of Gregory's morale precluded any thought of next time. He was recovering physically, but his emotional state frightened her. Robin dropped by but Gregory refused to talk about plans for IBC. He sat huddled in his bathrobe, staring vacantly out of the window.

When he was discharged from the hospital, he took to his bed at home and lay staring at the ceiling. He refused to believe the laboratory reports. He claimed he felt pains in his neck, in his hips. "It's all through me, I know it," he moaned.

And one morning he awoke and found himself completely paralyzed from the waist down. He couldn't move his legs or sit up. Dr. Lesgarn was summoned immediately. He stuck a pin in Gregory's leg, and when there was no reaction, he sent for an ambulance. Gregory was put through extensive tests. It was not a stroke, as Judith had feared: every test proved negative. A neurologist was called in.

Dr. Chase, a leading psychiatrist, talked to Gregory. Another internist was summoned. Their opinion was unanimous. There was no physical cause for Gregory's paralysis.

They met with Judith and explained their findings. She was terrified. She sat staring at them, mutely pleading for an explanation.

"I suggest hospitalization," the psychiatrist said.

"You mean he stays here?" Judith asked.

The psychiatrist shook his head. "No, I'm speaking of a psychiatric hospital. The New York branch of Payne Whitney or the Hartford Institute–"

Judith covered her face. "No, no, not Greg–he couldn't sit around with a bunch of idiots!"

The psychiatrist stiffened. "Mrs. Austin, most of the patients are men of high intelligence and sensitivity. An insensitive person rarely suffers a breakdown."

"I don't care. Gregory wouldn't want to live if word got out that he was there. It would ruin his life. And the IBC stockholders would panic–no, we can't risk that."

Dr. Lesgarn looked thoughtful. He turned to Dr. Chase. "What about that place in Switzerland? Gregory could go there under an assumed name. They also have bungalows where the wives can live with their husbands while the husband undergoes treatment. Gregory would receive excellent psychiatric care, and no one would know. Judith could release word to the newspapers that they were going on an extended trip to Europe."

He looked at her and managed a smile. "And you could even run over to Paris or London and send cards to your friends to keep up the pretense."

"This is ridiculous," Dr. Chase snorted. "There is nothing disgraceful about a man needing psychiatric care. There are wonderful places here in the States. And I seen no need for this ridiculous secrecy."

Dr. Lesgarn shook his head. "I understand Mrs. Austin's point. The publicity would not be good for the network. IBC is known as a one-man operation; if that man doesn't function, the stockholders might panic. Switzerland is the best bet." He turned to Judith. "But it might mean six months to a year or even longer."

"I'll chance it," she said firmly. She told Dr. Lesgarn to make immediate arrangements. Then she went home and made two calls. One to Cliff Dorne, the other to Robin Stone. She asked both men to come to see her immediately.

They arrived at six o'clock. Judith didn't offer them a drink. She received them in Gregory's den and told them the entire story. Then she said, "If one word of this gets out, I shall deny it, and as his wife, I will dismiss you both. Since he is unable to make any decisions, I have his power of attorney."

"No one is arguing that," Cliff said quietly. "I think your decision is right. The stock would drop ten points in one day if word got out. And in a very minor way, I am also a stockholder."

"Then we're in full accord." When both men nodded, she went on. "I want Robin Stone to be given full command. Cliff, I want Dan informed of this tomorrow. He is to be told that Gregory will be vacationing for an indefinite time, and that he is to report to Robin. Robin's decisions will be final."

She refused to meet the expression of disbelief in Cliff's eyes. She stood up as a signal that the meeting had ended.

"Robin, if you can stay, I'd like to talk to you," she said.

Cliff hesitated at the door. "I'll wait outside, then. There are certains things I want to discuss with you, Mrs. Austin."

"Can't they wait until tomorrow? I'm very tired."

"I'm afraid they can't. You're leaving tomorrow at midnight, and there are some urgent matters that need your attention now."

Robin walked to the door. "I'll talk to you tomorrow, Mrs. Austin. How about lunch?"

"Yes. Will you come here? I'll be terribly busy packing."

"One o'clock all right?" When she nodded, he left the room.

The moment the door closed, she turned on Cliff. She didn't try to hide her antagonism. "What's so urgent?"

"Does Gregory know about this move?"

"Gregory scarcely knows his own name! Can't you understand? He's lying there paralyzed. He's a vegetable!"

"Mrs. Austin, do you realize what you are doing?"

"I'm doing what Gregory would do."

"I don't agree. He put Robin in to control Danton's power. Now you are not only giving all the power to one man, but you are making him autonomous."

"If I divided the power, the network would crumble. Danton is jealous of Robin—he would fight any ideas Robin might have, then nothing would be decided. There has to be one head."

"Then why not Danton?"

"Because Gregory doesn't trust him."

"What makes you think he can trust Robin?"

"I had a D & B on him. Robin is a millionaire in his own right. That means he can't be gotten to."

Cliff shook his head. "Power is an acquired taste. Once you get it, you find you like it. Also, I happen to think Dan is better qualified for the job."

"Dan's a lush."

"But not on the job. He's brought some good shows to IBC. He also knows how to run a network. And how do you think Dan will take the idea of Robin being put over him?"

She shrugged. "That's his problem."

"His position will be intolerable," Cliff said. "He'll have to quit to save face."

"Will it be easier for him to face the loss of a job?" she asked.

"When someone makes an emotional decision, they rarely take time to logicize. Anger often breeds false courage."

"Well, that's his problem," she said with finality.

Cliff Dorne made the announcement at a full-scale meeting the following morning at nine. At nine thirty Danton Miller handed in his resignation. Cliff tried to talk him out of it: "Stick it out, Dan. This will blow over. Gregory will return. I thought you were the one man who was born with a built-in survival kit."

Dan managed a faint imitation of his normal smile. "Sometimes to survive, one must retreat. Don't worry about me, Cliff. Meanwhile, who are you planning to put in my place?"

Cliff shrugged. "George Anderson is the logical choice, but Robin has already sent for Sammy Tebet."

"Fight him on it!" Dan stated. "Sammy is a good man, but he's cut from the same cloth as Robin. Harvard, a society background –he'll go along with all of Robin's thinking."

Cliff smiled. "I have to survive too. And my idea of survival is being on the scene, keeping an eye on the store. At the moment I can't fight Robin. I can only watch him."

Robin was aware of Cliff Dorne's hostility. But he wasn't out to win any popularity contests. He worked well with Sammy Tebet, and after a few weeks most of the personnel at IBC had forgotten there had ever been a man named Danton Miller. Vice-presidents put their black suits and black ties in storage and began to emulate Robin's Oxford gray.

Robin worked hard. He watched television every night, and made only rare appearances at the Lancer Bar. Gradually he lost all contact with the world. Nothing existed but IBC and the competitive shows. He read every program idea and had a dozen new pilots lined up to view on the Coast.

He was just leaving for the airport when Dip called. He had forgotten about Dip in the frenetic activity of the past few weeks.

"How's my buddy, the big executive?" Dip's cheerful voice blasted through the wire. "I was going to call and congratulate you, but I've been so busy helping Pauli."

Robin smiled. "Seems the last time we spoke you were on your way to kill her."

"You know me, pal—I burn fast, then cool off. Besides, she can't get along without me. I cue her, work with her. It's a cinch that the way Diana Williams is hitting the sauce, Pauli will get a chance to play the part after it opens on Broadway. How's about coming to Philly with me tonight and catching the show?"

"I'm on my way to the Coast, Dip. I have to look at some pilots for next February's dropouts."

"Okay, and while you're out there, drop the word around that I'm up for something big."

"Are you?"

"Nah, but say it anyhow. They believe anything out there."

The flight to the Coast was tedious. He found himself thinking about Judith Austin. Their last lunch together had been all business, until the very end. Then she had looked into his eyes and said, "*Ciao*—for now." His first inclination had been to ignore the intimate urgency in her eyes, but she had seemed so helpless and vulnerable in that large house. For some crazy reason she had made him think of Kitty, and he had pressed her hand, forced an easy smile and said, "Yes, *ciao* for now."

Well, Gregory would be away for a long time, and Judith would probably find plenty of European companions. He pushed her from his mind and tried to watch the movie. And when it ended, he studied the presentations for the pilots he was going to view.

He was eager for the goddam plane to land, eager to stretch his legs, but most of all, he was eager to see Maggie Stewart.

He called her when he checked into the Beverly Hills Hotel. She was surprised to hear his voice and agreed to meet him at six o'clock at the Polo Lounge.

When she walked into the bar he realized he had forgotten how beautiful she was. She smiled as she slid into the booth. "I thought you'd never talk to me again, after that fire."

He reached out and squeezed her hand. "Are you kidding? I thought it was very funny."

"How is Diana's show doing?" she asked.

"I wouldn't know. I haven't seen the lady except on business–it seems someone turned our budding romance into ashes. How is your new picture, by the way?"

She grimaced. "I saw a rough cut of it last week." She drained her Scotch and ordered another.

He looked at her curiously. "Is it really that bad?"

"Worse. If I didn't have a contract for three more pictures, I'd be out of the business. It won't even get a first-run release–they'll open it at the showcase theaters."

"Anyone can do one bad picture."

She nodded. "I have a chance to bail out with the next. Adam Bergman is directing it."

"He's excellent."

"He sure is. He even makes me look like an actress."

"What's the hitch?"

"He won't give me the picture unless I marry him."

He was silent.

"I'm going to refuse. Oh, don't look guilty. I refused him before last Christmas." Then her eyes blazed as she turned to him. "Yes, maybe you *should* feel guilty. You son of a bitch! You've ruined it for me with any man."

His grin was easy. "Come on, now, I'm not that wonderful."

"You're *damn* right you're not. It's me–just like you said, I'm a nut. Anyway I've been going to a shrink and I've just learned that I like myself."

"A shrink? But what's liking yourself got to do with marrying Adam?"

"I refuse to slip into a Hollywood-type marriage, at least the kind Adam wants. When I lived with him on the beach, I found myself doing things I never believed I'd do. Funny, isn't it? When I'm on the couch, I say, 'Where did everyone go? Where is the Maggie who lived in Philadelphia and loved and hoped? This girl doing the crazy things, she isn't me–' "

"What sent you to the couch?"

"The fire. When I realized that people could have been killed, it terrified me."

"Well, I've got a brand-new bed," he said. "With an asbestos bedspread." He took her to Dominick's for dinner, then they went back to the Melton Towers. He spent three days viewing tapes, and three nights making love to Maggie. The day he was to leave, they met at the Polo Lounge for a drink. She handed him a little box. "Open it," she said. "It's a present."

He stared at the little gold ring in the velvet box. "What is it? It looks like a tiny gold tennis racket."

She threw back her head and laughed. "It's an ankh."

"A what?"

"It's an Egyptian tau symbol–Cleopatra carried one. It means enduring life and generation. And that's you! *You* endure–no girl can forget you, and I think you'll go on and on. It's a sex symbol to me, eternal sex." She slid it onto his little finger. "Slim and bright and beautiful, isn't it? Just like you, Mr. Stone. And I want you to wear it. In a way I'm branding you. Of course you'll toss it away as soon as you leave me–but I'm going to pretend you're wearing it, and every girl will look at it and ask what it means. Maybe you'll have guts enough to tell them."

"I never wear jewelry," he said slowly. "Half the time I don't even wear a watch. But I'll wear it, I really will."

"You know something?" she said slowly. "I've heard of love-hate relationships, but I never knew what they meant till I knew you."

"You don't hate me. And you don't love me."

"I do love you," she said quietly. "And I hate you for making me love you."

"How long have you got until you start the next picture?"

"Ten days."

"Come back to New York with me."

For a flash her eyes brightened. "You mean that? You *really* want me to come?"

"Sure. I have my own private jet, courtesy of IBC. There's even a bed on the plane—we can hump our way across the country."

She was silent.

"Come on, Maggie. We'll catch all the shows, even go out to the Hamptons if the weather is mild enough. Can you get away?"

"Robin, I'd dump my whole career if I thought you *needed* me. I'm not even talking about marriage. I'm talking about needing. God, I'd follow you anywhere."

He looked at her oddly. "Who said anything about needing? I asked you to come to New York. I thought a change of scene might do you good."

"Oh, a little pleasure junket?"

"That's what life is about, baby."

She stood up with such force that the drink spilled on the table. "I think I've just about had it with you. Oh I don't say I won't take your call when you come back. I'll probably even fall into bed with you. Because I'm sick. But my shrink will straighten me out, and one day you'll need *me*—only I won't be there!"

His eyes went cold. "I think you've got it all wrong, baby. *I* don't need anyone. But maybe you need Adam Bergman. It's a cinch you need him to help you make a decent picture."

She leaned over and looked into his eyes. "To use a phrase from my newly developed show-business vocabulary, Mr. Stone, I *dig* you—oh Jesus, how I dig you—but you're the prize shit of them all!"

Then she walked away. He finished his drink slowly and went to the airport. He was about to toss the ring in a refuse basket, but it was tight and wouldn't come off. He smiled. Maybe she really had branded him after all.

When he returned to New York he learned that Diana Williams had withdrawn from the show, Pauli had gone on in Philadelphia and received such an ovation that Ike Ryan was chancing coming into Broadway with her.

Dip commuted to Philadelphia and besieged Robin with daily bulletins. In an effort to salvage the Diana Williams Happening, Robin took a crew to Philadelphia and taped Pauli. When he viewed the tape he was amazed to find it had tremendous impact. The first half was Diana at rehearsal, Diana talking about her comeback, then the newspaper headlines about her "illness." The second half showed Pauli going on, the interview with Pauli as she took over the star dressing room. It sounded like a soap opera, but he knew it would draw ratings.

The show opened in New York and Pauli's reviews were fantastic. Yet oddly enough she received no film offers. Dip was outraged, and refused to accept her agent's explanation that Pauli was a stage personality, and would become a Broadway superstar. He was crushed when he learned that Hollywood had signed a movie name to play her role in the picture.

Robin ran the Happening in May. It came across exactly as he had predicted, and outrated everything in its time period.

It was a good summer for him. The replacements were going well. He dated some of the girls in Pauli's show. He even tried to be nice to Pauli, but her back always went up when he was around. He ignored her antagonistic attitude and sat in Sardi's with whatever girl Dip brought along. He was getting to like Sardi's but as the legend of his power grew, he stopped going there and holed up more than ever at the Lancer Bar. In order to avoid contact with agents, agency men or stars, he also stayed away from "21" and the Colony. He had quickly learned the value of a decisive "No," accompanied by a firm smile, when he rejected a show. He had made a pledge that he would never allow himself to get angry or lose his cool. He never said, "I'll think it over." It was always a clear-cut "Yes" or "No." Soon word went around that he was a cold-blooded son of a bitch whose nod could make or break a man. The rare times he did go to "21" he was amazed at the aura of fear his presence caused.

However he found that a curious phenomenon accompanied his new fame. For the first time in his life girls were hard to come by. Starlets were out–he couldn't afford to be "held up" for a job. He stuck to airline stewardesses, but he didn't keep them long. They'd arrive in their best dresses, expecting to go to El Morocco or

Voisin, but soon learned that his social life was confined to the Lancer Bar, a movie, or his apartment.

If it hadn't been for Dip he would have had no sex life at all—Dip kept a steady stream of young girls on tap. However Robin's work took up most of his time, and as long as he wound up with a girl two or three times a week, he wasn't concerned. And he wore the ankh ring. When a girl questioned him about it, he'd say, "It means I'm in love with *all* women: it's the symbol of eternal life, of eternal sex."

He received cards from Judith twice a week. Cliff Dorne meticulously saw to it that items appeared in various columns mentioning successive laps of the Austins' world tour.

The day before Labor Day, Dip Nelson tore into his office and said he was positive that Pauli was having an affair with her leading man, Lon Rogers. At the same moment, Cliff Dorne called and announced that Ethel and Christie Lane had welcomed the birth of a nine-pound baby boy.

He told Dip it was all just "Broadway talk," and he called Tiffany's and sent Christie's baby a silver orange-juice cup. That night he walked down Broadway alone and went to a dreadful movie starring Maggie Stewart.

TWENTY-NINE

ROBIN sat in his apartment waiting for *The Christie Lane Show* to start its new season. For the past few days the newspapers had hinted that the public was in for a big surprise on the opening. Robin's guess was that Christie was probably going to introduce his newborn baby to his public.

Without speaking, he handed his empty glass to Dip Nelson for a refill. "Make it a light Scotch, Dip." His eyes narrowed as Dip obediently went to the bar. He knew there was growing speculation about their friendship. Robin had smiled and offered no explanation when Jerry Moss told him the word around was that Dip procured for him. Actually he let Dip hang around because he felt sorry for him. He sensed that despite Dip's exhilaration about Pauli's success, he couldn't really enjoy his new role as "husband of the star." Yet Dip never complained.

Robin had booked Dip on two guest shots on an IBC variety show. Each appearance had drawn murderous reviews. One columnist even began carping about Dip's pull with a certain Mr. Big at IBC. Robin didn't give a damn about columns or rumors. If Dip had any talent, Robin would have seen to it that he worked on every IBC show. But Dip was God-awful on television: a handsome face was not enough. There were guys doing shaving commercials who were better-looking.

"Why Scotch tonight, buddy boy?" Dip asked, as he handed him the drink.

"Opening of a new season. I like to be sober when I view a show. We'll go to the Lancer Bar later and really tie one on."

"I wish you'd go to Danny's Hideaway with me, it would do me a lot of good."

"Why?" Robin asked as he tried to get the green out of the color set.

"Well, J. P. Morgan once said to a guy, 'If I walk through the stock exchange with my arm around you, that's the best collateral you can have.' "

Robin smiled. "Okay, we'll go there after the show."

Dip's eagerness was childlike as he dashed to the phone. Robin smiled as he heard him make detailed arrangements to get the proper table. Then he turned up the sound on the television set as *The Christie Lane Show* came on the air.

Robin couldn't believe what he was seeing. At first he thought it would turn into a gag–that any second Christie's white tie and tails would turn into a breakaway outfit and the slapstick comedy would begin. But when they stopped for the first commercial he realized the show was in earnest. They were actually trying to do a frothy drawing-room musical. It was so bad it was almost high camp; but unfortunately the girl playing opposite Christie was good enough to make it semiserious.

Dip went into the kitchen and got a beer. He watched the show casually, and wondered why Robin was suddenly so intent on it. He went into the den and turned on a Western on the small set. Robin would understand: it bugged him to have to watch a television show that consistently turned him down.

When it was over he returned to the living room. Robin appeared not even to have noticed his absence. He was standing in the middle of the room staring into space.

"How was it, buddy boy?" Dip asked cheerfully.

"It was terrible."

"Well, maybe it'll be better next week." Dip was eager to leave for Danny's.

"It was unbelievable." Robin seemed dazed. "NBC has a great comedy opposite it, CBS has a good action thriller. We *had* to lose half the audience during the second half–I know we'll come up lowest in the time period."

"Well, let's go to Danny's. We can't erase it, it happened–that's the way the cookie crumbles."

"My cookie doesn't crumble," Robin said coldly. He picked up his direct line to IBC. "This is Robin Stone. Get me Artie Rylander on the Coast. You have his home number. It's in Brentwood." He lit a cigarette and waited. "I don't give a damn who the hell is on the tie line. Cut in and tell them to get off."

When he reached Artie, his teeth were clamped in cold anger. "All right, Rylander—*explain*. How the hell did you let him do it? Couldn't you see it was going to bomb? . . . Well, then, why didn't you call me? . . . I don't give a damn about Noel Victor! He may be the best lyricist in the business for Tony Newley or Robert Goulet, but not for Christie Lane. . . . What do you mean, Chris threw out your writers? I know all about Chris owning the package now—but he owns it *with* IBC. And we're more than equal partners—we also own the air time. . . . What ballads? Listen, Artie, there is no such thing as good *new* music, there's only good *familiar* music—the public likes to hear something it knows. . . . Don't give me that crap about a Broadway show. Sure, a Broadway show comes up with a new score, and on opening night critics write about it, and the public digs it, *after* it's played on albums and on jukeboxes. We don't have time for that with a once-a-week shot on TV. And Chris Lane is not Rex Harrison! He's the All-American slob. In tails he looked like a fat blond penguin. You tell him to revamp the show and go right back to the old format. Hire back the plain-Jane girl singer who played in the sketches and the cornball announcer. And what genius dreamed up the line of ballet girls? Don't you know ballet is lost on a twenty-inch screen? And I'm afraid to look at the below-the-line costs. . . . I don't give a damn about Noel Victor's contract, hire back the old writers. . . . What do you mean, he *won't?* We can force him to. . . . No, I haven't looked at the contract, but I *will* tonight! And I'll be in touch with you first thing tomorrow." He slammed down the receiver.

"Robin—" It was Dip. "We'll lose the table at Danny's if we don't hurry."

Robin crossed the room and put on his jacket. "Dinner is the last thing on my mind." He went to the phone again. "Get me Cliff Dorne at home. It's in Rye." He snapped his fingers for Dip to bring his cigarettes. "Cliff? It's Robin Stone."

"Yes, Robin, hold it, will you? I'll take it in another room."

Robin lit a cigarette and waited. Cliff came back on the line. "Sorry, Robin, we're having a small family party."

"What did you think of the Chris Lane show?"

There was silence.

"You thought it was that bad, too." Robin said.

"Well, to be honest, I didn't see it. You see–"

"What do you mean, you didn't *see* it?"

"Robin, it's my mother-in-law's seventieth birthday. We have the family here. We're at the table."

"The show stinks," Robin said curtly.

"I'll look at the tape first thing tomorrow."

"Meet me at your office, right away."

"What?"

"Right away! You have the keys to the contract files, haven't you?"

"Robin–can't it keep until tomorrow? My wife's mother is here."

"I couldn't care if Whistler's mother was there–get into town as fast as you can."

"Robin, if it was *my* mother, I'd do it. But my wife will never believe this was necessary. I'm not too crazy about her mother as it is. For thirty years we've had an armed truce. If I walk out now–"

"You support her?"

"No, she's a garage mechanic. Of *course* I support her! I even bought her a mink stole for the occasion. Kind of silly to put such an investment into a lady of seventy, but if I know my mother-in-law she'll outlive the mink."

"Then stop shooting the breeze up my ass about sentiment. Get down to the office!"

"Robin, I'm afraid it will have to keep until tomorrow."

"If it does, there will be a new boy in your place."

There was a slight pause. Cliff's voice was cold when he answered. "I'll be there. But, Robin, I think you'd better also read over *my* contract. I don't work *for* you or *under* you. I'm head of the legal department at IBC. I am not a boy who can be replaced."

"If you're in the office within half an hour, your mother-in-law might be eligible for another stole next year. If not, you'd better take it back in the morning. *I'm* running IBC now, and there is no one who can't be replaced. We have a top show that's about to go down the drain if we don't do something fast. I want to find out if we can. And not tomorrow–right now."

"All right, Robin."

"And, Cliff, if you don't feel you can work with me you can clear out your desk while you're there tonight."

"Oh, I'll work with you, Robin," Cliff answered, "until Gregory returns. Then I think maybe we'd all better have a little talk."

"As you like. Meanwhile, blow out the candles, sing happy birthday, and get your ass over to IBC." He clicked the receiver and walked to the window and stared at the lights on the river.

Dip laughed. "Like I once said in a cornball movie, 'New York, I'll get you yet!' "

Robin turned. "What do you mean?"

"It's a cliché. The big daddy of them all. But that's how you looked–the giant who is going to rule Madison Avenue, bend buildings, kill, kill–!"

"I'm just doing my job."

"What about Danny's?"

"I haven't time."

"Robin, the man's coming down from Rye. He can't make it in half an hour. You can at least make an appearance with me at Danny's. . . ."

"I couldn't eat. I don't want to drink. We'll make it another night."

"But I happen to know some big agents are going to be there tonight. I even arranged to get the table next to them."

"Go to Danny's. Tell everyone I'll be there. Say I'm in your pocket, if you like–I hear that's what you say anyhow. Put in a call to me loud and clear from the table, call this number. There won't be any answer. Then you can say, 'Okay, Robin, I'll meet you.' That will cover you." He reached into his pocket and threw a fifty-dollar bill on the couch. "Use this to pay for the meal." He started for the door.

Dip picked up the money and followed him.

As Robin left in the cab, Dip called, "If you get through in time, pal, come over. I won't make the call for an hour."

It was four o'clock in the morning when Robin and Cliff finished poring over the contract. "Go home, Cliff," Robin said weakly. "We've gone through every clause, every word. We're in a bind."

Cliff put on his coat and straightened his tie. "When we gave him co-ownership of the package, we kept the right of talent approval, but we gave Christie artistic and creative control."

Robin lit his last cigarette and crumpled the empty pack. "Who was the genius who came up with that ambiguous language? Why do we have cast approval if we have no artistic control?"

"It's an old hangover from the *Red Channels* days. That's the only reason it's still in. Gives the agency or network the chance to knock out an actor who might be offensive to the sponsor and his image."

Robin looked thoughtful. "Couldn't we disapprove of his entire cast? Keep saying no, until he goes back to the old stock company idea?"

"We'd have to give a valid reason. We'd have to claim it went against the sponsor image. And from what you tell me, the show was an unmitigated bore, but done in impeccable taste. So we can't reject the talent, or we'd be infringing on Christie's control."

Robin crushed out his cigarette. "Well, there goes one of our top shows down the drain."

"Was it really that bad?" Cliff asked.

"You'll see the tape later today. And I can just bet on the overnight rating." He waved Cliff off wearily.

It was beginning to get light when he walked down Madison Avenue. He knew what had to be done. No use crying over *The Chris Lane Show*. That was a sure cancelation by the end of June. He had to go after new shows–more comedy shows and more violence. He would call a full-scale meeting in the morning, send out a rush call for every new pilot around, hire writers who would develop pilots and shows for IBC.

In January, Robin made television headlines when he announced that *The Christie Lane Show* would go off the air the end of June. He told Jerry to remain calm–he'd come up with a winner for the new time period and Jerry's sponsors would have first refusal.

Christie's cancelation caused headlines in all the trades as well as the television columns of the *Times* and *Tribune*. Two days after the announcement, Christie was offered shows by NBC and CBS for the following season.

Although Christie's ratings had fallen, he continued with the sleek format. His publicity was tremendous. Christie and Ethel attended all the right parties. In hiring Cully and Hayes and Noel Victor, Ethel had gotten into the Alfie set. Alfie confided in her, adored her—and Ethel went everywhere to act as a "beard" to cover whatever boy he was romancing. The threesome made all the openings together while Christie worked on his show.

Chris did have firm offers from NBC and CBS, but he held off signing. The shows they offered gave him little opportunity to do more than act as a glorified master of ceremonies. He came to New York in February in one last attempt to straighten things out with Robin and remain with IBC. He told the Johnson-Harris office to tell Robin he was willing to go back to the old format.

The "new" format had been Ethel's idea, so she could get in with Alfie's set. Noel Victor was one of Alfie's best friends. Well, they were *in!* Hell, Ethel was so *in* now that he never saw her. He *wanted* to go back to the old show—it was a lot easier singing songs he knew than memorizing a new score each week.

When he arrived he was stunned to learn that his agent had not been able to arrange an appointment with Robin. "Once he says no," the agent explained, "that's it. He doesn't give you a chance to argue, beg or plead."

Chris tried to reach Robin himself. Each time he was informed that Mr. Stone was "in a meeting."

He called Danton Miller. Dan was delighted to hear from him and suggested they meet at "21". It was four o'clock and the restaurant was almost empty. They sat at a front table at the bar area and for the first hour they tore Robin Stone to shreds. Chris began to feel better.

"At least you've got offers from the other networks. Now there's a guy who is a real loser." They both watched as Dip Nelson entered and ambled over to the bar.

Dan smiled. "He's been coming here almost every day, alone."

"Why?"

Dan shrugged. "What else can a guy do when his wife is a star and he has no job?"

"How are things going with you?" Chris asked.

"Well, let's put it this way: it is now survival time. And that blond ox standing at the bar may be my lifeline."

"Dip Nelson?"

"I think he's lonely enough. And I have a property . . . ."

"Dip Nelson is finished. Go after his wife."

"His wife hasn't got Robin Stone in her back pocket. For some incredible reason, Dip has."

"Yeah." Christie seemed thoughtful. "In California, everyone is talking about it. They even hint there's something funny going on between them–you know: Queersville."

"I don't care if they're secretly *married*. I just want to get this property on the air."

"You mean you'd go back as a producer?"

"Producer and packager," Dan stated. "There's nothing about this business I don't know–but I want to be at IBC. I want to be there when the great Love Machine explodes. Then I'll step back where I belong, bigger and stronger than before."

Chris nodded. "At least you've got your future planned."

Dan laughed. "Christie–you've got it made. A big home in California, all the money you'll ever need–and you run with the Alfie pack. You've got a great life."

"Ethel has the great life," Christie sighed. "She's got what she always wanted. But I don't fit. Every night I come home and we either have a date with Alfie or we're going to a party. I don't even have Eddie and Kenny now. They like New York. They got a job with that new variety show on CBS."

"Maybe you've outgrown them, Chris. You've gone up in the world."

"You call it going up in the world to sit around and laugh at Alfie's jokes and watch him make calf eyes at some actor he's in love with? We all have to do whatever Alfie says. Ethel gets mad when I call her 'doll.' I'm supposed to call everyone 'luv.' You like that? A group I'm traveling with where men call each other 'luv'?"

Suddenly Christie's homely face crinkled into a forced smile.

"Listen, I shouldn't kick. Like you said, I got all the money I'll ever need. But most of all, I got my son, Christie Lane, Jr." He drew out an accordion folder filled with smiling pictures of a plump little baby. "Look, if Ethel never does another thing, I'm still ahead. She gave me my baby and that's all that matters. I *live* for that kid–it's like getting an extra dividend in life." Then he looked at his watch. "Say, I got to be getting back to the hotel. The Plaza, yet. Alfie says that's where I should stay. You should see my suite, I think Lincoln was laid out in it. But Ethel is calling me at six thirty; she holds the baby to the phone and sometimes he gurgles or coos–what a kid!"

Dan watched him leave. He ordered another martini. Then he sent a note to Dip, who was still at the bar. Dip read it and walked over.

"No use both of us drinking alone," Dan said. "Thought we might sit together."

"Why should I?" Dip asked. "You're the character who raised hell when Robin put me on the Chris Lane show."

"Only because it prevented me from preparing a decent setup for you. I assure you, had I been given a few weeks' time, your notices would have been different."

Dip sat down. "People are always out to kill a movie star. They have to start out thinking he's a no-talent bum. But when I sing–especially to a live audience–pal, there's no one who can touch me."

"Let me buy you a drink," Dan said.

"Ah . . . I'm waiting for a call from Robin. I'm only nursing a ginger ale until he calls, see–then Robin and I will really go out and tie one on."

"You and Robin are still very close?"

"Like that." Dip entwined his fingers.

"Why doesn't he do something for you if you're so close?" Dan asked. "The word is out that you're really just his messenger boy."

Dip's eyes flashed in fury. "Don't you ever use a word like that about me! Robin relies on me for everything. As a matter of fact, it was *I* who told Robin he had to cancel Chris Lane! Yeah, and you want to know something? Robin was willing to let him go on next season, but I don't forget–Chris Lane treated me and Pauli like shit when we came on his show, and I got a long memory. I sit back and wait, buddy, then I send in the shiv!"

"How much longer does your wife's show run?"

"Until June in New York. Then it goes on the road for a year. I'm going too. They're building up the part of the brother. I'll play it."

"Why would you take a small role?" Dan asked.

"To be with Pauli. She needs me."

"She needs you like she needs extra teeth," Dan said.

"You looking to be slugged right here at '21'?"

"I'm looking to put some sense in your head."

"Meaning what?"

"Meaning that you're sitting around every night with the biggest power on television. No one in the business has the autonomy of Robin Stone. And you should latch on to it while it lasts. Because eventually it has to blow up in his face. I've been watching him. The way he acts, I feel he almost has a death wish–he seems to delight in making enemies. It's almost as if he's testing–seeing how far he can go, how far he can push everyone. There's some kind of a sickness behind his arrogance and drive. So if you're smart, you'll sit back and listen to me."

"I don't need advice from a has-been." Dip's voice was ugly.

Dan shot his old Cheshire-cat grin. "Perhaps two has-beens make for more strength than one. How would you like to be co-owner of a package?"

"I don't know about packages."

"What are you doing for dinner?" Dan asked.

"Nothing–that is, I'm supposed to check with Robin."

"Can you get out of it tonight?"

Dip smiled. "I can do anything I want."

"Then let's go. I have an appointment with Peter Kane from the Johnson-Harris office at Voisin. Oh–you haven't signed to go on Pauli's road tour yet, have you?"

"No. I'm waiting to see how they rewrite the part."

Dan scribbled his name on the check. "Then come with me. Listen, but keep your mouth shut."

"No one talks to me like that," Dip said.

"I can. Because I'm about to make you a very rich man." He

rose, and Dip followed him out of the restaurant.

Dip toyed with a bourbon-and-water at Voisin. Dan and Peter Kane had martinis.

Dan immediately steered the conversation to Dip's career. Oddly enough, Peter Kane was interested. Everyone agreed the critics had been vindictive because of their antipathy for Robin.

"This poor boy has inherited all of Robin's enemies and none of his friends," Dan explained.

"What friends has Robin got?" Peter Kane asked. "Not even a steady girl. I hear Ike Ryan sometimes fixes him up with a scene —he likes the three-way bit. Tell me, Dip, is he queer?"

"Queer for girls," Dip answered.

"Well, I think your acting career has gone down the drain because of Robin," Peter Kane said seriously. "Everyone in the business knows Robin Stone is your best friend, and if *he* won't use you, they have to figure you're pretty bad. So they have no interest. He's hurt you very badly in not giving you a big show."

"I never looked at it that way," Dip said slowly. "Maybe that's why I get no offers."

He sat quietly while the two men discussed various shows on different networks. When dinner was over, Peter Kane turned to Dan. "I have the viewing room booked for nine—we'd better get a move on."

Dan turned to Dip. "We have a new show. It's my package, and Peter is representing it. We've just made a pilot. It's a spy series, and we can bring it in cheap. Vic Grant is playing the lead. I want you to look at it and see if you like it."

Dip's spirits soared. Vic Grant was a contract player when he was a star. Vic hadn't made a decent picture in two years.

Dan signed the check and they went directly to the projection room at the Johnson-Harris office. Dip watched the show. It was a good shoot-'em-up. Vic wasn't bad, but Dip knew he could do better—the part was made to order for him. And it would really put him right back on top!

When the lights came up, Dan looked at him. "Like it?"

"I think it could be great," Dip said enthusiastically.

"Let's go downstairs. There's a bar across the street and it's quiet. We can discuss the mechanics of the thing," Peter suggested.

"I'm with you, pal," Dip said.

They sat at a back table. Dip ordered a bourbon and drank it straight. If Dan and Peter saw him as this fast-drinking, devil-may-care detective, he couldn't let them know he usually stuck to ginger ale or beer.

"We're planning to ask one hundred and twenty-five thousand for it," Dan explained. "We can bring it in at ninety, some weeks less. We'll add the ten-percent commision to the package, and that leaves us with a thirty-thousand-dollar profit, to be split three ways if necessary."

"You mean I'd get one third of the action, instead of salary?" Dip asked.

"Oh, I think we could also arrange a token salary–say a thousand a week, plus office expenses."

"What in hell would I need an office for?"

"You'll need it for your company. You can't take the money as salary, it would all go in taxes. My company is the Danmill–you get a name for yours. If you like, my lawyer can handle it all."

It was going too fast for Dip. "How would I know I could trust *your* lawyer?"

"Because your company will get all the profits and send Danmill its share."

"Where would we film it? Here or in L.A.?"

"Wherever IBC thinks best. They have big studios in L.A., but I'd rather get the action of the streets in New York, the feel of the city."

"Oh–has IBC bought it?" Dip asked.

"They will, I hope."

Dip nodded enthusiastically. "Well, I know I can play the hell out of the part."

Dan and Peter looked at one another. Dan spoke. "I'm sure you could, but we have Vic Grant tied up for two years. He did the pilot for scale, with the stipulation that he'd get the part if the show was sold."

"Then why am I here?" Dip asked.

"Because you can make Robin Stone buy it."

Dip started to rise, but Dan grabbed his arm. "Sit down! Tell me, would you rather be a ham actor all your life, or a millionaire?"

Dip glowered at him. "You know all evening you've been begging for a belt."

Peter cut in. "Dip, face it. You haven't *got* it. Not on television anyway. You've had every chance. Now why don't you get smart and make some *real* money? There's more prestige in being a package owner and a producer than in being an actor."

"What makes you so sure IBC will buy it?" Dip asked suddenly.

Dan's eyes narrowed. "It seems to me you sit around Danny's telling everyone you have Robin Stone in your pocket. Well, now's the time to prove it. Make him buy it. There will be a lot of dropouts in January. As further incentive, tell him that if he buys it, he gets one third of the profits. You can pay him any way he wants it —cash, trips, a house in the country."

"Isn't there trouble with the government?"

"We have an excellent tax man. There are ways to make Robin's third look like legitimate write-offs. If he wants a Cadillac, we use it in a few scenes and say it's for the show. The country home we buy because we shoot a lot of footage in it. We build sets and give him the furniture. If he wants cash, we find a million ways to build up dummy expenses. You let us worry about that."

"You mean I just go to him and tell him how it is?"

Dan shrugged. "Obviously you know the best way to handle him."

"And how much did you say there'd be in this for us?"

"With a three-way split, ten thousand apiece."

"What happens to Pete, here?"

"I just want the agency to get the commission," Peter said. "If I break through with a sale to Robin Stone, I'll get a vice-presidency out of it. That's all I care about."

Dip stared into space. "My name has to be on the screen as producer."

Dan laughed. "Everyone would know it was a phony."

"I don't give a damn. Pauli won't know. The public won't know. I want billing—bigger than Vic Grant. That'll impress Pauli."

"All right," Dan conceded. "I'll be executive producer. You'll have a frame for yourself as producer."

Dip smiled. "Give me a letter first, all signed and witnessed, saying I get two thirds of the action. After all, suppose I go in and make Robin take it and then you guys welsh?"

"I'll have the letter drawn up first thing in the morning," Dan said.

Dip met Robin at the Lancer Bar the following afternoon. He had Dan's letter in his pocket. He waited until Robin had started his second martini before he brought up the subject of the pilot. He described it graphically, acted out the role and finished with a flourish: "And one third of the profits goes right into your pocket, buddy boy."

Robin grabbed him by the coat and pulled him close. "Now you listen to me, you slob. Danton Miller got rich making deals like that when he ran IBC. I've thrown out every agent who ever dealt with him. Don't you ever toss my name around in a slimy deal like this."

"Then it's no dice?" Dip's voice was groveling.

"No dice regarding the kickback to me!" Then he turned to Dip. "Look, if you've got a good pilot, show it to me. If it's half-way good, it'll take precedence over any other show. If Dan wants to put your namc up, that's his business."

Dip's smile was broad with relief. "Then you're not mad?"

"Only when you put me in your league, chum. Look, I'm always looking for shows. There's no reason why you shouldn't go into the production end. You've got a gangsterlike intelligence that I admire. If I buy this show and they put your name up as producer, I know damn well Danton will do all the work. But if you just sit around and take bows, then I take back what I said about your intelligence. Hang around, learn everything there is to be learned, watch the cameramen, learn about below-the-line costs—that's the first place where your profits go. Watch out for musicians and overtime. But as for the three-way split—forget it. Cut up the gravy between yourself and Dan, and whatever you have to give the crummy agent."

Robin viewed the pilot with Dip. When it was over, he stood up. "It's not good—it's *great!* Tell Dan he's got a deal."

Dip took a long walk after he left Robin. He decided he despised Robin Stone. He also hated Danton Miller. He hated every mother-fucking son of a bitch in the world. How had he gotten into such a situation? A wife who was a star and treated him like he was her servant. Men like Robin and Dan, who blatantly told him he was a lousy actor. Where had all the sunshine gone? The days when he used to walk into a room and light it up? The days when women clamored around him? Now they ducked him. Pauli had told him to stay away from the girls in the show–none of them wanted to go out with Robin Stone. But he had to get Robin girls to stay on the right side of him. Anyway, Robin was a weirdo with the broads–he'd never forget that whore he had beaten up. And the girls complained that Robin was cheap–he wouldn't take them anywhere, just the Lancer Bar or the Steak Place and then a roll in the feathers. And if they didn't perform the way *he* wanted, he sent them home without taxi fare. Dip sighed, and headed for Sardi's. He had taken to dropping in for lunch, casing the place–trying to spot new eager young actresses he could get for Robin. Of course Robin never asked for a date, but he always seemed pleased when Dip winked and said, "Have I got a new number for you, buddy boy–this one really swings!"

How had he come to this? Well, from now on it would be different. He'd be big again. Thirty thousand a week split two ways. . . . Why *two* ways? How would Dan know whether or not Robin took a cut? He wouldn't. He'd take *two thirds,* plus his salary. He'd tell them Robin wanted it in cash, and let them and their fancy tax man figure a way to cover it. And he'd put those ten G's in a safe-deposit box each week. *Tax-free!* He'd be rich. But he was damned if he was going to sit around and watch cameras and learn how to be a producer–let the shmucks like Dan Miller do that for their shitty little one third. He'd take two thirds and have a ball. And in a subtle way he'd let word get around that Robin was on the take. Then every guy who wanted to sell a package would come to him and offer him two thirds–one for himself, one for Robin. He could become a real power. Pauli would be kissing his ass–she wouldn't give him the "too tired" jazz when he wanted to ball her. Soon he'd be in the position to give *her* a job! Suddenly his spirits dropped. Pauli! Jesus, she was like a sickness to him. He couldn't get her out of his system. Sometimes he wanted to kill her, but with all the gorgeous broads he met, she was the only one who turned him on. He had even tried the orgy route with Robin, one girl and the two of them. He had sat and watched Robin getting blown and it hadn't excited him. When it was his turn he had only been able to get it up by pretending the girl was Pauli. And she had been a real looker, too! Well, wait until the name Dip Nelson blazed across the television screen in living color, wait until he had a show on the air–two shows, maybe even three–then Pauli would realize he was the biggest man in town.

Robin slated Dip's pilot, *A Guy Called Jones,* to replace the first January casualty. The contract was worked out, Dan had agreed, and now Dip had nothing to do but wait until September and see what shows bombed.

Pauli went on tour in June and Dip remained in New York. Pauli's attitude had changed when she learned that Dip was going to make ten thousand a week. (He did not tell her about the other ten he intended to deposit in the vault.) She wrote him long letters from the road and never failed to tell him how much she missed him.

In September the new shows came on. IBC had an immediate winner in one series Robin had chosen. Two others were shaky, but he had a solid daytime schedule. The new soap opera was a smash, and both game shows were going to make it. Of the two doubtful shows, one was a cinch to be axed in January. He'd replace it with Dip's show–that would write off any obligation he owed for all time. He thought about Dip. . . . In the beginning he had really *liked* him. He had an openness and a zest for living that Robin found appealing. But as the months had passed and he watched Dip take the crap from Pauli, his respect for Dip gradually turned to revulsion. Dip *had* to know that Pauli was cheating on him. In the beginning he had tried to snap Dip to his senses and arouse the manhood in him by treating him as a servant. He felt that Dip would rebel, and once the rebellion began his strength might return. But Dip took it.

The more Robin thought of Dip's subservience to Pauli, the less he cared to become involved with any girl. The few times he had tried to start anything that resembled a romance, his thoughts automatically turned to Maggie, and the girl he was with suddenly seemed dull. No, it was easier to let Dip supply temporary entertainment. He cared so little about the girls that Dip or Ike brought around that he found himself requiring a three-way bit. If he watched Ike make love to the girl it aroused him, then he was able to jump her too. He was aware that in a subconscious way Maggie was always in his thoughts. And when he acknowledged this to himself, he became enraged. No girl was ever going to "get" to him! Running the network was a full-time job. He hadn't even gone near his book in a year—just the night before he had carefully put the three hundred yellow pages in a portfolio and stashed it in a filing case. He wondered when Gregory would return, if ever. . . . The last card from Judith had come from Cannes in August. Gregory was feeling fine, even playing *chemin de fer* for hours on end.

The Austins slipped into town quietly at the end of September. Judith planned it that way. Once she was settled, their "official" return would be heralded with a big splash. She didn't want to dissipate the impact with just the usual picture of them getting off the boat. It had to be done with a gigantic party. She might even take over the ballroom at the Plaza, invite all the exciting people, all the press. . . . Gregory was his old self, and convinced he didn't have cancer. He had even proven himself sporadically a few times in bed with her. Judith felt she deserved an Academy Award —she had acted wildly excited, told him he was the greatest lover in the world. She hadn't shown that much excitement during their honeymoon. But she was determined to do anything to get Gregory well—and most of all to get him back to New York. They had been gone a year and a half!

But she had used the time to advantage. The first three months at Lausanne, Gregory was too ill to see anyone. Forty shock treatments, then the dreadful regressive period when he even soiled himself. And then the slow process back. . . . She had taken a small apartment near the sanitarium, and during the first three months, when she had not been allowed to see him, she had put herself in the hands of an excellent plastic surgeon.

It was a miraculous job, though at first she had been disappointed. She had actually expected to look twenty again. She looked about thirty-eight, but a beautiful, well-taken-care-of thirty-eight. The doctor had been a genius. Of course there were tiny creases in front of her ears and heavy scars behind them, but she wore her hair down now, soft and *bouffant,* a few inches below her ears. Vidal Sassoon himself had styled it for her, and it was a smashing look. Gregory knew nothing of the operation. He said she looked marvelous and the new hairdo had done wonders. She smiled. Couldn't he notice how firm her jawline was? He hadn't even noticed her breast lift, or the tiny scars near her pelvis where her thighs had been tightened.

Gregory looked well too. The red was back in his hair, he was tan and lean, but he had no desire to go back to work. They had been home a week and he hadn't gone near the office. Each day he had come up with a different excuse. He had to see his tailor—he had lost ten pounds and none of his suits fitted. He had to drive out to see his horses. At the beginning of the second week she literally threw him out of the house, insisting he go to the office.

The moment he was gone, she placed a call to Robin. She had deliberately waited. He *knew* they were back—Gregory had talked to him several times on the phone. She knew he must wonder why she didn't call. By now he would be eager. . . .

His private line didn't answer. She was disappointed, but no use leaving a message. He was probably at a meeting. She finally reached him at three o'clock. He sounded delighted to hear from her. He had spent the morning with Gregory and remarked on how well he looked.

"When am I going to see you?" she asked.

"Anytime," he said easily. "As soon as Gregory feels up to it, I'd love to take you both to dinner."

"I don't mean it that way, Robin," she said quietly. "I want to see you alone."

He was silent.

"Are you there, Robin?"

"I'm here. . . ."

"When can I see you?"

"Tomorrow at six, at my place."

"I'll be there. I'll leave word for Gregory that I've gone to a charity cocktail party. I'll have no time limit and Gregory falls asleep right after dinner."

She went to a new beauty parlor in the East Sixties. She couldn't chance her regular place where all the operators knew her, unless she wanted those scars behind her ears to be the biggest news flash along Park Avenue. The operators had always told her who had gotten the latest "lift."

She sat in a cubicle at the new beauty parlor. She had given her name as Wright. She was positive that no one recognized her. God, why should they? It had been over a year since her picture had appeared on the front page of *Women's Wear*. Well, in a few weeks, she'd take over. She lay back and wished the woman wouldn't rub so hard. She knew the operator felt the lumpy scars. The bitch, she was jealous because she would never be able to afford such a luxury. She glanced at the operator. She was a woman in her middle thirties: broad hips, fingers permanently discolored from hair dye, white space shoes on feet that ached from too much standing–God, even varicose veins! Why shouldn't the poor creature hate and envy someone who could pay three thousand dollars just to get rid of some lines?

The woman smiled as she led Judith into another booth to await her hair set. As Judith thumbed through a back issue of *Harper's*, the woman whispered to the young man outside the booth, "You'll get a big tip from this one, Dickie–it's Mrs. Gregory Austin under a phony name with a brand-new set of scars. Take it easy with the clips."

Judith smoked nervously as the slim young man coiled her hair into the large rollers. She caught him looking at her ears. "I had mastoids last year," she said casually.

He nodded. "My roommate had them too." His voice was sympathetic.

She relaxed under the drier. She would go to the booth after Dickie combed her out, and put on fresh makeup. She was wearing that wonderful underwear she had picked up in Paris. Thank God the scars under her breasts didn't show. The breast and thigh lift had really been painful, but it was all worth it. Tonight she'd strip off her clothes and stand before Robin. She was a match for any airline hostess now!

She left the beauty parlor at five thirty. She didn't want to walk and ruin her hair. She looked marvelous–Vidal had cut her hair so well that even Dickie had been able to follow the line. She had given him a ten-dollar tip. She hadn't felt this exhilarated in years. She wanted to shout . . . to sing, but she merely went to a drugstore and had a cup of tea to kill the time. At five of six she took a cab to Robin's.

The doorman glanced at her casually, but she felt that her large sunglasses hid her identity. Of course he wouldn't recognize her–she had been away so long.

She felt short of breath from excitement and nerves as she buzzed Robin's door. He opened it and beckoned her in and returned to the telephone. God, this was an anticlimactic greeting! He was talking to California–he sounded like Gregory with all those damn ratings. She looked around the room. She had only been here once, but during the past year she had relived every second they had shared together. Every word, every piece of furniture in his apartment, was etched in her mind. She felt slightly uncomfortable in the new underwear. The naked beige bra and the tiny lace pants scratched. But any annoyance would be worth it when she watched his face as she undressed. She planned to do it slowly, deliberately. She was wearing a suit–Valentino had outdone himself on this one: the silk blouse buttoned down the front, nothing had to go over the head, and she had those marvelous individual false eyelashes–no worry about the stripped ones coming off.

Robin hung up, came and grasped her hands in welcome. He tried to smile but there were two lines between his eyes.

"Trouble?" she asked.

"Roddy Collins."

"Who is he?" she asked.

This time he really smiled. "Not only have you been away, but it's a cinch you haven't watched the box since you got back."

"No. And neither has Gregory, thanks to you."

He sat down and offered her a cigarette. The lines returned to his eyes. "Our new star, Roddy Collins–his series has zoomed to the top ten. It's a Western. He plays the fastest gun alive for law and order. A beautiful guy, six foot six and all brawn. I've just learned he's a flaming faggot."

She shrugged. She wanted Robin to take her into his arms. He was pacing the room and had scarcely looked at her. His mind was still on the phone call. "Isn't a star's private life supposed to be his own?" she asked.

"Sure, if he'd *keep* it private, I don't care who he goes to bed with. But it seems sleeping with a boy is not his bag. He likes to dress like a woman and go out cruising to pick up a *guy*. Do you get the picture–six foot six, the newest all-American sensation, sponsored by a family-type product, walking into a bar in drag trying to pick up a guy?"

She started to laugh.

"It's not funny, Judith. It seems a guy five foot eight took a poke at him and the cops arrived. Our lawyers rushed in. We got three people to swear he did it on a bet, and that they were following him. We covered it *this* time, but we can't keep a guard on him every second."

"Robin, I've been away from all this for so long. I know I've got to start living with it again soon. But not now, not our first time together?"

He looked at her as if seeing her for the first time. "Of course–would you like a drink?"

"Yes." God, anything to break the ice.

He mixed two Scotches. "Gregory looks good," he said as he handed her the drink. "I'm very pleased that he wants me to keep running things, but you've got to make him take some interest."

"Doesn't he?"

"No. He called a meeting today and told everyone how proud he was of me. Tomorrow he's playing golf. And the following day he's going to look at some new horses."

She shrugged. "It's your network now, Robin."

"Yes, it is," he said quietly.

"Then let Gregory play with his horses and golf clubs."

"Judith, I thought he'd come back and try and take over completely. I was prepared to fight him on that–thirty percent of the programming consists of shows I've personally brought in. But he has no interest at all, and that's not healthy. I like Gregory. I want to work with him hand in hand, toss ideas around, make him argue with me when he thinks I'm wrong. It will make for better programming. Besides, the word *is* around that it's my network—and I don't want him to be upset."

She put down her drink and stared at him intimately. "Let me take care of that. It's my network too, you know."

"Judith, it's easy for you to say that now, but wait until you get into the swim of things. I don't give interviews. I'm not the most lovable guy in the world, according to the press. And unless Gregory is in there punching with me, he's going to be the forgotten man. As long as he was away, it was okay, but if he comes back and doesn't roll up his sleeves, then the papers will have a field day and it will *really* be my network. There's one columnist in particular who hates my guts. I refused to let him be a panelist on one of our game shows—he's a fat slob who is a hater. He's been writing about me every day, calling me the Love Machine!"

Her eyes narrowed. "How about living up to the title?"

He swallowed his drink. "Give me a chance to get healthy. You've been swimming on the Riviera. I haven't even had time to catch a weekend at the Hamptons."

"You look strong enough to me, Robin."

He walked over and pulled her to her feet. Her arms went around his neck. Suddenly there was the shrill interruption of the telephone. "Don't answer it," she said.

"It's the IBC line!" He removed her arms from his neck gently and walked over and took the call. "Hello. Yes. Oh, no kidding, Dip. Did Dan see it? No, I've never heard of Preston Slavitt. Oh yes, he's that off-Broadway writer who looks like he never takes a bath. Well, his talent is in his ass. . . . Really great, huh? Well, how long have you got the viewing room? . . . Okay, in twenty minutes." He hung up.

"You don't have to go somewhere?" She couldn't believe it.

"Dip Nelson latched on to a pilot that just might be great." He picked up his glass and drained his drink. "Dip claims he can get me first crack at it tonight. The other networks are viewing it tomorrow."

She looked surprised. "Who is Dip Nelson?"

"It's a long story, baby. He's an ex-movie star turned producer. We bought a series from him and Dan Miller." He held out his hand to help her up from the couch. "Look, Judith, you better go down first. I'll follow in a few minutes."

"When will I see you?"

"I'll call you tomorrow, around eleven." Then he kissed her lightly and walked her to the door but she felt his thoughts were already at the viewing room. She went down in the elevator, took a cab, and got home in time to find Gregory mixing a martini. He looked at her with genuine pleasure. "I'm so glad you're back early. I found your message and was afraid I'd have to eat alone. God, you look beautiful."

She took the martini and sipped it absently. And suddenly it occurred to her that Robin Stone hadn't even commented on the change in her looks.

When he hadn't called by one, she was furious. He probably had a lunch date so that meant he probably wouldn't call till three. But he had said he'd call at eleven! Well, he could have gotten jammed up. She stalked around her bedroom. She was all made up, but still in her negligee. She had hoped he might invite her to lunch, a long quiet lunch where they could talk and catch up on the past. Now it would have to be cocktails. She could manage to stay with him until nine. Leave word for Gregory that something had come up regarding the Orphans' Ball.

She stretched across the bed and began playing solitaire–she told herself that if five cards came up, he would call at four, just to talk. If ten came out, he would call at three, just to talk. Fifteen, he would ask her for a drink. Twenty, he would ask her for the evening. And if the game came out he would tell her that he was really mad about her and the whole thing would be as she dreamed.

Eight cards came out. She tried again. Fifteen this time–no, that wasn't fair. This time she'd do it and take the results seriously. No cards came out. Good Lord, did that mean he wasn't going to call?

At five o'clock she was desperate. She put in a call to him on his private wire. There was no answer. That meant he wasn't at his desk. When Gregory came home at six she was still in her negligee. "Are we going somewhere?" he asked as he noticed her perfect makeup.

"I wish we *were*," she said.

He smiled faintly. "We've been away a long time. People don't know we're home yet."

"You're right. I guess I'd better start phoning around."

He sighed. "I like it like this. We can have a quiet dinner and watch TV."

"What do you think I've been doing for a year and a half?" she asked quietly.

He looked contrite. "All right, why don't you put on something nice and we'll go to the Colony."

"Alone?"

"Together," he said.

"How will that look?" she demanded.

"Like we're having dinner at the Colony."

"Also like we haven't a friend in the world."

"Maybe we haven't, Judith. Most people don't, you know."

"That's nonsense, we've always been invited everywhere."

"Invitations," he said wearily. "Invitations to openings, to parties after the theater. Returning the parties–I guess we've been out of circulation."

"Let's get back," she insisted.

He shrugged. "All right, you start things going–that's always been your end."

She thought about it that night as she lay in bed. How did one get things going again? She had no real close women friends, just women she knew well enough to lunch with, discuss clothes and charities and listen to *their* troubles. Judith had never made a confidante of anyone and she had never been *out* of circulation before. Invitations for dinner parties, openings, art shows, charity balls–they had always kept pouring in. Suddenly she realized that their entire social life had centered around Gregory's work. When a Broadway show opened, there were opening-night seats from the producer, because the producer or director hoped to work for Gregory or get one of his stars on an IBC show. When stars came to town they called Gregory and invited them out. The phone hadn't rung since she had returned. But it was her own fault. She had done nothing but center her thoughts and plans on Robin. Well, she'd start things going tomorrow. Perhaps she'd give a small dinner party. She'd call Dolores and John Tyron. They were always "in" on everything.

Dolores was delighted to hear from her. "Oh, Judith angel, how divine that you're back. Are you going to the party for Joan Sutherland next week?"

"Well, to tell the truth, Dolores, I haven't made any dates, you're the first person I've called. I'm barely unpacked."

"You must be exhausted, all those parties in Europe. I'm dying to hear about it. Did you see Grace when you were in the south of France? I heard she gave a marvelous gala."

"We were in Capri then."

"Oh, then you were at the Korda ball? Was it divine?"

"I'll tell you all the things we did when I see you. But I'm more interested in *you* and all the friends I haven't seen in so long."

"Well, you must really have had a tremendous time to stay away this long! And isn't Gregory lucky having that marvy man running things for him? Tell me, Judith, I hear such wild things about him—are they true?"

"What do you hear?"

"*Everything,* darling—orgies, and also that he's AC-DC. He's always with that handsome ex-movie star, Pauli Nelson's husband."

"Who is Pauli Nelson?"

"Darling, you *have* been away. She was the biggest sensation on Broadway last year. But Robin Stone sounds so wicked. I'd just *adore* to meet him."

"Well, I'm planning a small dinner party and I'll invite him along. How about one night this week?"

"Darling, we're dead until a week from next Thursday. But get Robin Stone and arrange your little dinner—say in two weeks. Call me back and give me the date and I'll put it right down in my little book. Oh, angel, my other phone is ringing, and Freddy has just come to comb my hair and—good Lord, look at the time, I'm due at La Grenouille in an hour."

Judith made several calls. Everyone was delighted she was back, but each woman was booked and chatted endlessly about the excitement of the new season, and everyone naturally assumed she and Gregory had been invited everywhere. Well, a small dinner party at the Colony wasn't going to work. The solution was a large black-tie party in her home.

She decided on October first. She called Dolores back. Dolores was flying out of the door, but of course she'd look at her appointment book. *"Angel–not* October first! That's the opening of the New Regal Club. You've joined of course? Well, look through your mail–it's a closed membership but I'm sure they've sent you an application. Why not make your party, let's see, how about October eighth? That's open for us–I'll pencil it in lightly and you call back and confirm. I've got to dash, angel, but of course I'll see you before then."

Judith tried Betsy Ecklund. October eighth! Wasn't Judith going to the private showing and black-tie dinner at the Berner Gallery? The Duchess of Windsor was supposed to be coming in for it. Judith should check her mail–her invitation had to be there.

She hung up and stared at the mail on her breakfast tray. Some assorted bills, an ad from Saks, a letter from her sister. It was unbelievable! She was out of everything. To have to check with Dolores and Betsy on *their* availability–! In the past, she had just picked a date and given the list to her secretary. When her invitations went out, everyone came. Now she had to make dates fit in with *their* social life. Could a year and a half change things so radically?

It was twelve thirty. She had nothing to do. She dialed Robin's number with new determination. He picked up on the third ring. She heard talking in the background–his office sounded as if several men were there. "Oh yes." He made his voice impersonal. "I'm sorry I didn't call, things have piled up. Can I get back to you, either late this afternoon or first thing tomorrow?"

She replaced the receiver. Now what? She was all made up. She had to see him. Once he saw her, he'd respond. She had seen the look of admiration in his eyes when she came to his apartment–until that damn phone call!

She'd run into him! Make it appear accidental! Yes, that was the thing to do. *Today*. Let's see–he'd probably go to lunch at one and return around two. She'd manage just accidentally to pass the IBC Building at that hour and bump into him.

She dressed carefully–no hat; the beige coat with the sable boa.

She arrived at IBC at ten minutes to two. She went to a phone booth and called his office. When his secretary asked who was calling, Judith said, "Miss Weston of the Nielsen office."

"May I have him return your call, Miss Weston? He's expected back shortly."

"No, I'll call back." Judith clicked the phone. Good, that meant he was still out for lunch. There was a bookstore next to the IBC Building. She took her post there and pretended to be looking at the titles. She'd stand there until Robin returned and then as soon as she spotted him, she'd pretend to be walking by and accidentally bump into him. She waited ten minutes. How long could you stare at books? And it was windy–thank God she had her hair loaded with spray net. She wondered if the doorman noticed or recognized her. It was getting chilly, downright cold. She felt her eyes tearing. Some of the mascara began to run. There was a mirror near the doorway, and she saw that the mascara specks dotted the whites of her eyes. Half her bottom lashes had disappeared. That was the awful part of having once been a natural blond–your hair darkened with age, but your lashes never did. She got out her handkerchief. The mascara had caked in small lines under her eye. She tried to wipe it away.

"Something in your eye?"

She turned. It was Robin.

In the daylight with his tanned face close to her own, she suddenly felt that the entire operation had been a farce. But she turned and managed a weak smile. "Just mascara and wind. I had a luncheon date and thought it was such a divine day I'd walk, so I dismissed my car. It suddenly seems to have turned into winter."

"Want me to hail a cab?"

"Please." She tried not to show her dismay.

He led her to the curb and signaled a taxi. "Judith, I meant to call you, but I got so bogged down."

"I understand, but . . ."

The cab arrived and she was furious–usually you could never find one, but this damn fool had driven up as if he was practicing for the Indianapolis 500. Robin opened the door. "I'll call you, Judith."

As soon as she got to her bedroom, she flung herself on the

bed, sobbing off all her brand-new false eyelashes.

At five o'clock she took one of Gregory's sleeping pills and left a note that she had a headache. And as she fell into a heavy sleep she wondered if Robin suspected she had planned their "accidental" meeting.

The "accidental" meeting had disturbed Robin. He thought about it off and on during the afternoon. He found himself snapping at his secretary, being more than curt with Andy Parino, and actually rude when he turned down Jerry's invitation for drinks at the Lancer Bar. When he got home he mixed himself a drink and tried to watch television. But Judith kept coming to his mind. She had looked so pathetic standing in front of the bookstore. Her feeble excuse had rocked him—the poor thing, to be so desperate, to stand there hoping to run into him. Holy God, how had this happened? Had Kitty felt this way about her young boys?

He picked up the newspaper. He was damned if he was going to worry about it. Amanda had wanted him, a lot of girls had waited for his call—girls who didn't have double town houses or husbands who owned television networks. . . . But they were *girls*. They weren't fifty-year-old women who had gone through a face job. . . . He had been stunned when he had seen her: the smooth tight skin, like Kitty's. . . . Dammit, plenty of fifty-year-old rich women had face jobs—why did he have to feel guilty about Judith's?

He leafed through the newspaper in an effort to clear his mind. Suddenly he came upon a grinning picture of Dip Nelson. The headline read: TV'S NEWEST TRANSFUSION. The interview was in Dip's inimitable style: "TV needs new blood," he was quoted as saying; "that's why Robin Stone rushed to buy the new pilot Danton Miller and I created. The trouble with TV is too many people are in it who have no knowledge of real show business."

Robin tossed the paper on the floor. He went to the phone and dialed Dip. "No more interviews," he snapped. "You talk too much! From now on, let your show talk for you. That's an order."

"Okay, buddy boy. But I still think you're wrong not to have bought the other pilot I showed you. It's a sure winner."

"It was a piece of shit."

"You're in an adorable mood tonight."

Robin clicked the phone. He poured himself a stiff drink. By eleven o'clock he was very drunk.

Judith awoke the following morning with the dull sense that something was very wrong. Then she recalled the events of the previous day and fresh tears came to her eyes. It was nine o'clock. Gregory was going to Westbury to look at some horses. The entire day stretched before her. She tiptoed into his bedroom. He was gone. He had a *reason* to get up–his horses and golf–but she had nothing. She opened his medicine chest. That green pill had been a real knockout drop. She took another. Why not? At least she'd sleep through the day–it was better than lying around waiting for a call that wouldn't come.

The pill worked quickly. She hadn't eaten dinner last night. She thought of ringing for some tea, but her head felt heavy and she drifted off to sleep.

She heard the phone ring. It sounded like it was coming from a distance, but as she shook herself awake, the sound became clear and insistent. She groped for it. . . . Good Lord, it was four thirty–she had slept the day away.

"Hello, Judith."

It was Robin. He was on the phone, calling her. And she was so heavy with drowsiness. . . .

"Did I disturb you?" he asked.

"No, no, I had a hectic day." Why didn't her head clear? "I just got home and was trying to get forty winks."

"Then I'll hang up."

"No, I'm really awake." She hoped she didn't sound as sluggish as she felt.

"I managed to get through most of my work and I thought you might feel in the mood for a drink."

"I'd adore a drink."

"Fine. My place in half an hour?"

"Make it an hour," she said quickly. "I'm expecting a few calls for some charity events."

She staggered out of bed and rang for the maid. A pot of black coffee might help. Oh God, why had she taken that pill! He had called her! He actually wanted to see her!

She sat before her dressing table and sipped the coffee. Three cups, and still she felt light-headed. Everything seemed to be coming to her from a distance. But at least her hand was steady and she was able to apply her makeup. Her hair was a mess but she pinned on a fall. The hairpins dug into her scalp, but she had to be positive it was secure. Of course they might not go to bed, still she was taking every precaution. But she wasn't going to push things. . . . He had called! He wanted to see her and that meant he'd call again.

She scribbled a note for Gregory explaining she had been called to a charity cocktail party and might be late.

She was still light-headed when she knocked on Robin's door. He was in his shirt and had loosened his tie. He took her hands and drew her into the room. Then he kissed her gently on the lips. Suddenly with an abandon she had never known, she threw her arms around him, and kissed him long and deep. Then he took her by the hand and led her into the bedroom. She felt as if she was moving in a dream. All sounds were muted, even her movements seemed slower—yet she was without any inhibitions. She undressed slowly and stood before him. He stretched out on the bed and pulled her down. Making love with Robin suddenly seemed the most natural thing in the world. And she accepted his embrace as if she had known it all her life.

It was nine thirty when she got home. Gregory was sitting in bed watching television. She threw her arms around him. "Oh darling, I'm so sorry I missed dinner with you."

He smiled and patted her head. "Getting back in the social swim?"

"A bit. The meeting dragged on forever, and several of us went to '21' for a drink and then before I knew it . . ."

"That's all right. Shall I ring for some dinner for you?"

She shook her head. "I had two Bloody Marys. I think I'll just go straight to bed."

She *was* hungry, but she wanted to be alone with her thoughts. And she also wanted to go right to sleep and get the evening over with, because tomorrow would bring Robin—and that was all that mattered.

In the weeks that followed, Judith's entire life centered around the telephone. Robin usually called at eleven. To avoid any possibility of running into Jerry or Dip, Robin switched from the Lancer Bar to his new hangout, Marsh's Steak Place. She thought of it as "our place." And on days when he couldn't see her, she'd walk past it—just seeing the restaurant made it all seem real. Sometimes they went to his apartment; and yesterday she had driven him to the airport because he had to make a quick trip to the Coast. She wore her new European clothes and began to plan her winter wardrobe. Gregory wanted to spend the winter at Palm Beach. Fine. She'd manage to need dental work, redecorate the house—she'd get in to town often, then she'd be able to spend entire nights with Robin. She had gotten some marvelous hormone pills from Dr. Spineck and the flashes had stopped. As for the snoring—well, she just wouldn't sleep. How could she sleep if she had the chance to spend an entire night in Robin's arms, and wake with him and have breakfast with him! Of course she'd have to pretend to wake before him and patch her makeup. She'd buy one of those new alligator bags that had room for everything in it. . . .

She hadn't done a thing to reactivate her social life. She didn't care about it . . . Robin's phone call was the only thing that mattered. Sometimes she grew frightened at the intensity of her feeling for him. She was really in love. The frightening thing about this romance was her compulsion to see him constantly. At night she lay awake and had fantasies—Gregory would drop dead, painlessly and quickly, Robin would console her, and after a suitable time they could marry.

Marry! She sat up in bed. *Marry Robin!* Oh Lord, to kill off poor Gregory, even in a daydream—that was awful, horrible! But she loved Robin. Yes, she loved him—this was really it. This was the kind of love novelists wrote about. It did exist. Her past "romances" paled in comparison. Everything paled in comparison to Robin. He was her whole life. And Gregory wasn't going to drop dead quietly—he was getting stronger every day.

Suppose she divorced Gregory? No, that wouldn't work, because Robin would have to quit IBC. Well, why not? He had told her he wanted to write a book—he had even finished the first draft. It was about the Great Men who made it back from failure to the top: General de Gaulle, Winston Churchill . . . Robin's theory was that a true winner is the man who comes back after he's been on top and hit rock bottom. It's easy to make it once. But making it twice is what separates the lucky ones from the great ones.

Well, she had plenty of money. Even if she took nothing from Gregory, her stocks and securities were worth more than half a million. And the D & B report stated that Robin had real money of his own. They could go to Majorca, take a house. . . . She would keep everyone away from him. They'd walk the beach, sail together, and at night they'd sit before a fire and he would read his manuscript to her. . . .

The more she thought about it, the more obsessed she became with the idea. Suddenly it was urgent that she talk it over with Robin. He loved her—she was positive of that. They had been seeing each other constantly for six weeks. And the nights he wasn't with her, he was home watching television. Often she would slip into her bedroom and call him. And there wasn't a night she went to sleep without calling him to say good night—and he was always there. It was so wonderful to lie in the darkness, with Gregory safely asleep in the other room, and pour out her love to Robin. Of course he never came out and said he loved her. Robin wasn't the type. But he always said, "Sleep well, my darling."

She looked at her watch. It was noon—that meant it was eleven o'clock in Chicago. She had talked to Robin in Los Angeles last night. He was flying back today. The plane stopped at Chicago to refuel at four.

Suddenly she sprang out of bed. She'd be at the airport in Chicago when he arrived. They'd fly back together and she'd tell him. She scribbled a note for Gregory explaining that she had to go to Darien for the day. . . . Thank God Gregory was always so tired when he came home that he fell asleep right after dinner.

She arrived in Chicago at four, went to the VIP lounge and had him paged. He arrived slightly breathless, and speechless with surprise when he saw her.

She rushed to his arms. She didn't give a damn if anyone knew

–from now on they were going to be together all the time. They had a drink while the plane was refueling. For the first time she was glad that Robin had the use of Gregory's company plane. He seemed slightly off balance at her surprise appearance but she felt he was delighted. She held off with her news until they were seated in the plane, heading for New York. Oddly enough, it was Robin who gave her the perfect opening.

He took her hands and said, "This is all very wonderful and exciting but you must never do it again. The pilot certainly recognized you, and we don't want to hurt Gregory."

"I care about Gregory–that's why I want it to be quick and clean-cut. Robin, I'm going to ask Gregory for a divorce."

He didn't answer, but turned his attention to the clouds that floated beneath the plane.

"You want me, don't you, Robin?"

"We have each other. Why hurt Gregory?"

"I want to marry you."

He took her hands. "Judith, I don't want to get married." Then as he saw the tears rush to her eyes, he said, "I've never wanted to get married. To you, or to anyone."

"Robin, it *would* work. You could leave IBC, you could write. I'd be with you. . . . We could have such a wonderful life, Robin. Please don't say no. Just think about it. That's all I ask –*think* about it!"

He smiled and took her hands. "All right, we'll both do a lot of thinking. No more talking." He stood up and crossed to the small bar and mixed two drinks.

"To us," she said, as she raised her glass.

"To you, Judith. I never want to hurt you. Please believe that."

She snuggled against him. "Oh, Robin, I wish this plane ride would never end."

He didn't call the following morning. At first she wasn't concerned. She sat in the bedroom and waited. At three thirty she called him. He picked up the phone on the second ring.

"I'm sorry I didn't get to you," he said, "but there were several meetings this morning that I had to attend. Things piled up while I was out of town."

She giggled. "I caught you with people in the office, right?"

"Yes."

"How long will they be there?"

"It looks like the entire afternoon is jammed up."

"What about my coming by at six o'clock tonight at your place?"

"Can't. All kinds of appointments until seven, then I have to watch one of our new shows. It starts tonight."

"I'd love to watch it with you."

"I'll be at a sponsor's home. Then there's some party or something later. May I get back to you?" He sounded slightly annoyed.

She hung up. He didn't call back. She and Gregory had dinner alone. He was tired. Soon the Miltown caught up with him. He dozed off while he was watching the new show. She watched aware that Robin was also watching–somehow it made her feel closer to him. He was probably bored, and the party would be dull. She had been to parties given by agency men. . . .

The next morning she read the reviews. IBC had another winner. The *Times* gave it an excellent review and also mentioned the shot of adrenalin Robin Stone had given the network. But it was the afternoon papers that really upset her. There certainly had been a party–but it was no little agency party. They had taken over the Rainbow Room and every top celebrity and socialite had been invited. The center fold was filled with pictures. There was a large picture of Robin seated between a musical comedy star and a model. He was grinning as he listened to something the musical comedy star was saying. But the thing that ripped at Judith's heart was the way his left hand was interlocked with the model's. That gesture spoke louder than any words–they were together!

She waited a week and he didn't call. He had to be busy–he couldn't intentionally be ignoring her. Finally in desperation she called his private line at the office. The impersonal voice of the operator answered on the second ring and told her it was no longer a working number. A slow creeping fear nagged at her–he wouldn't dare! He couldn't! She dialed his private number at home. The same impersonal voice came on. "Sorry, that number is no longer in use. No, we cannot give out the new number. It is unlisted."

Her rage made her weak. He had done this to avoid her! She burst into tears and buried her face in the pillow. That night she lay awake until dawn. She wanted to destroy him! She would make Gregory fire him!

She began her attack the following morning. "He's taken the network from you. We're outcasts—do you realize that? Robin Stone is getting all the invitations we should be getting!"

Gregory listened apathetically. Then he said, "Judith, I'm sixty-two. The stock has never been higher—it's going to go two-for-one next month. The network has never been in better shape. And I don't intend to tamper with success. To tell you the truth, I kind of like the idea of checking in, finding everything is going well and slipping off to play golf or go to the track."

"And what am I supposed to do while you go to the track—sit home all day? And you're tired at night. I'm dying to go somewhere."

"I thought you were busy with your charities. Seems you've been happy enough these past weeks."

She avoided his eyes. "How many charity luncheons can I go to?" (She hadn't been to any.) "I can't keep doing that. I've forced myself to make charity dates for cocktails, but that's all over—people are beginning to wonder whether my name means that much on a patron list! They never see us anywhere. I'm embarrassed to admit we're not invited to all the 'in' parties."

"Haven't you had your fill of that? The same people at every party, the women all wearing name gowns to prove something to the other women?"

"No—I *like* going out."

"Well, I think it's a big bore. I thought you were finally getting some sense these last few weeks. It's been relaxing staying in. Now you want me to fire Robin Stone because he's invited to parties instead of us. Judith, you're acting childish."

"I'm not sixty-two and impotent!" she shouted.

He walked out of the room. She sat very still. Then the tears slid down her nice new tight face. Oh God, she moaned to herself.

She had hurt Gregory. And for what? For Robin Stone, that's what! She ran into her bedroom and flung herself across the bed. Oh God, Robin was gone! He had intentionally let himself be photographed with that girl. He had walked out on her—on all her dreams. She'd never hold him in her arms again, never feel his body against her own. . . . Her sobs came out dry and harsh. Suddenly she felt her head being stroked—Gregory was sitting beside her. "Don't cry, honey, I'm not mad. I know you didn't mean it."

She turned and clung to him. "Oh, Gregory, I do love you."

"I know you do, and just let me get my sea legs back. I'm not ready yet to tear into the aggravation of running a network. We'll go to Palm Beach this winter. We'll have fun—I promise you."

She nodded slowly. "And, Greg, you're not impotent . . ."

Judith made a determined effort to reactivate her social life, but she met with complete failure. Her frustration and anger almost eased the pain she felt about Robin. But there wasn't a night that she didn't stare at her phone and recall all the wonderful nights when she had been able to call him and whisper endearments. The memory would make her dissolve in tears and hug the pillow to muffle her sobs.

She decided to go to Palm Beach before Christmas. She didn't dare give her usual eggnog party—everyone was going to Acapulco, the Bahamas, or to parties given by the new hostesses who suddenly seemed to dominate the social scene.

She thought about Robin with a mixture of hate and desire. And when she reached Palm Beach she sat listlessly on the patio, played solitaire and tortured herself envisioning him making love to some young and beautiful girl.

But there weren't any beautiful girls in Robin's life. He worked ten hours a day, and kept abreast of the competition on the other networks. Dip's show was slated for February. Each day he checked with Robin. "Want any action, buddy boy?" Sometimes he allowed Dip to trail him to the Lancer Bar. And sometimes at ten o'clock when the walls would close in on him, he'd call Dip. "Meet me in front of my building. I want to walk."

"Pal, it's twenty-eight degrees, and I'm in bed."

"Are you meeting me?"

"Okay, give me ten minutes to dress."

When Dip wasn't "on call" to Robin, he sat around Danny's with the agents fawning over him. Sure, he'd see what he could do for them—Robin Stone never bought a show without consulting him. Dip reveled in his new power. He got back at every agent who had snubbed him by telling one and all that none of their clients would ever appear on IBC. And most of them actually believed he had that kind of power over Robin Stone. As one agent put it, "A man will do anything for the man he loves."

Oddly enough, it was Dan who fought those rumors. He laughed openly at the suggestion of homosexuality between the two men. It wasn't love Dip Nelson was giving Robin, he'd explain: it was cash—a nice healthy kickback.

The rumors reached Gregory in Palm Beach. When he saw Danton Miller's new show with a separate frame for Dip Nelson as producer, he called Cliff Dorne.

"The show is pretty good," Gregory said. "But when that hambone of an actor who couldn't produce his way to the men's room winds up with billing there's got to be something to the gossip. I don't believe the fag stuff—but there has to be a kickback involved."

"I've gone over the contracts carefully," Cliff said wearily. "If there is any kickback, it's well concealed. I came right out and asked Robin how come he bought a pilot from Dip Nelson, and he said, 'Cliff, if *you* have a pilot that's any good, I'll even buy one from you!' "

Gregory hung up. Judith was sitting with him on the patio during the conversation. "Well, what are you going to do?" she asked.

He shrugged. "Right now, I'm going to play eighteen holes of golf."

Nothing seemed to be able to stop Robin Stone. *Life* magazine did a story on him, without his cooperation. They drew from opinions of people who worked with him and girls he had dated. One airline stewardess claimed he really was the Love Machine. A model said he was the most romantic man she had ever known. An aspiring actress said he was a big zero. Maggie Stewart was quoted as saying, "No comment." The publicity snowballed, but Robin ignored it. He went to movies with Dip, occasionally met Jerry at the Lancer Bar, ate solitary dinners at the Steak Place, but most of all he worked.

It was Jerry who brought Gregory's growing antagonism to Robin's attention. They were standing at the Lancer Bar, and Jerry said, "How often do you consult Gregory on shows that you buy?"

"Never," Robin said. "There hasn't been any need to. Right now I'm going through the pilots for the next mid-season drop-outs. I'll invite him to view the ones I've selected."

"That's big of you," Jerry said.

Robin didn't answer. He gave the ice in his drink his total concentration.

"He did give you your chance," Jerry persisted. "If you want to stay where you are, I'd advise you to pretend to ask his advice now and then."

"I suppose it's known as Robin Stone's network now," Robin said slowly.

"Yes, it is."

Robin smiled. "Then let Gregory take it away from me."

"Meaning what?"

"Meaning that I don't give a damn. I didn't go after the network–but now that I've got it, I'm not handing it back to Gregory on a silver platter. Let him come after me, let him fight me to get it back."

Jerry looked at him oddly. "Know something? Someone said you have a death wish. I think it's true."

Robin laughed. "You go to your couch and I'll go to mine."

By April the fall lineup was set. Robin was leaving his office when Dip Nelson came crashing in. "Listen, Pauli's winding up her road tour. She gets into New York tomorrow. I got a great idea I haven't discussed with Dan yet. Instead of using a different girl on the show each week, let's use Pauli, make her a permanent character. How does that grab you?"

"It doesn't." Robin sat down and with a rare show of tolerance said, "Look, Dip. Let's not fool around with a successful format. Pauli can have her pick of any Broadway musical–Ike Ryan is dying to get her for his new show next season."

"But Pauli *belongs* on TV."

"Look, worry about your own career. One television show doesn't last forever. You should be finding new properties. Dan Miller has a new idea for a pilot that sounds sensational."

Dip's eyes went dark. "You're kidding! That dirty bastard! Sneaking behind my back. We got a deal–we go halves on everything."

"Have you got it in writing?"

"No, we got a gentleman's agreement."

Robin laughed. "That certainly won't hold up with either of you."

Dip's eyes narrowed. "I'll get him for this." Then with a complete change of mood his boyish smile returned. "Hey, how's about going to Danny's with me? You haven't been anywhere. People are liable to forget we're buddies."

Robin shook his head. "I'm leaving for the Coast tonight. I want to find a movie name to do Dan's pilot. And Ike Ryan has a series I might buy if I can get the actor I want."

Dip's smile vanished. "What's Ike got on you?"

"Meaning what?"

Dip sat on the edge of Robin's desk and smiled. "Look, buddy, the Big Dipper *knows* how you operate. You don't give away ice in the winter unless you're obligated. Did you beat up another whore somewhere?"

Robin reached out and grabbed his tie. "Listen, you cheap son of a bitch–no one has anything on me, including you. If Dan Miller hadn't come up with a good show, it wouldn't have gotten on. I was glad you cut yourself into the action, I thought you might try for a new career. If Ike Ryan has a good show, I'll *buy* it! But if a friend's show slips, I'll cancel it just as fast as any outside show. And you *remember* that!"

He released his hold on Dip. Dip smiled and straightened his tie. "What are you getting so riled up for, pal? The Big Dipper loves you and would kill for you. Remember that—*kill* for you! You don't come by friends like me so easy."

Robin put in a call to Maggie as soon as he checked into the Beverly Hills Hotel.

"It's eleven o'clock," she said, "and whatever you want, I'm too tired to listen."

"It's two A.M. New York time," he said. "And if I'm not too tired to talk you can listen. Besides this is business. Will you meet me for breakfast in the Loggia Room tomorrow at nine?"

"Make it eleven and I'll think about it."

"I have to view two pilots between ten and eleven."

"Sorry, I don't like being sandwiched in."

"Maggie, this is business."

She yawned. "Then tell me now."

"Okay. Let's start with this: I saw your last picture."

Her husky laugh came fast. "You're right—maybe it *was* my last picture."

"It was awful. But you looked great. I want you for a new television series."

"Why?"

"Because you just might be right for it."

"In that case, call my agent. Maybe *he'll* have breakfast with you. His name is Hy Mandel and he's in the book." Then she clicked the phone.

He spent the next ten days viewing pilots. He decided to let Maggie cool down. But he wanted to see her. . . . Several times he actually reached for the phone, but he resisted—he sensed they couldn't meet, make love and part again. And he wasn't buying matrimony.

It was one of those nights . . . a restless lonely night. Robin decided nothing could be lonelier than a lonely night in Los Angeles. At least in New York he could always go out and walk. But if you walked down any of the tree-lined streets in Beverly Hills, a prowl car immediately approached you. No one walked in Los Angeles. During the week, the entire city folded at ten. Of course, he could always get a girl—the Polo Lounge was loaded with ambitious starlets and agents who were terrified of him, yet eager to catch his eye. Suddenly he was tired . . . fed up. Why the hell didn't he just hand Gregory back the network, and walk out? But walk out where, and to what?

The sound of the phone broke into his thoughts. He looked at his watch. Seven thirty–too late for a business call. The operator announced Mr. Milano. For a moment it failed to register. Suddenly Robin brightened. "Put the call through," he said eagerly.

"Robin! I am so glad to have gotten you."

"Sergio, it's good to hear your voice. Where in hell are you?"

"I just got back to town today and am reading the back trades and I learned you were here."

"God, you even talk like an actor. I read that you were doing a picture in Rome. What's happened since?"

"I am getting my big chance now–I start on a new picture here, next week. I play the lead. I am an actor, Robin. Isn't it wonderful?"

"What are you doing now?"

"I told you, I start a picture next week."

"No, I mean now, like this minute?"

There was a pause. "Robin, I have met someone I care a great deal about . . ."

"Oh, well, good luck. I'm glad for you, Sergio, I really am."

"I am having dinner with him tonight. His name is Alfie Knight."

"I think you two make a hell of a team," Robin said good-naturedly.

"But what about a drink tomorrow?" Sergio asked.

"That's a date. Five o'clock in the Polo Lounge."

"I'll be there," Sergio said.

Robin ordered dinner from Room Service and turned on the television set. Dip's show was on–he might as well catch it.

The commercial came on. The show started with the usual action teaser just as the waiter arrived with his food. Robin was just starting on his baked potato when he saw a close-up of Pauli. He almost choked on it. God damn Dip–he had *told* him not to use her! How had Dan gone for it? He pushed away the table and watched the show. It was bad. In an effort to build Pauli into a permanent character the entire show went down the drain. He put in a call to Dan immediately.

Dan was stupefied. "Dip told me it was a direct order from you. Next week's script is already taped. I gave her a contract for the rest of the season." Robin slammed the receiver and put in a call to Dip. The wire was busy. The idiot was probably busy taking bows. He made reservations on the midnight flight out. Suddenly he remembered his date with Sergio. He didn't even know his phone number–well, he'd leave a note with the captain in the Polo Lounge.

He arrived at Kennedy Airport at eight in the morning and went directly to his office. He called an immediate meeting with Dip and Dan Miller. Robin's expression was deadly as he demanded that Pauli be written out after the following show.

"I can't do it to her," Dip argued. "She has a big interview today. She's told all the press she's a regular on the show and if she got axed it would hurt her reputation."

"It's an *order,*" Robin stated.

"I own the package," Dip said stubbornly.

Robin turned to Dan. "You have equal say!"

Dan stared at him curiously. "I have one-third say, and I'm willing to side with you."

"Who has the other third?" Robin asked.

Everyone was silent.

Dan looked at him. "I thought you had it."

For a moment Dip looked frightened. Then his face went hard and his body tensed as if ready for physical action. "No, chum, I have two thirds, so I have the voting stock as you might say." Then he smiled. "So I guess that settles it. Pauli stays."

Robin stood up and faced him. "Dip, once you did me a big favor. Do me one more. Never come near me again."

Dip made a pretense at a pompous bow and left. Dan shifted his feet nervously as he waited for Robin's reaction. He was surprised when Robin turned to him coolly and said, "Well, it looks like you're stuck with Pauli. Good luck."

"You can't be angry at *me?"* Dan asked.

"I'm only angry that you thought I'd deal in on anything like this."

"How does this affect my new show?" Dan asked.
"Is Dip in on it?"
"No."
"Then you still have your deal."

The ratings slipped after Pauli went on the show. In June, Robin canceled it. Dip was out of a job. But oddly enough the television exposure helped Pauli and she was signed to do a movie. Dip followed her out to the Coast and Robin concentrated on the new fall season.

Gregory Austin had scheduled the November stockholders' meeting to be held on the Coast. Usually he made a quick three-day trip accompanied by Cliff Dorne, but this time he had decided to spend a full week there. Judith needed the excitement.

Gregory stared at Robin's picture on the cover of *Newsweek*. He realized the stockholders regarded Robin as their God, and to them Gregory was a semi-retired old man. But he had never felt better, and was now eager to resume command. He had made several subtle attempts to regain control, but so far all of his efforts had failed. Robin listened to his suggestions . . . but that was all he did—listen. Then he went on to do things in his own way. And so far, Robin's way was the right way. The ratings were at a new high. IBC was Robin Stone's network.

But Gregory hadn't given up. The summer at Quogue hadn't been too bad for him though Judith had been bored. Christ—a man spends thirty years to build up a network and a good life, then along comes one illness—a year and a half away from the scene and he comes back to find a new civilization.

His heart went out to Judith. He had seen the scars behind her ears. Jesus! Did she think he was idiot enough not to notice how her breasts suddenly stood up? He knew she must have done it while he was going through those weeks of shock treatment. She had been so great to him while he was ill. It was only natural that she had come back eager for excitement. And he had failed her. Yet he had to admit that he had enjoyed the idea of Robin's take-over when he returned. In the beginning it had been relaxing to have someone else making the decisions. He had even enjoyed the summer at Quogue and tried to ignore the heavy sighs that emanated from Judith each night as they watched television. But it was her attitude when they returned to the city that finally made him take action.

Judith began taking to her bed for days at a time. Some days she took sleeping pills every four hours. On these days Gregory brought in a nurse to watch over her and at night he slept in her room—he was terrified she'd set herself on fire as she staggered around hunting for a cigarette. When she wasn't in bed, she shuffled around the house without makeup, in an old dressing gown. She refused to go out. He even offered to take her to El Morocco. She didn't want to go alone. Okay, he'd ask Maurice Uchitel to give a party for her there—take over the upstairs room. This only caused her to go into a crying spell: "No one would come." In desperation he placed a call to Dr. Brugalov, his doctor in Switzerland, and explained that Judith was going through a delayed reaction to the strain of his illness and asked if he could recommend someone in the States to help her.

Dr. Brugalov recommended a Dr. Galens. When Gregory explained the situation, Dr. Galens wanted to see Gregory each day. Oddly enough, he didn't want to see Judith. Gregory was so desperate that he agreed. They went back to his paralysis, they discussed his sex life with Judith. He told Dr. Galens about the scars behind her ears, the small scars on her body. He felt sure she hadn't done it to attract other men—Judith wasn't like that and actually sex meant very little to her. Gregory felt she had gone through the operation to hold her position as the goddess on the front pages of *Women's Wear*.

But Dr. Galens kept returning to their sex life. One day in desperation Gregory snapped, "Look, this girl was a virgin when we got married—so I started very slowly with her. And she never showed any desire to experiment. And that's how it's always been. Lately she must have read some of those 'How To' books—you know, those marriage manuals—because in the past few years she's made some amateurish attempts to go down on me. I never would have dared to try it with her—she's just not that kind of a woman. I don't need outside sex. God knows I went through enough variations in my bachelor days to last me a lifetime. And if straight uncomplicated sex was what Judith wanted, it was okay with me. Besides, it was our *life* she loved: it was exciting, and –" He had stopped suddenly. Jesus Christ! That was it! The fear! His fear! All interwoven with IBC and Judith–Judith loved the life he gave her. He loved her–no, it was more than that: he *worshiped* her. Despite his grumbling about the eggnog parties, he was still so damned thrilled she belonged to him–thrilled with the elegance she brought into his life. When he used to survey the dinner parties and realized she had created this beautiful world for him, he had always nurtured a hidden fear that something might destroy it. Another man? No, Judith wasn't highly sexed. Money? He'd always have that. Illness? Yes–illness could destroy everything!

And now it had happened: he had lost Judith. She was courting self-destruction now. But hadn't he done the same in returning and pretending to enjoy the luxury of having Robin run the network? Suddenly it was clear to him. He could get Judith back on her feet! It wasn't going to be easy. But his fighting spirit had returned.

First he had to regain control of IBC. He took immediate action. He went to Robin and stated that the decisions for next year's lineup should be brought to him. Robin looked at him with that lopsided smile.

"Why?" Robin asked.

Gregory was embarrassed. He couldn't meet Robin's cool, direct gaze.

"Look, Robin, I promoted you from newsman to president of this network. I'm proud of you, I want to work with you–you're my boy." He had tried to be open and affectionate.

Robin's eyes had gone hard. "I'm nobody's boy!" He spat out the word. "I've been calling every shot around here for almost two years. I can't start asking your permission for every move I make. If you want someone to do that, get yourself another *boy!*"

Well, Gregory could *get* another boy but he couldn't let another network get Robin Stone. Nevertheless, each time he looked at Judith, his determination strengthened–his poor sad Judith who had gone through all those operations only to slip into oblivion because of him. He had to regain control of IBC.

He hoped the trip to Los Angeles would help. He didn't expect to stir up any real excitement with the stockholders–he had to play a waiting game. It was crazy but he had to hope that Robin's shows flopped, that the IBC stock went down. He had to root against himself and pray for big losses. It was the only way he could get his network back.

Dr. Galens felt the trip would be therapeutic for Judith, providing she didn't just sit in the hotel. Gregory had called Cully and Hayes and asked them to publicize their arrival on the Coast and get them invited to all the big parties. It galled him to have to take such measures, but Judith's well-being was all that mattered. And Cully and Hayes had come through: several invitations had already arrived by mail. And Judith had stopped taking Seconals, gone and had her hair touched up and bought an entire new wardrobe for California. Perhaps the week of excitement would snap her out of her lethargy for good.

They were due to leave on Sunday. The Friday before, he called and asked her what time she wanted to leave.

"Must I answer this very second?" she asked. "Just tell them to have the plane ready by noon."

He told his secretary to call his pilot and have him stand by. The secretary seemed surprised. "Mr. Stone took the plane two hours ago."

"He what?"

"He's flying to Las Vegas this weekend to catch some performer. Then he's going to the Coast to attend the board of directors meetings. I assumed you knew–"

"I forgot," Gregory said quickly. He sat back. How *dared* Robin take the plane! He sent for Cliff Dorne.

Cliff sighed. "Look, Gregory, what do you mean, 'how dared he?' It's the company plane, and he runs the company. You know what that plane has been nicknamed along Madison Avenue. The Flying Couch! Robin redecorated it so part of it has been turned into a bedroom with a wall-to-wall bed! And he rarely makes his flights without some girl–any girl to keep him company in that bed. I can't keep track of him. Half the time I never know where he is."

"We've got to stop him," Gregory said.

"Unfortunately when you were ill, Judith gave him complete power. I can't tell you how many times I wanted to walk out. But

I knew I'd be playing into his hands. If he'd put in his own man as legal head, we'd be dead."

"We're dead now," Gregory said quietly.

"No, he'll bury himself."

"What do you mean?" Gregory asked.

"It has to happen–especially the way he's going the last six months. He makes insane decisions, and takes unheard-of chances. He put on two shows that *had* to flop and instead they came off as 'high camp' successes!"

"He's like all the rest," Gregory said slowly. "Power-mad."

"No, I don't think it's power he wants. On the one hand, he seems to want his name to blaze like headlights–and at the same time, he throws mud at it. I'll be very frank and tell you I can't figure him out. There are even rumors that he's queer, yet he always has a girl. Then there were rumors that he was getting a kickback and I spent weeks checking that. He wasn't. There's only one funny wrinkle. There's an actor–Sergio Milano. Until recently, Robin sent him three hundred dollars a week. I know this because his tax man and my tax man are cousins and I checked it out. Sergio Milano is making it with Alfred Knight."

"Then you think Robin is AC-DC?"

"It looks that way. Sergio hasn't made it big yet, but he's been getting some good parts, and he's a sexy-looking Italian. Obviously he's making enough money so he doesn't need any from Robin. Or maybe he's stopped taking it because Alfred Knight is his new lover."

"Look, can we put someone on this thing? I don't know how it's done." Gregory looked embarrassed.

"I've done it already. I have a man who will tail Robin the second he hits the Coast. I figure we owe it to our stockholders, if we think we have a guy at the top who could get involved with a morals clause."

"Cliff, I don't want any scandal. It's one thing to get rid of Robin, but another to destroy a man's life. I won't do that."

Cliff smiled. "Gregory, all I want is a written report. We're bound to unearth plenty. Then we present it to Robin. He won't want scandal either. He's got family–a sister who's a big socialite in San Francisco–and he's bright enough to know any open scandal would finish him in the business. That's when we tell him we're putting in someone to 'help' him. We'll divide the power. You'll create another new title. Let Robin remain as President of IBC. We'll get Dan Miller back. Then the power will be divided and *you* will make all final decisions."

Gregory nodded. "I'd like Dan Miller back. I can control him. But will he accept Robin's having equal power? That's what made him walk out before."

"No, he walked because Robin had power *over* him."

"And suppose Robin walks–right to another network?" Gregory asked.

"He won't be able to, not if we have the kind of written report I think we'll have."

"Well, we can't make any move until we get such a report," Gregory said.

"We'll get *something*. If not on this trip, then on the next one. Maybe even in New York. I've hired a good outfit, they have men in every city. Meanwhile, we just have to be patient."

Gregory nodded. Then he began to plan how to break the news to Judith that they'd be flying on a commercial airliner to the Coast. Oddly enough, she took it well. "I hate that bloody plane. Sell it."

Robin landed in Los Angeles late Sunday afternoon. A stack of messages was waiting for him at the hotel. Agents, stars and affiliate station managers had called. Everyone had sent liquor–his suite looked like a well-stocked bar. He ruffled through the messages: one was a note from Sergio.

He poured himself a shot of vodka. The Polo Lounge would be crawling with IBC personnel, let alone the goddam stockholders. It was the one place he had to avoid. He called Sergio.

"Robin, I am sending you a check next month for all the 'allowances' you sent me. I have just signed a great contract with Century Pictures."

"Forget the money, you'll only screw up my taxes. You were a good friend to me when I needed one, and I knew that the money on the sale of Kitty's estate wouldn't last forever."

"The government took so much," Sergio said mournfully. Then his mood changed.

"Robin, tonight Alfie is throwing a big party. It starts at eight. Please come."

"I don't make those scenes."

"It's not that kind of a party. Everyone will be there." Sergio laughed. "Good Lord, Robin, I'm just making it now–I couldn't afford a drag party. And I have a morals clause in my contract. So has Alfie."

"I don't mean that, in fact it never occurred to me. I mean I don't make the Hollywood scene. Sorry, chum. You'll have to celebrate without me. By the way, are you shacking up with Alfie?"

"No, he has a small house. I live at the Melton Towers. Eventually perhaps we will buy a house together. It is my dream."

"Melton Towers. I know a girl who lives there–Maggie Stewart."

"Oh yes. We see one another in the elevator. She is very beautiful."

When Robin hung up he called the Melton Towers. Maggie answered on the first ring.

"Oh it's Superman and his Flying Couch. I read in the trades that you were due in town."

"Maggie, I want to see you."

"I just finished taping a game show. Three today, two more tomorrow. I bring five different sets of clothes and kill myself trying to be bright, perky and above all sparkling with daytime personality. I tell you there's nothing like a daytime personality to kill a girl's morale."

"I want to see you," he repeated.

"I heard you the first time."

"Then why are you rattling on about taping shows and all that crap?"

"Because I'm insane. Know why? Because I *want* to see you. That means I *have* to be crazy–like asking for punishment."

"Do you want to come here? We'll order room service. Or how about Matteo's?"

"You come here," she said slowly. "I've taken off my face, my hair is limp. I have some franks in the freezer and I make a wild can of baked beans."

"I'll be right over."

"Cool it for an hour. I want to take a shower and look halfway presentable."

He poured himself a vodka, switched on television and wondered if Gregory Austin had arrived. Perhaps he should call. Then he shrugged. The hell with it—he'd see him at the board of directors meeting on Tuesday.

Gregory sat in the large living room of bungalow eight at the Beverly Hills Hotel. Ordinarily he would have preferred the Bel Air. It was off the beaten track and he wouldn't run into all the network personnel. Like tonight—it was six o'clock, but his watch told him it was nine o'clock, New York time. He was beat, but Clint Murdock had just phoned. Clint was a retired general and a very important cog on the board of directors. *Mrs.* Murdock had seen them checking in—would they have dinner in the hotel dining room tonight? He had no choice . . . the general was too important to snub. Well, it would be a quick dinner. With luck he'd be back in the bungalow before midnight. He yawned. Maybe he'd have time for a short nap. . . . They weren't meeting the general until eight. He'd better tell Judith. Mrs. Murdock was a bore, but at least Judith could wear one of her new dresses. Maybe they'd even stop off at the Polo Lounge for a drink. And from tomorrow night on, they were booked for a party every night. Cully and Hayes had earned their thousand a week. He hoped it would make Judith happy.

She came into the living room. "I don't know what to do. The valet is closed."

"They'll open early enough tomorrow," he said.

She smiled. "Well, I'll just have to wear the gold lamé pajamas tonight. They're the only things that didn't crush."

"Tonight?"

She waved an invitation. "This was here when we arrived. Alfie Knight is throwing a big party—everyone will be there."

"Judith, starting tomorrow we have parties every night. But tonight I made a dinner date with General Murdock and his wife."

"General *Murdock?* I wouldn't want to have dinner with them if I had *Nothing* to do–let alone turn down Alfie Knight's party for them!"

He rose from his chair and tried to put his arm around her. "Judith, I *need* him. Murdock can help me with the board."

Her face went ugly with scorn. "Sure. We'll sit for hours and I'll have to make idiotic small talk with Mrs. Murdock, while you listen to the general's latest story about his fishing. Do you think Robin Stone would grovel like that? He'll be at Alfie Knight's party! *Everyone* will be there!" She broke from him and dashed into the bedroom.

He felt panic as he saw her head for the bathroom. "Judith, what are you doing?"

She held his bottle of sleeping pills. "I'm going to take two! I refuse to sit and listen to those dreary people. At least if I'm asleep I won't be miserable about missing one of the best parties in town."

He grabbed the bottle. "I can't break the date with the general. But if the party means so much to you, you go. I'll invent some story for the Murdocks."

"I can't walk in to a party like that unescorted." She reached for the bottle. "Let me take the pills, *please,* Greg. I just can't face an endless dinner with those people."

"No, I'll get someone to escort you." He suddenly turned to her. "Perhaps Robin Stone will take you."

Her face was expressionless. "I'm sure he has a date."

"He can still escort you, even with a date." He went to the phone. He hated to ask Robin for a favor–then he thought of Judith. Dammit, he wasn't going to have her taking to her bed.

When Robin came to the phone, Gregory plunged right in. "Robin, there's a party tonight at some movie star's home–Alfie Knight, I believe. Yes, well, Mrs. Austin has been invited and feels it might be amusing. She hasn't attended one of these Hollywood bashes for a long time. Unfortunately, I have a dinner engagement with some of the board of directors and I would consider it an enormous favor if you'd escort her."

Judith watched Gregory's face for some sign. The silence was ominous–she could tell that Robin was refusing. . . .

"I feel the same way," Gregory answered, "but it would be a personal favor to me. Oh, I see. Well, look, Robin, can't you still keep your dinner appointment and take Mrs. Austin to the party? I doubt whether those things get going much before nine or ten. I really would appreciate it. . . ."

"Oh for God's sake, stop begging!" Judith shouted. She rushed over and grabbed the phone. "Robin, this is Judith–forget it! It was Gregory's idea, not mine."

"Do you really want to go, Judith?" he asked.

"I thought it might be fun. And I think I need a bit of excitement. But I don't want to force you to go."

"I hate Hollywood parties. But look, Judith, will it be all right with you if we make it late–say ten o'clock?"

"Ten would be marvelous. That would give me a chance for a quick nap."

"Fine. I'll ring you from the lobby."

She hung up and tried to hide her happiness. He hadn't wanted to go, but he was doing it for her. That meant he still felt something. She had given him every chance to get out of it. And he probably had a date with a girl and was breaking away just to be with her. She walked over to Gregory and kissed him lightly. "Your poor hired help, they still jump to your bidding."

He felt relieved to see her happy again. "No, he wasn't jumping–not for me anyway. You were the one he melted for. But then, you've always had that power, Judith."

She was so happy that she wanted to be kind to everyone. "Are you sure you don't mind my skipping dinner with the Murdocks?"

"Of course not. I'll tell them the trip knocked you out. And they'll never know you went to Alfie's party. It's a cinch *they're* not invited."

She kissed his head. "I'm going to cream my face and take a long warm bath. Then a little nap–wake me when you leave."

She sang as she ran the bath water. She was going to see Robin again. And she felt he wanted to see her too. Of course he did. She had scared him off with that marriage talk. Well, she'd let him understand that from now on, it would be on his terms. No more ultimatums. She'd see him every night this week–they were bound to be invited to the same parties. And when they got back to New York they'd go to the Steak Place and . . . Oh Lord, it was wonderful to be alive!

Robin rented a car and drove to Maggie's apartment. It was almost seven o'clock. This was a hell of a mess, but Judith had sounded so desperate. He had stopped it cold after that marriage talk, and had assumed she had someone else by now. But that false surge of pride in her voice when she had told him he didn't have to take her–it had been a cry for help. He hadn't the heart to refuse.

He thought about it as he drove down Sunset Boulevard. He wondered why he felt compassion for Judith. He didn't feel anything for anyone. Except Maggie–hell, he *wanted* Maggie! It was a physical drive. As simple as that. Also he admired her spunk. She hit back at him. She was a challenge, not limp and sad-eyed like Amanda. Maggie was a fighter–his kind of girl. But Judith –what the hell did he owe to *her?* Why had he cut short his evening with Maggie? It bothered him. He pushed it from his mind as he eased the car into a small parking spot near the Melton Towers.

Maggie looked tired, but hauntingly beautiful. He noticed the purplish circles under her eyes. She was too thin, but for some reason she was more desirable to him than ever.

They ate on the coffee table. And when they finished he helped her with the dishes. Then with almost a shy smile she led him into the bedroom. He was amazed at the way she somehow brought out all the tenderness in him . . . and later when he held her in his arms he felt completely fulfilled for the first time in ages. God, if they could just find some kind of workable truce. He knew he wanted her with him, but he couldn't ask her just to live with him. He lay there stroking her hair, and for the first time he wondered about marriage. It might work–that is, if she could let him be free to take off whenever he wanted. Oddly enough he couldn't think of anyone he would *want* to take off with. Jesus, very shortly he'd have to take off and escort Judith to that damn party. He stole a look at his watch. Eight forty-five –he still had time.

"Maggie . . ."

"Mmm?" She stirred, and nuzzled her face into his neck.

"Have you any plans for your career? I mean aside from the game show?"

"Alfie Knight has a picture I want to do."

"My offer to star in a new television series still holds."

"I'd rather do the picture."

"Have you done anything about it?" he asked.

She stretched across him and reached for a cigarette on the night table. "I wrote Alfie a note, and Hy's been on his neck. He said he'd use me if he didn't get a jumbo. I hear he wants Elizabeth Taylor. I don't think I have much of a chance."

"I might be able to help. But why not take the television series? It would be great exposure for you, good money, and Alfie won't be doing the picture until next year."

She looked at him slowly. "And then you'll pop out here every few months and we'll meet, fuck and talk about my career?"

"I'll be out here a lot–"

"That means we'll fuck a lot and talk a lot." She got out of bed.

"What *do* you want, Maggie?"

She stood in the center of the room. The bathroom light spilled on her body. He could see the anger in her eyes. "I want *you!* Tonight was marvelous, but as always, I'll hate myself in the morning. I'll feel like an accommodation–your West Coast lay!"

He was out of bed in an instant and took her in his arms. "Dammit, you know that's not true. I could get any girl in this town just because I have jobs to give out."

"And you've just offered me the plum–the big job, a lead in a series. And for that I'm supposed to be ready to jump at a phone call! God, it sounds like a plot for a B picture. Tell me, who is the New York girl you've got stashed away, ready to rush to the Lancer Bar at a moment's notice? And is there one in Chicago? There would have to be–you have to stop and refuel the Flying Couch."

He broke away from her and put on his shorts. She reached for a robe and lit a cigarette. She watched him as he dressed.

Suddenly he smiled. "The Flying Couch–is that what they call my plane?"

"Didn't you read *Undercover* last month?"

"What the hell is that?"

"A scandal sheet. You were on the cover. You don't only make *Newsweek* and *Time*! You make a lot of magazines. And according to *Undercover* you don't care *what's* on that Flying Couch with you, man or woman, just as long as you can hump!"

He slapped her hard. She went limp and burst into tears. Then she fell into his arms. "Oh God, Robin, why do we try to destroy one another?" she sobbed.

"I care for you, Maggie, and I want you to take this job."

"I don't want a payoff!" The tears ran down her face. "Can't you understand? The only thing I want in this world is *you!*"

"You *have* me! More than any woman in the world has ever had me. I still wear your goddam faggy little ankh ring."

When she didn't answer, he said, "Does a wedding ring make all the difference?"

"Yes."

"Okay."

"Okay, what?" she asked.

"Okay, we'll get married." He looked at his watch. It was nine fifteen–he had to get to Judith but he wanted to settle it with Maggie. "It will mean you're Mrs. Robin Stone. But I have to be free to come and go. Like right now, I have to leave."

She stared at him. "You *what?*"

"I have to take a lady to a party."

For a moment she stared at him in disbelief. She backed away from him as if he had struck her. "You mean you came here, knowing you had a late date, knowing you were going to jump out of bed and go to another woman?"

"It's nothing like that. The lady is Mrs. Austin."

"That makes everything legal. She's not exactly Dame May Whitty."

"Maggie, let's not get Mrs. Austin involved with us."

"Oh, she's *above* all that!" She laughed. "You want to be free, yet you have to jump when Mrs. Austin snaps her fingers. Is that how you got to be head of IBC?"

"I'm going to leave, Maggie. I don't want you to say things you really don't mean. I'll call you tomorrow."

"There is no tomorrow for us." Her eyes blazed.

"You don't mean that, Maggie."

She turned away and he knew she was sobbing. He went to her and took her in his arms. "Maggie, I *care* for you. Good God, how else can I prove it? I'm asking you to *marry* me. If you want me for what I am, fine. I want you."

"I want you to *need me,* Robin," she sobbed. "I was married to a man who didn't need me, except for one thing–an heir. Robin, don't you understand? I love you so much that it scares me. I was hurt when Hudson cheated on me even though I never loved him. But I'd never survive if you let me down. Don't you think I've tried to forget you? With Andy, Adam, all my leading men. But it didn't work. I don't want you to marry me because you feel you're doing me a favor. I want you to marry me because you *want* me, because you want to share everything with me–your thoughts, your love, your problems. Not just your body. Can't you understand, Robin? *I want you to need me.*"

"Looks like we can't close the deal," he said slowly. Then he smiled oddly. "You see, baby, I don't need anyone."

She nodded slowly in defeat. "Dan Miller once said that about you."

"Then Dan is brighter than I thought." He started for the door. "Do you want the job?"

"No."

"Do you want marriage?"

She shook her head. "Not on your terms."

He opened the door. "I'll be here for four or five days. If you change your mind on either count . . ."

She stared at him, her eyes heavy with tears. "Don't call me anymore, Robin. Please. Never!"

"You really mean that?"

She nodded. "Not unless you can call and say you *need* me."

She waited until she heard the elevator close behind him before she fell on the bed and sobbed.

Robin entered the lobby of the Beverly Hills Hotel at one minute before ten. Five minutes later Judith swept down looking like shimmering gold. She had never looked better and she had never stirred more compassion within him. He thought of Maggie with her ponytail and the purple shadows under her eyes. And he knew that no matter how hard he tried, he could never make love to Judith again.

He managed a bright smile as he walked toward her. "You're going to put all the movie stars to shame," he said.

"It's the only thing that didn't wrinkle. And I've worn it to death at all the parties in New York."

"I only have a rented Rambler. It's not elegant enough for you," he said as he led her to his car.

She snuggled against him in the front seat. "I like this better than a limousine." She watched his profile as he drove up the sloping hills. "Robin, I've missed you," she said softly.

"A beautiful woman like you shouldn't miss anyone," he said easily. "Judith, watch for the signs on your side. Alfie's house is on Swallow Drive—all these damn streets have birds' names."

"We're on Doheny now," she said.

"That's where we're supposed to be. Somewhere near here we take a sharp turn."

She concentrated on the street signs.

"I acted like a child," she said slowly.

"When?"

"Flying to meet you in Chicago."

"I thought it was a bit reckless, but charming."

"I've done a lot of thinking, Robin. I can't hurt Gregory, he needs me."

"Good girl. And I think you need him, too."

"No, I need you."

"Ah—here's Swallow Drive. And that must be the house, where all the Rollses and Bentleys are parked."

A prowl car was just pulling up as Robin parked. "You going in there, mister?" the officer asked.

Robin nodded. "I believe there's a party."

The officer laughed. "This is the third time I've been sent here. Look, tell Alfie Knight I'm a fan and he's entitled to have some fun, but the lady down the street has a baby that's teething."

"I'll do my best," Robin promised. He helped Judith out of the car.

The officer stared at her, dismissed her as a civilian and then turned his attention back to Robin. "Say, don't I know you? You look familiar. Of course! I used to watch the *In Depth* show when you were on it. Robin Stone, *right?"*

"Right."

"Almost every celebrity in town is at that party. Say, you should be back doing that show. I liked you—you're almost as good as Huntley and Brinkley."

"He has the Happening show now," Judith said with a hint of possessive pride.

"No kidding. Well, I'm on night duty lately so I don't get to see much TV." He waited until Robin started up the path. Then in a low voice he called, "Mr. Stone, could I see you a second—alone?"

Robin hesitated. Judith smiled and nodded. He left her and returned to the prowl car.

"Listen, Mr. Stone. I know that broad with you isn't your wife. She's got too much mileage for that."

Robin's gaze was cold. He waited for the officer to go on.

"Look, I'm not butting in. I just want to tip you off—in case she's someone else's wife. . . ."

"I don't think I understand," Robin said.

"I don't miss anything, see. And while I was talking to you, I noticed a tail."

"A *what?"*

"A tail. I think you got a tail. Are you in any trouble or something?"

"Not any more than usual."

"Well, while we were talking a guy was driving around this street. He made a U-turn and went down, then came back, then went down again, and now he's parked down the road a piece. I just recognized him last time around. He's a private investigator."

"Maybe he's tailing someone inside. The lady I'm with is with me at her husband's request."

The officer shrugged. "Maybe he's eyeing one of the other big homes, waiting for someone's husband to come out. But he's a tail."

"Well, he's not mine," Robin said, "but thanks all the same!" Then he hurried up the path after Judith.

When they entered the house, the surprise and delight on Sergio's face made him almost happy that he had come. He recognized several top directors, a few big stars, and the usual assortment of starlets. Someone grabbed him and planted a wet kiss on his neck. It was Tina St. Claire. He introduced Judith to Sergio, Alfie and Tina. Then he got two drinks and steered Judith toward a couch. A large Siamese cat sauntered through the room and eyed him. It let out a low growl and leaped into his arms.

Alfie almost dropped his drink.

"God, have you got sex appeal! Slugger hates everyone."

"Slugger!" At the sound of Robin's voice the cat purred. Robin scratched its ear. "Where did you get it?"

"Ike Ryan gave it to me. It belonged to his wife. Ike travels so much that half the time the poor cat was in a kennel and I adore cats. He hates strangers but you're the exception."

"No, we're old friends, Slugger and I." He rubbed the cat's neck and noticed it still wore the little silver tag on its collar.

Tina St. Claire stood before the combo and began to gyrate suggestively, staring meaningfully at Robin.

"Better cut the drums," Robin said to Alfie. "I just headed off the prowl car."

"Oh, that divine officer. I think he just used the neighbors as an excuse to come here. Personally, I think he's gay," Alfie said.

Judith smiled at Robin. "We really don't have to stay," she whispered.

"Bored already?" he asked. "Or is this crowd too much for you?"

"Any crowd is too much when I'm with you. I'd rather have a nightcap in your suite."

"I thought you wanted to go to this party."

"I've been. Now I want to be with you."

"That would be rude to Alfie, and to Sergio. He's an old friend."

He drank slowly and steadily, talking to Sergio and Alfie while Judith was trapped in conversation with a group of actors. He was determined to make it a late night–too late to take her back to his suite for a nightcap.

It was close to midnight when the party began to thin out. Judith extricated herself and joined him at he bar. Her smile was forced. "Well, I've let you spend all your time with the two boys. Now it's my turn. How about that nightcap?"

"What are you drinking?"

"Whatever you have."

"Alfie has a well-stocked bar. Name it."

"I don't want a nightcap here," she said angrily.

Alfie ambled over. "What's the trouble, luv?"

Robin suppressed a grin. Alfie was one of the few holdouts on television. Mrs. Gregory Austin meant nothing to him.

She smiled. "No trouble. I was just telling Robin that it was high time we got home."

"If you're tired, mate, I can always have someone drop you off at your digs."

She ignored him and turned to Robin. This time her voice was firm. "Robin, I want to go home."

His grin was loose. "Alfie, you heard what the lady said. Who's got a car going toward the Beverly Hills Hotel?"

"Johnny there lives on North Canyon–hey, Johnny, when are you packing it in?"

The young man across the room signaled that he was on his way. "There's your ride, luv," Alfie said.

"How dare you!" She turned her back on Alfie. "Robin, take me home."

"Sure, but not this moment. I want to finish my drink."

Alfie went behind the bar and handed him the bottle of vodka. "Looks like it needs freshening."

Judith watched him refill his glass. "Robin, I want to leave –with you."

"Look, luv," Alfie said, "we all can't have just what we want. Now I'd like to marry Sergio and have babies. Unfortunately, it just can't work out."

Her eyes blazed as she stared at Robin. "You like being here with all these degenerates!"

"I like being with my friends." He left her and walked over to the couch. Alfie and Sergio followed.

Judith stood against the bar. Nothing like this had ever happened to her. Alfie's easy scorn . . . they treated her as if she was a common girl on the town. She was Mrs. Gregory Austin, but she had been pushed around and ignored. She poured herself a large Scotch. The clock hanging over the bar ticked loudly in the silence. Suddenly she was aware that almost everyone had gone. Only Robin and those two queers remained, huddled together on the couch. He was doing this to her intentionally, to make her feel cheap. She got off the bar stool and something on the floor caught her eye. It was a gold bracelet. She read the inscription and a slow smile came to her lips. She held it gingerly as if it would soil her fingers and approached the men on the couch.

"Now I see why I was told to leave. The three of you really do want to be alone, don't you?"

The men looked at her curiously. Alfie saw the bracelet and leaped to his feet. His hand automatically reached for his wrist. He lunged for her but she backed away. "You bitch–I had it on tonight. Where did you get it?"

"I found it on the floor behind the bar." She dangled it before him. "The catch must have broken. It's really a very interesting bracelet."

Sergio jumped up and headed toward her. "Give him back that bracelet."

With a quick motion she dropped it into her bra. Then she brushed her hands together. "Now it's where neither of you fairies have the nerve to go."

Robin got up slowly. "Maybe you forgot about *me*. I'm not afraid of tits."

"You're a fairy too." But she backed away from him. "The Love Machine–with you it's girls for your name, but men are your game. The bracelet proves it."

"What's Alfie's bracelet got to do with me?"

"You tell me," she said lightly. "It has Sergio's name on the front, and on the back it says *From Robin Stone, Christmas, Roma, 1962*. But Alfie was wearing it. Is that why you wanted to stay, Robin? So you could have it out with Alfie for taking your real lover away from you?"

Sergio turned to Robin pleadingly. "It's the bracelet I asked from you in Rome. Remember you said that I could have anything I wanted engraved on it? So I had your name put on the back. I wore it always. It was and is my dearest possession. But Alfie gave me his." He held out his arm showing a similar gold bracelet. "Alfie's mother gave him this. It was the closest possession *he* owned. So we exchanged bracelets."

Alfie nodded. "It was something I treasured, Robin."

Judith threw back her head and laughed. "This is the most touching scene I've ever witnessed. Well, I guess I'll be on my way. I think Gregory will be delighted with this bracelet. I think all the scandal sheets will enjoy it too. We might make it in time for the board of directors meeting on Tuesday. After all, Robin, we've got to see that you are–what's the word–oh yes, totally unemployable."

"Judith, I don't give a damn about the network. If you have a gripe against me–fine. But don't get Sergio or Alfie involved. You could hurt their careers."

She looked at him and laughed. "You're making it sound better and better." She turned to Alfie. "I think the scandal sheets would adore knowing about you, *luv!*" Her eyes blazed in anger. She started for the door.

Sergio lunged for her. Alfie grabbed her and pulled her to the center of the room. Robin started toward them to break it up, but Sergio was closing in. He had her trapped behind the bar. She looked around wildly, like a cornered animal. Suddenly she saw the gleaming Oscar. She picked it up, and as Sergio moved toward her, she brought it down on his head. He fell to the floor immediately.

"You bitch!" Alfie screamed. "He's unconscious–you've *killed* him! Oh God, Sergio. . . ." He was on his knees sobbing over the unconscious man.

Judith raced toward the door but Alfie leaped up and caught her. "Oh no you don't!" His hand lashed across her face. Robin picked up Sergio and placed him on the couch. He heard Judith scream. He knew Alfie was slapping her, but he was sure that nothing more than her dignity would be hurt. His main concern was for Sergio. He got some ice and put it to his head. "Be careful!" Alfie shouted. "His skull might be fractured."

Robin turned, took one look at Judith and rushed across the room. Her lip was cut, blood was streaming from her nose. Her hairpiece was askew and looked oddly comical against her battered face. Robin tried to intercede, but Alfie dragged her from his reach by the hair. Miraculously, it remained on. She screamed at the top of her lungs. Robin grabbed Alfie's arm and forced him to release her. Judith's pajamas were torn at the neckline, revealing part of her wired bra. The bracelet slipped out and clattered to the floor. Alfie grabbed it. Then, for good measure, he gave Judith another blinding slap across the face.

Robin grabbed her and she clung to him, sobbing. "I'm sorry, Judith," he whispered. "But when you play like an alley cat, sometimes you get *treated* like one."

They all froze when they heard the chimes and the pounding at the door. "Open up! It's the police," a loud voice called.

"Oh my God," Judith began to sob. "This will kill Gregory. Look at me."

"You! What about *me!*" Alfie screamed. "And Sergio! This kind of publicity can ruin us all . . . because of you–you bitch!"

Judith clung to Robin. "Get me out of this. Oh, God, please get me out of this and I'll never do anything wrong again."

"You'll never do anything wrong! You've got your millions to go back to. What about me? I've got a morals clause!" Alfie spat at her.

Robin held Judith against him, and grabbed Alfie with his free hand. "Alfie, I'll get you out of this–only I've got one condition: Maggie Stewart gets the lead in your new picture."

"What picture? We'll all be run out of town tomorrow."

"Judith!" Robin held her off and stared at her mottled face. "Your story is that I was drunk. I went on the make for you. I ripped at your dress. Sergio stepped in to help you. I went to hit him, he ducked and you got the blow–that explains your face–then I smashed Sergio."

"And what was *I* doing?" Alfie asked.

"You rushed to her defense and I clipped you." He reached out and gave Alfie a resounding punch on the jaw. Alfie yelled. Robin smiled slightly. "Sorry, chum, but if you're defending the lady you have to take your lumps." Robin noticed that the pounding at the door had stopped. He knew the police were trying to make a forced entrance from the back.

"Now, everyone know their lines? I hope so, because here comes the law–"

He turned around just as the police came in through the bedroom terrace. In panic, Judith dashed for the front door. She flung it open and faced a blinding flash of camera bulbs. The reporters tramped into the room. She dashed back to Robin, then, seeing the press and police, she backed away. Dimly she heard Alfie explaining, "It's just all a ghastly misunderstanding. Mr. Stone stayed to talk to me about Miss Maggie Stewart–I want her for my new picture–and we had a few drinks. Robin had one too many. He really didn't know what he was doing. Good God, he couldn't be on the make for Mrs. Austin if he was sober, she's old enough to be his mother."

Judith's swollen lips grimaced at him. "Why, you dreary little–"

"Easy," Robin said. "Let's just say this wasn't my night."

Then the ambulance arrived. They all watched the doctor kneeling over Sergio.

"How is he?" Alfie asked anxiously.

"Probably just a concussion," the ambulance attendant answered. "However they can't tell till they X-ray." Then he shook his head. "You movie characters sure play rough."

The policeman whom Robin had met earlier in the evening took him by the arm and stared at him with a wounded expression as if to say, "And I trusted you." Alfie was asked to come along as a witness. Judith refused to press charges, but she was taken along despite her objections.

It was all routine at the police station, except for the newspapermen. It seemed to Robin that every reporter in town was there, plus a television cameraman from a local station. Robin did not try to avoid the cameras, but he shielded Judith throughout. When one inventive cameraman darted between them and managed to get a shot of Judith's swollen face, Robin lunged after him and smashed his camera. The other cameras picked up this byplay, but order was instantly installed by the police. Alfie refused to press charges. "After all, I took a poke at him first. And he was drinking," Alfie said.

The doctor phoned in to say that Sergio was all right–it was only a mild concussion. Robin paid a fine for disturbing the peace and wrote a check to the newspaperman for destroying his camera and it wound up with everyone being released.

Then he drove Judith back to the hotel and parked near Crescent. "We can go in this way and avoid the lobby. I'll walk you to the bungalow."

"Robin–"

He looked at her. One eye was beginning to discolor and her lips looked raw and bloody.

"Put some cold compresses on your face," he said. "Tomorrow you're going to have a real mouse on that eye."

She touched her face gingerly. "What do I tell Gregory?"

"Exactly what you told the police."

She reached over and took his hand. "Robin, I know this will sound crazy to you, but I really loved you." Tears came to her eyes. "And now I've destroyed you."

"No, baby, *I've* done it myself–and maybe it's about time."

He walked her to the bungalow. It was dark inside.

"I won't wake Gregory," she said. "There will be plenty of time to tell him about it tomorrow."

"Sleep well, Judith."

She clung to him for a brief second. "Oh, Robin, why did all this have to happen?"

"Go into your bungalow," he whispered, "and stay there. Stay where you belong from now on." Then he walked away and went into the hotel. He turned off his phone, fell across the bed and went to sleep without even taking off his clothes.

Gregory Austin was awakened at seven in the morning by Cliff Dorne. "Jesus, Gregory," he said, "I almost fainted when I heard the news. How is she?"

"How is *who?*" Gregory tried to rouse himself into full consciousness.

"Judith."

Gregory stared at the clock on his night table. "What in hell are you talking about?"

"Gregory, the lobby is filled with reporters. You've got a 'Do not disturb' on your line, but I told the operator I'd take full responsibility for breaking it. Have you seen the morning papers?"

"For Christ's sake, man, I've just opened my eyes. What is all this talk? And what's Judith got to do with it?"

"Robin Stone beat her up."

"What!" Gregory dropped the phone and raced into Judith's bedroom. She was sleeping face down on the pillow. He tugged at her arm gently. She mumbled and gradually awoke. He stared at her in shock. "Judith–your face! You've got a black eye! What happened?"

"It's nothing." She tried to bury her face in the pillow.

He pulled her into a sitting position. "Cliff is on the phone. There are reporters in the lobby. There's supposed to be a story in the newspaper. *What happened?"*

"Get me some coffee," she said slowly. "It's not as serious as you think."

Gregory raced back to his bedroom. "Judith's all right. Get up here immediately, and bring all the newspapers." Then he sent for coffee. Judith finally got out of bed and came into the living room. "I look worse than I feel," she said with a wry smile.

"Tell me what happened."

"There isn't much to tell. Robin drank a lot. Suddenly he lunged for me. Sergio tried to protect me and then when Robin lunged for him he ducked and I caught the blow. Then Robin knocked Sergio out–and then the police arrived. That's all."

"That's *all?"* Gregory thundered. "Look at yourself! Why didn't you send for me? Or Cliff Dorne?"

Judith sipped at the coffee. "Oh, Greg, you're making too much of a fuss. The police let us all off. As a matter of fact, Robin brought me home."

"He brought you home!"

"Yes, he had sobered up." She heard the door chimes and rose hastily. "That's probably Cliff. I don't want him to see me." She disappeared into the bedroom.

Cliff had all the newspapers. Gregory winced as he stared at the front pages. The big black headlines were all variations of the same theme:

LOVE MACHINE TURNS INTO WRECKING MACHINE
OVER NETWORK CHIEF'S WIFE.
A STONE'S FIST IS GRANITE.
THE NIGHT THE LOVE MACHINE RAN AMOK.

And each story was the same. Gregory studied the pictures. Everyone looked ready to fold except Robin. He appeared oddly undisturbed. There was even a slight grin on his face.

Cliff sat looking like a pallbearer. The doorbell rang constantly as bellboys delivered telegrams for Judith from her New York friends. It was close to noon in the East–the story and pictures were all over the country by now.

Gregory paced the room. "How did the newspapers get into the act?"

"Our man tipped them off," Cliff said morosely. "He couldn't know Judith was involved. He's the one who's been tailing Robin since he arrived."

Judith emerged from the bedroom. She had put Covermark over the discoloration of her eye, and aside from her swollen lips she looked fairly presentable. She even managed a slight smile at Cliff. "Well, I've certainly seen how the other half lives. And every one of our friends has suddenly remembered we're alive. Greg, would you believe they all think I'm glamorous? You should read these wires. Peggy Ashton wants to throw a big bash in our honor. She said I'm the woman of the century–having a man fight two men to get at me." Her smile was actually one of childish delight.

"We've got to write some statement for the press," Cliff said. "Of course Robin goes. It's a shame it had to happen this way"–he tossed a glance toward Judith, who was busy opening the wires –"but at least we've got a legitimate excuse for the board of directors."

"No. He stays." Gregory said.

Both Judith and Cliff stared at him.

"We've got to clean this thing up. It has to be a big misunderstanding as far as we're concerned. We'll give out a statement that Robin never went after Judith, that she slipped and fell down the stairs. We'll think of something."

"We will not!" Judith stood up. "I'm not going to be written about as if I were some idiot and make Robin a hero. He went after me and that's that!" She stormed out of the room.

"She's right," Cliff said. "A denial will only give added life to the story. Fire Robin, and in a few days it will blow over."

"He stays! Put in a call to Danton Miller and offer him his old job back. Tell him he'll work with Robin. They'll both have equal power, and neither can make any decision without my approval. From here on I am in control."

"Gregory, you must be mad. You've been looking for the chance to get rid of Robin. This is it!" Cliff argued.

"I wanted my network back, and I've got it. Besides, I asked Robin to take Judith to this party because Judith *wanted* to go. At least now she'll stick with her own kind. But I'm not about to toss Robin to the wolves."

"I think you're making a big mistake," Cliff said. "No other network will touch him now–he's unemployable."

"I'm not paying you for opinions," Gregory snapped. "I pay you for legal advice. Robin Stone has contributed too much to IBC to be booted out for one crazy night. This will all cool down after a time. We'll switch the board of directors meeting to the day after tomorrow. By then I'll have boned up on the reports and *I* will present them! Have Dan fly in. He and Robin will sit behind me like two co-workers while *I* speak."

Robin awoke to the banging on the door. He looked around . . . he was still lying across the bed. He felt rocky, but he made his way to the door. Cliff Dorne stalked in and threw a batch of newspapers on the coffee table.

Robin picked them up. They were worse than he expected.

"I've just come from Gregory's bungalow," Cliff said.

Robin nodded. "I suppose he wants my resignation."

"He sure as hell does, but he feels sorry for you. He's hired Danton Miller to replace you, and you can stay on until you find something else. At least you'll save face that way."

Robin went to the desk and scratched out a few lines. "I think this is the way it's done," he said. "I have no contract. It ran out some time ago. . . . Here is my resignation. You can witness it." He handed Cliff the pen and the paper.

Cliff smiled. "May I say, I've waited a long time for this moment."

"I'll leave on the first flight I can catch. I'll go to my office in New York and clear out my desk. And, Cliff—here are all the charts for the spring shows. Everything's in there—ratings, future plans, the report I was going to give to the board of directors." He handed him the attaché case.

"I'll send the case back to you in New York," Cliff said.

"Keep it. You gave it to me as a Christmas present last year." Then Robin walked to the door and held it open.

Gregory Austin stared at Robin's resignation. He shook his head. "Did you tell him I wanted him to stay, Cliff?"

"He had it all written before I arrived," Cliff said.

Gregory shrugged. "Well, he's just signed himself out of television. Damn his pride. If he had stayed on and worked with Dan, this would have blown over. . . . Maybe I should talk to him."

"You do, and I'll walk out on you," Judith said suddenly.

Both men looked at her in surprise.

"I want him out of our lives. I mean it, Gregory."

Gregory nodded. "All right. Cliff, tell Dan everything is set. But I want Sammy Tebet to take Robin's place. Sammy's a good man—nothing like Robin, but then I doubt if there will ever be anyone like him."

"Then why have him if you have Dan?" Judith asked.

Gregory smiled. "I want two men there, two of them who will be at each other's throats."

Cliff nodded and left the suite.

Robin was packed. He started to leave, then came back and picked up the phone. The operator said, "Oh, Mr. Stone, there have been hundreds of calls for you. Every newspaper has called, and there's a man from *Time* with a photographer waiting in the lobby. If you like, there's a way out on Crescent Drive—you can duck them—"

"Thanks, honey. Will you get me the Melton Towers? It's an apartment house, but it has a switchboard."

"Yes, we know the number. And, Mr. Stone, I just want to tell you that I think you're wonderful no matter what the newspapers say. It's unusual these days to read about a man who fights two men to get a woman he wants. I think it's romantic." She giggled, then rang the Melton Towers.

Maggie came on after two rings. Her voice was heavy with sleep. He realized she had probably not heard the news. "Wake up, sleepyhead, you're supposed to be at the studio for the game shows, aren't you?"

"Not until one—*Robin!*" She was suddenly wide-awake. "You're calling. Does that mean—?"

"It means I'm leaving for New York, Maggie, on the one o'clock plane."

There was a long pause, then she said, "Is that what you're calling about?"

"Yes. And, well, I just wanted you to know I didn't—" He stopped.

Suddenly it didn't seem important to tell her he hadn't gone on the make for Judith or hit her. Somehow he knew Maggie would understand. He just wanted her to know he wasn't running off without saying goodbye. "Maggie, you see, I—"

But the phone was dead. She had hung up.

THIRTY

December 1968

Dip Nelson rushed off to lunch at Sardi's carrying *Variety*. As he entered, he felt a new sense of power. He was Dip Nelson, Broadway producer, and Robin Stone was just a name from the dim past; it was a year since the big scandal and no one knew what had happened to Robin. He had just vanished. But the Big Dipper never struck out. He had come back. Maybe not as a performer, but as a top Broadway producer. Joe Katz had no alternative but to make him co-producer if he wanted Pauli as the star. And they had the biggest hit on Broadway. He stopped at each table and showed everyone the grosses in *Variety*. Everyone at Sardi's listened. They had all seen the story in *Variety,* they all knew Pauli was the greatest, and they also knew she was having an affair with her leading man.

Christie Lane sat on the plane and looked at *Variety*. His face broke into a broad grin. Then he tore out the clipping. "What is it?" Ethel asked.

He showed it to her:

L.A. to N.Y.

Christie Lane
Ethel Lane
Christie Lane, Jr.

He folded it and put it in his wallet. "His first *Variety* clipping for his scrapbook. I'm putting it beside the clippings of his birth notices."

Ethel smiled as she held the child. "We're going to have a smash opening. Alfie and Sergio will fly in and so will half of Hollywood."

He nodded and lay back and tried to catch a nap. He was excited at the idea of doing a Broadway musical. He didn't even mind that it was for Ike Ryan. So far Ike hadn't had a loser. And Ike didn't take any shit from anyone. When Dip Nelson had tried to muscle in as co-producer, he had turned him down. Well, Dip had made a deal with Joe Katz. And Pauli had a big hit. Leave it to Dip—he had learned plenty from Robin Stone. Funny, Robin had been bigger than all of them, and wham, just like that he had disappeared from the scene. Suddenly he thought of Amanda—he could think of her now with no emotion; she was just a dim memory now. Ethel had given him the only thing he really wanted: his son. He smiled contentedly.

Ethel snuggled the baby and kissed his head. Funny, in the beginning she had only gotten knocked up to get her way with Christie. Now the baby was the most important thing in her life, the only thing she really cared about. All the frustrated love she had given the men who had passed through her life, she now lavished on the child. But she'd never make a mother's boy of him—she'd know when to let go. He was her kid and he was going to have the greatest life in the world. And now Christie's Broadway opening would be exciting. She had a good life—she was den mother for Alfie and Sergio, *the* hostess of Hollywood. Her Hamtramck dream had practically come true. Of course there was no handsome leading man—there was just Christie. She had plenty of time on her hands to play around, but she didn't get any offers. She was respected. She was *Mrs.* Christie Lane. Oh well, you couldn't have everything.

Danton Miller read the review of his new special in *Variety*. It was murderous. Dammit, the only shows that held up were the old ones. The shows chosen by Robin Stone. He had been a rocket all right, but like all rockets he had exploded into thin air. He drummed this into Sammy Tebet's head every time Sammy got high-handed. Sammy was bright and he'd have to keep an eye on him—he couldn't afford another Robin Stone in his life. But Gregory would see to that. Gregory was back, riding roughshod, and Gregory was going to cancel the new variety show Dan had put on in September. Dan could feel it in his bones. It would happen at tomorrow's weekly meeting. He lit a cigarette. His ulcer stabbed him. He looked up toward the ceiling and silently promised that he would never smoke again if he got through tomorrow's meeting with his job still intact. He wondered if Gregory had read *Variety*. . . .

Gregory *had* seen *Variety*. But he was looking at *Women's Wear*. Judith's picture was on the front page. He stared at it fondly. He shuddered every time he recalled her picture on the front pages of the Los Angeles newspapers. Oddly enough, it had made her a celebrity again when she returned. She had worn an eye patch for a week. And the fact that Robin Stone had gone off the deep end over her gave her new glamour among her friends. It just proved you could never figure women. Judith was right back in the swim. God, every night this week there was a party or an opening. He suddenly remembered that he had a five o'clock fitting for his new dress suit. And of course Judith insisted on his ordering a new velvet smoking jacket for their egg-nog party. It was going to be bigger than ever this year. He stared at her picture and smiled. She had never looked better, and she had never seemed happier. . . .

They all read *Variety*, but none of them read the "Literati" section, and none of them noticed the small paragraph that said, "Robin Stone, former IBC Network President, has just completed a book which Essandess will publish in the late spring."

Maggie Stewart boarded the BOAC plane for London. She was also carrying *Variety*. The big headline on the front page was a lead story about her walkout from the new Alfie Knight picture. But when the plane was airborne she wasn't reading *Variety*–she kept reading and rereading a cable:

DORCHESTER HOTEL LONDON ENGLAND

MISS MAGGIE STEWART MELTON TOWERS
BEVERLY HILLS, CALIF.

I NEED YOU.

ROBIN

Once is Not Enough

To Robert Susann, my father
who would understand *

*and to Irving,
who does understand

Prologue

Him

HE BURST upon the theatrical scene in 1945. He was Mike Wayne—a born winner. He had been known as the best crap shooter in the Air Force, and the thirteen thousand dollars in cash, strapped around his waist, proved the legend to be fact.

When he was in his late teens he had already figured the stock market and show business to be the two biggest crap games in the world. He was twenty-seven when he got out of the Air Force and crazy about girls, so he picked show business. He parlayed his thirteen thousand into sixty with five hot days at Aqueduct.

By investing it in a Broadway show he became co-producer. The show was a hit and he married Vicki Hill, the most beautiful girl in the chorus.

Vicki wanted to be a star, and he gave her the chance. In 1948 he produced his first big lavish musical on his own and starred his wife. It was a hit, in spite of her. The critics praised his theatrical know-how in surrounding her with talented performers, a foolproof book, and a hit score. But they all agreed that Vicki was less than adequate.

When the show ended its run, he "retired" her. ("Baby, you gotta know how to walk away from the table when the dice are cold. I gave you your shot. Now you give me a son.")

On New Year's Day, 1950, she presented him with a baby girl. He promptly named her January, and when the nurse put the baby in his arms, he silently swore he would give her the world.

When she was two, he greeted her before he greeted his wife.

When she was four, he went to California and produced his first movie.

When she was five, he produced two hit pictures in one year, and was nominated for an Oscar.

When she was six he won the Oscar and his name was linked with several beautiful stars. (That was when his wife began to drink and took a lover of her own.)

When she was seven, he named his private plane after her and his wife killed herself trying to abort their unborn son.

And then there were just the two of them.

He tried to explain things the day he drove her to the boarding school in Connecticut. "Now that Mommy's gone, this fancy joint will teach you to become a lovely lady."

"Why can't you teach me, Daddy?"

"Because I travel a lot. And besides, ladies are supposed to teach little girls."

"Why did Mommy die, Daddy?"

"I don't know, honey . . . Maybe because she wanted to be somebody."

"Is that bad?"

"Only when you aren't, and it eats away at your insides."

"Are you somebody, Daddy?"

"Me? I'm a super-somebody." He laughed.

"Then I'll be a somebody," she told him.

"Okay. But before you can be anybody, you have to be a lady."

So she had accepted Miss Haddon's school. And whenever he was in New York, they would spend the weekends together.

His fame grew, and like all good gamblers, he knew when to push his luck and when to quit. He had been known to change the odds at the track with one bet. Once he lost his plane on the roll of the dice, but he walked away with a grin because he knew there would be another time.

And if you asked him when his luck ran out, he could tell you the exact day.

Rome. June 20, 1967.

The day they told him about his daughter. . . .

Her

IF YOU ASKED her when her luck ran out, she wouldn't have been able to tell you because she only thought of herself as *his* daughter. And being *his* daughter was just about the most marvelous thing in the world.

From the start she had accepted Miss Haddon's school as merely something to "get through." The girls were all friendly and fell into two categories. The older girls worshipped Elvis and the younger girls were "Linda followers." Linda was Linda Riggs, a student. She was sixteen. She could sing and dance and her hyper-enthusiasm was noisy but infectious. (Years later when January came across some early school photographs, she was amazed at Linda's resemblance to Ringo Starr.) But at the time, when Linda was the undisputed star at Miss Haddon's, no one seemed to notice the skimpy shaggy hair, the broad nose, and the heavy silver braces on her teeth. It was an accepted fact that when Linda graduated she was going to become a top musical comedy star on Broadway.

In Linda's senior year, she starred in the school's watered-down version of *Annie Get Your Gun.* When rehearsals began, Linda singled out the eight-year-old January to be her "special little friend." This meant January would be given the privilege of running errands for her and of cueing her on her lines and lyrics of the songs. January had never been a "Linda follower," but she was pleased with the arrangement because most of Linda's conversation centered on Mike Wayne. Linda was a great admirer of his work. *Had January invited him to the school play? Was he coming? He* had *to come! After all, hadn't Linda seen to it that January had gotten into the chorus?*

He did come, and after the performance January watched the star of *Annie Get Your Gun* dissolve into a stammering blushing high school girl when Mike Wayne shook her hand.

"Wasn't she great?" January asked as they walked off together.

"She stank. You stood out more in the chorus than she did in all of her numbers."

"But she's so talented."

"She's a fat ugly broad."

"Really?"

"Really."

But when Linda was graduated, Miss Haddon's suddenly seemed empty. A beautiful girl named Angela starred in the school play the following season, but everyone agreed she was "no Linda."

Two years later, Linda jumped back into the news when one of the girls ran screaming down the hall with a copy of *Gloss* magazine. On the masthead, in small print, was the name Linda Riggs: junior editor. Everyone at Miss Haddon's was wildly impressed, but January was secretly disappointed. What had happened to Broadway?

When she told her father about it, he didn't seem surprised. "It's amazing that she even made it as a gofer on a fashion magazine."

"But she was so talented," January insisted.

"Talented for Miss Haddon's. But this is nineteen sixty, and there are girls who look like Liz Taylor and Marilyn Monroe pounding the pavements, hoping for a break in anything. I don't say beauty is everything . . . but it helps."

"Will I be beautiful?"

He grinned as he fingered her heavy brown hair. "You're gonna be more than beautiful. You've got your mother's brown eyes. Velvet eyes. The first thing that attracted me to her."

She didn't tell him that she'd rather have his eyes. They were so unbelievably blue against his perpetual tan and his black hair. She had never been able to take his extraordinary good looks for granted. Neither could her classmates, who saw their fathers as beleaguered men who sometimes needed a shave, worried about losing their hair or jobs, and constantly argued with a mother or a kid brother.

But the weekends January spent with her father in New York, she only saw a handsome man who lived to please her.

It was because of these weekends that January discouraged all attempts at any "buddy-buddy" relationships with the girls at school. Having a "buddy-buddy" meant holiday dinners at their homes and occasional weekend "sleepovers"—on a reciprocal basis. And January had no intention of sharing any of her weekends with her father. Of course, there were times when he was in Europe or on the Coast, but the weekends they spent together more than compensated for the lonely ones. Those Saturday mornings when the limousine would arrive and whisk her to New York . . . to the large corner suite at the Plaza which he kept on a year-round basis. Invariably he'd be having breakfast when she arrived. A secretary might be taking notes; a production assistant going over weekly grosses; a publicity man checking advertising copy; phones would be going, sometimes three at once. But when she entered the room it was as if an alarm went off. All activity stopped and he'd sweep her into his arms. The smell of his aftershave lotion was like pine . . . and the feel of his arms around her gave her a sense of all-encompassing security.

She would have some lunch while he quickly disposed of the business at hand. It never failed to fascinate her. The wheeling-dealing, his staccato decisions on the long-distance phone. She'd nibble at her food and watch him, trying to etch into her mind the way he hunched the phone between his shoulder and his ear as he made notes . . . and that warm feeling that shot through her when he looked at her in the midst of it all and winked. A wink that said, "No matter what I'm doing, I still stop and think of you."

And after lunch there were no more phones or interruptions. The rest of the day belonged to her. Sometimes he'd take her to Saks and buy her everything in sight. Other times they'd go ice-skating at Rockefeller Plaza (he'd sit inside and have a drink while the instructor took her around). If he was putting on a new show, they'd stop by and watch rehearsals. They saw every show on Broadway; sometimes they went to a matinee *and* an evening performance. And they'd always wind up at Sardi's and sit at the front table under his caricature.

But she hated Sundays. No matter how much fun they had at their Sunday brunch, there was always the shadow of that big black limousine that was waiting to take her back to Miss Haddon's. And she knew she had to go, just as she knew he had to return to his phones and his productions.

But his favorite "productions" were her birthdays. When she was five he had hired a small circus and invited her entire nursery school class. Her mother had been alive then, a vague lady with huge brown eyes who sat on the sidelines and watched everything without too much interest. When she was six there had been a sleigh ride to the Tavern On The Green in Central Park, with a Santa Claus and a bag of toys waiting. Another time there had been a magician, and a puppet show.

But on her eighth birthday there had been just the two of them. It was her first birthday since her mother's death. It fell on a weekday and the car had picked her up at Miss Haddon's and brought her to the Plaza. She had stood solemnly as he opened the bottle of champagne and poured her a quarter of a glass. "This is the best there is, babe." He raised his glass. "Here's to my lady . . . the only lady I'll ever love." That was how he introduced her to Dom Perignon and caviar.

And then he had taken her to the window and pointed toward the Goodyear Blimp that was passing by. But instead of "Goodyear," the huge red letters blazed "Happy Birthday, January!" And from that time on, Dom Perignon and caviar became a ritual for all important occasions.

On her thirteenth birthday, he took her to Madison Square Garden. The marquee was dark when they arrived, so she assumed they were late. He took her hand and led her inside. Oddly enough there were no ushers to help them. No attendants . . . no people . . . no lights. He led her down a ramp, into the cavernous darkness of the empty Garden. It was eerie as they walked hand in hand . . . down . . . down . . . deep into the belly of the Garden. Then he stopped; and when he spoke his voice was quiet. "Make a wish, baby, a big one, because right now you are standing on the exact spot where some of the biggest champions stood. Joe Louis, Sugar Ray, Marciano." He raised her hand in the fighter's victory pose and, mimicking the nasal tones of a referee, chanted, "And now Ladees and Gennelmen . . . introducing the greatest champion of them all . . . Miss January Wayne . . . who has now entered her teens!" Then he said, "That means you're in the heavyweight division now, babe."

She threw her arms around him and he leaned down to kiss her cheek, but in the darkness their lips met and held . . . and then the scoreboards all exploded with lights, sparkling, HAPPY BIRTHDAY, JANUARY. A table was set with caviar and champagne; a waiter was standing at attention to serve them, and an orchestra played and sang "Happy Birthday."

After the song, the musicians began a medley of her favorite show tunes. They sipped the champagne, and then Mike held out his arms and asked her to dance. At first she was nervous, but after the first few awkward steps she snuggled against him, and suddenly it felt as if she had been dancing with him all of her life. As they moved to the music, he whispered, "You're on your way to becoming a lady. One day a boy will come along who'll mean more than anything else in the world . . . and he'll hold you in his arms like this and you'll know what it means to be in love." She hadn't answered because she knew she was already in the arms of the only man she could ever love.

He was producing a picture in Rome when she was graduated from Miss Haddon's. She didn't mind his missing the graduation. She would have liked to skip it herself, but she had auditioned and been chosen to deliver the valedictory speech, and now there was no way out. But she was joining him in Rome for the summer.

And she had won the argument against college.

"Daddy, I've been away at school all my life."

"But college is important, baby."

"Why?"

"Well, to learn things, to meet the right kind of friends, to prepare you for—hell, I don't know. I just know it's the right thing. Why do other girls go to college?"

"Because they don't have you for a father."

"Well, what do you want to do?"

"Be an actress maybe."

"Well, if you're gonna be an actress, you have to study for that too!"

And so it had been arranged. Once he finished the picture in Rome, he was scheduled to do one in London. And he had managed to get her enrolled at the Royal Academy of Dramatic Art for the fall term. She wasn't dedicated to the idea of the Royal Academy. She wasn't even sure she really wanted to be an actress. . . .

But she was going to Rome! There were just the graduation exercises to get through. Under her cap and gown was a blue linen dress. Her plane ticket and passport were in her bag. And her luggage was already in the trunk of the limousine waiting outside the school. All she had to do was deliver the speech, get that diploma, and run!

And then it was all over and she was making her way up the aisle; accepting congratulations from parents of classmates; pushing through a wall of tearful farewells; promising to write. Goodbye! Goodbye! Tearing off the gown. Tossing the cap to Miss Hicks of the drama department. Goodbye! Goodbye! Into the limousine and on the way to Kennedy Airport.

704 . . . first class half empty . . . too excited to concentrate on food or the movie. Hours and hours of magazines, daydreams and Cokes . . . then finally the descent . . . seven o'clock in the morning, Rome time. And there he was . . . standing with some important-looking officials . . . right on the airfield . . . with a private car. Out of the plane . . . into his arms . . . the arms of the most fabulous man in the world . . . and he belonged to her!

The long black car drove them to customs . . . her passport was stamped . . . they entered the busy terminal where two attractive young Italian boys in skinny dark suits stood waiting to attend to her luggage.

"They don't speak English, but they're great kids," Mike said as he handed them some crinkly paper money. "They'll get your baggage and take it to the hotel." Then he led her outside to a long low-slung red Jaguar. The top was down and

Mike smiled at her obvious delight. "I thought it would be more fun if we drove ourselves. Get in, Cleopatra. You are about to make your entrance into Rome."

And that was how she saw Rome on that sparkling June morning. The wind was soft and the early morning sun warmed her face. A few shop people slowly raised their blinds. Young boys in aprons began washing down the streets of sidewalk cafés. An occasional timid horn squeaked off in the distance, a horn that would join a pack that would blend into a screaming crescendo when traffic reached its peak.

Mike pulled the car to a stop in front of a little restaurant. The proprietor ran out and embraced him and insisted on personally making them eggs and sausage, with the hot rolls his wife had just baked.

The city was bursting with noise when they finally reached the block of the Via Veneto that housed the Excelsior Hotel. January stared at the small expanse—the sidewalk cafés lining both sides of the street, tourists reading *The New York Times* and Paris edition of the *Tribune* as they tried to drink the heavy espresso.

"*This* is the Via Veneto?" January asked.

Mike grinned. "Yep, this is it. Sorry I couldn't arrange to have Sophia Loren passing by. The truth is, if you sat here for a year you might never see Sophia Loren on the Via Veneto. But in one hour, you will see every American who's in town."

She was overwhelmed with the enormous suite at the Excelsior. The ornate marble fireplaces, the dining room, the two large bedrooms—it was almost palatial.

"I left the room facing the American Embassy for you," Mike said. "I figured the street noises might not be as loud there." Then he pointed to her bags which had been delivered. "Unpack, take a bath and go to sleep. I'll send a car to pick you up around four. You can come to the studio and we'll drive home together."

"Can't I go to the studio with you now?" she asked.

He smiled. "Listen, I don't want you to be tired for your first night in Rome. Incidentally, we don't dine here until nine or ten."

He started for the door and stopped. He stared at her for

several seconds and shook his head. "Know something? You really are goddamned beautiful!"

They were still shooting when she arrived at the studio. She stood in the back and watched in the darkness. She recognized Mitch Nelson, the American actor whom the press releases billed as the new Gary Cooper. Through a granite jaw and seemingly immovable lips, he was playing a love scene with Melba Delitto. January had seen Melba only in foreign films. She was very beautiful, but her accent was heavy, and several times she fluffed her lines. Each time, Mike would smile, walk over to her, reassure her, and then start the scene again. After the fifteenth take, Mike yelled, "Print it," and the lights came up. When he saw January he broke into that special smile that belonged only to her, and he crossed the sound stage. He linked her arm through his. "How long you been standing there?"

"For about twelve takes. I didn't know you were also a director."

"Well, it's Melba's first English-speaking part, and the first few days were pistols. She would fluff . . . the director would scream at her in Italian . . . she'd scream back . . . he'd scream louder . . . she'd walk off the set in tears. That meant an hour for new makeup plus another half hour for her to accept the director's apologies. So I learned that if I just walk over and soothe the lady and tell her how well she's doing, we save a lot of time and money and finally get a decent take."

A young man came toward them eagerly. "Mr. Mike, I was through work two hours ago but I wait, because I so much wanted to meet your daughter."

"January, this is Franco Mellini," Mike said.

The young man was in his early twenties. His accent was heavy, but he was tall and undeniably handsome. "Okay, Franco, you've been presented. Now scram." Mike's voice was gruff, but he smiled as the boy bowed and backed away. "That kid has only a small part, but he may walk off with the whole ballgame," he said. "I found him in Milan when I was scouting locations. He was doubling as a singer and a bartender in a dive. He's a natural. It's wild to see the way he's charmed every broad on the set. Even Melba." Mike shook his head. "When an Italian has charm, forget it." They walked arm in arm. The studio was empty and she felt as if all of her unspoken prayers had been answered. This was the moment she had longed for, the moment she had dreamed about. Walking beside him . . . being a part of his life . . . his work . . . sharing his problems.

Suddenly he said, "By the way, I've lined up a bit for you in the picture. Just a few lines—hey." He tried to pull away from her embrace. "You're strangling me!"

Later, as they inched through the unbelievable traffic, he told her about his troubles with the picture. Melba's anxiety with her English . . . her antipathy toward Mitch Nelson . . . the language barrier he had with some of the crew. But most of all he groaned about the traffic. And she sat and listened and kept telling herself it wasn't a dream . . . she was really here . . . this wasn't just a Saturday . . . there would be no limousine to take her away from him tomorrow . . . she'd be with him like this every day . . . and she didn't care if the traffic took forever . . . she was with him in Rome . . . just the two of them!

When they finally reached the hotel another slim attractive young man was waiting in the lobby with several large boxes. January wondered how all the men stayed so thin. Didn't Italians eat their own food?

"This is Bruno," Mike said, as the grinning young man followed them to their suite. "I figured you might not have enough clothes, so I sent him out a few days ago. He shops for a lot of the V.I.P.'s. Take whatever you want, any or all of it. I'm going to shower, make some calls to the States—that is, if I can break through the language barrier with the operators here. Sometimes we never get past *Pronto*." He kissed her cheek. "See you at nine."

He was waiting for her when she walked into the living room at nine o'clock. He let out a low whistle. "Babe, you're built like a brick—" He stopped suddenly and smiled. "Well . . . let's say you're better than any top fashion model."

"Meaning I really haven't got enough on top." She laughed. "That's why I adore this Pucci. It clings and makes me look—"

"Fantastic," he said.

"I took this and a skirt, some shirts and a pants suit."

"That's all?" Then he shrugged. "Maybe you'll have more fun finding all those hidden little shops the dames all talk about. I'll have Melba tell you where to look."

"Daddy, I'm not here for a fashion collection. I want to watch you make the film."

"Are you kidding? Jesus, babe . . . you're seventeen. You're in Rome! You don't want to stick around on a hot movie set."

"That's exactly what I want to do. I also want that bit part you promised me."

He laughed. "Maybe you will be an actress at that. At least you're beginning to sound like one. Come on. Let's get going. I'm starving."

They went to a restaurant in the old ghetto section of Rome. January adored the old buildings . . . the quiet streets. They went to a place called Angelino's. Dinner was served by candlelight in a Renaissance piazza. There were even strolling musicians. The entire evening took on a feeling of beautiful unreality. She sat back and watched Mike pour her some wine. She realized that another of her favorite fantasies was actually unfolding . . . she was alone with Mike in a storybook setting . . . he was pouring the wine . . . women were looking at him with admiration but he belonged to her. No phones could take him away, no long black limousines could take her away. She watched him light his cigarette. The waiter was just pouring their espresso when Franco and Melba came into the restaurant. Mike waved them over to the table and ordered another bottle of wine. Melba began talking about one of her scenes in the picture. When her English failed, which was often, she got her point across with gestures. Franco laughed and turned to January. "I speak the English language very poor. You will help me?"

"Well, I—"

"Your father, he all the time talk about you. He count the hours until you come."

"He did?"

"Of course. Just like I count the hours until I meet you tonight." He reached out and touched her hand. She pulled it away and turned toward her father, but he was whispering something into Melba's ear. The actress giggled and rubbed her cheek against his.

January looked away, but Franco smiled. "Maybe love needs no language, right?"

"I think your English is excellent," she said stiffly. She tried not to stare at Melba's hand, which was resting on her father's thigh.

"Oh, I learned from G.I. uncles." Franco laughed. "My mother was widowed from war. She was very young . . . *multa bella* . . . she speak no English then, but she learn and teach me. And G.I. uncles good to my mama. But she's fat now and I send her money because now no G.I.'s to help out. Just Franco."

January was relieved when Mike signaled for the check. He left a pile of bills on the table and they all stood up. Then he turned to January with a smile. "Well, I guess I've hogged you enough, babe. Besides, a beautiful young girl should spend her first night in Rome with a handsome young Italian. At least that's what it says in all the movie scripts I've ever done." He winked at Franco. Then he put his arm around Melba as they walked out of the restaurant.

For a moment they all stood together on the narrow cobbled street. Then Mike said, "Okay, Franco. I'm gonna let you show my daughter some of the night life in this town. But take it easy. After all, we're all gonna be here two months." Then he took Melba's arm and headed for his car. January watched them drive off. It all happened so fast she couldn't believe it. Her father was gone and she was standing on a strange street in Rome with a handsome young Italian, courtesy of Mike Wayne.

Franco took her arm and led her down the street to a tiny car. They squeezed into it, and with skillful maneuvering he managed to dart in and out of the crowded traffic. She was silent during the drive. Her first inclination had been to ask him to take her back to the hotel. But then what? Sit there and wait . . . and wonder what they were doing? *No!* Let *him* sit and wait and wonder what *she* was doing. He had walked out on her . . . left her with this boy. Okay. She'd show him how it felt.

"Small car only thing to use in Roma," he said. They went through winding streets and stopped at an outdoor ice cream parlor. "We go downstairs," Franco said. They climbed out of the car, and he led her down a dark narrow staircase. "You'll like . . . best discotheque in Roma."

The entire building looked as if it were ready for the demolition ball, but they entered a cavernous expanse that was packed with couples gyrating to blasting music and psychedelic lighting. Franco seemed to know everyone in the place, including the waiter, who led them to a choice table in an alcove. He ordered some wine and then pulled her onto the floor against her will. She was embarrassed because she didn't know the new dances. She looked around. All the girls seemed to be undulating, oblivious of their partners. The entire floor looked like a mass of worms . . . wriggling . . . squirming . . . twisting. She had never tried it. Her last term at Miss Haddon's had been dateless by choice, because Mike had been in New York and she had spent every weekend with him.

But Franco laughed away her doubts. The beat of the music was strong, and under his guidance she began to move slowly . . . tentatively. Franco nodded encouragement and swayed to the tempo. His smile radiated confidence and approval. She found herself falling into a modified imitation of the other girls on the floor. Franco nodded . . . his arms waved in the air . . . his hips slithered . . . she followed his pace . . . the beat of the music grew louder . . . soon she was dancing with complete abandon. They fell into each other's arms from exhaustion when the music stopped. He led her back to the table and she drank an entire glass of wine in one long swallow. Franco ordered a bottle and refilled her glass. Several of his friends came to the table, and soon a large group of young people had gathered. Very few spoke English, but they all danced with her, smiled easily, and even the girls seemed warm and friendly. She would actually have enjoyed herself except for the nagging thought of Melba and her father. She had seen the way Mike had looked at Melba . . . the way their eyes had held. She drank another glass of wine. Melba meant nothing to her father. She was just the star of the picture. He wanted to keep her happy. Hadn't he explained that was why he went over and whispered to her between each take? But what had he whispered? She took another long swallow of wine and nodded in agreement when another handsome young man asked her to dance. The music was blasting. She was moving with the exact precision of the other dancers. (Were Melba and her father sitting somewhere listening to good music—music for lovers—sitting alone in some quiet place with violins?) She suddenly stopped dancing and walked off the floor. The boy hurried after her, jabbering in Italian, waving his arms questioningly.

"Tell him I'm tired, that's all," January told Franco. She sat down and listened to the exchange of Italian. The boy stopped frowning, smiled, shrugged, and asked another girl to dance. At one o'clock the group began to disband. She wondered if Mike was home. Was he worried that she was out this late? Maybe he wasn't home yet. She finished her glass of wine and reached for the bottle. It was empty, and Franco immediately ordered another bottle, but the waiter shook his head. A heated argument began. Finally Franco stood up and tossed some money on the table. "They are closing. Come, we go somewhere else."

She followed him up the steps. "Where does everyone go now?" she asked. "I mean, people who want to stay up late? Is there a place . . . well, like in New York we have P.J.'s . . ."

"Oh, you mean meeting place? No, only Americans meet late here. Italians don't stay up or go to late clubs. They have home-type social life."

"But—" She stopped as they reached the street. That would mean Mike was coming home just about now.

"I tell you what," Franco said. "We go to my place. I have the same wine." He turned to another couple who were standing with them on the street. "You come too, Vincente and Maria."

Vincente shook his head with a wink and walked off with his arm around the girl. Franco led January to his car. Suddenly she said, "I think I'd better go home, too. I've enjoyed it very much, Franco . . . honestly. It's been really neat."

"No. We have nightcap. Your papa think I am very bad escort if I bring you home so early."

She laughed. "Is that what you are? An escort? Courtesy of my father?"

His face went dark. He stepped on the gas of the small car and it careened through the streets, swerving, taking corners at an unnerving speed.

"Franco, we'll get killed. Please. Have I insulted you?"

"Yes. You call me a gigolo."

"No . . . really . . . I was just kidding. . . ."

He pulled to a stop on a small side street. "Look, one thing we get straight. Your papa important man. But I am good actor. I am superb in film. I see rushes. I know. Zeffirelli wants me to read for part in his new film. I will get it. You see. Most of my part is finished in your papa's picture so I am not playing the politic. I take you out tonight because you are beautiful. Because I want to see you. Your papa talk much about you, but I did not believe. But when I see you this afternoon . . . ah . . . then I believe."

"Okay, Franco." She laughed. "But one thing . . . there's no such thing as gigolos anymore. And you've got to learn not to be so touchy."

"What you call a man who is bought?" he asked.

She shrugged. "No *man* is ever bought . . . or kept. The ones that are . . . I suppose you'd call them escorts, or fags, or muscle-beach types . . . male whores."

"I am not male whore."

"No one said you were."

He started the car but he drove slowly. "In Naples where I was born, we learn we have to fight for what we want. Women, money—even to stay alive. But we cannot be bought by women. We are maschio." Then he smiled. "Okay . . . I forgive you . . . if you come back for some wine."

"But—"

"Or maybe I feel you are only with me to please your papa unless we have one glass of wine."

"All right. One glass of wine."

He drove through winding streets . . . over cobblestones

. . . past massive dark buildings with courtyards. Finally he pulled up in front of an imposing old house. "Way back this was private palazzo of rich old lady. Mussolini once stayed here with his mistress. Now it is run down and made into apartments."

She followed him through a dark courtyard with cracked marble benches and a broken unworkable marble fountain. He fitted his key into a massive oak door. "Come in. This is my place. Not neat . . . but nice . . . yes?"

The living room was a wild contrast of modern disorder against old-world antiquity. High ceilings . . . worn marble floors . . . sofa strewn with newspapers . . . littered tin ashtrays . . . tiny kitchen stacked with dirty dishes . . . bedroom door ajar, with unmade bed. Here he lived in typical bachelor chaos.

He seemed unabashed by the appearance of the apartment. He flicked on the hi-fi and suddenly music seemed to be coming from everywhere. What he lacked in furniture he made up for in speakers. She studied the moldings and fine marble while he worked on the cork of the bottle of wine.

"This is same like we had," he said as he came to her with the glasses. Then he led her to the couch, swept the newspapers to the floor and motioned for her to sit. The stuffing and some springs were leaking through the bottom, but there was pride in his voice when he said, "All my furniture donated by friends."

"This is a marvelous couch," she said. "If you had it redone and—"

He shrugged. "When I become big star I furnish place good. Maybe."

"Maybe?"

"Well, if I'm big star enough, they send for me to come to America. That is where the real money is, no?"

"Melba Delitto is a big star and she stays here."

He laughed. "Melba is already very rich. Besides, she is thirty-one . . . too old to go."

"But she made all that money here."

"No. From lovers. She has had many lovers . . . many

diamonds. She make good money in films but more from lovers. See, is different for a woman. Your papa already give her big pin with diamonds."

She stood up. "I think I'd better get home."

"You just arrive. You didn't drink the wine. I opened whole bottle."

"Franco, it's getting late, and—"

He pulled her back on the couch. "First drink your wine." He handed her the glass. She sipped it slowly. His hand dropped from the back of the sofa onto her shoulders. She pretended not to notice, but it felt heavy, as if it had a life of its own. The fingers began to play with the back of her neck.

She made an effort and swallowed some of the wine. Then she stood up. "Franco, I think I'd like to go."

He stood up but held out his arms. "Come. We dance. Old-fashioned style."

"I really don't want . . ."

But his arms went around her and he held her close as he led her into a slow dance. She felt the hardness of his body . . . the bulge in his pants . . . he was pressing against her . . . moving his body to the rhythm of the music. Her thin Pucci dress felt like paper. Suddenly he kissed her. His tongue pressed her lips apart. She tried to pull away, but he held her head with one hand and with the other he began caressing her breasts. She kept trying to get away from him, but he laughed at her efforts. Then, with one quick move, he lifted her up and carried her into the bedroom and tossed her lightly on the unmade bed. Before she could move, he had her dress up and was pulling at her pants. She screamed when she felt his hands on her bare buttocks.

He stared at her. "What is it? What is wrong?"

She jumped off the bed, pulling down her dress. She was too angry for tears. "How dare you! How *dare* you!" She ran into the living room, grabbed her purse and ran toward the door. He leaped in front of her and blocked her way. "January—is something wrong?"

"Is something wrong!" she said hoarsely. "You ask me here for a drink and then try to rape me."

"Rape?" He stared at her. "I try to make love to you."

"To you, it's obviously the same thing."

"What same thing? Rape is crime. Making love is two people whose bodies long for one another. You agreed to come here no?"

"For a drink . . . and to . . . Well, I thought your feelings were hurt."

"Maybe I have big temper," he said. "But you are acting like spoiled American girl."

"Well, I am an American girl."

"Ah yes. But you are maschio's daughter. That is the big difference. See, they say American girls . . . have rules. First date . . . maybe goodnight kiss. Second date, maybe a little feel. Third date more touching and feeling. But never no lovemaking until after fourth or fifth date. And American men follow these rules. But Mike Wayne makes his own rules. I thought his daughter would be like him."

"You mean . . . just like that . . . you thought I'd go to bed with you!"

He laughed. "Well . . . just like that . . . you went for drinks with me. You danced with me. It's all very natural and very good. Making love follows." He leaned over and stroked her breasts. "See. Nipples are hard. Right through your dress. Your lovely little breasts want Franco . . . even if you don't. Why not let me just make love to them?"

She pushed his hands away. "Franco, take me home."

He leaned over and kissed her, pinning her against the door. She fought violently . . . kicking . . . pulling at his hair, but he only laughed as if it were part of a game. With one hand he took her arms and pinned them behind her. With the other hand he tried to pull down the zipper in the back of her dress. In the midst of her panic she remembered to be grateful that it was only a six-inch zipper. He tugged and tugged. Then, quickly, he reached down and pulled thc dress up around her head. It trapped her arms against her head and muffled her screams. She wasn't wearing a bra and suddenly she felt his lips against her breasts and in spite of her fury she felt a strange sensation in her groin. He slid one hand under her pants and groped between her legs. "See, my little January. You are moist with love . . . waiting for me."

With one frantic burst of strength she broke away and blindly groped at her dress. As she pulled it down she gasped between sobs, "Please . . . please let me go."

"Why are you crying?" His amazement was real. He tried to put his arms around her again and she screamed.

"January, what is wrong? I will be a good lover. Please. Take off your clothes and come to bed with me." He was fidgeting with the buckle of his belt. He stepped out of his pants. His grin was boyish, as if he were cajoling a stubborn child. "Come. Look how very much I want you. Please look." He was standing before her in brief shorts.

She tried not to stare . . . but she was hypnotized. He smiled modestly. "Franco is like a stallion. You will be pleased. Come . . ." He held out his arms. "We make love. Your body is calling out to me. Why you try to deny this happiness to us both?"

He took her hands and shoved them under his shorts. "Feel how much I want you. Can't you see it has to be?"

"No . . ." It was a plea mixed with a moan. "Oh, God, no. Not like this . . ."

He looked bewildered. Then he looked toward the bedroom. "You mean because of bed? Look. I never made love on those sheets. I just slept on them."

"Please! Please let me go!" Tears were blurring her vision. She hugged herself protectively and tried not to look at him. Suddenly he stared at her closely and reached out and touched her cheek as if he could not believe her tears. A curious expression came on his face. "January . . . you have made love before?" he asked quietly.

She shook her head.

For a moment he was silent. Then he came to her, smoothed her dress, and brushed the tears off her face. "I am sorry," he whispered. "I had no idea. You are what . . . twenty-one . . . twenty-two?"

"Seventeen and a half."

"*Mama mia!*" He slapped his forehead. "You look so . . . so filled with knowing . . . so . . . like the Americans say . . . so cool. Mike Wayne's daughter a virgin." Again he slapped his forehead.

"Please take me home."

"Right away." He got into his pants, grabbed his shirt and jacket, and opened the door. He took her arm and led her through the garden to his car. They drove in silence through the deserted streets. He didn't speak until they reached the Via Veneto. Then he said, "There is someone you care about in the States."

"No."

He turned to her. "Then let me . . . oh, not tonight . . . not tomorrow . . . not until you want me. I won't touch you until you ask me. I promise." When she didn't answer, he said, "You do not trust me?"

"No."

He laughed. "Listen, little beautiful American virgin. In Roma there are much beautiful Italian girls. Actresses, models, married women. All want Franco. They even make my bed, cook for me, bring me wine. Know why? Because Franco is good lover. So when Franco asks to see you and says nothing will happen, you must believe. Hah! I do not have to fight to have love. It is all around. But I want to apologize. We start fresh. Like this never happened."

She was silent. She didn't want to say anything to make him angry; they were close to the hotel. She just wanted to get out of that car and get away from him.

"It is very sad that you do not want me," he said quietly. "Especially because you are a virgin. You see, my little January, the first time a girl gives herself to a man it is not always enjoyable . . . to her or to the man. Unless the man is expert and gentle. I would be very tender. I would take you so carefully. Make you very happy. I will even get you the pills."

He was so serious that her fear began to dissolve. And the wild part was he actually felt he had done nothing wrong.

"I upset things tonight," he went on. "I fight you because I think maybe it is part of your game. One American lady I met —she made me chase her around her suite at the Hassler and then she lock bedroom door. I start to leave and she holler, 'No, Franco, you must break down door and tear off my clothes.'" Again he slapped his forehead, but he was grinning. "Ever try breaking down door in Italian hotel? Like iron. She finally open it and I chase her again and then I tear off her clothes. Whooey . . . buttons . . . lace . . . stocking pants ripped . . . everything torn . . . and it was crazy . . . we make love all night. She married to very big American star so I don't tell you her name. But he like to do it that way too. But see . . . I am gentleman . . . I never tell who I sleep with. Not right. Yes?"

She found herself smiling. Then she caught herself and stared ahead. It was insane. This man had just torn at her clothes, tried to rape her, and now he was asking for approval of his past exploits. Obviously he sensed her mood, because he smiled and patted her hand almost condescendingly. "You will ask me to make love to you. I know. Even now I can see your nipples harden through your dress. You have much sexual desire."

She folded her arms across her chest. She should have worn a bra. She hadn't realized the dress was so thin.

"You're not too big on top," he said pleasantly. "I like that."

"Franco . . . Stop it!"

Once again the familiar slap against his brow. "Whooey . . . how can Mike Wayne's daughter be so . . . such prude?"

"I'm not a prude." She felt safe at last. He was pulling into the driveway of the Excelsior.

"I have no call tomorrow," he said as he sprang out of the car and opened the door. He helped her out. "We see each other . . . no?"

"No."

"Why? You are not angry?"

"Not angry? Franco, you treated me like . . . like . . ."

"Like a beautiful woman," he said with a smile. "Please. Tell you what . . . You have good night's sleep. I call tomorrow and we spend day together." He held his arms open. "No touch, I swear. We take ride on my motorcycle. I show you Roma."

"No."

"I call tomorrow. *Ciao.*"

She turned and walked into the deserted lobby. It was almost three o'clock. Mike would be frantic . . . probably waiting and tapping his foot. Well, she wouldn't tell him the truth.

She'd just say she didn't want to be stuck with Franco again. She'd tell him he made a slight pass. She thought about it as she rode up the creaky elevator with the sleepy attendant.

She put the oversized key into the door. He was up. She could see the streak of light under the door. She walked in. "Mike . . ." Then she looked around. The door to his bedroom was shut. There was a pile of paper money and a note propped up against the lamp on her desk.

> "Waited until two, Princess. Hope you had fun. Sleep late. Remember the shops all close between one and four. So just see some sights in the early part of the afternoon. Visit the Spanish Steps. A guy named Axel Munthe once used the little house down there to take in stray animals. Also a guy named Keats lived there too. You can visit his apartment. After four go to the Via Sistina. Melba says there are some great shops there. If you run out of money you can always send things to the hotel C.O.D. Sleep well, Angel. Love, Daddy."

She stared at the note . . . then at his closed door. He was asleep! He wasn't even concerned about her! But then, he probably never dreamed Franco would dare to come on so strong.

She went to her bedroom. Some of her anger evaporated. If he had waited up until two . . . that meant he had gotten home around one . . . maybe earlier. So he probably really just had a nightcap with Melba. Nothing more. The big love affair was all in Franco's mind. Melba was old . . . well, old for a movie star . . . in her thirties . . . she needed sleep. She couldn't take a chance of staying up late with Mike. She was too career-minded. She walked into the bathroom and ran the bath. But what about the diamond pin? Well, what about it? Mike always gave the stars of his productions lavish gifts. Of course . . . It was all in Franco's mind. The entire evening was like a dream. She took off her clothes and stared at her breasts. But the evening *had* happened. Franco had touched her breasts . . . sucked at them. His fingers had been between her legs. She got into the tub and scrubbed herself violently.

Later as she lay in bed in the strange room, she felt wide awake. She stared at the dim outline of her bedroom door. Outside was the living room . . . and then there was his door.

He was sleeping in there. Oh God, if she could only slip in there and climb into his arms the way she used to do when she was little and had a bad dream. Why couldn't she slip into his arms and tell him all the terrible things that had happened tonight? Let him hold her close and tell her it would be all right. He was still her father. Why was it wrong now? And yet . . . she felt she couldn't do it. Was it because she *wanted* to feel Mike's body against her own? Yes. But in the nicest of ways. She wanted the soothing strength of his arms. She wanted to kiss his cheek, especially the side where the dimple almost formed. She wanted to hear him say, "It's all right, baby."

There was nothing wrong in it. She got out of bed quietly and opened the door. She crossed the large living room and turned the handle of his door gently. It opened easily. At first, she saw only the darkness. But gradually she saw the dim outline of the bed across the room. She tiptoed over, feeling her away along the wall. She reached the bed and pulled aside the sheet and slid in. Her side of the bed was cool and crisp with clean sheets. She inched over and reached for him. But her hand touched another cool crisp pillow. The bed was empty!

She sat up and switched on the lamp on the night table. The bed was turned down . . . the linens were clean. He wasn't there! She got out of bed and walked back into the living room. She stared at the note and the money.

Everything Franco said was true . . . he was with Melba. But why didn't he tell her . . . why did he have to lie to her . . . leave the note about waiting up for her. She went back to the desk and reread the note. But he hadn't said he had waited *up* for her. He had said, "Waited until two." Sure . . . he and Melba had waited until two . . . and then gone off together. Right now they were probably making love.

She went back to her bedroom. He had every right to be with Melba. Why was she so upset? He always had girls. But she was the only one he really loved. Their love was beyond sex . . . people had sex without love. Animals had sex . . . and they weren't in love. They mated, that was all. Like the time when she was five and she had a poodle. It had been mated and it wouldn't even look at the male after it was over. And then when it had puppies . . . it had loved them . . . *until* they were three months olds. She had been so amazed when her mother told her they had to give away the male because to the girl poodle he was no longer a son . . . just another male. And that was all Melba was to her father . . . just someone to have sex with.

She got into bed and tried to sleep. She held the pillow in her arms as she often had at school when she was lonely. But suddenly she pushed it away. The pillow had always been a symbol of Mike, of comfort. But now Mike had Melba in his arms. . . . She had to stop thinking this way! After all, what did she think he had been doing all these years since her mother died? But she had never been *there*. Okay, now she was *there*. And she must get him used to the idea that she was an adult, that she could be a great companion, a help to him. He had been alone so much. He was used to latching on to anyone.

When she did fall asleep her dreams were strange and disjointed. She dreamed she was at the funhouse in Coney Island where her father had taken her when she was small. Only there was jarring blasting discotheque music now. She looked at herself in the mirror and laughed . . . first she was long and skinny . . . then short and squat . . . over her shoulder she saw Melba . . . only Melba's face wasn't distorted . . . it was beautiful . . . and she was laughing . . . her face grew larger and larger until it covered the mirror. Melba kept laughing . . . then she heard Franco laughing . . . his face was on the mirror with Melba's and they were both pointing at her grotesque foreshortened image and laughing. Why was the funhouse mirror making her look so funny when it let Melba and Franco look beautiful? She looked around for Mike. He was at the shooting gallery. Melba walked over and stood close to him, her hand on his leg. "Daddy—" January cried out. "Come and take me away from the mirror." But he laughed and said, "Let Franco help you. Besides, I'm shooting all the clay ducks and pipes. I'm doing it all for you, baby. I'm winning all the prizes to lay at your feet." And he kept shooting and each time he shot he hit the bull's-eye and the bell rang and rang.

She opened her eyes. Coney Island and the funhouse were gone. A blotch of sunlight had found its way onto the rug through the drapes. As she came fully awake she was aware of the shrill cacophony of Rome's famed traffic. Horns of all ranges screamed their demands. Soprano horns . . . tinny horns . . . bass horns . . . And through it all there was still the sound of a bell ringing. It was coming from the phone in the living room. She stumbled in. The marble clock on the mantel chimed softly—eleven o'clock. She picked up the phone.

"Franco here," the cheerful voice called out.

She hung up.

Then she called room service and ordered coffee. The door to her father's bedroom was ajar. The light on the night table was still on, just the way she had left it. She turned it off, and on sudden impulse ruffled up the bed. She didn't want the hotel maid to know he hadn't come home. But that was ridiculous. Probably there were a lot of nights when his bed was unused. Or maybe it had been used . . . by Melba.

The phone rang again. She hoped it was Mike. She must sound as if nothing had happened. Cheerful. Or sleepy. Yes, sleepy, as if she had really had a marvelous evening. She picked up the phone.

"Franco here. We were snipped off."

"Oh . . ." She didn't even try to hide her disappointment.

"Dumb operator. She snip us off."

"No, I hung up."

"Why you do that?"

"Because I haven't even had my coffee yet and—" She paused. "Well, golly . . . why shouldn't I hang up on you?"

"Because it is a beautiful day. I pick you up. We go to lunch in a cozy little place—"

"Listen, Franco . . ." She began to sputter. "What you did last night was . . . well, it was terrible, and I don't ever want to see you again."

"But last night I didn't know you were a child. Today I treat you like a child. Okay?"

"No."

"But you get mad if I treat you like a beautiful woman. Look, I have been shining up my Honda for two hours. It is so beautiful . . . Tell you what. No cozy little place for lunch. We go to Doney's. Like tourist. We sit right out in the open.

I buy you your coffee, then we take ride. *Ciao.*" He hung up before she could answer.

Her coffee from room service never arrived, and when Franco called from the lobby she decided she might as well go with him to Doney's. After all, she had to have coffee. She scooped up the money Mike had left. Then on an impulse she put it back . . . along with the note. She called the hotel maid and told her to make up her room immediately. Let him come back and wonder whether *she* had slept home last night!

It was impossible to remain angry at Franco. He ordered her coffee and croissants. He was warm and volatile. And it seemed half of Rome stopped at the table to talk to him. His boundless enthusiasm gradually melted her reserve, and she found herself laughing and enjoying her breakfast. This sunny, easygoing boy almost made her forget the Franco of last night. She realized he was trying to apologize, trying to please her, and it would be fun to see Rome with him. She was wearing dungarees, and she realized that subconsciously she had intended to go on the motorcycle with him.

The Honda was bright red. He gave her a pair of oversized goggles and told her to sit behind him. "This time you must hug me." He laughed.

He drove through the traffic carefully and pointed out churches and important buildings. "Next week we see the Vatican," he told her. "And I also take you into some churches. Michelangelo's work in marble you must see."

After a short time they left the city and headed for the Appian Way. He did not speed. He let her get the feel of the seat, of the wind blowing through her hair and cooling her face. He pointed out important villas . . . bits of ruins . . . the house of a movie star. Then he cut off and went down a winding country road. They stopped at a small family-run restaurant. Everyone including a barking dog greeted Franco eagerly. They called him by his first name . . . beamed radiantly at January and brought out bread, cheese, and red wine.

"The Appian Way is the road to Naples," he said. "We must go there someday. And Capri." He kissed his fingers to the sky. "Tomorrow I have filming, but I take you to Capri on Sunday.

See Grotto Azura and . . . oh, we have so many places to see."

Later as they walked back to the Honda he put his arm around her shoulders in a brotherly fashion. As they were about to get on the bike she turned to him suddenly. "Franco, I want you to know that this has been a fabulous day. Really neat. Thank you so much."

"Tonight I take you to a great place for dinner. Ever eat clams Posillipo?"

"No . . . but I can't have dinner with you."

"Why? I took promise I won't touch you."

"It isn't that. I . . . want to be with my father."

"You what?"

"My father . . . I haven't seen him since last night."

"Okay, you see him when you go home now. Then at nine o'clock you have dinner with me."

"I want to have dinner with my father."

"Perhaps your papa has other plans." He climbed on the motorcycle.

"No. I'm sure he expects to have dinner with me."

"Before you come . . . every night he take Melba to dinner."

"But I'm here now."

"And you expect to eat dinner every night with your papa?" He was no longer smiling.

"Perhaps."

He started to rev the motor. "Get on. I see everything now."

"What do you see?"

"No girl wants to eat with her papa. You must have other date."

"Franco, for heaven's sake. I don't have another date."

He grabbed her wrist. "Then you have dinner with me tonight like I say."

"No."

He released her hand. "Get on," he snapped. "I take you home. Hah! And I believed the virgin story. Now I know. You just don't dig Franco."

They started down the country road. He drove quickly, bouncing over potholes and rocks. Several times she was almost hurled off. She clung to him as they turned onto the Appian Way. A sightseeing bus filled with Japanese tourists passed. He careened past, almost skinning its wheels. The driver screamed some profanities . . . Franco shook his fist at the driver and went faster. She shouted for him to be careful. But her voice was lost in the noise of the motor and the wind. She was frightened now. There was violence in his driving. She pleaded with him to slow down until she was hoarse. Finally she could do nothing but cling to him and pray. As they rounded a curve she saw a car trying to pass another. He saw it too and tried to swerve the motorcycle off the road. It seemed to rear on its hind legs like a horse . . . she felt herself going through the air . . . and in that split second before she lost consciousness, she felt only a sense of amazement that there was no pain when her body was flung against the stone wall.

When she opened her eyes she saw her father. Two of him . . . three of him . . . She closed her eyes because everything blurred. She tried to reach out for him, but her arm felt like lead. She opened her eyes again. Through the haze she saw the dim outline of her leg raised in traction. Then she remembered the crash. The wild drive . . . the white stone wall . . . and now she was in a hospital with a broken leg. It would ruin the summer, but she felt lucky to be alive. But these days they fixed it so you could walk with your leg in a cast, didn't they? She tried to move, but her entire body felt like cement. She forced her eyes open again, but the lights made them tear. Why was her body so taut? Why couldn't she feel anything in her right arm? Oh God, maybe it was more than just a broken leg.

Mike was standing across the room talking to several doctors. A nurse was bustling about. They were whispering. She wanted him to know she was awake.

She called out, "Daddy . . ."

She tried again. It seemed as if she were shouting. But he didn't move. No one moved. She was screaming but no words were coming out. She was screaming but her mouth wasn't moving. She was screaming inside! She tried to move her left arm . . . she wriggled the fingers, and then everything blurred into a soft gray sleep.

When she opened her eyes again, there was just a small light in the far corner of the room. A nurse was reading a magazine. It was night now. The door opened. Her father and the nurse began to whisper.

He dismissed the nurse and pulled a chair to the side of her bed. He stroked her hand. "Don't worry, baby. Everything will be all right."

She tried to move her mouth. She strained every muscle, but no words would come. He went on talking. "They tell me that even when you open your eyes you don't see me. But they don't know everything. You're gonna make it . . . for me!"

"Make it!" What was he talking about? She had to tell him she'd be fine. A broken leg would heal. She felt awful. Here she was causing him all this trouble. She had probably made him lose a whole day's shooting just because Franco had lost his temper this afternoon. But it was ridiculous for him to be so worried. But why couldn't she talk? She wriggled the fingers of her left hand . . . that worked. She tried raising it. That worked too. He was staring off into space. She reached out and touched his shoulder. He almost leaped off the chair.

"January! NURSE! Oh, babe . . . you moved! You moved your arm! NURSE!"

She tried to tell him she was fine, but suddenly she felt herself falling through space . . . and the thick gray sleep was trying to take over. She didn't want to sleep! She fought against it. The room was suddenly crowded. She saw two white-coated men closing in on her. One white coat raised her right arm and let it drop. Another stuck a needle into it. She saw it rather than felt it. That was odd . . . she felt nothing. Another doctor stuck a needle into her left ankle. Wow! She felt that! And then the gray sleep took over.

When she opened her eyes she saw a big jar of fluid hanging over her ankle. The doctors were all gone but her father was bending over her.

"Nod if you understand me, baby."

She tried. Oh, God. Did they have her head strapped down? It was like a rock.

"Blink your eyes, January. Blink if you understand."

She blinked her eyes.

"Oh, baby—" He buried his head in her shoulder. "I promise you everything is going to be fine." Then she felt the dampness on her neck. Tears. His tears. She had never seen Mike Wayne shed a tear in his life. No one had. And he was crying over her. And suddenly for that one second she was happier than she had ever been. She wasn't worried about her leg or her arm. He loved her . . . he cared for her this much . . . she would get well . . . she would heal so fast . . . they'd have their summer together . . . on crutches . . . with a cast . . . it didn't matter.

She reached out to touch his head . . . to stroke him . . . but her gauge of distance was suddenly crazy and she touched her own head. It felt like stone. Mike stood up. His face was composed. He saw her left arm flailing toward her head.

Her head! What was wrong with her head? Maybe her face was hurt, too. The panic shot through her; a sudden wrench of nausea twisted her stomach. But she forced herself to touch her face.

He understood her frantic gesture immediately. "Your face is fine, baby. They had to shave your head, but your hair will grow back."

THEY HAD SHAVED HER HEAD!

He read the panic in her eyes, and took her hand and held it tight. "Look, I'm gonna give it to you straight because you're gonna have to do a lot of fighting. We both will. So I'll give you the bottom line. You have a fractured skull along with a brain concussion. They had to operate to release some blood. They were afraid of clotting or something. It's all right now. The operation was a complete success. Your back is broken. Two vertebrae, but they'll mend. You also have what they call multiple breaks in your leg. You've got casts all over you . . . that's why you can't move. You can't move your right arm because of the brain concussion. But they say that will all come back." He tried to smile. "Outside of that, baby, you're in great shape." Then he leaned over and kissed her. "You don't know how great it is to see you look at me. It's the first time you've really looked at me in ten days . . ."

TEN DAYS! Ten days since she had fallen off the motorcycle!

Was Franco hurt? How long would she have to be here? Once again she tried to talk, but no words came out. He held her hand and said, "That's part of the concussion, baby. The side of your head that was hit affects the speech area. Don't panic. It will all come back. I swear to you. . . ."

She wanted to tell him she wouldn't panic. As long as he was there, everything was okay. She wanted to tell him to go back to the studio . . . he had a picture to do . . . she wanted to let him know these things . . . that as long as they were a team . . . as long as she knew she'd see him the end of each day and that he loved her and was thinking about her—nothing would stand in her way. She scratched furiously with her left hand. She wanted a pencil. She had to tell him these things. Tears of frustration streamed down her face. She wanted a pencil. But he didn't understand.

"Nurse!" he called out. "Come here quick . . . maybe she's in pain!"

(Daddy, I'm not in pain . . . I just want a pencil.)

The nurse was all starched efficiency. January felt the needle go into her arm . . the numbness began to seep through her and in the distance she heard her father's voice . . . "Just relax, babe . . . everything's gonna be all right. . . ."

One

September, 1970

When Mike Wayne walked into the V.I.P. Lounge at Kennedy Airport, the hostess was positive he was a movie star. He had that look of someone you've seen many times but know you've never met.

"Is Flight Seven, Swissair, still scheduled for a five o'clock arrival?" he asked as he signed the guest book.

"I'll check," she said, flooding him with one of her warmest smiles. He smiled back, but experience told her it was the smile of a man who already had a girl. A girl arriving on Flight Seven. Probably one of those Swiss-German beauties that were crowding the market lately. It was getting so a domestic stewardess didn't have a chance.

"Half an hour late. Due at five-thirty." Her smile was apologetic.

He nodded and walked to one of the leather chairs by the window. She studied his scrawl on the book. Michael Wayne. She had heard the name, and she *knew* his face, but she couldn't place him. Maybe he was on one of those television series . . . like that dreamy fellow on *Mannix* whom she watched whenever she was dateless on Saturday nights. He was older than the men she usually dated, maybe in his forties. But for Mr. Michael Wayne with the Paul Newman blue eyes she could easily forget the generation gap. In a final bid for attention, she came over with some magazines, but he shook his head and continued to stare at the planes being serviced on the ground. She sighed as she returned to her desk. *No way!* This one really had something on his mind.

Mike Wayne had plenty on his mind. She was coming back! After three years and three months of hospitals and therapy . . . she was coming back.

When she crashed on that motorcycle, his own crash dive had begun. It started with the flop of Melba's picture. He took the blame for that himself. When your kid is busted into pieces, you can't worry about a spaghetti western. And January's prognosis had been dismal. In the beginning none of the surgeons held any hope that she would ever walk again.

The paralysis was due to the concussion and called for immediate physical therapy. For weeks he studied X rays he didn't understand . . . electroencephalograms . . . spinal pictures.

He flew in two surgeons from London and a top neurologist from Germany. They agreed with the specialists in Rome—the delay in physical therapy lessened the chances of recovery from paralysis, yet nothing could be done until the broken bones healed.

He spent most of his time at the hospital, going to the studio to make sure that most of Franco's scenes were cut from the picture. He didn't buy Franco's story—that January had insisted he drive faster—and when he put it to January she had refused to deny or confirm it. But he threw Franco off the set and let the director cut and edit the picture. He wanted to get out of Rome . . . and take January with him.

But three months later she was still in a partial cast and unable to talk. The picture opened in Rome to murderous reviews and tepid business.

In New York it was yanked out of a first-run house after one week and went straight to Forty-second Street on the bottom half of a double bill. In Europe the press labeled Mike Wayne the only man who ever made Melba Delitto look sexless.

He tried to be philosophical. Everyone had to have one flop. And this was long overdue. He had been on a winning streak since 1947. He told it to himself. He told it to the press. Yet as he sat beside his daughter's bed, the thought nagged like an exposed nerve. *Was* it just one flop—or had his luck run out?

He had two more pictures to release through Century, and he could amortize the loss of this picture against the profits of the others. And he didn't see how the next picture could miss. It was a spy story from a best-selling novel. He started principal photography in London, in October. Each weekend he flew back to Rome; forcing himself to walk into that hospital room with a smile to match the one she always had for him. He tried not to be disheartened at her lack of progress. She would make it. She had to! On her eighteenth birthday she surprised him by taking a few laborious steps with the aid of the therapist and crutches. Her right arm had improved, but she still dragged her right leg. Her speech was coming back. There were times she halted or stuttered on a word. But he knew that was just a matter of time. But damn it! If she could talk and use her right arm, what was holding up the progress of the leg? Certainly not the concussion anymore. But her smile was so bright and victorious. Her hair had grown back short and shaggy—she looked like a frail little boy. His throat felt dry. He felt it tighten as he forced a smile. Eighteen years old, and so many months lost.

After her birthday he had to go to the States to film the chase scenes in New York and San Francisco. Then there was the editing and final scoring in Los Angeles. He had high hopes for the picture; it had the smell of a winner. And somehow he tied up his hopes for the success of the picture with January's recovery. Like a mind bet. If the picture made it big—her recovery would be rapid.

It opened with a big charity premiere in New York. The klieg-light bit; the celebrities; Barry Gray interviewing the V.I.P.'s. The audience applauded and laughed in the right places. When the lights came up, the heads of Century walked up the aisle with him . . . back-slapping . . . smiling. Then on to the party at the Americana, where they heard that the first reviews on TV had been bad. But everyone said it didn't matter. *The New York Times* was all that counted. At midnight they learned the *Times* had murdered it (that was when the heads of the studio left the party). The head of Century publicity, an optimistic man named Sid Goff, shrugged it off. "Ah, who reads the *Times*? For movies, it's the *Daily News* that counts." Twenty minutes later they learned the *News* had only given it two stars, but Sid Goff was still optimistic. "I hear the guy at the *Post* loved it. Besides, word of mouth will make the picture."

But neither the *Post* nor word of mouth was good. Business was weak, but Sid Goff was still cheerful. "Wait till it plays across the country. The people will love it. That's where it counts."

It received a lukewarm reception at the Chinese in Los Angeles. It limped along in Detroit. In Chicago it bombed completely. And Philadelphia and other key cities refused it at first-run houses.

He couldn't believe it. He had been so sure of the picture. Two flops in a row. And now he faced the old show business superstition. Everything bad comes in threes. Deaths . . . plane crashes . . . earthquakes—and flop pictures. Obviously the heads of Century pictures felt the same way, because when he called, everyone was always busy in meetings or had "just stepped out of the office." And the final clincher was when word came from the New York office that they would allot him only two million dollars (including advertising) for his third picture.

He couldn't bring it in on that kind of a budget unless he settled for actors whose names went under the title and a new director or an old one with a long backlog of flops. But he had no choice. He had to do the picture; it was part of his contract. He had a three-picture deal. Well, if that's the way the cards were stacked he'd get the third flop out of the way, pack it in, go back to New York, and do a smash Broadway show. The more he thought about it, the more his confidence grew. His return to Broadway would be an event. Money would be no problem. Hell, he'd back it himself. He was worth several million. What was a few hundred thousand bucks? The only thing—he had to come up with a hot script.

These were his emotions that summer of '68 as he started his third picture. He was in high spirits when he flew to Rome to see January, but when he saw her hobble toward him, still dragging her leg, it hit him for the first time that she just might not walk again. Her bright smile and eager excitement only added to his feeling of despair. She wanted to know all about the new picture. Why had he picked unknowns? Who was the leading man? When could she read the final shooting script? He forced himself to invent stories and gossip with an enthusiasm that came hard. He held his panic until he was alone with the doctors. Then his rage and fear exploded. What was all this crap about her making steady progress? All the good reports he had received during the past few months? She hadn't improved one iota.

They admitted she was not responding as quickly as they had hoped. But he must realize . . . They had not been able to start the physical therapy as soon as they should. Then they told him the facts. She would improve. But she would always limp and possibly have to use a cane.

That night he went on a wild drunk with Melba Delitto. And when they wound up at her apartment, he paced and raged about the doctors, the hospital, the hopelessness of it all.

Melba tried to calm him. "Mike, I adore you. I not even hold my one big flop against you. But now you have done another bad picture. You must not let your daughter's misfortune destroy your life. This next one must be good."

"What do you want me to do? Just go to work and forget about her?"

"No, not forget. But you have your own life to live. Stop fighting for the impossible."

His anger made him suddenly sober. His whole life had been a fight to attain the impossible. Son of a mother who deserted him when he was three. Father, an Irish prizefighter who died from a lucky punch from a third-rate kid. A life of growing up on his own in South Philadelphia. Enlisting in the Air Force at seventeen because anything seemed better than the world he knew. And then the war . . . being in the midst of it . . . seeing guys you lived with and slept with catch a bullet at your side . . . wondering why *they* got it and not you. *They* had families who were waiting for them to come home. Families and sweethearts who wrote long letters and sent food packages. And gradually the idea hits you that maybe they got *your* bullet because there was something back there, waiting to be done . . . by *you*. And it's your job to go back and do it. He felt he had been given luck—luck to accomplish the impossible. And he had to make good so that the guy who got his bullet would understand. He wasn't religious, but he believed in paying his dues. That had always been his philosophy, and it still was.

"My kid will walk," he said quietly.

Melba shrugged. "Then try Lourdes. Or if you really want to spend money, take her to the Clinique of Miracles."

"What's that?"

"In Switzerland, in a remote section of the Alps. It is very expensive, but they have accomplished great things. I know a racing driver who crashed at the Monte. They said he'd be paralyzed for life. He went to the Clinique of Miracles—they made him walk."

The next day Mike flew to Zurich, then drove to a rambling château hidden in the mountains and met with Dr. Peterson, a fragile-looking man who seemed incapable of creating even the smallest miracle.

It was just another wild chase. Another blind alley. But he was there. So he toured the Clinique with Dr. Peterson. He saw old people who had suffered strokes wave cheerfully at the doctor as they struggled with crutches and braces. He followed the doctor into a room where small children were singing. At first glance, it appeared to be an ordinary songfest, until he realized that every child was performing against odds. Some had cleft palates . . . some wore earphones . . . some had facial paralysis. But they all smiled and forced some sounds through their lips. In another wing there were Thalidomide children working with their artificial limbs, smiling as they made some slight progress with a new and cumbersome prosthesis. Mike felt his mood changing. At first he didn't quite understand. But then it hit him. Everywhere he went, there was an absence of despair. Everywhere he looked was an attempt at accomplishment. The fight to attain the impossible.

"You see," Dr. Peterson explained, "every waking moment is spent in therapy. In striving to get well. We have one little boy who lost both his arms in an accident with a tractor on a farm. With his prosthesis he has learned to play the guitar. We have songfests every night. Sometimes we put on plays and ballets—all part of the therapy. But there is no television or radio."

"But why cut out the outside world?" Mike asked. "Aren't they segrated from life as it is by their illnesses?"

Dr. Peterson smiled. "The Clinique is a world of its own. A world where each patient helps the other. News from the outside world concerns wars, strikes, pollution, riots. . . . If it is not a world that healthy people enjoy, why should our patients want to fight insurmountable obstacles just to return to it? Also, a child born without legs who has worked six months to take two steps can be disheartened if he sees the violence or apathy of people born more fortunate. The Clinique of Miracles is a world of hope and the will to recover."

Mike looked thoughtful. "But there is no one here my daughter could relate to. Everyone is very old . . . or very very young."

"Who is she relating to in her hospital room in Rome?"

"No one. But she's not surrounded by sickness and mutilation."

Dr. Peterson looked thoughtful. "Sometimes seeing others less fortunate helps one to recover. A boy comes here with one arm and sees a boy without any arms. Suddenly, having one arm is not the end of everything. And the boy missing two arms takes great pride helping the boy without legs. And that is how it happens here."

"One question, Dr. Peterson . . . do you really think you can help my daughter?"

"First I must study her records and the reports from the attending physicians. We accept no one whom we cannot help. And even then we cannot always promise a complete cure."

Three weeks later Mike chartered a plane and flew January to the Clinique of Miracles. He had not spared her. He told her what she would find, the condition of some of the patients. But at least—here—she had a shot at getting well. He did not tell her that Dr. Peterson had some reservations about her complete recovery.

The nearest village was five miles from the Clinique. He checked into the inn and remained a week to see how she would take it. If she felt any revulsion she did not show it. Her smile was always bright, and she praised everyone at the Clinique.

He returned to the Coast and went through the motions of making the final picture. It was a dog and nothing could save it. But he had already started the publicity going on his "return to Broadway." Agents, actors and directors began calling. Each night he holed up in his bungalow at the Beverly Hills Hotel and read scripts. Scripts from established playwrights, new authors, amateurs. He read everything, including galleys of new novels. His attaché case was stacked with them when he flew to Switzerland. January had been at the Clinique two months. Her speech was perfect. Her right arm was as strong as it had ever been. But her leg still presented a problem. She was walking better, but with a decided limp.

The picture was finished in December. He gave it to the director to edit and score and walked away from it. He had a long meeting with his business manager. He sold his plane and some stocks. But he refused to relinquish the suite at the Plaza.

On the day before Christmas he flew to Switzerland five hundred dollars in overweight, with three suitcases loaded with toys for the children. He brought January a record player and albums of all the show tunes of the past ten years.

They celebrated her nineteenth birthday in the little dining room at the inn. She chattered about the albums—how much she liked them, how she wished she hadn't missed the shows of the past year. Then her face grew serious and she reached out and took his hand. "Tell you what. Next time you come, I'm going to be able to dance with you. That's a promise."

"Take it easy." He laughed. "I haven't danced in a long time."

"Well, brush up," she said. "Because I'll be waiting." Then she smiled. "I don't mean discotheque stuff. But maybe a quiet little waltz. At least it's something to shoot for."

He nodded and managed a smile. Just that day he had a long talk with Dr. Peterson, who also was concerned over the lack of improvement of her leg. Dr. Peterson suggested they send for one of the top orthopedic surgeons in London for consultation.

A few days later Mike met with Dr. Peterson and Sir Arthur Rylander, the English surgeon. After Sir Arthur studied the X rays, it was his opinion that the bone had healed improperly. The only chance for a cure was to rebreak it and reset it.

When Mike put it to January, she didn't hesitate. "Let's break it. I've always thought wearing a cast in the Alps was rather chic. Didn't you do a picture like that, where the heroine sat in après-ski clothes and looked beautiful?"

"I've done three of them." Mike laughed. "And all my heroines always recovered. Remember that."

The operation was performed in a hospital in Zurich. Two weeks later she was back at the Clinique of Miracles. Those who were able signed her cast, and her unbelievable spunk sent Mike Wayne back to the States with fresh determination. Anyone with her guts deserved to have a kingdom waiting on her return. Nothing could stop him now.

He went to the Coast, cleared out his office at Century pictures, and went to the races at Santa Anita. He bet a long shot. It came in and he won five thousand dollars. He wasn't really surprised, because he knew his luck had changed. And that night he read a script from a new author, and knew he had found his play. He decided to back it himself. He went to New York, put extra phones in his suite at the Plaza, took a lavish office in the Getty building, and called a press conference. Michael Wayne was back on Broadway!

For the next few months he was an explosion of frenetic energy. There were discussions with set designers, directors, actors, interviews at Sardi's, appearances on the talk shows, quick dinners at Danny's Hide-a-Way to unwind with the comedians, dropping by and sitting up half the night with Long John Nebel on his radio show. His return generated the excitement of a superstar. He was well liked by the press . . . his enthusiasm and "rough cut" charm were infectious to everyone around him. When rehearsals began he sent daily reports to January. He sent her the script; the newspaper stories; wrote to her about rehearsals; and kept her informed on every development of "their" propect. The only thing he neglected to tell her about was the ingenue who had moved in with him after the first week of rehearsal.

The play opened in October in Philadelphia and got mixed notices. Revisions were made and the ingenue lost two of her best scenes and stopped talking to him. It went on to Boston, where it received excellent notices. Three weeks later it opened in New York to a rousing ovation and murderous reviews. The consensus was "Old hat" . . . "Cumbersome" . . . "Badly cast." The playwright went on talk shows and said Mike had changed his original conception, taken away all the mystical quality. The ingenue went on talk shows and said the playwright was a genius and Mike had ruined his work (she had already moved out of the Plaza and in with the playwright).

He refused to close it. The cast took cuts and went on minimum salary. He poured another two hundred thousand dollars into signs on buses and subways, full-page ads in *The New York Times,* radio and television spots, full-page ads in the trades, in weekly *Variety.* He reprinted the Boston notice in full-page ads in out-of-town newspapers. He papered the house and gave it the razzle-dazzle he had always given his hits. He flew to Switzerland and told January it was a smash —it would run forever and he would have at least three companies on tour.

Two months later, after a long session with his accountant, he was forced to close. The market was down, but he sold more stock and arrived in Switzerland for her twentieth birthday, walking like a winner, and carrying the usual amount of overweight in gifts.

And when January walked into the reception room without crutches and without a trace of a limp, he felt like the winner of all time. Her steps were slow and measured, but she was walking. He clamped his jaw and swallowed hard. She was so damned beautiful with those great brown eyes and her hair hanging to her shoulders.

And then she was in his arms, both of them talking and laughing at once. Later, over dinner at the inn, she said, "Why did you tell me the show was such a hit?"

"It was . . . with me. Just had too much class for the public."

"But you put your own money into it . . ."
"So?"
"Well, you've had three flop pictures . . ."
"Who says?"
"*Variety* says."
"Where in hell did you get *Variety*?"
"You left it here last time. Dr. Peterson gave it to me, thinking you might want it back. I devoured it. But why did you tell me it was a hit?"
"It was . . . in Boston. Look, forget the play. Let's talk about important things. The Doc says you'll be ready to leave in six months."
"Daddy—" She leaned across the table and looked into his eyes. "Remember when I entered my teens, you said that was a special night. Well, tonight I've left my teens. I'm twenty. I'm a big girl now. I know the clinic costs over three thousand a month. Erik, the little boy who taught me to play guitar, had to leave because it was too expensive . . . so I've been thinking . . ."
"The only thing you've got to think about is getting well."
"What about money?"
"Hell, I made money from the flop pictures. I was on a percentage of the gross, baby—got it right off the top."
"Honest?"
"Honest."
He had gone back on the plane determined to knock down windmills. His talk with Dr. Peterson had been unsettling. ("Mr. Wayne, you must think of January's future with much care. She is so very beautiful but also so very innocent. She talks of being an actress, which is natural because it is your business. But you must realize how protected she has been in the world of our Clinique. She must be eased back into your world, not thrown into it.")
He thought about it on the plane. Somehow he'd manage to have one hell of a world waiting for her. When they ran into some rough weather, he was hit with the crazy idea that a plane crash might solve everything, until he realized he had already cashed in his insurance.
A hit picture was the only solution. Maybe with the three

bad ones behind him, the curse was off. He returned to Los Angeles and once again holed up at the Beverly Hills Hotel reading scenarios and treatments. Oddly enough he found one almost immediately. It was from a writer who had not had a hit in the past ten years. But in the fifties, he had one blockbuster after another. He had Oscars for doorstops. And this one would get him another. It had everything. Big love interest, action, a violent chase scene. He met with the author and paid him a thousand dollars for a month's option.

Then he went to the heads of the big studios.

To his amazement, he couldn't raise any money or any interest in the script. The answer was the same everywhere. The industry was in a slump. A scenario from a screenwriter meant nothing. Now if he had a best-selling novel . . . perhaps. But scenarios were flooding the studios. And everyone seemed in a state of quiet panic. Changes were happening everywhere. Studio heads had come and gone. At some studios he didn't even know the new people in charge. The top independent film-makers also refused to back him. They felt he was a bad risk and the author was old hat. At the end of the month he was forced to relinquish the property. Three days later, two kids in their twenties who had come up with a sleeper the year before grabbed it and got immediate backing from a major studio.

He returned to New York in a frantic search for some action. He invested a hundred thousand in a show a top producer had in rehearsal. The trouble began when the leading man quit the second week of rehearsal. The out-of-town tryout was a nightmare—eight weeks of hysteria, fights, cast replacements, and finally his decision to close the show without bringing it in.

After that he spent two months pouring money into an idea for a television series. He worked with the writers; he paid for the pilot himself, spent over three hundred thousand dollars. The networks looked at it, but "passed." His only chance to recoup some of the money would be as a one-shot slot filler in the summer.

A few weeks later he went to a private screening of the picture he had lost. The production room was filled with young men with beards, tank shirts, and hair hanging from their armpits. The girls wore tank tops and no bras and their hair was either Afro or long and stringy. He felt sick as he watched the picture. They had ruined a great script. Put the ending at the beginning, flooded it with flashbacks and out-of-focus camera work, made the love scene a psychedelic dream sequence with hand-held cameras—the *cinéma-vérité* crap. Sure, they had to play it that way with the beasts who were passing as actors and actresses today. There were no more faces around like Garbo's or Crawford's, or actors like Gable and Cary. . . . Today was the world of the Uglies. That's what everything seemed to be, and he didn't understand it.

A week later he went to a sneak preview on Eighty-sixth Street. The same crowd was there, along with college kids and young married advertising executives. The audience cheered.

Three weeks later it opened, and broke box-office records all over the country. That really rocked him. Because it meant he really didn't know what was good or bad. Not in today's market. Three years ago he could call the shots. Studios had believed in him . . . and more important, he had believed in himself.

It was time to walk away from the table. Mike Wayne was tapped out. How had the chemistry changed in such a short time? He looked the same, thought the same. Maybe that was it. He hadn't gone along with all the changes, the nudity, plays and movies without plots, the new trend of Unisex. Well, he was fifty-two. He had lived through some great times. He had known what it was like to walk down Broadway without worrying about getting mugged. He had known New York when it had nightclubs and lines of beautiful girls, not just porno movies and massage parlors. But most of all he was sad —because this was the world she was coming back to.

He sat in the V.I.P. Lounge and stared at the gray sky. She was flying home through that leaden muck. He had always promised her a bright shining world. Well, goddammit, he was keeping that promise.

The smiling hostess was back. She announced that Flight Seven was arriving. He had arranged for January to receive courtesy of the port. An official would be waiting to whisk her through customs. Hell, what could a kid who had spent three years in hospitals have to declare? He walked out of the lounge and never noticed that the hostess had leaped up to say good-bye. Ordinarily he would have turned on the charm because she was a pretty girl. But for the first time in his life, Mike Wayne was scared.

He spotted her the moment she walked into the airport. Hell, you couldn't miss her. Tall, tan, long hair swinging—she would have caught his eye even if she wasn't his daughter. She seemed oblivious of the men who turned to look at her. A little man was walking double time to keep up with her long strides as her eyes scanned the airport. Then she saw Mike and suddenly he was enveloped in bear hugs, kisses, and she was laughing and crying together.

"Oh, Daddy, you look super! Do you realize I haven't seen you since June? Oh, wow! It's so wonderful to be home again . . . to be with you."

"You look great, babe."

"You too! And . . . oh . . . this is Mr. Higgens." She turned and introduced the little man. "He's been so nice to me. I never even had to open my bag and . . ."

Mike shook hands with the customs official, who was carrying her overnight case. "I'm very grateful, Mr. Higgens." He took the bag. "Now if you'll tell me where the rest of my daughter's luggage is, I'll arrange to have it brought to the car."

"That's all there is, Mr. Wayne. And it was a pleasure. And such a pleasure to meet you, Miss Wayne." He shook hands with both of them and disappeared into the crowd.

Mike held up the overnight bag. "This is it?"

"Yup! I'm wearing my best outfit . . . do you like it?" She stood off and spun around. "I got it in Zurich. They said everyone was wearing pants suits and this suede outfit cost me three hundred dollars."

"It's beautiful. But—" He stared down at the small bag he was carrying. "No other clothes?"

She laughed. "Oh, that's loaded with clothes. Like three

pairs of jeans, a couple of faded shirts, some sweaters, sneakers, and oh . . . a gorgeous shortie nightgown I got in Zurich. I ran out of money or I would have bought the robe to go with it. But other than that little omission, I'm practically set for any emergency."

"We'll take care of the clothes tomorrow."

She tucked her arm through his as they walked to the exit. "I saw so many different skirt lengths on the plane. Mike, what *are* people wearing?"

"Mike?" He stared at her. "Where did *Daddy* go?"

"Oh, you're too gorgeous to be called Daddy. You are gorgeous, you know. I like the sideburns . . . and the gray in them."

"They're white; and I'm a dignified elderly gentleman."

"That'll be the day. Hey, look, that girl is wearing an Indian outfit. Think she's part of some act or something—with the headband and the braids and all?"

"Come on, you know how kooky everyone is dressing today," he said.

"How would I know? Most of my friends wore bathrobes."

He stopped suddenly and looked at her. "Holy Christ, that's right. No TV . . . no nothing?"

"No nothing."

He led her outside to the car. "Well, everyone dresses like they're going to a costume party today. That is, kids your age." But she wasn't listening. She was staring at the car. Then she let out a low whistle. "Wow . . . I'm impressed."

"You've been in limos before."

"I spent my life in them. But this is not just a limo—this is really super." She tossed him a smile of approval. "A silver Rolls-Royce—the *only* way a girl should travel." She got in and nodded. "Pret-ty nice . . . chauffeur's uniform matches upholstery . . . a telephone . . . a bar . . . all the necessities of life *if* you're Mike Wayne." Then she threw her arms around him. "Oh, Daddy . . . I'm so glad for you." She leaned back as the car inched its way out of the airport. She sighed. "It's so great to be back. If you only knew how many times I've dreamed of this moment. Even when I felt it could never happen, I kept dreaming the dream—of *walking* into your arms, of us together in New York. And it's all happening just as I dreamed it. Nothing's changed."

"You're wrong, baby. A lot has changed. Especially New York."

She pointed to the traffic as their car slipped into the speed lane. "This hasn't changed. And I love it all—the traffic, the noise, the crowds, even the smog. It's just so wonderful after all that sanitary snow in Switzerland. I can't wait until we go to the theater. I want to walk through Shubert Alley . . . see the trucks pull out of the Times Building . . . I want to get my nice clean lungs all polluted."

"That'll happen. But first we have a lot of catching up to do."

She nestled against him. "We sure do. I want to sit at our table at Sardi's . . . I can't wait to see *Hair* . . . I want to walk down Fifth Avenue . . . see the clothes. But tonight, I just want to stay in and do the caviar and champagne scene. I know it's no birthday. But you've got to admit it's one hell of an occasion. And most of all I want to know all about your big hit picture."

"My hit picture? Who told you that?"

"No one. But I know how you operate. When I got all those postcards from Spain this summer with mysterious hints of a big new project . . . well, I knew it had to be a picture and you were afraid of jinxing it by telling me. But now . . . when I see all this—" she waved her hand. "Well, come on—tell me about it."

He looked at her. And this time he didn't smile. "You tell *me* something. Are you still the most resilient girl in the world? Because you're gonna find a lot of changes and—"

"We're together," she said. "And as long as that never changes, nothing else matters. Now tell me—is it a movie or a play? And can I work with you? In any capacity—a walk-on, a script girl, a gofer . . ."

"January, did it ever occur to you that there are better things in life than the theater and tagging along after me?"

"Name one."

"Well, like you finding the right guy . . . getting married . . . making me a proud grandpa . . ."

She laughed. "Not for a long time. Listen—beside you sits a lady who has spent three years just learning to walk and talk again." She reached out and touched his face tenderly. "Oh, Mike . . ." Her sigh was happy. "I want to do all the things we've always dreamed of doing together."

"Sometimes we change our dreams," he said. "Or perhaps I should say . . . exchange them."

"Fine. What have you in mind?"

"Well, as you know, I was in Spain," he said slowly. "But it wasn't for a movie."

"A TV series," she said. "That's what it is! Right?"

He looked out of the window. His words were measured. "I've made some pretty good moves in my life and this is about the best I've ever made. I've got some big surprises for you. Tonight you're going to—"

She cut in. "Oh, Mike, please, no surprises tonight. Just us and the champagne. If you knew how many months I've dreamed of being with you in our suite at the Plaza, looking out at the park, seeing my old wishing hill and toasting to—"

"Will you settle for the Pierre?"

"What happened to the Plaza?"

"Mayor Lindsay donated it to the pigeons."

She smiled, but he saw the disappointment in her eyes. "The view is almost the same," he said quickly. "But I'm afraid you'll have to forget about your wishing hill. Drunks and junkies have claimed it now. Along with a few large dogs who use it as a lavatory. Everyone has large dogs now. Not for pets—for protection." He knew he was talking too much. He stopped and stared at the approaching skyline, the uneven beauty of the buildings shrouded in smog. Lights beginning to glow in tiny square windows . . . evening in New York.

And then the skyline was gone and they merged into New York's traffic. As they made their way down Sixtieth Street, Mike called out to the driver. "Stop at that cigar store on the corner opposite Bloomingdale's." They pulled up and before the chauffeur could get out, Mike jumped out of the car. "I'm out of cigarettes." He turned to the chauffeur. "You can't double-park here. Drive Miss Wayne around the block. I'll be out by then."

He was standing on the corner when the car rounded the block. He lit a cigarette when he got into the car. Suddenly he extended the pack as an afterthought. "Do you?"

"No, I don't. But did you?"

"Did I what?"

"Make the call."

"What call?"

She laughed. "Oh, Mike . . . there's a whole carton of cigarettes right here in the bar area of the car."

His jaw tightened. "Okay . . what call did I make?"

She slipped her arm through his. "To order the caviar and champagne. I could tell by your face that you forgot."

He sighed. "Maybe I forgot a lot of things."

She put her fingers across his lips. "Just tell me one thing. Did I guess right about your call?"

"Yep, you guessed right."

Her voice was soft. "Mike, you haven't forgotten anything."

When she opened her eyes, she thought she was still at the Clinique. But the darkness in the room was unfamiliar; the dark shapes of the furniture were different. And then consciousness took over and she realized she was in her new bedroom at the Pierre. She switched on the lamp on the night table. Midnight. That meant she had been asleep only two hours. She stretched and looked around the bedroom. It really was beautiful. It didn't look like a hotel bedroom at all. The entire suite was luxurious and huge. Bigger than anything Mike had ever had. He had explained the hotel had co-op apartments and some people sublet their suites. Well, the people who owned this one sure had taste. The living room had been so beautiful when she arrived. Candlelight, caviar, and champagne all iced, the velvet darkness of the park so many stories below. Then they had toasted one another, eaten the caviar . . . And, after just one glass of champagne she had suddenly gotten drowsy. He had noticed it immediately. "Look, babe, it's only nine o'clock here, but by Swiss time it's two or three in the morning. You go right to bed. I'll take a little walk . . get the papers . . . watch some TV and turn in early too."

"But we haven't talked about you . . . what you're doing . . . or anything."

"Tomorrow." His voice had been firm. "We meet in the living room at nine and have breakfast together and do a *lot* of talking."

"But Mike—"

"Tomorrow." Again that strange quality in his voice. Almost like a cut-off. An odd new hardness. The way it had been with the photographer in the lobby who had snapped a picture of them. He had seemed like a nice young man. He had followed them to the elevator and said, "Tell me, Mr. Wayne, how does your daughter feel being the—"

But he had never finished the question. Mike Wayne pushed January into the elevator and snapped, "Beat it. This is no time for any on-the-spot interview."

She thought about the incident now. The whole thing had been so unlike her father. To him publicity had always been a way of life. She had been on the cover of a national magazine with him when she was nine. And she had felt so sorry for the young man in the lobby.

When she had asked her father about it, he shrugged. "Maybe Rome did it to me. I don't go for these guys who take pictures on spec—pictures that can turn up anywhere, in any cheap magazine. I'm all for giving an authorized interview or posing for a photographer for pictures to *accompany* a story. But I don't like guys popping out from dark corners at me."

"But he was waiting in the lobby. He looked very nice."

"Forget it." (Again that cold determined cut-off tone.) Then he had opened the champagne. When she toasted and said, "To us," he shook his head. "No . . . to *you*. It's your time now, and I'm here to see that you get it."

She lay in the dark bedroom. She had the whole night ahead of her. She should try to go back to sleep. But she was wide awake and thirsty. She was always thirsty after caviar. She slipped out of bed and went to the bathroom. The tap water was lukewarm. She decided to forget it and got back into bed. She switched on the dial of the radio beside her bed to an album station. She was just drifting off to sleep when the commercial break came, and an enthusiatic announcer began his pitch on a new diet cola. The way he began to sell that damn soda—suddenly she *had* to have a glass of cold water!

She got out of bed. There was a big kitchen in the suite. She could get some ice . . . She started for the door and stopped. She had no robe! And she was wearing the short see-through nightgown. She opened the bedroom door cautiously and called out, "Daddy?"

The living room was empty. She tiptoed out. She looked into the darkness of the dining room . . . the large den . . . and down some long corridor off the kitchen. Mike had said there were servants' quarters. But the apartment was empty. She went to his bedroom door and knocked. Then she opened it. Empty. For a fleeting second she thought of Rome . . . and Melba. But he wouldn't do that, not on her first night home. He had probably gone for a walk and run into some friends. She went into the kitchen. The refrigerator was stacked with Cokes, 7-Up, ginger ale, along with every kind of sugar-free diet soda. She took a Coke and poured it into a glass. Then she ambled into the living room. She stood staring out at the park. The tiny sparkling lights gave it a Christmas-tree effect. It was impossible to believe there was anything to fear in that soft darkness.

Then she heard the click. Her father was fitting the key into the lock. Her first impulse was to run and greet him. Then she looked down at her nightgown. It was ridiculous to have bought something so short and sheer. But after three years of flannel pajamas at the Clinique, the sheer gown had been a symbol. Part of being well . . . and leaving. Well, she'd better tell him to keep his eyes closed and lend her one of his robes.

The door opened and she heard the woman's voice. Oh, good Lord . . . he had company. She looked frantically across the long living room. If she tried to make it back to her bedroom, she'd have to pass the foyer and run right into them. The nearest door led to his bedroom. She dashed inside just as they came into the living room. His bedroom was dark. Oh, God . . . where was the light? She groped along the wall searching for the switch.

"Mike, this is absolutely ridiculous for me to have to sneak in here." The woman's voice was petulant. "After all, she's not a child."

"Dee"—his voice was firm but cajoling. "You've got to understand. For three years she looked forward to the way she wanted to spend her first night back."

The woman sighed. "But how do you think I felt when you called and told me to get out of the apartment after I had gone to such pains, getting the best caviar, the right champagne. It was going to be my 'getting to know January night.' Instead I'm dismissed like some chorus girl. Thank God I was able to catch David. We sat in that bar at the Sherry for hours. I'm sure I dragged him out of the arms of some beautiful young thing—"

"Come here," Mike said softly.

There was silence, and January knew he was kissing the woman. She didn't know what to do. It was wrong to stand in the darkness and listen. If only she had a robe.

Her father spoke softly. "January and I are having breakfast tomorrow. I want to have a long talk with her before you two meet. But believe me, I was right . . . handling it the way I did tonight."

"But Mike—"

"No buts. Come on, we've wasted too much time already."

The woman laughed. "Oh, Mike, you've ruined my hair. Oh, would you be a love and pick up my purse . . . I left it on the table near the hall."

January stood very still. They were coming into the bedroom! The door opened and there was a sudden burst of light as the woman flicked on the wall switch. For a split second they both stared at one another. For some reason January felt she looked strangely familiar. She was tall and slim with frosted hair and incredibly beautiful skin. The woman recovered first and called out, "Mike . . . come on in. We seem to have company."

January didn't move. She didn't like the funny smile of composure on the woman's face, as if she had the situation well in hand and had her next move planned.

Mike's first reaction was surprise. Then an expression came

to his eyes that she had never seen before. Annoyance. And when he spoke his voice was cold. "January, what the hell are you doing snooping around in here?"

"I . . . I was having a Coke—" She pointed toward the living room where she had left her drink.

"But what are you doing in here . . . in the dark . . . *without* the drink?" the woman asked.

January looked toward her father, waiting for him to end this horrible scene. But he stood beside the woman, waiting for the answer.

Her throat was dry. "I heard the door . . . and voices . . ." She forced the words out. "I had no robe, so I dashed in here."

For the first time they both stared at the filmy nightgown. Her father walked into the bathroom quickly and returned with one of his dressing gowns. He tossed it to her without glancing up. She struggled into it and started for the door. The woman's soft voice called out, "Stay a moment, January. Mike, you can't let your daughter go without introducing us."

January stood with her back to them waiting for her release.

"January—" her father's voice suddenly seemed weary. "This is Dee."

January forced a slight nod in the woman's direction.

"Oh, come now, Mike," the woman slipped her arm through his. "That's not really a proper introduction."

Mike looked at his daughter and said quietly, "January . . . Dee is my wife. We got married last week."

She heard herself congratulating them. Her legs felt like weights, but somehow she managed to walk out of that room . . . through the living room and into the safety of her own bedroom. Only then did her knees begin to shake . . . and she rushed to the bathroom and was violently ill.

Two

SHE SAT by the window for the rest of the night. No wonder the woman looked familiar. Dee wasn't just Dee. She was Deirdre Milford Granger, often reported as the sixth richest woman in the world! No one really knew whether she was the sixth or sixtieth. It was obviously a tag some reporter had dreamed up, and it stuck. The girls at Miss Haddon's used to kid about the title whenever her picture appeared in the newspapers or magazines. And in those days, Deirdre's marriages kept her in print constantly. First there had been an opera singer. Then an author, followed by a top designer. That marriage had made *Vogue* in January's time. He had been killed four years ago in an automobile accident in Monte Carlo. There had been newsreel pictures of Deirdre in heavy widow's weeds at the funeral, tearfully claiming the dead man to be the only man she had ever loved, swearing she'd never marry again. Unfortunately, she had changed her mind.

Or had Mike changed her mind! Of course! She had been his big new project. All those postcards from Spain. Dee had a house in Marbella—she had seen that in *Vogue*. Dee also had a Palm Beach estate where she kept forty in help—she had seen that in *Ladies' Home Journal*. And there was a yacht in Cannes—that had come into the news when Karla had been Dee's guest at sea. Karla had retired from the screen in 1960 and was more of a recluse than Garbo or Howard Hughes. So much so that her appearance as a guest on someone's yacht made *Time* magazine. All of the girls at Miss Haddon's had been fans of the Polish actress. In 1963 January's biggest claim to fame came when her father offered the great Karla a million dollars to come out of retirement. She never accepted or declined, but it had gotten Mike a great deal of publicity. Later her father had told her that it had been one of his big dreams just to meet the great Karla.

Well, he'd probably meet her now. Maybe he had already.

So the big new project was Deirdre Granger! In a porcelain-muted way, Dee was beautiful. But she seemed bloodless and fragile. Could Mike really love her? She seemed so cold, so unable to give affection. But maybe that was the fascination. Mike always loved a challenge.

She sat at the window until the first hint of light filtered through the darkness. She watched the black sky turn gray. She knew the sunlight was beginning to creep over the tall apartment buildings on upper Fifth Avenue. Everything was so silent—that intermediate time between night and morning.

She put on a pair of jeans, a sweater, and sneakers and slipped out of the apartment. The elevator man's greeting was a cross between a yawn and a nod. The desk clerk looked up with weary disinterest. A man in coveralls was mopping the floor of the lobby. He stopped to let her pass.

New York was still shadowy. Empty, desolate—a vacant city. In the gray morning light the streets seemed curiously clean. She walked to the Plaza and stood for a moment looking up toward the corner suite. Then she cut across the street and walked into the park. A bedraggled woman, wearing a man's overcoat, was poking into a trashcan. Her legs, swollen to twice their size, were swathed in dirty rags. Drunks were sleeping on benches, empty liquor bottles smashed on the ground at their sides. Others slept in fetal positions on the grass. She walked quickly—to the Zoo, back toward the Carousel. The sun worked its way through the smog and fought to clear the sky. Two young men dressed in sweatshirts jogged by. Pigeons began to cluster on the grass, searching for breakfast. A squirrel came right up to her, cupping its paws, its bright little eyes demanding a nut. She shrugged and held out her empty hands and it scampered off. Three black girls on bicycles waved, holding up their fingers in the Peace sign. She continued to walk. The sleeping drunks began to stir. A woman came into the park carrying an elderly dachshund. She placed it on the ground gently and said, "Come on, Baby . . . make ca-ca." Neither the woman nor the dog looked at January. The dog performed—the woman praised it, picked it up, and left the park.

The drunks were pulling themselves to a standing position now. Those who staggered were helped by others. Suddenly the park became alive with dogs: a professional walker with six dogs of assorted breeds, a man with a schnauzer, a woman with rollers in her hair and a fat cocker on a leash. The park that looked like velvet in the darkness last night was now harsh and dirty. The sunlight seemed to spotlight the beer cans, the broken bottles and sandwich papers. A wind stirred the trees, and the sighs of the leaves dropping to their death seemed despairing and gentle against the belching snorts of the huge buses. There were sounds of horns, riveting, blasting —the monolithic monster was awake.

Babies were coming into the park now. Babies in strollers, pushed by young mothers who looked pale and weary. Sometimes an elderly dog tagged jealously along, attached to the stroller, thinking of fonder days when *he* was the main concern of the family. There were other carriages where an infant slept while a two-year-old perched perilously on a jump seat as the mother trudged them toward the playground.

And then the Fifth Avenue brigade entered. A stream of large English prams, with pure silk initialed blanket covers concealing the tiny babies inside. Nurses in stiff uniforms wheeled these sparkling carriages to nearby benches, where they gathered and talked while their tiny charges slept.

January glanced at them enviously. Those tiny bits of life . . . yet each one felt at home in this park. They belonged in this city. Each one had an identity, a name, a home.

She walked with no real direction and found herself heading toward the wishing hill. It was such a small hill. But it had seemed like a mountain when she was little. When she was five she had climbed to the top of it triumphantly, and her father had raised her arm in victory and said, "Now this is your own hill. Close your eyes and make any wish . . . and it will come true." She had silently wished for a doll. Then he took her to Rumpelmayer's for hot chocolate, and as they were leaving he bought her the biggest doll in the place. From that moment on it became the wishing hill.

But now the hill seemed so bare and ugly. She kicked through dead leaves as she walked to the top. She sat down, drew her knees up to her chin, hugged them, and closed her eyes. Oddly enough it seemed as if the sounds of life around her were suddenly intensified—the noise of the traffic below, the barking of dogs in the distance. . . . Then she heard leaves crackle, and she knew someone was approaching. All the stories of violence she had heard rushed to her. Perhaps it was someone with a knife. She didn't move. Maybe if she just kept her eyes shut it would all be over. Quickly and painlessly.

"January . . ."

Her father was standing beside her. He held out his hand and she struggled to her feet.

"This is the third time I've come back to this hill in the past half hour," he said. "I figured you'd come here." He took her arm and led her out of the park. They crossed the street and he stopped in front of the Essex House. "They make pretty good coffee here. C'mon, let's have some breakfast."

They sat in the impersonal dining room without speaking; the untouched eggs before them. Suddenly he said, "Okay. Yell, get mad . . . but say something."

She started to speak, but the maitre d' appeared and asked if anything was wrong with the eggs.

"No. We weren't hungry," Mike said. "Take them away and just leave the pot of coffee." He waited until the waiter left, then turned to her. "Why the park? My God, why? You could have been killed."

"I couldn't sleep," she said.

"Who could! Even Dee had to take an extra sleeping pill. But no one goes walking around New York at dawn. I sat up all night just waiting till morning. I smoked two packs of cigarettes waiting—"

"You shouldn't," she said tonelessly. "Cigarettes are bad for you."

"Look, let's not worry about my health right now. Christ,

when I found your room empty . . . I went crazy. Dee woke up just as I was calling the police. She calmed me down and said you were probably walking to think things out. That's when I got the idea of the wishing hill."

She didn't answer, and he reached out and grabbed her hand. "January, let's talk it out." When she didn't answer, he looked at her and said quietly, "Please, don't make me beg."

"I wasn't snooping or intentionally eavesdropping last night," she said.

"I know. I was just caught off guard. I was angry at myself, not you. I—" He hesitated and lit another cigarette. "I wanted to write to you about Dee—"

"Oh, Mike, why didn't you?"

"Because until the very end, I didn't think I'd actually marry her. And when our seeing one another began to break in all the newspapers, I was worried it might leak to you. Thank God for Dr. Peterson and his rules about keeping the world locked out. Because this was something I felt I had to tell you in person. I had intended to tell you on the ride back from the airport. But when you said you had waited so long, that you wanted to be with me alone, well, Christ, I felt you rated having your first night the way you planned it. So I made the phone call and told Dee she had to get out. I figured I'd tell you at breakfast today."

"When did you fall in love with her?"

"Who's talking about love?" He looked directly at her. "Look, for the record, the only broad I ever loved in my whole life—or ever will love—is you!"

"Then why? *Why?*

"Because I was tapped out. Through!"

"What are you talking about?"

"Through. Finished. After three years of straight flops, I couldn't raise a dime for even an Off Broadway show. On the Coast they treated me like I had some communicable disease. And then the Clinique gave me the great news. They were releasing you in September. Jesus, here was the moment we had both lived for . . . and I was wiped out. Know where I was when I got the great news? Shacked up with Tina St. Claire on the Coast."

"You used her in a picture once."

"Yeah, I used her when she was seventeen. No talent, but beautiful. She still has no talent, but she's on a television series that's in the top ten and will keep going for a long time. She's got a big house filled with servants and hangers-on. That was me—prize hanger-on number one. Why not? She had a nice house, a well-stocked bar, and all I had to do was accommodate Tina." He paused. "This is a lousy way for a father to talk to a daughter, but there's no time for a dress rehearsal. I've got to give you the script . . . cold." He stabbed out his cigarette. "Okay, so there I was at the pool at Tina's, sopping up the sun like a beach boy. A Chinese houseman to bring me drinks, a sauna to relax in. I've got everything any man can want except cash. It's July. And I get the news that you can leave by September. And like I said, I'm just sitting there getting a tan and wondering what to do. And wham! That night, I get the idea from Tina. We're at an opening. The old klieg light bit doesn't mean a thing anymore, but they make the effort once in a while, and like a jackass I'm walking down that red carpet with her—as *her* escort—and as she snuggles in the seat next to me, she starts telling me how she wouldn't know what to do if I ever left. She kept rambling on about how hard men were to find, that she hadn't had sex for a month until I arrived. Then suddenly she says, 'We look so great together and I have enough money for both of us. How about getting married? Then at least I'll be sure of having someone to take me to next year's Emmy Awards.'"

He looked past his daughter. "I realized at that moment that I was at the bottom of the barrel. She was only in her late twenties and she wanted to keep me. I began to feel like the movie *Sunset Boulevard* in reverse. The next day I took my usual spot at the pool and tried to find the answers. I decided if I was gonna be kept it wasn't going to be for meals and a swimming pool from a Tina St. Claire. If this was the last port of call, at least I'd go down first class. So I began to think. Barbara Hutton was married. Doris Duke I didn't know about. The Baroness de Fallon was a beast . . . And then I thought of Deirdre Milford Granger. We had met once when I was riding high and she had been good-looking in a faded way." He stopped. "Nice story, huh? But at least I'm giving it to you straight. Not the 'I-met-this-broad-and-fell-madly-in-love-and-I'm-giving-up-my-career-just-to-make-her-happy' jazz. Oh, no . . . I made her a project. I learned she was in Marbella. I sold everything I owned. My car . . . the Patek Philippe watches . . . the last of the IBM stock. All together it gave me forty-three thousand bucks. It was a big roll of the dice and I was putting it all on the line. I went to Marbella to court the lady . . ." He frowned at the memory.

"I didn't know that after our first date she had a Dun and Bradstreet on me. She sat back and played it cool while I handed out twenty-buck tips to captains . . . picked up eight-hundred-dollar tabs for groups of her friends in nightclubs. Three weeks of this and I couldn't even get close enough to kiss her goodnight, let alone even have dinner for two by candlelight. No, we traveled in packs. During the day I mixed drinks for everyone and watched her play backgammon. Then just as I was beginning to get flop sweat, I arrived at her villa at cocktail time, expecting to find the usual crowd, but she was alone. She handed me a drink and said, 'Mike, I think you'd better get around to asking me to marry you because you only have twenty-six hundred dollars to your name.'"

He smiled at January's expression. "Yep, she knew my bank balance almost to the penny. Then she said, 'But first I want you to know that I will never back any of your projects—pictures *or* plays. Now, do you still want to marry me?'"

He lit another cigarette. "Oh, it gets even better," he said with a grim attempt to smile. "Once the lady let me know how much she despised show business and everything it stood for, I naturally came up with all the stock lines, like 'Look, Dee, maybe that was what I had in mind when it started, but now I've really fallen for you and I wish I had three hits running on Broadway now because then I could ask you to marry me.'" He paused. "Does it make you sick? Because it does me . . . just in repeating it."

"Go on," January said. "Did she believe you?"

"Well, at least she didn't stick to the script and simper and go coy. Oh, she's nothing if not original. She smiled and said, 'Well, Mr. Mike Wayne, if you had those three hits, you probably never would have even gotten a date with me.'" He paused thoughtfully. "I don't know what it is. She has some hang-up about show business. Maybe way back she was rejected by an actor or maybe it's just snobbism, but I had to promise not to go back in show business if she'd marry me. So there I sat, with her calling the shots. Before I accepted I told her about you. But of course she already knew all about that too. I explained that your future was the most important thing. And when she agreed, that was it!"

"Where was the wedding?" she asked.

"We got married the end of August, quietly and secretly in London. But the news got out and then the parties in our honor began. Suddenly *Sunset Boulevard* turned into a Fellini movie. Contessas, semi-royalty, top international models, a few real princesses thrown in. It's a world where the women are all thin, gorgeous, and titless, the men have no asses, and English is everyone's second language. She runs with that crowd in New York, too. No one plays golf; tennis is the *in* game and gin rummy is for peasants. Backgammon is their game." He sighed. "Okay, that's the whole ballgame. Any questions?"

"Just one. Do we both stand in line every Friday and get our allowances?"

Their eyes met and he said, "Where did you learn to hit so hard?"

She fought back tears but held her gaze. "Well, it's true, isn't it? Dee supports you—as you said—in style."

"Real style, honey." His voice was hard. "But she does it with class. She's made me a director of one of her companies. Sure, it's just a title. What in hell do I know about real estate or oil tankers? But I sign things once a week; and everyone in my office acts like I'm needed." He smiled. "Every man needs an office to go to. You'd be surprised how it breaks up the day. I go there and close the door so my secretary will think I'm busy. Then I read the trades. Wednesday is the big day—*Variety* comes out, so that takes up the whole morning. Then I stop down at the brokerage office in the same building, have a shoe-shine, and on to the Friars Club for lunch and a game of gin. And I get a salary too—one thousand a week. I used to spend more than that on tips—but it's a great life. I've got the New York apartment, the houses, a chauffeur . . . I've got everything any man would want."

"Stop it," she moaned. "Oh God, stop it! I'm sorry for what I said. I know you did it for me." She felt her throat close with tears but she forced herself to go on. "Couldn't we have gotten a small apartment somewhere? Maybe I could have gotten a job."

"Doing what?"

"Acting maybe, or even working for a producer . . . reading scripts."

He shook his head. "The whole business has changed. Some of the top playwrights refuse to write for the theater now. Why should they? Work their asses off for two years and have a guy on the *Times* close it in one night. Sure there's Neil Simon who rarely misses; but even stars stand in line to get into one of his plays. Then there's Off Broadway . . . and even Off Off Broadway. But that's another civilization. I know nothing about it. And it's not what I want for you."

"What do you want for me?" she asked quietly.

"To hand you the world."

"And by marrying Deirdre Granger do you think you've given me that?"

"At least I'm handing you a bright new world. A world where people talk about something else besides theater or box-office grosses. Look, for you, show business can be like a great dessert. Something you enjoy maybe a few evenings a week. But it shouldn't be your whole life. Besides, you saw it as Mike Wayne's daughter. When you went backstage you only saw the star's dressing room. Never the drafty ones on the third floor in Baltimore or Philadelphia. You saw success, baby. The bright side of the moon. It's only normal for you to think that it's your world. What other world have I ever given you?"

"But why should I want another world? You loved show business. I know you did."

"Nah, I loved the horses just as much. I loved the gamble of doing a show or a picture. I loved the money, the fame the broads. Look, you don't think I took you to the theater every Saturday because I loved it, do you? Hell, I took you there because I didn't know what else to do with you. Now don't get angry," he said as he saw the color come to her face. "But what does a man do with a little girl every weekend? I had no real social life. Only broads who I shacked up with. Some of them were divorcées with kids your age who called me Uncle Daddy. That would have made a big hit with you, right? Jesus, it's a wonder you turned out as perfect as you did. Because I sure as hell gave you nothing. But that's all changed now. At least I can give you a chance at another kind of life. All I ask is that you try it this way."

"And what is this way?"

"See how other people live. Meet Dee's friends. Give it a shot. If you don't, then I've struck out all around."

She managed a smile. "Of course I'll try."

"And try to give Dee a chance, too. She's a great broad. I don't know what she ever wanted with me."

"The same thing Tina St. Claire wanted," January said. "And Melba Delitto . . . and probably every girl you meet."

He shook his head. "Sex isn't all that important to Dee." He looked thoughtful. "I get the feeling that she wants something more than that with me. Companionship maybe . . . a togetherness . . . to be part of a team. I don't know too much about that kind of life. But please give Dee a chance. If you could see all the trouble she went to arranging tonight's dinner party. And she's invited her cousin, David Milford, as your escort."

"Is David Milford also one of the six richest people in the world?"

"No. Dee's father had all the big money. And—"

"And he died when Dee was ten," January chanted. "And six months later Dee's beautiful young mother committed suicide because of his death. Oh, Daddy, at Miss Haddon's we all read about Dee's life story every time she got married. The magazines called her 'The Lonely Little Princess' always seeking happiness." She stopped. "That sounds bitchy, and I didn't mean it that way. It's just that I may have been out of touch with the world during the past three years, but at Miss Haddon's Deirdre Milford Granger was like an institution. Some of the girls had mothers who knew someone who knew her. I grew up knowing everything about her—except that one day my father would marry her."

He was silent and waved to the waiter for the check. She tried to smile. "Mike, I'm sorry." She made her voice soft and traced his fingers with her fingertips. "Come on, tell me about David. Have you met him?"

"Several times," he said slowly. "He's good-looking. In his late twenties. Dee never had any children. Her mother and David's father were brother and sister. The Milfords have no real money. Oh, they live well. In fact, they do very well." He paid the check. "He works at a brokerage house. He handles Dee's accounts. His father is a lawyer with his own firm and David is Dee's principal heir and—"

"Wow," January said softly. "You really made a package deal. A girl for you . . . a boy for me . . ."

His eyes flashed. "Boy, you sure as hell are my daughter. Always a direct hit. But first . . . I haven't got David lined up for you. I think David has his own idea of who *he* wants to marry. But I'd be a goddamned liar if I didn't admit that through Dee I hope you meet someone with class. David probably has a lot of friends. He'll introduce you around. In that way maybe you'll meet someone you really like, someone you'll eventually marry. I'd love to have a grandchild, maybe two . . . three. Sure, I'd like it. But I'll tell you what I wouldn't like—to have you wind up a female version of me."

"That's too bad." she said softly. "Because that's exactly what I am. And what's more, I planned it that way."

"Why?" His voice was almost a snarl. "What kind of a model am I? I've never given a woman a fair shake in my life. But I'm gonna play it straight with Dee. It's about time I started paying my dues. And between you and me, I owe plenty."

She was silent for a moment. When she spoke she looked off into space. "But my dues are paid in full. Maybe I could have brought us some luck. We could have tried it together." Then she smiled. "But that's in the past. I'm sure I'll like David Milford and I'll do my best to charm him so he'll introduce me to all his fancy friends. So the first thing I'd better do is buy something dreamy to wear tonight." She stopped suddenly.

"Don't worry. That's all arranged. No, not what you think." He dug into his pocket and took out a card. "Here, go to this bank and ask for a Miss Anna Cole. You'll have to sign some things. There's money in trust for you. You can open a checking account right away."

"Mike, I don't–"

"It's not Dee's money," he snapped. "When your mother died, she left a small insurance policy–fifteen thousand dollars. I stuck it in trust for you. Thank God I did . . . or I would have gone through that, too. With the interest and all, there should be close to twenty-two or twenty-three thousand bucks waiting for you. Now go buy out Bonwit's and Saks."

They walked down the street and stopped in front of the Pierre. Subconsciously they both looked up half expecting to see Dee at the window. Mike laughed. "She took another sleeping pill when I left. Besides, she rarely gets up before noon. Oh . . . here's a key to the suite. You're registered, so always check at the desk for your messages."

She laughed. "Mike, you're the only person I know in New York. So maybe you ought to leave me a message–"

"I don't have to. I think you got it." Then he turned and walked into the building.

Three

SHE WAS EXHAUSTED when she returned to the Pierre. It was almost four o'clock and she was carrying only one large box. And it hadn't been easy to decide on that! She didn't know *what* to wear to a dinner party with Dee. At Bergdorf's, a saleslady told her *midi* skirts were *in* and *mini* skirts were *out*. But at noon, as girls poured out of office buildings on their lunch breaks, Fifth Avenue became flooded with minis and *micro minis*. On Lexington Avenue she saw Indian headbands, blue jeans, knickers, and long granny skirts. It was like a costume parade. She finally settled on the long patchwork skirt and red jersey blouse she saw on the mannequin in Bloomingdale's window. The saleslady assured her it would fit any occasion.

When she walked into the hotel she stopped at the desk on a whim and asked if there were any messages. To her amazement the clerk handed her two slips of paper. Balancing the box under her chin and one arm, she studied them as she rang for the elevator. One had come at three, the other at three-thirty. Both asked her to call the same Plaza number and ask for Extension 36. She looked at the name on the message form. It was for her, all right. Suddenly she smiled. Of course . . . the Plaza number was probably Mike's office.

When she came into the apartment, a maid was dusting some little jade elephants on the mantel. In the daylight the apartment looked even more beautiful. The sunlight mirrored itself on the silver frames that covered the top of the piano. There were so many pictures. She recognized a United States Senator,

Nureyev, an Ambassador, and the remarkable face of Karla. She walked over and studied the childish scrawl in faded ink. "To Deirdre . . . Karla." January stared at the high cheekbones, the fantastic eyes. The maid came over. "There are three princes on the left. And a Rajah."

January nodded. "I was looking at Karla."

"Yes, she's very beautiful," the maid said. "Oh, by the way, I'm Sadie. And I'm glad to meet you, Miss January."

January smiled. The woman was in her mid-sixties and looked Scandinavian. Her light faded hair was pulled into a tiny skimpy knot and her face was clean and shiny. She looked spare, bony and strong. "Miss Deirdre told me to hang your things. I took the liberty of rearranging your drawer space. When do your trunks arrive?"

"They don't," January said. "There's just what you saw. And now this new outfit from Bloomingdale's."

"I'll press it out. Miss Deirdre is out now, but if you want anything, there is a button beside your bed. It connects with the kitchen and my bedroom out back. I'll hear it wherever I am. And I didn't know if you smoked, but I put cigarettes in all the boxes in your room. If you prefer a certain brand, let me know."

"Thank you, no. I think I'll take a bath and rest."

"Be sure and ring if you need anything. I also left all the latest fashion magazines in your room. Miss Deirdre thought you might like them. She said something about you had a lot of catching up to do." Then Sadie took the Bloomingdale box and left the room. In less than a second she had popped back. "And Ernest comes at six if you need him."

"Ernest?"

"Miss Deirdre's hairdresser . . . every night at six."

January suddenly remembered the phone messages she was holding. She went into her bedroom, flopped on the bed and gave the number to the operator. After three rings a switchboard operator answered. January dutifully asked for Extension 36.

There was a pause . . . a click . . . another voice. "Miss Riggs' office."

"Who?" January sat up.

"Who are you?" The voice was annoyed.

"I'm January Wayne. And who is Miss Riggs?"

"Oh, I'm Miss Riggs' secretary. One moment, Miss Wayne. We called you. I'll connect you." There was some more clicking. Then a voice drawled, "January, is that really you?" It was a sleek voice, aristocratic, smooth and cool.

January tried to place it. "Who is this?" she asked.

"Good God, January. It's me . . . Linda. Linda Riggs!"

"Linda . . . you mean from Miss Haddon's?"

"Of course. You think there's another?"

"Oh, wow! Well, it's been so long. How are you, Linda? How did you find me? And what've you been doing?"

Linda laughed. "I should ask you that. But first things first. Why was your father so snotty to Keith Winters?"

"Keith?"

"Keith Winters . . . the photographer . . ."

"Oh, you mean last night?" (Good Lord, was it *just* last night?)

"Yes, I sent him down to get a picture of you for our magazine."

"What magazine?"

There was a slight pause. Then in a voice tinged with annoyance, Linda said, "Well, I am editor-in-chief of *Gloss*, you know, and—"

"Editor-in-chief!"

"January, where on earth have you been? I was a smash on the Mike Douglas show last month. And I've been asked to do the Merv Griffin show the next time I'm on the Coast."

"Oh, well. I've been in Europe and—"

"But everyone knows what I've done for *Gloss* magazine. I'm one of the youngest and most famous editors-in-chief in the world. Of course, I'm not Helen Gurley Brown. But then *Gloss* is no *Cosmopolitan*. But give me time. I'm going to make this magazine the biggest thing going."

"That's marvelous, Linda. I remember after you left Miss Haddon's. I was about ten. And we all went crazy when we saw you were a . . . a . . ."

"Junior editor," Linda finished the sentence for her. "It might have looked impressive to everyone at Miss Haddon's, but it was just a fancy label for slave. My God, I ran all over town sixteen hours a day. Tracking down jewelry for fashion layouts . . . getting coffee for photographers and models . . . running errands for people in the art department . . . returning an earring left by a fashion director—all this for seventy-five dollars a week. But at eighteen it seemed like a lark. I'd get four hours' sleep and still manage to get to Le Club every night and dance. God, I'm weary just thinking about it now. Incidentally . . . how old are you?"

"I'll be twenty-one in January."

"That's right. I'm twenty-eight. Funny how it evens out now. The age thing. When I was sixteen and you were about eight, I didn't think you were even human. I mean, as I recall, you were one of the moppets who followed me around at Miss Haddon's, weren't you?"

"I suppose so." January saw no reason to tell her she had never been a "Linda follower."

"That's why I sent Keith Winters to the Pierre. Celebrity Service had it that you were arriving from Europe and I thought I'd run a picture of you and Daddy in *Gloss* along with a cute story about Daddy's young lady meeting Daddy's new lady. Your father was a real horror to Keith, but the picture turned out fine. Either you're very photogenic or you've turned into a real tearing beauty. Listen, why not pop in tomorrow . . . say about three-ish. I'll dream up some kind of story and we'll take some good pictures."

"I'd love to see you, Linda, but I don't know about a story."

"We'll talk about it tomorrow. You know where the Mosler building is, don't you? Fifty-second, near Madison. We have the entire top three floors. Come to the executive penthouse. See you then. *Ciao.*"

January ran the bath and got into the tub and closed her eyes. She hadn't realized how tired she was. She thought about Linda—so ugly, so eager, so energetic . . . And now she was . . . well, she sounded important. January felt so tired. She knew she was falling asleep. It seemed just seconds later when she heard Sadie whisper, "Miss January, wake up."

She sat up. The water was tepid. Good Lord, it was six o'clock!

"Miss Deirdre says it's time for you to dress for dinner," Sadie explained. "I pressed your dress. It's hanging in the bedroom closet."

She was dressed when Dee knocked on her door and swept into the bedroom. For a moment they both stared at one another. Then, self-consciously, January held out her hand. "Congratulations. I'm afraid I forgot to say that last night."

Dee pressed her cheek against January's cheek. "I don't think either of us said too much last night. It wasn't exactly the best way to become acquainted."

"I–oh, good Lord . . ."

"What's wrong?" Dee asked.

"I forgot to buy a robe!"

Dee laughed. "Keep Mike's. It looked marvelous on you. Some women look fabulous in men's robes. I'm not one of them."

January decided Dee was more attractive than she had originally thought. Tonight she wore the frosted hair in a Gibson-girl style. And January knew the globs of diamonds on Dee's ears were real. She looked very feminine in black silk harem pants, and January suddenly wondered if the patchwork skirt was right.

Dee stood back and appraised her. "I like it . . . but I think we need a bit of jewelry." She buzzed Sadie who appeared instantly. "Get my box of gold jewelry, Sadie."

Sadie returned with a huge leather jewel case, and Dee began draping gold chains around January's neck. She insisted January wear gold hoop earrings. ("Darling, with your tan it's perfect . . . gives you a gypsy effect.")

January felt weighted down with four chains, a jade figa, and a lion's tooth set in gold. (Dee explained she had shot the lion herself on a safari).

"I like your makeup," Dee said as she came up close. "They're your own lashes. Fan*tas*tic! I love that no-lipstick look you young girls affect. And your hair . . . well, it's marvelous. Today you young things have it made, wearing it just long and straight. When I was your age, I was all clipped and permanented for the bloody Italian cut. That was the rage in the early fifties. I always told Gina I could kill her for starting that style. I have straight hair, and it seems to me I've spent half my life in rollers under driers. And now that long straight hair is in . . . well, one really can't wear it hanging down to her shoulders after thirty-five. At least I don't think one should

. . . although God knows Karla hasn't changed her hair style since she was eighteen."

"What is she like?"

Dee shrugged. "Karla is one of my oldest and dearest friends . . . although God knows why I put up with her eccentricities."

"At Miss Haddon's," January said, "we all watched her movies on television. To me she is even greater than Garbo or Dietrich because she moves like a dancer. Imagine having the guts to retire at forty-two and stay retired."

Dee reached over and lit a cigarette. "She never cared about acting. She always said that as soon as she made enough money she would quit. And she's got the first dime she ever made!"

"Where is she now?" January asked.

"I believe she's back in town. She'll get around to calling soon. She keeps an apartment at the East River View. Marvelous building, but aside from a few good paintings that were gifts and some good rugs—also gifts—the apartment is barely furnished. Karla has a sickness about spending money. She was supposed to come to Marbella. Your father was so disappointed . . . I know he wanted to meet her. Good Lord, until this summer she was always around. Last spring poor David was stuck taking both of us around. Not that she gads about, but she adores the ballet. Other than that, Karla still sticks to her old movie routine—up at seven, four hours of ballet exercises, long walks, bed at ten. But she will go to dinner with a close friend and she adores watching television. Actually, she's quite dreary once you get to know her. And then there's her disappearing act. She does that. Like last June—she just goes off without so much as an 'I'll see you.' Personally"—Dee lowered her voice—"I think she went off to have her face done. She was just beginning to sag a bit . . . and God forbid anything happened to hurt that Polish bone structure that is now so immortal."

January laughed. "Now I'm really nervous about meeting David."

"Good Lord, why?"

"Well, if David felt 'stuck' taking Karla around as a favor to you, then taking me out must be the Big Daddy of all favors."

Dee smiled. "You darling child. Look in the mirror. Karla is over fifty and David is twenty-eight." She put out her cigarette. "And now it's time I checked on your father. If I know him he's watching the news and still hasn't shaved. Why do men hate shaving twice a day? Women put on makeup at least that many times. Oh, by the way, I've told everyone, including David, that you've been away at school in Switzerland at the Institut International. It's an excellent college."

"But why?"

"You do speak French, don't you?"

"Yes, but—"

"My dear, trust me. There's just no point in bringing up the accident. Why have anyone think you might have brain damage? And some people get sticky the moment they hear one has been at a sanitarium. Now we want you to meet the right people and have a wonderful life . . . so we mustn't handicap ourself with a past illness."

"But a brain concussion and broken bones isn't an illness—"

"My dear, anything with the brain throws people off. I remember Kurt . . . I almost married him until he told me he had a steel plate in his head from a skiing accident." She shuddered. "I just couldn't bear the thought of touching a man's head with steel in it. There was something Frankensteinish about the whole thing. Besides, if one has a piece of steel against one's brain . . . well, it stands to reason the pressure *must* do something. Do it my way, dear. Now then . . . I've asked David to come twenty minutes before the others. You stay in your room until he arrives. I'll give you the signal when to come out. One must always make an entrance." She started for the door and turned. "You'll fall in love with David. Every woman does. Even Karla found him a little more than entertaining; and Karla's not capable of falling in love with anyone. So don't let his good looks throw you. Just play it cool and pour on the charm. I'm sure you have some. After all, your father has almost too much." She opened the door, and stopped just as January was about to sink on the edge of the bed. "No . . . no. Mustn't sit. You'll crease your skirt. One must be perfect for an entrance. Now I must dash. Ernest is waiting to put the final spray to my hair. You just stay here . . . until it's time to meet David."

Four

At six-thirty, David Milford rushed to his apartment to change his clothes. He jammed in the plug of his electric razor. Goddammit but he hated Dee! But anything Cousin Deirdre wanted—Cousin Deirdre got! The acceptance of her autonomy had come into full cognizance with his promotion to a vice-presidency at Herbert, Chasin and Arthur. In a down market, with most brokerage houses cutting back—*he* had been promoted. And his future with the firm was assured—just so long as he handled Dee's stocks. Damn Dee! And damn his father for not having his own fortune. No, he didn't mean that. After all, the old man worked hard, made close to a hundred and fifty thousand a year. But with his mother insisting on the ten-room Fifth Avenue co-op, three in help, and the house in Southampton . . . well, there certainly wasn't going to be anything left for him to inherit. But then no one was expected to amass a fortune; because Cousin Dee had enough for them all.

Her marriage to Mike Wayne had thrown them into shock. His mother went into one of her major traumas—three days of Librium and tears. Dee's past husbands had never been a threat. They had all been of the same cut. Charming, well-bred lightweights. But Mike Wayne was no lightweight. And his past record indicated that his romantic affiliations had always been with girls half Dee's age. But their major concern was the absence of the "will ritual." His father handled that end of her business. Dee had what the family jokingly referred to as the "loose-leaf will." Before every marriage, she and her "husband-to-be" would arrive at his father's office, and Dee would dictate a new will with a generous inheritance for her new groom. On the day of the wedding, a signed copy was presented to him. The following day, Dee would return to the office alone, draw up a new will, allotting a nominal sum to the new husband *if* he was still her husband at the time of her death.

She had been married to Mike almost a month. And Mike's name hadn't been entered in the loose-leaf will. As it now stood, he and his father and Cliff (his mother's younger brother, who was also in the law firm) would serve as executors of her estate. Each of them would wind up with several million on that end alone. The bulk of the estate would go to the Granger Foundation, and he would be designated to officiate as president at a salary of one hundred thousand a year.

Of course, Dee was still very much alive, and fifty was not old. But Dee's prospects for a golden age didn't seem very likely. For years the newspapers had given extensive coverage to her consistent bouts of illnesses. First there were the fainting attacks which medical tests diagnosed as an organic heart murmur and chronic high blood pressure (but Dee refused to give up the strong diet pills and reveled in her high-fashion gauntness). There were also several operations . . . female stuff. And the "influenza" that had almost killed her a few years ago (that had really been an overdose of sleeping pills over some mysterious love affair). Odd, he had never thought Dee capable of feeling any desperate emotion. But why not? He had never thought he could ever feel any real emotion either.

He pulled out the plug of the razor and slapped some after-shave lotion on his face. Might as well look at the cheerful side. So far as the will was concerned—maybe Mike wasn't playing the super-operator, maybe he was really in love with Dee. Maybe he didn't care about her money. Hell, there was enough for everyone as long as Wayne didn't get greedy. But why did he have to have a daughter to complicate things! No one knew she even existed until a week ago when Dee's call came. "David, darling. Mike has this divine daughter who is arriving any day. You've got to help me out and take her around. It would please me to know she was taken care of by someone *I* care about. I'd consider it *such* a favor."

Favor? It was a command!

And once again he swore softly. Goddammit but he hated Dee. But hell, he hated everything and everyone these days. Everything and everyone who kept him away from Karla.

Karla! For a moment he stood and stared at himself in the mirror. It didn't seem possible. He, David Milford, was Karla's lover! He wanted to shout it to the world, to stop people on the street and tell them. But he knew that absolute silence was the major law in his relationship with Karla.

Karla! At fourteen, he had masturbated with her picture propped up before him. His friends had their school lockers loaded with pinups of Doris Day, Marilyn, Ava, and other glamor girls of the fifties. But with him it had always been Karla. At seventeen, the first girl he had gone to bed with was a horse-faced debutante who had hair like Karla's. In the years that followed he often found a girl who had a quality that was reminiscent of Karla. But as he matured he accepted each girl on her own individual charm, and the image of Karla receded into some kind of mystic dream.

And then, eight years ago, he had come across a newspaper picture of Karla on Dee's yacht. He had immediately written Dee an impassioned letter pleading for an introduction. She had ignored it. But he never failed to renew the request every time he saw Dee. And then, last spring, when he had all but given up, Dee had casually said, "Oh, by the way, David, Karla is in town. Would you care to take us to the ballet?"

He had been like an idiot that first night. He hadn't done any work at the office all day. He had rushed home and changed suits three times before he decided which one would be proper. And then . . . Dee's casual introduction . . . Karla's firm handshake . . . he knew he had stood there just staring at that wonderful face . . . listening to the low voice he had heard so often on the screen. He had moved about in a catatonic state that night, unable to comprehend that he was actually sitting beside her, unable to concentrate on the ballet on the stage, unable to believe the casual way Dee behaved in the presence of this magnificent woman. But then, when you had Dee's kind of money maybe nothing really turned you on. To Dee, even Karla was just another "fun" person, a name to encase in a silver frame to join the exclusive gallery on the piano.

The day after the ballet he had sent Karla three dozen roses. His office number was on his card, but he also added his unlisted apartment number. She called just as he was leaving the office. The cool low voice thanked him but told him firmly never to do that again as she was allergic to flowers. She had already sent them off with her maid. When he began to stutter, she laughed and said, "But in return, I will give you a drink. Come to my apartment this afternoon at five."

He was shaking like a schoolboy when he rang her bell.

She opened the door herself and greeted him with outstretched hands. "My so very young admirer. Come in. Come in. And please do not be so nervous, because I want you to make love to me."

She had led him into the apartment as she spoke. His eyes never left her face. But he was aware of an empty spaciousness to the room. A few paintings, a TV set, a large couch, a woodburning fireplace that looked as if it had never been used, a staircase that obviously led to a second floor—but most of all, he felt no reflection of Karla's personality in the apartment. It was almost as if she had "borrowed" it. For a moment they looked at one another. Then she held out her arms and the schoolboy vanished. And when their bodies came together, David suddenly knew the difference between sex and making love. On that late spring afternoon, his one wish was to please her . . . and when he did, oddly enough his own gratification seemed intensified.

It was later when they were lying together that she gave him the rules. "Dee must never know. If you want to go on seeing me, *no one* must know." He agreed. He held her close and poured out devotion and promises. And he heard himself say, "Any way you want it, Karla. You see, I'm in love with you."

Her sigh was tremulous. "I am fifty-two. Too old for love . . . and much too old for you."

"I'm twenty-eight. That's not exactly a boy."

She laughed. "Twenty-eight, and so very handsome." She

stroked his cheek. "A very young twenty-eight. But . . . perhaps we can be happy for a time. That is, if you behave."

"How do you want me to behave?"

"I have told you. Also, you must promise never to try to reach me. I shall not give you my phone number and you must never come here unless I invite you."

"Then how do I see you?"

"I will call you when I want you. And you must not speak of love. You must not imagine yourself in love with me or you will be very unhappy."

He smiled. "I'm afraid that happened when I was fourteen . . ." He stopped. Goddammit, that was wrong, showing the disparity of their ages. But she had smiled.

"You love the Karla you saw in movies; you do not know the real Karla."

He had held her close and knew a strange excitement as he felt her small flat breasts against his body. He liked breasts. But oddly enough it hadn't bothered him that she had none. Her body was strong and firm. A dancer's body. He had read stories about her early training in Poland for the ballet—how she had been forced to escape to London during the war and went directly into pictures as an actress. How she still worked out on the bar four hours a day. She had changed studios many times because of photographers who learned the address and waited to catch her. He had also heard that she had been a lesbian during her early days in Hollywood. All these thoughts came to him as he held her in his arms. But these stories were part of the legend . . . the woman of mystery . . . the woman photographers still chased everywhere. But at that moment she seemed to belong to him completely . . . her ardor and passion were young . . . she clung to him when they made love. Yet when it was over, a curtain came down, and Karla, the legend, returned.

That had been last spring. They had spent a fantastic month together. A month in which he wandered around feeling everything was unreal except his meetings with Karla. A month when he awoke each day not really believing this miracle was happening to him. But there was always the frustration of not being able to call, of having a sandwich sent in at lunch for fear of missing her call, of walking through all work and conversation until the call finally came.

And then one day there was no call. He tried not to panic. Perhaps she didn't feel well. Maybe she had the curse. Hell, did women of fifty-two still get the curse?

The following day there were the familiar pictures in the newspaper. Karla ducking photographers at Kennedy Airport. She was off to Europe, destination unknown. He had tried to check her plane reservations, but it was obvious she had used another name. One enterprising reporter claimed a ticket agent thought she was going to South America. But it was all just speculation. She was gone. That was all he knew.

He had tried to sound casual when he phoned Dee that night. He had talked about stocks, the weather, about her plans for Marbella . . . And when he finally managed to bring up Karla's disappearance, Dee had laughed. "Oh, dear boy, she always does that. Karla refuses to have roots. That's why her apartment is hardly furnished. If it were too comfortable, she might feel she actually lives there."

"Has she always been like this?"

Dee sounded bored. "Always. I met Karla in California at the height of her fame. I was married to Emery then, and his book had just been bought by Karla's studio. Naturally, Emery was frantic to meet her—most people still are—but you can imagine what it was like then. Well, Emery knew a director who knew Karla, and one great day—for Emery, that is—Karla actually appeared at a Sunday brunch. That was about 1954. Karla was at the peak of her fame and beauty. I must say she did generate a certain magnetism when she entered that room. She was painfully shy . . ." Dee laughed and he realized she was warming to the subject. "But she gravitated to me that day because she has an animal cunning and she knew I was the only one in that room that wasn't impressed and it amused her. I was nice to her for Emery's sake. And she actually invited us to her place for a drink the following week." Dee sighed. "Talk about Falcon's Lair. This was it. Not in the chic part of Beverly Hills, but way up in some godforsaken hills, surrounded by a twelve-foot stone wall she had had built. The house was barely furnished. It looked as if she had just moved in. I swear there were still crates in the halls, and she had lived there five years. No one ever saw the rest of the house, but I understand that aside from the living room and bedroom, it was empty. She didn't do Emery's picture, and years later after I had divorced Emery and Karla had retired, we met and became friends. But one must take Karla as she is. The key to her personality is the three S's. Secretive, stingy, and stupid! Once you realize that—you understand Karla."

Dee had gone off to Marbella and he had tried to put Karla out of his mind. He had gone back to the models he had been dating. He got involved with Kim Voren, a gorgeous Dutch model who adored him but told him he was an unsatisfactory, selfish lover. That had rattled him. He had always been a good lover. But with Karla on his mind . . . perhaps something was missing in his lovemaking. On top of this came the explosive news of Dee's marriage, which threw the family into panic and jolted him back to reality. Dee was their security. Karla was gone, and he had to get back to the business of everyday living.

He gave his full attention to his work. He turned on the charm for Kim, and within a few days she exuberantly retracted her opinion of his lovemaking. And as he settled into his normal routine he almost appreciated the security of knowing what each day would bring. No wild highs . . . but also no agonizing lows. No sitting and waiting for the private phone in his office to ring.

And then, eight days ago, it rang again. Right in the middle of an active trading session. The low voice . . . the heavy accent. She was back! Ten minutes later he was ringing the bell of her apartment. When she greeted him he had not been able to conceal his amazement. It was as if she had stepped out of one of her old movies. She looked barely thirty. The magnificent face had no lines . . . the skin was taut across the cheekbones. She had laughed as she grasped his hands. "I am not going to tell you Karla had a long rest," she said. "I will tell you the truth. I was so tired of my face not matching the firmness of my body. So I had something done. A wonderful man in Brazil. . . ."

She had not called Dee and she told him to keep her arrival

secret. "I am not up to Dee's questions about my face. Or her gossip with her friends."

And now it was as if she had never left. They saw each other every day. He would either go to her apartment at five, or they would meet and go to a ballet picture or a foreign movie. Then they would return to her apartment and make love. Afterward they would go to her kitchen and watch television as they ate the steaks they cooked together. Karla had no servants—she hated strangers to be around her. A maid came in every few days at nine, and left at noon.

She also adored television. She had a set in every room. She wasn't interested in the news . . . she hated the war . . . pictures of it made her shudder. David realized she had lived through World War II in an occupied country. She refused to talk about it and he never pressed it. He was not eager to remind her that in 1939, when Poland was occupied, he had not even been born.

He finished dressing and looked at his watch. Six forty-five. He walked into the living room and mixed himself a short martini. In less than an hour he had to be at Dee's to meet this stepdaughter she had inherited. Dee hadn't sprung this dinner engagement on him until yesterday. And when he told Karla about it last night, she had smiled and said she understood. "Do not be upset. I shall invite an old friend over to eat your steak tomorrow."

She hadn't called today. Because she had no reason to call. She had told him to come by at the usual time tomorrow. If only he could call her now. This was the most frustrating part of their relationship. How could he play the man if he had to sit like a love-sick girl and wait for her to call the shots? He sat back and sipped his drink. He felt oddly unsettled. He wasn't quite sure what bothered him the most—the idea that he wasn't going to see her tonight, or the realization that she wasn't in the least upset. And now he was racked with a frantic kind of desperation, a sensation he had never known until he met Karla. If only he could call her and tell her he missed her, that perhaps it would be an early evening and they could still be together. He swallowed his drink. It was an impossible situation, not being able to call her; she had even taken the precaution of removing the number from the dial of her phones. It robbed the affair of some of its intimacy. What intimacy? He made love to her and she enjoyed it. *He* was the one who was emotionally involved. Actually she didn't give a damn. But it didn't matter. All he lived for was to be with her, and tonight *he* had been forced to break the date because of Dee. Dee didn't know what it meant to feel like this. Goddammit but he hated Dee!

His mood was still heavy when he pressed the buzzer to Dee's apartment. Mario, who doubled as chauffeur and butler when Dee was in New York, answered the door. Mike greeted him, and Mario set about to fix him a martini.

"Dee's having her hair combed," Mike said. "One of those guys with the tight pants comes up every night." Then the door opened and Dee swept into the room. She put her cheek to Mike, who dutifully kissed it, floated over to David and told him how perfectly marvelous he was looking, and he in turn kissed her cheek and told her how marvelous she looked. Then he sat on the edge of the couch; made the proper small talk with Mike and wondered where in hell the daughter was.

He had almost finished his martini when she came into the room. He heard himself accepting the introduction, asking the stock questions—How was her trip? Did she feel the jet lag everyone talked about? But he knew he was staring like an idiot. Holy God! She was a real knockout!

He heard himself promising to take her to Le Club, to Maxwell's Plum, Daly's Dandelion—to all the places she hadn't seen. Good God, he was saying he'd get tickets for *Hair*. He lit a cigarette and wondered how he would ever manage to extricate himself from all these offers he had suddenly made. He had been talking from nerves. Well, he was plenty unnerved. He hadn't expected anything like this. He sat back and tried to think rationally. Okay, January was an exceptionally beautiful young girl. But she wasn't Karla. Yet one day Karla would pick up and leave again. He must realize that. Karla was just something insane and wonderful that was happening in his life.

Suddenly he realized he was just staring. He had to say something.

"Do you play backgammon?" he asked.

"No, but I'd like to learn," January said.

"Fine. I'd be delighted to teach you." He finished his drink. (Oh, great! Now he was going to teach her backgammon!) He'd better shut up and go easy on the martinis. He decided to keep it impersonal and began talking about the backgammon tournaments in Vegas, London, and Los Angeles. Dee was their family champ. She always did well. He heard himself explaining how the tournaments went, about the betting . . . Suddenly he stopped. He had a feeling that she really didn't give a damn about backgammon and was just listening to please him. This couldn't be happening! He was Karla's lover. And this young girl was throwing him off base. It was her incredible cool. That easy half smile that was making him run off at the mouth like an idiot.

The doorbell rang and Mario admitted two couples who had arrived together. David found himself accepting another martini. He knew he shouldn't, but the girl had a disconcerting effect on him. He watched the easy nonchalance with which she accepted the introductions. And always that quick smile . . .

He also noticed that her constant focal point was her father. Her eyes followed him wherever he moved, and occasionally they would exchange a wink as if they shared some private joke.

Dee's guests were paying January extravagant compliments. She accepted them quietly, but he could tell she wasn't impressed. Then it hit him that maybe she wasn't overly impressed with him either. This was a new experience. Like when the Dutch girl told him he wasn't great in bed. Was he allowing Karla to swallow him alive? Drain him of all of his personality? For the rest of the evening he made a concerted effort to put Karla out of his mind and concentrated on January. Yet as the evening progressed, he had the uneasy feeling that he wasn't reaching her in any way.

Actually he was having an extremely disconcerting effect on her. After Dee's "selling job" she had been prepared to dislike him on sight. Instead she found this marvelous-looking young man who didn't seem at all taken with himself. He was very tall. Ordinarily she didn't like blond men, but David's hair was dark brown and sun-streaked. He was tanned and his eyes were brown.

She liked him. She really did. And that half smile that bothered him had been the nearest thing to a mask that she could manage. The muscles of her face actually ached, trying to hold that smile as she watched Mike in the role of "Dee's husband." Because from the attitude of everyone—Dee's friends, even the waiters and maitre d' at the restaurant—she was still Deirdre Milford Granger . . . and Mike was just her newest husband.

They had gone to dinner at Raffles, a discotheque restaurant next door to the Pierre. Dee directed the seating arrangements at the large round table. Mike was wedged in between two women: a Rosa Contalba, a middle-aged Spanish lady whose escort was a young Yugoslavian artist she was sponsoring, the other woman was plain and a bit on the large side. Her diamonds were also large. And her husband was enormous. He sat to the left of January and felt it was his duty to make small talk. He went into an endless story about their ranch in Montana. At first she tried to appear interested but soon realized that an "Oh, really!" or "That's very interesting!" was all he seemed to need. There was cross-talk back and forth—summer vacations and winter plans. Rosa was going on a photographic safari to Africa. The stout woman was too tired after the season in East Hampton to even *think* of the winter yet. And everyone asked Dee when she was opening the Winter Palace in Palm Beach.

"In November. But I'll play it loose with houseguests. They'll have to understand that we're going to pop off for all the backgammon tournaments. Of course, we'll always be in residence for the holidays. January will probably come down for Thanksgiving and Christmas, but I imagine she'll spend most of her time in New York on a fun job."

Fun job? Before January could speak, the large man said, "Now Dee, don't tell me this gorgeous creature is going to work."

Dee smiled. "Stanford, you don't realize. Today the young people want to do things—"

"Oh, no," Stanford groaned. "Don't tell me she's one of those types who wants to change the world. Give the land back to the Indians, or march demanding equality for females and blacks."

"What about those religious nuts who paint their faces and shave their heads?" the large woman added. "I saw a group of them beating tom-toms and chanting. Right on Fifth Avenue in front of Doubleday's."

"They're no worse than the weird types we see on newsreels on the college campus," Rosa cut in. "And they march, too. Arms around each other . . . boys and girls . . . boys and boys . . . you can't tell the difference unless one of them has a beard."

"Oh, that reminds me"—the stout woman leaned into the table and everyone knew a choice bit of gossip was coming. "Pressy Mathews is *not* really at a spa at all. She's having a complete nervous breakdown at some sanitarium in Connecticut. It seems that this summer her daughter ran off with a Jewish boy. They bought a secondhand truck and loaded it with supplies and a big mongrel dog and traveled across the country, staying at communes. Pressy's psychiatrist told her to be permissive about it, that little Pressy would get the rebellion out of her system. But this fall little Pressy will not return to Finch. She's having a baby with this Jewish boy and they're not going to get married until *after* the baby is born because little Pressy wants the baby at the wedding. Well, you can imagine! Big Pressy just collapsed . . . they're trying to keep it a secret . . . including the sanitarium thing . . . so let's keep this among ourselves."

Then the stout man said, "Well, at least, it's not all guitars and hard rock. Look at January."

Everyone murmured that January was indeed a beauty, but then as Dee pointed out, January had studied abroad. Rosa asked her what she had majored in, and Dee quickly said, "Languages. January speaks French fluently." Then Dee launched into a story about some darling little nursery school where the wee ones were taught languages immediately. January watched her father snap to attention with his gold Dunhill lighter every time one of the women on either side of him picked up a cigarette. He was even nodding and smiling at a story the Yugoslav artist was telling. He sure was paying his dues. She watched the way he leaned his handsome head in a listening pose as the large woman rambled on and on. Once he caught her staring and their eyes met. He winked and she managed a smile. Then he went back to his work. Suddenly she heard Dee saying, "And January will love it."

January will love what? (You couldn't leave this conversation for a second.)

Dee was smiling and explaining in detail about the nursery school. "The idea is—teach the tots early. Make them bilingual. That's why Mary Ann Stokes had made such a hit out of La Petite École. Mary Ann and I went to Smith together. The poor girl got polio in her junior year. Then her family lost everything . . . and with no money and a shriveled arm . . . Well, naturally poor Mary Ann's chances of a decent marriage were nil. So when she wanted to start this school some years ago, I agreed to back her. It's practically self-supporting now."

"Oh, Dee, darling," the stout woman boomed, "you are so modest. All these years . . . I never knew you started Mary Ann. It's a divine school. My grandniece goes there."

Dee nodded. "And of course the minute I told her that French was January's second language, she leaped. After all, that's part of the premise—beautiful socialites teaching the tots. They'll adore January."

"Me teach?" January knew her voice had actually cracked.

David was watching her carefully. "When does she start?" he asked.

Dee smiled. "Well, as I told Mary Ann, it will take at least two weeks to get January's wardrobe in shape. I'd say we'll shoot for the beginning of October. Mary Ann is coming by for tea tomorrow. We'll settle it then."

The music switched from rock into standards. January looked toward Mike. Their eyes met. He gave her a slight nod and stood up. But Dee rose at the same moment. "Oh, Mike . . . and I was afraid you wouldn't remember. They're playing our song."

Mike looked slightly startled, but he managed a smile. Dee turned to the table as she led him toward the floor. " 'Three Coins in a Fountain.' They were playing it in a little restaurant in Marbella when we first met."

Everyone watched them leave. Suddenly David stood up. He tapped January on the shoulder. "Hey, I'm your date." He led her out to the floor. The crowded floor made actual dancing impossible. They moved among the other couples. David held her close and whispered, "This will be over soon, and then we'll cut out."

"I don't think I can." She glanced toward her father who was whispering into Dee's ear.

"I think you'd better," he said evenly.

He led her back to the table when the set was over. There was espresso, after-dinner drinks, more talk and somehow the evening finally ground to an end and everyone was standing up telling Dee how marvelous it had all been.

"I'm taking January for a nightcap," David said. Then he quickly thanked Dee and Mike for the evening, and before January could voice any objections, they were in a cab, heading for Le Club.

The place was jammed, the music was loud. David knew almost everyone in the room. There were several couples who were friends of his, standing at the bar. David suggested they join them. "We're not staying long, so we really don't need a table."

She accepted introductions, danced with some of his friends. Dee's chains felt like an anchor, but it seemed every girl on the dance floor wore them. Some wore twice the amount of chains, but they didn't appear cumbersome. The girls' long hair swished as they moved, and the necklaces clinked in rhythm. She was in the midst of being shoved around the floor by an effeminate-looking boy who held her too close and insisted on making a date for the following night. She was trying to be politely evasive when David cut in. "I had to save you from Ned," he said. "He's a real closet queen but feels he has to score with all the beautiful girls to prove otherwise."

Miraculously the music changed and some Bacharach-David songs came on. They moved closer. He obviously felt her relax, because he whispered, "I like this kind of music too. I have most of these records at home."

She nodded and felt his hand stroke the back of her neck. "I'd like to sleep with you," he said.

They continued to dance. She couldn't believe the matter-of-fact tone he had used. No ardent pleading like Franco. No promises. Just a statement. Weren't you supposed to be insulted if a man said this on a first date? At Miss Haddon's, you were. But this wasn't Miss Haddon's. This was Le Club, and David was a sought-after, sophisticated man. Besides, the way he had said it—not like a question, but almost like a compliment. She decided that no answer was the best course.

When he led her back to the bar he joined in the conversation, and everything seemed casual and impersonal. They talked about the upcoming World Series. The girls discussed their summer vacations, how the "season" was really on, the cost of lengthening a sable coat—*Women's Wear* said the mini definitely was *not* coming back . . .

January smiled and tried to appear interested, but she was suddenly very tired. She was relieved when David finished his drink and suggested they leave. Once they were in the cab she kept up a steady barrage of conversation—How interesting Le Club was . . . How nice his friends seemed to be . . . Why did they play the music so loud? . . . She never stopped until she saw the canopy of the Pierre. David told the driver to hold the clock. And he walked her to the door.

"I had a wonderful time," she said.

"We'll have a lot of them," he said. Then, without any warning, he pulled her to him and gave her a long kiss. She felt his tongue prying her lips apart. She knew the doorman was tactfully looking the other way. And she was dismayed that she felt the same revulsion she had always felt when a man tried to kiss her.

When he broke the embrace, he smiled. "It's going to be great between us. I can feel it." Then he turned and walked back to the cab.

Mike and Dee were huddled over the backgammon board when she came in. "I beat her," he called out. "For the first time, I beat her!"

"He broke every rule," Dee drawled. "He just had incredible luck with the dice."

"I always break rules." Mike grinned.

Dee turned her full attention toward January. "Isn't David divine?"

Mike stood up. "While you two broads rehash the evening, I'm going to get a beer. Anyone want anything. A Coke, January?"

"No thanks." She began taking off Dee's jewelry.

The moment Mike left the room Dee said, "Wasn't I right about David? He is beautiful, isn't he? When are you seeing him again?"

January suddenly realized he hadn't actually made a date. She handed Dee the earrings and began taking off the chains. "I want to thank you for the jewelry . . ."

"Anytime. Now tell me about David. Where did you go?"

"To Le Club."

"Oh, that's a fun place. What did you two young things talk about?"

January laughed. "Dee, no one talks at Le Club. Unless you use sign language. We danced, and I met a lot of his friends."

"I'm so glad. David knows all the right young people and . . ."

"Dee, I've got to talk to you about the tots."

Mike walked into the room. "What tots?"

Dee wandered back to the backgammon board. "Oh, January and I have a project in mind. Now set up the board, Mike. I've got to beat you before we go to bed to prove you don't really know the game at all. Run off to sleep, January. We've got a lot of chitchatting to do tomorrow."

She blew a kiss at her father and slipped into the bedroom. For a moment she stared at the closed door. Mike Wayne . . . sitting up playing backgammon. She thought of David . . . Maybe he had just meant the "I want to sleep with you" as a compliment. And she had gotten all uptight over it. After all, it wasn't as if he had tried to grope her, or said it in a slimy way.

But it still wasn't right!

Or was it?

Things had changed since Miss Haddon's. Mike had changed, the whole world had changed. Maybe it was time for her to change.

And David was so nice. He was so good-looking. Maybe she had turned him off. Maybe he had felt her stiffen when he said that. But then, he *had* kissed her goodnight. Only she hadn't been exactly wildly responsive. But maybe he hadn't noticed that.

Or had he?

He hadn't asked her for another date. But then maybe he had just forgotten. After all, she hadn't realized it either until Dee brought it up.

The phone rang. She reached for it so eagerly she almost knocked down the lamp.

"Hi, babe." It was Mike's muffled voice.

"Oh, hi, Daddy."

"Dee's in the bathroom. I figured we've got a few things to talk over. How about meeting in the living room for coffee tomorrow morning at nine?"

"Okay."

"And don't sound so blue. I promise you—you're not gonna teach any tots."

"Oh." She managed a slight laugh.

"See. I'm always there to fix things. Right?"

"Right."

"Goodnight, babe."

"Goodnight, Daddy."

Mike was sitting on the sofa drinking coffee and reading the *Times* when she came into the living room the next morning. Without saying a word, he poured a cup and held it out to her. "Sadie sets this up before she goes to bed," he said. "Dee usually sleeps until noon, so there's not too much action for breakfast around here."

"Do you always get up this early?" she asked.

"Only since you came to town."

She sat down and sipped her coffee. "Mike, we have to talk."

He smiled. "What the hell do you think I'm doing here?"

She fastened her eyes on the coffee cup. "Mike . . . I—"

"You don't want to teach at La Petite École."

She looked at him. "You knew about that?"

"Not until you did. And I settled it with Dee last night. No Petite École. Next?"

"I can't live here."

His eyes narrowed. "Why not?"

She got up and walked to the window. "Oh, look, I can see my hill from here. There's a large French poodle on it and . . ."

He came to her side. "Why can't you live here?"

She tried to smile. "Maybe it's because I can't stand sharing you."

"Come on. You know damn well you're not sharing me. What we have together belongs to us."

"No." She shook her head. "It won't work. I can't stand to see—" She stopped. "Forget it."

"What can't you stand to see?" he asked quietly.

"I . . . I can't stand to see you play backgammon!"

For a moment neither of them spoke. He looked at her and forced a smile. "It's not a bad game . . . really." He took her hands. "Look, she redid that bedroom for you—new wallpaper, special hangers in the closets, all that jazz. I think she'd be hurt if you didn't at least give it a try. Besides, we're going to Palm Beach the beginning of November. In six weeks you'll have the whole place to yourself. Try it for a while anyway. Then, if you want to move—okay. But at least give it a shot. Please?"

She managed a smile. "Okay, Mike."

He walked over and poured himself another cup of coffee. "What did you think of David?"

"I thought he was . . . well . . . very groovy-looking." She caught his look of surprise. "You wanted me to like him, didn't you?"

"Sure. But I guess I'm like all fathers. I know one day you'll fall in love—I want you to fall in love—yet when I hear about it, I'll probably hate the whole idea." He laughed. "Don't pay any attention to me. I never was any good in the morning. Now, what's on your schedule? Want to meet me for lunch?"

"I'd love lunch . . . another day. I've got to get some clothes. David said the kind of places I'd like are on Third Avenue. So I'm heading there. And I have a three o'clock appointment with Linda Riggs."

"What's a Linda Riggs?"

"She's the girl from Miss Haddon's—the one we all thought would be a star. That is, everyone but you. She's editor-in-chief at *Gloss* magazine now."

"Okay. That takes care of your day. Now tonight Dee is

having some people in for cocktails at seven, and then we're going to "21." Do you want to join us? Or are you all set with David?"

She laughed. "Last night we went to Le Club. It was mobbed . . . the music was so loud . . . David knew everyone there. It was impossible to talk. And . . .. well . . . we just forgot about making a date. That's crazy, isn't it?"

He lit a cigarette. "No, it happens." He paused. "Look, babe, don't go off the deep end for him. Take it real slow and easy."

"Mike, you wanted me to like David. Something is bothering you. What is it?"

"Well, I can see right now that you're in a pretty vulnerable spot. You come back . . . New York is strange . . . I've got a new wife . . . you're at loose ends . . . a sitting duck for the first halfway attractive guy who comes along. I like the idea that you like him, but there are a lot of beautiful broads in this town, and he's a very eligible guy."

"And?"

"Well, he might not have *forgotten* to make a date. He might just be booked up for the time being."

"Mike, you know something?"

He got up and walked to the window. "I know nothing. I saw him coming out of an art movie with Karla last week. I have to admit I was very impressed, because that's one lady I want to meet. I wouldn't have thought anything of it. But two days ago, I also saw him standing on Fifty-seventh Street outside of Carnegie Hall. Dee tells me Karla rents a studio there. And sure enough, down she comes, and they go off. He didn't see me. And I've said nothing to Dee."

"Are you trying to tell me he goes with Karla?"

"I'm also trying to tell you there's a gorgeous Dutch model named Kim Voren. She's on the cover of *Vogue* this month. Maybe I gave you the idea that we were serving David to you on a silver platter. Dee would like it that way. But David is his own man. And I don't want you to be hurt. I would like to plunk the world in your lap. Last night I did a lot of thinking, maybe because I saw you for the first time as a gorgeous girl out on a date. A gorgeous vulnerable girl. And I don't want you sitting around just waiting for this guy to call."

"I have no intention of doing that. I want to work."

He walked over and poured himself another cup of coffee and lit a fresh cigarette. "What do you want to do?"

She shrugged. "Until now I always assumed I'd be in show business because of you. In some way, I guess I've felt as if I've been in it all of my life. I think I can act. But I've had no experience. And I know there aren't many jobs open. But there's Off Broadway. Maybe I could try for an assistant stage manager . . . or an understudy . . . a walk-on . . . anything. Dee was right about one thing—I do want to do something."

He looked thoughtful. "Most of the producers and directors I know are on the Coast now. As for Off Broadway, that's a whole new breed. Tell you what—I'll call the Johnson Harris agency. It's a hell of a good talent agency. Sammy Tebet is vice-president in charge of motion pictures. He owes me a few favors. I'll get him to introduce you to whoever runs the legit department there." He looked at his watch. "I'll try them in about an hour."

"That would be great. Maybe they can see me tomorrow." She stood up. "And now I'm off to buy out New York—like you told me to do yesterday."

He smiled. "Only today . . . you really feel like doing it."

She nodded. "Just shows you what a good night's sleep will do."

Five

THIRD AVENUE WAS a whole new world. She had dropped off boxes at the Pierre loaded with pants, long skirts, shirts, dungarees—enough to fill most of those heavy brass hangers Dee had put in her closets. Now her wardrobe was as freaked-out as everyone else's in New York.

Gloss was a factory of mod clothes and frenetic activity. The receptionist announced her, then pointed the way down a long hall. People stood in clusters studying layouts. Young men carried art portfolios. Girls rushed about carrying sketches. Bright simulated daylight flooded most of the windowless offices. There was a "now" look about everyone, from the skinny girls with the long hair and tinted glasses to the young men with the well trimmed beards. She was glad she was wearing one of her new outfits.

She stopped at the end of the hall before a large lacquered white door with the name LINDA RIGGS in impressive block wooden letters. The secretary, sitting in the small cubicle outside, led January into a striking corner office with windows from floor to ceiling. A beautiful young woman was sitting at the desk, a phone cradled against her shoulder, making notes as she listened. The office was colorfully modern. White walls . . . orange rugs on stained black wooden floors . . . paintings that looked like colored Rorschach tests . . . white leather chairs . . . a black velvet couch . . . plexiglass tables . . . copies of *Gloss* everywhere. In spite of the decor, there was a worked-in feeling about the office. January sat down and waited until the woman got off the phone. It was incredible to envision Linda of the shaggy hair and funny face in this sleek setup.

The woman on the phone smiled, and signaled that she was trying to get off. January returned an understanding smile and stared at the manuscripts that lay piled on the windowsill. *Ladies' Home Journal, Cosmopolitan, Vogue,* and other rival magazines lay on a table.

The woman got off the phone. "I'm sorry. That call was endless." Then she looked at January and smiled. "Well, you really are quite a beauty. But then why not—with a father like Mike Wayne."

January smiled politely and wondered where Linda was. This smooth attractive woman was staring at her as if she were some kind of a specimen. January stood up. "I'm supposed to see Miss Riggs at three and—"

The woman laughed. "January! Who do you think *I* am!"

January looked bewildered. But Linda only laughed. "I forgot. Good Lord! How long has it been?"

"About ten years." January finally managed to speak.

Linda nodded. "That's right! Well, you didn't think I intended to stay stuck with that face all of my life, did you? The braces came off, a few caps were added, and of course the nose job—that was my graduation present—and I've lost about twenty pounds of what we used to call baby fat . . ."

"It's unbelievable," January said. "Linda, you're beautiful. I mean . . . your personality was always so great that people thought you were beautiful, but—"

"I was kinky-looking—before it was 'in' to look kinky. Now that I've gone all through this, the uglies have come in. I swear, sometimes I wish I had my old nose back. Incidentally, Keith doesn't know about the nose job or the teeth or anything." She pressed a buzzer and the receptionist's voice came through the box on her desk. "Norma, when Keith Winters arrives, send him right in." Then she turned to January. "I wish you had worn something with more color. I love those pants, and the suede jacket is divine . . . but it's all so beigy and Keith is coming with reams of color film."

"Linda, I didn't come here to be photographed. I came to see you. I want to hear all about you and the magazine. I think it's just fabulous."

Linda came out from behind the desk and sat on the couch.

She reached for a pack of cigarettes in a large glass bowl. "We've got just about every brand here . . . except grass . . . so help yourself."

"I don't smoke."

"I wish I didn't. How do you manage to stay so thin without it? I worry sometimes with all that cancer talk, but they say until women have the menopause, they have some secret ingredient that protects them. Speaking of menopause, tell me about Deirdre Milford Granger."

"She's Mrs. Michael Wayne now."

"Of course." Linda smiled. "I'd love to get a story on her and your father. We cater to the twenty-to-thirty crowd, but *everyone* loves to read about the really filthy rich. We've tried and tried, but she's always turned us down. That's why I'm keen to do a story on you. It will really grab our readers. I'm surprised Helen Gurley Brown or Lenore Hershey hasn't gotten to you. Although it's more of a *Cosmo* story than *Ladies' Home Journal.* I swear that Helen Gurley Brown will drive me back to my analyst."

"Why?"

"She's so damned successful. And it all started from writing about how a single girl landed a divine husband. And the wild part is, no one gets married anymore . . . except older people. Anyway, that's going to be my angle. Stories don't drop in your lap. You've got to find them . . . be first. That's why I'm in my office from eight in the morning until eight at night. It's not easy. But it's the only way. Because I intend to make *Gloss* bigger than *Cosmo*. Bigger than them all one day."

"Don't you believe in marriage?" January asked.

"Of course not. I live with Keith and we're divinely happy. We live for today. Because nothing is permanent . . . not even life."

"He's the photographer?"

Linda smiled. "Actually he's really an actor. He moonlights as a photographer. I give him all the jobs I can. He's damn good. Of course he's no Halsman or Scavullo. He could be, if he dedicated himself to it, but he's determined to become the Marlon Brando of the seventies. He's really marvelous. I saw him do *Streetcar* in an Equity Library thing. But there are just no jobs. And he hasn't really ever had a break on Broadway."

"I thought you'd be the big star," January said. "We all did at Miss Haddon's."

Linda shook her head. "I tried. But even with the nose job and all . . . nothing really happened. I mean it was all so tacky—girls working as waitresses at night so they could study and job hunt during the day. I tried it for a while. I even got a job as a waitress in a coffeehouse. And then one day I saw a girl applying for a job who was also an actress, only she was in her thirties. That's when I quit . . . and got the job on *Gloss*. The magazine was on the verge of folding, and I had a lot of ideas of things that could make it go. But no one would listen to me. I stayed on as a gofer for about two years. And then someone in the advertising department dropped it to me that John Hamer was going to close *Gloss* down. He's chairman of the board of Jenrose—they own *Gloss* and several other publications. Everyone was already looking for other jobs. So on a wild chance I went to him and told him my ideas. I told him it should stop competing with *Vogue* for high fashion . . . to gear it to the younger woman . . . the working girl . . . or housewife . . . to go after ads for new bras . . . buy stories that didn't all have an 'up' ending. To do articles on marriages that *couldn't* be saved by a pastor or a marriage counselor . . . stories about the 'other woman' who suffered while the wife who didn't give a damn had a ball. He took a chance and made me editor of special subjects. After a year we had doubled our circulation. At the end of that year I became editor-in-chief. We were the first to do a photo layout on the topless beach at the Riviera. I also did articles for and against natural childbirth, for and against children . . . We've done great and we're still climbing in circulation. But if I want to beat out *Ladies' Home Journal* and *Cosmo,* I have to keep coming up with firsts. And if I can't get Deirdre Milford Granger *Wayne* . . . then I want January Wayne. I want to run a picture layout of you in our January issue, with the heading: 'January is not a month. She's a girl who has everything.'"

"Linda, I don't want a story done on me."

For a moment Linda stared. "Then why did you come to see me?"

"Because . . . well . . . I had hoped we could be friends. I . . . don't really know anyone in New York."

"The lonely little princess? Come on, that's your stepmother's bag. Or at least it was until she married your father. He must be a great stud. Know something? I've always had a thing for him."

January stood up, but Linda grabbed her arm. "Oh, for God's sake. Don't take it that way. Look . . . okay . . . so you're lonely. Everyone's lonely. And the only way not to be lonely is to go to bed with the man you care about . . . and waking up the next morning and finding yourself still in his arms. I've got that with Keith, and that's one of the reasons I want this story. Because I'll be able to give him some decent money on the assignment. You see, I feel that if he got some real recognition for his photography he'd take it more seriously. Then I wouldn't have to worry that he might take off for six months with a bus and truck company of some show." The intensity of Linda's feelings changed her entire face, and suddenly January was looking at the Linda of Miss Haddon's. The Linda who was raucous. The Linda of *Annie Get Your Gun*.

They were both silent. Then January said, "Linda, if you care this much for Keith, why don't you get married?"

"Because as I told you—we don't believe in it." She was Linda Riggs of *Gloss* magazine again. "He's my mate and we live together and it's fine and . . ."

They both looked up as the door swung open and Keith Winters walked into the room. January recognized him immediately as the photographer in the Pierre lobby. His hair was long and shaggy, he wore a Dutch boy cap, an army surplus jacket, a T-shirt, sneakers, and dungarees.

"Sorry, Keith," Linda said. "I'm afraid there is no assignment. The lady says no."

He shrugged and took off the camera he had slung across his shoulder. He also had one around his neck. January began to feel slightly guilty.

Keith reached for a pack of cigarettes from the bowl. Then he turned to Linda. "Listen, you better not plan on me for dinner tonight."

"But this is the day Evie comes to clean. I told her to make a big meat loaf—the kind you adore."

He shook his head. "I have an appointment with Milos Doklov. I have to be downtown at five thirty."

"Who is he?" Linda asked.

"Just one of the best Off Broadway directors there is. He was nominated twice for an Obie." He looked at January. "That's an Off Broadway Tony."

She smiled faintly. "Oh. I didn't know."

"Cheer up. Neither does Linda."

"Keith, I have nothing against Off Broadway."

"How could you? You've never been there."

"I'll come for the opening of this."

"Cool it," he said. "This is for Off Off Broadway. But it's good enough for Milos to have done it, so it's good enough for me."

"Why, that's wonderful," Linda said with a forced enthusiasm. "Tell me about it. What's the part like? When does it open?"

"It's opened and is a hit—by Off Off Broadway standards. The leading man is splitting to do another show. So I may replace him."

"Well . . . that's marvelous. I'll freeze the meat loaf and wait up for you. We'll have pâté and wine to celebrate."

"I don't like pâté." He looked at January. "Sorry you're goofing out on us. I could use the bread and my old lady needs a good story. She doesn't sleep nights unless the circulation climbs."

January felt an undercurrent of hostility between them. Linda's smile was forced and her hands fumbled as she tried to light a cigarette. Suddenly January felt Linda needed this story desperately—and not just for the magazine.

"Linda, maybe if I phoned my father and asked him . . ."

"Asked him what?" Linda was staring at Keith.

"About the story . . . I mean, what you suggested doing on me . . ."

Linda brightened. "Oh, January, do. Call him now. Use that phone on my desk."

January realized she didn't know her father's office number.

Maybe Sadie would know. She called the Pierre. Sadie knew the number and also told her two dozen roses had arrived. She waited while Sadie read the card. "It's from Mr. Milford. It's on his business card. It says, 'Thank you for a lovely evening. Will call you in a few days. D.' "

She thanked Sadie and dialed her father's office. His secretary told her to try him at the Friars Club. She thought about the flowers as she waited for them to page him at the Friars Club. "Will call you in a few days." Well, as Mike said, he hadn't been just sitting around waiting for her to arrive. He probably was dated up. And the flowers were to show her he was thinking of her.

When her father came on the phone, he sounded breathless. "What's up, babe?"

"Did I get you away from something important?"

"Yeah. A hot gin game and a double Schneid–"

"Oh, I'm sorry."

"Well, look, sweetheart, from where I'm standing I can see the guy I've got on the blitz trying to sneak a look through the pack. You want something special? Or is this a social call?"

"I'm at *Gloss* magazine and Linda wants to do a story on me."

"So?"

"Is it okay?"

"Sure . . ." He paused. "That is, if it's a story on *you*. I don't want Dee kicked around. Look, get it in writing that you have complete approval of the story before it goes into the magazine."

"Okay."

"Oh . . . and listen . . . you're all set with Sammy Tebet tomorrow at the Johnson Harris office. Ten A.M."

"Thanks, Mike!"

"See you later, babe."

She hung up and told them Mike's demands. Linda nodded. "Fair enough. I'll have a letter drawn up immediately. I'll put Sara Kurtz on the story. Keith, you can start right in with the pictures." She pushed an intercom buzzer. "Send Ruth in to take some notes." She pushed another buzzer. "Janie, hold all calls. Unless Wilhelmina calls back. I want that new German model she has for the February cover . . . Shotzie something. Good Lord, you know I'm bad on names. What? No. And tell

Leon to leave the artwork for the new novel excerpt. I've got to see it before I leave tonight. Yes, that's about it." She looked up as an ugly birdlike girl timidly entered the room clutching a notebook. Linda gave her a brief nod and then hung up.

"Sit down, Ruth. This is January Wayne. Ruth is gorgeous at shorthand. I'll ask questions, because I know the way the story should go. Then in a few days we'll set up a date to put you and Sara together . . ."

Keith had finished loading his cameras. He took out his light meter, changed a lamp, then took a quick shot with a Polaroid to check composition. He stared at it, nodded, and started snapping with another camera.

Linda's smile was all business. "Okay, January. After Miss Haddon's, where did you go to school?"

"Switzerland."

"What was the name of the college?"

January saw Ruth making all funny curlicues on the pad. She hesitated. She couldn't remember the name Dee had given her. What Dee wanted to tell her friends was one thing. But she didn't want to lie about it in print. Besides, it might get Linda in trouble. And to add to her personal confusion, Keith was suddenly all over the place, taking shots of her at crazy angles. She turned to Linda. "Look, let's concentrate on *now*. I don't want any stuff on Miss Haddon's or Dee or Switzerland. I'm going to start job hunting tomorrow, and . . . well, let's go from there."

"Job hunting?" Linda laughed. "You?"

Keith came up close and snapped his camera. January jumped. "Ignore me," he pleaded. "You and Linda keep talking. I shoot better that way."

"If you want a job," Linda said, "come work for me."

"Here?" January was getting jittery. Keith's clicking was nerve-racking.

"Sure, I'd love a name like yours on the masthead. You could be a junior editor. Only you wouldn't be a slavey or a gofer. I'll pay you one hundred and twenty-five a week and let you do some pieces."

"But I can't write!"

"Neither could I," Linda answered. "But I learned. And now

I don't have to. I have plenty of rewrite people. But all *you* have to do is get the interviews, go out on them, take notes or use a tape recorder. Then I'll assign someone to rewrite them."

"But why would you want me?"

"For your muscle, January. Look, last year Sammy Davis Junior was in town and there was no way I could get to him. Now if you had been working for us then, it would have been just one telephone call from your father to Sammy. Mike Wayne may have retired, but he still has entrée to people we could never reach. Right now we're going after the young beautiful-people readers. You could do a monthly column—what's doing with that set, where do they go. Also, your new stepmother knows the great Karla. Now—if we could get a story on her!"

"Karla's never given an interview in her life," Keith said.

"Of course not," Linda agreed. "But who's talking about an interview? If January happens to see her at one of Dee's dinner parties and just happens to overhear some pearls dropping from that beautiful Polish mouth . . ."

"January, I've got six shots of you frowning," Keith said. "Give me a different mood."

January got up and walked out of camera range. "This is wild . . . the way you two are going on. I come to see an old friend and wind up doing an interview. I say I want to work, and you ask me to be Mata Hari. As you would say, Linda, NO WAY!"

"What kind of work do you want to do?" Linda asked.

"Act."

"Oh, God," Linda groaned.

"Any experience?" Keith asked.

"Not really. But I spent my life watching and listening. And at the—in Switzerland—I used to read aloud a lot. Every day for two hours. Shakespeare . . . Marlowe . . . Shaw . . . Ibsen."

Keith clicked as she spoke. "Come along with me this afternoon. I'll introduce you to Milos Doklov—he always has some project going. He may know someone else who might be doing something you could audition for. Do you sing or dance?"

"No, I—"

"That's a great idea," Linda said. "And Keith, see if you can get some pictures of January with this Milos. Also get some background shots of her in the Village . . ." Then as Keith started packing his camera, Linda said, "I'll check with you in a day or so, January. I'll have the letter your father wanted drawn up and I'll set up an appointment for you and Sara Kurtz." She looked at Keith. "I'll keep the meat loaf hot until eight. Try to get back by then."

"I'll try. But don't count on it," he said. "Come on, actress," he took January's arm. "You're on your way."

When they got outside, Keith said, "Well, rich girl, you're about to travel out-of-work-actor style."

"How's that?"

"On the subway—Dutch Treat. Got thirty cents?"

"Yes, sure. Know what? I've never been on a subway."

He laughed as he led her down the steps. "Keep talking, baby. You're blowing my mind."

She sat beside Keith fighting off a queasy feeling as the train rattled its way downtown. She decided there was nothing wonderful or colorful about poverty. The man sitting near her had body odor. A woman across from her had a large shopping bag cradled between her legs and was working diligently at picking her nose. There was a dank feeling in the car and the walls were covered with names and graffiti. She sat very straight and tried not to show her revulsion as Keith chattered through the noise of the car. At one point he almost broke his neck trying to stand on a seat across the aisle to get her picture. The train lurched and he sprawled across the floor. His camera slid down to the other end of the train. January ran down the car to help. It struck her as odd that no one else bothered to help or even seemed to notice. She was relieved when they got off.

They walked two blocks to a dingy building. Then they climbed five steep flights. "Milos keeps his office up in a loft," Keith explained. They both stopped several times for breath before they reached a wet-looking steel door. Keith rang the bell and a strong voice boomed, "It's unlocked. Enter."

The voice was the only strong thing about Milos Doklov. He was a skinny, dirty-looking little man with long thin hair that only partially covered a shiny scalp. His fingernails were long and dirty and his smile revealed decayed teeth.

"Hi, man. Who's the chick?"

"January Wayne. January, this is Milos Doklov."

"So you've come home to Daddy," Milos said, ignoring January.

Keith took out his camera and snapped January, who was openly staring at the place. "I didn't get the job with Hal Prince, if that's what you mean," Keith answered as he tore open a new role of film with his teeth.

"Baby . . . baby . . ." Milos sprang to his feet like a cat. "That Broadway shit will kill your potential. After you make it here and find out what it all means, then you can go uptown for a season to make some bread. But always remember—this is the scene, this is where it's at."

"Cut the sales pitch, Milos . . . I'll take the job."

Milos smiled sadly. "You could have had the part originally . . . gotten all the reviews. Look what's happened to Baxter —he's going into *Ashes and Jazz*."

Keith clicked the camera again. "That's still Off Broadway."

"Yes, but he's up for an Obie."

"Look, I said I'll take the part."

"Split with the fashion lady?"

"No."

"Then why the change of heart? Seems to me that was the main reason you wouldn't take the part before."

Keith began to reload his second camera. He checked the light meter. "I was still hoping for the Hal Prince deal. Let's cut it. When do rehearsals start?"

"We'll have just two days. Maybe next Monday and Tuesday. You watch the performance every night—learn the part and the moves. No sweat."

"Okay, Milos." He took a final shot of January.

"Why the pictures?" Milos asked.

"Doing a setup on the lady."

"You a model?" Milo asked.

"Nope." Keith strapped his camera back in its case. "She's an actress. Know anyone who needs someone who looks like her?"

"Are you any good?" Milos asked her.

"I think so. That is, I feel I am," she said.

Milos rubbed his chin. "Look, one of the Muses is leaving the same time as Baxter. I was going to call Liza Kilandos. It's only ten lines and pays . . . ah . . . are you Equity?"

"Not yet."

"Fine. Go see the show tonight with Keith. It's the part Irma Davidson plays." He tossed the script to Keith. "Bone up on it, man. And January, you come back tomorrow at four and read for the part."

When they got out on the street she grabbed Keith. "Did he mean it? I mean, that I might have a job right away? Wouldn't that be fabulous?"

The weather had changed. There was a sudden rumble of thunder. Keith looked at the sky. "It's going to come down like bullets, but it won't last. Let's go in for some coffee." He led her to a little cellar. "We can have a sandwich here and kill time until we go to the theater. No point in spending money going back uptown. Do you have to call anyone to say you're not coming back?"

She called the Pierre. Her father wasn't home and Dee was resting. "Tell them I can't have dinner with them," she told Sadie. "I—I have a date." It wasn't exactly the truth. But it was better than a long explanation.

She walked back to the table. The rain was slicing across the pavement. They both sat in the small booth and stared out at the wet gray street. They ordered hamburgers and Keith took a few more shots of her in the restaurant.

"Linda says you're a good photographer," January said.

"I get by."

"She said you could be one of the best."

"Look, I'd rather be a half-ass actor than the best photographer in the world."

She was silent. Then he said, "The lady makes thirty thousand a year. I don't want any more mercy jobs!"

"But she says you're good."

"Yes, but not with the camera."

She knew she had blushed and she busied herself adding more relish to her hamburger. He began telling her about his career—the few decent roles he had in summer stock . . . his roles Off Broadway . . . the Industrials . . . the one TV commercial which kept him going for a year. "But that's run out . . . my unemployment insurance is out too . . . and I have no intention of trying to be better than Avedon and all the others."

"But you could learn," January said.

He looked at her. "Why?"

"Why?"

He nodded. "Yeah. Why? Why should I kill myself trying to learn something I don't enjoy doing? Sure there's rejection in the theater. But it's like getting a turn-down from a chick you got a hard-on for. At least you keep trying because you got a chance she might say Yes. The other way you're working just as hard to settle for a chick who doesn't turn you on. Dig?"

"But you'd be with Linda."

He stared into his coffee cup. "No rule says I can't be with her as an actor."

"But . . . I mean . . . as an actor you have to tour a lot and be away from her."

"Ever hear of a thing called self-respect? Before you can be with someone every night you want them to respect you. And for them to respect you, you got to respect yourself. I know too many actors who sold out . . . turned queer to get a job . . . or got kept by someone . . . And know something? They never really make it, because it kills something inside of them."

She was silent. Suddenly he said, "What about you? What's your scene?"

"What do you mean?"

"You love someone?"

"Yes. I mean, no."

"How can you mean yes . . . and then no?"

"Well, I love my father. I know that. But that's not being in love, right?"

"I should hope not."

"And then I've met someone. But when I think about love—" She shook her head. "I mean, I'm not quite sure how you're supposed to feel when you're in love. I like him, but—"

"You're not in love. That's the story of my life. I've never been *in* love."

"You haven't?"

He shook his head. "To me love will be when I stand on that stage and know the whole fucking audience is there just to see me. That's the real orgasm. What I feel for a chick—" He shrugged. "That's like eating a good meal. I love good food . . . I love life . . . . I love tasting new things . . . new sensations." He stopped. "Look . . . don't look so shocked. Linda knows the score. She's been my old lady for a long time, yet she knows I might split at any time. But if I do, it won't be because I've fallen in love with some chick. It'll be for some other experience. For some other scene. Dig?"

"No."

"You're a real put-on, aren't you? I mean no one, like no one can be this straight. Look, I'm a life freak. I want to wring it dry. Linda only pretends she is. But she isn't. She lives only for that magazine. Sure, she digs me. But I'm not the first man in her life. I think she'd feel worse losing a big story than losing a guy. Dig?"

"The rain's stopped," she said.

He stood up. "Your end is ninety cents. That means we're leaving a thirty-cent tip—fifteen apiece. Okay?"

"Okay."

The streets were wet and a few occasional drops fell from the trees. They walked the few blocks in silence. January dredged her mind trying to think of something to say that would put Keith into a more romantic frame of mind toward Linda. He seemed so turned off. . . . Maybe he was just talking, maybe he was nervous. After all, a lot of people said things they didn't really mean when they were nervous. He was attractive in an earthy kind of way and Linda was really in love with him. Maybe after he got in the show things would change. Mike always said he was more relaxed when things were going great.

Suddenly it began to rain. Keith grabbed her hand and they ran the rest of the way, ducking under awnings and trees. They were breathless when Keith stopped in front of a store.

"Well, here we are."

"But . . . Where's the theater?"

"Follow me." He led her through the store, which was empty except for a few wooden plank tables with lemonade and peanut butter crackers stacked in readiness for the intermission break. A girl stood beside a homemade ticket box. She waved when she saw Keith. He led January past her into a long narrow room. There were rows and rows of hard-looking folding chairs. Up front was a stage without a curtain. Keith led her to the third row. "These are house seats," he said with a grin.

"This is the theater?" she asked.

"It was an old store. But they've turned it into a playhouse. The dressing rooms are upstairs, and Milos keeps a pad on the third floor for starving actors. It's like a dorm . . . co-ed . . . and they live there rent-free if they're out of a job."

By eight o'clock the house was full, and to January's amazement extra chairs were being jammed into every available spot.

"It's a real hit, isn't it?" she asked.

"It's caught on pretty big . . . mostly word of mouth. I see a lot of uptown people. Maybe some of the producers will come down at that."

The lights dimmed and the entire cast came on. They bowed, introduced themselves and exited. Three girls remained. "The one on the left—that's the one you're replacing," Keith whispered. "They stay on stage all the time. They're the Greek chorus."

The three girls were dressed in gray coveralls. They chanted a few lines and then the young man they were talking about came on. He looked like Keith. He had a long diatribe which January barely understood. The Greek chorus cut in occasionally with an "Amen, brother." Then a girl came on. There was a violent argument. They sat down and went through the elaborate motions of smoking pot. The stage filled with artificial smoke.

"This is a hash-dream sequence," Keith said. "They're using a smoke screen now. This is the scene that's bringing them down from uptown."

When the smoke cleared, the two leads were nude. The Greek chorus was also nude. Then actual lovemaking began on the stage between the boy and girl. At first it was slow . . . almost like a dance . . . the Greek chorus hummed to background music that came from an offstage speaker. As the music grew louder, the chorus grew louder . . . everyone moved faster . . . the dance turned into a frenzy as the leading man broke into a song and began stroking the breasts of the Greek chorus and the leading lady, while the leading lady in turn stroked everyone. Then the Greek chorus began stroking each other until everyone was intertwined in a song called "Move, Touch, Feel . . . That's Love."

Then the stage went dark and the house lights came up and it was intermission.

January suddenly scrambled to her feet. "I'm leaving."

"But there's another act. Your big scene is in it." He laughed. "You have ten lines alone."

"With or without clothes?" she asked.

"Say . . . are you uptight about frontal nudity?" He grabbed her arm as she pushed her way up the aisle. "I mean, nudity is a natural thing. To hide the body is an idea planted in our mind from birth. I guess it started when Eve ate the apple. But a baby has genitals . . . yet everyone loves a bare-assed baby. Our body is part of the expression of love. Do we cover our faces because our eyes send out signals of love or because our mouth talks of love? Our tongues caress someone's lips . . yet is a tongue obscene?"

"We see with our eyes and talk with our tongue," she said.

"Yeah . . . and we pee with our pricks and our cunts but we also make love with them."

She broke away from him and ran outside. People were crowded in front waiting to pay a dollar for a cup of lemonade. There were limousines parked outside. Keith reached the street and grabbed her by the arm.

"Okay, so maybe I'm not crazy about doing a sex number right on the stage either. Why do you think I didn't take the job when the play first opened? I knew Linda would blow her top. But it's the way things are today. If I'm not uptight about nudity, then I shouldn't be uptight about the sex act. It's a normal function."

"So is throwing up, but no one wants to pay to watch it!"

"Look, January, the play has caught on. It's a big chance for me. Besides, everyone is doing it. Big-name movie stars are doing nude scenes. It's just a matter of time before they'll go all the way. And it's not Keith the man they'll be looking at on that stage. It'll be Keith the actor. And that's all I care about. I'd rather live in Milos' dormitory and do hard-core porno *acting* than sit around in a Park Avenue penthouse holding a camera."

They had walked halfway down the block. A light misty rain was falling. The trees that lined the street partially shielded them. Keith tried to smile. "Come on. The second act is starting. Let's go back."

She continued to walk in the opposite direction. For a moment he hesitated. Then he shouted, "Go on. Run home. Go back to the Pierre where your father is being kept by a dame. At least *I'm* trying! If guys like your father hadn't thrown in the towel, maybe we wouldn't have to do this kind of shit. But it's guys like him who played it safe and refused to experiment. Well, fuck them! And fuck you! And fuck Linda too!" He turned and ran back to the theater. For a moment she stood very still. There had been tears in his anger. She wanted to tell him that she understood . . . that she wasn't angry. But he was gone. People were returning to the theater. The second act was beginning. And suddenly she was alone on a deserted street. There wasn't a sign of a cab. She walked back to the theater and looked at the license plates of the limousines. Several had X's, indicating they were rentals. She walked over to one chauffeur. "The play won't break for another hour. I wonder if you'd like—"

"Beat it, hippie!" He turned up his radio.

Her face burned. She dug into her bag, took out a ten-dollar bill, and approached the next car. "Sir—" She held up the money. "Could you drive me home? You'll get back in time for the break."

"Where's home?" The driver was staring at the bill.

"The Pierre."

He nodded, took the bill and unlocked the door. "Hop in."

As they drove uptown he said, "What happened? Fight with your boyfriend, or did the play turn you off?"

"Both."

"They're all coming down. Just to see bare boobs, heh? I mean, that's what they show, isn't it?"

"More," January said quietly.

"No kidding. Know something? I'm married and have three kids. But I once wanted to be a performer. I still sing occasionally at friends' weddings in the Bronx. I do Irish ballads. I'm also great with Rodgers and Hammerstein. But they don't write songs like that no more. No more Sinatras coming up. No more Perry Comos. Now *they* were singers . . . not the stuff I hear my daughter play on her record player."

They finally pulled up in front of the Pierre. He waited until she walked in, then his car disappeared into the traffic. She was relieved to find the apartment empty. She went to her room and stood in the dark. Things didn't seem so glaringly real in the dark. She thought of Linda, transferring her personal desires for success to the magazine, making it her symbol of life. She also thought of Keith going into that dreadful show . . . of the limousine driver who once wanted to be a singer . . . of her father probably sitting in some restaurant with Dee and her friends.

She stood very still. Where did everybody go? Where was all the fun and happiness she had hoped for? All those long snow-filled days when she had worked so hard just to walk . . . for what? She snapped on the lights. The room felt so empty. The whole apartment felt empty. Then she saw the roses on her bureau.

She thought of David—and suddenly the dirty theater and the entire evening seemed far away. There still was a world with clean beautiful people. And there still were stages on Broadway with beautiful settings and talented actors.

She would get into that world, and she would make Mike proud . . . and David would be as proud to be with her as he was with Karla or the Dutch model. Because from now on she would not be just Dee's new stepdaughter—or just Mike Wayne's daughter—from now on she was January Wayne.

A lady on her own.

Six

SAMMY TEBET'S GREETING was warm and expansive. He asked about Mike. Called him a lucky devil to be out of the rat race and said a beautiful girl like January should find a nice boy, get married and forget about show business. But if she insisted, he would do what he could.

Then he took her down the hall and introduced her to a bright young man who looked barely old enough to shave. The bright young man had his own office and sat behind a large desk. He had a telephone with five buttons, and each time one lit up a harassed secretary who looked old enough to be his grandmother poked her head in the door and pleaded, "Mr. Copeland . . . *please* pick up on two. It's the Coast." He would toss her a smile and say, "Cool it, Rhoda." Then with a bored but apologetic glance toward January he would push down the button and in a voice charged with animation launch into a multi-figured business discussion.

Between these calls he managed to set up some appointments for her. He knew of two shows that were being cast. She was too tall for the ingenue, but she might as well go and read anyway. Maybe the understudy was open. The other was a musical. Could she sing? No . . . well, go anyway. Sometimes they took a beautiful girl with no voice if they had enough dogs with strong voices to carry her. If not, nothing was lost. At least she would get to meet Merrick. He might remember her when he was doing something else. He gave her a list of producers to visit—"Just for contacts." They'd be active later in the season. He also set up an appointment at an advertising agency for a commercial. Commercials weren't his line, but it just so happened that at P.J.'s last night he had run into the director who told him they were looking for girls with great hair. When she thanked him, he held up his hand in a pontifical manner. "Cool it, sweetheart. Sammy Tebet asked me to do this. Sam's the man. Love him. Love *him*! Beautiful person. Said your father was once right up there with David Merrick. Well, let's hope you can make the old boy proud. That's part of the fun of making it. Gives them something to live for. Now you check in with me once a week and leave your phone number with Rhoda." Then he went back to his phone with the lights, and she gave her number to the hysterical Rhoda.

She followed all the leads he had given her. She read for one play. She hadn't been very good and she knew it. She was dismissed with the usual "Thank-you-very-much." She hiked over to Madison Avenue to the advertising agency and spent an hour waiting in an office along with thirty girls with hair down to their waists. When she finally met the director she learned that it was a cigarette commercial. The beautiful hair was a "must," as it was important to give the image that *young healthy* people smoked. They liked her hair, told her to learn how to inhale and come back in two days. She bought a pack of cigarettes, went back to the Pierre, locked herself in her room, and practiced. After a few puffs, the room began to spin. She lay very still and knew she was going to be sick. But after a time it passed and she tried again. This time she rushed to the bathroom and was really sick. Then she fell back on the bed and wondered why people *enjoyed* smoking.

Dee and Mike invited her to dinner. She begged off, explaining she had an audition the following morning and had to bone up on a script for a "reading." She spent the rest of the evening alternating between trying to inhale and fighting off bouts of nausea.

At eleven o'clock at night she finally stood in front of the mirror, inhaled and managed not to feel faint. As if to punctuate her accomplishment, the phone rang!

It was David. "I expected to leave a message. I didn't think I'd find you at home."

"I've been practicing inhaling."
"Inhaling what?"
"Cigarettes."
"What kind of cigarettes?"
She looked at the pack. "True."
"Oh . . . why?"
"Why True? I just liked the name."
"No, why the inhaling?"
He listened carefully as she explained about the commercial. Then he said, "Look, try not to take it any farther than your throat. The effect will be the same. No use lousing up your lungs. And after you get the commercial—throw away the cigarettes."
She laughed. "I bet you think I'm some kind of a nut sitting here and getting sick, just for a commercial."
"No, I think you're a girl with determination. I like that in you."
"Oh . . . well . . . yes." She knew she sounded flustered.
"Are you busy tomorrow night?" he asked.
"No."
"Well, how about having dinner with me? I'll coach you while you smoke. Maybe even teach you to blow some rings."
"Oh, great! What time?"
"I'll leave a message for you during the day."
"Okay . . . Goodnight David."
She was up early the next morning. Rhoda had called telling her to be at a producer's office at eleven for a reading. She was really excited. Rhoda said that Mr. Copeland said she was a natural for the part. Maybe this was really going to be her day. She'd think positive. She was going to get the part. After all, *someone* had to get it. And tonight she was seeing David.
As she dressed she thought about the evening. She had worn the gypsy outfit with David. What should she wear tonight? The long suede skirt with boots? Or should she wear the wet look—the black pants and jacket that were featured in *Vogue*? The man in the Third Avenue shop had said this was a perfect "rip-off!" Well, she had all day to think about it.
Her sense of well-being persisted even as she sat in the crowded office, waiting to see the producer. But Keith was

right. There was so little casting . . . and so *many* actors. Actors who had experience. As she waited she heard bits of their conversation. They talked about residuals, unemployment insurance. And some even joked about their experiences modeling at body-painting parlors. Nothing was demeaning if it brought in the rent and enabled the actor to job hunt and study. She marveled at their attitude. In spite of all the rejections they received, none of them seemed depressed. They were actors, and all the letdowns and disappointments were part of it. They might not have money for food all the time, but they all managed to go to classes. She heard snatches of conversation about Uta . . . Stella . . . the Studio . . . And she noticed they all had picture composites with their credits Xeroxed on the back. Another staple was the "Week-at-a-Glance" book, dogeared and crammed with appointments for "go-sees," auditions, and lessons.

She waited two hours, and was finally ushered in to see a tired man who looked at her and sighed, "Who sent you here?"

"Mr. Copeland."

Another sigh. "Why does Sheldon do this? I told him yesterday—we need a tired-looking blonde in her late twenties. It's not fair to you . . . it's not fair to me. He thinks he's keeping you busy by sending you around, but he's wasting your time . . . and mine. Okay, honey, better luck on your next stop." Then he turned to his secretary. "How many more are waiting?"

January walked out as a tall red-haired girl went in. She wondered if Sheldon had sent her also. Did he think just seeing a weary producer at the end of his day would make an "impression" on him for another time? Maybe she should tell all this to "Sheldon." She walked outside. A little whirlpool of a wind blew some dust in her eyes. Her mascara began to run as she dabbed at her eye. She hailed a cab, but it passed her by. Every cab she hailed seemed to have an OFF DUTY sign on it. She began to walk toward the Pierre. Mike was right. It was not the sparkling world she had seen on her weekends from Miss Haddon's. She walked up Broadway. The afternoon was ending. Prostitutes in their oversized wigs were beginning to take their positions on the corners. A blind man with a sad-looking dog shuffled along. A group of young Japanese men with cameras were taking pictures of the street. She wanted to shout, "It wasn't always like this." But maybe it was, maybe from her seat in the limousine with Mike it had just seemed different. And now, after two days of job hunting, it hit her that she really didn't give a damn about the theater—not without Mike.

It was four-thirty when she reached the Pierre. She would soak in the bathtub and wash away all the discouragement and grime of the day. Tonight she would feel fresh and wonderful for her dinner with David. She felt better just thinking about it. She wanted to go to some quiet candlelit place and talk. She wanted to learn more about him. Somehow she felt he would understand the confusion she was feeling. Mike would only say, "I told you so." Because he had been right.

There was a message in her box. She stared at it with disbelief. It was from David. He would pick her up at five-thirty. Five-thirty! Why five-thirty? Maybe it was a cocktail party. Yes, that was probably it. She dashed into the apartment, took a quick shower, and got into the long skirt. She was just putting on her lipstick when he called from the lobby.

"Come on up," she said. "I can't make a martini. But Mario is here. And Mike should be home any second."

"No. We have to hurry. You come down."

She grabbed a woolen shawl and went down to meet him. He looked at her and frowned. "I'm stupid. I should have told you to wear dungarees." She noticed he was wearing an old pair of corduroy pants and a jacket and sport shirt.

He took her arm. "There's a great espionage movie at the Baronet. I never get to see the movies I want to see, and there's always a line for this one. So I figured if we caught the six o'clock show we'd get in. We can grab a bite afterward."

The evening had been a total disaster. She thought about it as she lay soaking in the tub. David had adored the movie, and when it was over, they had walked to a restaurant called Maxwell's Plum. It was mobbed, but David knew the captain, and they were immediately wedged into a small table against the wall. David also knew the people at the next table. He made the introductions, ordered her a hamburger, and then talked to his friends throughout dinner. At ten o'clock they left the restaurant.

"Will you come home with me?" he asked.

"What?"

"Come home with me." He held her hand as he signaled for a cab.

"Why don't you come back to the Pierre?" she said.

"Dee and Mike might be there. Besides, I'd be uncomfortable sleeping with you knowing they might be in the same apartment." The cab pulled up before she could answer and he helped her in. Then he leaned across and she heard him give the driver an address in the East Seventies.

"David, I'm not going to bed with you!" She had almost shouted it. Then in a lower voice she said, "Please take me home."

"Change of plans," he called out to the driver. "Make it the Pierre Hotel." Then he turned to her with a tight smile. "Okay. Let's talk about more important things. How'd you do on the commercial? Did you get it?"

"That's not until tomorrow. David, don't be angry. But I . . . well . . . I just can't go to bed with someone I barely know."

"Forget it," he said quietly. "It was just a suggestion."

"I do like you, David." (Why was she apologizing! After all, it wasn't as if she had turned him down for a dance.)

"Fine, January. I understand." His voice was cold. "Oh, here we are." And when he walked her to the door and kissed her on the brow she felt as if she had been slapped across the face.

She got into bed and turned the radio to an album station. She liked David. That is, she *could* like David—if only he gave her a chance to *learn* to like him. She needed to like him, she wanted to like him, because she suddenly felt so lonely.

It seemed she had just fallen asleep when the phone rang.

"Did I wake you?" Linda said cheerfully.

"What time is it?"

"Seven-thirty in the morning . . . sixty-eight degrees . . . air quality acceptable, and I'm sitting at my desk and have already done an hour of yoga."

January switched on the lamp. "My drapes are closed. It still looks like midnight in here."

"January, I've got to see you. It's important." Linda was still cheerful but there was an urgency in her voice. "How about throwing on a pair of slacks and coming up here for breakfast? I'll send out for it."

"I can't. I have a nine o'clock appointment at the Landis agency. Hey, congratulate me. I've learned to smoke."

"Quit before it grabs you."

"Oh, I'm only doing it for the commercial. Although I must admit it helped get me through a dilly of an evening last night. When you're staring into space and your date is talking to the next table . . . a cigarette can be a girl's best friend."

"January, I've got to see you."

"Is it about the story?"

There was a split second of silence before Linda said, "Of course! Listen, you wouldn't by any chance be free for dinner?"

"Very free."

"Fine . . . then come by around five-thirty. We'll sit with Sara Kurtz and discuss the story. Then we can go to Louise's. It's a good Italian place where two ladies can go without people thinking they're trying to score. See you later. . . ."

Linda was just ending an editorial meeting when January arrived. She motioned for her to sit on the couch in the back of the room. Linda was sitting at her desk. Her editors and assistant editors sat in a semicircle surrounding her.

"I think that'll about wrap up most of the plans for the February issue," she said. There was a slight scuffling of chairs as everyone began to rise. Suddenly Linda said, "Oh, Carol, check on John Weitz. He said he might take over the Colony and give a Valentine's Day party. Find out if he is. Maybe we could simulate some shots of the decor so we could run it in the February issue. Also, if he has any idea of his guest list . . . I know it's early, but he must have about ten or twelve names that he knows he's going to invite." She stood up, signifying the meeting had come to an official end. Her hint of a weary smile conveyed that a real smile would take too much out of her. Her eyes clocked the group who were hastily disbanding. "Where's Sara Kurtz?" she demanded.

"She's on the phone with London," a young man answered. "She's trying to track down an idea she has that the Bow Bell Boys are not really English."

"That's ridiculous," Linda snapped. "They're the biggest sensation to hit the States since the Rolling Stones."

The young man nodded almost apologetically. "Yes, but Sara swears she saw the lead singer doing a disc jockey gig in Cleveland in 1965. She claims he's straight from Shaker Heights. And you know Sara—she never forgets a face."

"Well, send her in. I need her now."

Everyone left in little groups. Linda walked over to January and flopped down on the couch. "And this was an easy day," she sighed. She watched January light a cigarette. "Oh, you got the commercial, I see."

"Wrong. I was among the last three to be eliminated. Seems I inhale like a champ . . . but my exhaling needs work."

Linda laughed and walked to her desk. She pressed an intercom buzzer. "Tell Sara Kurtz to come here immediately. I can't wait all night while she tracks down one of her neuroses."

"Do you think the boy really comes from Cleveland?"

Linda shrugged. "Sara digs disc jockeys. The boy in Cleveland probably gave her a real brush. And she won't rest until she gets even. Gold help him if he *is* one of the Bow Bell Boys."

"She sounds dreadful . . ."

"She is. We'll get this over with. Then we'll talk."

Within seconds, an enormously tall girl, bearing an uncanny resemblance to Tiny Tim, loped into the room. Linda introduced Sara Kurtz, who stooped over as she shook hands with January. Then she pulled a crumpled pad out of a beat-up denim bag and began scratching away. She was mostly concerned with the spelling of January's name and was amazed to learn it was spelled like the month. After a few more questions, she uncoiled herself and backed out of the room.

"She's a beast," Linda said. "Keith claims she looks as if she could play for the New York Knicks, but her father was a good newspaperman, and oddly enough she's inherited a kind of style by osmosis. We save her for our shaft pieces. She gets her orgasms doing them. I told her that this has to be an 'up' piece—that's why she looks even more miserable than usual."

"Why does she like to shaft people?" January asked. "I would think she wouldn't be able to face them afterwards."

"Maybe when you look like Sara you just naturally hate the world."

"But I thought you said being ugly was in."

"I did. But there's an 'In' ugly and an 'Out' ugly. Sara is definitely out. But don't worry. You have complete approval of the article. Here's the paper . . . all signed." She handed January an envelope. "Tell Daddy he doesn't have to worry."

January put it in her bag. Linda stared at her closely. "Hey, does losing that commercial really bug you?"

"Of course not. Why?"

"For a second there . . . you looked like it was the end of the world."

January forced a smile. "That's ridiculous. I've got everything to be happy about. I'm in New York . . . my father has a wonderful wife . . . I have a beautiful room all redecorated for me at the Pierre."

"Bullshit!"

"What?"

"I said bullshit. January, who are you trying to con? You hate living there and you can't stand seeing your father with Deirdre Milford Granger."

January shrugged. "That's not true. Besides I rarely see them. But I do feel funny about living there. I mean, it's her apartment and I feel like an interloper."

"Then move."

"He doesn't want me to."

"Look, when you try to please everyone, you wind up pleasing no one."

January stubbed out her cigarette. "Trouble is, I don't really know what I want. Probably because all my life I never really thought about anything except being with my father. And now I find when I go out on a date it's like . . . I don't know what to do . . . how to act."

Linda whistled. "Boy, do you need a shrink!"

"I had enough of that at the Clinique."

"What?"

"Oh, Linda . . . it's a long story. But look. When you grow up without a mother, it's a natural thing to make your father the major thing in your life. And when you have a father like Mike . . . why not?"

"I agree," Linda said. "Your father is damned attractive. But then, so is David Milford. Ronnie Wolfe had it in his column that you were at Raffles with him the other night. I don't dig that phony social scene. But if you have to go that route, going with David Milford is the only way to go."

"That was Dee's party. We also had a date last night. He asked me back to his apartment, but I wouldn't go. When he took me home he didn't even try to kiss me goodnight."

Linda stood up. "Let's go to Louise's. We both could use a drink."

January liked the restaurant. Louise was a warm motherly woman who brought them a plate of her homemade chicken liver. She welcomed January to New York and told her she looked like a movie star. The whole atmosphere was home-like, and January began to relax. She ordered a glass of white wine, and Linda ordered a double Tanqueray martini on the rocks. For a few moments they both sat in silence.

Linda took a long swallow of her drink and swished it around on the ice. Then she said, "What did you think of Keith?"

"He's very nice."

"Have you seen him since?"

"Me? Why would I see him?"

"Well, *I* haven't," Linda snapped. Then she took another long swallow of the martini. "Tell me, please. Tell me the truth. Did he come on to you?"

"Did he what?"

"Make a pass . . ."

"Of course not! We went to see the show and–"

"And what?"

"I walked out on it . . . and him, I guess."

They were both silent. Then January said, "Look, Linda, maybe I'm old-fashioned. But I was shocked and–"

"Well, I have nothing against nudity," Linda said. "But–" She stopped. "What is this bullshit I'm giving you? I sound as brainwashed as Keith. Sure, we're the big liberated generation. The body is beautiful–so show it. Well, I went down there last night. Keith was sitting in the audience. He didn't see me. But you tell me what's beautiful about a bunch of ugly people rubbing their bodies against one another in a dirty theater on a dirty stage. Their feet were black with dirt–it was revolting. And don't think those people with the limos come to see art! They come to see a lot of starving actors demean themselves. God, an actor has to go through enough rejection in his life . . . at least, let him have *some* personal privacy. But no, there's no such thing as personal dignity anymore. That's for squares. We're the new generation. We're liberated. Marriage is out . . . bastards are in. . . ."

"But yesterday you said you didn't believe in marriage."

Linda shook her head. "I don't know what I believe anymore. Look, my mother has had four husbands and is working on getting her fifth. My father had three wives. Between them I have seven half-brothers and sisters, whom I hardly know. They're all off in some version of Miss Haddon's. But they were born in wedlock so everything's all very proper. At least my mother thinks so–because that's what she was taught. But now our generation is against marriage–because that's what we've been taught."

"By whom?"

"By the people we meet and care about."

"Linda, you *do* want to marry Keith, don't you?"

"Maybe. But if he thought I felt that way I'd lose him. That is, if I haven't already."

"But what's happened?"

"He never came home that night. He called and said he's decided to live at that filthy commune for a while so he can think things out. He knows I'm against his being in that play. He hadn't told me which play it was that day in the office. Look, if nudity is important to a plot, if it's realism, then okay. But the way they're doing it in that play–" She shook her head. "But I know what's really bugging Keith. It's the fact that I earn thirty-five thousand a year plus a Christmas bonus and he earns thirty-five hundred a year including his unemployment insurance. To him I'm Establishment. I'm so mixed up. Look, I've tried to do it his way. I've sat with his friends. I've drunk beer instead of martinis. I've worn dungarees instead of slacks. But there's no law that says I have to live like a pig. I pay four hundred a month for my apartment. It's in a good neighborhood, in a good building, with a doorman and elevator operators. I'm in my office every morning before eight and sometimes I don't leave until midnight. I've earned the right to have a nice place to come home to. Why should I give it up and work on some underground newspaper for fifty bucks an article?"

"Is that what he wants you to do?"

"All I know is he's always putting down me, *Gloss* and every article I dream up. But he raves about a guy he knows who sells dirty poems to newspapers that run pictures of a man's penis on the cover. He claims the man is writing because he has something to say and isn't looking for plastic glory. I tell you I'm so sick of all these phrases. But I love him and I want him. It's not that I'm forcing him to do things my way . . . but if only we could compromise. I know we could have a great life together. I want it. Oh, God, I want it!"

"It must be a good feeling to really know what you want." January said.

"Don't you? Didn't they give you any direction at that fancy Swiss University? By the way, what was the name of the school? Sara will at least want your college credits."

"Linda, I'll tell you all about it . . . after dinner."

They sat over coffee and Linda listened silently as January told her about the Clinique. She sipped some brandy and tears came to her eyes when January had finished. "Jesus," she said softly. "You really had the shit kicked out of you. Three years out of your life . . . three years of waiting to come back to Daddy Dream Man. And then to find him married . . ."

January managed a smile. "Well, it's not as if he's deserted me. He isn't my lover."

"Isn't he?"

"Linda!"

"Oh, come on, January. You didn't sleep with that divine Italian who was responsible for you breaking your skull. You rejected David Milford. Any psychiatrist would tell you that on your second date with David you had a subconscious desire to cool the relationship because you liked him too much. You had the guilts. It was like cheating on Daddy."

"That's not true. Look at how he arranged the date. Our first time alone together. No candlelight and wine . . . no small talk . . . he arrives at five-thirty . . . calls me from the lobby . . . won't even come up for a drink. Then we sprint five blocks to the movie. Then he rushes me to Maxwell's Plum. It's a great swinging place. But you don't take a girl there when you want to talk and get really acquainted. *Then* he suddenly asks me up to his apartment."

Linda looked thoughtful. "I agree. There must be some conversation before you leap into bed. And when a man invites you to his apartment, it is usually for just one thing. Somehow it's different if *you* invite him up for a nightcap to your apartment. You're in control, and whatever happens seems natural and not planned. But you can't very well invite him up to the Pierre. Really, January, the first thing you've got to do is find an apartment of your own."

"I'd like to, but—"

"But what? Look, whether you realize it or not, you're eating your heart out every time you see your father with Dee. It's not fair to you . . . or them. Take my word for it—you're never going to have an affair until you move out on Daddy. And as for your career in the theater . . . well, I'm the last one to give you any advice there. . . ."

"I'm not Keith. I realize I'm not serious about acting," January said. "But I know I want to do something. To be part of the scene. I don't want to be like my mother."

"Why? What did she do besides die when you were young?"

"Oh, she . . . well, she sat around on the sidelines . . . with her big brown eyes just watching life. Watching . . . while Mike was *doing*. I want to *do* too!"

"Well, as I said, there's always an opening at *Gloss* for you."

"I don't want an 'in-name-only' job, Linda."

"It wouldn't be that kind of a job. I'd really put you to work."

"Are you serious?"

Linda nodded. "And so what if I asked you to use whatever

pull you could to get to certain people—or to get a story? I do that myself. My mother's sister is married to a golf pro. I used her to get me permission to travel on a big tournament. That's how I did my story on how the golf wives live. Now the money won't be too great to start with."

"I have over fifteen thousand of my own," January said. "And you're right—I'm going to get out of the Pierre."

"Listen." Linda snapped her fingers. "There's a bachelor in my building. Edgar Bailey. I think he's a closet queen. Anyway, he teaches at Columbia and he's going to Europe on a year's sabbatical. He asked me just the other day if I knew anyone who wanted to sublet. It's only one room . . . a studio job. He pays nothing for it. His rent's frozen. In fact, I think they built the building around him. Want me to find out the price?"

January looked at her watch. "It's only nine o'clock. Call him now. Maybe we could go over."

Edgar Bailey was enchanted with January. Her name enthralled him. He showed her the large walk-in closet, the small dressing room, the *marvelous* Castro Convertible, and the kitchen with a window. He said he paid one seventy-nine, but because of his furnishings he would have to ask two hundred and seventy-five.

"Come on, Mr. Bailey," Linda cut in. "You're paying one thirty-nine. I know from the super. They'd like to bomb you out of here. January will pay you two twenty-five a month—that's all it's worth. There isn't a stick of furniture that costs anything. Including the Castro. It's over ten years old."

He pursed his lips for a moment. Then he reached for a bottle of sherry and three tiny glasses. "To my new tenant. I know I could get much more, but I'll feel better knowing someone lovely will take care of my little home."

Linda raised her glass. "You also know you have to leave in ten days and you're getting panicky."

January raised her glass and smiled. "To your trip, Mr. Bailey. And to you, Linda."

Linda shook her head. "No, this one's for you. Here's to Ms. January."

Seven

January sat propped up in the Castro bed, surrounded by a pile of back issues of *Gloss*. She was working on her first assignment, an article called "Breakfasts of the 'B.T.W.'" B.T.W. stood for Beautiful Thin Women. She hadn't been able to get to Babe Paley or Lee Radziwill. But Dee had given permission to quote her as saying, "*Who* gets up before lunch! Only children eat breakfast." She also had quotes from a skinny lady poet, a skinny screen starlet, and a writer who was a militant member of Women's Lib. She was still trying to contact Bess Meyerson and Barbara Walters. Did Barbara Walters eat breakfast *before* or *after* the *Today* show? Just trying to reach these people was practically a full-time assignment.

She had made a careful study of all the current articles in the leading magazines and found the stories that caught her attention had openings that hooked the reader. She had tried ten different approaches, but none of them seemed right. Of course Linda expected to put a rewrite girl on it, but January wanted to surprise her and have the article stand on its own. Working on the magazine had given her the first identity she had ever known. The little windowless cubbyhole she went to every day was *her* office. Mr. Bailey's sublet was now *her* apartment. She paid the rent with money *she* earned.

The past three weeks had been hectic. But they had been three weeks of being on her own; making her own decisions. Getting through the first week had been the roughest. Especially breaking the news to Mike and Dee that she was moving. Dee's eyes had narrowed angrily, but before she could voice any objection, Mike had cut in and said, "I figured you'd want your own pad. Most girls do. And if that's what you really want . . . well, you sure as hell are entitled to it."

Dee insisted on looking at the apartment before January signed the lease. Edgar Bailey seemed stunned when she walked in. "Oh, Miss Granger . . . I mean Mrs. Wayne . . . Oh . . . I had no idea January was your daughter." January knew he was ready to collapse for settling for two hundred and twenty-five dollars.

"You mean it only has *one* room?" Dee asked.

"But it's so spacious," Edgar Bailey insisted. "And I'm so pleased to have someone like January live among my things in my little home."

Dee walked past him, pulled the drapes and groaned. "Good Lord, January. It's on the court!"

"A garden?" Edgar Bailey said timidly.

"No sunlight and only one room. But I suppose this is the new generation." Dee sighed. "Leave a luxury apartment for a slum."

Edgar Bailey came to life. "Mrs. Wayne, this is a very fine building."

Dee waved him off. "Well, I suppose we could make it more cheerful. Get rid of those awful drapes . . . change the rug . . . get some new throw pillows—"

"Mrs. Wayne." Mr. Bailey's voice cracked in near hysteria. "Nothing can be changed. Those drapes were made for me by—"

But Dee had already disappeared into the kitchen, and January followed her after quickly assuring Mr. Bailey that everything would stay intact and that she adored venetian blinds and his flowered drapes.

She had signed the lease and moved in October first. David sent her a Dracaena plant. Mr. Bailey had left a small bunch of rosebuds (which never did bloom), along with a little note wishing her luck. Linda sent her notepaper from Bergdorf's engraved with her name and her address. And at five o'clock, Mike arrived with a bottle of champagne. They drank it over the rocks, and Mike looked at the apartment with a smile. "Know something? I think it's great. You've been living with people all your life. In school, at the hospital. It's time you had some privacy."

Dee arrived at seven to pick him up. They were going to an exhibition at an art gallery, but she brought a basket of cocktail hors d'oeuvres. "You never know when you might need them. There are several tins of smoked oysters . . . now don't make a face. David adores them. You just put them on these little imported crackers. By the way, David also adores what I call rat cheese. Cut it in cubes and put toothpicks in it and he's happy as a clam. Which reminds me—how are you two getting on?"

"He sent that plant," January answered.

Dee smiled complacently. "Mike and I are leaving for a quick trip to Europe. There's a backgammon tournament in London that I'm entering. We'll be back soon. But we feel dreadful leaving you here with this grubby little apartment and job. Before I leave, is there anything I can do, other than reveal for your magazine that I don't eat breakfast?"

January hesitated. "Is . . . is Karla in town?"

"Why do you ask?"

"I'd love to do an interview with her."

Dee's laugh was cold. "She never does interviews. And it's not that she's pulling a Garbo or a Howard Hughes. She's just a stupid Polack. Oh, come now, January. Don't give me one of those 'everyone is equal' looks. I know Karla, and she is stupid. She's never read a book. She's never voted. She isn't aware of anything that's going on except her own creature comforts. She's in town. She called the other day. But to tell you the truth I've been too busy to see her. A little bit of Karla goes a long way. I mean, she won't lunch anywhere civilized. If she comes to dinner one must give her the entire guest list. It's ridiculous. It's not as if she's Nureyev or Princess Grace. She's just a has-been actress who for some insane reason still attracts incredible publicity."

So much for an interview with Karla.

She had written David a note thanking him for the plant. He had called and told her he was going out of town on business but would call her as soon as he returned. That was ten days ago. She went to dinner with Linda or some of the other girls at the office. But she was perfectly content to come home and work on her article and read. She bought a portable typewriter and taught herself to type with two fingers. Linda saw Keith occasionally, but they weren't officially "back together." He stayed at her apartment most of the time but insisted on keeping his things at the "commune." "Personally, I think he only stays with me because he likes my stall shower," Linda confided. "We're together . . . but it's just not the same." She refused to go downtown to see the show, but she did go along with the new health kick Keith was on. Organic food, twenty different vitamins a day, plus massive vitamin shots twice a week from a new doctor Keith swore was a genius. Obviously it worked, because Linda, who had always been enthusiastically energetic, was now supercharged. She never seemed to sleep. Sometimes she'd call January at three in the morning and shout, "Hey, don't tell me you're asleep! There's a divine Bogart movie on Channel Nine."

Mike had sent a card announcing that Dee was in the finals of the tournament. Somehow it didn't sit right. Mike, the gambler of all time, standing by, watching his wife throw the dice.

Now as she sat in the Castro bed, trying to get an opening paragraph, she found herself wondering if it was possible to write an amusing article without being bitchy. She stared at the quote she had from the vapid-faced model turned actress who had just made her first (and last) movie. Her part had been cut to ribbons because of her flat delivery, but she didn't seem to mind. "Oh, they were so nice to me out there. They got me real calves' liver for breakfast and I've never been more thinner." God, what Sara Kurtz would do with a quote like that.

She sighed and went to her typewriter. Even Dee's quote sounded snide. Yet when she had said it in her lazy way it had been amusing.

She put a fresh piece of paper into the machine and made a stab at a new opening. Maybe if she said the model was anemic and *had* to have liver . . . or maybe if she started it with, "The reason Deirdre Wayne is so beautiful . . ." No. She tore the paper out. There had to be a better way to get into it.

She was just putting in a fresh piece of paper when the phone rang. The sound vibrated through the room. She had forgotten to turn the bell to low. Probably Linda with another flash about a Bogart picture. She couldn't believe it when she heard the familiar, "Hi, babe!"

"Daddy! Where are you?"

"P. J. Clarke's!"

"What!"

"We just got off the plane, and I had a big yen for chili. So we came here right from the airport. How about joining us? I'll send the car for you."

"Oh, I'd love to. But I'm undressed and I'm working on a story that has to be done by the end of the week."

"You really writing it?"

"Yes. And I think it's going to be all right."

"Hey, that's really great. Well, I'd better get back to Nick the Greek—that's my new name for Dee. The broad came in third and won fifteen thousand dollars. How about having lunch with me tomorrow? Just the two of us." He was shouting above the noise in the restaurant.

"Oh, Mike, I'd love it."

"Well, you dream up wherever you want to go. I'll call you at the magazine at noon. Oh, wait a second. Dee's coming over. I think she wants to say Hello."

"January . . ." It was Dee's crisp voice.

"Congratulations! I'm very impressed," January said.

"Oh, we had a marvelous time. Are you coming here?"

"No. I told Mike . . . I'm all piled up here with work."

Dee laughed. "Oh, you big career girl. Oh, Mike . . ." Dee's voice went off the phone. "Better get back to our table. Someone might grab it. Order your bloody chili and a spinach salad for me. January, are you still there?"

"Yes, and you're making me hungry."

"It's a mob scene here tonight. I don't know why everyone is suddenly staring at the door. Someone must be coming in. Probably Onassis and Jackie. Tell me, January. Are you having a marvelous time living your career-girl life?"

"I'm enjoying it, Dee. I think I can really write . . . a little."

"Well, that's nice and—" Dee's voice had suddenly trailed off.

At the same time January heard a great swell of voices from the people at P.J.'s."

"Dee . . . are you still there?"

"Yes . . ." Dee's voice seemed strained.

"Are you all right?"

"Yes . . . I'm fine. Tell me, January. When was the last time you saw David?"

"Why, I—"

"There's a near riot here—he's just walked in with my old friend Karla."

"Karla at P.J.'s?"

"Oh, she does that now and then—pops up where no one would ever expect her." Dee's voice was easy. "But don't you fret, darling. Karla's no competition for you."

"I'm not fretting, Dee. Actually I'm very impressed with David."

"You go back to . . . whatever you're doing, angel. I'll take care of things. It will take me a few days to get organized now that I'm back. So why don't we plan on brunch . . . Sunday . . . around one-ish."

January hung up. She wasn't bothered about David being with Karla. But she was bothered that he was back in town and hadn't called her. She went back to her typewriter, but she couldn't concentrate on the article. She got up and went to the kitchen for a Coke. She saw the new watering can she had bought for David's Dracaena. She had just watered it yesterday. The florist said it should only be watered twice a week. She grabbed the can and filled it. Then she marched into the living room and poured it on the plant. "Drown, you bastard," she said. "Drown! Drown!!"

When Dee came out of the phone booth she managed to collide accidentally with David and Karla who were heading toward a small table in the back of the room.

"Karla, I can't believe it. You, braving P.J.'s," Dee said lightly.

Karla smiled. "There was a showing of *Red Shoes* at a little movie house near here. I have seen it so many many times, and always it is entrancing. And it was such a beautiful night

I wanted to walk. And then I got hungry." She turned and looked at Mike, who had left the table and come to Dee's side. "And is this your handsome new husband?"

"Yes, and you are a lady I've always wanted to meet," Mike said.

Karla held out her hand. "And now . . . you see how easily it has happened."

"How long are you staying in town?" Dee asked.

Karla shrugged her broad shoulders. "That is the lovely part about not working. I stay where I like . . . as long as I like."

"We're opening the house in Palm Beach in about ten days. Perhaps you'd like to come down. I can give you the east wing you had before."

Karla smiled. "That is so kind. Perhaps I shall . . . Or perhaps I go to Gstaad to ski. Who knows? But even ten days is so far off. Right now I can only think of my stomach and I am very hungry." She turned to Mike. "It was so very nice to meet you." Then she smiled and walked off to her table with David following.

Dee sat down with Mike and rummaged through her bag for her cigarette case. "Mike, I don't like to pry, but do you think January has discouraged David?"

He smiled. "Karla is heavy competition."

"Ridiculous. Karla is old enough to be David's mother." Dee sighed. "I thought David would be mad for January. They look so perfect together."

"Dee, I learned a long time ago that looking the part doesn't always mean you can play it."

"But January should try to encourage him. After all, she's not a baby. She'll be twenty-one in a few months."

He laughed. "That's not exactly over the hill. Besides, the girls of today don't rush into marriage. Half of them don't even believe in it."

"January is not today's girl. She's caught between two worlds. The isolated one she just left . . . and the new one she doesn't quite know how to enter. If she ever really fell in love and it didn't work out, she could crack up."

"She's not going to crack up, and it seems to me she's adjusted just great. She's got a job, her own apartment. What more do you want? She's only been here a little over a month. Look, you can't wrap people up like Christmas packages. And that goes for David as well as January." He looked toward the back of the room. "Karla is one hell of an exciting woman."

"She's a stupid uneducated peasant."

He shook his head. "You dames really kill me. She's been to your place in Marbella, she's been on your yacht, you've just invited her to Palm Beach . . ."

"Darling, I always have houseguests. It's always good to have a 'live-in' celebrity. Besides, I feel sorry for Karla. She's really a very lonely lost soul."

He started to laugh. "What strikes you so funny?" Dee demanded.

"You women, the way you waste your pity. Worrying about January 'getting on,' Karla being lost and lonely. Look, my daughter will find her own way. And as for Karla, she's far from being lost. It's easy to see why David would go for her."

"Really?" Dee's voice was cold. "Then why did you ever wind up with plain old me?"

He reached out and patted her hand. "Sweetheart, I cut my teeth on the top beauties in Hollywood. And you're something special. The question is . . . why did you want me?"

"Because–" and her eyes grew distant.

"Because what?"

"Because I loved you," she said seriously. "Oh, I know we could have been together without marriage. But I think that kind of thing is grubby. I'm not old-fashioned. God, the way things are today, you're labeled archaic if you have *any* standards. If you have money you're supposed to play it down. If you have a luxurious home you're committing some kind of crime. But what's wrong with having a big estate? I keep a full staff of servants at all my places all year round. I'm giving these people work. The pilots of my plane have families. I'm responsible for their children being able to go to college. The captain of my boat gets paid fifty-two weeks a year and so does the crew. When I give big parties in Palm Beach I'm giving work to caterers, musicians, designers . . . I like to wear beautiful clothes . . . I like to see other people wearing them. I like gracious dining and pretty people. I hate this place and all places like it that people claim are so 'in.' And when I see Karla walk in here I know it's not just a casual evening with David. Even a woman like Karla gets lonely. It's no fun living alone. David could offer Karla an exciting life, sex, good companionship—all the things I want for your daughter."

Mike glanced over at Karla. David was whispering something in her ear. "Well, it looks like David has his own ideas."

Dee stared staright ahead. "It's up to January to change his ideas."

"Really?"

"Oh, Mike, don't you know that a woman can make a man think her idea was really *his*?"

"She can?"

"I bet you thought you wooed and won me," she said.

"Well, if I didn't, I sure wasted a lot of money in Marbella."

"I'll tell you a secret," she said. "I decided to marry you the second evening we spent together. I just had to let you go through the motions."

He laughed and signaled for the check. "I still don't know how I got so lucky." He leaned across the table and took her hands. "Why, Dee? I mean, why did you pick me?"

Her eyes met his and held them. "Because I wanted you. And I always try to get what I want."

David arrived at the Côte Basque at one the following day. Dee's call had come at ten that morning. "David darling, I'd love to see you. How about having lunch today?" For the rest of the morning he had definite signs of an ulcer attack.

They sat at a banquette table. He asked all the proper questions. About the backgammon tournament, about London, about the new shows she had seen in the West End. He sat there with a forced smile, waiting for the whiplash. But when they finished lunch and her conversation drifted to the current state of the market, he lit a cigarette and began to relax. Maybe she just had no luncheon date. Maybe it was just his own guilt that made him so uptight. He signaled for the check. In a few more minutes it would all be over. He'd walk through that door and out into the sunlight.

She struck just as he was signing the check. "David . . . what is this thing with you and Karla?"

He kept his hand steady as he continued to write. (Two dollars for the captain . . . four dollars for the waiter.) He felt a pulse beat in his neck and wondered if she could see it. He took longer than was necessary to put away his pen, and when he spoke he hoped his voice sounded casual and light. "I think she's great fun to be with . . . we have a lot of laughs."

"Oh, come off it, dear boy. Karla is anything but a bundle of laughs. In fact she can be quite dreary." She shook her head. "I can understand that thing you had with that divine Dutch girl—Kim something or other—even if she does walk into Raffles with a see-through blouse. At least *she* has something to show. But when a young man is seen tagging around after an older woman . . . people do talk."

"Oh . . . what do they say?"

"That she's giving him money, that he's impotent and is just her escort—or that he's gay." Dee's smile was almost melancholy. "I don't have to tell you, because we've all said the same thing about others."

"That's ridiculous," he said.

"*You* know it's ridiculous and *I* know it's ridiculous. But people do talk."

"We just have fun together, that's all. She likes being with me," he said doggedly.

Dee's laugh was merry, but her eyes were cold. "Don't be ridiculous. She's not capable of enjoying anyone's company. But she just might be interested in a young man who she thinks will wind up with a big inheritance." She opened her cigarette case and waited while David fumbled for a match. She exhaled the smoke slowly and stared at the cigarette. "I really should give these things up . . . I hear Nina Creopopolis has emphysema . . . which reminds me . . . what do you think of Becker, Neiman and Boyd?"

"They're a pretty fair law firm. Why?"

"I'm thinking of using them. I want to draw up a new will."

"Why? I mean, I thought Dad handled everything like that for you. Look, not just because he's my father . . . but you can't compare Becker, Neiman and Boyd to Dad's firm."

"You're prejudiced, darling." She patted his hand. "But I like that. God knows, no one is more family-oriented than I. But I should get an outside opinion. This change in my will isn't like the others. I need some very sophisticated advice. After all, I have a husband and a stepdaughter. I care about them, David. I really do. I must see that they are provided for."

"Of course." (Oh God, his voice had cracked. Now she knew he was scared. He turned to her with his best "young and earnest" look.) "Dee, you know it would break Dad's heart if you switched to another firm."

"And would it break your heart if I switched to another brokerage house?"

He didn't even try to answer. His hand shook as he lit his own cigarette. No more playing cat and mouse. The mouse was caught and the cat was beginning the game of teasing it to death.

She leaned over and kissed his cheek. "Well, so far I'm just thinking. That's all. Just thinking."

He walked her to her car, and she pretended not to notice the photographer from *Women's Wear* who snapped her. She held her cheek for him to kiss and said, "I've enjoyed our lunch, David. It's good to keep in touch like this. I like to keep my family happy . . . and together."

He stared after her until her car disappeared into traffic. Then he went to the nearest phone booth and called January.

Eight

MIKE WAS MIXING Bloody Marys when January arrived at the Pierre for Sunday brunch. She had seen Mike, but this was the first time she had seen Dee since her return from London. Dee put down the *Times* crossword puzzle and held her cheek to January. "I don't know why I bother with this damn thing," she said. "I started it last night, and I actually lose sleep over it. And really there's no great achievement in getting it done. I know some of the dreariest people who whizz through it. Of course, most of them use a dictionary. But that's cheating. Now . . . sit down, and tell us all about the job. Is it fun?"

"Yes, they accepted my article. I'm really excited about it. Of course, it has to be edited—I don't punctuate too well—but Linda and the whole staff said it was really good. I hope you both like it."

Dee smiled. "I hope you aren't taking this job so seriously that you're neglecting your social life."

"Well, I do get up every morning at seven. And I rarely leave the office before seven at night."

"Why, that's slave labor," Dee said.

"You're much too skinny," Mike said as he handed her the drink. "I bet you're skipping meals."

"Oh, I eat a lot. Last night I had a fabulous meal . . . even cherries jubilee. I was with David."

Dee's reaction was merely polite interest. "And how is my handsome young cousin?"

"Fine. We went to the St. Regis to see Veronique."

"Veronique? Is she still around doing her third-rate Edith Piaf act?" Dee asked.

January shrugged. "I never saw her before. But she has a great act. She has three Russian dancers with her. Young men. And one of them had the sex change operation . . . in reverse. I mean, he *was* a girl—now she's a man."

"Now, January—" Dee's tone was a gentle reprimand. "One mustn't give lip service to dirty little rumors like that. I know they're the kind of stories your magazine likes to play up, but—"

"You're so right. I wish I could get a story on 'Nina into Nicholas.' I tried my damnedest last night!"

"Don't tell me you actually talked to this creature."

"Of course. Upstairs in Veronique's suite."

Dee put down her drink. "But how did you get to her suite? Is Veronique a friend of David's?"

"No . . . Karla's."

"Karla!" Dee's voice went up an octave.

"Yes. You see, David had a reservation for a table for two and when we got there they had us stuck behind a post. Then this young Greek man came over and introduced himself and said he and his friend were with Karla and that Karla would like us to join them. She had a wonderful table in a secluded alcove but with a perfect view of the floor. And she is so beautiful. In fact I was so busy staring at her that I almost missed seeing Nina-Nicholas. Then after the show Karla took us up to Veronique's suite and Nina-Nicholas was there. She . . . or he . . . talks about it openly. Linda says she'll raise my salary if I can get an interview for *Gloss*. But Nina-Nicholas says all the magazines have asked her . . . even offered to pay for her story."

"I think vanity might be the key," Mike said. "Tell him or her that you'll do a color photo layout by a top man and give him the pictures and the color plates. And maybe spring for some wardrobe like a Cardin outfit . . . there are a lot of ways to soften someone."

January sighed. "That's just it—we haven't got that kind of a budget."

"January," Dee cut in. "Tell me—what happened after the show?"

"Well . . . we had a drink in Veronique's suite and—"

Sadie came in and announced that brunch was served. They went into the dining room. Mario served them, and Mike insisted January take some sausage. "You can use it. I don't like you this thin."

Dee smiled with a show of good nature. Then she said, "You were telling us about Veronique."

"Oh . . . well." January swallowed the sausage. "It was as if we were suddenly transported into a foreign country. Everyone had a different accent. Veronique is French, Karla's accent is sort of Middle-European, the two Greek boys had accents, and Nina-Nicholas is Russian. So everyone used French as the common denominator, which was fine for me. Only poor David didn't understand a word."

"Where did you go after that?" Dee asked.

"Nowhere. Karla went off with the Greek boys and David took me home because he's playing squash this morning at nine."

Dee was silent for a moment. She stabbed at her eggs, then put down her fork. "I'm so furious I can't eat."

"What's wrong?" Mike went on buttering his toast.

"Your daughter being dumped before midnight so David could go off to Westport with Karla."

"What makes you say that?" Mike asked.

"I talked to Karla yesterday. She told me she was leaving for Westport last night for one last weekend in the country before it gets too cold. Don't you see . . . this was all planned. Karla never goes to a supper club. She never goes anywhere. Sure, she knows Veronique . . . but she refused to go to a party honoring Nureyev, whom she really admires, because of her fetish about crowds. But because David obviously felt he had to see January, they decided this whole thing between them—a lovely way to kill two birds with one stone. Karla would see Veronique for old times' sake, and at the same time David could take January on a date. Then January would be dumped . . . and the two of them drive off to Westport."

Mike's jaw tightened but he continued to eat. "If David wants to go off for a weekend, I think that's his business."

"And make a fool of your daughter for a woman more than twice her age."

Mike stopped eating and pushed his plate away. His voice was quiet and even. "Dee, I think you ought to let people make their own decisions and live their own lives."

January wished she could suddenly vanish. Dee was actually angry, and Mike's jaw was getting that clenched look. In an effort to break the mood, she said lightly, "Listen, both of you . . . I had a marvelous time . . . really. David and I got on just fine and—"

"Then why did you let that Polack walk off with him?" Dee demanded.

January held on to the table until her knuckles went white. She had enjoyed the evening with David . . . he had been warm and attentive. And now Dee was ruining it. It had never entered her mind that the Karla thing had been prearranged. David had seemed genuinely surprised to see her, and Karla had gone out of her way to be gracious and warm to her. She had asked about her job and given her permission to quote her as saying she ate oatmeal every morning for breakfast.

Now she suddenly had doubts. Had it all been arranged? Was David really in love with Karla? All this flashed through her mind as she watched the tension between Mike and Dee. Suddenly she knew she had to get out of there. It was dreadful enough to learn that she had been a "mercy date" with David. But to have Mike and Dee fight . . . over her! Talking about her as if she wasn't there. And how must she look to Mike? A real zero!

Her father's anger made Dee suddenly back down. Her lips trembled and she tried to manage a smile. A pleading tone crept into her voice. "Mike . . . I'm only trying to do things for her sake. Wasn't that your main concern when we got married? Didn't you tell me you wanted to be sure January had everything because of what she had gone through? All the good times she had missed?"

"That doesn't mean you have the right to run her life—to force her to date a man who obviously has other inclinations."

"Oh, good Lord. David told me that January was one of the most beautiful girls he had ever seen." She sighed. "Maybe I've tried too hard, because nothing seems to have worked. I planned that beautiful bedroom for January and she walked out on it. I had planned we'd all spend the holidays together in Palm Beach. I thought I'd send the plane for January and David and we'd have a family thing there on Thanksgiving. And then on Christmas I want to give a big ball, as I did a few years ago. Fly in someone like Peter Duchin. Invite Mayor Lindsay, Lenny, Rex . . . all the fun people. And I had hoped that January and David would announce their engagement by then–"

"That's all very nice," Mike said. "But maybe it's not what January wants."

"How can she know what she wants?" Dee's voice went cold. "She's got to be taught to want the right things."

"For three years she had to be taught just to walk and talk," Mike shouted. "From now on it's her ballgame."

Dee's eyes narrowed. "All right! Let her work at that dingy magazine. Let her live in that third-rate apartment house. I'm not going to try anymore. Why should I knock myself out when you're both such ingrates? Neither of you even knows how to enjoy the nice things in life. Let her freeze in New York this winter. I'm not going to beg her to come to Palm Beach."

"Maybe I won't go to Palm Beach either," Mike said.

"Oh really?" Dee said softly. "Tell me, Mike, what will you do? Move out of here? Find a big apartment for yourself and your daughter. Produce a hit Broadway show. Amass a fortune to leave her from all your *hits*! Go ahead. Why should I even bother to try to get her married. *You* can give her the world. Go on! Produce a show . . . a picture . . . give her back her dreams."

January saw the color drain from her father's face. She stood up. "Mike . . . you've made all my dreams come true. You don't have to do another thing. I'm a big girl now. I love my work on the magazine. And from now on, I have to make my dreams come true on my own. I'd love to come to Palm Beach on Thanksgiving. Really, I'm looking forward to it. And Dee . . . honest . . . I appreciate all you've done. I loved the room you offered me. It's just that–well–I have to be on my own now. And David is very nice. In fact, he's one of the nicest people I've ever met . . . and you both mustn't quarrel over me." She stopped. They were sitting, stiff and motionless, staring at each other. She backed away from the table. "Look, I have to run. I promised Linda I'd help on the planning of some new articles for the magazine." She kissed her father. His cheek felt as if it had turned to stone. Then she dashed out of the apartment.

Mike never looked after her. He stared at Dee, frozen with rage. When he spoke his voice was low and controlled. "You just cut off my balls in front of my daughter."

Dee laughed nervously. "Oh, stop it, Mike . . . let's not fight. We never have before."

"And never will again!"

She came to him and put her arms around him. Her voice was silky but her eyes were frightened. "Mike, you know I love you . . ."

He shoved her away and left the table. She ran after him as he headed for the bedroom. "I'll be packed and out in an hour."

"Mike!" She grabbed his arm as he pulled a suitcase from the closet. But he shook her off. "Mike—" she pleaded. "Forgive me . . . please . . . please forgive me . . . don't go. Please don't go!"

He stopped and looked at her curiously. "Tell me something, Dee . . . why *did* you marry me?"

"Because I love you." She wound her arms around his neck. "Oh, Mike . . . our first quarrel and it's my fault. Forgive me. Please, angel. It's not right for us to fight. It's because of your daughter." He pulled away but she ran after him. "Mike, I never had a child . . . I'm probably stepping out of line because of my eagerness to treat January like a daughter. I'm probably going about it all wrong . . . saying all the wrong things . . . being overbearing . . . overprotective . . . as I am with David. I never had a brother or sister . . . he's been like a son to me. And now with January . . . I guess I pushed too hard. It's just that I want her to be happy. And for us to fight is ridiculous. We both say things we don't mean. It's David and Karla I'm angry at . . . not you." Her panic mounted as he continued to throw things into his bag. "Mike . . . don't . . . please! I love you. How can I prove it? I'll call January and apologize. I'll do anything!"

He stopped and looked at her. "Anything?"

"Yes."

"Okay. I never asked you for a thing, did I? I even signed a premarital agreement that if I divorced you I wouldn't get a dime. Right?"

"I'll tear it up," she said.

"No, keep it. I don't want a cent. But from now on—cut all this talk about how you love January and how concerned you are about her future. Put your money where your mouth is!"

"What do you mean?"

"I want to know that if some day I drop dead watching you play backgammon, my daughter is going to be a rich young lady."

"I promise. I'll do it tomorrow. I'll leave her a million dollars in trust."

He stared at her and his eyes were hard. "That's chicken shit."

"What do you want?"

"Ten million."

She hesitated a moment, then nodded slowly. "All right . . . I promise. Ten million."

He smiled slightly. "And from now on, cool it on David. That's an order. If he has a thing for Karla, it will have to burn out on its own and not because you demand it. But in any event, I'm not having January shoved at him. Remember that!"

"I promise."

"And I don't want any cracks about her job. Goddammit, she's trying. She's got ambition, and when you lose that, baby, you've really cashed in your chips."

"I promise, Mike." She put her arms around him and kissed his neck. "Now come on . . . smile. Don't be angry."

"You gonna stay out of her life and not butt in?"

"I'll never mention her name to David again."

"And the ten million you promised to lay on her is also a deal."

She nodded.

He stared at her for a moment, then he swept her up and tossed her on the bed. "Okay. Now that we've had our first fight . . . let's fuck and make up."

David arrived at the Racquet Club five minutes early. His father's voice had sounded urgent. That meant trouble. Just when everything was going so great. Usually he hated Mondays, but he had awakened this morning feeling he owned the world. His date with January at the St. Regis had gone off without a hitch. She had bought the idea that running into Karla was an accident. She was even pleased about it . . . like a fan. And she certainly had no inkling that at midnight he and Karla had driven to Westport. Even now, he felt light-headed just thinking about it. It was the first time he had ever spent an entire night with her. He'd never get over the unbelievable sight of Karla in the kitchen the following morning, making him bacon and eggs. It had been the greatest twenty-four hours of his life. She had borrowed the country place from a friend and their privacy was perfect. The house was set back in the midst of six acres of its own property. Even the weather had cooperated. Sunday had been one of those rare days when autumn lives up to all of its poetic descriptions. To him autumn had always meant the beginning of winter. Early dusk; a gray rainy day on Wall Street; a dusty wind and no taxis. But autumn on a country road in Westport was an explosion of colored leaves that crunched underfoot, clear air and the feeling of complete isolation from the world.

And this had been a good Monday. The good weather had followed them into the city. Even New York's rancid air seemed cleaner. The market had closed up three points for a change, and at three o'clock she had called to tell him he could escort her to Boris Grostoff's. That meant he had really made her inner circle. Boris had been her favorite director and his small intimate dinners numbered among the few parties Karla attended.

He saw his father enter and rose to greet him. The old man waited until their drinks arrived. Then he came right to the point.

"What does January Wayne look like?"

David was startled by the question. "January? Why . . . she's beautiful."

"Really?" His father seemed surprised. He sipped his Scotch thoughtfully. "Then why is Dee so frantic about her?"

"I don't understand, sir."

"She was in my office this morning to change her will. Her main concern seems to get this stepdaughter married. I figured the girl might be awkward-looking . . . or unattractive."

David shook his head. "Actually she's one of the most beautiful girls I've ever seen."

His father reached into his pocket and took out a slim leather-bound notebook. "I jotted down some of the changes she wants in the will. It's in the process of being drawn up."

"Do they concern me?"

"Very much. You are no longer an executor of the estate."

David felt the blood rush to his face. "She cut me out!"

"I've been bruised also. Our office is now sharing the executor powers along with Yale Becker of Becker, Neiman and Boyd. But the door is still open for you, my boy—there's a provision that *if* before Dee's death, David Milford is married to someone who has met with her approval, he will then become an executor and head the foundation."

"Why, that bitch," David said softly.

"Oh, there's more," his father answered. "Her stepdaughter, January Wayne, will inherit one million dollars *when* she marries, and *ten* million is to be put in trust for her, to be paid out on the occasion of her father's death—or Dee's, should she predecease him."

"I can't believe it," David said.

"I can't either," his father said. "Of course, it's not an irrevocable trust. Dee can always change it. Odd that Mike Wayne didn't think about that. Well, I guess it's obvious that the man's sophistication does not extend to the drawing up of a will. I find his faith rather childlike, especially knowing Dee. But for the moment it will probably stand because it looks to me as if she's really in love with this man. This amazing generosity toward the daughter is pretty good insurance on his staying with her. One thing for sure—Mike Wayne seems to be running this marriage. And here's the odd part—he wants nothing for himself, just this unbelievable inheritance for his daughter. It made me think the girl was totally unmarriageable and that the money was the only way to buy her a husband."

David frowned. "She's shoved January at me right from the start. She wants the girl married and out of the way. I think for the first time in her life, Dee is really in love. Also, she likes to run things, likes to feel her power. And with Mike Wayne she has no power—just through his daughter."

"And she figured by getting her married to you, that would please him?"

"No. I think she wants January married because she thinks of her as a rival for Mike's affections."

"David, what on God's earth are you talking about?"

"I can't put my finger on it," David said slowly. "But that first night—several times I caught them looking at each other. January and her father. And there was an intimacy in their eyes . . . not like a father and daughter. I was January's date, but I actually felt he was my competition. Dee must have felt it too."

"But why would she cut you out as executor of her will?"

David smiled. "It's obvious she wants me to be the one to remove her competition. The bait is there . . . in black and white."

"Good Lord. Do you have a chance? I mean, has the girl taken a shine to you?"

"I don't know. I've taken her out. But—"

"Well, would you like to bring her to the house for dinner?"

"No, let me do it my way." He sighed. "Well, I guess men have given up more for ten million dollars."

"What are you giving up?" his father asked.

"Karla."

His father stared. "Good God! I was smitten with her when I was your age. Never missed one of her films. Twenty-five years ago I used to moon over her. But now . . . good Lord . . . she has to be your mother's age."

"Karla is only fifty-two."

"Your mother won't be fifty until February."

"I don't think of age when I'm with Karla. And it's not as if I intend to marry her. Look, Dad . . . I know it has to end. I know one day I'll wake up and suddenly I'll be bored with eating steaks in her kitchen and rushing to movies that I hate. And on that day I'll break all records with a fifty-yard dash to January Wayne."

"And do you think she'll be there waiting?"

David sighed. "I try to keep my hand in. I really do. But right now I can't give up Karla. Not yet . . ."

"Do many people know about this Karla affair?"

"No. She never socializes, except on rare occasions, like tonight. I'm escorting her to a director's house for dinner."

"That's exactly how you'll be known if this affair continues. An escort . . . to an ex-movie queen." His father leaned across the table. "Suppose keeping your hand in isn't enough for January. While you're busy with Karla, suppose January meets another man, a man who meets with Dee's approval. Perhaps even a broker at another brokerage house. And would this woman—Karla—place her money in your hands and allow you to manage her funds?"

David shook his head. "She's known to be the tightest woman in the world."

His father nodded. "Then let's say she wouldn't exactly be an asset to you at the brokerage house."

David nodded. "You've made your point. And I have the distinct feeling that if I don't start really romancing little January, Cousin Dee's next move will be to change brokerage houses, too."

His father raised his glass. "Well, hop to it, son. Hop to it."

Nine

THE DANCE FLOOR at Le Club was crowded. David held January close and inched her around the floor. He had taken her to Le Mistral for dinner. Several times he had held her hand and had been agreeably surprised at her response. Dee and Mike would be leaving for Palm Beach in less than a week, and he was determined to have January report the wonderful turn their relationship had taken. And once Dee was gone, it would be harder for her to keep track of just how *many* glowing evenings they had together. But at least she'd know he was in there pitching.

Of course a great deal depended on January's reactions. He had to make her really fall in love with him. She was no Kim Voren. To Kim he represented not only a great stud, but security and a place in society. January didn't need any of that. No, he had to come on strong with her . . . in bed. Once you hooked them in the feathers, the rest was easy. He could leave Kim alone for ten days and she'd still jump when he called.

All he needed was time. He had told Karla that Dee was forcing him to take January around occasionally. Karla understood. He had a bad moment when he hinted that he might have to go to Palm Beach over the Thanksgiving holidays. And Karla had said, "Yes, Dee invited me too."

For a moment he had panicked. He could never manage that. In Karla's presence he acted like one possessed. Dee and January would spot it immediately. "Would you come?" he had tried to make his voice sound as enthusiastic as usual.

"No. Thanksgiving is not my holiday. Even though I became a citizen, I never quite got used to it. It is such an American holiday—like the Fourth of July."

But lately he had noticed a slight restlessness in her attitude. When she spoke of Europe, which she did quite frequently now, he felt a sick feeling of foreboding. Yet deep down he knew his only salvation would be if she suddenly disappeared off the face of the earth. Because he now realized that this affair was never going to burn itself out . . . on his part. Sometimes he even had fantasies of her death. If she was irrevocably gone—only then could he settle down to the business of living his own life.

And even now as he held this beautiful girl in his arms on the crowded dance floor, he was thinking of Karla. It was wrong . . . sick. He'd always had complete control before. No woman had ever dominated him. Even in his wildest affairs he might have been carried away for a few weeks . . . that was part of the fun and excitement of a new romance, but eventually he always got the upper hand and the woman began to want him more than he wanted her, and he, in turn, cooled off. But it hadn't happened with Karla. And he knew it never would.

But he had to become all-important to January. He had to make this girl want him, and need him, and *wait* for him. He wanted a little more time. He looked at her and smiled. She was really beautiful, even more beautiful than Kim. If he made his move tonight . . . would that be rushing her? *Rushing her!* It was November. He had known her almost two months. Kim had gone to bed with him the first night. And Karla the next afternoon. He had planned it for tonight. He had even bought the albums she liked.

Suddenly he felt slightly nervous. He hadn't gone after a girl in ages. They had always come after him! Suddenly he didn't quite know how to put it. Maybe he was out of practice. Or maybe it was because January was a cut above the girls around town. She didn't grope for him under the table or say, "Let's go home and make love."

He snapped to attention. She had asked him something.

"I hear it's always sold out, but if you have any problems,

Keith Winters—he's a friend of Linda's—well, he knows a boy in *Hair* who could get us house seats."

Hair! Christ, he had promised to take her to see that show when she first came to New York. He smiled. "I'll get a pair for next week. Our office has a good ticket broker. Don't worry."

He had to score with her . . . tonight. It had to be all set by the time they went to Palm Beach. His father said Dee's new will had been all signed and witnessed. It was now official. Of course if he married January everything would probably be changed . . . or even if they got engaged. He was possessed with a sudden feeling of urgency. He took her arm and led her off the floor. "It's impossible to talk here," he said. "Somehow we never get to talk. We're always with people."

He helped her to her seat. Then she said, "We could always go to Louise's."

He laughed. "No. Carmen the bartender and I are both football nuts. We'd wind up discussing next Sunday's game. Look, why not come back to my apartment? I have all the albums you said you like. Plenty of Sinatra and Ella. We can have champagne and really talk."

To his amazement, she agreed without any pressure. He signed the check and led her outside. Several people he knew stared at her and signaled their approval to him. Well, why not. She was goddamned beautiful! Tall and streamlined and young and—young! He *had* to stop thinking of Karla. Otherwise he just might not be all that great tonight. After all, he probably had to follow some pretty tough competition. She must have had plenty of fancy European lovers when she was at that Swiss college. Hell, she probably knew plenty before she went there. Any girl who grew up around Mike Wayne had to be a swinger. Look how fast she got a pad of her own. And that artsy crowd she ran with at the magazine . . . people like that reminded him of a plate of worms—eventually everyone got around to doing it with everyone else.

Well, he'd get her hooked tonight. Then perhaps he could manage it so they saw each other maybe two or three nights a week. And maybe by spring become unofficially engaged. But he had to hold her off as long as he could . . . *why* did he have to hold her off! Karla didn't really give a damn about his future. January *was* his future! All right. But first things first. He'd make good tonight. And he'd still have Karla. All he had to do was keep his head.

January sat beside him in the cab as it sped up Park Avenue. She knew he was going to try to make love to her. And she was going to let him. She was curious about the whole thing now. She was positive that once he held her in his arms something marvelous would happen. They'd ignite . . . and maybe she'd really fall in love. She felt a certain attraction toward him, and Linda had sworn that once he made love to her, everything would be different. Linda had been stunned to learn she was a virgin. And from the attitude of all the other girls on the magazine, she was beginning to feel that virginity was nothing to be proud of. It was almost like no one had asked you to dance. She had taken her own private poll: there was not one virgin at *Gloss*. Except the thirty-one-year-old male theater critic; he had a German accent and always had an eighteen-year old girl on his arm, but Linda had said the word was out that he was a "self-satisfaction man."

Linda was sleeping with the art director now. Keith hadn't called in a week and, as she put it, she had to have a body next to her.

The cab stopped at Seventy-third Street. When they reached his apartment, David seemed nervous as he fitted the keys in all the safety locks on his door. Finally he led her inside and switched on the lights. She took off her coat and looked around. The living room was nice enough—phony fireplace, lots of hi-fi speakers. The bedroom door was open . . . Oh sweet Lord! A round bed and red walls! She wanted to laugh. The jock's idea of a bordello.

He turned on the hi-fi, and the velvet voice of Nat King Cole floated through the room. Then he went to the bar and held up a bottle of Dom Perignon triumphantly. "When I heard you say you liked this, I bought a bottle the very next day. It's been waiting for you ever since." He began working with the cork. "I didn't really expect you tonight, so it isn't cold—we'll have to have it on the rocks." He walked over with the glass. "Well, what do you think of the apartment? No, don't answer. I know. The living room is Macy's version of Park

Avenue and the bedroom is the socially correct young man's fantasy room." He stopped as he realized that Karla had never been to his apartment, and that the greatest fantasies of his life had been realized in Karla's bare bedroom in her prim narrow maple bed. He pushed her from his thoughts and managed a smile. "You know, when I grew up I had the typical boy's bedroom, decorated by my mother. Pennants on the wall, bunk beds until I was twelve, though God knows I was an only child and the only time the other bunk bed was occupied was when a cousin slept over."

He led her over to the couch and they sat down. Now Nat King Cole was singing "Darling, Je Vous Aime Beaucoup" softly and beguilingly. She stared at the champagne. Dom Perignon was for special occasions . . . She took a long swallow. Well, this was a damn big occasion, wasn't it? She was going to get laid!

She took another gulp from the large old-fashioned glass he had poured the champagne in. He was drinking from a smaller glass. She felt a stab of disappointment. She hadn't expected him to be so obvious . . . to try to get her drunk. No, she mustn't think like that. She wanted to fan the glimmer of attraction David held for her, not dissolve it. But Mike would never handle a woman in such an obvious way. Oh God! This was no time to think of him. She'd ruin the whole thing. She could just see his frown—"January, I wanted you to like the man but not this . . ." She wanted to run. Franco had been more attractive than David, yet when he had touched her she had panicked. Oh, Lord. What was she doing here? She could still leave . . . But then what? Remain a virgin all her life? Tell Linda she had walked out on David and Nat King Cole and Dom Perignon and a round bed and red walls? She swallowed the rest of the champagne. David jumped up to refill her glass. This was crazy. Was she going to bed with David just because Linda thought it was the thing to do? Or to show Mike that she was a match for Karla. *Why* was she doing this? Certainly not because she was in love with him. But what did she know about love? What was her basis of comparison? Linda said the kind of love she was looking for only happened between Ingrid Bergman and Bogie on the late show. Today that kind of love didn't exist. Even her father had said he had never *loved*—he *loved* sex. That's what it was all about. And she was *his* daughter. She took the glass David offered her and sipped it slowly. David was handsome. And once it got started . . . she *would* enjoy it . . . and love him . . . and . . . She smiled and held out her empty glass again. Well, he wanted her to get tight, didn't he? He seemed elated as he refilled her glass. But he still seemed slightly nervous. He had finished his glass and now *he* was getting a larger glass and was pouring champagne . . . to the top.

The bottle was empty when Nat finished singing and Dionne Warwick began purring the Bacharach-David songs. January leaned her head back against the couch and shut her eyes. She felt David kissing her neck. Dionne was singing "Say a Little Prayer for Me." Yes, Dionne. Say it for me . . . for January . . . I'm that girl you met with my father in 1965. I was only fifteen then and you told my father I was lovely. Tell me, Dionne—were you in love the first time you did it? You *had* to be to sing like this . . .

David was leaning over her now. He had finished with her neck. Now he was nibbling at her ear. Oh God . . . his tongue was in her ear. Was she supposed to like *that*! It just felt cold and wet. Then he started on her mouth, his tongue forcing her lips apart. She began to panic when she realized she didn't like the sensation. His tongue tasted rough. His hands were groping her breasts, fumbling for the buttons on her blouse. She hoped he didn't break them . . . it was her new Valentino shirt. But how do you tell a man you'll open your own blouse—you're supposed to be so carried away with passion that you're not supposed to even be noticing what he's doing.

When was she going to feel something? She tried to respond . . . she stroked his hair . . . it was stiff. He used hair spray! She mustn't think of things like that now. She opened her eyes to look at him. After all, he was good-looking. But he looked ridiculous with his eyes closed, sprawling all over the couch. Why couldn't they act sensible and walk into that horrible bedroom and get undressed and . . . and then what? Wasn't he supposed to hold her close and tell her he loved her instead of just biting her lips and tearing away at her best shirt? She noticed that the gold trim on his Gucci shoes had ripped his silk couch. For some reason that pleased her. Hey, she'd better get with it. . . . She closed her eyes . . . she wanted to feel romantic . . . she wanted to feel . . oh, thank God, he had finally gotten her blouse open without breaking the buttons. Now he was fumbling with the back of her bra. He had real expertise there . . . only now it was up somewhere around her neck. Was she supposed to make some sort of a token protest—or pitch in and help him? She decided to pull away.

"Relax, little baby," David whispered as his head went to her breasts. He began licking each one gently and she felt her nipples harden . . . and the odd sensation in her pelvic area. He pulled her to her feet, took off her blouse with one hand and fumbled with the zipper on her skirt with the other. Ah, he was good at that too . . . it dropped to the floor. He took off her bra. She was standing in her boots and stocking pants. He lifted her up and carried her into the bedroom. She could have walked. She would have preferred to walk. Five foot seven and weighed a hundred and ten. That was bone-thin according to fashion. But a hundred and ten plus boots must feel like a ton to a man trying to be Romeo. She tried not to think of her long silk skirt lying in a heap on the living room floor. Of her bra beside it. And her silk shirt crumpled somewhere on the couch. What did she do when it was over? Walk out there stark naked and start picking up her things? He tossed her on the bed. Then he pulled off her boots and her panty hose.

And then she was lying there completely nude and he was telling her she was beautiful. Now he was undressing. She watched him take off his pants . . . she saw the large bulge in his jockey shorts. He almost strangled himself as he tore off his tie. He took off his shirt—and then, triumphantly, his shorts. He smiled with pride and came to the bed. She stared at the huge angry penis standing erect against his stomach.

"It's a beauty, isn't it?" he asked.

She couldn't answer. It was the ugliest thing she had ever seen. All red . . . all those veins . . . it looked like it would burst.

"Kiss it . . ." He pushed it toward her face. She turned

away. He laughed. "Okay . . . You'll want to kiss it before we're through . . ."

She fought off a feeling of hysteria. Where was this romantic sensation she had expected to feel? Why was she feeling only revulsion and panic?

He lay on top of her, supporting his weight on his elbows and mouthed her breasts. Then his hands began to explore between her legs. Involuntarily she clamped them together. He looked at her in surprise. "Is something wrong?"

"It's . . . it's just so light in here and . . ."

He laughed. "Don't you like to make love with the lights on?"

"No."

"The lady commands, I oblige." He went to the switch and turned off the lights. She stared at him as he walked toward her. This wasn't really happening. She wasn't lying on this bed, waiting to be taken by this . . . this stranger. Suddenly she realized she hadn't gone to the doctor Linda had suggested and gotten pills or a coil.

"David . . ." she began, but suddenly he was stabbing that throbbing thing between her legs. Pushing . . . pushing . . . she felt his fingers everywhere . . . on her breasts . . between her legs . . . pulling her legs apart . . . pushing into her. . . .

"David, I'm not on the pill," she said in a muffled voice as he tried to kiss her.

"Okay. I'll pull out in time," he muttered. He was breathing hard. Perspiration made his chest damp. And all the while he was trying to push that big thing into her. She felt its repeated thrust, repelled each time by its impact against a solid wall of muscle and tissue within her. Couldn't he see that it was impossible? But the thing only became more demanding . . . again and again. It was ripping her apart. Oh God, he was killing her! She bit her lips to keep from screaming and dug her nails into his back. She heard him mutter, "Great, eh, baby. Fuck me . . . Come on . . . fuck me!" Then there was a blinding pain as he finally tore through her. Unbearable pain as if he was crunching bone and muscle. Suddenly he pulled out of her and she felt a hot sticky liquid shoot onto her stomach.

Then he fell on his back, holding his chest . . . gasping. The thing between his legs lay crumped and inert like a dead bird.

Gradually his breathing came back to normal. He turned toward her and rumpled her hair. "Well . . . was it great, darling?" He reached for some Kleenex on the night table and put it on her stomach.

She was afraid to move. The pain was so intense she was frightened. Perhaps he had torn her apart. Linda had said it hurt a little in the beginning; she never said it would be agony. Like a robot she wiped her stomach. It was gooey. She longed to rush into a hot shower. But most of all she wanted to get away. He stroked her hair. "How about giving me some head, baby? Then we can do it again."

"Head?"

"Go down. . . . " He pushed her head toward the limp thing that now rested on the inside of his leg.

She jumped out of bed. "I'm going home!" Then she stopped when she saw the blood. It had made a violent blotch on the sheets and was running down her legs.

He sat up. "For God's sake, January, why didn't you tell me you had the curse!" He jumped out of bed and ripped off the sheet. "Oh, Christ . . . right through to the mattress."

She stood very still with her hand clamped between her legs. She felt that if she moved her hand, her insides would fall out. He turned and looked at her. "For God's sake, don't drip blood on the rug. There's some Tampax in the medicine closet."

She raced into the bathroom and locked the door. She took her hand away and nothing drastic happened. The bleeding had stopped. She took a towel and washed the blood off her legs. She felt sore and torn inside. The bright light over the medicine chest gave her face a yellow cast. She stared at herself in the mirror. Her eye makeup was streaked, her hair was a mess. She must dress and get out. She washed the makeup off her eyes. Then, draping another towel around her, she opened the bathroom door and dashed into the living room. He didn't even look up. He was still naked, but he had stripped the bed and was working furiously with cleaning fluid on the mattress.

She grabbed her clothes from the living room, picked up her

boots and stocking pants from the bedroom, and rushed back to the bathroom. When she came out, the bed was still stripped, but he was dressed.

"Well, I'll just have to wait until it dries before I can tell," he said. "I'll probably have to call a cleaning service. Come on, I'll take you home."

He didn't speak until they were in the cab. Then he put his arm around her. Involuntarily she pulled away. He took her hand. "Look, I'm sorry if I was cross about the sheets. But they're Porthault, and you should have told me you had the curse. I know you've lived in Europe and some of those foreign characters like it. But I never wade through the red sea. Did you find the Tampax all right?"

"I don't have the curse," she said.

For a second he didn't understand. Then it hit him and he slumped in his seat. "Oh, my God! January, you aren't . . . I mean you weren't . . . oh, Christ! But whoever heard of a twenty-year-old virgin? Especially one who looks like you. I mean, you felt tight, but I figured because you were so slim and . . . oh, Jesus . . ." He wound up with a groan.

They drove for a few blocks while he sat and silently stared into space.

"Why are you so upset?" she asked.

"Because, dammit, I don't go around taking virgins."

"Unfortunately, someone has to," she said. "I remember a boy in Italy telling me that."

When they reached the corner of her street, he asked the driver to stop. "Look, let's go into that bar for a nightcap. I want to talk to you."

They both ordered a Scotch. She hated the taste of it but hoped it would make her sleepy. God, how she wanted to fall into a dead sleep tonight.

David made rings on the napkin with his glass. "I'm still in shock. But . . . look . . . I'm really proud that you selected me to be the first. And you won't be sorry. Next time I'll really make you happy. January . . . I . . . I really care for you a great deal."

"You do?"

"Yes."

"Well, that's fine. I mean I'm very flattered."

He reached over and took her hand. "Is that all you feel?"

"Well, David—I—" She stopped. She had been about to say, "I don't know you very well." That was wild. She had just gone to bed with him.

"January . . . I want to marry you. You know that, don't you?"

"No."

"No what?"

"No, I didn't know you wanted to marry me. I know that Dee wants you to marry me. But I didn't know you wanted to. I mean, this is all ridiculous, isn't it, David? We're strangers. We've been to bed together but we're strangers. We sit here trying to find things to say to one another and it shouldn't be like this. I mean, aren't you supposed to want to shout . . . to sing . . . when you've had your first love affair? When you're in love isn't something marvelous supposed to happen?"

He looked past her and said quietly, "Tell me what you think it's supposed to feel like?"

"I don't know. But . . . well . . ."

"Like you never want the night to end?" he asked.

"Yes, I suppose so."

"And that you're afraid to leave because it's so wonderful that you want to own the person . . . be together every second."

She smiled. "Sounds like we've both been watching the same late movies on TV."

"January, will you marry me?"

She stared at her drink. Then she took a long swallow. She shook her head helplessly. "I don't know, David. I didn't feel anything for you and—"

"Look," he cut in. "Those things we both talked about. They don't really happen. Maybe for one night with kids strung out on pot . . . or people enmeshed in a clandestine love affair . . . or—"

"Or?" she asked.

"Or . . . well . . . if a teeny bopper meets her hero . . . someone she's always worshipped. I suppose every girl has her dream man . . . just as some men have dream girls. Most of us go through life never meeting or realizing our dream."

"Must we?" she asked.

He sighed. "Maybe it's better that way. Because if you ever get it, you might find it impossible to let go. And you can't hold a dream forever. You can't marry a dream. Marriage is something different—it takes two people who want the same things, two people who like one another." When she remained silent he said, "I . . . I love you, January. There . . . I've said it."

She smiled. "Saying it and meaning it are two different things."

"Don't you believe me?"

"I believe you're trying to sell yourself almost as hard as you're trying to sell me."

"Do you love me?" he asked.

"No."

"No? Then why did you come back with me tonight?"

"I wanted to fall in love with you, David. I thought maybe this would do it. But it hasn't . . ."

"Look . . . it's my fault. I didn't know you were a virgin . . . Next time it will be different. I swear."

"There won't be a next time, David."

For a moment he looked nonplussed. "You mean you don't want to see me again?"

"I'll see you . . . but I'm not going to bed with you."

He motioned for the waiter and paid the check. "Look, this is just a normal reaction after what's happened."

She stood up and he helped her into her coat. He held her arm as they walked down the street. "January, I'm not going to crowd you. I won't ask you to go to bed with me. I don't care if we wait months. Maybe you're right . . . let's get to know each other better. But I promise you—you're going to marry me. You're going to love me and want me . . . But we'll take it step by step. We'll spend Thanksgiving together in Palm Beach. We'll have four days and nights together. At least that will be a good start. And I promise—I'll never ask you to go to bed. When it happens, it will happen the way you want it. And as you fall asleep tonight . . . remember, I love you."

When she let herself into her apartment she ran the tub and tore off her clothes. She eased herself into the warm water . . . and tried to think of all the things David had said.

And it wasn't until later, as she lay in bed, trying to sleep, that she realized he had not even bothered to kiss her good-night.

When she awoke the following morning, she found she had hemorrhaged during the night. Her first thought was to call Linda. But she realized she wasn't up to Linda at the moment. She could just see Linda's expression if she heard the story. She tore through the phone book and found the number of Dr. Davis, the gynecologist Linda had told her about. When she explained she was hemorrhaging, she was told to come right over.

Oddly enough the examination itself was easier than sitting before his desk, fully clothed, and telling him the cause of her condition. To her relief he explained that although it was rare to experience this kind of bleeding, nothing was really wrong. He gave her a prescription for the pill, and also for a sedative. Then he told her to go home and stay in bed for the rest of the day.

When she got back to her apartment there was a messenger ringing her doorbell. He had a small package from Cartier's for her. She signed for it, and went inside. It was a hand-carved ivory and gold rose attached to a heavy gold chain. The note read, "Real ones die. This will last much longer—to remind you that my feelings are also lasting. David."

She put it in her drawer. It was beautiful, but at the moment she didn't feel like thinking about David. She had stopped and gotten the prescriptions filled. The way she felt now, she had no desire to start on the pill. She put them away, beside the Cartier box. But she took one of the sedatives. Then she called Linda and said she had spent the morning at the dentist's and wouldn't be in.

She got into bed and tried to read . . . then the pill took its effect. She was in a heavy sleep when the phone rang at five o'clock. It was David. She thanked him for the necklace. "Could we have a quick drink this afternoon?" he asked.

"I'm afraid not. I'm . . . I'm piled up with assignments," she said.

He paused. "Well, there's going to be a Securities Analysts' meeting on the Coast in a few weeks, and several heads of companies are in town now. I'm afraid I'll be tied up with meetings the next few nights."

"That's all right, David."

"But I'll call you each day. And the first free night, we'll have dinner. I'm getting tickets for *Hair* next week."

"That's fine, David."

Then she hung up and lay in the semidarkness. It was a peaceful feeling of half wakefulness, half sleep. But at nine o'clock the sedative wore off and she sat up and turned on the lights. The whole night stretched out. She thought about food; but she wasn't particularly hungry.

She had made a list of subjects that might make interesting articles. She had intended to submit them to Linda today. She studied them now. Perhaps she should try to start one. She was particularly intrigued with the idea: "Is there life after thirty?"

It had come to her when Linda turned down a secretary who had top references and accepted a nineteen-year-old girl who just barely got by with shorthand. "January, I don't want a woman of forty-three to be a secretary at *Gloss*. I don't care if she was secretary to a president of an oil company for twenty years. *Gloss* is a swinging *young* magazine. I want shiny beautiful *young* people in this office."

January had noticed when she had gone for her "commercial" that most of the girls who worked as secretaries and receptionists at the advertising agency were all in the nineteen-to-twenty-nine age bracket. Of course it didn't apply to executives, or the woman who was head copywriter. Linda was pushing thirty—but for her job, she was young.

She liked Linda. But aside from their mutual enthusiasm for the magazine, they were worlds apart. At *Gloss*, Linda was "Power." When she walked through the halls, everyone snapped to attention. Linda at the weekly editorial meeting was cool and beautiful—in total command. Every editor and junior editor admired her almost classic elegance in looks and style. Yet Linda away from the office, with a man—any man—was devoid of any stature. She couldn't understand Linda's attitude about having a "body" next to her. Being able to enjoy sex with a man even if you didn't particularly like him. Last night had been dreadful . . . even before the pain. She hadn't felt any desire for David's body. Was something wrong with her?

She had to talk it out with someone. Not Linda! Linda would immediately suggest vitamins or a psychiatrist.

Suddenly she felt she had to see Mike. Maybe they could have lunch tomorrow. She couldn't really tell him what happened. But just talking to him might help. It was only nine thirty. He wouldn't be in, but she could leave a message.

She couldn't believe it when he answered the phone. (Oh, God, maybe she had interrupted him and Dee. . . .) She tried to make her voice light. "I can call back if you're playing backgammon."

"No. As a matter of fact you woke me."

"Oh . . . I'm sorry. Apologize to Dee . . ."

"No, wait a minute. What time is it?"

"Nine-thirty."

"I'm wide awake now and I'm starving," he said. "Hey, how's about if I jump into a cab and pick you up. We'll have a hamburger."

"Where's Dee?"

"I shot her. She's hanging in the closet."

"MIKE!"

He laughed. "Be downstairs in front of your building in fifteen minutes. I'll tell you the gory details."

They went to the bar down the street and she studiously avoided the table she had sat at with David the previous night.

"Your old man is slowing up," Mike said. "Played eighteen holes of golf, came home at five, and fell into a dead sleep. Dee wanted to go to dinner and a movie, but I couldn't budge. She must have tried . . . but obviously I slept on. She left me a note that she was off to play backgammon at a girlfriend's. I guess she thought I'd sleep through the night."

"And I woke you. I'm sorry."

"No, I'm glad." The waiter brought their hamburgers. He bit into his eagerly. "I was starving . . . as you can see. My stomach would have gotten me up around midnight, but I would have missed seeing you." Suddenly his eyes narrowed. "How come you were sitting home tonight?"

"Oh . . . I had a date with David last night. Tonight he's at some kind of a meeting."

He nodded. "Translated—things aren't going right."

"He gave me a necklace from Cartier's," she said suddenly.

He pushed his beer away. He lit a cigarette and said casually, "A little early for Christmas, isn't it?"

"He wants to marry me."

His expression relaxed. Suddenly he smiled. "Well, Jesus, that's a whole different story. Why didn't you give me the bottom line right away?"

"I'm not in love with him."

"You're sure about that? I mean . . . you've known him only a short time. You're positive it's no deal?"

"Positive."

She reached out and took one of his cigarettes. His eyebrows went up. "Since when?"

"I learned when I was trying for a commercial." After a moment she said, "I'm sorry about David."

He laughed. "Tell that to him . . . not me. Hell, nothing's lost. So you dated him and he proposed. Give him back his goddamn necklace and that's it."

She stared down at her half-eaten hamburger. Suddenly she realized that he didn't want to believe there had been any intimacy between her and David. He wanted to think the necklace was just a "courting present." Mike, the sophisticate, was completely old-fashioned about her.

"Mike . . . do I have sex appeal?"

"What an insane question."

"Do I?"

"How the hell would I know? I can tell you that you're beautiful . . . that you've got a great figure . . . but sex appeal is a one-to-one relationship. A broad who would have sex appeal for me might not have it for the next guy."

"You have sex appeal for me," she said.

He looked at her. Then he shook his head. "And David doesn't."

"David doesn't."

"Oh, boy—" He whistled under his breath. "Here's a guy that every broad in New York would dig, including the most talked-about movie star in the world. And he has no sex appeal for you . . . but I have."

She tried to make her voice light. "Well, maybe I'll just have to meet someone who looks like you."

"Don't talk like that," he said roughly. "Jesus, you acted like you really dug the guy."

"I liked David," she said. "I still do *like* him. But as far as romance goes . . . he turns me off." She tried to laugh. "Maybe it's his blond hair."

He pushed his glass of beer away. "This is gonna be great! Every guy who comes along is going to lose out at the last minute on account of me . . . right?"

"Look, there's no reason to be upset just because I changed my mind about David."

"If we don't straighten this out, you'll change your mind every time. You'll get right up to the altar and change your mind. That can happen . . . hell, it has happened. And it ends up in disaster. Listen—" His voice was low. "Don't build up any false images about me. Images that other men can't follow. I'm no big deal. You only know me as Daddy . . . and Daddy is the dream man. Well, get this straight. There is no dream man. It's the woman who creates that dream image. And it's time you learned that Daddy Mike is a hell of a lot different from Mike the man."

"I see Mike the man and I love him."

"You only see what I've let you see. But now I'll give it to you straight. I was a lousy father and an even worse husband. I've never made any woman really happy. I loved sex . . . but I never loved. I still don't."

"You loved me . . . you always have."

"That's true. But I didn't hang around every night and tuck you in your crib. I lived my own life. I always have."

"That's because Mother died."

"Died? She killed herself, goddammit!"

January shook her head . . . yet somehow she knew he was telling the truth. He sipped his beer and stared at the glass. "Yep . . . she was pregnant and I was running around. So one night she got drunk and left a note saying this was her way of getting even. When I came home I found her on the bathroom floor. She had stuck a kitchen knife up her to dislodge the baby. It was there too . . . lying in the blood. It was scarcely a baby . . . maybe five months . . . a boy. I had enough clout to keep it quiet, make it look like her death came from a natural miscarriage . . . but—" He stopped and stared at her. "Now you know . . ."

"Why did you tell me this?" she asked.

"Because I want you to get a little tough. Learn how to handle yourself. Be *my* daughter. If you love me so damn much, love me for what I am. And if you accept what I really am instead of what you dream I am, then you'll find your own man and you'll fall in love with him. Hell, you'll fall in love a dozen times. But only if you learn to face reality. Go after what you want. Don't live in a dream world. Don't be a loser like your mother. She skulked around with those great brown eyes, never openly accusing me, yet damning me with every silent look. Christ, I almost respected her when I learned she had another guy. I even got a little jealous and was going to try and romance her back—then I learned she couldn't even hold him. She'd get drunk when she was with him and cry over me. And every time I looked at her there was always those sighs." He turned on her. "Don't ever sigh. That's the worst. God knows there are times right now that I want to sigh . . . But every time I start, I remember that I got into this thing for us."

"Us?" she said. "In the beginning it was just for me."

"Okay . . . Okay. Maybe it was the only way out for me, too. But I did try to give you the works. A great apartment, a maid, a car . . . Okay, so you walked away from it. But you *know* it's always there, so you're not gambling with scared money. Dee tried to give you a guy, but you don't like the color of his hair. Okay, so he's said he wants to marry you. But we both know that doesn't mean a guy is madly in love with a woman. It's a cinch he's not foaming to see you. I don't buy business meetings at night. I've used that excuse too many times myself."

"You think he's with Karla?"

He shrugged. "If he's lucky . . . maybe he is. In my book, any guy who gets a shot with Karla has to flip out over her. I know I would." He paused and looked at her thoughtfully. "Say, maybe you're not in love with David because he doesn't want you to be . . . at the moment. Let's face it, he wouldn't want you all turned on over him while he was in the midst of making it with Karla." He grinned. "Ever think of that? Maybe he's holding you off. After all, if a guy doesn't get romantic with a girl, how *can* she be in love with him?" He seemed relieved at his new analysis. "Wait till he turns on the high voltage. I bet it'll be a whole new ballgame."

"You would flip out for Karla?" she asked.

"What?"

"You said you would flip out for Karla."

"Haven't you heard anything else I've said since then?"

She nodded. "I heard it. But I'm asking you a question."

"Sure I would." He finished his beer.

"And you really think she's too much competition for me?"

He smiled and patted her hand. "You're a girl, she's a woman. But don't worry—David asked you to marry him. That means that you're the girl he really wants—later." He was grinning. "When *he* wants."

"When *he* wants . . ." She laughed. "Oh, Mike, do you actually think David hasn't come on strong for me and . . ."

He slammed his fist on the table. "Has that sonofabitch tried anything?" His jaw tightened. "I'll kill him. Don't tell me he's tried to . . . to get intimate with you."

She couldn't believe it. Mike, who had all the women . . . Mike, who told her about Tina St. Claire and Melba . . . Mike, suddenly switching their relationship to outraged father and innocent daughter. It was crazy . . . insane . . . yet something told her not to tell him the truth.

"David has been a gentleman in every way," she said. "But I know that I could have him any way I want him."

"Any woman can have any man if she'll spread her legs," he said coldly. "But you're different. David knows that too."

"David!" She almost spit the name out. "Dee comes up with a nice presentable cousin, and I'm supposed to act like a Barbie doll and fall in love with him and live happily ever after. And you know something? I tried . . . and I almost brainwashed myself into believing it. Tell me—is that what you wanted for me? To fall in love with a nice plastic man, wear a white bridal gown, settle down and maybe raise a daughter and find a David for her to marry? I mean—like the song says—'Is that all there is, my friend . . . is that all there is?'"

He called for the check. Then he stood up and left some bills on the table. They walked out into the night. Two boys with long hair with red butterflies sewn on the backs of their dungarees passed. They stopped at a street light and began to kiss.

"Looks like love is everywhere these days," Mike said.

"They're Red Butterflies," January said.

"They're what?"

"It's a Communist Gay Liberation group that operates in Canada. A few of them are in town for recruits. Linda thought of doing a story on them. But it's not for *Gloss*."

Mike shook his head. "Know something? When you asked me in there, 'Is that all there is?' I can't tell you whether that's all there is or not. Because I don't know anymore. I don't know what *is*—in life, in show business . . . in anything. The whole world has changed. In my movies and all the movies of my day . . . the villain had to die. The hero won the gunfight, and ten years ago if I had a twenty-year-old daughter who was dating a David, I'd have said, 'What's your rush? The world is your oyster. And I'll give it to you.' But I'm not the way I was any more than the world is the way it was. So maybe I am looking for a quick solid soft berth for you. Because I look at this bright permissive world of today and in my book it stinks! But I can afford to turn my back on it because I'm fifty-two. I've lived a good hunk of my life. But you can't . . . because it's all you've got. And I can't turn it back to what it was. The corner suite at the Plaza belongs to someone else now. The Capitol Theater is now an office building. The Stork Club is Paley Park. That world is gone. You can only see it on the Late Show. Unfortunately you've got to face the world as it is now. So try to enjoy it. Because suddenly one day you wake up and find you're played out. It happens overnight. So grab every brass ring you can, because when you look back, it seems like a hell of a short ride." He put his arm around her. "Look. I just saw a shooting star. Make a wish, babe."

They were standing in front of her building now. She shut her eyes, but she couldn't think of anything she really wanted. And when she opened her eyes he was gone. She watched him walk down the street. He still walked like a winner.

Later, as she lay awake in the darkness, she thought about the things her father had said. He was afraid of the world now—afraid for her . . . and afraid for himself. Well, as he said, it was her world now—the only one she had—and it was up to her to go out and squeeze it and make it fit. She would be a winner . . . and prove to him that it could be done.

She smiled as she stretched in the darkness. "Daddy," she whispered, "when Dee comes home from her backgammon game, you two better not sit up and worry about me and my future. Because, Daddy . . . I'm smiling . . . not sighing."

Ten

But Dee was not home waiting to discuss January's problems with Mike. When she saw he had fallen into a heavy sleep after his golf game, she had slipped into the study and made a quick phone call. Then she scribbled a note, propped it on the phone by his bed, explaining she had tried to awaken him but he had looked so peaceful that she left him to sleep and had gone off to play backgammon.

She got into the car and told Mario to take her to the Waldorf. "I'll be visiting a friend for several hours. Come back to the Park Avenue entrance at eleven o'clock." Then she entered the Waldorf, walked through the lobby and came out on the Lexington Avenue exit. She hailed a cab. It was only a few blocks; she could walk, but she was too eager to get there. It was only six o'clock. She had said she'd get there at six-thirty. Well, they'd have an extra half-hour together.

When she arrived at the large building, the doorman was busy piling luggage into a cab for a tenant. She walked right past him and into the elevator. The elevator operator was a new man who had never seen her before, but he merely nodded when she told him the floor. Some security in these luxury buildings nowadays!

She got off the elevator, walked to the end of the floor and rang the buzzer. The elevator man hadn't even bothered to wait to see what apartment she was going to. She rang the buzzer again. She looked at her watch. Six-fifteen. Where could one go at an hour like this? She reached into her bag and took out a key. She entered the apartment and switched on the lamps in the living room. She lit a cigarette and made herself a drink.

Then she went to the mirror and combed her hair. Thank God she had had Ernest set it in a soft pageboy today—the Gibson-Girl style got messed up in bed. Today's girls, with their loose swinging hair—how she envied them. She looked at the new individual eyelashes Elizabeth Arden had applied. Yes, they were marvelous. She turned off one of the lamps, then went back and looked in the mirror. Yes, that was better . . .

She sat in the club chair and sipped her drink. Her heart was pounding. No matter how many times she came here, she always felt the breathless anticipation of a schoolgirl.

It was five after seven when she finally heard the key in the lock. She crushed out her freshly lit cigarette and stood up. "Where the hell have you been?" she demanded.

Karla dropped her shoulder bag to the chair and took off her raincoat. "Am I late?" she said easily.

"You know damn well you're late. Where have you been?"

Karla smiled. "Just walking. I always like to walk at dusk. Besides, I did only two hours at the bar today. I needed the exercise."

"You didn't need to walk. You did it intentionally . . . just so I would be sitting here waiting!" She paused because she knew her voice had risen. "Oh, Karla! Why do you do everything to bring out the worst in me!"

With a slow smile Karla held out her arms. Dee hesitated for a second, then rushed to her. And Karla's kiss silenced any further protests.

Later, when they were locked in one another's arms in the cool dark of the bedroom, Dee clung to Karla and said, "Oh God, if we could only be together forever."

"Only death is forever," Karla said. She pulled away and reached for one of Dee's cigarettes. She snapped open the gold case and stared at it. "Very beautiful."

"Mike gave it to me . . . or I'd give it to you. But I've given you three cases. And you always lose them."

Karla shrugged as she exhaled the smoke. "Perhaps it is some inner instinct that is trying to tell me I must stop smoking. I am down to ten a day . . ."

"You're such a health fiend. All that walking and those ballet exercises—" Dee paused as she lit a cigarette. "Oh, by the way—I made out a new will."

Karla laughed. "Dee, you're not ever going to die. You're too mean to die."

"I also put ten thousand dollars into your savings account today."

Karla laughed. "The joint savings account of Connie and Ronnie Smith. Connie puts in . . . Ronnie takes it out. I'm sure everyone in the bank is onto it."

"They don't recognize me," Dee said quickly.

Karla jumped out of bed and did an arabesque. "But can I help it if I am so magnificent that everyone recognizes me!" she said, mocking her own fame.

"You nut." Dee laughed. "Come back here."

Karla slipped into a dressing gown and switched on the television set. She climbed back on the bed, sat cross-legged, and worked the remote control, clicking the channels until she came to a movie. It was *Grand Hotel* starring Garbo, Barrymore, and Joan Crawford.

"What time do you have to be home, Dee?" she said.

Dee snuggled against Karla. "No time, especially. He played eighteen holes of golf and will probably sleep through the night. Just in case, I left a note saying I was playing backgammon with Joyce."

"Who is Joyce?"

"Someone I invented. This way he can never check."

"Mike Wayne is very attractive," Karla said slowly.

"I only married him because of you."

Karla leaned back and laughed. "Oh, Dee, I know the press thinks I am not very bright because I will not give interviews. But you know better than to think I really believe that."

"It's true! I told you before I married Mike . . . before I ever met him, that I was going to get married. That I *had* to get married. All last spring when I had David take us around . . . I knew people were beginning to wonder . . . not about you . . . but me . . . like why was I tagging along? You're famous for wanting to live your own life Everyone knows how you fight for your privacy. But they're accustomed to seeing me in all the newspapers—at the opening of the opera season, the ballet, opening nights of certain Broadway shows, especially when there's a charity benefit. Then there're the Balls . . . I'm on the boards of three big charity organizations . . . and there are my business affiliations. I'm chairman of the board of two corporations. There are dinners I must attend. I need a presentable escort. I need to make appearances at the proper places with a *man*. A hospital is being dedicated in my name in Spain. Next spring, when I go there, the Monsignor will officiate. Can't you see? I can't risk any scandal."

"Why not donate the money and stay away from all these public functions?" Karla suggested.

"Turn away from the world? The way you try to do?" Dee looked at her. "If I did . . . would you promise to move in with me and stay with me forever?"

Karla's laugh was low. "Unfortunately, the only person I must be with forever is myself."

"But you don't mind being alone. I'm terrified. I've always hated it. But it didn't turn into terror until you came into my life. The first time you disappeared I swallowed a whole bottle of Seconals. I'll still suffer when you go off . . . but at least I'm not alone."

"This kind of fear I cannot understand," Karla said, as she watched the movie.

"Maybe it's because loneliness is something I grew up with. My parents died so early and I grew up with just banks and trustees and the knowledge that I wasn't a beautiful little girl, but it wouldn't matter because I was so very very rich. Do you know what that's like? To feel that every man you meet only flatters you and acts as if he cares about you because of your money."

"Dee, that is ridiculous. You are very beautiful."

Dee smiled. "I have the kind of beauty that comes with money, grooming and dieting. I wasn't born beautiful like Jackie Onassis or Babe Paley."

"I think you are." Karla stared at the close-up of Joan Crawford.

Dee stared at the television screen. "She's beautiful," she said. "And her beauty got her money, and men who loved her. While my money got me beauty and men who professed to love me. But I've always known it . . . and I never really let myself feel anything for any man. Basically I hate men. Women are different. And I've always picked women who had plenty of money so I would know they wanted me for myself. They all did. But I never really loved any of them. I didn't think I was capable of really being in love until I met you. Karla . . . do you realize you're the only person I've ever loved in my whole life?"

"You know, this picture still holds up," Karla said.

"For God's sake, will you turn that damn thing off?"

Karla turned down the sound and smiled at Dee. "Now, are you happy?"

Dee looked at her. "Know something? I don't think I've actually had a happy day since we met."

"But I thought you said you loved me." Karla was watching the movie without sound.

"That's why I'm so unhappy! Oh, Karla, can't you understand? As close as we are . . . like right now . . ." Her hand went under Karla's robe and stroked her body. "Right now, touching you where I am touching you now—I don't feel as if you really belong to me, or that I'm really reaching you in anything I say . . . or do."

"You are making me feel very sexy right now . . . and I think maybe I better take my robe off and we make love."

And once again Dee felt the indescribable perfection of their physical intimacy. And when it was over she clung to her and she said, "Karla, I worship you. Please . . . please . . . don't make me unhappy."

"I thought I had just made you very happy."

Dee turned away. "I'm not talking about just sex. Can't you understand what you do to me! The times you disappear—"

"But now you know I always come back," Karla said.

"How can I *know* that for sure . . . any more than I can know when you are going to pick up and go off again? Karla, do you realize that I've loved you for almost nine years and yet if we added up all the times we've been together, it would be no more than a few months?"

Karla turned up the sound. Garbo was in the midst of her love scene with Barrymore. "You'd get tired of me if I stayed too long," Karla said.

"Never."

Karla kept her eyes on the screen. "My sweet little Dee, just as you cannot be alone, there are times Karla *must* go off alone."

Dee reached over and grabbed the remote control and switched it off. "Karla . . . you know about the sleeping pills I took the first time. Well, I swore to myself that would never happen again. I suffered each time you took off . . . but each time I told myself I was getting stronger . . . that you would come back . . . But last spring, after you took off again, I . . . I cut my wrists. Oh, it was kept quiet. I was in Marbella and I have several friends there who are doctors. But that's when I knew . . . I had to get married . . . to save my sanity."

Karla's large gray eyes looked at her with compassion. "You say things like that—it makes me very sad. Perhaps I should go out of your life for good."

"Oh, God! Don't you understand?" Dee clung to her. "I can't live without you. And I also know that if I cause too many scenes like this, you'll leave me. That's another reason I married Mike Wayne. He's not like the others. I can't walk all over him, or push him around. I have to play the game of being his wife. I must answer to him. And the discipline of it will keep me from going off the deep end over you. And I know that as long as I act like a wife, he'll stay . . . because he has no money . . . and because I just created a ten-million-dollar trust fund for his daughter."

"Isn't that unlike you?" Karla asked. "Uusually you hold strings over someone's head."

Dee smiled. "It's not an irrevocable trust. I can always change it." Then she looked at Karla pleadingly. "You must come to Palm Beach. Mike will play golf all day . . . we can be together . . . and we'll even have nights together . . . like this. The place is so huge he'd never find us—"

Karla laughed. "What was all that talk about appearances? For me to houseguest with a newlywed couple would most certainly cause talk."

"Not if you come down during the holidays. Everyone has houseguests then . . . and if you stayed on . . . no one would talk."

"We shall see." Karla took the remote control from Dee, and

walked over and turned on the set. Then she got into bed and clicked the channels. She came in on the middle of a Cary Grant picture. She settled back happily. "A wonderful man . . . I almost did a picture with him. We couldn't get together on terms."

Dee lay back and watched Karla's perfect profile. She saw the fresh scars behind Karla's ears and suddenly she wondered why Karla had done it. Dee had gone through a face-lift seven years ago. But she had done it to stay beautiful for Karla. She had gone through another a year ago. Again, just to hold Karla. And last spring when she had seen the beginning of the tiny lines under Karla's eyes . . . the slight slack along her jaw . . . she found herself praying it would happen fast . . . that the magnificent face would fall apart so no one else would want her. And now—during this last disappearance, Karla had gone and done it. Why? She wasn't interested in going back to work. Every time anyone came to her with an offer she turned it down. Then *why* had she done it? Suddenly she felt weak inside. Could Karla really be serious about David? Until this very moment, she had thought it just flattered her ego to have David hanging around. But now the fear began to take hold, because suddenly she realized it was possible. Karla was a homosexual . . . she had told that to Dee. Once she had said she knew it when she was a little girl. She never elaborated on it . . . but Dee assumed it must have happened in some ballet company. But Karla had also had some well-publicized love affairs with men. And Karla had admitted she had felt genuine attraction toward the men. Dee closed her eyes as a wave of despair hit her. Twenty years ago in Hollywood, Christopher Kelly, the actor Karla almost eloped with, looked very much like David. Maybe there was a certain type man who turned her on. She looked at Karla. Karla tossed her a bright smile and returned her attention to the TV set. She wanted to scream. Here they were . . . lying together . . . yet she didn't dare ask or pry into Karla's personal emotions. She had learned that no amount of physical intimacy gave her permission to invade Karla's privacy. The part of herself she held remote could not be penetrated by tears, threats, or even money. Long ago she had discovered Karla's pathological stinginess. The woman was a millionaire . . . yet the nearest thing to a display of devotion came when Karla was the recipient of a large amount of money. But tonight even the ten thousand hadn't brought more than a polite smile. She seemed preoccupied. Maybe Karla was really in love with David. Her panic suddenly made her forget all rules but she kept her voice even.

"Karla, have you been seeing much of David?"

Karla kept watching the television screen. "Yes."

"I think he likes my stepdaughter."

Karla smiled. "I think you would like him to like your stepdaughter."

"Well, he doesn't really mean anything to you, does he?"

"Of course he does. Why else would I see him?"

Dee jumped out of bed. "You bitch!"

Karla lay back and smiled. "You will catch cold if you stand without your clothes. And, Dee, you really should take ballet exercises. You need it in your thighs."

Dee dashed into the bathroom and Karla turned up the sound on the television. She seemed completely engrossed in the picture when Dee came out of the bathroom. Dee dressed in silence. Then she walked over to the bed. "Karla, why do you do these things to torment me?"

"How do I torment you?" Karla's voice was cold. "You have a husband . . . and so very very much money. You enjoy running people's lives, controlling them and frightening them with your money. But you cannot control or frighten Karla."

Dee sank down on the edge of the bed. "Do you know how rotten it is to have my kind of money?"

Karla sighed. "Oh, my poor Dee. You suffer because you wonder whether people really care for *you*. You say that has left a deep scar within you. But we all have scars." Karla turned off the television set. "Unfortunately—or fortunately—you have never known the scars of working to get to become a star . . . and the harder work of staying there . . . remembering all the time what it was like *not* to have money—"

"But that was a challenge and fun—"

"Fun?" Karla smiled.

"You don't talk about your early days. But I've read everything that was ever written about you. Sure, you were growing up in Europe during the war. It must have been dreadful. I remember I was about twenty when Pearl Harbor happened. I joined committees and knitted for the English, the Russians—yes, they were our allies then—but we only read about the fighting. There was no TV that brought the war into our living room as it does today. It's horrible." She shuddered.

Karla stared into space. "You shudder because TV brings it into your living room. But in Poland we had it walk right into our living room."

"In your living room?"

Karla smiled. "I was twenty when Germany and Russia were allies. In 1939 Hitler invaded Poland and divided it between them."

"Is that when you went to London?"

"No . . . first Sweden . . . then London. . . . But this is not bedtime conversation and I am suddenly very tired."

Dee knew she was expected to leave. Karla was dismissing her. She hesitated. She could walk out and threaten to never see her again. But she'd only crawl back. They both knew that.

"Karla, we're leaving for Palm Beach next week. Please come down."

"Perhaps."

"Shall I send the plane for you?"

Karla stretched out. "I'll let you know." (Dee realized she was actually falling asleep.)

Dee leaned down. "I'll call you tomorrow. And Karla . . . I love you."

When Dee reached the Pierre, Mike was just coming in. He threw his arm around her shoulder. "I went for a hamburger. Did you have a good game?"

He opened the door of the apartment and she tossed her coat on the couch. He came to her and put his arms around her. "Sorry the old man fell asleep." He grinned. "But I'm up now . . . in every way."

She pulled away. "No . . . not tonight, Mike . . . please!"

He stood very still for a moment. Then he forced a smile. "What happened? Did you lose in backgammon?"

"Yes. A little. But I'll get it back. I've got to—" She turned to him with a tight smile. "You see, it's a matter of pride."

Eleven

AT MIDNIGHT, on the Tuesday before Thanksgiving, Linda sat in the middle of her bed (with January as her captive audience), damning the hypocrisy of the holiday. "Just what are we celebrating?" she demanded. "The fact that some emotionally disturbed people, who called themselves 'Settlers,' came here, met some friendly Indians, and then proceeded to take the whole country away from them."

"Oh, Linda, they were friendly with the Indians. The fighting came later. In fact, Thanksgiving was to celebrate a year of good crops and friendship with the Indians."

"Bullshit. And besides, what smartass settler decided to make the celebration come on a Thursday and screw up a whole business week? It'd be different if it was summer and you could go to the Hamptons. But what am I going to do with a long weekend in November?"

"What about your family?" January asked.

"What about them? My father's new wife is like twenty-five and she just had another baby and the last thing he wants around is a daughter who is older than his wife. Might remind him how old he is. And my mother is on the verge of splitting with her husband. She caught him at a cocktail party groping her best friend in the powder room—so she's not exactly hanging over a turkey. You're lucky . . . four glorious days at Palm Beach in a beach-front palace . . . going there in your own jet . . . with two guys in attendance as you soak up the sun . . . Daddy and David. Or is it still just Daddy and will David be in the way?"

January walked to the window. She had been ready to go to bed when Linda called and insisted that she come up to her apartment. She had said it was urgent, but for the last twenty minutes, she had been holding forth on Thanksgiving.

Actually January was looking forward to the trip. Mike had been gone ten days. David had taken her out twice since the dreadful night. They had gone to see *Hair* (he had loathed it . . . she adored it). The next time they had done the early movie and Maxwell's Plum evening. And both times he had taken her home, held the cab, and said goodnight with that "*I'll*-wait-until-*you*-ask-*me*" smile.

She realized the remark about David and Daddy had stemmed from Linda's own loneliness. Linda was wearing an old pajama top that had belonged to Keith. Suddenly she realized January was staring at it. She smiled. "Every girl has an ex-lover's old pajama top, that she wears on special occasions . . . to remind her that, at heart, every man is a shit heel."

"Oh, come on—" January tried to change her mood. "With Keith it's a career problem."

"I'm not talking about Keith," Linda said. "I am talking about Leon . . . *the* asshole of all time. At exactly five o'clock this afternoon he announced that he was going back to his wife. He loves me, but his psychiatrist thinks I'm castrating him. Also, it seems he can't afford the alimony he would have to pay her, along with the occasional dinners he bought me. And, of course, he's got his psychiatrist three times a week." She shrugged. "It's just as well—he never really appealed to me."

"Then why did you sleep with him?"

"Darling, Leon is a brilliant art director. He could get much more at another magazine. . . ."

"You mean he's staying on?"

"Of course. We'll still be friends. Maybe even sleep together occasionally. Look, one of the main reasons I started the relationship, was to keep him on the job. This way, *he's* walked out on me to go back to his wife. And I've had enough therapy myself to know just how to handle it. I cried . . . told him I really loved him . . . made him promise me he'd enjoy his Thanksgiving . . . that I understood . . . he had a wife and a kid . . . In short, I laid such a guilt trip on him—he'll *never* leave the magazine."

"Is that all that matters to you—the magazine?"

Linda lit a cigarette. "When I was at Miss Haddon's, all the girls there adored me because I was always on, always with it, right? And the boys dated me because I went all the way. But even by going all the way, I was never sure they'd call again, or for how long I'd hold them. Because I guess I knew there would always be someone they'd meet who would go all the way better than I. And when I got out of Miss Haddon's and had the nose job and tried to be an actress, I saw how girls humiliated themselves auditioning. And I was one of them—singing your guts out on a dark empty stage and then hearing a disembodied voice call out, 'Thank you very much.' And even if you were lucky enough to get a job . . . the following season you were back, groveling, begging, walking, trying . . . praying . . . for another chance to stand on some dark stage and hear 'Thank you very much.' But when I got hired on at *Gloss*, I knew I'd only have to jump, run, fetch and carry, *once*—on my way up. And if I made it, *Gloss* would always be there. Not like a show that closed after a season . . . not like a man who leaves your bed and doesn't come back. There will be plenty of Leons . . . maybe even a few more Keiths."

"Keith . . . wasn't he the big love?"

Linda smiled. "Oh, come on, January. Do you think he's the first man I almost died over? I just cared for him in a different way from Leon."

"But you told me you wanted to marry him. That Keith was—"

"Was important then," Linda cut in. "Look, I'll be twenty-nine next week. That's a shitty age. Because when you say it no one believes you. Like, twenty-seven they'll believe. But twenty-eight and twenty-nine both sound phony. And twenty-nine is over the hill to have not even had a *bad* marriage. But it isn't over the hill when you're editor-in-chief of *Gloss*. When you're the youngest editor-in-chief in New York. So you don't cry yourself to sleep when you realize Keith is gone forever."

"But how do you know he is?"

"He's shacked up with an older woman. I mean a really older woman. Would you believe Christina Spencer?" When she saw no sign of recognition on January's face, she said, "She's rich

. . . Oh, not in Dee's class, she never gets full pages in *Vogue* like Dee. This one's the type that sometimes makes the centerfold of *Women's Wear,* in one of those tiny pictures coming out of restaurant X, Y, or Z. But she's got a few million–" Linda put out her cigarette. "God, these women with money. They buy themselves younger faces, younger boyfriends . . . A few days ago I saw a picture of Keith in a new Cardin jacket, escorting her to a Save the Children ball at the Plaza. There they were, right in the centerfold of *Women's Wear,* only Keith was half cut off and *Women's Wear* called him an unidentified escort."

"But what would he want with her?" January asked.

"Christina Spencer's been taking pieces of Broadway shows for the past ten years. This morning I read in the *Times* that she was a major backer of the new rock musical *Caterpillar* and that Keith Winters has been signed for a featured role."

"Do you feel bad?" January asked softly.

Linda shook her head. "I haven't really felt bad since Tony."

"Tony?"

"Yes, he was the big one. When he split, I took five red dolls and two yellow jackets. I was twenty and thought our love was forever. Well, I survived. Both Tony and the pills. Then there were a lot of quickies. You know–you latch on to someone because he's available, because you want to show Tony that you aren't dying, you want to show yourself that it's 'Right on, baby . . . all the way.' But it never becomes a meaningful relationship, because no matter how attractive he is, he isn't Tony. Oh, it can last several months. Sometimes a year. But something's wrong with it–maybe it's because you generate a negative reaction because suddenly he stops calling. He even forgets he's got three shirts at your place all nice and fresh from the laundry that *you've* paid for. I guess that was when I began picking people who could help the magazine. And most of the time, there isn't even any sex involved. Like right now, a big advertising agency buys full-page color ads for their clients. The president of this agency, Jerry Moss, lives in Darien, has a lovely wife and two children and has been a closet queen all of his life. But a year ago he fell in love with Ted Grant, a male model I know. And I'm their beard. Sometimes I go out with the two of them. Naturally the wife thinks it's business. I even went to their house in Darien on Christmas Eve with Ted as *my* date and sat with the wife in the living room making small talk for forty minutes while they did their number in the upstairs john. Then there's a designer and his wife—they're both gay. She has her girl, he has his boy, and I'm there to make it a fivesome—confusing to everyone but the principals involved. The designer has been a big help, and his wife gives lovely dinner parties and I go and meet all the best people. Yes . . . I love *Gloss*. It's been good to me. I can hold its sales growth in my hand better than a penis that goes limp on me. Oh, that's happened too. When they can't get it up and the guy just lies there with his limp cock and looks at you like *you're* the one who's made him impotent. He lies there and defies you to make him hard. You get a bellyful of them. And then along comes a Keith and you begin to think maybe . . . and you con yourself that it *can* happen. But you know it can't. And when he splits . . . you don't really cry."

"Well . . . I'm sorry." January started for the door.

"Sit down, you idiot. I didn't get you here to talk about my sex life. Or to torch over Keith. I'm resilient. And besides, I read my own Tarot cards the other day and they said something big was going to happen in 1971. So tonight when Leon gave me the news, I came home, took a lamb chop out of the freezer, and while I was waiting for it to thaw, I started reading the galleys of Tom Colt's new novel."

"Is it as good as some of his others?"

"Better. More commercial. His last few were too good. I mean he went literary. No one but the critics dug him. They didn't sell at all. But this one is going to be a rocket. That's why I'm a fatalist. If Leon had been here, we would have had sex and I wouldn't have gotten to the galleys."

"What do you want to do?" January asked. "Bid for serial rights?"

"Are you kidding? I hear *Ladies' Home Journal* has bid up to twenty-five thousand just for two excerpts. We can't get his book, but we can get him. Understand?"

"Linda, I'm tired and I haven't packed yet. Let's not play games. No, I don't understand."

Linda's eyes narrowed. "Listen, you've been acting spooky lately. I'm telling you, you better make it with someone or the next thing you know . . . your skin will go."

"That's a fallacy, and—" January stopped.

"And what?" She looked at January. "Hey . . . you're blushing. You've made it with David! Well, thank God! Are you on the pill? Is everything divine? No wonder you're so thrilled about Palm Beach—four long days and nights of sand and love and—"

"Linda! We did it only once, and it was awful."

Linda paused. "You mean he couldn't get it up?"

"No . . . he . . . well . . . he was fine . . . I guess. It was awful for me."

Linda laughed in relief. "It always is . . . the first time. For the woman that is . . . but never for the man. From what I hear, those bastards come like crazy the first time, even if they're thirteen and do it in a dark hallway with the local 'bad girl.' *She* may not come—and they may come before they even get it into her bird—but goddamn it . . . *they come*! And that's something Women's Liberation is never going to be able to change. A virgin lady is all tight inside even if she's been finger-fucked. A virgin lady hurts when the glorious prick enters. And a virgin lady—whether you call her Ms., Miss, or Mrs.—rarely comes until she's properly stretched and oiled with passion. Thank God you're no longer a virgin lady . . . Only it's a shame you lost it with David."

January nodded. "That's the way I feel . . . I think maybe I should have waited."

"Sure. I could have fixed you up with someone . . . even Leon."

"Are you insane!"

"Never do it the first time with someone you care about. As I said, the first fuck is usually awful and you can lose the guy. Did you turn David off completely?"

"I don't think so, really . . . He says he loves me and wants to marry me."

Linda stared at her. "Then why are we sitting here having a wake for your lost hymen? You sneaky elegant ones—you're always the wild women in the kip. Now look—congratulations and all that. But let's get back to Tom Colt. From what I hear, he needs money and he's consented to do the grand tour."

"But he's very rich," January insisted. "I met him when I was little. He had a town house here with one of his wives and my father was buying one of his books for a picture. He's written about fifteen big novels . . . he has plenty of money."

"So did your father once. Maybe the dice got cold for Tom Colt too. He's married . . . pays alimony to three ex-wives . . . gave the fourth a huge settlement. His new wife just presented him with a baby boy. Imagine, at his age . . . he's never had kids till now. But as I said, his last few books didn't do well. And when you live in a big home in Beverly Hills, with a Rolls, servants, a projection room—the works—you can't have three non-selling books and still be solvent. Not with all the upkeep he's got. He also hasn't had a picture sale since 1964—and that's where the big money is, that and paperback. But on this new one he's back to his old hard-hitting style. Claims he stopped writing for the critics and wants to reach the people again. There was that interview in *Paris Review* a few months ago where he said he doesn't care if the artsy crowd says he sold out—he wants to be number one, and he wants a big picture sale, so . . ."

"So?"

"So he will need all the publicity he can get. And he may ask big money for an excerpt from his book. But he could come absolutely free if we offer to do a cover story on him."

"And what's to keep Helen Gurley Brown from getting the same idea, if she hasn't already?" January asked.

"Oh, she probably has . . . but *we* have *you*!"

"Me?"

"*You* know Tom Colt."

"Oh, Linda . . . I met him when I was about five years old. What do I do? Send him my baby pictures and say, 'Guess who?' and let's get together for old time's sake. Besides, you said, he lives in Beverly Hills."

"If necessary, I'll send you there. First class. Look, the book doesn't come out until February or March. All you have to do is ask him for an interview . . . for Daddy's sake."

January stood up. "I'm tired, Linda. And I have to pack . . ."

"Okay. Have a marvelous time. And while you're basking in the sun and making love, see if you can't frame up a good letter to send to Tom Colt. Maybe you could even get Daddy to add a few lines . . ."

Twelve

Mike was waiting at the airport when the Grumman jet landed. He watched January come down the steps, with David at her elbow. She hadn't spotted him yet, and for a brief moment he reveled in the pleasure of watching her unobserved. Each time he saw her, there was some almost imperceptible change. A new facet of beauty seemed to emerge. He approved of her casual "today" look. The wide slacks, floppy hat, and long straight hair. She looked like one of those new breed fashion models. And then she saw him, and raced toward him, shouting, "Daddy . . . oh, Daddy . . . I'm so glad to see you." He smiled when he realized that in an emotional moment she always reverted to *Daddy* instead of *Mike.*

"I left Mario making drinks. I'm your chauffeur," he explained as David sat in the back of the convertible, wedged in between the luggage.

"How many houseguests this time?" David asked.

"Maybe about eight or ten. But you lose count because she gives those lunches for thirty or forty every day. I go off for golf at nine and when I get back at four, half of them are still here. And then at seven the cocktail group arrives. But Dee has decided that the Thanksgiving dinner itself will be an intimate affair. Just two tables of twelve. Meanwhile let's hope we stay lucky with the sun. You both could use some color."

The good weather held throughout the weekend. There were always two or three backgammon games going at poolside. Hot and cold buffets were wheeled out by an endless stream of servants. Mike and January sat together; soaked up the sun; walked on the beach and swam together. And when she played tennis with David, Mike watched with amazement as she outwitted him on every volley. Where had she learned to play so well? And then like flash bulbs . . . the memory of all those tennis tournaments he had never attended flashed through his mind. All those scrawled little notes he had received in Los Angeles, Madrid, or London! "Am playing for the Junior Cup. Wish you could come." "Am representing Miss Haddon's in the Eastern division. Wish you could be here." "I won." "Am sending cup to the Plaza." "I won." "Sending cup to Plaza." "I came in second." "I won." "Did you get trophy? This one is real silver." "I won." "I won!"

God, how little of himself he had actually given her. And suddenly he found himself wondering what had become of all those cups and trophies. She had never asked him about them. They were probably in some storage place along with the typewriters, the piano, the filing cabinets, and the office furniture he had collected on all those "Comebacks." And he didn't even know where the storage slips were.

How much of her childhood he had missed. And how much of her teens *she* had missed. And now she was hitting her best years and he had to miss them too. He was married . . . only this was one flop he couldn't just close the office and walk away from.

And suddenly as he sat watching his daughter playing tennis, he was hit with panic at the thought that had just slipped through his subconscious. He had thought of his marriage as a flop. Yet actually nothing had changed. Dee still smiled at him across the table each night. She still slipped her arm through his when they greeted guests. He still went to bed with her twice a week . . . There! That was it! He had just touched the exposed nerve. *He* went to bed with *her*. Lately, he had the feeling that she was accommodating him, putting up with him. She wasn't "acting" anymore. When was the last time she had moaned and clung to him and told him how wonderful it all was? But maybe it was his fault. Maybe because he felt he was accommodating her . . . she sensed it. Things like that can be felt. Yes, it was his fault. The poor broad probably resented that he spent so much time at the club. God knows he certainly wasn't paying much attention to her. Golf all morning, gin games in the afternoon (he had found a few good pigeons) . . . Sure, he got back only in time to join her in the martini bit. And the evenings were always filled with dinner parties.

Well, from now on things were going to be different. The moment January left, he'd give Dee the old razzle-dazzle. And he'd cut down on the gin games every afternoon. Nothing wrong in spending a few afternoons with her. But he wouldn't be *with* her. He'd be hanging around having lunch with all those friends of hers, watching them play backgammon. No, he'd stick to the golf club. Besides, so far he had won close to five thousand bucks at gin. He had opened a savings account. Five thousand was a joke, of course. But it was *his* money, money *he* had earned, or won. What the hell, when you earn it in gin, you shoot the same kind of adrenalin you shoot when you earn it anywhere else! But he had to pay more attention to her in the kip. Maybe he was being too perfunctory about it. Well, Sunday, after January and all the houseguests left, the new romantic regime would begin. Suddenly he felt better. It was necessary to take stock of things like this every now and then. Here he had been sitting around thinking something was missing in their relationship when actually he was the one at fault. Hell, she had the same crowds hanging around at Marbella, and she'd have them in Greece next August—and wherever else she decided to go. In London there were never fewer than twenty for cocktails, at the Dorchester. This was her way of life. He knew it when he went into it. He was supposed to supply the romance. That's what he had done when they first met, and she had flipped out for him, and that's what he would do now—starting Sunday.

But for the next few days he concentrated on enjoying his daughter. He watched her turn golden brown, watched the marvelous body in the bikini (Dee was so goddamned white), the way her hair swung, the way Dee's was always in place. Her crazy denims—Dee's perfect white sharkskin pants. The little silver rings on all of her fingers—Dee's David Webb jewelry. They were such wild opposites. Dee was a beauty. Yet he was glad his daughter looked the way she did.

There was something so clean and sparkling about her. And he liked her keen interest in everything. Vital interest in *Gloss* magazine. Casual interest in David. "Pretended" interest in Dee's small talk about the current romantic affiliations of some of the local socialites. The names all had to be a maze to her, but she listened attentively.

It was hard for him to evaluate David. He was always there . . . smiling . . . the perfect escort. You could tell he and Dee were first cousins. They were cut from the same cloth. The aristocracy was all there. The excellent manners—the way he tirelessly played backgammon with Dee's guests, his proper clothes for every occasion. His tennis shorts were just the right cut, his sweater was casual and right, even his perspiration was classy, just a little on the brow, the better to make his suntan glisten. But wasn't that what he wanted for January? Long before he had ever met Dee, he knew he wanted something better than a show business life for his daughter. That's why he had chosen the fancy school in Connecticut. That had been on advice from his business manager: "She'll get to know classy girls, meet their brothers—that's how it all happens. That's what good schools are for."

Well, the only thing she had gotten out of that school was a lot of tennis trophies and a job on a magazine. Of all the girls there, she had to tie up with Linda, a real barracuda, the kind that leaped in and out of a different bed each night. But then, wasn't that part of the new permissiveness of today? He stared at his daughter on the tennis court. Had she? Nah! Not that he expected her to remain a virgin forever. But she was the kind who would probably do it with a guy after they got engaged. Or maybe just before . . . just to make sure. Right now she was all involved with the magazine. But like Dee said, she'd probably play around with being the career girl for a short time and then marry David.

He wondered why he felt depressed. This was what he wanted for her, wasn't it? But did he want her to turn into a young Dee? Well, why not? It would be a hell of a lot better than having her go the route some of the other kids went. Moving in with some guy, going funky and East Village. Or suppose she had been more like him—intent on becoming a superstar. Then what? Suppose she made it. She'd catch herself a few hot years on Cloud Nine, but the eventual end for any superstar, including himself, was loneliness and defeat. If a man had money, he lasted a little longer. But for a woman, even with money, the loneliness came quicker. Age was a woman's defeat. Even a legend like Karla—what kind of a life did she have? Still with the ballet exercises! But without them, where else would she have to go each day? And most of the superstars weren't lucky enough to be born stupid like Karla, content to go walking and practicing ballet. The more emotional ones—they were the bleeders, sitting home alone in a mansion in Beverly Hills, taking sleeping pills or booze. Anything to get rid of the night so they could wake up to an endless day that stretched before them, to meals served on a tray while they sat alone watching daytime soap operas on television. No, it was turning out right for January. She had learned all the basic things at Miss Haddon's—and now he had supplied the rest. A place like this to come to—sun in the winter, snow in the summer. Anything she wanted.

And he had gotten it for her. He watched her walk off the tennis court with David. She had beaten him again. That was his daughter—a champion. But David was also a champion. Losing gracefully was a hard art to come by. And David had mastered it. The way he leaped over the net to congratulate her, the way he put his arm around her shoulders while the other guests applauded. But most of all, Mike admired the charm and enthusiasm he engendered at all the endless parties they attended each night.

But January had seemed to enjoy the weekend too. Maybe he had done it all right. Maybe it was all working out as he had hoped it would. Maybe when they came back to Palm Beach for the Christmas holidays they'd be really serious about each other. Dee would like that. But hell . . . not yet. She wouldn't be twenty-one until January. She deserved some free time.

Free time for what? She was a girl . . . he was thinking of her subjectively. Girls didn't need to play the field. They were content to settle for one man for life. She wasn't one of those half-baked Women's Liberationists. Anyhow, he didn't even believe them. Sometimes when he saw them on TV, he'd talk back to the screen. "Yeah, baby . . . just one good fuck and you'd sing a different tune." That's all they were—broads without a guy. And his daughter would never have to worry about that.

He got up early on Sunday. He had promised to have an early breakfast with her at the pool. She was leaving around four. Then he and Dee would be alone. And he was determined to keep his vow. He hadn't been to bed with Dee in a week. He wondered if she noticed it. They both had their own rooms here. Rooms! His bedroom was forty feet by thirty five, facing the ocean. He also had a sauna, a shower and a black marble bathroom with a sunken tub. His bedroom adjoined hers, but as he put it, it was a sleeper jump to get there. First he had to walk through her dressing room . . . and her bathroom—a huge white and gold marble affair with a real tree growing in it and one whole wall filled with tropical fish. That wall was also a wall of her bedroom; it was slightly smaller than his, but its ocean-front terrace was almost the size of a ballroom. They breakfasted there occasionally under an umbrella.

Today he started his training—no Bloody Marys at lunch, no martinis at cocktails . . . Tonight he'd make love to her with his old passion.

He spent the morning with January. She glanced through the magazine section of the *Times*, and he went for the sports pages. That was another great thing they had together—they didn't feel conversation was necessary for communication. It wasn't until he had finished the sports section and the theatrical section that he noticed she was reading a set of galleys.

"Any good?" he asked.

"Very good." She looked up and pushed her sunglasses up into her hair. "Tom Colt . . . remember him?"

"How could I forget?" he said. "I made a three-million-dollar profit on the picture I did of his book."

"I meant, do you remember the time you took me to his house?"

"I did? Oh, of course. A brownstone in the East Sixties, wasn't it?"

"*Gloss* may do an article on him. What's he like?"

"He was having a love affair with himself in those days. He had won a Pulitzer Prize with his first novel, but instead of being impressed with it, he blandly told me he was after the big one. The Nobel. He had written only about six books when he told me that, and the way he figured it, ten more prolific years would do it. But I guess all those marriages and bar fights killed that dream." Mike looked thoughtful. "I know his last books haven't been selling well. But I still didn't think he'd panic enough to go for an interview with a magazine like *Gloss*."

"Mike! Have you ever read *Gloss*?"

"From cover to cover, when you said you were going to work there. And it's not for Tom Colt. Look, babe, remember about six years ago when all the newspapers carried the story of how he had a dogfight with a shark? When the fishing boat he was on capsized, he had been the one to swim under water and actually punch the sharks on their snouts and kept them at bay until help arrived for the others."

"He did?"

"He also fought a bull in Spain. Knocked out a professional fighter in a bar. When his plane crashed, he walked a mile into town with a broken leg. He can also drink any man under the table and he can knock out Muhammad Ali with one hand tied behind him."

"He can?"

Mike laughed. "No . . . but that's the kind of publicity he wants. He did knock out a lot of guys in barroom fights, only no one knows if he knocked out a fighter. The shark story is true . . . so is the bull. Everyone says it was a tired bull, but the fact is, he did go in the ring and try it. And what I'm getting to is . . . *that's* the kind of publicity he goes after. And I can't see him holding still for a story in *Gloss*."

"Well, we're hoping to get one."

"Oh, you mean you haven't really got it?"

January stared at her tanned legs. "I'm supposed to write him a letter."

"And casually mention that I'm your father?"

"Yeah . . . real casual. Like have you write a P.S. at the bottom."

"No way," he said. "It's not that I wouldn't do it for you. Hell, I'd crawl on my belly if it would help you in any way. But your best chance of getting an interview with him is *not* to mention that I'm your father."

"Why?"

"Well, like I said, when I knew him, he was thinking 'Nobel.' And to make a big commercial hit picture out of his book, I had to leave out a lot of key scenes and characters; otherwise we'd have had a six-hour picture. He never forgave me for it."

"But if the picture made money—"

"It did—for me and the studio. He had just gotten a flat fee—like two hundred thousand—but no percentage. So he was looking at it artistically. Let's say . . . we're not enemies but we're really not exactly buddy chum pals."

"How old is he?"

Mike wrinkled his brow. "About five or six years older than me . . . maybe fifty-seven or fifty-eight. But from what I hear, he's still boozing and making the scene with young broads." He sighed. "Know something? There's nothing worse than an overaged stud. It's like a forty-year-old woman trying to look like a teeny bopper."

"What would you suggest I do about getting the interview?"

"Forget it . . ."

And then the butler announced lunch was being served, guests began arriving at the pool, Dee made her entrance in flowing pajamas and a large hat, and the ornate buffet lunch had officially begun.

After that he didn't get too much chance to talk to January. There were at least fifty guests. Several of the young men gave David rough competition for her attention. Mike noticed this. And he also noticed David's confident attitude. Why not? The bum was gonna have her all to himself on the plane ride home. But Mike was beginning to like him better. The few times they had talked during the week, he had detected a warmth that the boy hadn't shown before. Probably being with January had drawn him out, made him loose. Or maybe just because he felt that David might become a permanent fixture, he was *looking* to like him. Anyway, he wasn't in the mood to analyze his thoughts. She was leaving soon, the whole caboodle would soon leave—and he'd be alone with Dee tonight. Tomorrow the luncheons would begin again . . . And then there would be the start of parties before the final Christmas rush. She had said something about going to Palm Springs for a week in January—a backgammon tournament—and they would be houseguesting with friends. Maybe after that they could go back to New York. He liked the sun and golf—but enough was enough. Even though he just played gin and goofed in New York, it was different. There was something invigorating about New York, about the cold weather. It was his town. He could still walk down Fifth Avenue and run into someone he knew . . . talk shop at the Friars Club . . . see the Broadway shows . . . go to Danny's Hide-a-Way for dinner with January when Dee played backgammon. He remembered the old days when Danny's was his second home. He'd sit at that front table with the girl of the moment—and most of the time he knew everyone in the room. But lately . . . he didn't see the same faces anywhere. Where did everyone go? At "21" and at Danny's, new faces sat at the front tables . . . TV stars, recording artists, Society Charlies. But he still wanted to get back to New York. And tonight he'd ball Dee, make her happy, dependent on him—and then suggest a stopover in New York for a few weeks after Palm Springs.

He drove January and David to the airport and watched them climb into the plane. He walked back to his car. They looked so young and beautiful. When did he get so old? He stared at himself in the rear view mirror as he drove. He was going to be fifty-three. Hell, that wasn't old. He was in his prime. And he looked good. He didn't have an extra ounce of flesh on him. Dames still gave him the look. Of course they were Dee's friends—all in their forties—but at the club some of the younger women who played golf gave him the eye. But he always kept his smile open and friendly, nothing more, even though there were a few he would have liked . . . that daughter of Dee's banker friend . . . Monica. Yeah, Monica was about thirty-two, a divorcee. She was suddenly taking golf lessons every day. One of his gin-playing friends said it was because of him. Monica . . . yeah . . . That'd be real nice. But he wouldn't. He had made a deal with himself—if he married Dee and if she laid enough money on January, he'd play it straight. Besides, there was nothing wrong with Dee's looks. She was slim. A little soft in spots . . . but good-looking. Hell, plenty of men would give anything to be able to have her whenever they wanted . . . and he had only "wanted" twice a week lately. That was all wrong. She couldn't come to him and ask. She wasn't like Tina St. Claire, who would say, "Hey, lover, let's fuck." No. The Dees waited. And they didn't fuck . . . they made love. And you courted them. He had let it get cut and dried, he had to change all that. If this was the life he was stuck with, he could at least make it interesting.

It was almost six o'clock when he got back to the house. Everyone had gone. One of the butlers was restocking the bar on the terrace. "Where is Mrs. Wayne?" he asked. For a moment the butler stared at him vacantly. Mike swore softly—the dumb sonofabitch was one of the help who still thought of her as *Miss Granger*—well, he wasn't going to say it, he'd never say, "Where is Miss Granger?" Not if they stood all day and had a staring contest. The old butler blinked a moment—then a happy smile spread across his features as his memory rewarded him. "Madam is upstairs resting, I believe."

Mike nodded and started toward the massive flight of stairs. He looked at them for a moment, turned around, took the elevator down to the wine cellar. He selected a bottle of champagne and took it to the kitchen and waited while the maid set it up with glasses and put caviar on an iced dish.

She was lying on the chaise longue when he came in carrying the tray. Her phone book was in her lap and he realized she was setting her appointments for the following week. He walked over with the tray and set it on a table.

"What's the occasion?" she asked.

"Us . . . we're alone . . . and I dig you." He walked over and took the phone book out of her lap. He sat on the edge of the chaise. "We have no dates tonight, have we?"

"Several parties we can drop in on if we like. Vera is in town and the Arnold Ardens are giving a party for her. Then there's—"

He leaned over and kissed her. "How's about blowing them all. . . ." His hand went under her dressing gown. She pushed him away. "Mike, it's only six o'clock."

He laughed. "Where is there a rule that sex has to happen on specific hours? Now, let's get a little high . . . and make love right over there on that big bed where we see the ocean and maybe if we're lucky . . . the moon will come up. Twilight fucking is just great, Dee."

"Mike!" She jumped up and walked across the room. "Who do you think you're talking to . . . one of those chorus girls you used to date?"

He came to her. "Oh, Dee . . . that's part of love talk. I meant no harm."

"Well, it's vulgar."

He grinned. "Come on. I've said that word when we were in bed."

"That's different. I mean, when you're actually doing it, well, I can't stop you from saying those words, but . . . well, I don't like them. Oh, I know some men get a kick out of using them . . . but why? Does it excite them, does it make them feel more of a man? One of my husbands couldn't even get an erection until he forced me to say that word, to say I wanted him to . . . you know."

He managed to force a smile. "All right. I'll try and watch my language in the kip . . ." He came to her but she turned away. "Now what?"

"Oh, Mike, don't be ridiculous. This is not the time for—" She turned away.

He stared at her back for a moment. Then he picked up the champagne and started for the door.

She turned around. "Now, Mike . . . don't be angry. It's just that I'm not in the mood."

"Okay. I understand." He saluted her with the bottle. "I think I'll have this all by myself. Because it is an occasion, you know . . . It's the first time I ever got a turn-down. But like they say—there's always a first . . ." He closed the door.

Dee stood very still when he left the room. That had been a wrong move. She should have given in . . . but she just couldn't. She was exhausted. Exhausted from smiling and floating from party to party, playing the role of the beautiful cool Dee Milford Granger Wayne. Lucky Dee Milford Granger Wayne, married to such an attractive man. Poor, poor Dee Milford Granger Wayne, heartbroken because that slob of a Polack didn't show up. Karla had practically promised that she would come. Oh, God, how she had wanted Karla to be there. She had especially wanted Karla to see January and David together. To see them swimming together, dancing together, playing tennis together . . . to see that they were young and belonged together. And when she had spoken to Karla on Tuesday, Karla had said "perhaps." She had even promised that if she decided to come she'd be at the airport at four. Dee had told the pilot to wait until four thirty.

She had masked her disappointment when she saw David and January arrive alone. She was delighted they were getting on so well. That had been the only bright spot of the weekend. David seemed to really like January. If only Karla had been there to see it. Why *hadn't* she come! Just plain perverseness. After all, everyone in New York had gone away. What would Karla do with herself during the long weekend?

David had also thought about Karla. He had thought about her the entire weekend. And he was thinking about her now as he sat in the plane watching it make its approach to Butler Jetport, the private field at La Guardia. He suddenly realized he had barely talked to January during the flight. But she had been reading some galleys, and when she had put them away she had just sat staring out the window. He wondered what she was thinking about. But he didn't really care.

Actually January was thinking about David. She had finished the book and had decided to send Tom Colt a letter on her own as assistant editor of *Gloss*. She wouldn't tell Linda that Mike would be no help to them. She watched David's tanned face staring out his window at the bright lights below. He had been so nice during the holiday. Always ready to play tennis or go for a swim. That faint glimmer of something she had begun to feel for him had been snuffed out after their awful night together. Perhaps it could be fanned back to life. Perhaps if they had a drink together, talked a bit—maybe they might even make love again. And this time it might be all right. But she couldn't face that horrible red bedroom of his . . . ever.

David had ordered a car. It was waiting on the airfield. They piled their suitcases in the trunk and headed toward January's building. David helped the chauffeur give her bags to her doorman. She smiled. "I've enjoyed the four days together," she said. "Really enjoyed it."

"I have too . . ."

She looked at her watch. "It's only nine o'clock. Want to come up for a drink? You've never seen my sumptuous apartment."

He smiled. "Will you promise me one thing? Give me a raincheck the very next time. I have so many business calls to make when I get home . . . and I know my service is jammed with messages. I'll phone you tomorrow. First thing."

She stared after him as he got back into the car. Wow! Now she knew how Linda felt . . . what a turn-down.

David had no idea he was turning her down. He thought her invitation had been extended out of politeness. And he had no intention of wasting an hour sitting around having a drink with her. He got home, dismissed the car, and checked with his service immediately. There were a few messages. Kim was at a party at Monique's—please come . . . Princess Delmanio had called—she was having a backgammon party . . . His maid had called—she couldn't come in on Monday, but would Tuesday be all right . . . there was a number to call her. There were a few more messages, but none that he cared about. Nothing from Karla. Well, why should there be? She knew he wasn't coming back until tonight. She'd call him tomorrow at his office.

Suddenly he kicked the wastebasket near him. This was ridiculous. It was only nine-thirty. Karla was the woman he loved. He had the whole evening free—they could be together. Yet he had no way of calling her. He couldn't go on like this, sitting around like a girl, waiting to be called. He grabbed his coat, raced out of his building and hailed a cab. He would go to her . . . bang on her door and demand that she give him her phone number. He didn't care if she was asleep. He was going to assert himself. If he wanted her to treat him like a man, he'd better start acting like one. He would stand his ground tonight, even if it meant their first fight. But more than anything he wanted to take her in his arms . . . to look into her eyes . . . feel her strong arms around him . . . listen to the husky laugh.

The cab pulled up. David paid the driver and sprang out. Ernest, the cheerful and polite doorman, was on. He gave him the usual friendly nod, but instead of saying, "Good evening to you, Mr. Milford," he said, "Where are you going, Mr. Milford?"

"To see Miss Karla."

"But she left Friday morning."

"Left!"

"That she did . . . with two suitcases."

"Where? I mean . . . she didn't move . . . or—"

The doorman saw the panic on David's face. "Now come on, son . . . nothing to be so upset about. Of course she didn't move. You know Miss Karla. She always takes off on a moment's notice. None of us here knew she intended to leave. But on Friday morning down she comes at nine, huddled in that big fur coat and dark glasses, only instead of taking her usual walk to her dancing studio, she asks for a cab. And like I said, she's got them suitcases. She tells me she left word for them to hold her mail and stop her *Wall Street Journal*. That's the only newspaper she ever reads . . . but she told me to check on it and make sure. Then she told the driver Kennedy Airport. That's all I know."

"I . . . I was away myself," David said in an attempt at recovery. He couldn't bear the sympathetic look in the doorman's eyes. "I was in Palm Beach . . . you can see by my tan . . . and I haven't checked with my service. Afraid I took off without giving Miss Karla any notice myself and I called from the airport and when her phone didn't answer . . . well, you know how phones are today . . . you never can tell . . . so I thought I'd come around. But I'll probably find a message from her on my service."

"Of course you will, my lad."

David turned and walked away. She was gone. No more of those "Good evenings to you," from the doorman. God, they had been such *good* evenings! Those evenings when he sailed in, confident and happy, smiling at the doorman who knew he was expected, nodding to the elevator man who also knew he was expected. And now she was gone again. For how long? And why? The lights of the street were blurring now . . . he began to run. She was gone . . . without even saying goodbye. He kept running . . . it was the only way to keep from cracking up. He ran all the way to his apartment. And when he let himself in, he called out to the empty walls: "OH GOD . . . KARLA! WHY?"

And then he stood there and sobbed . . . great dry sobs . . . the first time he had sobbed since the day he was cut from the football squad at Andover.

Thirteen

Karla sat huddled in the front seat of the jet. After calling all the airlines she had settled on TWA's eleven o'clock flight to London when they had assured her that no one would share her seat.

She was still wearing her oversized dark glasses. So far the young stewardesses had not recognized her. Some of them were only children when she had retired. But these same children were members of the new cult who had discovered her on the Late Show. She watched them giggling together, preparing hors d'oeuvres and drinks, always smiling as they flashed up and down the aisle serving people. They were so young. And so very happy. Had she ever been that young or giggled like that? No . . . it was not possible. Not when you grew up in a village near Wilno.

WILNO. A mistake of migration by her father . . . a mistake made by so many Poles. In 1920, Poland had launched a successful attack on Russia and seized Wilno, the capital of Lithuania. And to this new state came farmers eager for new acres. In 1921, Andrzej Karlowski, his wife, his baby daughter, and their two small sons arrived. He came from a village near Bialystok hoping to make his fortune in Wilno; to send his sons to the university when they were grown. Instead he found a land that was scourged. His neighbors were Ukrainians and Rutherians who retained their national characteristics. There was a small Catholic church in the nearest village, a state school where the nuns taught, and Andrzej and his wife had no choice but to work fifteen hours a day to farm their barren land. There was no time to miss the old life or friends. The farm took all their energy—that and the dream of the university for their sons. And it was in this desolate atmosphere that Natalia Maria Karlowski was raised.

It was a placid unemotional childhood. She grew up with no laughter, no imagination, no dreams, and no ambitions other than to marry a boy with a nice piece of land.

The Karlowskis were good Catholics, and the only day she could remember seeing her mother sitting without peeling potatoes was Sunday, when she attended Mass. On that day her mother exchanged the babushka for the black hat with the large hatpin, the apron for the shiny black dress, and the rosary replaced the paring knife in her rough calloused hands. Her father wore his one black suit, the suit he wore to church, weddings, and funerals.

She attended the state school, and her first few years were as calm and as unemotional as her days on the farm. She was nine when Sister Thérèse arrived, bringing the first bit of beauty and excitement into the lives of the drab little students.

Sister Thérèse was from Warsaw. She had been to Moscow and Paris. She had studied for the ballet and had suddenly gotten the "calling." She gave it all up and entered a convent. The little school had been her first assignment. She told this to her spellbound pupils in a quiet direct way. They stared like mutes—it was the first time any of them had seen a beautiful woman, a woman without weather-beaten skin and red hands. The hard Polish winter robbed young women of their beauty before it blossomed.

All of the girls worshipped Sister Thérèse. But little Natalia was enraptured. And when Sister Thérèse offered to teach some ballet exercises in the gym class, Natalia worked with demoniac energy. At home she spent hours in her small room practicing every exercise because she noticed how pleased Sister Thérèse was when any of the girls displayed the least bit of grace. And a word of praise from Sister Thérèse sent her home with vaguely disquieting, yet hauntingly wonderful daydreams. And then one afternoon, Sister Thérèse asked her to wait after class. Her palms were wet and her heart seemed to be beating in her neck and throat as she waited. Sister Thérèse came to her with a smile. "Natalia, I think you have the makings of a real ballerina. I have talked with the Mother Superior, and if it meets with your family's approval, I would like to try to get you a scholarship at the Prasinski School of Ballet. You will have to live there, and your school work will continue there, but you will receive five hours of ballet a day."

Her mother and father agreed immediately. They knew nothing about ballet; but if a nun had suggested it . . . then it was right. Natalia was torn. She realized it was a great opportunity, except it would mean leaving Sister Thérèse. But when the Sister told her she would visit the school and watch her progress, Natalia felt better. All of the students picked names to use when they danced in the school recitals. Natalia had no imagination. She was enrolled as Natalia Karlowska and that was her name.

For the next seven years her entire life was centered around the ballet and Sister Thérèse. Every Saturday afternoon the students performed a ballet in the little theater in the school. The money for the tickets helped toward running the company. During the first few years of recital, Natalia helped with scenery, makeup, and sewing costumes for the girls who performed. When she was twelve she made the corps de ballet. And each week Sister Thérèse would sit in the audience, and Natalia would dance her heart out to her.

Her mother and father had come to the first recital in their church clothes, looking uncomfortable and warm in the auditorium. Her father fell asleep during the second act and her mother had to pinch him to stop his snoring. They never came again—too long a trip, too much work to be done at home . . .

When Natalia got her first solo, and all the girls insisted she pick a name, it was Sister Thérèse who suggested "Karla." And after the performance when she flung herself into the nun's arms and Sister Thérèse whispered, "Congratulations . . . Karla," she never thought of herself as anything but Karla again. She had been rechristened and reborn.

One day after a recital, Sister Thérèse requested to visit her parents. "You are nineteen. It is time to talk about your future. May I come next Sunday . . . after Mass?"

She would never forget that Sunday. She had left ballet school on an early train. When she reached the house, her parents were still at church, but she smelled the goose and the apple pie. She stood in the small living room. Suddenly it looked so shoddy. It was immaculate . . . but so very poor. It was June, and she rushed outside and picked some spring flowers. She put them around the room and tried to cover the worn spots on the chairs with the doilies. But when Sister Thérèse arrived she seemed unaware of the poverty. She admired the andirons at the fireplace . . . the pewter mugs . . . she moved about like a beautiful porcelain goddess. Sister Thérèse praised the goose and red cabbage and knedlicky. Her mother's round face beamed, and it was the first time Karla realized her mother had dimples . . . or that her father's gray eyes were so beautiful when he smiled. She sat in silence as Sister Thérèse explained to her family that she would like to send Natalia to Warsaw.

"My family is very wealthy," Sister Thérèse said softly. "And my mother's brother, my Uncle Otto, lives in London. He is also a big merchant. They will do for Natalia what they hoped to do for me. She could stay with my family in Warsaw while she auditions for the ballet. Later perhaps she could stay with Uncle Otto if she tries out for the Sadlers Wells in London . . . but do I have your permission?"

Her parents nodded in unison. It was too much for them to fathom. Warsaw . . . London . . . anything the Sister wished was acceptable—only there was no way they could repay her.

Later Natalia and Sister Thérèse had taken a walk. The moment they were outside, Natalia said, "I am not going to Warsaw. I am not leaving you."

Sister Thérèse had laughed. "In time you will be very happy there. Very shortly our little Prasinski Ballet will not be able to teach you anything more. You are almost ready." Suddenly she pointed toward a tree. "And what is that?"

Karla blushed. "I made that for you when I was nine."

Sister Thérèse walked over to it. Some planks were built

around a tree forming a seat, and a crude picket fence surrounded the tree. Karla laughed with embarrassment. "You brought not only dancing, but poetry into my life. One day at school you talked about a beautiful gazebo . . . you made it so real . . . I could almost see you sitting in it. So I came home and built it. I used to dream that one day I would show it to you—and now I see how very ugly it is."

Sister Thérèse entered and sat down. "It's lovely, my little Karla. Come sit with me." Sister Thérèse smelled of clean soap and violets. Suddenly Karla threw her arms around the Sister and said, "I love you. I have loved you since I first saw you."

Sister Thérèse disengaged herself carefully. "I love you, too."

"You do! Oh, then let me kiss you and hold you and—" She reached out and touched the Sister's cheek . . . and held her hand.

But once again Sister Thérèse calmly extricated herself from the girl's embrace. "You must not touch me. It is wrong."

"It is wrong to love?"

"Love is never wrong," Sister Thérèse said. "But physical love between us is wrong. You cannot kiss me or touch me."

"But I want to. Can't you understand? Oh, Sister, I know nothing about the ways of making love. I talk very little to the girls at school. But sometimes at night as I lie in bed in my cubicle, I hear them sneak into bed with one another and I know they are caressing. I have been approached . . . but I turn away. No one matters but you. I lie there alone and dream that you are in a nightgown and coming to me and taking me in your arms and then—"

"And then?" Sister Thérèse asked.

"And then I hold you close and kiss you . . . and touch you—" She paused. "Oh, Sister, I want you close to me. Is that really wrong?"

Sister Thérèse fingered the rosary that hung from her habit. "Yes, Karla, it is wrong. You see, when I studied ballet in Warsaw, I too paired off at night with other girls. It is something that happens . . . girls reach puberty . . . they only have one another . . . there is no time to meet young men. So they love one another. I did it, but I knew it was wrong . . . and it tormented me. And I also knew I was not as fine a dancer as some of the others, that I had been accepted because of my family's money and prestige. And one day after I had just been given a role that another girl had tried out for, I heard someone whisper, 'It is her face that got her the role . . . not her feet.' And the girl who did not get the role ran off sobbing, saying my beauty was evil—that it got me things I did not deserve." Sister Thérèse's face was drawn as she forced the unpleasant memory into words. "That night I fell to my knees and prayed for help. And suddenly it was as if I had been released from a prison. I realized I didn't want to be a great ballerina. I found I wanted only to serve and love *Him* . . . my sweet Jesus. I spent days meditating. I read the lives of all the Saints, read about how *they* had gotten the calling, and suddenly when I read the life of the Little Flower—Saint Thérèse who just wanted to do 'little things'—I knew then that I must become a nun. I knew I could never bring about any big miracles . . . but I could make people happy by doing little things. And the first little thing happened when I left the ballet. The girl who had run off sobbing got my part. And believe me, Karla, it was the first genuine happiness I had known. And when I came here, and saw all the serious little faces, I knew that the years of study had not been in vain . . . not if they could bring some little bit of happiness to the children of Wilno . . . and to you, my little Karla. And you must work hard at your dancing . . . and always remember *He* is watching and that it is a mortal sin to make love with a woman. One day a man will come along . . . and then you will understand true love."

"Why didn't that man come along for you?"

"He did. His name is Jesus."

Then they left the gazebo, and they never spoke about love again. As the summer drew to an end, Sister Thérèse changed the plans about the Warsaw trip. "We must arrange for you to go to England. . . ."

"When?"

"Immediately. I have written to Uncle Otto in London about you. Today I received an answer. He and Tante Bosha will be delighted to have you stay with them while you audition for the Sadlers Wells."

Karla tried to put her off. "Not for a while. Next year perhaps."

But Sister Thérèse was insistent. "You must make your plans to leave in ten days. Here is your plane ticket to London."

Karla stared at the ticket Sister Thérèse had placed in her hand. She shook her head. "No . . . no . . . I don't want to go."

"Karla, you must listen to me. War is just seconds away. Germany has signed the nonaggression pact with Russia. Von Ribbentrop went to Moscow last week. Why do you think I said you must not go to Warsaw? You will only be safe in London."

"But what about you? If it is so dangerous . . . why are you staying?"

"I am protected. I am in the church. Even in wars, the church is not molested. God will protect me. Jesus watches over us all."

"Then let Him watch over me."

"No. You have your own calling."

The following day there were no classes as all the students and teachers huddled around the radio and listened to the news that Hitler had served notice on England and France that Germany wanted Danzig and the Polish Corridor. There was talk . . . groups huddled together—how would war affect the ballet? But the following day all the students were back to their bar work and rehearsals went on as usual. But reality and fear hit the Prasinski Ballet on August 31, when Hitler offered Poland sixteen conditions of peace and Poland rejected the terms. Suddenly there was frenzied activity at Prasinski. Classes ended. Suitcases were dragged out. Instructors tried to get train reservations to get back to their homes. That night everyone gathered in nervous little groups, whispering together. Students who had to part to return to homes in distant cities sat together, their arms around each other, openly professing their love. Karla sat alone and thought about Sister Thérèse. What was she doing? Praying with the other nuns? Was she thinking about her?

The following morning at dawn, without any formal notice of war, Germany invaded Poland. Students no longer waited for proper trains. They left on foot. They sat at railroad stations waiting for any train. Karla was fortunate. She managed to get a lift from a milk farmer who had land near her parents.

When she finally reached the farm, she found her parents sitting in front of the radio in a somnambulistic stupor. Their sons had left the university to join the army . . . everything they had worked for was gone. Karla had never read newspapers, but now she went to the village to buy the daily paper. She read about things she couldn't understand. She suddenly realized she knew so little about anything other than ballet. She knew all about Nijinsky—his wife, his manager, his instructors. But she knew nothing of the world she lived in. She had been aware of the peril of Hitler . . . but the full impact of war had never permeated the Prasinski Ballet.

Now the most important moments were the broadcasts from Radio Warsaw—listening to it sign on with the first few notes of the Chopin Polonaise in A Major. When she learned German mechanized units had reached the outskirts of the capital and had opened fire on Warsaw, she knew it was time to leave. She must get to London and Uncle Otto. She packed her bag, kissed her parents goodbye, and walked the two miles to the convent to tell Sister Thérèse.

When she arrived, Sister Thérèse was sitting at the radio, fingering her rosary, her eyes staring into space. All night she had tried to get through to her parents in Warsaw, but the lines were down. When she saw Natalia's bag and heard she planned to go to London, she shook her head with a sad smile. "It is too late for that. No planes . . . no trains . . . no more ballet . . . the dream has ended."

Secretly, Karla was relieved that she would not have to leave Wilno and Sister Thérèse. For the next week she alternated between visiting the convent and sitting with her mother and father at the farm, listening to the radio. The radio became a way of life. Her family couldn't get through to their relatives in Bialystok . . . obviously they had fled. The escape route was through Rumania. In the village a mass exodus had begun. A constant flow of people carrying bundles, bits of valuable furniture, and even some livestock, were trying to make their way to Rumania. The Polish army was fighting valiantly, but on the seventeenth of September the Russians began to invade from the east. Andrzej told his wife and daughter to seek refuge at the convent. Maria, fear turning the blue eyes glassy in her round weather-beaten face, refused to leave her husband and their land. But she insisted Karla must go. She stared at the girl as if seeing her for the first time. "You are tall . . . you will be a strong beautiful woman. Go to the convent. Even the Russians will not harm the church."

Somehow Karla knew it was the end of the only life she had known. These two strangers were her parents . . . yet she didn't know them. She clung to them, but they barely responded. They stood like petrified images of people. They did not know how to give affection . . . or to accept it. They raised their children because they were there. They farmed the barren land because it was there. And now the two sons had vanished from the university . . . and with them went all hope of any tomorrow. Nothing was left but the land.

Sister Thérèse welcomed Karla into the convent. As people fled they left their dogs, cats and even baby lambs on the street. Each day Karla went out and collected the homeless animals. She took them all into the convent. But as the days passed and the Russians drew closer, the Mother Superior said they must be turned out. They were running low on supplies themselves . . . they were God's creatures, she claimed, and the Lord would take care of them. Karla had pleaded . . . she had grown to love the kittens and the dogs. She begged to be allowed to keep the smallest, but the Mother Superior was adamant. Another nun collected them and turned them out. When Sister Thérèse came to her room, she found Karla sobbing. She looked up and shouted, "I am never going to love anyone . . . not even an animal. It hurts too much when it's taken away from you."

Sister Thérèse stroked her hair. "Love the Lord. He will never desert you or be taken away from you. He will be with you throughout eternity."

"He'll never leave me?"

"Never. This life is just something to get through as well as we can. But it is only the preparation for the real world—the life we have after death—when we go to Him."

"Perhaps I could become a nun," Karla suggested.

Sister Thérèse looked at the girl seriously. "It is too big a decision to make in such a short time. I do not feel you have the calling. You are coming to this decision from fear. But pray to Him . . . ask Him to show you the way."

And so Karla spent the long days with the Sisters, ate with them, and went to early Mass and evening Chapel with them while the Polish army fought on. After nineteen days of unbelievable resistance to the bombardment of Germany's superior forces, the battered and heroic defenders of Warsaw surrendered to the Germans. Until the last hour, Radio Warsaw continued to identify itself with the first three notes of the Polonaise.

A few days later several Russian officers arrived at the convent and informed them that they were now living in Russian-occupied territory. Schools were closed, and the remaining citizens were notified that an immediate Sovietization of the Russian occupied areas had begun. Tales began to trickle into the convent of midnight arrests by the Soviet officers. At first they were made on the charge of subversiveness to the new government. By September 30, President Moxcicki had crossed the border into Rumania with the entire government, and the exiles formed a provisional government in exile in Paris.

General Sikorsky, also in exile, acted through some high-ranking Polish officers who had remained in the country, and gradually the Polish Underground began. It was a ground swell that grew larger and larger despite cruel and barbaric reprisals. It became known as the Polish home army—ARMIA KRAJOWS, whispered among the Poles as the A.K.

No one bothered the nuns, but for safety's sake, after hearing rumors of rape by drunken army privates, the Mother Superior allowed Karla to wear the habit. Each weekend Karla drove the battered convent car to her parents' farm and brought them any news that she heard. And she would return to the convent with fresh eggs, which her parents insisted she give to the Sisters. The Soviets had reopened elementary and secondary schools. Nuns were no longer allowed to teach, and the Polish universities at Lwow and Wilno were transformed into centers designated to convert the population to the Soviet order. Although the convents and churches were not desecrated, religion was frowned upon.

One weekend, just before Christmas, she drove to the farm, just as her mother and father were being herded into a jeep by two Russian officers. She was wearing her nun's habit and was about to rush to them, but her mother merely nodded and said distantly, "Hello, Sister. Take the eggs for the convent. They are in the kitchen." She started toward them, but the fear in her father's eyes also shot her a warning not to speak. The Russian soldiers ignored her, made some jokes among themselves about the ugly black habit, and drove away in the jeep with her parents. She felt helpless. But if she rushed after them and declared they were her parents . . . then what? Be taken off with them and shipped to a labor camp.

She drove back to the convent, and as she got out of the car, she noticed a good-looking young Russian officer turn to stare at her on the street. She rushed inside and bolted the door, and that night when she looked at herself in the small bathroom mirror she realized that although the coif hid her hair, it only served to make her prominent cheekbones and large eyes more effective. She stared at herself from every angle. Yes . . . she was beautiful . . . not petitely beautiful like Sister Thérèse . . . but the way the Russian officer had stared . . . she knew a man would find her desirable. But she was now serious about becoming a nun, and in her daily prayers she asked guidance and pleaded for the Lord to make her love Him more and Sister Thérèse less. But as arrests grew more frequent, her days became too busy for daydreams about Sister Thérèse. Half of the chapel had now been converted into bedspace for the children found wandering in the streets . . . children whose parents had been taken off in the night. And the library which had been the Mother Superior's office held cribs with five infants. Mothers who knew they were being taken away hid their children in closets and warned them against crying out. They often bundled up their infants and hid them in the yard, praying a more fortunate neighbor would care for them. The neighbors invariably brought them to the convent. And as the days passed, more children streamed into the convents. People who had been arrested as "political" prisoners were now arrested for being nothing other than Poles and were forced into slave labor.

As the stories of rape grew, women began to wear thick glasses to make themselves unattractive to the Russian soldiers. Some carried a handkerchief and a small penknife. If a soldier approached, they cut their finger and let the fresh blood stain the handkerchief. Then if the soldier reached for them, they'd pretend to cough into the handkerchief, show the fresh blood, and say "Tuberculosis." It was an effective ruse, and it forced many soldiers into an abrupt change of mind.

Both Sister Thérèse and Karla had acquired thick glasses brought to them by the children. They came with their pitiful possessions. A lock of the mother's hair . . . the father's glasses . . . the family Bible.

Winter came early the year of 1939. By October there was snow on the ground, and when dusk came they could hear the soldiers singing songs of their homeland. But when they were drunk, their songs were raucous and often they loitered near the convent. Many nuns grew frightened, but Sister Thérèse would constantly remind them, "They are God's children too. It is a war between countries . . . not *people*. Remember, they are in a strange land . . . away from their loved ones. Conquerors can be the loneliest of all."

A few weeks later, Karla was in the children's dormitory, hearing the children's prayers. She was about to turn out the lights when she heard the thundering noise downstairs at the front door of the convent. The children began to scream when they heard the sounds of Russian voices and heavy boots. She quickly put on her thick glasses and commanded the children to be quiet. She slipped out of the dormitory and tiptoed down the stairs. The sight in the reception room turned her rigid with terror. A surge of nausea ripped through her, and she clamped her hand over her mouth to kill the scream that started in her throat. She wanted to run, but she was paralyzed as she clung to the wall in the safe darkness. She wanted to cover her eyes but her horror held her transfixed.

The Mother Superior was naked. She had always seemed such a powerful and domineering figure as she marched into Chapel, shrouded in the thick black habit with the massive silver cross hanging down her ample front. But stripped of her habit, she had diminished into a skinny old woman, with long flat hanging breasts, blue-veined legs, a quivering object of ridicule to the drunken soldiers who laughed every time they glanced her way. She stood huddled in a corner, praying, as the Russian soldiers boisterously and methodically raped all the other nuns who were lying nude on the floor, their helpless arms and legs flapping under the weight of their merciless captors.

And then Karla saw Sister Thérèse. Blood was smeared between her thighs as one Russian got off her. Another picked her up by the neck and kissed her violently. Then his mouth began to ravage her body, beginning at the breasts as he chewed away on each of them, his dirty fingers groping between her legs. While he was enjoying himself, slobbering down her body, another soldier approached her from the back, spread her buttocks apart and rammed into her. At the same moment, the soldier in front opened his pants and also rammed into her. Karla couldn't believe it—two men tearing at her insides . . . one from the front . . . one inside her back! Mercifully, Sister Thérèse passed out.

Karla stood crouched in the darkness for half an hour. She counted ten of them who had attacked Sister Thérèse alone. Suddenly she heard footsteps behind her. It was Eva, the thirteen-year-old who helped her with the smaller children. Karla tried to motion her away, but it was too late. The child saw the nude bodies on the floor and screamed. The soldiers looked toward the dark hall. "Run, Eva," Karla commanded. "Run and get into bed." But the child stood frozen as the soldier approached.

He grabbed Karla and Eva by the arms and shoved them into the room. One soldier looked up at Karla and saw the thick glasses. He shrugged with distaste, but snatched off the white starched bib and pulled her habit apart. He looked at her flat chest, and at the glasses, and pushed her away and reached out for the screaming Eva. Karla rushed over to protect the child, but she was thrown across the room where she fell against the naked and shivering Mother Superior mumbling bits of prayers. Karla adjusted her habit, stood in front of the older nun, and clenched her teeth as the tormented Eva's screams filled the room. Sister Thérèse was still mercifully unconscious.

The bedlam began to abate after another half hour. The soldiers were satisfied. They adjusted their belts and pants and stared at the limp naked bodies on the floor like diners who have eaten their fill at a banquet but are still loath to leave food on a table. One who was obviously in command pointed at Sister Thérèse, Eva, and three other nuns and shouted a command. Blankets were thrown around them, and the soldiers threw them over their shoulders like potato sacks and carried them outside. Karla broke away from the icy grip of the Mother Superior. "Where are you taking them?"

One soldier who spoke Polish said, "To our camp. Do not worry, ugly one. We only want the beauties. We leave you and the others to stay and take care of the children."

She stood at the door helplessly as the jeeps rolled away into the cold night. As the last sounds of the raucous laughter faded away, the Mother Superior began to move like a sleepwalker. She groped around the floor for parts of her habit as other nuns picked up broken rosary beads that were strewn across the room. Prayer books that had been torn from the nuns' hands lay abandoned on the floor. Karla saw Sister Thérèse's prayer book and rosary near the spot where she had lain. She knelt down and touched the blood. She put her fingers to it and touched her lips. She pressed the prayer book to her cheek. Then she set about helping the other ravaged nuns. She ran baths for them, put ice on swollen lips, prayed with them and for them. By dawn some semblance of order was restored. Shrouded in a new habit, the Mother Superior seemed to take on at least a shadow of her old strength.

A week later the same soldiers returned. They were more raucous than before. And this time Karla did not escape. They pulled off her glasses and her clothes. She was thrown on the floor and her head struck against a chair. She prayed for unconsciousness but was jolted into awareness with the knifelike pain as her legs were forced apart and the soldier ripped into her. Rhythmically, roughly, they rode her, one after another—

five, six, seven, eight . . . her blood mixed with their orgasms . . . their wet mouths biting at her lips, her breasts.

And then she saw the heaviest man coming toward her. He looked like a giant. He fell on top of her . . . his breath was foul and he slopped some kisses on her lips . . . she prayed for death . . . then she heard the door open and more voices. Oh, God . . . more soldiers. But suddenly the man was dragged off her. There were angry voices . . . the soldiers were scrambling to their feet. And then, almost gently, an officer was helping her up. It was the same young Russian captain she had seen on the street. Blond and brown-eyed . . . and it seemed as if there was sadness in his eyes as he handed her part of her torn habit to cover herself. Then he snapped orders at the men . . . another officer herded them off. He spoke to Karla in Polish. "I am sorry for what these men have done. They will be punished. We are soldiers, not animals. I shall return tomorrow and see what reparation can be done."

When they were gone, Karla and the other sisters gradually got to their feet. They moved slowly . . . silently . . . and hopelessly. Some of the sisters went to a small chapel they had erected in one of the rooms and prayed. Karla went to her bed and lay very still. She thought about taking her life . . . but then she would spend the rest of eternity in Purgatory. She thought about Sister Thérèse. And for the first time in her fear and loneliness, she found herself thinking of her mother, and as she listened in the darkness of the night, she heard muffled sobs coming from many of the other small cubicles . . . only they were calling for Jesus . . . and suddenly she realized she had no one.

The following morning, the blond young captain arrived and apologized again and promised complete protection for the convent. His name was Gregory Sokoyen. His father was General Alexis Sokoyen . . . and he had just married a beautiful girl whose father was an important government official. He was lonesome for his young wife and took to visiting Karla several nights a week. He would sit in the reception parlor while she sewed and tell her stories of his boyhood, of the children he and his young wife hoped to have.

She listened politely. He was attractive and he was also the first young man she had ever known. He made no improper advances and always brought the nuns provisions along with candy for the children.

It was toward the end of November when Karla noticed her waist was growing thick. She had never been too regular with her periods, but suddenly she realized she was overdue. She was terrified, but she methodically went about her work. When the children went outdoors to play and she noticed some soldiers look with interest toward the ten- and eleven-year-old girls, she immediately cut off their hair and bound their chests and had them dress like boys. And every night, in the secrecy of her bedroom, she did the most strenuous ballet exercises, hoping to dislodge the baby that was forming inside. After a time she realized it was hopeless. Her waist was thick and her stomach was taut.

One morning the young captain arrived unexpectedly with some provisions. He had warm blankets and several pounds of cereal. She helped him unload them and was suddenly seized with an attack of nausea. She rushed to the sink and he held her head as she threw up. "You are sick. You must go to bed," he said.

She managed a smile as she sat down. "I am all right—it has passed."

"What causes your illness?" he asked.

"The Russian soldiers," she said tonelessly.

His eyes shot to her stomach which was hidden by the voluminous folds of her habit. "A baby?" He paused. "Do you want it?"

"Want it . . . how can I want it . . . knowing it came from one of those beasts?"

"But it is also yours. It is your body that is forming it . . . your blood . . . it might be a little girl who would look just like you."

She wrung her hands. "And then what could I do for her? How could I raise her? And besides, how do I know it would not be a boy who would look like Rudolph or Leopold or Nicholas or Igor or Sversky or—"

"You know all their names?"

"When you are lying on the floor and they are calling out to one another . . . you remember. You remember the bad breath, the hairs on their noses, the decayed teeth . . . and their names. Oh God—if there is a God—how can I rid myself of this thing growing in me?"

He colored slightly. "I know of a way that might work. I . . . I saw it happen one night last week. Some soldiers were searching some homes . . . looking for some escaped prisoners from work camps. Suddenly I heard a scream . . . I rushed upstairs . . . one of the soldiers had raped a woman—" He sighed. "You must understand, some of these men are peasants . . . they are lonely . . . they have never been away from the farm . . . they have never had much to drink . . . suddenly they have Polish vodka . . . there are pretty women. And—" He shrugged. "They rape. This man . . . he raped a girl in your condition. Only it was a baby she wanted . . . from her husband. She had pleaded with him . . . told him she was three months' pregnant . . . that she might lose it." He shuddered. "I heard her begging . . . but when I got to the room it was too late . . . and she lost the baby . . . or what was the beginning of the baby. I shot him." Then he stood up. "Think about it . . . I shall come by tonight at eleven. You can give me your decision then."

When he arrived, the convent was dark, but she was waiting at the door. She led him quietly to her small bedroom. With a sense of urgency and no shame, she took off her robe. He undressed quickly. In the dim light she saw his young body, he said, "Sister Karla, are you sure? It could be a little boy with gray eyes like yours."

"Let us get it done," she said.

He lay beside her on the bed and stroked her body. She was rigid. When his lips went to her breast she pushed him away. "Please . . . do your business and be done with it."

"No . . . first I make love to you." And against her will he gently caressed her . . . kissed her lips . . . her neck . . . her breasts . . . And soon she found herself relaxing. And when he lay on top of her and took her smoothly, rhythmically and fiercely, she suddenly felt an odd sensation. She held him close, and when the unbelievable explosion shot through her, she cried out in agonized delight because she knew she had lost the baby. When he fell off her, she jumped out of bed and hid in the corner, covering her eyes. "Don't tell me what it was . . . just clean it up and take it away before I see it," she begged.

"There is nothing . . . come look."

"No . . . because if it looks human I will feel that I have done murder."

"Come, Sister . . . obviously God intends for you to have it as there is nothing there. The baby is still inside of you."

"But I felt . . . my whole insides had turned upside down."

He smiled. "You had an orgasm, my sweet Karla."

Later, as they lay beside one another, he said, "You must think of your future now . . . you and the child."

"There must be others like me. What are they doing?"

"The mothers are sent to Russian labor camps. Doctors deliver their babies and they are sent to an orphanage. The children will be raised by the state. Siberia needs young settlers . . . eventually the orphans will be sent there when they come of age."

"And what about the children here in the convent?"

He sighed. "As long as I am here they will be safe. But any day my orders can change. And how long will our peace with Germany last? Already there are rumblings—"

"Then I must try and reach the A.K."

He put his hand over her lips. "I do not want to know anything. But I will get you some money. What you plan to do . . . I must not know."

"I must get the children out of the country first."

"Please, Karla, do not tell me."

Each day he arrived with money. She never asked where he got it, and he never asked what she did with it. If he noticed there were fewer children at the convent each time, he never mentioned it. Until one night when he arrived and she was alone. She had candles on the table and had cooked the meal herself. She had discarded the habit and was wearing a dress. He stared in disbelief as she handed him a glass of wine.

"Are you allowed not to wear the habit?" he asked.

"I am not a nun," she said. "Sit down, Gregory. There are so many things I want to tell you."

Throughout dinner, she told him the events that had led to her coming to the convent. It seemed such a short uneventful life in the telling . . . so little had actually happened to her . . . and now, she sat alone in the convent with the handsome young Russian soldier and there was a baby growing inside.

"What about the baby?" he asked.

"The A.K. will take care of it. I will manage to get to Sweden, I hope . . . have it there . . . and put it with a family."

"And then?" he asked.

"And then, I will get to London. Sister Thérèse had an uncle there. Uncle Otto. I have his address."

"And the baby?"

She shrugged. "It will be placed with a family. Somehow I shall send money back to support the child."

"But why go to all that trouble for a bastard you don't want? If you have it here, it can always be placed in an orphanage."

Karla's eyes flashed. "Because it will still be half mine. And it is such a cruel world. I must give it some kind of a chance. But I would never want the child to know that I was its mother. I would just send money for its support."

"Then eventually you will send for the child?"

She shook her head. "I am going to be a ballerina. It is hard work. I will give the child money . . . not love. In that way he cannot ever miss what he has never had." She touched her stomach wistfully. "It is not good to grow up knowing someone does not want you. It is better to think the parents are dead."

He held her close that night. And she looked at him intently, as if trying to imprint his image on her mind.

"I shall never forget you, Karla," he said as they made love.

She clung to him, because although she knew she could never really love a man, she was grateful for all he had done . . . and his body felt so young and strong.

Karla closed her eyes as the plane began its descent to Heathrow Airport in London. She had sent Jeremy a cable. But would he be there? He was getting so old. Each time she saw him, he seemed to have shrunk a little more. What would she ever do when the day came that Jeremy would not be there?

The plane landed. . . . There were photographers on the airfield. Karla covered her face and followed the waiting airline official who led her to the limousine. Jeremy Haskins was waiting inside the car. She sat beside him and squeezed his hand. "It was nice of you to come and meet me."

The old man managed a smile. "I'll be eighty next month, Karla. As long as there's a breath inside of me, I shall consider it an honor to meet any plane, boat, or train that you choose to take."

She sat back in the car and closed her eyes. "We've traveled a long road together, Jeremy."

He nodded. "The moment I met you, I felt that we would. . . ."

They had met in a bomb shelter. She had been terrified. She had just arrived that day, and was met by a smiling Uncle Otto who welcomed her to his home. She had a nice room. Tante Bosha was warm and jolly and for the entire morning they had sat and talked about Poland, about the hazards of her escape. She tried not to dwell on it, even though they were anxious for details. She omitted the gory parts—the rape, the Russian soldiers, her own pregnancy. She just spoke glowingly of the A.K. Uncle Otto had heard nothing from Sister Thérèse or her family, and without actually saying it, Karla insinuated that Sister Thérèse and the other nuns, along with the orphans, were safe.

At dusk she had gone for a walk. Uncle Otto had warned her not to go far. At any time the air raids might begin. London was in the midst of Germany's blitz, and the British people were growing accustomed to spending many a night in an air raid shelter. The Nazis had given up daylight raids the past October when the RAF in an enormous counterattack took too big a toll on their Luftwaffe invaders. But they still continued their night attacks on London, which spread panic and destruction but had little military value.

She had walked about ten blocks when she heard the first siren. She stood rooted to the spot as people came pouring from their homes heading for the nearest Underground. She started back toward the house but stopped when she realized she'd never make it in time, and that Uncle Otto and Tante Bosha were probably in a shelter themselves. So she turned and followed the stream of people. She found a spot and sat with her hands over her ears as she heard the sounds of destruction overhead.

"Child, you act as if this is your first air raid."

She looked up at the smiling man. She found herself smiling back. "It is in a way."

"Where are you from?"

"Wilno . . . Poland. Is my English that bad?"

"Dreadful. But then, I don't even speak a word of Polish so you're way ahead of me. What's your name? I'm Jeremy Haskins."

He forced her to talk as the bombs fell and she told him about Uncle Otto and Tante Bosha . . . and how she intended to try out for the Sadlers Wells Ballet. Of course that would not be for some time . . . it was so long since she had practiced . . . she would have to get a job in a factory or something first . . . and work out each day to get into shape.

"I can't really see you in the darkness," he said. "Are you beautiful?"

"I am a fine dancer," she said.

When the All Clear sounded they came outside. He walked her home and told her about himself. He was a publicist for J. Arthur Rank films. His wife was an invalid and his daughter had been killed in a bombing raid. They reached the block Uncle Otto's house was on and for a moment she thought they had come to the wrong place. A street that had held a row of houses an hour ago was now just a smoldering ruin. Fire trucks were still hosing down some charcoaled skeletons of buildings. There were moans of people who were being taken to ambulances . . . cries of young babies . . . and the muted sobs of the women as they plowed among the ruins of their homes, searching for things dear to them.

Suddenly she saw Uncle Otto, holding Tante Bosha's hand. She dashed after them. Tears were streaming down his face. "Our money . . . so much of it . . . we had in there. All burned . . . gone. Bosha's pearls . . . everything is gone." He looked at Jeremy in a daze. "Such beautiful things we had from the old country . . . things I was hoping to sell to give my relatives in Poland a chance when all this is over. Tapestry . . . fine laces . . . paintings . . . all gone. A Goya . . . gone! No money can replace that." He looked toward the sky. "Why? This is no military target . . . this is plain vandalism . . . destruction without reason." Suddenly he seemed to remember Karla. "Your clothes . . . they are all gone. I will get some money from the bank tomorrow . . . tonight we are to stay with a neighbor in the next block . . . they have no extra room for you, but perhaps if I ask around someone will put you up."

"She can come stay with us . . . in our daughter's room," Jeremy Haskins said quickly.

Uncle Otto frowned. He looked at Jeremy Haskins as if suddenly seeing him for the first time. Then he stared toward the charred ruins of his house, and heaved a lumbering sigh, a sigh that signified he felt too old, too tired, and too despondent to take on the added responsibility of the morals of a strange Polish girl. He nodded with a vague relief, and Karla found herself meekly following Jeremy Haskins to the Underground. They got into a crowded train and rode in silence. After a time she felt he was staring at her. Her face flushed and she looked down at her plain hands.

He reached over and patted them. "They could do with a little manicuring. But you know, you are really quite beautiful."

She kept staring at her hands. This nice man who had comforted her during the air raid, who had convinced Uncle Otto he was sincere—who was he really, and where were they going? There probably never had been a daughter who died . . . or a sick wife. He was probably taking her off to some dreadful little room and . . . she stared down at her mud-spattered shoes. Did it really matter? Where did she have to go? And after the Russians . . . what could this poor little Englishman do? Force her to spread her legs . . . what did it matter?

Suddenly he spoke. "Look, my girl, there's a part in a film that a friend of mine is producing. It's not a large part, but it would put you over. It's a Nazi spy, and I was just thinking—your accent would be perfect. Can you act at all?"

"I don't know . . . my English is bad."

"Of course. But it will be perfect for the role. Tomorrow we shall have you meet him. And look, old girl—it may not be Sadlers Wells, but it's certainly better than the factory."

He had a nice little house and she met the invalid wife, a lovely tissue-paper-looking lady named Helen, who looked at her husband as he made the tea, her eyes filled with gratitude and death. She was delighted that Karla had come to stay. Her pride was mingled with sadness as she offered her their daughter's room. Karla had never had such a nice room, and as she fell asleep, she felt safe . . . and knew that once again she had found someone who would think for her.

She had gotten the part . . . and suddenly the acceleration of the pace of her life was like a movie running in double time. Makeup tests, costume fittings, nights of working on her heavy accent . . . and the final discussion . . . the argument over her name. She insisted on being called Karla . . . just one name. Karla. Arnold Malcolm, the producer, finally agreed. He also sensed the stubborn Polish girl had something that would register on the screen. And as Arnold Malcolm predicted, it happened. The newspapers all singled out the new foreign discovery. She caused a small sensation when the picture came out, and the only thing that made her sad was Helen's death, which occurred a week before the picture was finished. Once again Karla realized the danger of growing attached to someone. She had cared about the delicate woman who bore her suffering so silently, who had helped her with her English, and encouraged her each day. They buried her silently and without tears. And that same day she took the Underground back to work at the studio. Karla sat stoically, and when she got off she said, "I hate movie making. I hate the English language which I will never be able to learn. I hate the waiting, the lights—but most of all, I hate this train."

And Jeremy had managed a tight smile and said, "One day you will understand English with ease and you shall ride in a limousine."

Jeremy had sold the house and taken a flat for himself and Karla in Kensington. He gave up his job with J. Arthur Rank and became her manager. The newspapers all hinted that he was her lover, but actually they had only gone to bed once. She had done it out of gratitude and he had realized it. "I was silly to hope . . . I am too old for you." He sighed.

"No," she said, looking at him directly. "It is not your fault. You see, I am a lesbian."

Her tone was so matter-of-fact that he found himself accepting it as just another fragment of information about her life. And then, as they lay in the darkness, holding hands like two good friends, she told him everything about herself. About the men who had raped her . . . about Gregory . . . about the baby, who was living with a Swedish couple. She sent money to them every month now. And when he asked why the baby was never to know she was its mother, she had answered, "What you never have, you cannot lose. It was still such a little baby when I left—it didn't know me, I didn't know it. Neither of us will feel pain or disappointment in one another this way. Why should my child wonder which bastard was the father—or feel neglected because I am not there?"

When he tried to probe her about Gregory—or force her to admit she really cared for him—she shrugged. "Perhaps I did. I will never know. I was so filled with hate for what the Russians had done to Sister Thérèse, to the others . . . I never let myself feel." And then she went on to tell of a short but tender love affair she had had with a woman resistance worker in the A.K. A woman who had been beautiful, considerate and kind, who had helped her with her escape, helped her get the baby to Sweden. No, it was the tenderness of a woman that she loved. She could never really love a man.

So they became good friends. Together they worked on her English, on the parts she played. In her fourth picture she received star billing. Each day she'd sit with Jeremy in the darkened studio and stare at the daily rushes on the screen. She couldn't believe that she was that exciting woman on the screen.

It was Jeremy who decided against interviews. "We shall not allow any. Your English is not good enough, you might not understand some of their questions, you would be misquoted, and–"

"And I am stupid and dull."

"No, that isn't true. You are still very young. On the screen you come across worldly . . . as a woman of mystery. But to know you . . . is to know a child."

"No, Jeremy. I am stupid. I know it. You do not have to pretend. I hear other actresses talking. They speak of Shakespeare . . . they can quote him. They talk about books written by Maugham, Colette, even American writers like Hemingway. Some of them ask me about Polish writers. I know none of them . . . but *they* do. They speak of art . . . I know nothing."

"You may lack education," he said. "But you are not stupid. To realize there are things you don't know only proves you are most intelligent. If you like, I can help you learn about these things."

"Will they help me make more money?"

"No . . . but they–"

"Forget it," she said.

Karla was terrified about going to California, but Jeremy had signed the contract with Century. And then, on the day she was supposed to leave for Hollywood, the Swedish couple had cabled that they didn't want to take care of the child any longer. Jeremy sent her to California alone, in spite of her protests, while he remained and arranged to have the child brought to London. He hated to trust her away from him for the six weeks it took to get things settled with the child and bring it to London. When he got to California, he found his premonitions had not been groundless. She was living in a huge partially furnished mansion the studio had found for her and was enmeshed in an ecstatic love affair with Heidi Lanz.

"Karla, you cannot afford this kind of gossip. It could ruin you. Heidi is a big star with a husband and three children. The public would never believe it of her."

"Tell me about my child."

"Everything is fine. I have found a perfectly marvelous couple–John and Mary. They think the child is a distant relative of mine and your interest is due to our relationship. The child is a little slow—the doctors say it has something to do with not getting enough oxygen at birth—but I think it was the Swedish couple. They scarcely ever spoke. John and Mary are marvelous. Everything will be fine. Naturally they think we are lovers."

"Wait until you meet Heidi . . ."

"Karla, you must be more discreet."

"I will be a star after this picture in America. An international star. Already they compare me with Garbo and Dietrich . . . they say I am bringing back the lost glamor. Here, look at my pictures—on *Photoplay, Modern Screen, Movie Mirror* . . . all of them. Wonderful stories about the great Karla. So do not worry—my publicity has been excellent. I have obeyed you to the letter. No interviews, closed set, lunch alone in my dressing room. No one can see me except Heidi."

He sighed. "Karla, already in London there have been pictures of the two of you in pants, ducking cameramen."

Karla shrugged. "Out here everyone wears pants . . . and many people duck cameramen."

"Are you saving money—remember—for your child? You want the best schools . . . everything you missed—"

"Am I saving?" She threw her back her head and the throaty laugh filled the room. "I have been here almost seven weeks and have only cashed one paycheck. Heidi pays for everything!"

The romance between Karla and the German star didn't last long. But Jeremy was amazed at how the top lesbians of the film colony came after her. He wondered if there was some sort of radar that passed among them—like a neon sign lighting on their forehead that only they could see. But Karla refused to mingle with them.

Byron Masters was cast opposite her in her third picture. He was dashing, handsome, did his own stunts, had been married three times, and was bisexual. And to Karla his resemblance to Gregory was startling. She suddenly grew coy. And when she learned he was currently living with another male star, the challenge appealed to her. Suddenly she wanted a young man's strong body in her arms.

They began filming, and after the first week, Byron moved out on his roommate . . . fell insanely in love with her . . . to the extent that he allowed her to dominate the entire picture. She emerged a full-fledged star, and stories of their romance flooded every movie magazine.

For a few months she reveled in her love affair with Byron. She had him come to dinner at her sparsely furnished home. They cooked steaks and ate in the kitchen. Jeremy had discreetly moved to a furnished apartment and grown interested in a divorced real estate lady.

But Byron loved the excitement of Hollywood—the large parties, the klieg-light openings. Karla refused to attend them. In her own home when she picked up the steak with her fingers, he laughed—they were two kids on a picnic. But she knew her table manners were bad (Jeremy had given up on pleading with her about the slurping noises she made with soup or tea), and she was terrified of crowds, and of the brittle small talk that went with big parties. She was afraid they would laugh at her accent. So gradually her affair with Byron ended, and he fell in love with his new leading lady.

Karla took it very philosophically. There was always an ingenue who went into raptures at the idea of coming to the great Karla's home. On the set Karla never even acknowledged the girl . . . so if the girl did talk about her "romance" with the great Karla, there would be no credence to her stories. And every so often there was a young man who reminded her of Gregory, and she allowed him to come and make love to her and eat steak in the kitchen. The press always lunged at these romances and blew them up. Fan magazines were screaming for stories on Karla . . . but the romances were usually over before the story got into print.

And then in 1952, Karla co-starred with Christopher Kelly. He was of Dutch and French extraction and had the combination of blond hair and brown eyes that always attracted her. Christopher's popularity was also at its crest. He ate steak in her kitchen the first week they worked together. And throughout the three months it took to film the picture, the romance grew in intensity.

She learned she was pregnant the last week of shooting. She

thought about it coldly and unemotionally. Theoretically, the practical thing would be to rid herself of it *and* Christopher. But for the first time she found she couldn't just walk away. It caught her by surprise. She had never become involved with a man to the extent that she didn't want him to leave her. Oddly enough she found it easier to handle her romances with women. She could make all the rules. She felt no fear of being hurt with women. They loved her. With women her problem was to ease them out of her life and cause as little pain as possible to the girl she was rejecting. And most men had also fallen into line, becoming almost effeminate in their desire to please . . . to acquiesce . . . to hold her.

But Christopher was different. He had actually dragged her to his palatial house with all the servants and taught her to swim. He tried to teach her tennis but she never got further than volleying the ball across the net.

And now the picture was almost over. In six weeks she was to start another. She could have him as her leading man if she wished. Century had already signed someone else—a newcomer. They didn't feel the need of paying out two star salaries. Karla could carry a picture alone. But if she demanded Christopher, they would get him.

Christopher didn't care one way or another. He was one of the new breed of stars who worked without a studio contract. His fee was two hundred thousand a picture, and he'd work for Twentieth, Metro, Century—any studio that gave him his fee, and offered a starring role and co-star billing.

She waited until the picture was finished. Then one night as they were taking a drive she told him about her pregnancy. "I am seven weeks late," she said. He almost veered off the road. "Karla . . . it's fabulous! We'll head right now for Tia Juana . . . we'll get married . . . keep it secret . . . then in about a week we'll tell everyone we got married before the picture. Your little man Jeremy can fix everything."

She agreed and watched him turn the car around and whip down from the mountains. "It will be great. We'll give up both our homes . . . get a huge showcase . . . maybe have it built. There's a great piece of property up on Crescent. I've got two alimonies to pay. But what the hell . . . I make two hundred thousand a picture, and with what you make we can live like royalty. We'll call our home Karl-Kel . . . we'll be the new royalty . . . we'll entertain. Karl-Kel will be like Pickfair was in the old days, and we'll be the new royal couple. We'll live to the hilt!"

Live to the hilt!

"Turn back," she said harshly.

"What's the matter?"

"Turn back. I am not going to Mexico. If you dare to take me there I'll accuse you of kidnapping me."

They drove back to her house in silence. Live to the hilt! Have another baby! How had she allowed herself to think that way? She already had one child to support . . . one huge obligation. She could never live his way—sit back and watch people coming in and drinking *her* liquor . . eating *her* food. It would be like seeing them take *her* money . . . when she had worked so hard to earn it.

The next day Jeremy arranged for an abortion, and she changed her phone number. A week later Christopher Kelly attempted suicide. He recovered . . . but even this dramatic act could not get Karla to answer his telegrams.

She spent a great deal of money trying to trace Sister Thérèse. But there was no sign of her . . . or of her family. Finally she gave up and concentrated only on her work.

In the middle fifties, Karla was now firmly entrenched as "Karla, the living legend!" But her salary in no way matched her fame. Her contract with Century had originally started at five hundred a week. With raises and "holdouts" she had worked up to three thousand during the last two years. She knew she was underpaid, but in 1960 the contract would expire, and Jeremy said then they would make their real money.

Jeremy was rich. He had invested in the market and had tripled his money several times over. He had begged and pleaded with Karla to be allowed to invest her money or put her with an investment counselor. But she clung to it and deposited it in savings accounts, never allowing one to exceed ten thousand in any given bank.

She ran into a bad cycle of pictures in 1957 and 1958. But her personal publicity carried her through. The legend grew, and her isolation from the studio heads kept her totally unaware of the box-office receipts. Jeremy saw to it that the public was also unaware of any slip in Karla's popularity. The announcement of her retirement in 1960 caused headlines and shock waves throughout the motion picture industry—throughout the world. Neither Karla nor Jeremy had intended the retirement to become permanent. It began when Jeremy went to renegotiate her contract with the head of Century.

"I hear Elizabeth Taylor is getting a million dollars for *Cleopatra,*" Karla said. "I want a million one hundred thousand. Tell the Head I will give him a three-picture deal at three million, three hundred thousand."

While Jeremy was negotiating with the studio, a negotiation that took several weeks, she busied herself building a ballet bar in one of the empty rooms of her house, doing four hours a day of bar exercises, and taking long walks.

Then one night Jeremy came to her house for dinner. He told her he had a deal, but that they would discuss it after dinner. She nodded with her usual detachment. They sat in the kitchen, and he watched her plough into the steak, the gravy running down the chin of the magnificent face so many people worshipped. "Karla, you know the book *The Emperor*?" He sighed as he said it. How could she know it? He knew and she knew that she never read books. "It's number one on all the lists," he went on. "And the Head is trying to get Marlon Brando or Tony Quinn to play the Emperor."

"So . . . ?" She gnawed at the bone of the steak.

"They want you for the Empress."

"So? Is it a right kind of part for Karla?"

"Marvelous."

"And the money?"

"Very little."

She stopped eating. "I thought we were getting a million."

And then in the brightly lit kitchen he explained the facts—how her last few pictures had died at the box office. But her legend was so strong that no one except the top people in the industry realized it. She was to get a hundred thousand for the picture, and, after the break-even point, 2½ percent of the profits . . . which could only mean something after the picture grossed ten million dollars.

She was silent. Then he said, "We have no alternative."

She pushed away her plate. "If I take so little money, then *everyone* will know I have fallen. But if I retire, no one will know."

Jeremy stared. "You're forty-two years old . . . at your peak."

"Oh, I retire . . . but only for a year. Then they come after me. You'll see. And each offer will get bigger."

He stared at her. It was a brilliant move . . . but could she hold out financially? "You only have two hundred and fifty thousand dollars," he said.

"Invest it in bonds at six percent. I will not touch it."

"But what will you live on?"

Karla crossed the room and stared out at the stone fence she had erected around the house. "It's damp out tonight. But I think I will take a walk." She threw on a coat and left.

Jeremy was in the living room watching the news on television when she came in.

He clicked off the set. "Have you made your decision?"

She nodded. "Have you ever heard of a woman named Blinky Giles?"

"Yes . . . she's a millionaire from Texas or somewhere."

"She is also a big bull dyke. For a year now she has let it be known among the girls that she'd drop a hundred thousand dollars at my feet if I would let her be my lover for one night. I will tell Sonya Kinella . . . she has those Sunday brunches that all the gay set attend. I shall tell her to allow Blinky to visit me this weekend."

Blinky Giles . . . the fat heavy-breathing bull dyke. But she had entered the house and tossed the money at her feet. One hundred thousand tax-free dollars. It had been unbelievable. She thought of it now as Jeremy sat at her side. And after Blinky there had been the Countess. . . .

And as her retirement continued, the legend grew. And the offers also grew until one day, three years after her retirement, Jeremy came to her with a contract . . . one million dollars against 10 percent of the gross.

To his amazement, she refused. She openly admitted she was

frightened about coming back. She had just met Dee Milford Granger, the "sixth richest woman in the world." Dee was in love with Karla, the legend. What would happen if the picture failed? The legend would be smashed! Why chance it by making a comeback? By remaining a lègend, there would always be women like Dee who would offer anything just to be with her. In the last three years she had managed to save almost half a million dollars *without* working. Dee had her own plane, a yacht, and a fag husband who didn't care what she did. Dee wasn't as generous as the others. She had that "prove-you-really-love-me-for-myself" attitude that some rich people get. But at least Dee was beautiful and Dee was security. So she refused the million-dollar offer. And all the ensuing offers. Because she felt secure in the knowledge that she controlled Dee . . . and could have her as long as she wished, on any terms that she wished. And everything had gone just as she had planned . . . until Dee's fag husband got killed in an automobile race, which forced Dee to drag out David as their escort.

David . . . she had thought she was too old for all that. David with the blond hair and brown eyes. David, as young as Gregory . . . and she was so old. But a women never gets old. It's only the years that mount up. Inside she is still eternally eighteen . . . and she felt young and foolish and wonderful when she was with David.

The car was approaching Park Lane. Jeremy was talking about her latest offer. (They still filtered in, no longer for a million dollars, but big money for a cameo "starring" role.) The latest was for half a million, two weeks' work, and a thousand dollars a day expenses. She smiled as she shook her head. Why bother? What was she trying to prove? She had never really believed in herself as an actress . . . She had never even really believed in herself as a dancer. She had done that just to incur Sister Thérèse's favor. Perhaps that was why she kept up with the ballet exercises—somehow she felt as if she was paying off a debt when she did them. She was not a religious person—she never went to Mass—yet each night she got on her knees and said a prayer in Polish that she had said since she had learned to talk. And often in the darkness, she felt God about her . . . and she hid her head under the pillow and silently told Him she was doing her best.

She entered the Dorchester Hotel and huddled her face in the sable coat that Dee had given her. She knew her future was with Dee . . . and that the affair with David had grown too important. It was time to leave, time to settle some business . . . And thank God for Jeremy.

But that night, long after Jeremy had left, she sat staring out at Hyde Park. She knew that Jeremy had noticed her unlined face. When she had left David to have her face done, she had prayed David would be waiting. Because for the first time, she had known that she wasn't really a lesbian. In his arms she felt safe and happy. Each time they were together, it made it more difficult to be with Dee. A woman's soft body after David's strong lean one suddenly was beginning to repel her. And when she got on her knees to say her prayers, she found herself also praying that David would be waiting again. . . .

Fourteen

JANUARY SAT in Linda's office drinking lukewarm coffee from a plastic container. Linda was in one of her down moods. Linda was always morose on Mondays. But a rainy Monday in February was, as she put it, the "mother of them all." January was cheerful in spite of the weather. After all, February only had twenty-eight days. And the twenty-first of March was officially spring. So once you cracked February, winter was practically over.

She had always hated winter. Winter had meant school. Summer and holidays had meant Mike. But now holidays meant Palm Beach. She had gone there Christmas Eve and stayed through New Year's. But before Palm Beach there had been . . .

THAT WEEK BEFORE CHRISTMAS IN NEW YORK!

Holly and fake Christmas trees at the office even though everyone is working on the layout for the April issue.

The sudden change of attitude of all the employees at the apartment building. The doorman springing to open the door. The elevator man's newly acquired talent of leveling the car with the floor. The fifteen names of hitherto invisible employees that suddenly crop up on the "Christmas list" the super slides under the door.

Sloshing through the rain. People on every corner weighted with shopping bags, futilely signaling at the empty taxis that flashed by flaunting their OFF DUTY signs. Dismal men in Santa outfits, their arms jerking with a spastic reflex as they rang their tinny bells. "Merry Christmas. Help the needy."

Fighting through Saks—a madhouse encased with silver decorations. A cashmere scarf for David; squashing into the elevator to the third floor to get a Pucci bag for Linda, which Linda promptly returned. ("January, I've told you a million times . . . it's *Gucci* that's *in* . . . *Pucci* is *out*!")

At least Mike had been easy. Two dozen golf balls with his name engraved on them. But Dee! What can you buy for a Dee? (And this was before she learned that the crystal icicles on Dee's Christmas tree were from Steuben.) You couldn't get Dee perfume. She had a closet full. At Palm Beach *and* the Pierre. Probably in Marbella, too. The salesgirl at Bonwit's recommended a "Fun" present, like red flannel booties. She finally wound up buying some imported linen handkerchiefs at a shop on Madison Avenue. Dee could always give them to someone else as a gift.

CHRISTMAS IN PALM BEACH!

The twelve-foot Christmas tree! Massive and shimmering with its silver balls and crystal icicles. A displaced giant in a glass-encased room overlooking the swimming pool. It stood like an angry sentry. Uprooted, disoriented, its cold silver silence protesting the tropical atmosphere.

And there was Mike, tan and beautiful. Dee, white and beautiful. Parties . . . backgammon . . . gossip. A ten-day extension of the Thanksgiving holiday. Going to the track with Mike and wanting to sob at his indifference as he walked to the ten-dollar window to place a bet. Because she could remember the old days when he'd pick up a phone and bet five thousand on one race. Yes, she could remember. And so could he. After the first party, every other party seemed like an instant replay. And then there was the surprise party Dee threw for her twenty-first birthday. Five thousand dollars in floral arrangements, a dance floor covering the Olympic-sized swimming pool. Two orchestras—one indoors, one outdoors. David arriving to celebrate. Both of them dancing together, playing the "Hello, Young Lovers" bit for Dee. The guests were all the same people she had seen throughout the week. There were just more of them. They all brought "just a teensy remembrance" from their own Christmas surplus. (She was now set for life with silk scarves.) Some came towing lantern-jawed daughters or an uncommunicative son. And always the omnipresent photographers, shooting the same people they had shot at the last party . . . and the same people they'd shoot in the parties to come.

AFTER CHRISTMAS IN NEW YORK!

Finding the first cockroach in the sink. Sure it's dead, but what about its brothers and sisters? It couldn't be a lone spinster roach.

A frantic call to Linda. "Relax, January. They're everywhere in New York. Call the super. You gave him a generous Christmas present. He'll get the exterminator."

The super thanked her for the twenty dollars but explained that the exterminator had gone to Puerto Rico for the holidays and couldn't be reached for another ten days.

David took her out several times. Each time they joined another couple or a group at Raffles or Le Club where the music was too loud for any real conversation, so everyone danced, smiled, and waved at people across the room. And then one evening he took her home and dismissed the cab. For a moment they both stood in front of her apartment building. After an uneasy silence, he said, "Aren't you going to at least ask me up to look at the plant I gave you?"

"Oh, it's doing fine. They say I should prune it in the spring."

Her breath smoked the cold air. There was another awkward silence. Then she said, "Look, David, I like you. I really do. But what happened between us that one night was a mistake. So as they say in the movies—'Let's be friends.'"

He smiled. "I'm not going to rape you. I like you too. I more than like you. I . . . I . . . well at the moment, I happen to be freezing . . . and we haven't had a chance to talk all evening."

January wondered why this evening should be different from all the other evenings. "Okay, but it's really just one large room." Once again there was an uncomfortable silence as they went up in the elevator. She suddenly realized they had nothing to say to one another. Absolutely nothing. And for some insane reason she felt off balance. She found herself chattering nervously as she opened the door. "It's not too neat. Linda and I share a maid who has a violent love life. Half the time she comes in sniveling with a black eye. But that's when things are good. When things are bad, she just doesn't show. Linda says that means he is gone and she is sitting home drinking and waiting for him." She knew he didn't give a damn about her maid. "Well . . . this is it. And look at your tree. It's grown two inches and has three new branches."

"Why don't you get rid of her?" he said as he stood standing stiffly in the center of the room.

"Get rid of what?"

"The maid." He unbuttoned his coat and took off the scarf she had given him.

"Oh, well, Linda has empathy for anyone who is a loser in love. And I have empathy for anyone who survives all those black eyes." She sat on the couch. He sat on the club chair near her, and stared at the floor, his hands folded between his knees.

"January . . . I want to talk to you about—" He looked up. "Do we have to have that thing on?"

"You mean you don't like Mr. Edgar Bailey's Tiffany-type lamp?"

"I feel as if I'm in a bowling alley with all these lights."

She jumped up and put off the overhead light. "Can I get you some wine . . . or a Coke? That's all I have."

"January . . . sit down. I don't want anything. I want to talk about us."

"Okay, David." She sat quietly and waited.

"I guess you've been wondering about me . . . about us," he began. "Well, I've had some personal problems and . . ."

She smiled. "David, I told you before—we're friends. You don't owe me any explanations."

He stood up and fished for a cigarette in his pocket. Suddenly he spun around and faced her. "We're not friends. I . . . I love you. I meant everything I said that night. We *are* going to get married. But not . . . not for a while. I've got something I have to work out . . . business-wise. I'd appreciate it if you didn't mention it to Dee. She gets worried if she thinks I have any problems with my work." He attempted to smile and shrug it off. "She actually tries to mother me. I love her for it, but I want her to enjoy herself with your father. He's really a great guy, and I can work out my own problems. So just trust in me, January . . . trust in me and be patient. We're going to get married . . . eventually. Will you remember that . . . even if there are times I don't call?"

She looked at him and shook her head slowly. "Wow! You blow my mind. You really do! I mean, how many ways do I have to put it to you that *I* have no intention of marrying *you*? But if it will make you feel any better, I'll let Dee and my father assume that we're seeing a great deal of one another."

He turned on her angrily. "What makes you think I care about their opinion?"

"Because you do. And, look, it will be easier for me too. As long as we do see one another occasionally, and they think it's . . . well, like steady . . . why not?"

He dropped into the club chair and stared into space. He looked like a giant rubber toy that had suddenly sprung a leak. She could almost see his body deflating. "It's such rotten timing," he sighed. "I mean, ordinarily we'd have been so great together." He stared at the floor for a moment, then looked up and managed a smile. "Know something? You're a good kid, January. Okay. We'll let them think we're dating a lot, if it will help you. And when you grow up a little, I think we'll be just fine together. Just fine."

He called her at the end of the week to announce that he was going to California to attend the Securities Analysts meeting he had been telling her about. She wasn't quite sure there really was such a thing as a Securities Analysts meeting in California . . . but she did know that Karla had arrived in Los Angeles from Europe via the Polar route. The newspapers had carried the usual pictures of her, holding a magazine in front of her face as she tried to avoid the photographers. One of the columnists reported she had come to visit Sonya Kinella, the wealthy Italian socialite and dilettante poet. They were old friends from Karla's early picture days.

But January had no time to wonder about David or Karla. Thomas Colt was due in town February 5 to attend a big publication day party his publishers were given him. That was less than a week away, and as January sat drinking the lukewarm coffee on the bleak Monday in February, Linda was fuming at the impertinence of a Ms. Rita Lewis who had not answered any of her calls.

"I've put in five in the last three days," she said as she slammed down the phone. "I even talked to Mr. Lawrence's secretary."

"Who's he?"

"The publisher himself. I said that *Gloss* had not received its invitation to the party at the St. Regis and was it an oversight? She gave me the real private 'secretary to the President voice' and said, 'Well, really, Miss Riggs, it's not actually a press party. Oh, no doubt some of the press will be there, but actually it's more of a welcome to New York party for Mr. Colt. The Mayor will be there . . . all of the top celebrities.' I got the distinct impression that *Gloss* just isn't chic enough to rate. It wound up with her promising to give Rita my message."

"Well, we still have four more days," January said optimistically. "Maybe she'll call."

Four days passed and there was still no word. January sat in Linda's office trying to cheer her. "Come on, Linda. He's going to be in New York for quite a time. There must be another way to get to him."

Linda sighed. She glanced at the gray window. "Is it still raining?"

"No, it's snowing." January said.

"Good!" Linda said cheerfully. "I hope it turns into a blizzard. Then maybe half the people won't show . . . and the other half will be all wet and in a lousy mood. Honestly, January, everyone I know who has ever met your father says he was divine to work with . . . how colorful he was . . . everyone adored him—except Tom Colt!"

"Maybe they were both too strong for each other. Or maybe it was just Tom Colt being Tom Colt. Look, I sent in my first team. I wrote him a letter in November. I didn't say I was related to Mike, because I knew that would kill any chance we had. So I just signed it J. Wayne. Then I followed it up with another letter two weeks later. When I didn't hear, I called

Jay Allen, his press agent in Los Angeles. Jay had done some work for my father, so he was real nice and gave me Tom Colt's beach house address. I wrote a letter there. Nothing! Then I followed it up with a Christmas card, with a 'Hope to see you when you get to New York' little note on it. Then three weeks later I wrote another glowing letter telling him I had read the galleys and knew he had a big hit." January leaned forward. "Linda . . . be realistic. Tom Colt wouldn't attend the Oscar ceremonies of the picture my father made of his book. It won in five categories. Of course he didn't write the screenplay . . . he felt that was beneath him. So you start out knowing what kind of a snob he is. Mike told me how everyone had pleaded with him to attend. But he refused. Know why? Because he said he was a serious writer, not part of a circus. He also said he had nothing to do with the crummy commercial picture Hollywood made of his book. So why on earth should we even think he'd do a story for us?"

Linda nodded slowly. "Everything you say is right. But then, who would have believed he'd consent to do a publicity tour? That's a real circus. He probably doesn't know what he's getting into. And as for magazine publicity, he probably never heard of it in connection with a serious novel. Oh, I'm sure he expects *Life* to do a a story on him. And *Time*. And *Newsweek*. But *Gloss*? He probably never heard of it. Or thinks it's some new kind of toothpaste. But I won't give up. If I have to be a panzer division. I did that with Dr. Blowacek from Yugoslavia. I hounded him and actually got him before anyone else. That was the story that helped get me promoted to editor-in-chief. January—*Gloss* is my life! As it grows, so do I! And I've got to get Tom Colt for *Gloss*! I've got to!" Her expression was grim. The blood actually seemed to drain from her face. Then she sighed. "The Dr. Blowacek story elevated me in the eyes of my publisher. And since then I've been running stories geared for circulation and advertising. Now it's time for me to go after stories to elevate *Gloss* in the eyes of the trade. If I get an interview or story on Tom Colt, that would help turn *Gloss* into something pretty heavy. That's why I can't take no for an answer. Sure he'll be in New York for some time, but *Gloss* has to get him first. And getting to this cocktail party would have been a big help. He digs beautiful girls. That's why Rita Lewis hasn't invited me. She doesn't want him to do a story for *Gloss*. She's very into the literary thing . . . like she'd rather get him a paragraph in *The New York Review of Books* than a cover story with us. That's why I wanted to go to the party. I figured if we could just see him . . . we could convince him."

"Then let's go," January said.

"You mean crash?"

"Why not?"

Linda shook her head. "Too important a party. With this kind of an 'A' list, they'll have people at the door, checking off every name."

"Let's try it anyway," January insisted. "We'll dress our best, hire a limo, and go—"

"Hire a limo? January, what a smashing idea!"

"It's the only way. With this weather there won't be a cab in sight. Everyone will arrive as you predicted . . . wet and looking slightly beat. If we're going to crash, we're going to crash with style."

Linda laughed nervously. "Do you really think a limo will give us enough style to bring it off?"

"Well, Ernest Hemingway once defined style as grace under pressure. And arriving in a limousine is certainly a step in the right direction."

The party was held in a small ballroom. Judging from the noise of the crowd, the weather had been no deterrent. People spilled out into the hallway, forming their own small noisy cliques. A long sheet of paper with guests listed in alphabetical order lay deserted on a table outside the door. Linda's theory about arriving late had been right. Once the V.I.P.'s were checked in, the people at the door would duck inside to mingle with the celebrities and grab free drinks.

They pushed their way into the main room. January recognized several authors, some press, several Broadway stars, a few Hollywood personalities, and the usual inveterate partygoers.

There was a bar at the end of the room. They spotted Tom Colt immediately. He was much better looking than the picture on his jacket cover. He had a strong face, dark hair, pugilistic features. A man who looked as if he had lived through much of the violence and action he wrote about.

"He scares me," January whispered. "You go up to him if you like. . . . I'll just stand back here and watch."

"He's gorgeous," Linda whispered.

"Sure he is. But so is a rattlesnake if it's in a glass cage. I mean . . . Linda, you can't mention *Gloss* magazine to a man like that."

"Well, I'm going to . . . and you're going with me. Come on." She grabbed January's arm and pulled her through the crowd toward the bar.

Tom Colt was encircled by an admiring group that seemed to be trying to close in on him. But he stood erect, with a bottle of Jack Daniels in front of him, pouring his own drinks. He took a long swallow as he stared at the plump little man who had written a best seller five years ago. He hadn't written anything since, but he was making a career out of going on talk shows and attending celebrity parties. He had also turned into a lush. Suddenly he clamped his pudgy hand on Tom Colt's arm. "I read everything you write," he squeaked. He smacked his lips in ecstasy and rolled his eyes heavenward. "My God, but I adore your work. But be careful about getting caught up in the rat race of television." He giggled. "Look what a whore it's made out of me."

Tom Colt pulled his arm away and looked at the damp-looking group around him. His dark eyes seemed angry as they quickly surveyed the crowd. Suddenly they rested on January and Linda. "Excuse me," he said to the plump little writer, "but my two cousins from Iowa just walked in. And they've come all the way by bus." He took the stunned girls by their arms and led them across the room. "Thank God for the pair of you . . . whoever you are. I was stuck with that bore for twenty minutes and no one came to rescue me because they thought I was being amused."

Linda was staring at him in a glazed way. January found him completely overpowering. She managed to loosen his grip on her arm and said, "I'm glad if we were able to help you, and—"

Linda suddenly came to life. "And now you can help us."

His eyes narrowed. "I've got a feeling that maybe I should have stayed at the bar."

"I'm Linda Riggs, editor-in-chief of *Gloss* magazine, and this is my assistant editor, January Wayne. She's written to you several times about an interview."

He turned to January. "Holy Christ! Are you the J. Wayne with the letters and the Christmas card?"

She nodded and for some strange reason found herself blushing. He laughed, as if it was some private joke. "So you're J. Wayne." He laughed again. "And all the time I kept thinking the letters were from some skinny fag. Well, glad to meet you, J. Wayne. I'm glad you're not a fag . . . but it's *no* on the interview. My publisher has too many lined up as it is." He turned and looked at her again. "But why the J. Wayne? Is that part of this Ms. business? At least I might have answered you if I had known you were a girl."

"Well, January Wayne wouldn't have given you any lead on my sex either."

"No, it wouldn't. It's a crazy name, it's—" He stopped. Then he pointed a finger at her accusingly. "You wouldn't by any chance be the daughter of that sonofabitch Mike Wayne!"

She started to walk away but he yanked her back by the arm. "Listen, he fucked up one of my best books."

"Don't you dare use that language when you're talking about my father! He got an Academy Award with that picture."

"January . . ." Linda's voice was a whispered plea.

"Let her rave on." Tom Colt laughed. "I have a six-month-old son. One day when someone pans his old man's book, he'll hit out for me." He smiled and held out his hand. "Truce?"

January looked at him and held out her hand. Then he locked his arms through theirs. "Okay, now that we're all friends, let's the three of us cut out. Where can we go for a few quiet blasts?"

"There's Elaine's," Linda said. "A lot of writers go there and—"

"Yeah, I heard about it. But not tonight. The little capon at the bar told me he's winding up at Elaine's. Let's go to Toots'!"

"Where?" Linda asked.

"Toots Shor's—the only place to go for some serious drinking." Still holding them by the arms he started for the door. A harassed young woman with long stringy hair rushed to him. "Mr. Colt, where are you going?"

"Out."

"But you can't leave. Ronnie Wolfe hasn't gotten here yet, and—"

He patted her on the head. "Relax, press lady. You've done a fine job. The booze is flowing. I've been here for two hours and talked to everyone you put with me. My deal was that I'd attend a press party. No one said how long I'd have to stay. Oh, by the way . . . do you know my cousins from Iowa?"

"I know Rita Lewis," Linda said, not able to hide her delight. "We've never actually been introduced. But no doubt she's seen some of my messages this week."

"I told my secretary to send you the invitation," Rita said, rising to the occasion. "I see you got it."

"No, we crashed," January said happily.

"But you can make it up," Linda added. "All we want is an in-depth interview with Mr. Colt. We'd give you the cover for that."

"No way," Rita Lewis said. "Mr. Colt is lined up with interviews all next week. All the major magazines, plus the A.P., U.P.I.—"

"But our story would be different," Linda pleaded.

"Yes," January added. "We'd sit in on some of his other interviews, like the talk shows; we'd cover the Green Room backstage; we'd even go to some of the other cities."

"Forget it," Rita said. "I don't want him to be in *Gloss*." She looked at Linda and added, "And don't start harassing him with phone calls."

Tom Colt, who had been watching the cross-talk like a tennis match, cut in. "Wait a minute! What are you, some kind of a Nazi general? Telling people it's off limits to phone me?"

"Of course not, Mr. Colt. I didn't mean it that way. But I know how persistent Linda can be. And I'm sure she's trained January well. It's just that our schedule is set . . . and *Gloss* is out. I don't care what you do in your personal life with either of them . . . but you can't give them any interview. I've made commitments that might be endangered if you did their story."

His eyes grew cruel as he looked at the publicist. "Look, baby. Let's get things set from the very beginning. You can make appointments for me . . . and like a nice little trained dog, I'll go through all the paces. I made a deal. And I always keep my word. But don't ever tell me what I *can't* do." He put his arm around January protectively. "I've known this little girl since she was a baby. Her father's my buddy chum pal. He made a hell of a picture out of one of my books. And you're going to stand there and tell me I can't do an interview for her magazine!"

Rita Lewis looked at Linda pleadingly. "Well . . . make it a small one, Linda . . . please. Otherwise I'll lose *McCall's* and *Esquire*. No in-depth thing, no following him around—"

"They can follow me into the can if they want," he stormed. "But right now, we're going out to booze a little." Then he took each girl by the arm and propelled them through the room.

January opened her eyes slowly. She was asleep in the club chair. Why hadn't she opened the bed? Why was she sleeping with her clothes on? She stood up, but the floor began to slant crazily. She fell back on the chair. It was seven o'clock in the morning! She had only been asleep two hours.

She stood up and struggled to get out of her clothes. Several times she had to grab the chair for support. She managed to pull out the bed, then rushed to the bathroom and threw up. She came back and fell across the bed. The events of the entire evening floated back to her. The abrupt change of heart Tom Colt had about her father . . . the three of them leaving the St. Regis while the bewildered Rita Lewis stood by, glaring helplessly. His amazement at their having their *own* limousine. He liked that . . . said it was the first time he had ever heard of gate-crashers coming in a limo. Then there had been his entrance in Toots Shor's . . . Toots back-slapping him . . . sitting with them at the front table. Only no one mentioned food. It was Jack Daniels all the way. When he had stated that no one could really be his friend unless he drank Jack Daniels, she and Linda had hesitated for a split second, and then instantly announced they adored bourbon.

She had found the first drink heavy going, but the second went down much easier. And the third brought a strange lightness to her head along with a marvelous sense of good will. And when Tom Colt leaned over and kissed each of them on the cheek and called them his Chocolate and Vanilla girls (January still had her Palm Beach tan and Linda had streaked her hair blonde this month), January felt they were a hilarious threesome. People drifted over to the table. There was much back-slapping—"Sit down, you crum bum" (this was Toots); sports writers who knew her father joined them; Tom kept refilling everyone's glass. At midnight, Tom insisted on stopping off at "21" for a nightcap. They closed "21" and went to P.J. Clarke's. At four in the morning they had all stumbled out of P.J.'s—she could remember that. She remembered weaving into the lobby with Linda, both of them giggling . . . But everything that was said or done from P.J.'s on was a haze.

She stumbled into the bathroom and took some aspirin. Then she made it back to the bed. When she closed her eyes the room begin to spin. She opened her eyes and tried to fix her attention on a stationary object. Mr. Bailey's Tiffany lamp. She must have finally fallen asleep, because suddenly she was in the middle of a dream. She was aware that she was dreaming. She was enough awake to know it was a dream, but enough asleep to allow the dream to propel itself. A man was bending over her. He was about to take her. Any moment he would enter her, yet she experienced no panic. She wanted him, even though his face was a blur . . . She looked closer . . . it was Mike. But then as his lips touched hers she realized it was Tom Colt. Only his eyes weren't black like Tom's . . . they were blue. But not blue like Mike's . . . they were aquamarine! She reached out for him . . . and then she woke up. She lay back against the pillows trying to determine whose face it was—Mike's or Tom's—but all she could remember was the color of those amazing eyes.

She forced herself back to sleep, searching for those eyes. But it was a soft dreamless sleep, dissolved suddenly by the telephone. It was Linda. "January, are you up?"

There was a throbbing in the back of her head but her stomach had settled some. "What time is it?" she asked slowly, afraid of any sudden movement.

"Eleven o'clock and I have a godawful hangover."

"Is that what it is?" January asked. "I thought I was dying."

"Take some milk."

"Oh my God . . ." January suddenly felt a wave of nausea.

"Look, eat a piece of bread and take some milk. Right now! It will absorb any liquor left. Do that and call me back. We have to make our plans."

"What plans?"

"To go on with Thomas Colt."

"Oh, God . . . must we?"

"Last night you told me you adored him."

"That was probably after I met his friend, Jack Daniels."

"We're not going to do that tonight," Linda said.

"Do what?"

"Drink when we go with him. We take a firm stand. We'll sip Scotch. He can drink all he wants to. But if we want to write this story we have to stay sober. We don't tell him that. We just don't try to match him drink for drink."

"Is that what we did?"

"We damn well tried."

"Linda . . . I'm going to be sick."

"Eat the bread. I'll throw on some slacks and come to your apartment and we can plan our strategy."

She managed to get down half a glass of milk, and she watched Linda make the coffee. Linda finally settled in the club chair and smiled happily. "Now sit up . . . come to life . . . you've got to make the call to Tom Colt."

"Why me?"

"Because even though I intend to sleep with this man tonight, I have a distinct feeling that this morning he will not remember my name. But your name will strike a bell. It has to after that big love he suddenly developed for Daddy."

"I still feel he's not exactly wild about Mike. He was just furious at Rita Lewis for giving him orders."

Linda lit a cigarette and sipped her coffee. "January, this instant stuff is awful. You've got to learn to make real coffee."

January shrugged. "It suits me."

Linda shook her head. "But it won't suit your man."

"What man?"

"Any man who stays over. That's the one thing they usually demand the next morning—decent coffee."

"You mean you have to make coffee for them too?"

"Sometimes even eggs. And if you have a health freak like Keith used to be, it's Granola or one of those nutsy raisiny cereals and Vitamin E and . . . oh, Lord, thank God that's all out of my life."

"Don't you ever think of Keith or miss him?"

Linda shook her head. "When *Caterpillar* opened I almost sent him a wire. But I figured the hell with it. It's over. I'm glad for Keith the show's a hit, because he sure has to pay big dues sleeping with Christina. Besides, it takes a man like Tom Colt to make you realize that Keith is just a boy."

"But Linda . . . he's married, he has a six-month-old baby."

"But his wife and baby are on the Coast . . . and I'm here. Besides I'm not looking to take him away from his wife or child."

"Then why are you after him?"

"Because he turns me on . . . he's beautiful . . . I want to go to bed with him. And so do you. At least you acted that way last night."

"I did?"

"January, your sign should be Gemini instead of Capricorn—you really are twins. I mean, when you drink, you really become another person. Last night he was kissing us both at P.J.'s . . . like taking turns . . . real deep kisses . . . calling me Vanilla . . . and you Chocolate."

"He was kissing us at P.J.'s?"

"That he was."

"Really kissing?"

"Well, he had his tongue down my throat. I don't know about you."

"Oh, my God."

"And what about going home?" Linda asked.

"What about going home?" January sat up straight.

"He reached over, slipped his hand under your top, and said. 'Tiny buds. But I like them.'"

January buried her head in the pillow. "Linda . . . I don't believe it."

"Sure . . . then he kissed my boobs and said they were really wild."

"What was the driver doing?"

"Watching the rear view mirror like mad, I suppose. But they're used to everything, including actual rape, I'm told."

"Linda—" January's voice was weak. "It's all gradually coming back to me. I remember thinking as he slipped his hand under my blouse that it was the most natural thing in the world. Oh, good Lord . . . how could I?"

"Because you're finally turning into a nice normal girl."

"Is that what being normal is . . . to have a man you've just met touch you, in front of another girl?"

"Oh, come on. I've never played the three-way scene in my life. When I'm in bed with a man I've always felt anything goes as long as there's just the two of us in that bed. And last night was all in fun. It was nothing to get uptight about."

January got out of bed and wobbled across the room to get a cigarette. She lit it slowly, inhaled deeply, then she turned to Linda. "Okay, I know I've been away from it all, and I know things have changed. Like, you don't have to be married to love someone . . . or to go to bed with someone. I know that's the way everyone thinks. But there's no rule that says I have to think that way. I thought of myself as some kind of freak because I was a virgin. I literally talked myself into thinking I was stuck on David. And it was awful—" She shuddered as she ground out the freshly lit cigarette. "Linda, I want to fall in love. Oh God, how I want to fall in love. And I'll even go along that marriage isn't necessary right off. But when I'm in love, and the man I love . . . touches me . . . I want it to be something wonderful between *us* . . . and not just 'all in fun.' "

"January, when people get high—whether it's on bourbon, wine, or pot—the things they do . . . or feel . . . are usually true. Drinking just releases the inhibitions. If you let Tom Colt touch you and if as you say you thought it was so natural at the time, then it means deep down, you *wanted* him to touch you."

January lit another cigarette. "That's not true. I admire his work . . . I admire his strength . . . but Holy God, what must he think of us? Two gate-crashers, coming after a man in our own limousine . . . allowing him to–" She stopped as she stubbed out her cigarette. "Oh, Linda, what *can* he think of us?"

"January, stop torturing yourself about what he thinks of us. Do you realize how many bourbons he had and how many breasts he's fondled? He probably doesn't even remember those little gems of yours. Now, for God's sake, it's almost noon. Call him."

"No."

"Please . . . for my sake. Let him take us both out and in the middle of the evening you can say you're not feeling well . . . and leave. But please make the call. I really want him. I mean, there's no one around quite like him, is there? He looks so mean at times. Yet when he smiles or looks you in the eye, you could die."

"You mean you want to go to bed with Tom Colt, knowing there's no future in it? Knowing that he has a good marriage–"

"What are you trying to do to my head? Lay a guilt trip on me? If I dig Tom Colt and he digs me, what's wrong with us having a few marvelous evenings together? Who is it going to hurt? There are no next-door neighbors who are going to laugh at the poor unsuspecting wife as she hangs out the wash. *His* wife is young and gorgeous and is roughing it at Malibu with a nurse for the baby and probably some big Hollywood celebrities as neighbors. What am I taking from her! She isn't here, is she? Now . . . will you call him?"

"No. And even if he didn't have a wife, I wouldn't call him."

"Why?"

January walked over to the window and rolled up the blinds. "Looks like snow again. Thank goodness last night's stuff didn't stick."

"Why wouldn't you call him even if he didn't have a wife?" Linda demanded.

"Because . . . well . . . you don't just go calling men. They should call you."

"Oh, my God . . . I don't believe it. You sound like something out of a Priscilla Lane movie. Like Saturday night dates, and little gardenia corsages. Today women don't have to sit around and wait for a man to call. Besides, Tom Colt isn't just a man—he's a superstar—and we're doing a story on him." Linda picked up the phone and dialed the Plaza. "I know eventually we'll have to put that beast Sara Kurtz with him a few times, so she can catch his style . . . Hello . . . Oh, Mr. Tom Colt, please . . ."

"Why Sara Kurtz?" January asked.

"Because this is just about the most important story *Gloss* has ever done. And she is the best writer I've got . . . Hello . . . what? . . . Oh . . . Miss January Wayne calling! Yes . . . January . . . like the month."

"Linda!"

"Hello, Mr. Colt . . . No, this isn't January. It's Linda Riggs . . . But January's sitting right here beside me . . . Yes, we're fine . . . Well, a little . . . Oh well, we both want to see you. . . . Who? *Hugh Robertson.* Honestly? . . . Oh, great. We'd adore it . . . Fine. Your place at seven . . . the tenth floor . . ." She scribbed down the suite number on a pad. "We'll be there." Linda hung up with a beautiful smile. "Hugh Robertson is coming up to his suite for drinks this afternoon. And we're all to have dinner together. And Tom is sending *his* limousine for us."

"Why did you call him Mr. Colt on the phone?" January asked.

"Isn't that wild? But I suddenly got scared. He sounded so cold at first. But after two drinks tonight, it'll be Tommy. And imagine having Hugh Robertson along as an added starter. I wonder what it would be like to make love to an astronaut."

"Looks like you're going to have your chance," January said. "At least he's divorced."

"*You* take Hugh . . . I want Tom."

"Why are you dismissing Hugh?" January asked. "He's a superstar in his own right. I mean he has made the cover of *Time* and *Newsweek.*"

"Look, January, I am not a superstar groupie . . . in fact I've never balled a star, let alone a superstar. Keith got into *Caterpillar after* we broke up, and he's still no star. He never even got mentioned in the notices. So when I say I want Tom Colt, it's because he has something special . . . I mean, he'd turn me on even if he were an out-of-work accountant. He's so strong . . . so completely his own . . . Yet at times, there's something gentle and melancholy about him. Haven't you noticed it?"

"No. Unfortunately I got involved with Jack Daniels, and after that I couldn't see anyone's eyes. But I'll look tonight."

"No, tonight you look into Hugh Robertson's eyes. *I'm* with Tom. Just think . . . tomorrow at this time, I'll probably be having breakfast in bed with him at the Plaza."

Fifteen

THEY ARRIVED at the Plaza at five after seven, looking like two eager schoolgirls on an outing. When they walked into the lobby, January suddenly stood motionless. The place held so many memories. Linda pulled her toward the elevator. "Come on. We'll be late."

"Linda, I haven't been here since—"

"January, this is not back-to-daddy time. This is now! Tom Colt . . . Hugh Robertson . . . Remember?" She dragged January into the elevator.

Hugh Robertson opened the door. January recognized him from his pictures. He introduced himself and invited them in. "Tom is on the phóne in the bedroom talking to his agent in Munich about foreign sales. I'm supposed to make the drinks. I can't ask what will you have because all we seem to have is Jack Daniels."

Linda took a drink but January "passed." She walked over to the window. It was unbelievable . . . Tom Colt in *this* suite. The suite Mike had kept on a year-round basis. Even the same table near the windows. She touched it lightly, almost expecting some kind of a vision to materialize. How many times she had sat there, watching him wheeling and dealing. Sometimes all the phones would ring at once. She turned away. It was spooky, because now all the phones were ringing at once and Tom Colt walked into the room and said, "To hell with them . . . let them ring . . . it's Saturday and I don't have to work." Then he walked over to her and took her hands. "Hello, Princess Feel okay after last night?"

"Yes." She suddenly felt self-conscious and off balance as she watched him cross the room to greet Linda.

They went to "21." Tom remained reasonably sober. When he noticed January wasn't drinking the bourbon he had ordered for her, he sent for a wine list. "White wine, I bet. Is that it?"

"But you said last night—" Linda began.

"This is tonight," Tom said. "I say different things every night."

It was a relaxed evening, but January suddenly found herself unable to direct any conversation to Tom. She weighed everything before she said it, then rephrased it in her mind, and then the moment had passed so she didn't say it. She felt like an idiot. Linda was chattering so easily, telling them about how she had started at *Gloss*, about the miracle she had wrought. January tried to think of something to say. Why did she suddenly feel shy and look away whenever he looked at her? Maybe she should tell him she enjoyed his book. How should she phrase it: "Mr. Colt, I think . . ." *No* . . . "Tom, I adored your book . . ." No, that sounded inane. "Tom, your book has to make number one on the list . . ."—too presumptuous. Who was she to tell him how it would rate with the public? How about . . .

"Oh, Tom," Linda said. "I must get you to autograph your book for me. It's so sensational."

(Well, that polished off the book as conversational opener.)

Tom was promising to get them each a copy at Doubleday's. "They're open at night. I'm glad you like it. Lawrence and Company tell me it makes *The New York Times* list in number six spot next week. Actually this book isn't half as good as some of the others that bombed. But it's commercial . . . and today that's the name of the game." Then, dismissing his book, he turned to Hugh and demanded to know what he was doing holed up in Westhampton. "Has to be a lady involved," Tom said.

"It's a very big lady," Hugh said. "Mother Nature."

"You mean the ecology thing?" Linda asked.

"No, I'm worried about dear old Mother's body. She's liable to fall apart in spots from shock. It's the faults of our earth I'm interested in. The San Andreas is the best-known, what with all the mystics predicting that California might sink under the ocean this year. I think Los Angeles is long overdue for an earthquake, but I don't believe tidal waves will turn it into another Atlantis. It's the other faults I'm interested in—we have so damn many in our earth. I'm especially interested in finding out whether any new ones have been created. So I've gotten a grant, and I'm trying to prove a few theories that in the end might make our tiny little world last a few years longer."

"Well, if we don't use the bomb or foul up the air, won't the world just keep going?" Linda asked.

Hugh smiled. "Linda, the other night when I lay out on the dunes in my sleeping bag and—"

"You lie out on the dunes in February?" Linda asked.

"I have a one-bedroom house smack dab on the beach," Hugh said. "But I don't think I spend more than a few hours a day inside. I have my thermal underwear, my sleeping bag . . . I get myself nestled between a couple of dunes to protect me from the wind. Of course it's much nicer in the summer, but the sky is fascinating in all seasons . . . kind of cuts you down to size. Especially when you realize that in the theory of the universe, our world is just one little cinder. Just think—there are millions of suns out there, maybe breeding the same kind of life. And when you look up there, you realize that there may be worlds fifty million years ahead of us."

"I was in my second year at Miss Haddon's when I first learned the stars were huge and could be other worlds," January said. "Until then I had always thought of them as tiny, warm, comforting . . . God's lights—" She paused. "I can't remember who told me that, but I do recall the terrible shock I had when I learned the truth. I lived in constant terror that they might drop on us, crush us. When I told my father about it, he told me every star had its special spot. And that when people died they went on other stars to live."

"Nice theory," said Hugh. "He sounds like a good man. I mean, it's a good story to tell a little girl. Makes her believe in eternal life and takes away the fear of the unknown." Then he went on to explain about the solar systems and his firm belief that one day there would be interstellar communication.

Tom seemed fascinated with Hugh's theory and kept throwing questions at him. January listened with interest, but Linda was bored. After making several attempts to get the conversation on a more personal level, Linda gave up and sat back. She shot a murderous glance at January when she asked Hugh a question that set him off on another long explanation.

But January was genuinely interested. Also she found it easy to talk to Hugh. And when she talked to Hugh, she felt she was also communicating with Tom. She was even able to make them both laugh—as long as she directed her conversation toward Hugh. The one time Tom said something directly to her, she found herself tightening up, choosing words, withdrawing.

She watched Tom covertly as Hugh explained something about the moon and the tides. He looked so intense, like a man molded in granite. Yet she felt there was a vulnerability about him, a quality Mike never had. Mike was always a winner. You knew when you looked at Mike that no one could ever hurt him. Yet oddly enough, you felt that with all of his toughness, Tom had been hurt. Tom wasn't as strong as Mike. Yet, perhaps in some ways he was stronger. He admitted that some of his best books had bombed, the last four . . . Yet he had sat down and written another. Mike had quit because he was positive the dice had grown cold. Tom Colt obviously didn't believe in dice.

"Are you a gambler?" she asked suddenly.

Both men stopped speaking and looked at her. She wanted to dive under the table. The question had just slipped out. Tom stared at her for a second and then said, "Only if the odds are in my favor. Why?"

"No real reason. I . . . you remind me of someone."

"A long-lost love?" Tom asked.

"Yes . . . her father!" Linda snapped.

Tom laughed. "Well, that's a pretty good bringdown for any man. And when a guy is in his late fifties and thinks he can entertain two beautiful young girls, he should be brought back to reality."

"You can't be in your late fifties," Linda said.

"Don't try to make it up to me," Tom said with a smile. "Yep, I'm fifty-seven, a few years older than Mike Wayne. Right, January? And Hugh, you're young enough to know we've been boring these ladies with all the talk about stars. The only stars they're interested in are Paul Newman, or Steve McQueen."

"I wasn't bored at all," Linda insisted. "It was fascinating."

They left "21" at eleven. The weather was clear and there was very little wind. "Let's walk the girls home," he said. "They share a pad."

"We live in the same apartment building, but we each have our own apartment," Linda said pointedly.

Tom dismissed the car and they walked to Doubleday's. The sales people all greeted him; he bought books for January and Linda, autographed them, and grudgingly autographed a few for the store, then quickly cut out. They walked east. Linda tried to steer January and Hugh up front as she held on to Tom's arm, but he kept talking to Hugh, and when they could, the foursome walked abreast. They finally reached a narrow block and were forced to separate into couples. Linda and Tom walked ahead. January noticed he was holding Linda's hand. Suddenly she realized Hugh had asked her a question.

"I'm sorry . . . I didn't hear you," she said. "That taxi was making so much noise . . . I . . ."

He smiled. "Don't let your girlfriend bug you. Tom is married . . . and you don't look to be the type for a quickie romance."

"I'm not bugged. What makes you think I am?"

"The way you've been staring at them holding hands while I was talking. No cab was making any noise."

"Actually . . . I suppose I was daydreaming. That's a bad habit of mine. And really, Hugh, I'm delighted to be walking with you."

"We're both deadbeats . . . romance-wise . . . me and Tom. Me, I've got the stars and the ocean . . . and Tom's got himself a new wife and a new baby. He never had a baby before . . . you realize that? Four marriages and gets his first baby at fifty-seven. So if your little friend has any serious ideas beyond—"

"No, Linda knows the score."

"That kind of talk doesn't sound like you," he said.

"How do you know what I sound like?"

"Because I know who you are and what you are. Just like I know what Linda is. Tom always winds up with the Lindas. He even married a couple of them. Know why? Because he doesn't go after any girl. He's a lazy sonofabitch—he takes the ones that come after him. It's easier that way. Besides, I don't think he's capable of being in love . . . except maybe with the characters he creates in his books. So to him, it's whichever girl chooses *him*. Only now that's he's got a son . . . he'll stick with this new little wife forever."

"What's she like?" January asked.

"Beautiful . . . red hair . . . had a kind of a career going in pictures for a few years. Didn't ever get beyond doing bits. But she was pretty. And she met Tom . . . went after him . . . gave up her career and gave him a son."

"What was her name . . . I mean as an actress."

He stopped in the darkness and stared at her. "January," he said softly. "Lady, want some advice? Leave him to the Lindas. You'll get hurt."

Before she could answer, Tom suddenly called out, "Hey, Hugh, you still want me to come out and spend the day at the beach tomorrow?"

"Sure, all set. The freezer is loaded with steaks."

"Well, how about inviting the girls to come along and cook the steaks?"

"We'd adore it," Linda said quickly. "I've never been to the beach in February."

They had reached the apartment building. Linda looked at Tom. "Can I invite you all up for a nightcap? I have no bourbon, but I've got rye—"

"No, we want to start early," Tom said. "I dig the beach in gray weather . . . even in cold weather. It belongs to you then. At Malibu I do my best writing when it's cold and the fog rolls in."

Sunday was cold, and rain was predicted, but they all left for the beach at ten-thirty in the morning. Everyone wore heavy slacks and sweaters and old jackets. Tom Colt looked truly relaxed for the first time.

It did rain, but the house was warm and they kept the fireplace going all day. January felt at times that they were the only people left in the world as they sat before the fire. It was a strong little house. A large living room, a big kitchen, a big bedroom upstairs with its own sundeck. "Perfect for a bachelor," Hugh said.

"Perfect for a couple in love," Linda said, gazing at Tom. "Do you like our beaches in New York as much as Malibu, Tommy?"

He smiled and yanked at her hair. "Linda, you can call me shit heel . . . sonofabitch . . . or whatever—but never call me Tommy."

The limousine returned at ten o'clock to take them back to the city. Hugh was remaining behind. As they left, Tom reached out and grabbed a bottle of bourbon. "Provisions for the road."

Linda tucked her arm through Tom's as they walked down the path to the car. Hugh walked the short distance with January. A light rain whipped their faces. "Looks like the match has been made," he said. "So now it's up to you to watch out over them on the tour."

"Tour?"

"Linda says you both are going with him to write the story. And this tour . . . it's not for Tom. He'll drink too much. Basically he's very shy. I've only known him for six years, so I don't know what his private demon is. God knows women love him and men are equally attracted to him. But it seems as though he has to prove something every second. Maybe that's what the drinking is all about. Maybe after each book he feels he's said all he has to say. Yet he knows he has to do it again. This tour could hurt him—his psyche, that is. That's why I say watch out over him. He needs someone who will help make it all not seem too honky-tonk."

January smiled. Linda and Tom had already gotten into the car. "I like you, Mr. Hugh Robertson," she said.

"I like you, too, January Wayne. I think you're very special."

"Thank you."

He took her hand. "I mean that . . . in the best of ways. I'm a friend."

She nodded and held out her hand. "Friend."

They both smiled and she climbed into the car. Tom opened the bottle and took a long swallow. He handed it to Linda. She managed to take a big gulp. Then he offered it to January. She hesitated . . . their eyes met and held in the semi-darkness . . . for a moment everything seemed suspended . . . like a motion picture when the frame suddenly freezes. She reached for the bottle slowly . . . their eyes still together . . . and suddenly with a quick movement he pulled it away. "No. I've changed my mind. No more refreshments on the way home. Tomorrow is a working day."

The moment was gone. He discussed the interviews that were set up—the appearances he was to make on the *Today* show, the Johnny Carson show, the quick trips he would take to Boston, Philadelphia, and Washington before starting on the tour across country.

"I guess we better stay away from your interviews," Linda said. "Rita would really do a number if we showed up for any of them. But if it's all right we'll cover your TV appearances and some of the out-of-town shows and press conferences."

"Come along. But I can't see why it will make that interesting a story."

"Have you ever been on a tour?"

"Of course not."

Linda smiled. "It will be very interesting. I promise you."

When the car pulled up in front of their apartment, he got out and walked them to the door. He leaned down and kissed them both on the cheek and started toward his car. For a split second, Linda was speechless . . . then through her teeth she hissed, "Go on in, January . . . now." She pushed January through the door and rushed back to the limousine just as Tom was getting in. "Tom . . . I know you're doing the *Life* thing tomorrow . . . but what time does . . ."

January didn't hear the rest. She went directly to the elevator and went to her apartment. Her emotions were scrambled. . . .

She undressed and got into bed. She wondered if Linda had made it back to the Plaza . . . to the bedroom that once belonged to Mike. She tried not to think about it.

If Linda wanted to have a romance with Tom Colt, why not?

She punched up the pillow and tried to will herself to sleep. Everything seemed too quiet. She could hear the clock . . . the television set next door . . . a couple arguing across the court. . . . Then the phone rang.

It was so unexpected that she jumped when she heard it. She picked it up on the second ring.

"I didn't wake you, did I?"

She stared into the phone dumbly. It was Tom Colt.

"January . . . are you there?"

"No . . . I mean yes, I'm here . . . no, you didn't wake me."

"Good," he said. "I was just about to leave my wake-up call and I suddenly realized I'm free tomorrow night. Have you seen *Gingerbread Lady*?"

"No."

"Well, I'm a big fan of Maureen Stapleton, so I'll get three tickets and we can go tomorrow. You tell Linda."

"She might have seen it," January said.

"So what? We haven't. That makes it two out of three. That's the way we'll have to work things between the three of us. Majority rule. I'll pick you both up at seven. Goodnight."

She stared into the phone for a moment, after she heard the click. Then she hung up slowly. Linda wasn't with him. She lay in the darkness and thought about it . . . Linda wasn't with him! But why was she so happy about it? *Because she wanted him herself*! She lay very still, almost in shock at this sudden revelation. But it was true . . . She was falling in love with a man older than her father. A man who had a wife and a baby! And he felt something for her!

Otherwise, why had he called her and not Linda about *Gingerbread Lady*? Could he feel something for her? But hadn't Hugh said he was lazy . . . that he allowed the girl to pick him . . . rather than make the effort to go after the girl. And hadn't Linda very definitely picked him? Yet he had called *her*. She stretched out and allowed herself the freedom of a dream, like suppose his wife suddenly came to him and wanted a divorce, or suppose . . . suppose she suddenly died and . . . no . . . that wasn't right . . . she couldn't kill her off. . . . Well, suppose he did fall really in love and wanted a divorce

. . . no . . . he wouldn't give up his son . . . Tom Colt, Jr., was a big thing to him. . . . Well, suppose the beautiful young wife came to him and said it wasn't really his baby . . . that it belonged to some beachboy . . . and she wanted a divorce. And then he'd have no guilt . . . he would support the child . . . because it had his name . . . and then he could marry January . . . and they could live in the beach house together . . . and she'd type his manuscripts and . . . it would be wonderful . . . and . . .

IT WAS INSANE!

Yes . . . it was insane . . . but she hugged the pillow and went to sleep thinking about the way he had looked at her for that one instant in the car.

Sixteen

SHE DIDN'T SLEEP well. But when the alarm went off, she sprang out of bed, eager for the day to begin. She stood under the shower and found herself singing, "I'm in love, I'm in love, I'm in love with a wonderful guy!" Then she remembered another Rodgers and Hammerstein song: "The gentleman is a dope, he's not my cup of tea, but why am I crying my eyes out, he doesn't belong to me." Only she wasn't crying her eyes out. She was standing in the shower like an idiot, singing old show tunes . . . and she never felt better in her life.

But he *was* married. She thought about it as she dressed. Where was her conscience? Look how her mother had suffered when her father had affairs with women. But she wasn't going to go to bed with Tom Colt. It was just so wonderful to feel something for a man . . . other than Mike. To want to *be* with another man . . . to want his admiration. Could that be so wrong? Just wanting to be with him. Especially if no one ever knew how she felt . . .

It had been murder trying to be casual with Linda. "What do you mean *we're* going to see *Gingerbread Lady*!" she had screamed. "I'd much rather see *No, No, Nanette.* Besides, why did he call *you*?"

"I don't know. . . . Maybe because there's always been the three of us. Maybe he thought it would look better if he was impartial."

"Well, this threesome is going to split into a twosome . . . like after tonight!"

"What about us working together on the article?"

"That's all changed. As of now, you are off it."

"But why?"

"Look, January, Sara Kurtz will do all the rewriting anyhow. And when it gets time to go on the road, only two of us are going—Tom and me. I'll tell him that when the time comes . . . and explain I had to put you on something else. I'll even introduce him to Sara and tell him I'll be sending tapes back to her. I'm sure one look at Sara and he won't want her to go on the road."

January hesitated. "Linda, let me try to write the story. I really feel I can do it. Let me just go along with you on the tour. I won't be in the way. I promise."

"Darling, you're in the way right now. Unfortunately there's nothing I can do about it tonight . . . but enjoy it for all it's worth. Because suddenly three is getting to be quite a crowd."

They sat in the darkness of the theater. Tom had told them that Maureen Stapleton was his idea of the best actress around. She had seen Maureen in several shows and agreed with him. But this was the first time in her life she couldn't concentrate on what was happening on the stage. She was too acutely conscious of the man sitting beside her. Although his entire attention was focused on the play, she felt a peculiar sense of intimacy, sitting beside him in the darkness of a theater. Several times when his arm accidentally brushed hers, she had an insane urge to reach out and touch him. His hands were so strong . . . and clean . . . she liked the shape of his fingers. He smelled of something faintly reminiscent. She sniffed, trying to place it. He turned to her. "It's Chanel Number Five cologne," he said. "I always use it after shaving. Some people get the wrong idea."

"No, I like it," she said.

"Good. I'll get you some." Then he returned his attention to the stage.

They went backstage after the show and visited Miss Stapleton, who joined them at Sardi's. Tom told her that if he ever took a crack at writing for the stage, he'd write something for her. They began talking about shows . . . past and present . . . making comparisons. January came up with the names of some shows that amazed Tom. "But you couldn't have been around

then," he said. "That was probably before you were born."
She nodded. "It was . . . but from the time I was eight, I not only saw every show on Broadway, but I used to sit in this restaurant and listen to talk about shows from the forties."

She realized they were all into a world that Linda couldn't enter. January tried to pull her into the conversation. "Linda and I went to school together. She was our star. You should have seen her in *Annie Get Your Gun*."

Linda began to spark a bit, and before the evening was over she was talking to Maureen Stapleton about doing an interview for *Gloss*.

When Tom Colt dropped Linda and January off together, Linda made no attempt to invite him up. "I've decided to save it all for the road tour. I think he feels the same way. It'll all be so natural then."

The doorbell rang just as the alarm was going off the following morning. January slipped into a robe and looked through the peephole in the door. It was a messenger with a package. She opened the door cautiously, keeping the safety chain on. She signed for it, gave him a tip, told him to leave the package on the floor. She didn't remove the chain until the messenger had gone down in the elevator. (This was a rule Mike had forced on her—part of the survival kit of a girl living alone in New York.) The moment the elevator door closed, she opened the door and grabbed the package. She took it inside and opened it carefully. It was the largest bottle of Chanel No. 5 she had ever seen. There was no note. She held the bottle to her cheek—he had actually thought of her—and where had he gotten a bottle this size at eight-thirty in the morning? Had he sent two of them? Was the messenger on his way to Linda's right now?

She arrived at the office reeking of perfume. Linda smelled it immediately. "What have you got on?"

"Chanel Number Five." January waited for Linda's answer.

She merely shrugged. "I left a short story on your desk. Read it . . . I like it. Let me know what you think. I may be too close to it. It's about a girl who has her nose done to hold her boyfriend . . . comes out looking gorgeous . . . and loses him to a girl who looked like she did *before* the nose job. It's a funny story . . . and it came in over the transom."

"Over the transom?"

"Unsolicited . . . no agent . . . by an author I've never heard of . . . with a self-addressed return envelope to the Bronx. It's a pretty dog-eared script, so I gather Ms. Debbie Mallon has gathered a lot of rejection slips . . . it doesn't figure she'd send it to us before *Ladies' Home Journal, Cosmo, Redbook* or the others. See what you think."

January took the manuscript into her office. She sat down and lit a cigarette and began to read the manuscript.

He hadn't sent Linda any Chanel . . .

She re-read the first paragraph of the manuscript. She couldn't concentrate. She went back and read it again.

But maybe he also felt three was a crowd . . . and this was like a "kiss-off" present.

She went back to the first paragraph of the story. She glanced at her watch. Yesterday Tom had called her at home . . . in the morning. It was almost ten o'clock now . . . maybe he had called her again. She should get an answering service. But until now, there just hadn't been any need for one. Mike always knew where to find her. He usually called her at the office every day after golf. Even David knew how to find her. So if Tom Colt wanted to find her, he certainly would know enough to look up *Gloss* magazine. He had found her home number and she wasn't listed yet in the phone book. That meant he had to call Information to get it. Maybe he had called Linda . . . and Linda was telling him that January was on another story and too tied up to go along with them.

She stared at the manuscript, "Nose Job" by Debbie Mallon. Probably the girl's own story. Had to be . . . poor Debbie Mallon . . . poor Debbie Mallon's unsolicited manuscript . . . being given to her to read. She felt a jolt of conscience. She *must* read about Debbie's nose or else God wouldn't be on her side . . . He wouldn't make Tom call. This was ridiculous! Of course God wasn't on her side. Why should he be? Why should He help her by making a married man call her? "But it's just to be with him," she whispered as she stared toward the ceiling. "Just to maybe hold his hand . . ." Would that be wrong?

. . . She forced herself to read the manuscript . . . "I looked like a parrot but Charlie loved me. And Charlie looked like Warren Beatty. That's enough to give any girl a complex. . . ."

She forced herself to read on. Debbie was being very clinical about the whole operation. Even to getting all those needles jabbed in her nose. She shuddered. And the chin . . . they were adding something to her chin . . . All this and she was going to lose Charlie at the end of page ten. She stopped in the middle of the operation. Ten fifteen. Maybe he had called Linda. Well, she couldn't go back to Linda's office until she got through with Debbie's nose.

At ten-thirty she had finished the story. She was undecided. But why not give Debbie a break? She put the manuscript back into the manila envelope and walked down the hall to Linda's office.

"It's good," she told Linda as she handed her the story.

Linda nodded. "I think so too. Sara's got the biggest nose in town, so if it gets by her, we'll use 'Nose Job' in the August issue. We can use a piece of short fiction from an unknown, because that will be the issue we use the story on Tom Colt. I intend to get a lot of good pictures of him on tour . . . Shit, if only Keith weren't in *Caterpillar* . . ."

"You would want him on tour with you and Tom Colt!"

"Yes . . . but only because I could afford him. Any other photographer is going to be expensive, real expensive. Oh, I know. I'll call Jerry Coulson. He's great and he doesn't know just how good he is yet. I probably can make a good deal with him."

"Has Tom okayed the pictures?"

"I haven't asked him. And I don't intend to. Look, by then we'll be a big hot romance. Last night in the theater he kept pressing his leg against mine. And he did the same thing in Sardi's while you all were talking theater."

"Oh . . . well . . . I guess I'll go back to my office . . ."

"Sit down. The coffee wagon is due."

"No. I've got the article on Celebrity Cats to do. Do you realize how few celebrities have cats? They all seem to have dogs."

"That's ridiculous. Pam Mason has a thousand cats."

"But she's in California! Say, do you think Maureen Stapleton has a cat?" (January knew she was talking too fast.)

"I don't know . . ." The phone rang on Linda's desk. "Maybe that's Tom. I'll get Maureen's number from him." She pressed the button. "Hello . . . What? . . . Sure, Sherry . . . You're kidding! I want to hear. Come to my office and tell me." She hung up. "Don't leave, January. This will be some real dirt. Sherry said Rita is splitting a gut over something. I've put two calls in for Tom already, but his suite doesn't answer."

Sherry Margolis, an attractive girl who headed the magazine's Public Relations, came in. Linda motioned her to sit. "You said Rita Lewis is blowing a fuse over me?" Linda's smile was almost unctuously complacent.

Sherry nodded. "She asked if you had heard from Tom Colt. She's a wreck. Seems she arrived at the Plaza to pick him up at seven for the *Today* show and he was still asleep. And he was due on it at eight. He claimed he didn't know it was for *this* Tuesday. She sat in the lobby almost having a fainting spell until he calmly walked down at ten minutes to eight. She had a car, so they just about made it. After the show, he was talking to Barbara Walters, so she took time out to go to the john. And when she came out he was gone. Someone said he was in the News Room. There was a big commotion going on. She saw Tom using their telephone. She figured he was talking to you. Then he bolted out. She called . . . ran after him, but the elevator door closed just as she got there. She didn't panic because she assumed he had gone back to his hotel. He knew he had a ten o'clock breakfast interview. But he's not there, and she's been cooling it for half an hour with a guy from *Playboy* who's on his third Bloody Mary. One more and he won't be able to do an interview if Tom Colt *does* show. His suite doesn't answer and she even went up and banged on the door. The maid said she had just made up the room and no one was there. Rita kind of intimated that he wound up with you over the weekend and figured *you* might know where he is. . . ."

Linda smiled again. "That's exactly right. Only tell Rita that I left him safe and sound at the Plaza last night . . . all tucked in."

Sherry stared with open admiration. "Well, that beats Group Therapy . . . and that's where Rita Lewis spends four nights a week. I'll be delighted to give her the message."

When Sherry left the room Linda looked at January and winked. "This will kill Rita. She's had her eye on Tom from the beginning. Wait until she gets to Group Therapy tonight and they start telling her she's not rejected . . . that *they* love her and she's to be happy with *their* love . . ."

"How do you know?"

"Because I've played that scene myself. Thank God I was able to afford my own private shrink three times a week."

January shook her head. "Honestly, Linda, I just don't understand. Why would you want Sherry to think you went to bed with someone when you didn't? I mean, is there some kind of an honor in having a high score? Is it like a batting average?"

Linda yawned. "When you go to bed with a Leon, you keep it a private matter. But with a Tom Colt you make it a headline."

Suddenly Sherry came dashing back. "Linda, turn on the television set. There's an earthquake in California. A real one!"

"Did you call Rita and tell her what I told you?" Linda asked.

"Yes, and she took it beautifully—three gasps and a choked sob." Sherry had turned on the set. People were pouring in from the other offices.

Within seconds everyone was huddled around the set. They sat stupefied as the newscaster announced that the first violent tremor had hit forty miles away from the downtown area of Los Angeles at five fifty-nine Pacific Coast time . . . eight fifty-nine New York time. It registered 6.5 on the Richter scale and was felt over a three-hundred-mile area from Fresno to the Mexican border and as far east as Las Vegas. News reports stated that the initial shock was equivalent to an explosion of a million tons of TNT.

They switched to all the stations. Bulletins were interrupting regular shows . . . announcements of new tremors . . . fires. In New York, Kennedy Airport was a madhouse.

A roving reporter went around . . . asking questions . . . one man said his house had collapsed but thank God his wife and children were unharmed.

Suddenly Sherry screamed. "There's Tom Colt!"

The reporter had seen him too. He pushed through the crowd and shoved a hand mike in Tom Colt's face. "Why are you rushing back to Los Angeles, Mr. Colt?"

"To be with my wife and baby." He turned away.

"Are they all right?" the reporter asked.

Tom Colt nodded. "Yes, I called her right after I did the *Today* show. The big shot had just hit, and there was another while I was talking to her."

"Aren't you here in the east to publicize your new book?"

"Book?" Tom Colt looked vague. "Look, right now there's an earthquake going on. I have a wife and son, and all I'm interested in is making sure they're safe." Then he pushed past the reporter and got on the plane.

Linda suddenly stood up and snapped off the set. "Well . . . we've got to get back to work. The worst is over. Los Angeles may have its problems with property damage, but at least it's not going to sink under the sea and disappear." Everyone quickly dispersed. There were murmurings. "Come to my office . . . I have a radio." "We can always catch it during lunch hour at a bar!" When they were alone, Linda looked out the window and whispered, "I can't believe it!" Then she spun her chair around and said, "I mean, I really can't believe it. My love life is doomed. Even nature is against me. It's hard enough to hold a man against the usual competition. But *I* have to have an earthquake!" She sighed. "Well, as long as I'm obviously free tonight, how about going to Louise's for dinner?"

"No, I think I'll stay in and work on the cat article." Then January dashed back to her office. He was gone. Friday, Saturday, Sunday and Monday. Four nights of her life . . . four nights with Tom Colt. And even though nothing had happened between them, it had been wonderful . . . And it was still wonderful to have someone to think about. Even if he never came back. . . .

The next day she got an answering service. But when a

week passed without word from him, even Linda grew discouraged. "I guess I blew it. His book is up to number four spot in *Time*. I guess he'll do his shows from out there. Why not? Johnny Carson goes out there enough. Merv Griffin is there . . . Steve Allen . . . He's got enough to keep him busy for a month. But the least the man could have done was call and tell me that."

January decided to try to put Tom Colt out of her thoughts. She told herself it was a sign. Maybe God was telling her, "Stop before anything happens." Maybe it was His way of telling her He disapproved. She wasn't particularly religious. But at times she found herself speaking to the God of her childhood, the wonderful old man with the long white beard who presided over all the heavens with his big book, like a ledger—keeping score, marking down the good deeds on one page, the sins on the other.

But each day she checked with her answering service and found excuses to duck going to dinner with Linda. She spent another dreary evening at Le Club with David. Everyone was talking about the upcoming backgammon tournament at Gstaad. Dee was going . . . it was a three-day affair . . . David couldn't take the time off from work . . . but he envied Mike . . . Gstaad was great at this time of the year . . . everyone would be at the Palace Hotel . . . then the Eagle Club.

David dropped her home at eleven-thirty and didn't even ask to come up for a nightcap. But she was excited. If Dee and Mike were going to Gstaad, they'd come through to New York first. She'd see Mike. It was just what she needed—a long lunch with him, a good long talk . . . She'd tell him about her mixed-up feelings about Tom Colt. He'd help set her straight, and he'd understand. After all, he had been there so many times himself.

She called Palm Beach the following morning. When the butler said Mr. and Mrs. Granger had left for Gstaad three days ago, she hung up and sat staring dumbly at the phone. He had been in New York and hadn't called. There had to be some explanation. She had talked to Mike just a few days ago . . . Suddenly she began to panic. Maybe something had happened. But that was ridiculous. Nothing could have happened. It would be in the newspapers. Unless he was sick . . . Maybe he was lying in a hospital with a heart attack or something. And Dee was playing backgammon. She placed a call to the Palace Hotel. Then she dressed and sat waiting for the call to be completed. Ten minutes later Mike's voice sounded as if it were in the next room.

"How are you?" she yelled.

"Just great. Anything wrong! You okay?"

"Yes . . ." She sighed. "Oh, Mike, I was frightened."

"About what?"

"Well, last night David told me where you were. And I knew you'd have to come through to New York. And I called Palm Beach and they told me you had gone . . . and I thought that . . ."

"Hold it." He laughed. "First, we arrived at the airport at five in the morning. Stayed just long enough for the plane to be refueled. I didn't want to wake you. And I figured we'd stop over a few days on the way back. Listen, I've got great news—I finally broke the back of this idiotic game. I won a few bucks the last few weeks in Palm Beach. I'm not up to playing in *this* yet. But at the Calcutta auction, I'll buy me a player. It's a great game, babe . . . wait till you get the hang of it."

"Yes, Mike . . ."

"Listen, you're paying for this. Jiggle the operator, tell her to reverse the charges to me."

"No, Mike. It's my nickel. I want it that way."

"Okay. Listen, I got to run. I've got me a pigeon for gin. While we were waiting for the plane to be refueled, I beat Freddie out of three big ones . . . in one hour. And he's come on this trip with us, and I got him eager to play every day."

"Who's Freddie?"

"Oh, some young schmuck married to a rich broad. I thought you met him in Palm Beach . . . sure you did."

"Okay, Mike. Good luck with Freddie."

"Bye, baby. See you soon."

That night she accepted an invitation to go to dinner with

Linda and a friend of hers who was bringing along a "friend." They went to a small restaurant on Fifty-sixth Street and Linda warned her to pick the cheapest thing on the menu. "Mine is paying two alimonies and yours is paying alimony plus shrink fees for his son."

January decided her date looked like a long skinny pig. He was tall and thin, but from there on all resemblance to a man ended. His face was pink and his nose was absolutely a snout. He had wisps of pink hair that barely covered his scalp, and patchy little sideburns that refused to grow. He talked about his squash game and his jogging and the ulcerous work of Madison Avenue. Both men worked at the same advertising agency and during the better part of the evening they discussed their accounts and inside gossip at the office. It was obvious from their conversation that they lunched together every day. Why talk about it now? But she realized they were nervous . . . and they were, as Mike would put it, born losers. They were with two girls they hoped to impress, and somehow they felt "big business" talk was the key. She marveled at the unreality of it all. Didn't they look in the mirror when they shaved? If the pig (who answered to the name of Wally) *owned* the advertising agency, he couldn't impress her. She was sorry she had accepted the date. At the moment she would rather be home eating a TV dinner and reading a good book. At ten-thirty the dinner finally dragged to a finish. It was freezing, but the pig said he hadn't done all of his jogging so they walked home. Linda immediately invited everyone up for a nightcap, but January said she was tired.

The pig insisted on going into the building and escorting her to her door. When she put the key in the lock and turned to say goodnight, he stared at her. "You must be kidding."

"No. Goodnight and thanks for a very nice dinner."

"But what about us?"

"Well . . . what about us?" she asked.

"Don't tell me you're one of those frigid types?"

"No . . . right now, I'm just a tired type."

"Well, let's fix that." He leaned over and immediately his tongue was pushing its way down her throat and his hands were all over her body . . . groping under her coat . . . trying to slide up her blouse. In a burst of anger she lifted her knee and it made its mark. He leaped away with a groan. For a split second his little pig eyes smarted with tears of pain. Then his mouth went ugly. She was frightened now and tried to open the door and get inside, but he pulled her around and slapped her across the face. "You lousy little cunt! You stone-assed virgin types kill me. Well, I'll show you." He grabbed for her. She was now more angry than frightened, and with a sudden surge of strength, she shoved him away, pushed open the door, slipped inside and slammed it in his face. For a moment she stood trembling from anger and shock. He had expected her to go to bed with him for a $3.95 table d'hôte dinner.

She undressed slowly and turned on the bath. She needed a lot of bubbles and perfume to wash away the ugly evening. She was just about to get into the tub when the phone rang. It was Linda in a muffled voice. "January . . . is Wally there?"

"Of course not!"

"Oh. Well, listen. Steve is in the bathroom. I just checked with my service. And guess what. Tom Colt called!"

"He did!"

"Yes. He's in town. My service said he called at ten thirty. Call him now. He's at the Plaza."

"Me? But he called you."

"January . . . I can't. I'm in bed with Steve—that is, I will be when he gets out of the bathroom. Look, tell him you're calling for me . . . that I'm having a late conference . . . you know . . . but find out if he plans to see me tomorrow."

"I can't. Honestly, Linda."

"Do it. Come on, now. I'll tell you what . . . you can even cut yourself in on the date."

"No."

"Please! Oh, hi . . . Steve . . . I was just checking with my service." There was a pause, then Linda said in an impersonal tone, "All right, Miss Green. Thank you for my messages, and *please* make that call for me."

January sat on the bed. The water in the bath had cooled. Twenty minutes had passed and she still hadn't made the call. She couldn't. How *could* she call him? But then she owed it to Linda. She was letting her own feelings hold her back. She picked up the phone.

The night operator at the Plaza said Mr. Colt had left a DO NOT DISTURB. She left a message that Miss Linda Riggs had returned his call. Then she hung up and wondered whether she was disappointed at not being able to talk to him . . . or grateful that he'd never know she had called.

Linda's call came before the alarm went off. "January . . . wake up. I only have a second. Steve's in the john. Then he's going to give me an early morning fuck. Tell me . . . did you talk to Tom?"

"Oh, my God. What time is it?"

"Seven o'clock. Did you talk to him?"

"No, he had his phone turned off, but I left a message saying you had returned his call."

"Good girrrl! Talk to you later."

At eleven-thirty Linda summoned January into her office. "I just spoke to him," she said. "And I'm keeping my word. We're all going to see *No, No, Nanette* tonight."

"Oh . . ."

"Aren't you going to thank me?"

"Linda, I don't have to go really. In fact I think I'd rather not."

"No. It's all right. He said, 'Last time *I* picked the show . . . now what do you want to see?' And when I said *No, No, Nanette*, he said, great, because Patsy Kelly has always been a favorite of his. Then he said, 'Do you want to ask January along?' and I said, 'Yes, I think it looks better. After all, you are married. On the road it won't matter because everyone will know I'm there to do the story.' So that's how we left it. Only tonight, I think I want to clinch it. So let's not do the Sardi's bit. Let's make it some place where he'll really drink. Then at the proper time you can cut out. Or if I get him to come up to my place for a nightcap . . . you don't come."

"Linda, maybe he'll invite Patsy to Sardi's . . ."

"Oh shit. That means we sit and talk theater and everyone is very proper like last time."

"He obviously likes the theater."

"Well, let's play it by ear. We're to meet in his suite at six. He said he'd have some hors d'oeuvres and a drink to hold us until after the show. Now if I can just get him drinking on an empty stomach . . . I'll score . . ."

They arrived at the Plaza at six. Rita Lewis was there, along with a subdued young man from *Life* magazine. Tom was holding a glass of bourbon and made the introductions. Rita went into a state of shock when she saw Linda and January. Tom fixed them a drink and they both sat quietly while the interview continued. January noticed that Tom looked at the clock on the mantle several times. At six-thirty, the young man was still asking questions. At quarter to seven, Tom said, "How much longer will this take? We have tickets for a show."

"Mr. Colt," Rita's voice veered on quiet hysteria. "This is for *Life* magazine. Mr. Harvey will be here for quite some time. I mean . . . there is no time limit. And a photographer is coming at eight thirty."

"Looks like we'll have to postpone the session," Tom said. He turned to the reporter. "I'm sorry, young man, but—"

Rita jumped up. "Mr. Colt . . . you can't do this. You've already upset our schedule by two weeks. I had to change all the bookings—the Mike Douglas show, Kup in Chicago . . ."

"Well, next time when you say I have a five o'clock interview, don't spring any surprises on me."

"But I left an envelope with your schedule for you last night. It distinctly said, '*Life* reporter and pictures at five . . . first session.' Anyone knows that a session means several hours. And a photographer can't be rushed either. We've got Rocco Garazzo—he's one of the best."

"Sorry, kid . . ." Tom said. "We'll do it another time. Look, the booze is all set up over there. Enjoy yourself."

"Mr. Colt . . ." Rita's voice broke. Her eyes were glassy with tears. "You're going to make me lose my job. They'll say

I goofed. And it would keep me from getting other jobs because the word would go out that I wasn't competent enough to handle a star author. I'll also blow all my personal contacts . . . like with *Life* magazine . . . because what you're doing is insulting to the reporter. He's a writer . . . doing his best, and–"

"Cut it," he said quietly. "You've made your point." He turned to Linda. "The tickets are in my name. You kids go see the show. Come back here when it's over. Use my car. It's out front." Then he took off his jacket, poured himself a stiff drink and said to the reporter, "Okay, Mr. Harvey. I'm sorry about the misunderstanding. Let's have a few blasts together, and take all the time you want."

As they drove to the theater, Linda rhapsodized over the turn of events. "He's drinking. And now there's no chance of Sardi's. But I'm going back alone. I feel the timing is right."

After the show, Linda lost some of her nerve. "Maybe Rita and the *Life* people are still with him. You better come back. If he's alone, stay for one drink, and then split. I'll give you the cue. When I say, 'January, I think your cat article is going to be great,' then you can say, 'That reminds me, I have some work I need to do on it tonight. I'd better go.' Okay?"

"Okay. But Linda, aren't you? . . ." She stopped.

"Aren't I what?"

"Aren't you kind of going after him like a man should go after a girl?"

Linda laughed. "January, I bet if you balled a man, you'd expect him to send you flowers the next morning."

"Well . . . yes . . . David did."

"Maybe that's why David only comes around every ten days. But I happen to know that model whom he balls quite often not only doesn't get flowers from him, but she makes him breakfast and brings it to him in bed. And considering that Kim only eats maybe one stalk of celery every other day to keep nice and consumptive-looking . . . it's not easy to watch a guy eat bacon and eggs when you are starving."

"Meaning what?"

"Meaning, there is no boy-girl thing anymore. The girl can

be as aggressive as she wants. She can call the man. She can ask him to go to bed. That's the way it is today. This is the seventies. *Not* the fifties."

"There's one thing I'm curious about—if you dig Tom Colt this much, why would you go to bed with Steve last night?"

"Last night, I didn't know that Tom was coming back until after I had already told Steve I wanted him. I couldn't throw him out, could I? Besides, he's very good in bed and I hadn't had sex for quite a while."

"But don't you have to *feel* something to go to bed with a man?"

"Yes . . . horny."

"Linda!"

Linda stared at her in the darkness of the limousine. "Know something, January? Tom Colt is fifty-seven, but he's with it. *You* are the generation gap."

Rita Lewis and the reporter were just leaving when January and Linda returned. Tom greeted both girls expansively, asked about the show, and insisted everyone, including the harassed Rita Lewis, have a drink. Rita had to leave. The *Life* journalist stayed for one nightcap. Then he said, "I've really got to go. I told my wife I'd be home by ten. She's holding some food for me."

Tom shook his head sadly. "Why didn't you speak up, man? Just because I forget about food when I'm drinking. Christ, I starved you . . . and that poor P.R. lady from the publishers. Where do you live?"

"Down near Gramercy Park."

"Well, the car is outside. Take it. Then send it back and it can take the girls home."

"January, I just love that cat article you're working on," Linda said.

January started for the door. "It needs work. In fact, I had intended to work on it a bit tonight . . . I'll leave with Mr. Harvey . . . he can drop me."

"The poor guy is starving," Tom said. "And he goes in the opposite direction. You gonna make him go uptown first, then backtrack downtown just for a cat story. Can't it wait until tomorrow?"

"Well, I really should—"

"January does some of her best work at night," Linda said quickly.

"Don't we all. But this time her genius will have to wait. Go on, Bob."

The young man hesitated. "It's really all right. I don't mind . . ."

"Beat it," Tom said good-naturedly. "Get home to your wife and dinner." Then he turned to Linda and held out his glass. "Want to freshen up this one, baby? And pour some ginger ale for our cat girl."

Tom had two quick drinks. Then he noticed an envelope on the table. He picked it up. "Tomorrow's instructions from the Press Lady."

"You'd better read them," January said. "I mean . . . you might have an early call."

"Oh, I know about the call. It's Philadelphia . . . the Mike Douglas show. Then Washington."

"You're leaving?" Linda asked.

"Just for two days. Then I'm back here for a week. Then Chicago, Cleveland, Detroit . . . Then back here for another few days. Then Los Angeles."

"What time are you leaving tomorrow?" Linda asked.

He nodded toward the envelope. "Open it and see."

Linda ripped it open. "You don't leave until noon. It says the limo will pick you up then. But you have a nine o'clock breakfast date with Donald Zec."

"Yes. He's from London . . . doing a story on me for the London *Daily Mirror*." He stood up. "I'd better get to bed. I want to be awake for Donald. He's a buddy of mine." He started for the bedroom.

"January, I think your cat story is—"

"I've got to leave. I can take a cab," January said.

He turned on them. "You'll both leave together with the car. I'm going to get undressed, and when I call, you both can come and tuck me in, and we'll have one for the road together."

He disappeared into the bedroom. January looked at Linda and shrugged helplessly. Linda was furious. "I've got to find out when he leaves for the Chicago, Cleveland, Detroit tour. Because I'm going to be on it with him. I can't go to Philadelphia and Washington . . . it's too late to make reservations for hotels and all. Besides, I think he'll probably have the *Life* people with him." Suddenly she looked at January. "Look . . . get out . . . now."

"You mean, just leave?"

"Yes. And when I go in I'll say you really wanted to split."

"But Linda, that's so rude . . ."

"He doesn't really want you. He's just being polite. And you never really insisted on going. Bob Harvey was willing to go the few blocks out of his way, but you certainly didn't fight very hard."

"Well, holy smoke, Linda. I don't want Tom Colt to think I hate him. If I accept a theater invitation from him, I can't act as if he's suddenly contaminated. He'll think I'm rude."

"What do you care what he thinks? After he's in bed with me, he won't be doing any thinking. Come on, January—get your coat and go."

Suddenly Tom's voice bellowed from the bedroom. "Hey, girls, bring in the bottle and three glasses."

"Go on," Linda hissed.

"Linda, will you really tell him I *had* to work? Please."

"Yes . . . For God's sake, just get going!"

Suddenly he walked into the room. He was in a dressing gown. It was obvious he had nothing under it. "Hey, why are you both standing there like bookends? Get the booze and come on in."

Linda glared at January and took the bottle. They both went into the bedroom. Tom Colt propped himself up on the bed on top of the covers. "Now, we'll all have one for the road. Then you both can tiptoe out and put off the lights." When he saw Linda had only two glasses, he pointed toward the bathroom. "There's a glass in there. I want you to have a drink this time, January. To toast my road tour."

She went into the bathroom and obediently returned with the glass. He poured a good shot for each of them, and then poured half a glass full of straight bourbon for himself.

"Now . . . sit on each side of me." He patted the bed. Both girls sat down. He rumpled Linda's hair teasingly. "Now, we drink to the big author who is about to go out and sell himself like breakfast food. Step right this way, folks . . . come see the writer . . . laugh at him . . . hiss at him . . . do anything . . . as long as you *buy* him." He tossed half the drink down in one gulp. Linda finished hers in one swallow and stared at Tom for approval.

He winked, and refilled her glass. He freshened his own, then looked toward January. She had taken a sip . . . suddenly she bolted it down. He grinned and refilled her glass. Her throat was burning. For one second she thought this is how people must feel when they swallow poison. Then the burning gave way to a slight glow in her chest. She sipped the second drink . . . and once again, found the second went down easier. She kept taking small sips. It was better than burning her throat with one big gulp. She wondered if Tom realized that she and Linda also had not eaten any dinner. She felt giddy, as if she were outside, watching herself. She edged toward the end of the bed. Linda had put her head on Tom's chest. Almost absentmindedly, he was stroking her hair. He lifted her chin. Their eyes were close. January wondered how she could slip out. He leaned over and kissed Linda's brow. "You're a beautiful girl," he said slowly.

January knew she should leave . . . but she was paralyzed. Linda was staring into Tom's eyes. She looked as if she were about to dissolve.

"Linda," he said slowly. "You've got to help me."

Linda nodded dumbly.

He stroked her hair. "Linda . . . I'm kind of crazy about January. What shall I do?" For a moment the room was very still. It was as if time had suddenly stopped . . . like a wax museum with everyone frozen into position. Linda was still leaning close, staring into his eyes. January was sitting at the foot of the bed, still holding her glass. Seconds passed. Then she snapped into action. She jumped off the bed.

"The bathroom," she said suddenly. "I have to go." She dashed in and sank to the floor, resting her head in her arm on the bathtub. The whole tableau was unreal. Was Linda still sitting there gazing at Tom? How could he have said that? Or was it a gag . . . a private joke between them? Of course!

That was it! Right now they were probably in each other's arms laughing at the way she had fallen for it. Well . . . she hadn't fallen for it. She'd pretend to go along with it. Pretend she really had to go to the bathroom. She flushed the toilet several times. She let the water run in the sink and made a good deal of noise washing her hands. Then she opened the door and walked resolutely into the room.

Tom was sitting propped up against the pillows, staring at her. There was no sign of Linda. For a moment they both looked at one another. Then with almost a sad smile, he motioned her over. She moved slowly and gingerly sat on the edge of the bed.

"Where's Linda?" she asked.

"I sent her home."

She started to rise but he pulled her hand gently and she sat down again. "Don't be so uptight. I'm not going to rape you. I don't usually go around falling for a girl who has a father younger than I am. I can get all the girls I want . . . uncomplicated girls. I even marry them. Too often . . . That's my trouble. I think the kids today have the right idea about abolishing marriage. People should be together as long as they care about one another, not because it's a law, like a prison sentence. Now, here's the answers up front. No, I'm not wildly in love with my wife. I never really was, except she gave me a child and that was something I wanted. If I left her, she'd keep the baby. So I'll never let that happen. It's crazy . . . my wanting you. Linda would have been easier. No questions . . . just balling together. I tried to want Linda . . . but you got in the way. I found myself thinking about you all the time. I really didn't have to come back here and do the eastern part of the tour. The book is selling great—over fifty thousand copies so far and going into another twenty-five thousand printing. But I came here and agreed to go on with the tour because of you." He pulled her to him and kissed her on the lips gently. "Nothing is going to happen tonight, January. In fact nothing is going to happen until you feel the same way about me . . ."

"Tom. I . . . Oh, Tom, I do care for you . . . and I was horrified when I realized it . . . because you do have a wife and a child."

"But what we feel for one another has nothing to do with my child. I've already told you how I feel about my wife."

"Tom, I couldn't take it for just a week . . . or just for now . . . don't you understand?"

"January . . . love is never forever. Thank the fates and take it wherever you find it."

She looked at him steadily. "Do you love me, Tom?"

He looked thoughtful. "That's a heavy word. And I have to admit I've used it many times and never really meant it. But I kind of get the idea that if I use it with you, it'll have to be for real."

"Yes . . . it's the only way I could . . ." She tried desperately to find the right words. "You see I'd feel so guilty . . . I mean, I even feel guilty sitting here talking like this with you, knowing you are married, that you have a child. What we are doing is wrong . . . completely wrong . . . But if I felt you really loved me . . . and that no one could get hurt . . . except us . . . well, that's the only way we'd have a chance for anything at all. I'd figure maybe God wouldn't be too angry because we both are really in love—" She knew she was blushing and looked down at her hands. "I know I must sound like an idiot to you . . . and . . ."

He lifted her face and his eyes were gentle. "January, you're even more wonderful than I thought you'd be." Then he took her in his arms and stroked her hair as if he were comforting a child. After a few moments, he broke the embrace gently and got off the bed and led her into the living room. He picked up her coat and suddenly she flung herself into his arms. The coat dropped to the floor as he held her close and kissed her. And for the first time she understood the intimacy of a real kiss. Their bodies were close. She pressed against him, wanting to become part of him . . . Suddenly the phone jangled. It was the driver announcing he had returned.

"Time for you to go," he said as he picked up her coat.

"Oh God, Tom, I wish you weren't leaving."

"It's just for a few days. Maybe it's for the best . . . it will give us both a chance to think." Then he kissed her lightly and watched her go down the hall until she reached the elevator.

She felt elation . . . fear and excitement. It couldn't be

wrong. It had to be Fate . . . to have Tom live in Mike's suite. She would have her first real love affair in Mike's bed.

She sat back in the limousine and thought about it. She relived every event of the evening . . . everything he said. Then something bothered her. At first it was just a nagging thought that cut into her happiness. But by the time she got home, she was almost in panic. What had he meant when he said the two days would give them both a chance to think? Oh God, did that mean he was going to change his mind? Had she scared him off, talking about love and guilt? Would he come back and say, "I've thought about it, January . . . And we'd better not let anything happen." No, he wouldn't do that. He cared about her. And then in the darkness of the limousine, it suddenly occurred to her that when their bodies had been pressed together . . . he hadn't even had the slightest erection. Absolutely nothing! Oh God, maybe she didn't really turn him on . . . maybe she had really frightened him away!

Seventeen

SHE DIDN'T SLEEP all night. In some ways it was a more tormented night than the night she had learned Mike was married. That night she had just sat by the window in a stupor, unable to feel any distinct emotion other than a sense of loss. This sleepless night had been different. She had smoked an entire pack of cigarettes. *"It's just for a few days . . . Maybe it's for the best . . . It will give us both a chance to think."* The words haunted her. *Think about what?* Think about ending it before it really started. How could she have been so stupid? Demanding that he love her . . . What was it he had said? He had lied about love many times, but with her it would be a heavy word. Of course—she had scared him off. You don't go asking a man if he really loves you right off, not if you're cool. But she wasn't cool. She didn't want to play games with Tom. If they had anything between them, it would be rough enough because of his marriage . . . let alone playing games. She wanted an honest relationship with him, she wanted to be able to tell him how she felt, how much she loved him. . . .

At nine o'clock she dragged herself to the office. She had toyed with the idea of calling in sick to avoid the confrontation with Linda. But Linda had to be faced . . . sooner or later. She decided to get it over with and went directly to Linda's office.

To her amazement, Linda was smiling when she walked in. "Sit down. Have some coffee and give me the fabulous details."

"Linda . . . about last night . . . I—"

"January, I'm not upset," Linda said cheerfully. "At least,

not now. I must admit that I did contemplate various forms of suicide last night. But this morning I was back at my shrink's, sitting out in front of his office, at seven-thirty, waiting for him to come and open shop. I made him give me twenty minutes, even though there was a hysterical menopausal lady waiting in the outer office. And I told him everything. And by the time I finished I was sobbing louder than the menopausal lady. Then he said, 'Linda, I usually wait for you to find your own solutions. But for now, I will tell you that Tom Colt is not in love with you or January. For a man his age to have had so many women means he has to constantly prove something to himself. And for him to choose January definitely relates to her father.' Then he explained how in taking you, Tom Colt is getting back at your father."

"Wow," January said softly. "Remind me never to get involved with a shrink."

"You had one at that Clinique in Switzerland, didn't you?"

"Yes, but we never talked about anything personal. I mean he would just talk to give me confidence that I would walk and get back into the world and be with my father again. But that was all. I mean, how can you sit there and tell your innermost thoughts to a strange man, even if he is a psychiatrist?"

"Dr. Galens is not a strange man. He's a Freudian analyst, but he does believe in therapy for situational problems. Like me getting tossed out of bed for you. Later on, he'll still deal with it in a Freudian way and prove how it all relates back to my past. You see, even with my nose job and all, inside there is still an ugly little girl screaming to get out. That's why I need sex–to prove I'm attractive. And with you . . . everything relates to your father. Like even in the accident on the motorcycle. You got on the damn thing just to punish your father for going with Melba."

"You mean you told him about me!"

"Yes. He said you had an Electra complex. That's why you can't dig David. He's too young and handsome."

"Linda, you didn't tell him about that too!"

"Of course. He's my shrink, and he not only has to know everything about me, but also about the people I associate with. And as you can see, he's just great. You see, basically I'm a very shallow person . . . Oh, don't look shocked. I know I am. I have a superstar complex. Unfortunately, I can't sing as well as Barbra Streisand. As an actress, I'm not exactly Glenda Jackson. And Ann-Margret doesn't have to worry about me crowding her as a sex symbol. So how do I go about becoming a superstar? With *Gloss* magazine. Dr. Galens forced me to admit that my dedication to the magazine is not because I believe in it . . . but because I AM *Gloss*. And if *Gloss* makes it, so do I. I'm not a Democrat or a Republican. But in Seventy-two, no matter what the publisher says, *Gloss* will go all-out for the Democratic candidate, because I want to be part of the political picture. I don't know whether it's going to be Muskie, Lindsay, Humphrey, or Ted Kennedy. But nothing is going to stop me."

Then she smiled. "But the hell with that. I pay Dr. Galens to put my head in order. Tell me about last night. Was it great?"

"We didn't do anything. I mean . . . we just talked."

"You what?"

"Because—Linda, I'd rather not talk about it."

Linda nodded good-naturedly. "Don't feel bad. He was probably too drunk." Her voice changed and became all business. "Look, do you know how to work a tape recorder?"

"Yes."

"Okay. Take this." She handed January a small compact machine. "I guess it's obvious who is going to tour with Tom Colt. So each night, or each morning, or whatever . . . talk into it and tell about the tour. Tell everything as you see it. And from your tapes, Sara will write the story. Talk into the machine as if it were a diary. Don't leave anything out—"

"Linda, I can't."

"I don't mean your sex life. I just want you to tell *me* about that. Although from your track record, it could be a total disaster."

"What do you mean?"

"Look what happened with David."

"But I didn't love him. I . . . I care about Tom Colt."

Linda sighed. "Look, loving a guy, or caring about him, doesn't necessarily mean you're going to be great in the kip.

Some of the biggest courtesans in the world were lesbians, yet they made men go out of their minds. It takes finesse, not just love. And this isn't just a man. This is Tom Colt—a legend in his own lifetime and all that jazz."

"I've lived with a legend. And they're human."

"Oh, is that it? So that's why you've fallen for him. Because your father has shown his cracks you're looking for someone who is bigger and better. Your own private superman. Right?"

"Linda . . . know what? I think you're over-analyzed."

"Okay. But take this tape machine. And maybe in the end when we play them back, we'll not only find out what Tom Colt is like . . . but maybe we'll find the real January Wayne."

She tried talking into the tape—about Tom . . . her first impressions of him . . . the cocktail party . . . his strength . . . his gentleness. But when she played it back, it sounded like a high school girl's diary.

She spent a murderous day. Suppose Tom never called again. Suppose he decided he wanted out. Had she really bungled it? At four o'clock she left the office. Maybe if she tried to write about it, if she faced a typewriter and a blank piece of paper she might be able to write dispassionately of her meeting with Tom . . . and then read it off to the tape machine. She decided to walk home to clear her head. She tried to tell herself everything would be all right. But she kept hearing the words—*Perhaps it's for the best. It will give us both time to think things over.*

"Think things over." What did that mean? It had to mean that he wanted to pull out. Oh God, if only Mike were here, if only there was someone she could talk to . . .

She got home and checked with her message service. Nothing. Suddenly the room seemed to close in on her. Empty Coke bottles, littered ashtrays . . . Remnants of last night's ordeal were strewn around the apartment. She began to clean up. Suddenly she felt she had to get out of that room. She had to talk to someone.

She rushed to the phone and called David. He answered on the second ring. "January, this is a nice surprise. It goes down with all of the big firsts in my life. This is the first time you've called me."

"I . . . well . . . I've been working hard on a story, and I'm afraid I'm stumped. I need a man's point of view. David . . . could you take me to dinner tonight? I need to talk things out with someone."

"Oh, my poor angel . . . of all nights. I have a seven-thirty dinner date with a client. But look . . . I'm free until then. Want me to come up for a drink? It's only five-thirty."

"No, let me meet you somewhere. I've got to get out of here."

"January . . . is anything wrong?"

"No, it's just that I've been cooped up in the apartment writing."

He laughed. "I'm very impressed. Look, I have to be somewhere on the East Side at seven-thirty. Could we meet at the Unicorn? That way it will give us more time."

"Yes, David. I can be there in ten minutes."

"Make it fifteen," he laughed. "I just got home and I want to give my face a fast runover with the electric shaver."

They sat in the Unicorn at a small table. David stared in amazement when she ordered a Jack Daniels. She hated the drink, but somehow it made her feel close to Tom.

"All right." He smiled. "Now, tell me what's the big hang-up with America's newest and most beautiful writer."

"Well, it's a short story I'm trying my hand at. And I just realized I'm writing it all from the woman's angle and I've got to get the man's point of view."

He nodded seriously. "Good thinking." He looked at his watch. "Go ahead. Tell me about it."

"Well, I have my heroine in love with a married man, a man much older than she is . . ."

"Oh, he's got grandchildren and all that?"

"No, he has a baby . . . and a wife. No grandchildren."

"How old is he?"

"In his late fifties."

"Then you're writing it wrong. A man in his late fifties should have grandchildren, not a baby. Make it grandchildren . . . more pathos already."

"That's not important. The crux of my story is the relationship between the man and the girl."

"How old is the girl?"

She took a good swallow of the bourbon. "She's . . . I haven't really decided."

"Make her around thirty-two. A man in his fifties rarely marries anyone younger. Otherwise it won't work. And if he has a baby with the other woman . . . well, she has to be in her thirties, too."

"Why couldn't the girl be in her twenties?"

"Well, only if the man is an unmitigated louse. Then you could even make her fourteen. But if he has a wife and baby and falls in love with another woman—she has to be a woman, not a girl."

"All right, suppose she is in her thirties, and they fall in love and she has a guilt feeling about the wife and baby . . . and refuses to go along with it for like a one-night stand. But she's mad about him, and tells him she doesn't expect to break up his marriage or anything like that, but if they have a relationship it has to be love . . ."

"So, what's your problem?"

"Do you think she would be wrong in telling him that?"

He looked at his drink. "Why would she be wrong? Every girl says that, even if it's a one-night stand."

"I don't mean it that way, David. I mean, what if they were together for several days . . . no sex . . . just thrown together . . . then separated. And when he came back, he told her he wanted her, and she said, 'You'll have to say you love me, and—' "

"Oh, no," he groaned. "January, what are you writing for, *Screen Romances*? A girl knows better than to demand that a guy says he loves her."

"She does?"

"Of course. That's the quickest way to scare him off."

"Okay. The girl in my story is kind of an idiot. And what's more, she says it just before he goes off on a business trip. She tells him she won't settle for less than love, and also that she'll miss him the few days that he's gone. And he says, 'It's just for a few days. Maybe it's for the best. It will give us both a chance to think.' "

He was silent for a second. Then he smiled. "Beautiful!"

"What?"

"January, maybe you can really write at that. What a finish. I can see it. That's your last line, followed by dot dot dot. And then you leave it to your reader. Does he . . . or doesn't he come back!"

She took another sip of the bourbon. "As a reader, what would you think?"

He laughed as he waved for the check. "She's blown it. She'll never see him again."

"Will everyone feel that way?"

He scribbled his name on the check and shook his head. "No, that's why it's great. Women will probably feel he will, but a man will understand. It's the biggest cop-out line in the world. That 'Give us both a chance to think' bit."

"You make it all seem so final," she said.

He stood up and helped her with her coat.

"Well, honey, you're the one who wrote it."

Eighteen

THE FOLLOWING NIGHT she accepted a date from Ned Crane, a dull but attractive young man she had met with David. He had called her several times, and she had always refused. But suddenly anything seemed preferable to another long, sleepless night. They went to Le Club, joined up with a group of his friends, and for a short time she almost welcomed the noise and frenzied activity. She sipped white wine, allowed herself to be pushed around the floor, and even tried to join in the conversation. By eleven o'clock, she suddenly felt drained. She fought to hide her yawns and wondered how she could break away. She was saved at eleven-thirty when someone suggested going over to Vera's for backgammon. January said she didn't know Vera and she didn't play backgammon, and she finally convinced Ned that she would be perfectly safe taking a cab home.

She fell into bed at midnight and was so exhausted that she slept. She was still asleep when her phone service rang her at eight-thirty.

"Miss Wayne, I just came on duty and I notice you didn't call in and get your messages last night."

"Oh. Holy smoke. I was so tired . . . I even forgot to set the alarm. Thanks for calling. I've got to get up anyway."

"Don't you want your messages?"

"Oh . . . oh, sure . . . yes."

"Sara Kurtz called. Said she expects some tapes by this afternoon. That you would understand."

"Oh, yes. Thank you."

"And a Mr. Colt called from Washington."

"*What?*"

"A Mr. Colt called from Washington at eight-thirty P.M., and again at ten. He wanted you to call him at the Shoreham Hotel."

"Oh, thank you. Thank you!"

"I'm sorry if I woke you."

"No . . . no, it's wonderful. I . . . I should be up anyhow. Thank you so much!"

She caught Tom at the Shoreham just as he was leaving. "Oh, Tom . . . I came home at twelve and forgot all about checking with my service. I'm so sorry."

"Wait a minute." He laughed. "First . . . how are you?"

"I'm fine . . . no, I'm not . . . I miss you. How are you? Do you miss me?"

"Yes . . . to everything."

"When will you be back?"

"Friday night. Will you have dinner with me?"

"Will I . . . oh wow . . . I mean . . . yes, I'd adore it."

"Okay. I'll call you as soon as I get in."

"Okay. Look, Tom. Maybe I should call you . . . you know . . . I could keep checking at the Plaza . . . because you might miss me between the office and my apartment."

"I'll find you, January. Don't worry." And then he hung up.

She spent the morning trying to tape an unemotional account of the cocktail party for Tom Colt. His attitude, the people who were there, the trapped feeling an author has when he's spotlighted as guest of honor.

Linda played it and nodded. "Sounds okay. I'll give it to Sara." Then she stared at January. "What's the matter with you? You look awful."

She was silent for a moment, then she said, "Linda, I don't know what to do . . . I'm so scared."

"Of what?"

"Well, Tom gets in tomorrow—"

"Don't tell me you're still going to play the virgin queen."

"No . . . I . . . I want to go to bed with him. But suppose I don't arouse him."

"A man like Tom Colt will be aroused. Don't worry."

January stared at her hands in her lap. "Linda, when he held me close that night at the Plaza . . . he . . . he wasn't wearing anything under the robe . . . and . . ."

"And?"

"There was nothing," January said.

Linda whistled. "I forgot. Sure. He's in his late fifties and he drinks. That combination is murder. You'll have to start right off by giving him head."

"I don't think I could. I . . . I don't even know how."

"Pretend it's a popsicle—pretend—oh, hell . . . that's something that takes practice. If I say so myself, I give the best head in town. Every man says that. But you've got to get started. Part of it is instinctive. And a man like Tom will guide you . . ."

"But . . . what happens if he comes?"

"You swallow it."

"*What!*"

Linda groaned. "January, when you're making love with someone you really care about, it's the ultimate fulfillment and expression of love. The man ejaculating it . . . you taking it . . . and swallowing it. Swallowing part of him."

"Linda, I may throw up! That's the most revolting thing I've ever heard."

Linda laughed. "Listen, stone-age lady. It's also very good for you. It's loaded with hormones. It's also great for your skin. I use it as a facial mask whenever I can."

"*You what!*"

"I use it as a mask. When Keith was living with me and we were doing it every night, I'd do the hand bit maybe three times a week, and just before the explosion came, I'd be ready with a glass. Then I poured it into a bottle and put it in the refrigerator. It's great for a facial mask. It's like egg white . . . only better. You leave it on ten minutes until it stiffens, then wash it off with cold water. Why do you think I let that jerk from the advertising agency stay . . . I got half a glass from him."

"Linda, that's the most awful thing I ever heard. I just couldn't. I'm nauseous. It's—"

"Well, when you go down on Tom, if you can't get yourself

to swallow it, let it come all over your face . . . rub it into your skin and . . ."

January jumped up. "Linda, I can't listen! I—"

"Sit down! Jesus, I realize you spent three years away from everyone and everybody in Switzerland. And Miss Haddon's wasn't exactly a place Masters and Johnson would go for research. No one is telling you that you *have* to do any of the things I tell you. But it's time you learned people who do these things are not degenerates . . . and the least you can do is listen!"

"All right. But I don't want to rub, swallow, or package any of that stuff."

"Okay. But you also can't just lie back and give him the pleasure of allowing him to enter you. It *is* a two-way thing."

"But what do I do?"

"Respond!"

"How?"

"Oh Jesus!" Linda got up and paced the room. Then she leaned over the desk, her eyes level with January's. "You did kiss back when he kissed you, didn't you?"

"Yes."

"And then what! Did you respond?"

"Yes."

"Good girrrl! Now, when you're in bed with him and when he kisses your boobs, start feeling him."

"Where?"

"Oh God, January . . . anywhere. Start rubbing the back of his head. Kiss his neck . . . his ears, . . . his cheek . . . just to let him know you're alive. That you *like* what he's doing. Move and groan in pleasure, bite him—"

"Bite him?"

"Oh, not to draw blood . . . playful bites . . . like a kitten . . . scratch his back . . . then let your hands travel . . . then later your tongue . . ."

"Oh my God—" January leaned back in the chair. "Linda, suppose I can't. Suppose I suddenly get uptight when I actually am in bed with him."

Linda stared at her for a moment. "I know." She snapped her fingers. "What time are you seeing him tomorrow?"

"When he gets back from Washington. For dinner."

"Then at four, you take a vitamin shot."

"A vitamin shot?"

Linda was spinning her rolodex. She stopped at a card and scribbled down a name and address. "Here. Dr. Simon Alpert. He and his brother Preston are fantastic. Keith took me to him a few times when he was on the health kick. He's still on it, I guess. He has to be to get it up for Christina Spencer."

"But how will vitamin shots make me feel sexy about Tom Colt?"

"Look, all I know is that when Keith made me take one of those shots, the whole world exploded . . . everything became technicolor. I worked twenty hours a day. I had orgasms with Keith that seemed to last an hour. I was great in bed without being too aggressive. Keith always said I was too aggressive because I was always directing him. That's his male chauvinism. I mean, when he's going down on me, what's wrong if I say . . . go more to the left . . . or harder . . . or lighter. Some men feel that if they dive, we're supposed to be grateful. The ones who make a token dive are the ones who kill me. You know . . . touch it with their tongues for one second and then look at you as if they have given you the Kohinoor diamond. And for that, you are then supposed to flip out and go down on them for hours . . . even if their dingle is like spaghetti. But, anyway, when I had a vitamin shot it seems I adored everything he did without once being a stage manager. They're really fabulous. It's some kind of a combination of the Vitamin B's plus some E. Dr. Alpert mixes it in front of you. Try to get Dr. Simon Alpert rather than Preston—he's got a gentler touch with the needle. But they're dynamite. Listen, they have to be great—they cost twenty-five bucks a shot. And if Keith shelled out that kind of money . . . well, you know. I took about three of them . . . I think they also have some appetite depressant in them because I didn't even want to touch food. A lot of women who are overweight go there. In fact, a lot of doctors give them. There's one who's supposed to give them to big stars, some Washington big shots, a big composer, and several Hollywood producers."

"Why didn't you keep taking them?"

"At twenty-five a shot? They last about three days. One

woman I met in the waiting room told me she took four shots a week. But then I broke up with Keith, so I didn't need all that energy. Certainly not for the Leons who come into my life."

"But isn't it dangerous?"

"Listen, January, you're twenty-one, you've had one affair that you hated. With a dreamy guy . . . that you didn't dig. So David went down the drain. Now you've got a shot at Tom Colt . . . and you sit here and tell me you're afraid of failing. God, if I had a date with him coming up, I'd be rushing up Madison Avenue to find some divine outfit, not sitting and wondering how I was going to make him get a hard on. *That's* the only thing I'd be sure of . . ."

January smiled. "You make me sound like I'm retarded . . . sexually."

Linda laughed. "Listen, there's nothing wrong with you that a good fuck won't cure. Now call Dr. Alpert and make the appointment for this afternoon. You'll never get out of bed. Oh . . . and stop into Leon's office and ask him to get you a popper."

"What's that?"

"Ammies. You put it in a Benzedrex inhaler and leave it on the night table. Then you each take a sniff just as you are about to come. It's wild!"

"Linda, can I ask you something? Tell me. Doesn't anyone just go to bed with someone they care about and have a real good old-fashioned affair?"

"Of course, darling—that's what you had with David!"

She left the office at five and rushed home. She took a long bath. Then she doused herself with perfume. She laid out two outfits. Slacks and a shirt; a long skirt and silk blouse—depending on where he wanted to go. She put on her new Pucci bra; she wondered if Linda would say Pucci bras were out. But then Linda said all bras were out.

At seven, she was still sitting in her bra staring at the phone. She had smoked half a pack of cigarettes and had taken a sip of Jack Daniels. She had bought a bottle in case he came over. She had also bought real coffee and some eggs. She didn't know what she expected—but she just wanted to be prepared.

By eight o'clock she had called the Plaza three times. Each time, the operator confirmed: Yes, they were holding a reservation for Mr. Colt, but he had not checked in.

His call came at nine. "January . . . forgive me. The planes weren't going because of weather. So I had to take the train. It was supposed to get in at six. That's why I didn't call. But there was an hour wait in Baltimore. And would you believe it? We had to stop in Trenton for half an hour because a woman was in labor—"

"Oh, Tom . . . no!" She was so relieved to hear from him that she was actually laughing.

"Look, I'm beat . . ." (Her heart dropped.) "Would it be all right with you if we just had some room service here at the Plaza?"

"Look, Tom . . . if you're too tired to see me, I understand." (What was she saying!)

"No, I've got to eat. And I'm starving . . . unless it's too late for you."

"I'll be right there."

"Good. You'll find my car in front of your place."

"You mean . . . you knew I would come."

"Of course. Weren't you the one who said . . . no games?"

He was waiting at the door when she came down the hall. She flung herself into his arms and he kissed her lightly. "God, you look great," he said. "Come on in . . . the steaks are on their way. I figured a girl in love wouldn't care what she ate."

He was full of his trip. He had hated every minute of it. He felt like a trained monkey, especially on TV. The performers all told him they were his fans, yet he admired the ease with which they went on, their cool as they sat under the lights and ad-libbed with one another. When he came on, he felt like a prehistoric animal—oversized, out of context, out of place. But the hosts of the shows had all helped him, and somehow he had gotten through. "You earn every book you sell," he said. Then he added that he had hit number three on *The New York Times* Best Seller list.

They had dinner, and then they sat together on the couch watching the late news as he drank bourbon. She sipped at hers slowly. Tom seemed surprised that she wanted one. But she knew that if they were going into that bedroom she had to feel relaxed. Suddenly he turned to her and said, "Listen . . . how would you feel about the beach?"

"Westhampton?"

"Yes. Hugh invited me up. We can stay over. He sleeps out on the beach half the night anyway. And he said he'd bunk down on the couch if he wanted to come in."

"When?" she asked.

"Tomorrow. We could leave at three. I have two interviews in the morning."

"I'd love it," she said.

He stood up and took her into his arms and kissed her gently. His hands slipped under her shirt and under the bra. She remembered what Linda had said—"Do something. Show him you care!" Tentatively she let her hand roam . . . down his back . . . toward the front. Suddenly he pulled away. "Look, it's late and I'm beat. We'll have the weekend together."

He got her coat and walked her to the door. "January," he said, "you haven't mentioned it once all evening."

"Mentioned what?"

"Love." He smiled. "Do you still love me?"

"Oh God, Tom . . . you know I do."

He smiled and kissed her lips lightly. She wondered why he had said that. Suddenly she looked up at him. "Tom . . . do you love me?"

He nodded slowly. "I think I do . . . I really think I do."

She was at Dr. Alpert's office at nine o'clock the following morning. She filled out the card the receptionist gave her. She was a bit apprehensive. But she realized she needed something. Last night Tom had broken the embrace . . . because he had not had an erection. He had pulled away because he hadn't wanted her to know. She had not aroused him. All the Fracas perfume, the Pucci bra—a waste.

She had called Linda at midnight. And when Linda yelled, "What happened?" and she had answered, "Nothing," Linda advised her to get to Dr. Alpert's unless she wanted to blow the whole weekend.

"But is it possible for a man to love you and not get an erection?"

"Oh Jesus, January, do you know how many guys come to

me in wild heat, leap on me, and then their cock turns to rubber and we practically have to fold it in."

"Linda!"

"Will you stop yelling 'Linda' and get with it? This man has had every kind of woman in the world. He's also fifty-seven and slightly weary. You've got to turn him on. The sight of that nymphet body of yours isn't going to turn him on. *You've* got to do it."

She sat in Dr. Alpert's office and filled out all the questions on the card. Then the receptionist took her to a private cubicle equipped with just an examining table. There were at least seven cubicles in the office. And they were all filled. The waiting room had already begun to get crowded when she left it. The receptionist pointed to the paper coat and said, "Take everything off and then go to the end of the hall." She wrapped the crinkly examining robe around her and went to the room down the hall. A nurse was waiting with a cardiograph machine. She motioned for January to lie on the couch. Then she attached the electrodes.

When the test was over, the nurse led her to another room. "And now, Miss Wayne, we'll take some blood samples."

"But I'm just here for a vitamin shot. I told that to Dr. Alpert on the phone this morning."

"Dr. Alpert always wants a complete examination on the first visit."

January held out her arm. She winced as the nurse took the blood. And even more when she pricked her finger. But it gave her a sense of confidence. This was really a doctor to be reckoned with. He was thorough. No wonder his shots were good.

Finally she was led back to her cubicle. She sat on the edge of the examining table and waited. His office had been crowded. But she had purposely come early, explaining, as Linda had told her to say, that she was making a plane and had to be out by noon.

After about fifteen minutes a middle-aged man with a stethoscope hanging around his neck, entered the room. His smile was warm. "I'm Dr. Simon Alpert. Now, what's your problem? Feel listless? I noted your blood count is only ten. That's slightly anemic. Nothing to worry about. But you should be twelve."

She noticed his collar was frayed and his fingernails were dirty. It seemed impossible that this man was responsible for the beautiful Park Avenue office, the efficient antiseptic nurse and receptionist. Perhaps he was like Einstein who never combed his hair and walked around in sneakers. His teeth were tartar-stained, and since his smile was perpetual, she found herself studying the discolored teeth. His gums weren't good either. He certainly looked as if he could use some vitamins.

"Now just exactly what is it that brings you here? I understand Miss Riggs, a former patient, recommended you."

She looked away, then studied her own immaculate nails. "Well . . . I . . . there's a man I've been seeing and—"

"We don't handle abortions here . . . and we don't give the pill."

"No, it's nothing like that. You see this man is divine, every woman finds him attractive, and I—"

"Say no more." He smiled knowingly. "I get the picture. He's walked out on you. You're depressed. Uptight. Stay there." He waddled out of the room.

In less than five minutes he returned with a syringe. "This will make you feel like a new woman. You'll get him back. I know." He was adjusting the needle. She hoped he had washed his hands. "Young things like you, you fall in love, give too much of yourselves. The man gets bored, and then you start phoning him . . . right?" He went on before she could answer. "Sure, it's the same story . . . phoning him . . . begging him . . . pleading . . . driving him farther away. It's the same story all the time."

He untied the string of her examining robe. It fell to her waist, but he barely noticed her nudity. He put the stethoscope between her breasts, listened, seemed content with what he heard. Then he swabbed the vein of her arm. "Listen, don't call him. Promise Uncle Simon . . . don't call the bastard." She felt the needle go into her vein. She looked away. Amazingly enough he did have a light touch . . . no real pain. She turned and saw her own blood floating back into the syringe . . . then watched it gradually return to her arm along with the contents of the syringe. He smiled. "Now, hold your arm up like this." He placed a piece of cotton on the needle mark. "Just hold it like that for a second. You have beautiful veins."

She couldn't believe it. But she felt an instant reaction. A slight sense of floating . . . light-headed . . . but a nice feeling. Then suddenly a wonderful feeling of warmth shot through her . . . like when she got sodium pentothal in Rome . . . that amazing fluidity that went through her entire body. Only instead of the nothingness and sleep the pentothal caused, she felt crackling with life. She had a wild urge to touch herself between her legs because that's where she was vibrating with a pulsing sensation.

Dr. Alpert smiled. "Feel better?" He tweaked the tip of one of her breasts and she laughed. Because it wasn't the gesture of a dirty old man. It was just a nice gesture of friendship by Uncle Simon.

"You'll be fine," he said. "We'll have your blood up to twelve or thirteen in no time. Maybe you'll want a shot a week . . . or sign up for a series. Take that up with Miss Sutton, my receptionist. Some people like them twice a week . . . or milder forms every day. I have a man whose blood is fifteen, but he takes one every day. He's a famous composer and he works eighteen hours a day. He pours energy into his work so he needs them often. And so do you skinny little things who make love all night and work all day." Then he tweaked her breast again and waddled out of the room.

She leaped off the examining table and the white robe fell to the floor. She ran her fingers down her breasts. She did it again. The nipples hardened. She felt that divine unbelievable feeling between her legs. She touched herself. Oh, how glorious. Oh, beautiful Dr. Alpert with the dirty fingernails and the wonderful vitamins. She realized with a new clarity that she had probably only been half functioning until now. Maybe she had been anemic all her life. That is, since the accident. Of course . . . before that . . . she always felt alive like this when she was with Mike. And now, she felt alive again . . . aware. The world was waiting to belong to her!

She dressed quickly and wrote a check for one hundred and twenty dollars for the cardiogram and blood tests and the shot. The receptionist explained from here on the shot would cost twenty-five dollars unless she wanted a series of twenty; then it would cost four hundred dollars payable in advance. January smiled. She'd take them as she needed them and pay twenty-five.

She stopped off at Saks and bought Tom a tie. She went to Gucci's and sent Linda a belt she had admired, and wrote on the note, "Thank you for Dr. Alpert." Then she rushed home and packed. And when the buzzer rang at three and the chauffeur announced the car was waiting, she floated down in the elevator eager for the weekend ahead.

She couldn't wait to see Tom. And she also looked forward to seeing Hugh . . . he was wonderful, too! The whole world was wonderful!

Nineteen

Tom loved the tie. "I'll wear it on all my TV appearances," he said. He had a bottle in the car and offered her a drink. She shook her head. "You're my high," she insisted. And when they arrived at Westhampton, she flung herself into Hugh Robertson's arms. If he was surprised at the exuberance of her greeting, he did not show it. But she had thought about that day they had all spent at Westhampton so many times that her return felt like a homecoming. The oversized couch and fireplace were exactly as she remembered them. The sound of the surf seemed far away, even though she could see the ocean through the picture window in the living room. They sat around the fire. Tom sipped at his drink and Hugh cooked the steaks. She cuddled against Tom on the huge sofa, leaping up now and then to help Hugh with the food.

At ten o'clock, Hugh stood up. "Well, it's time for me to hit the dunes."

"You'll freeze," January said.

"Oh, I won't stay long tonight. I've got a workroom behind the kitchen with a studio bed in there. I often sleep there. Sometimes I just don't feel like going to all the trouble of climbing the stairs to go to bed. So you both enjoy the room with a clear conscience."

After Hugh left, January and Tom sat watching the crackling of the logs on the fire and listening to the rumble of the waves lapping at the shore. January never grew tired of watching the waves—there was something stubborn in the way they would rise in strength, dissipate themselves against the beach, and then regroup and try again. They reminded her of mischievous little children, scampering to the beach, only to be dragged back by their mother.

She snuggled closer to Tom and traced his profile with her fingertips. He leaned over and kissed her. Then he picked up the bottle of bourbon, took her by the hand, and led her upstairs.

The room was a reconverted attic. The owner was obviously very patriotic. It was painted white and the furniture was bright blue and red enamel. A huge feather bed dominated the center of the room. January flopped on it, kicked off her shoes, and jumped up and down. "Tom . . . come on in . . . wow . . . no springs. It's like floating." Then she leaped off the bed and came to him. "I love you," she said as she unbuttoned her blouse. Their eyes met and held as she dropped her jeans to the floor. Slowly she unhooked her bra and stepped out of her pants. "Here I am," she said softly.

He stared at her for a moment with a slow smile. She put her arms around his neck. "Come on, lazy," she whispered as she unbuttoned his shirt. "Let's go to bed."

He turned toward the bureau and poured himself a drink. He swallowed it quickly, then reached out and switched off the light. She lay on the bed and watched him undress in the darkness. She could see the contrast of his buttocks against his tanned shoulders and back. His thighs were strong . . . then he turned and jumped on the bed with such force that it creaked. They both laughed and hugged one another. He was on top of her, resting his weight on his arms. He stroked her hair and in the darkness he whispered, "Oh, baby, I want to make you happy."

"I am happy, Tom." She put her arms around his neck and pulled him down to kiss her. He rolled to his side and held her close as they kissed. She ran her fingers down his back. She felt relaxed and at ease, as if their bodies had always been close like this. She was eager to touch him . . . to be taken by him . . . to belong to him.

Then he eased away and she felt his tongue streaking across her body . . . on her breasts . . . her stomach . . . she clutched his head . . . the feeling was so warm and wonderful. But she wanted to please *him* . . . to do anything he wished . . . his tongue was on her thigh . . . his fingers were exploring her . . . every nerve of her body was responding . . . his tongue seemed everywhere . . . and then she felt an insane sensation . . . so unbearably wonderful. She couldn't believe what was happening . . . she had never felt anything like it. She moaned. Her entire body was dissolving into an explosion of ecstasy . . . she held his head and shivered . . . and finally fell back wrung out and exhausted. He came up and lay beside her and stroked her breasts. "Did I make you happy?"

"Oh God, Tom . . . I never felt anything like that . . . but . . . we didn't do it . . . I mean . . . you—"

"I wanted to make you happy," he said

"And now—" Her strength was returning. Now he would enter her.

"And now we'll just hold one another in our arms."

She lay very still. Something was wrong. He held her close . . . but she felt sick with panic. She hadn't aroused him. She began kissing his neck . . . stroking his body. She wasn't quite sure how to go about it . . . but perhaps if she imitated him. She got on top of him and began kissing his chest. Then she slid down. But there was no big throbbing thing like David had thrust at her . . . something inert lay between his legs. It was about the size of a man's thumb. She couldn't believe it. How could a man Tom Colt's size—a man as virile as Tom—have such a tiny penis? She began to stroke it, but there was no reaction. Then she put her lips to it. She felt a sudden surge of protective tenderness toward him. Tom Colt, whose fiction exploded with volatile sex . . . Tom Colt, the man women worshipped, the man other men looked up to . . . Tom Colt, the living symbol of man—with a boy's penis! God, how this must have haunted him throughout his life. She had worried at school when her breasts didn't grow large enough . . . but at least she had something. But for a man to have nothing . . . the penis was his entire sex object. Oh God, so this was the reason for all the prizefights . . . the scuba diving . . . the championship golf and tennis . . . the barroom brawls. She made love to him with an added tenderness. Poor, poor Tom

. . . to have to write his sex fantasies because he couldn't live them.

He suddenly pulled her up to him. "January . . . don't feel you've failed me. My pleasure is in making you happy."

She lay very still. She wondered how many other women he had said the same thing to. And suddenly she was determined to make him feel like a man. She began to stroke him. She let her tongue run up and down his arm . . . his hips . . . She tantalized him . . . coming closer to him . . . then stroking him and pulling away . . . and she saw the small penis begin to stiffen . . . she kept playing the game . . . letting her lips brush against it . . . then darting off to another part of his body . . . her fingers explored him . . . suddenly he rolled her over and got on top of her . . . he began to move steadily . . . faster . . . and with urgency . . . and then she heard him moan and felt his body go limp. He stayed on top of her for a few seconds. Then he looked into her eyes and said, "Thank you, January."

"Thank you, Tom."

He pulled away from her and took her into his arms. "January . . . I love you."

"And I love you," she whispered.

He stroked her hair. "Do you know what you've done for me?" he said. "This is the first time I've made it in ten years."

"I'm so glad, Tom." She kissed his cheek and it was wet. Then she saw the tears in his eyes. "Tom . . . is anything wrong?" He buried his head against her neck and she held him close and comforted him as she would a child. After a few minutes, he got out of bed and walked to the bureau. He took a long swig of bourbon and kept his back to her. "January, I'm sorry–I–"

She jumped out of bed and went to him. "Tom . . . I love you."

He turned and looked at her. "I'm sorry about letting go like that. I don't think I've shed a tear in twenty years."

"Did I do anything to cause it?" she asked.

He stroked her head. "No, baby . . ." He led her back to bed and they lay beside one another. He held her close and said, "You've made me very happy, January. I think the tears were for both of us. For me because I've found a girl with such class . . . and for you because you're only getting the remnants of Tom Colt. Not that my equipment was any better . . . a man can only use what he's got . . . but at least it was always workable. For the last ten years it's been call girls, aphrodisiacs . . . you name it—nothing worked. Until tonight . . . with you."

"But Tom . . . You have a baby."

"I want you to know the truth. You see, all my life women went along with me . . . accepted the fact that I wasn't built like a stallion. But they wanted to be seen with me. And hell, I could satisfy them in other ways. But a few years ago I got to thinking . . . all the years of writing, all my body of work . . . who was I leaving it to . . . who would care? I had no one. I lost two brothers in World War Two. I have an older sister who has no children. And suddenly I realized I wanted a kid. So I decided to adopt one. But you have to be married to adopt a child. So I started casing all the women I knew, trying to figure out which one would make the best mother. None of them fit. Either they had kids of their own from another husband . . . or they frankly stated they hated kids. There was just no one around who fit the bill. Then about a year and a half ago I ran into Nina Lou Brown, a little starlet type at a party at Malibu. She was slightly over the hill for a starlet . . . twenty-seven at the time . . . and she had just about given up. She was doing some TV commercials. She came on strong and we got to talking. She told me she was from Georgia and had twelve brothers and sisters and hadn't worn shoes until she was twelve. She loved kids and said she was even thinking of marrying a cameraman she knew because she wanted kids and at twenty-seven she felt she was getting on. At first it all sounded too good to be true . . . but I realized it was no put on because she didn't know I wanted a kid. Our host had two little boys and later in the afternoon, the youngest one, he was about five, got a splinter in his foot. A big angry-looking thing from some driftwood. He wouldn't let his mother touch him. Suddenly Nina Lou moved in. She began to play a game with him. Told him she bet he could help her get it out. She asked for a glass of Scotch. She made him stick the needle into the Scotch to sterilize it. But she told him she was going to get his foot drunk. Well, believe it or not, he allowed her to pick that damn thing out . . . and it was wedged in there deep as hell. When it was over, he kissed her. And I knew right then that she would be the mother of my kid.

"We dated for about a month. And I never went to bed with her. But I asked her to marry me and I explained about my problem. And it was Nina Lou who came up with the idea. Artificial insemination. It had never occurred to me. We got married . . . went straight to a doctor . . . it took several months . . . but it worked. And six months ago she bore me a son."

January lay very still. Tom lit a cigarette and handed it to her. "Now you know the story of my life."

"Wow," January said softly. "Then you really must be in love with her."

"Grateful is the word. I was never in love with her. But I love her for what she gave me. In exchange, I've given her sexual freedom . . . as long as she's discreet. She's got a young actor type who comes and services her now and then. But she's a hell of a mother to Tom, Junior. And she likes being Mrs. Tom Colt—she likes the prestige, the parties she's invited to, the house at Malibu . . . And the marriage is working, if you can call it a marriage. But hell, I can't expect a girl of twenty-nine to give up normal sex for the rest of her life. She loves the baby and—"

"Tom . . . it happened with us tonight. Did you ever really try with her? It seems to me you weren't even going to try with me."

He shook his head. "Of course I tried. She was positive she could work miracles. I suffered the humiliation of letting her try . . . night after night . . . until we finally agreed there was no chance. I never expected anything to happen with us tonight . . . but I cared for you enough to let you know the score—" He held her closer. "January, you can see what you've done for me. Even if it never happens again . . . I'll be grateful for the rest of my life."

"It will happen again."

"January, I can't get a divorce. Nina Lou would never give

it to me . . . and I can't give up my son. I want him to have everything. That's why I agreed to do the tour bit. I have enough money to live fine for the rest of my life. But I want to leave a bundle to her and my son." He got off the bed and brought the bottle back. "Shall we have a nightcap?"

She shook her head. "I'm happy this way," she whispered.

He took a long drink. "I don't know how to put it in words . . . I love you . . . like I've never loved any woman. I never leveled with any woman except you and Nina Lou. I had to with her, but I wanted to with you. I've been a heel with most women. I just tell them *they* don't turn me on. I act like maybe with the right woman my pecker grows six feet. Look, I don't know how long you'll want me, but as long as you do . . . it's going to be your way . . . no games. I'll love you all the way . . . and if you want what there is of me . . . then . . . I belong to you."

She held him close. "Oh, Tom . . . I love you. And I want you . . . and I'll be with you whenever you want me . . . and for as long as you want me . . . forever . . . we *are* forever. I swear it."

They lay together for a while, and after a time his even breathing told her he was asleep. She was still wide awake and longed for a cigarette. She also wanted to think things out. She loved him—the size of a man's penis wasn't a barometer for love. She had to convince him of this. She slid out of bed, careful not to disturb him, put on her robe and tiptoed down the steps. The living room was deserted and the fire was just about dying. She put some newspaper on it and added another log. Soon it was crackling and warm. She sat on the couch, her legs curled under her, and stared into the fire and thought about Tom. She had always thought all men were built pretty much alike. Oh, she knew some were larger than others . . . but she never knew anyone could be like Tom. Suddenly she wondered about her father. Was he a stallion like David? Of course. He would have to be. But poor Tom. Her emotions were confused. She thought of him protectively, yet with tenderness and desire. It was the desire to be in his arms . . . to feel his bare chest against her breasts . . . to feel the closeness of him . . . to feel his lips on hers—that was what love was all about.

She heard the door open and she knew Hugh was standing behind her. He came around and stared at her. Then he glanced upstairs.

"He's asleep," she said. "He's finished the bottle of Jack Daniels."

He went to the wooden table that served as the bar and poured himself a Scotch. "Want one?"

She shook her head. "I'll take a Coke though."

He handed her the drink. "Want some cold steak? You must be starving. You didn't eat a thing at dinner."

She stretched. "I feel marvelous. Just marvelous. I don't need food."

He looked concerned. "January, I don't know how good his marriage is, but he loves that baby and—"

"Hugh, I know he'll never marry me. Don't worry about it."

"You're in love with him?"

"Yes."

He sat beside her. "I've seen girls fall in love with him before. And they all say they can handle it. But when he decided to walk . . . several of them reached for the pills."

"Hugh . . . how well do you know Tom?"

"Does anyone really know Tom? I've known him for six years. We met when he was writing something about space in one of his novels. He came to Houston for research. We buddy-buddied together. And when I came to Los Angeles, he was just getting a divorce, so I shacked up with him. He fixed me up with some of his rejects and I had me quite a time. My own marriage was coming apart, but I had that thing about divorce . . . you know the bit . . . wait until the kids can understand. Hell, they never really understand . . . even when they're grown and have kids of their own. My daughter, God love her, has a three-year-old, and she says, 'Dad, why are you and Mother splitting . . . after all these years!' Well, hell—" he stopped suddenly. "What am I doing, rambling on like this? You ask me a simple question and I give you my life's story . . . when it's really Tom's you want. Okay. How well do I know

Tom? I don't. It's not easy to know Tom. We're friends, good friends—I know if I ever needed him, I could call on him. And he knows the same about me. We're a lot alike in some ways. A man like Tom gets lost in his writing, the characters become him, or vice versa. I get lost in my work . . . I never even got to really know my kids . . ."

Then he began talking about his children, about his early days of flying. She listened carefully, realizing he was unburdening his own guilts—his wrecked marriage, the loss of contact with his children. She told him not to feel guilty, that he was only following his destiny. "You really think that people should do their own thing?" he asked. She nodded, and it never once struck her as odd that she was offering Hugh Robertson advice, because at that moment she felt she could solve anything. They talked about the mystery of life . . . the solar system . . . infinity. He explained that the concept of intelligent life existing beyond our own solar system was now an accepted fact. He felt that in centuries to come there would be communication between solar systems. There would be telstars and satellite planets . . . chains of them . . . stretching out into space like a giant bridge connecting the planets and the solar systems.

"But how will we communicate with the little green men?" she asked.

"What makes you think they'll be green? If a planet is adjacent to another sun in the same position earth is to our sun, it has to breed the same kind of being."

"You mean there could be another earth? With a superior race?"

"Millions of them. Some, billions of years ahead of us . . . and of course some, billions of years behind."

They were both silent after that. Then she smiled sadly. "It makes everything we do or think about seem awfully small in comparison. I mean, when you think that on all those other worlds there are people like us, praying to God. Like when I think of how I used to pray to Him to help me to walk . . ."

"Walk?"

They both turned, and it was Tom coming down the steps.

He had on a robe and he was carrying an empty bottle. "I woke up and found both my girl and my booze gone." He came and sat beside January. "Did I hear you two say something about a walk? It's almost two in the morning."

"No," Hugh said. "January was saying how she prayed to God to learn to walk."

"I couldn't sleep," she said as she snuggled against him. "Hugh and I have been talking about the stars."

"What about the walking?" Hugh asked.

"It's a long story."

"It seems to me I've told you some pretty long stories tonight," Tom said. "Now it's your turn."

She began to talk, hesitantly at first. And then she found herself reliving those long hopeless months. The fire died out, but neither of the men seemed to notice. And as she talked Tom's dark eyes held her, offering silent compassion and admiration. She realized she had never told anyone how much she had really endured. She had told Linda just the facts. Even Mike never knew the total desolation she had felt, because she always put on a brave front with him. But sitting in the darkness with Tom's arm around her, all the suffering and loneliness she had known suddenly spilled out. When she finished, neither man spoke. Then Tom stood up. "I think we all need a drink now."

Hugh poured himself a Scotch. "Can you use this? We're clean out of bourbon."

"I came prepared," Tom said. "I had the driver put a case in the kitchen. I'll be right back."

Hugh watched him leave the room. Then he raised his glass to January who was still huddled on the couch. "I get a whole new picture of you now. You know, I think everything's going to be fine with you and Tom. Looks like he found himself a real hunk of woman in a skinny little girl."

The front door opened so quietly that neither of them heard the two men enter. January turned just as a hand clamped over her mouth. She saw the gleam of the knife that was held at her throat. At the same moment, the other man flashed a light in Hugh's face. "Okay, Mister . . . if you don't want your old lady killed, give us your jewelry and the money. If you shout or try to get help, your old lady gets her throat slashed."

"There is no money or jewelry," Hugh said hoarsely.

"Come on, Mister . . ." The man towered over Hugh. He was close to seven feet. "Last week we hit someone down on the beach. A weekend couple like you. Had to threaten to cut his balls off before his old lady coughed over her rings. You people who come out for weekends on the beach . . . you always got cash and jewelry."

"She's got no rings or anything," whispered the one with the knife at January's throat.

Hugh emptied his pockets. Some change . . . two fives . . . a few singles and keys came spilling out.

"That's chicken shit, man," the giant said. Then he glanced at the stairs. "You hold the girl," he called out. "I'll take him upstairs. Maybe I can convince him to show me where he keeps things."

January was left alone with the man with the knife. Where was Tom! The kitchen was behind the workroom. Unless she screamed he wouldn't be able to hear her. She stared at the man, who was breathing heavily and smirking at her. He was a little man, he hardly reached her shoulder. But he had a knife and it was at her throat.

One of his hands reached out and untied the sash of her robe. It fell open, and he stared at her nude body. His smirk became an evil grin. "Oh . . . Caught you and the old man ready for a little action."

She shut her eyes and tried not to scream as his rough hand touched her breasts. Then he unzipped his pants and exposed himself. "Pretty good for a little guy like me. But like I always say, you got to have your weight somewhere. Now my friend up there"—he nodded toward the steps—"he's all business. But me, I like to combine business with pleasure. So you and me is gonna have ourselves a little fuck." He wrenched the robe off her. "Turn around!"

"Please . . ." she begged.

"Oh. Maybe you'd like it all romantic. On the nice soft couch over there with me on top of you. Sure, and give you a chance to grab for the knife. Oh, no, sister. You're gonna take it doggie style. That way I got you in no position to fight. Now turn around and bend over!" he snarled.

"Please . . . I won't take your knife. Please . . ."

"You bet your ass you won't. And because you gave me some lip—I'm gonna make you use it. Your lips. Hey, that's a joke. Get it? Now before I give it to you, you do a little ground work." He pushed her to her knees and shoved his penis in her face. Her revulsion made her forget fear, and she suddenly jumped away and raced across the room. In an instant he had her by the arm and slapped her across the face. Then he pushed her on the floor. "Get on your knees, you cunt. No more games. I'm gonna ram my joint so far up your ass it'll come out through your throat!"

As he leaned close to her, she screamed. His reflexes caused him to jump away. Then she felt the cold blade of the knife at the black of her neck. "Trying to wake the neighbors? Well, nobody's home . . . on both sides of you. We hit them for some transistor radios. Nothing worthwhile. But don't try any more screaming. It would take the enjoyment out of it all for me and might make me cut you up before I fuck you."

But she continued to struggle as he pushed her into a kneeling position on the floor. Then she saw Tom's shadow in the doorway. He had heard her scream! With one last burst of strength, she twisted and managed to pull away. But the little man grabbed her. He was breathing hard, and she felt him against her as he made a futile attempt to penetrate her. She knew Tom was creeping around the room. She made one final effort and wrenched herself from his grasp. He clawed at her breast in anger as he tried to pull her toward him. Tom was behind the man now. And then she heard the thump as the bottle hit his head. The man gasped, released her, and slipped to the floor. Tom pulled her into his arms. She was sobbing hysterically. "Oh, Tom! He was trying to . . . Oh, God! If you hadn't come in time . . ."

He picked up her robe and helped her into it. Her teeth were chattering, but she pointed upstairs. "There's another one. A giant. And he's with Hugh . . ."

Tom looked at the unconscious man on the floor. He handed

her the bottle. "Now, look, if the bastard even stirs, hit him with this. Don't spare him. Just remember what he wanted to do to you."

Then he started for the stairs. There were sounds of a scuffle. Obviously the giant was beginning to rough up Hugh. Tom crept up the stairs, one at a time. A board creaked. She held her breath. The little man on the floor stirred slightly. January wavered as she held the bottle. But the man merely moaned and slipped back into unconsciousness. She was relieved. Somehow she felt she couldn't have hit him. Not with him lying there like that. If he was attacking her it would have been different. She stared at him. He was an ugly little man with two days' growth of beard. There was a smell of decay about him. Yet with his eyes shut and his mouth open there was something oddly pathetic and innocent about him.

She turned and watched Tom inch his way up the stairs. There was another sound of scuffling in the room. Furniture scraped, and it seemed as if the ceiling would come down. Tom took two steps at a time. He had just reached the top when the door opened and the giant appeared. He stood there for a split second, taken off guard at seeing another man. His eyes went from Tom to his unconscious accomplice on the floor. With a guttural curse he leaped at Tom and they both rolled down the steps. Tom was the first to scramble to his feet, but the huge man lumbered after him. "I left your friend half dead in the bedroom," he snarled. "But with you, I'm gonna finish the job." His fist crashed into Tom's stomach. Tom doubled over but staggered to his feet. This time the man lunged for his jaw. Tom ducked. He was stalling for time to get his breath back. But the huge man gave him no chance. He came at him with another smashing blow to the stomach, and Tom went down. January stood riveted in one spot as he approached her. Then she saw the knife lying on the floor. She grabbed it and raced across the room. The giant laughed. "Oh, want to play games? Want Big Henry to try and get the knifey away from the little girl?"

He started toward her. She leaped behind the couch. He came after her and she ran to the other side. "TOM . . . HUGH . . . HELP!" she screamed.

The man laughed. "No one awake but just us chickens."

Then he laughed heartily at his joke. He was coming closer. She hesitated. If she stabbed at him and missed, it would be all over for everyone. She had to stall for time. She ran around to the other side of the couch. The giant was laughing. "Come on. You're a cute piece. Wish I had the time to give it to you." He came closer. She backed away and almost tripped over the man on the floor. She heard Tom begin to stir. The giant heard it too. His smile disappeared. "Okay, you bitch. No more fun and games." He jumped across the couch and grabbed her. She tried to slash at him with the knife, but he twisted her arm. She cried out in pain as the knife fell to the floor. He picked it up, shoved her across the room, and started toward Tom, who was standing now.

"Okay, Mister. This is one time you're gonna wish you never woke up." He lunged at Tom to slash at his throat, but Tom ducked. Then Tom connected with a punch on his jaw. But the man seemed to barely feel it. He came at Tom, grinning, stalking. Tom kept backing away. Then he crouched like a cat, waiting. The man approached, brandishing the knife. Tom didn't move. The man came closer. And suddenly Tom leaped up like a panther, smashing the side of his hand against the man's windpipe, following with his fist to the man's jaw. It all happened so quickly that January couldn't believe her eyes as the huge man crumpled to the floor like a paper bag. Then Tom raced up the stairs for Hugh. January followed. Hugh was on the floor, just beginning to regain consciousness. His jaw was beginning to swell. One eye was shut, but he forced a slight smile. "I'm gonna live . . . guess I wasn't much help . . . I'm not in very good fighting shape these days."

They went downstairs. The little man was beginning to come around. Hugh went to the phone. Tom stopped him. "What do you think you're doing?"

"Calling the police. They're junkies. Look at that one's arm —loaded with needle marks."

"Put that phone down," Tom commanded. "We'll get some rope and tie them together and I'll drive them a mile off and dump them. If we have the police, then January gets involved. You know how the papers will play that up."

Hugh went to get the rope while Tom tried to slap some life into the face of the bigger man. When Hugh came back

Tom was still working feverishly on the man, massaging the back of his neck. But he lay like a rag doll. "We can't dump them," Tom said. "They'd never make it. They'd freeze to death."

"They'll make it," Hugh said as he bound them together. "They're junkies . . . junkies don't feel weather."

"Hugh, I think this man is dead." Tom stood up and stared at the limp figure of the huge man.

Hugh leaned over him, felt his wrists, his neck. "I feel a slight pulse."

"Then we've got to get him to the hospital. Hugh, you're going to drive January back to New York. January, get dressed immediately." It was a command and January ran up the stairs.

"But what will you do?" Hugh asked.

"As soon as you both get out, I'll call the police and tell them to send an ambulance. I'll say I wanted to do some writing and you loaned me the place. Then I'll tell it like it was—that I was out in the kitchen . . . I surprised them. . . ."

"Why don't you drive January back to New York? I'll call the ambulance and give the same story. I think January would prefer it that way."

"I would, too," Tom said. "But look, man. You're five foot ten. There's no way you could have hit that guy in the windpipe or on the jaw unless he bent down to let you." He looked at his raw fist. "And I've got the skinned knuckles to prove I did it."

January came down with her bag. Her face was white and she clung to Tom while Hugh went out to start the car. "I heard your plans. But what if the men talk? What if they say there were three people here?"

"They're junkies, so they saw double, or triple—it's my word against theirs. Don't worry." They heard Hugh's horn. He led her to the door. "Oh, Tom." She clung to him. "I thought we'd have the whole weekend together. Not just one night."

He looked at her and managed a wry smile. "I know. But you have to admit . . . it's been one hell of a night."

Twenty

January and Hugh had been silent on the drive back, both immersed in their own thoughts. The night had faded into a slate-colored dawn when they reached New York. The heater in the car was uncomfortably warm, but January suddenly shivered. Everything about New York seemed so dismal and gray. Westhampton and the violence that had occurred suddenly seemed unreal. Hugh pulled up in front of her apartment building. The streets were empty. A chill wind sent small bits of paper skimming across the sidewalk. Her mood was as heavy as the soot-stained canopies of the unattended apartment buildings along the street. "Buildings look dead without doormen," she said.

Hugh smiled and patted her hand. "Go grab yourself some rest, January." He helped her out of the car and they stood in front of her building. Her teeth chattered from the early morning cold. "You must be tired and stiff from driving," she said. "I make lousy instant coffee . . . but if you want some—"

"No. The police at Westhampton are very polite but also very thorough. Tom can handle just about anything, but I think he'd feel better if I was there." He leaned over and kissed her cheek. "Look, I want to take back a lot of the warnings I handed out so freely in the beginning. There's something that's clicked between you and Tom that's never happened with any other girl before. I'm not just saying this because you're a woman in love. I'm saying it from watching Tom, the way he looked at you tonight, his attitude—it's a whole different thing. Now you get some rest and we'll call you as soon as everything is settled."

When she entered her apartment it was as if time had stood still. Remnants of her packing lay strewn about. Slacks across the chair, shirt on the bed—inert signs of a distant past. A lifetime had happened in twenty-four hours.

She went to the refrigerator and poured herself a Coke. It suddenly occurred to her that she hadn't eaten anything. Hugh had teased her about not liking his cooking. Perhaps she should scramble some eggs. But for some reason the thought of food repelled her. She felt crystal clear . . . wide awake . . . charged with energy. She longed to go out into the lonely morning and walk. She leaned out the window. A heavy mist coated the air. She felt that if she walked . . . she could dispel it . . . like a magic genie . . . wave her arms and scatter sunshine everywhere. She was stronger than the mist . . . stronger than any element . . . Because as Hugh had put it, she was a woman in love. But she couldn't leave, she had to wait for Tom's call.

She chain-smoked, drank another Coke . . . It was still too early to call Linda, and besides she didn't want to keep her phone busy in case Tom called. She turned on the television set. There was a sermon on one channel. She switched to another channel—a children's cartoon. Then there was an early movie, an old Van Johnson picture with the sound so bad on the print that she couldn't listen—she couldn't listen to anything. She turned off the set. Suddenly she thought of her answering service. She had forgotten to check. Not that anyone important would call.

The woman on the service was disgruntled. "Miss Wayne, you must remember to check in with us. Or at least leave a number if you're going away for a long stretch of time. Your father was very angry. He acted as if it was our fault that we couldn't find you. After all, we're just an answering service, not a—"

"When did he call?" January asked.

"Friday night at ten. He had checked into the Plaza and wanted you to call." (*Friday night at ten . . . she was* at *the Plaza . . . and of course she had forgotten to check in with her service.*) "And then again Saturday morning at nine-thirty," the woman continued. "He wanted you to have lunch with him." (*She had been at Dr. Alpert's.*) "Then again at noon." (*She was at Saks on her shopping spree.*) "And then at five . . . at seven . . . and finally at ten o'clock last night. He left for Palm Beach and wants you to call him there."

She looked at the clock. Eight-ten. She waited until nine, then called Palm Beach.

"Where in hell have you been?" Mike demanded.

She managed to laugh. "Mike, you won't believe it, but I keep forgetting about checking with the answering service. I was out in the morning . . . shopping. I forgot to check. I went out again in the afternoon, and must have just missed your call, and then I was out for dinner. It's awful . . . I'm so sorry. But how was Gstaad?"

"Great. Dee came in second in the tournament. She flew right back to Palm Beach, but I stopped off in New York to see you. And instead of going to our place at the Pierre, I checked into the Plaza because I thought you'd get a kick out of it. I couldn't get my old suite . . . Hey, guess who has it . . . Tom Colt. But I got an identical one on a lower floor. And there I sat—like a groom left at the altar—waiting for my girl."

"Oh, Mike. . . ."

He laughed. "It was okay. Listen, I didn't tell Dee. I said we saw each other. I didn't want to look like a damn fool."

"Of course, Mike."

"Now listen, we're staying here until Easter. And we expect you and David to come down for that weekend. That's when Dee gives her last big bash. Then . . . I have a real surprise for you."

"What?"

"The Cannes film festival."

"The what?"

"Remember how we talked about it in Switzerland, how you dreamed of going? Well, there's a backgammon tournament in Monte Carlo just about that time, so I've convinced Dee to go. We'll stay at the Carlton Hotel in Cannes—you're twenty-one now, so I can take you to the Casino, teach you Chemin de Fer, Baccarat . . . We'll see all the pictures . . . all my old friends

. . . And I may just have a few other surprises for you, too."

"Mike, when is all this?"

"It starts in May. But I figure if we hit it around the fifteenth, we'll get all the action we want. That'll give Dee a chance to come back to New York from Palm Beach, open the suite at the Pierre—I think it's probably all covered with sheets and stuff. And I'll catch up on the shows. Maybe you'll go with me if David can spare you. But I've got to teach you backgammon. I'm on a hot streak with it, and eventually I'll play big. Right now I'm still playing for five bucks a point. But it's just a matter of time . . ."

"You're happy, aren't you, Mike?"

"I'm gambling, and I'm hot, and that's what it's all about—for me anyway."

"I'm glad."

"How is it with you and David?"

"He's really a very nice man."

"That's it."

"I'm afraid it is . . ."

"Anyone else on the scene?"

"Yes . . . Mike . . ." Suddenly she knew she was going to tell him. He would understand. "Mike . . . I met someone . . . I think . . . I mean I know—"

"Who is he?"

"Mike, he's married."

"Go on." His voice was suddenly hard and ugly.

"Don't tell me that shocks you?"

"It disgusts me. When I played around, I played around with bums. That's exactly what I thought of them, even if they were stars, because they all started off knowing I was married and had a kid. So when you . . . at twenty-one . . . a girl who has everything . . . who has a guy like David in love with you—"

"Love has to be a two-way deal, Mike."

"You mean to tell me with all the guys you could meet, you could only hook up with a married one. And, of course, he has kids."

"He has one."

"Can he get a divorce?"

"I don't know. He's—"

"Don't tell me. I can see the scene. An advertising guy . . . maybe in his thirties . . . tired of the girl he married on the way up . . . has her stashed in Westchester . . ."

"Mike . . . it's nothing like that."

"January, tell me one thing. Have you . . . have you been intimate with this man?"

She stared at the phone. She couldn't believe it. She couldn't believe the phrase—"have you been intimate"—or the faltering way he asked. He sounded like a preacher . . . not like Mike. She *couldn't* tell him. He really wouldn't understand. It was awful—to have to hide this from Mike—but she heard herself saying, "Now, Mike, it's not that serious. I just said I met someone and—"

"January, have I ever steered you wrong? Now listen to me . . . please. Don't see him again. He can't respect you if he thinks you'll go with him when he's married . . ."

"Mike, you're talking like . . . well . . . like three generation gaps . . ."

"I'm talking to my daughter. And I don't give a damn about how things have changed. Sure there's more sexual freedom. I wouldn't be shocked if you told me you went to bed with David . . . say . . . a few months before you married him. Or that you had gone to bed with him already and he left you cold. That's Today. That's the new freedom. That's the big change. But men don't change as far as their emotions go, and let me tell you, they don't respect a broad who goes to bed with them when they have a wife. Because no matter what kind of a story they give you . . . how the wife is a wife in name only . . . or that they have separate bedrooms . . . or an arrangement—you better believe that the nights they don't see you and have to go home, they're still going to bed with their wives. Even if it's a mercy hump. I know . . . because I've been there. And they still respect their wives because of their guilt. In fact, she almost gets to be a madonna because of it. And the better the lay the girl is, the more guilt they feel toward their wives. And when the guilt gets too heavy and when the girl wants more than a few nights a week . . . or a stolen trip . . . or gets too demanding—they drop her and go back to their wives for a few weeks until they find a new girl. Don't give me this liberated jazz. A married man is a married man—in nineteen fifty . . . sixty . . . or seventy. Laws and morals might change, but emotions remain the same."

"Okay, Mike. Please. Cool it. I'm fine . . ."

"All right. Now get back to David or some guy like him. Make your old man happy. I'll talk to you later in the week. I've got to run off for golf. I'm playing that game for big money —because like I said, when your luck is good, you've got to push it." He clicked the phone.

She hung up and walked to the window and stared aimlessly at the barren courtyard. She had been insane to think Mike would understand. Even if he hadn't sounded off on it, she could never have told him the entire story. And unless he knew about Tom's problem, there would be no way she could convince Mike that Tom really loved her, that their love was different from the affairs he had had. She thought of Tom . . . and the love and tenderness she felt constricted her chest. This great strong wonder of a man . . . and she had been able to make him happy.

The phone jangled. She almost turned her ankle rushing to it. "Hello—" She stopped. She had been about to say, "Hello, Tom." But it was Mike.

"Listen, I can't go off to play golf leaving it like this between us. Look, if this joker you say you like is really a good Joe and wants to get a divorce and you really love him and—"

"Oh, Mike, it's not anything like that . . . really."

"I have a hell of a nerve sounding off like that. I'm sorry."

"It's all right, Mike."

"I love you, babe. And remember—there's nothing you can't tell your old man. You know that, don't you?"

"Yes, Mike."

"Love me?"

"Of course."

"Okay. Call you in a few days."

She sat by the phone the rest of the day. Tom's call finally came at five o'clock. "I've sent the car for you. Will you come to the Plaza?"

"Of course, Tom. Are you all right?"

"I will be . . . as soon as I see you."

The traffic was heavy and she felt jittery as the car inched its way toward the Plaza. When she reached the hotel she actually ran down the hall to his suite.

He looked drawn and weary, but his smile was bright as he took her in his arms. He sat on the couch and sipped bourbon as he told her how everything stood. The man was in a coma, but no charges would be filed. The man had a long record of arrests. The police were still checking on his accomplice.

"I don't know how you did it," she said. "You were drinking a good bit."

His smile was sad. "I fight for blood when I fight."

"Have you ever lost?"

"A few teeth at times. But there's a killer instinct in me that always makes me win. It worries me at times, because I could kill. That was a karate chop I gave the big guy. I tried to miss his windpipe. Thank God I did. Otherwise he'd have been dead. I once promised myself I'd never do it unless my life was threatened."

"But it was."

"No, I could have beat him with my fists. The karate thing"—he showed her the motion with the side of his hand—"you hit a man in the right place with that . . . it's over."

She spent the night with him and once again she managed to arouse him into actual intercourse. His gratitude was overwhelming, and when he held her and told her he loved her, she knew he meant it.

The next day he was deluged with reporters. The story at Westhampton broke in all the papers. It was the kind of story the press associated with Tom Colt. At noon, the police got a "make" on the little man. He was wanted in Chicago for raping and killing three women. Now the story took on national importance. The Chicago police had arrived. The phones were going. The suite was cluttered with police and reporters.

Rita Lewis was ecstatic as she directed the traffic of the news media. January had slipped out at eight-thirty in the morning just before his first scheduled interview . . . before the news had broken. That afternoon he called her at the office and said, "The place is a madhouse. Now the FBI is in on it. I may have to go to Washington tomorrow—something about testimony on the little guy—and added to everything, his accomplice, the big guy, his name is Henry Morse. Well, Henry has a common-law wife and two kids and she's got herself a lawyer who's slapped me with a million-dollar assault charge."

"She can't do anything to you, can she?" January asked.

"No. Just take up my time. In the end, she'll settle for a few hundred bucks."

"But why should you have to pay her anything? That man was out to kill us all."

"It's easier than going through pre-trial examinations. Her lawyer knows that. Unfortunately, that's the way it works. The people who have plenty of time and nothing to lose figure their nuisance value will make you pay off . . . and you do."

"Oh, Tom . . . how awful."

"Anyway, you better play a low profile as far as I'm concerned for the next few days. The little guy—his name is Buck Brown—he's already mumbling about a girl with long brown hair being there. No one believes him. But it's just as well that no one see me with you until this blows over."

"Well, how long will it be?"

"Just for a few days. My publisher is jubilant. He acts as if I planned this whole setup just to help the book. We had over eight thousand reorders in the last twenty-four hours. They're going into another big printing. Everyone seems to think I'm a cinch for number one."

"Oh, Tom, how wonderful!"

"I was getting there on my own." His voice was grim. "Number three this week. I'd hate to think a fist fight could put me to the top."

"If the book wasn't there, all the fights in the world couldn't make it sell. You know that."

"January, tell me something—how did I ever live without you?"

"I'm just wondering how I'm going to get through today without you."

"I'll keep in touch by phone. And the first chance I get, we'll be together."

He left for Washington that afternoon and called her at midnight. "I'll be here for a few days. I'm also doing some book stuff, so it works out fine. That little Buck Brown—the one that was holding the knife at your throat—he would have killed you. That's his pattern. Rape, then kill. He just hooked up with the big guy a few weeks ago on a dope score. They're both involved with drugs. They're pushers and users. But the little guy is paranoid. Now it seems he's killed six women, and the list seems to be growing—once he rapes, he must kill, he's admitted that." His voice went low. "Know something, baby? I may just give up drinking. Suppose I had been more sloshed . . . and had slept through it all . . . You'd be—" He stopped. "Look, I'll be back at the end of the week. You get some rest. Then we'll spend the weekend together."

"Not at Westhampton," she said.

"No. At the Plaza. All safe and sound in Fun City. And, January, for God's sake, never let on to Linda that you were there when all this happened. After all . . . I am under oath."

It hadn't been easy. When the story broke, Linda had turned into a Torquemada.

"Where were you when all this happened? I thought you were spending the weekend at West Hampton with him?"

"No, I just went for the day. He sent me back so he could work."

"And nothing happened?"

"Well, it looks like plenty happened after I left."

"I mean . . . with the bed department."

"Linda, everything is fine."

"January, are you leveling with me?"

"Yes."

"But when did you do it?"

"Linda, for heaven's sake! I didn't leave there until around ten."

"Was he great?"

"Yes . . ."

"You don't sound very enthusiastic."

"I'm just tired . . . I haven't slept very much."

"You look awful. You're getting too thin, January."

"I know. I'm going to eat a big dinner and go to bed early."

But she hadn't eaten. And after she had talked to Tom, she hadn't been able to sleep either. A whole week without him

. . . suddenly all of her sense of well-being vanished. The following morning she woke up stiff and her neck was sore. She went to the office, and at three o'clock she was positive she was coming down with a virus. Linda told her to go home. "Honestly, January. Most girls who are in love bloom . . . you wilt!"

She got into bed. But she had chills and began to shake. She didn't know any doctor and she didn't want to bother Linda. Then she thought of Dr. Alpert. Of course. He certainly was a good doctor. Look at all the tests she had gone through before he gave her the shot. She phoned him, but his receptionist told her he didn't make any house calls and advised her to come over immediately.

The office was crowded, but the receptionist slipped her into a small examining room. "I'll get him to you," she promised.

Five minutes later Dr. Alpert shuffled in. He looked at her, nodded, shuffled out and returned with the syringe.

"Shouldn't you take my temperature?" she asked. "I mean . . . I know vitamins help everyone. But I feel sick. Like I'm coming down with something."

He felt her brow. "No sleep . . . no food . . . too much energy. When did you eat last?"

"Why I . . . " She tried to think. Tom had berated her for leaving her steak the night before, and she had barely gotten a piece of toast down this morning. "Not since . . . well . . . maybe Friday. I've been nibbling. But I'm not hungry."

He nodded. "This will set you right, I promise."

She was sitting in dungarees and a shirt. She rolled up the sleeve and extended her arm, but he shook his head. "Take off the pants . . . this is an intramuscular shot."

She pulled down her dungarees and lay on her side. The needle went into her buttock with ease. But there was no rush of exhilaration. She sat up and pulled on her pants. "I don't feel anything," she said.

"You didn't come here to feel something. You came here because you were sick," he said gruffly.

"Yes, but last time the vitamin shot made me feel marvelous."

"When you feel good, the shot makes you feel marvelous. When you feel sick, it makes you feel better."

She sat on the edge of the table and stared at him. She had to admit that the stiffness had left her neck. But there was no sign of that glorious euphoria she had experienced before. She walked into the outer office and paid the receptionist twenty-five dollars. As she walked home, she realized the shivering had stopped. She was feeling stronger and the pains in her back and neck were gone. But she didn't have that "go out and conquer the world" feeling.

Tom returned Friday afternoon, and she rushed to the Plaza to meet him. He looked strong and somewhat less harassed. And when he opened the bottle of Jack Daniels, he insisted she join him. "I know I said I might give it up, and I have cut down . . . but we have to celebrate. I just got the news—a week from Sunday, I'm number one. And it looks as if I'm making a big picture sale. Right now Columbia, Metro, Century, and Twentieth are all bidding, plus a few good independent producers. And the best news of all—the big guy is going to make it, he's out of the coma—so I won't have to carry that guilt on my back." Then he reached into his pocket and handed her a gift-wrapped box. "It's not really a present. It's just something I saw in a window and couldn't resist getting for you."

She opened the package. It was a beautiful silk scarf emblazoned with the word Capricorn. "Oh, Tom . . . I love it . . . But more than that . . . I love the idea that you thought of it."

But that night when they went to bed, she was unable to arouse him. He held her close and tried to pass it off. "I'm overtired," he said. "And maybe I didn't cut down on the drinking like I promised. Let's both get a good night's sleep. Tomorrow will be different."

The following morning she told him she had a dentist appointment. He told her to cancel it, but she promised to be back in the early afternoon.

She rushed directly to Dr. Alpert's office withcut calling for an appointment. Fortunately the office was not crowded, and Dr. Alpert was smiling again. He told her she looked better, and she told him she had eaten and kept regular hours. Almost as if she were reporting to a teacher for good marks. (See how good I am. *Now* will you give me the real vitamin shot?) She waited hopefully while he went out to get the needle. Her heart beat fast when she saw him shuffle back with the big syringe. She had not changed into the examining gown, but in a flash she had taken off her blouse and held out her arm. "You promise to eat . . . even if you aren't hungry?" She nodded eagerly as he tied the rubber tubing around her upper arm. She watched the needle go into the vein. Once again she saw the rush of her own blood fill the syringe . . . then pump back into her arm. And once again the fantastic surge of electric excitement charged through her. She felt reborn. Fully alive for the first time . . . her senses were alert to colors . . . to smells . . . And above all there was the sense of power . . . there was nothing she couldn't accomplish . . . her body tingled . . . suddenly she felt as if she was having an orgasm. She longed to get back to Tom. She threw on her blouse . . . hugged the doctor, scribbled a check for the receptionist, and rushed outside. It was cold again; but she knew spring was coming. She felt it. Everything good was coming . . . The Plaza was only a few blocks away, but she hailed a cab. She couldn't wait until she was in Tom's arms.

He was on the phone when she arrived. It was a long-distance interview, and she sat patiently as he answered the usual questions. Occasionally he'd look over at her and smile. Then he sighed; the man was going into questions about context against literary quality of today's novel. Tom tried to be polite. "Look, I don't think I want to get into that area. I don't ever criticize any other writers. Hell, it's even hard work to write a bad novel." But the man was persistent. January got up and put her arms around him. He was still in his robe. She began kissing his neck. Then she swung around and got on his lap and cradled herself in his arms under the phone. Her hands slid under his robe. He grinned but grabbed her with one hand and tried to continue his interview. She began to kiss his cheek. Finally he said, "Look, I think we've covered everything and I've got another appointment. In fact it's kind of urgent, so if you don't mind, let's cut it off here." Then he hung up and held her in his arms. "You have just destroyed an interview." He laughed.

"You were trying to end it."

"I tried . . . but you finished it."

She encircled his bare waist . . . then she opened her blouse and unhooked her bra . . . she pressed her breasts against him.

"I love you, Tom. I really do." Then she stood up and led him into the bedroom.

Later when they were lying together, he said, "How do I thank you?"

She snuggled against him. "For what?"

"For not giving me a chance to worry about last night. For turning me on this morning . . . right now . . . and having it turn out to be the best we've had so far."

She kissed him violently. "Oh God! It was wonderful!"

"Was it for you? It was for me because I functioned normally . . . but nothing happened with you."

"Yes, it did, Tom."

"January—" He leaned over her, and his eyes were stern. "Wasn't that part of our deal? Complete honesty. Don't ever lie to me . . ."

She held him close. "Tom, a woman isn't like a man. I don't have to come all the time. Just holding you in my arms and knowing I make you happy makes me more of a woman than I've ever felt before."

His dark eyes glowed in the semidarkness of the bedroom. "January, I can never be without you again . . . never."

"You won't have to be, Tom. I'll always be waiting . . . whenever you want me."

Then he smacked her across the bottom. "Okay. Let's take a shower together. Hey, do you bike?"

"Do I what?"

"Ride a bike?"

"I don't know . . . no . . . I never rode one."

"Well, today, you're going to learn."

They rented bicycles and spent the afternoon in Central Park. She caught on immediately. Her balance was good, and soon she was whizzing past him on the bicycle lanes. They went to a movie on Third Avenue . . . ate pizza . . . and went back to the Plaza. And when they made love again, it was perfect, and Tom insisted on satisfying her until she had to cry out.

The following day they rode downtown on their bicycles. He took her to Irving Place and showed her where Mark Twain had lived. He pointed out the brownstone house where Oscar

Wilde had lived when he was in this country. They went to a little French restaurant and he told her stories about Sinclair Lewis—he had been a young man then, and "Red" Lewis had been on an acting kick—he told her about meeting Hemingway . . . how he had met Tom Wolfe when he was teaching at N.Y.U. He told her about his early days. He was born in St. Louis and came to New York and got a job on the *Sun*. Then a short stint in Hollywood. He had met them all out there—when writers were looked down upon by the movie industry. "That's why I never do a screen treatment of any of my books no matter what they offer me. I wrote too many pieces of junk tailored to fit the stars during the forties, and I promised myself—if I ever got to be a novelist, I'd never write a movie script again."

During the next two weeks, time and days fused into a meaningless maze for January. She forced herself to try to concentrate at the office. But her life only had content when she was with Tom. Mornings of waking up in his arms, having a quick breakfast together, escaping just before Rita Lewis arrived, rushing to her apartment to change, running to Dr. Alpert's for shots every third day, returning to the magazine and accomplishing a day's work in two hours. She did five tapes in one day after a vitamin shot, and even Sara Kurtz had to admit they were good. She told about the loneliness of a writer like Tom Colt . . . the demands on his time . . . his feelings about the circus atmosphere of today's promotional efforts for a book. How he understood that the media had changed—New York had only three newspapers. She drew a fine impersonal picture of Tom Colt—she called it "Echo of a Lion"—and compared him to the lion coming out of the jungle to face civilization. At the end of the two weeks Sara said she had enough for a good story.

But it was at night that she really came alive. Bursting with this new incredible energy, she'd tear back to her apartment, shower and change, and rush to the Plaza. Sometimes they'd go to a show and stop off at Sardi's. Once he took her to Danny's Hide-a-Way for dinner and they sat at the front table . . . Mike's old table. And sometimes if he'd had a rough day, they'd just stay in and have room service and she'd listen to his gripes about the interviews . . . the television shows . . . his agents . . . and then there would always be the wonderful tenderness of his arms when they lay in bed together. There were some nights they didn't make love, when he said, "I'm fifty-seven, baby. And I'm tired. But I want you to be with me." Those were some of the best nights. And when she got the curse and told him, and asked if she should sleep home, he had looked at her in amazement. "I want you in my arms at night, not just to hump you . . . but because I love you. I want to wake up and find you there, to reach out during the night and be able to hold you—isn't that what it's all about?"

Then there were nights when he wanted only to satisfy her . . . when he made love to her until she was limp with exhaustion.

And then there was always Linda. Always questioning. Always watchful. Growing slightly resentful because January had developed an expertise in evading personal questions.

At the end of March, Tom had to leave for another short promotional trip. Detroit, Chicago, Cleveland. "I don't think you should come," he said. "Why cause a lot of talk? I don't care for myself. It's you I'm concerned about. It'll only be for five days."

When he saw the tears in her eyes, he grabbed her in his arms. "January, for God's sake, of course you can come. Please, baby, don't cry."

She shook her head. "It isn't that. Of course you're right. It's only five days. And you will come back. But it just suddenly hit me that there will be a time when you'll have to leave for much longer than five days, when you won't be coming back . . ."

"I've thought about that, too," he said slowly. "Much more than you would believe. It's something I've got to think out while I'm gone. I told you once—I can never be without you. I mean it. I've also been thinking about the next book I want to write. The idea finally crystallized in my mind. And when that happens I can't wait until I go off to write. Only it's not quite happening that way now. I think of the book . . . and you come through. Before, a new book always took precedence over anything. I'd lock out the world and the book became my new mistress. But it's not like that now."

"That's wrong, Tom. You've got to write."

"I know . . . and I'll have to figure it out. Look, we'll talk about it when I get back."

When he was gone, it was as if all the oxygen had been taken out of the air. She skipped her usual appointment with Dr. Alpert. After two days she felt nervous and listless, but she forced herself to have dinner with Linda, who was now in love with one Donald Oakland, a newscaster on a local television show. They went to Louise's, and January listened while Linda gave explicit details of her sex life with Donald. "He doesn't give good head . . . but that's because he's Jewish. Jewish boys never really think it's proper to give head. But he's learning. I've assigned Sara to do a story on him," she said as she chewed on a piece of celery. "He's on local news right now, but when the story comes out and he gets a taste of real fame and realizes what I can do for him, he'll unload his wife and stick with me. I can't stand this three-evenings-and-one-afternoon-a-week scene."

"Do you want to get married?"

Linda shrugged. "I'm pushing thirty . . . so why not? Or at least I'd like him to live with me. And I'm also learning a lot from him. His I.Q. is 155—that's near genius. And I've just realized how little I know about politics. He's been explaining things to me. I don't dare tell him I've never voted. He's given me a lot of books to read. He's a big hot Democrat. I want to be able to hold my own with him and his friends so I'm reading *The New Republic* and *The Nation* like they're *Cosmo* or *Vogue*. Until now I was always busy watching my competition and trying to make *Gloss* as good. But I suddenly realize that while *Gloss* has grown, I haven't. I mean, like I don't know anything except things that concern the magazine. Donald thinks Women's Lib is great, so maybe I'll join one of the groups . . ." She laughed. "Except when he stays over he forgets all about Women's Lib and even expects me to wash out his underwear."

"Do you?" January asked.

"Of course. I even bought him a toothbrush and his favorite

mouthwash to keep at my place. I make him breakfast when he stays over . . . a good breakfast, better than that wife of his makes. She wants to be a poet, so she's up writing half the night and is always asleep when he leaves Riverdale. And some nights I cook dinner—almost cordon bleu type because he really can't afford to take me out each time. I mean he's paying for his house in Riverdale . . . and his wife just put in a pool . . . and he's putting his brother through college and—"

"Linda, can't you ever find a nice available man?"

"No. Can you?"

Twenty-one

TOM CALLED every night. They discussed the shows he had done, the hassle he had gotten into with a critic on Kup's show, the endless interviews he had given, the mixed reviews his book had received. He was still number one, but he was concerned about the new books coming out on the spring list. He mentioned nothing about his future plans.

By the middle of the week January began to feel unstrung, physically and emotionally. Tom was due back Friday night. He had said he could never be without her. But he was without her now. And he had admitted that his work had always come first. Had this brief separation given him time to have second thoughts?

The following morning she was at Dr. Alpert's office before he arrived. Once again the receptionist slipped her into a booth without an appointment, and once again Dr. Alpert came shuffling in, and when that needle went into her vein, every doubt about her future with Tom vanished, and she floated out of the office with a golden feeling of confidence.

He returned Friday night and stopped off at her apartment without calling her. She let out a shriek of delight and fell into his arms. They clung together, both talking at once, both insisting each had missed the other more. And as he held her, she knew that her worries had been groundless. He would never leave her.

When he broke the embrace, he turned and looked at the apartment. He was so massive; the room seemed to shrink.

"How long is your lease?"

"It's a sublet. I have it until August. But Mr. Bailey wrote and said that if I wanted it for another year, he would stay on in Europe."

"Get rid of it. I'm going to buy us an apartment. You're going to pick it out. I want it to be on the river, with a wood-burning fireplace, a bedroom, a living room, and another room for me to work in, because that's where I'm going to write my new book."

"But what about California?"

"What about it?"

"Don't you have to go there?"

"Yes. We're leaving next week."

"We?"

He looked at her earnestly. "Look, I don't know about you . . . But these last five days seemed like five years. I did a lot of thinking. In a couple of years I'll be sixty. You'll be—well, you'll still be a child. So we've only got now. I don't know how long 'now' will last. But let's grab it. I love you. I want you with me. I've got a final two-week blast of publicity to do out on the Coast. I can't afford to be separated from you for that long. I called Nina Lou and told her about you. I didn't tell her your name, but I leveled with her and explained how it was with us. I told her I was bringing you out . . . and that as long as you'd have me, I was going to be with you. I told her I'd check into a bungalow at the Beverly Hills Hotel—the publisher is paying for that. And to make things look okay, I'll get you a room at the hotel which you won't use. And for all concerned, you are out there to do the story on me for your magazine. I'll go to the beach to see my kid. But that's the extent of it. Nina Lou says it's fine. She's pretty hung up on some actor, so as long as I don't make her look bad to her friends, she couldn't care less."

It was all going too fast for January. But she was light-headed with the knowledge that she hadn't lost him.

"We'll be in New York for another week now," he went on. "So your job will be to find the apartment. Get one all set, so we can move into it when we come back. I know it's short notice. But a good renting agent should be able to swing it. You go see them all. Then when you've narrowed it down to maybe two or three that you like, I'll come and see them. And we'll decide together."

"But Tom, if you live in New York with me . . . what about seeing your son?"

"I'll fly to the Coast every other weekend. Don't worry. It'll work out. I just know I can't be without you."

She spent eight hours a day looking at apartments. Linda was carried away with the idea. She was so expansive she told January to count the trip to the Coast as a paid vacation. "It's a bonus. You rate it. And remember . . . don't worry about a thing, just keep the genius happy. And we've got to find you the greatest apartment in New York. January, just think—as Tom Colt's girl, you can run a salon. With his muscle, all the 'In' people will come. We can start a whole new thing. Like maybe Sunday brunches. I'll write them up for *Gloss*. Wow! It's out of sight! We'll be the new 'A' group in town. *We'll* make the news . . . set the pace. And will I have muscle with Mr. Donald Oakland! He's impressed as it is that I know Tom Colt. But when he comes to your salon and sees all the important men I'll be able to meet . . . January, the timing is perfect. New York is ready for something like this. Now, it has to have a huge living room, one that opens on a dining room preferably, and . . ."

She was amused at Linda's enthusiasm and felt it was best just to let her ramble on. The apartment was going to be a fortress. Just for Tom. No guests, no parties—just the two of them. But she allowed Linda to come along and visit some of the apartments because she was slightly terrified of the efficient real estate lady who took them around. After four days, January was positive she had been in every great building in New York, and the search had finally narrowed down to an apartment at the U.N. Plaza or a ground floor apartment with a huge terrace hanging over the river on Sutton Place. Linda liked the U.N. building, but Tom was enthusiastic about the Sutton Place apartment.

It was a co-op, and the price of one hundred and ten thousand didn't seem to bother him. He was pleased with the relatively low monthly maintenance, the ninety-year ground lease—he kept nodding as the woman reeled off all the selling points of the apartment. Finally he said, "It's a deal. Draw up the contract and send it to my lawyer on the Coast. He'll send the check." He gave the ecstatic real estate lady all the necessary addresses and phone numbers. Then he took January to the nearest bar. He toasted their new apartment with a sad smile. "I like her talk about the ninety-year lease. January, for a man my age to expect this thing to last with a child like you—" He shook his head. "I know I'm crazy . . . but let's give it a real try. And no matter how long it lasts . . . let's make it a happy time."

"Tom, it will last forever."

He raised his glass. "To forever. I'll settle for five good years."

She spent the rest of the days buying clothes for California, cleaning up last-minute things at the office . . . And each night she rushed to the Plaza exhilarated. Her energy was boundless.

They were due to leave for California on a Wednesday afternoon. That morning she visited Dr. Alpert. When he saw her, he seemed surprised. "You were here just two days ago . . . you're not due until tomorrow."

"I'm leaving for Los Angeles today," she said as she watched him fix the syringe. "Dr. Alpert. I'm going to be away for a week at least. Can you give me some long-lasting shot?"

"Where will you be in Los Angeles?"

"The Beverly Hills Hotel."

He smiled. "You are a lucky girl. My brother, Dr. Preston Alpert, flew out there a week ago. An important singer is out there to make a comeback at some big club, and he must have a vitamin shot every day, so my brother is staying with him throughout the engagement. You call him at the Beverly Hills Hotel."

"Dr. Alpert . . ." She felt a sudden rush of fear. "Are these injections addictive?"

"Why should they be?"

"I mean, if the singer has to have them every day . . ."

"He drinks two quarts of brandy a day . . . doesn't eat . . . sleeps with a lady every night—of course he needs vitamin shots. You also have a great need for vitamins. Tell me, before you came to me . . . was there some traumatic thing in your life?"

She smiled. "Like three years of trauma . . . and then a kind of shock. But that was back in September. And everything worked out fine."

He shook his head. "Delayed reaction. Look, my little girl. There are doctors who treat the head. And why? Because something that happened twenty years ago hurts the mind today. So why do patients feel that things that happened to them some months ago can't hurt the body? If you're run down, what's wrong with taking vitamin shots three times a week if they make you function and feel good? Don't you have your teeth cleaned every few months . . . don't you brush them three times a day . . . don't you use eye lotion at night? Why not help your tired young blood? Today with the food you girls eat . . . or better yet, don't eat . . ."

He was right. This dear sweet man, taking all this time explaining things to her when he had an office filled with patients. His smile was benevolent. "Have a good time . . . call my brother. And when you get back, make your next appointment in advance."

She walked home. She knew she would be able to pack in no time at all. It was one of those rare April days—clear and cool, no smog, a Wedgwood sky. She wondered why the New Year always began in the middle of winter when everything was dead. The new year should start in April, on a day like this when new young life was just beginning. She saw it everywhere—a lady walking a tiny puppy, wobbly with its training leash; tiny buds breaking through the bare branches of the new young trees propped up with sticks and braces, burlap around their slim bodies to help them survive in a small patch of earth on a New York City street. Then she saw an old woman, the stockings slipping down her frail legs, walking an arthritic dog—the two of them inching down the street. Tears came to her eyes. She felt sorry for anyone who wasn't young. In fact, she felt sorry for everyone who wasn't going to California and for everyone who didn't know a man like Tom Colt.

As the day progressed her state of euphoria grew. She had never felt so complete and aware of everything around her. She sat beside Tom on the 747. The ride was smooth, the service perfect. Everything was perfect! Until the hostess placed the small glacéed Easter eggs on their dessert plates.

Easter eggs!

This was Wednesday.

Sunday was Easter!

And tomorrow Dee's plane would be waiting to take her to Palm Beach for the Easter weekend.

She wired her father the moment she reached the hotel. "AM IN LOS ANGELES AT THE BEVERLY HILLS HOTEL DOING A STORY ON TOM COLT. WILL HAVE TO MISS EASTER. LOVE, YOUR CAREER GIRL."

She hoped that by keeping it light, it would sound like a last-minute assignment rather than complete thoughtlessness on her part. She had checked into her "own room" in the main building, but her luggage went to Tom's bungalow. "I'll go there each day and muss up the bed for appearance's sake," she said. He laughed and shook his head. "With everyone living together, stars publicly having babies out of wedlock . . . do you really think anyone gives a damn about where you sleep?"

"I do," she said.

The publisher had set up a tight schedule for the next two days. Breakfast interviews, luncheon interviews, the Merv Griffin show, a news show, and a seven o'clock morning show. She accompanied him everywhere, carrying a notebook and playing Girl Reporter from *Gloss* magazine.

On Saturday Tom sent her to sit at the pool while he went to Malibu to visit his son. Sven, the attractive young man who managed the cabanas, offered her a comfortable chair in the sun. He gave her suntan lotion and brought her some magazines. But she couldn't relax. After an hour she began to feel nervous. She forced herself to stay at the pool; she could use some sun. Tom had admired her tan when they first met. She clenched her hands and gripped the arms of the chair. She felt she had to hold on. It was as if she was coming unhinged. She told herself she was just restless because Tom was away.

But soon she was forced to admit that the pains in her neck were very real and she had the beginnings of a blinding headache. All of the unmistakable signs . . . it was time to call Dr. Alpert's brother.

She left the pool and went to her own room. It was a nice room, but even with the nightgown and robe she had hung in the bathroom, it was still obvious that no one used it. She wondered what the maid thought. She lit a cigarette and picked up the phone and asked for Dr. Preston Alpert. The operator said he was expected back at six. He was at Malibu. God, was everyone at Malibu!

It was only three o'clock. How was she going to get through the rest of the afternoon! She lay back on the bed to ease the hammering inside her head. By four o'clock she was hanging over the sink, letting cold water fall on the back of her neck. Two more hours to go. She left the room and went to the bungalow. She changed into slacks and a shirt. Her hands were shaking as she poured some bourbon into a glass. She almost gagged but forced some down. It always seemed to do so much for Tom; maybe it would help her head. She took another swallow. Her throat burned, but the headache didn't seem quite as intense. She slipped the bottle into her pouch bag and returned to her room. She stretched out on the bed and began drinking the bourbon. It was a restful room. It was sad to keep it and not use it. "I'm sorry, room," she said aloud. "It's nothing personal . . . just that my man lives in a bungalow."

She continued to sip the bourbon. It dulled the headache, but she knew she was getting drunk. She didn't want Tom to come home and find her that way. Maybe a warm bath would help. At least it would pass the time. She forced herself to stay in the tub until the skin of her fingers began to crinkle. Then she fixed her makeup and looked at her watch. Five-fifteen. She checked Dr. Alpert's room again. The message was the same. Dr. Alpert was expected back at six.

Her head was aching again, even worse than before. Her neck felt as if it were packed with swollen glands. Oh God. She was probably really anemic now. She hadn't eaten a thing today, just coffee with Tom in the morning. Dr. Alpert had warned her she must eat. And she had lost more weight. Even her hip-huggers were slipping down.

The next half hour was interminable. She felt warm and turned on the air-conditioning. Then she felt cold and turned it off. At five forty-five she left another message for Dr. Alpert, adding that it was urgent. At six-fifteen he still hadn't returned. Oh, God . . . suppose he didn't get back at all. Suppose he decided to spend the whole weekend at Malibu. She had run out of cigarettes and began smoking the butts. Tom was due back at seven. She wanted to feel great when she saw him. After all, his wife was probably very beautiful. She had to be if she had been a starlet. There weren't any starlets anymore! She poured herself another drink. She was a bit player! That's what she was. Just a girl who did extra work, an overaged bit player. So there was no reason to get uptight about her. But even an overaged bit player could be attractive. Look at how many were becoming stars on television. But this was silly . . . Tom had gone to see the baby. But how could you spend a whole day with an eight-month-old baby? It had to sleep a lot, didn't it?

It was six-thirty and she had gone through the last decent butt. The drugstore was just downstairs, but she was afraid to leave her room, afraid of missing the call. She sent for a pack and tipped the bellman a dollar. At quarter to seven she tried Dr. Alpert again. His line was busy! She sat by the phone, drumming her fingers on the table. Why was his wire busy? Hadn't she left word that her call was urgent? Five minutes later she tried again. A calm lethargic voice said, "Yesssss?"

"Is this Dr. Preston Alpert?"

"Who is calling?" the quiet drawl asked.

"January Wayne."

"What is it in reference to?"

"Oh, for God's sake! Are you Dr. Alpert?"

"I asked, what is this call in reference to?"

"I'm a patient of Dr. Simon Alpert. He told me you would be here, taking care of—"

"Never mind." The voice suddenly became firm and clipped. "What do you want?"

"A vitamin shot."

"When did you have the last one?"

"Wednesday morning."

"And you need another so soon?"

"I do . . . Honestly, Doctor, I do . . ."

He paused. "I'll be speaking to my brother later this evening. Suppose you call me tomorrow at noon."

"Oh no! Please . . . not then . . . I need it now. Look, I write for *Gloss* magazine. I'm here doing an in-depth piece on Tom Colt, and—"

"Tom Colt?" The voice was impressed.

"Yes. And you see I have to be alert all the time and watch everything and remember . . . because I don't take shorthand."

"Oh . . . I see . . . well . . . I'll check with my brother and find out what vitamins you take. Mr. Colt is in Bungalow Five, isn't he?"

"Yes . . . but I'm not there . . . I'm in room one twenty-three."

"Oh, then you're not the girl who's staying with him?"

"No girl is staying with him!"

"My dear girl, if you're really interviewing him, you must know he has a beautiful young girl with him . . . young enough to be his daughter. Everyone at the hotel knows it."

She paused. Then she said, "Thanks. But she won't be young and beautiful if you don't get here pretty soon. For God's sake . . . it's five of seven now."

"I'll be right there."

Ten minutes later he knocked at the door. She hated him on sight. He was tall, with heavy sandy hair and a hawk-like nose. His skin was bad and his long skinny fingers were clean but bloodless-looking. She preferred his brother. At least there was some warmth about Dr. Simon Alpert. He might not be as sanitary-looking, but he was warm and friendly. This one was like an immaculate antiseptic fish. She rolled up her sleeve as he fixed the syringe. Then without looking at her, he said, "Lie down on your side and take down your pants."

"I take it I.V."

He seemed surprised but wrapped the rubber tubing around her arm and proceeded to mix the solution. She winced when the needle went in. She fell back against the pillow. She had never had a shot like this one. She felt dizzy, as if she were rocketing to the sky. Her heart was pounding . . . her throat closed . . . she kept going up . . . up . . . Then she felt as if she were falling through an enormous air shaft . . . with no bottom. . . . For a moment she panicked. Then everything leveled off, and she felt nothing but a golden glow of life flowing through her entire body. She rolled down her sleeve after he had placed a bandaid on her arm. "How much do I owe you?" she asked.

"It's a gift."

"What?"

"Any girl who attracts a man like Tom Colt deserves a free vitamin shot."

"Well, thanks . . . thanks a lot."

"How long are you both going to be here?" he asked.

"For another week. He's been working very hard. He has a few more interviews next week, then two days in San Francisco, then back to New York and he—" She paused.

"And he goes back to his wife?"

She had been about to tell this dreadful man that they were going to sign the lease for their apartment. That was the danger of the shot—you felt so good you wanted to talk to everyone . . . trust everyone.

"I think I'd better get back to the bungalow," she said.

He nodded. "A man like Mr. Colt . . . with all that work . . . he certainly could use a series of shots."

She smiled faintly. "He doesn't need them. He has Jack Daniels."

"You know about the singer I'm treating?"

She walked to the bureau and pretended to comb her hair. His unctuous manner bothered her. Yet she couldn't afford to completely alienate him . . . she might need him again.

"I also treat a very famous composer; he takes a shot every day. And then there are several TV personalities that have started their injections. A man Tom Colt's age—granted he is a very virile-looking man—but he certainly could use some vitamins. Any man going at his pace—writing a book, promoting it, making love to a young girl." His gray eyes were glassy with what was supposed to be sexual innuendo.

It was all she could do to keep from throwing him out, but she turned and managed a faint smile. "I'll suggest it to him," she said. "And now . . . I've really got to dress."

He packed his case and left the room. She waited until he was gone, and then dashed to the bungalow. Tom hadn't returned. She felt wonderful. Dr. Preston Alpert's shot was much more powerful than his brother's. She poured herself another glass of bourbon. Tom would be pleased if he found her drinking it. Good Lord, the bottle was almost empty. It had been three-quarters full when she took it to her room.

She walked to the bar and opened another bottle. She thought of Tom and suddenly put the bottle to her mouth and took a long swallow. She gagged a bit, but it went down. She tried it again. Suddenly the entire room began to float. She realized she was very drunk. Roaring drunk. It struck her as very funny. She began to laugh. She kept laughing until the tears rolled down her face. Until her stomach actually ached. She wanted to stop . . . but she couldn't. Her body felt lighter than air. She was still laughing when the phone rang.

She looked at the clock. Almost eight o'clock. It had to be Tom . . . offering some explanation for being so late. She reached for it but changed her mind. No. She had waited all day. Let Tom and the operator have a little trouble finding her. She knew how it worked. Now they'd try the Polo Lounge, then page the lobby . . . Okay. Now she'd let them find her. She picked up the phone. "Hello . . . Operator, this is Miss Wayne. You have a call for me?" She began to laugh again. The whole thing seemed so terribly funny.

There was a pause while the operator connected the call. Then she heard Mike's voice. "January . . ."

"Mike." She began to laugh harder. It was Mike . . . not

Tom. She kept laughing. But it wasn't funny . . . only she couldn't stop laughing. She wanted to stop . . .

"January, what is it? What's the big joke?"

"Nothing . . ." She was doubled over now. "Nothing. It's just that I had a shot and some bourbon and I . . . I feel . . . so marvelous . . . and . . . " She broke into spasms of laughter again.

"What kind of a shot?"

"Vitamins. They're . . . heaven–ly . . ." Now she had stopped laughing and felt she was drifting on a cloud. The vitamins had conquered the bourbon. She felt silken inside . . . the bed was a cloud floating in space . . .

"January, are you all right?"

"Oh, my beloved father . . . I've never been better. Never . . . never . . . never . . ."

"Who are you with right now?"

"No one. I'm just waiting for Tom."

"Tell me something," he said. "How come the magazine sent *you* to do this interview? Since when did you become their star reporter?"

She began to laugh again. Mike sounded so serious. So stern. If he only knew how happy she was. How happy everyone should be. She wanted him to be happy. She wanted him to know how it felt to float. "Mike . . . are you happy?" she asked.

"What are you talking about?"

"Happiness. It's the only thing that matters. Are you happy with Dee?"

"Never mind about me. What are you doing there? What are these shots you're talking about?"

"Just vitamins. Heavenly wonderful vitamins. Oh, Mike, there're palm trees out here, better than the palm trees in Florida. And Bungalow Five is like my own private home. Did you ever stay at Bungalow Five when you were here? I bet you did . . . because you and he are a lot alike. After all, he even had our suite at the Plaza."

His voice was hard. "I want you to leave Los Angeles immediately."

"No way. And after Los Angeles I go to my big new apartment with a garden terrace on the river and—" She suddenly couldn't remember what she had been talking about. "What was I just saying?" she said.

"Too much. Goodbye, January."

"Goodbye, my magnificent father . . . my lord . . . my handsome one . . . my. . . ." But he had hung up.

She was stretched out on the bed without any clothes when Tom came in at nine. He stared at her for a moment, then smiled. "Now this is what I call a real greeting." She held out her arms but he shook his head as he sat on the edge of the bed. "I'm too weary. It's been a rough trip. And today was another ball-breaker."

"You mean you're tired from playing with the baby?"

He laughed. "Actually, I held the baby for exactly twenty minutes. Then he threw up and the nurse gave me a dirty look and whisked him off. I got to see him once again after his bath."

"Then what did you do all this time?"

He stood up and took off his jacket. "You're making noises like a jealous wife. And you have no cause to be. I told you it was part of my deal to keep up a semblance of a marriage. So today I had to be nice to a lot of people that Nina Lou had in for brunch, cocktails and . . . well . . . the whole deal was like a twenty-four-hour open house—welcoming the big author bit."

"I feel shut out," she said suddenly. "Like you have a whole other life going for you. And to me, you're my whole life."

He sat down on the edge of the bed again. "Look, baby, writing is my life. Right now you've come into it in a very big way and you can stay as long as you like. I love you. But no woman can be my whole life. Except for now while I'm on this circus of promoting. Because through all this you're the only thing that is real. But once I start writing—you're going to have to accept the fact that the writing comes first."

"But no other woman."

"No other woman. I swear to that."

She grinned happily and jumped off the bed. "I accept those terms and now you must accept mine . . . for tonight." She pulled him to his feet and began unbuttoning his shirt. "And now that you've done your husbandly duties, your loving geisha girl awaits." She stroked his chest and ran her fingers up his back. He took her hands and held them.

"Baby . . . I'm not up to it. I'm just too tired. But if you want, I'll make love to you."

"No . . . Let's just stay up all night and talk and be together in each other's arms."

"Fine. But I think I'd better order some dinner for you."

"I don't need food . . . I've got you."

He smiled. "I wish I knew what you were sniffing. I'd like some too."

"Vitamins," she said. "You should try them."

He laughed. "God, it's wonderful to be young. You can turn on and recharge yourself. I could do it too when I was your age." He sighed heavily. "It's rotten getting old. I never thought it would happen to me. I felt I'd always be strong . . . always be young . . . able to get by with too much booze and too little sleep. Health and stamina were just things I took for granted. But it creeps up on you—" He sighed again. "It's hell to know you're creeping up to sixty."

"You're not old," she said. "And I do take vitamins. Shots . . . here . . . look at my arm." She held it out and pulled off the adhesive. He saw the tiny prick on her arm. "What the hell are you doing?" he demanded.

"It's a vitamin shot."

"You get them in the ass."

"I got one that way once . . . but it didn't work as well. That's intramuscular. This is intravenous."

"Okay, Dr. Kildare. Now tell me something. Where did you get this shot?"

"Dr. Preston Alpert. He's out here now. In New York his brother takes care of me."

"And just what do these shots do for you?"

"Make you feel like you own the world."

"Send for him," he demanded.

They reached Dr. Alpert in the Polo Lounge. Within fifteen minutes he was at their bungalow. When he met Tom he was so visibly impressed that his hand shook as he attached the disposable needle to the syringe. January sat huddled on the bed in one of Tom's robes. Tom was shirtless . . . still in his white denim pants. He was tanned from the beach. In contrast Dr. Alpert looked like a spindly green grasshopper as he bent over his syringe. Tom watched the doctor carefully. January looked away as Dr. Preston plunged the needle into his arm. But if Tom felt anything, his expression never changed. He waited silently until Dr. Alpert finished. He stared at the small bandaid on his arm and reached into his pocket. "What do I owe you?"

"One hundred dollars."

"One hundred dollars!" January shouted. "Why that's crazy. Your brother only charges me twenty-five."

Dr. Alpert looked at her nastily. "That's an office visit. This is a house call. And after hours at that."

Tom slammed the money into his hand. "Look, take your money. And if I ever see you around here, I'll break every bottle you've got in that case."

Dr. Alpert was stunned. "You mean you're not pleased with the shot? Don't you feel anything?"

"I feel plenty. Too much for just a vitamin shot. That shot is loaded with some kind of speed."

Dr. Alpert started for the door. Tom went after him and grabbed him by the jacket. "Remember, I don't want you to go near her or I'll run you out of town."

Dr. Alpert pulled himself together. "Mr. Colt, if they did a blood analysis on you right now, they'd find heavy doses of Vitamin A, E, C, and all the B's."

"And some meth as well, I'm sure. I don't doubt that you've got some vitamins in it. But it's the speed that makes the patient feel good."

Dr. Alpert tripped over the door ledge in his hurry to leave the bungalow. Tom turned to January. "How long have you been on these things?"

"I'm not really on anything, Tom. I mean . . . I've taken a few shots . . . Linda told me about it. . . ." Then she went on to explain about Keith and all the important people who used the two Dr. Alperts.

Tom took her in his arms and held her close. "Look, baby, right now I feel like I could make love to you all night. That I could start writing my next book and never stop . . . that I could dive off the highest hill at Miramar in Acapulco . . . catch the current as well as any of the professional Mexican divers. It's a great feeling. And I've had it before. I was a correspondent during World War Two. I used to take bennies and get a little of this kind of jolt. The bomber pilots who made the early morning raids ate them like gumdrops. Maybe they hadn't slept too well the night before, figuring it might be their last. But they popped those bennies in their mouth at four A.M., and an hour later, when they took off, they were soaring into that wild blue yonder positive that no bullet could hit them. Hell, half of them felt as if they didn't even need the plane. I feel the same way now. I could . . . well . . . hell . . . let's not waste the shot." And he threw her on the bed.

The following morning, the effect of the shot seemed to have worn off for Tom. But January was still in a constant state of enthusiastic energy. Tom sat her down and tried to explain the danger. "Look, I'm six foot two and weigh a hundred and ninety pounds. So my system absorbed it quickly. But you . . . you can't weigh more than a hundred pounds, and that shot is loaded with methamphetamine, I'm sure. It's not addictive like the hard stuff . . . but when it wears off, the withdrawal signs are like a bitch of a hangover."

"But can they really hurt me?"

"As a steady diet they could kill you. It races the pulse . . . makes your heart beat triple . . . Now look, if you want to get high, do it with booze. You can't drink enough to hurt you. I can—and do—but then I've lived my life. Now, no more shots . . . Promise?"

"I promise."

That night they had room service and they had barely finished dinner when he jumped up and pulled her toward the bedroom. "Tom." She laughed as she followed him. "The waiter will come in . . ."

"Let him. We'll close the bedroom door. Maybe it's the

bourbon activating what's left of the shot. But whatever it is, I don't want to blow it."

They didn't hear the doorbell. They didn't even hear the bedroom door open. Then everything happened so fast that she could barely put things together. She was aware of the lights going on. Someone pulling Tom off her. Seeing a fist send a bone-crunching blow to Tom's jaw. Tom staggering and spitting blood. Then she gasped. It was Mike! . . . standing there . . . his fists clenched . . . staring at them both.

"Mike!" The word stuck in her throat.

Tom had recovered and lunged after Mike, but Mike's fist slammed into his face again. Tom struck back, but Mike crouched like a street fighter. Tom wasn't able to touch him, and Mike came after Tom with a maniacal fury. His fist smashed into Tom's face again and again. She tried to scream, but no sound came out. Tom stood up as Mike pummeled into him. He tried to lash out, but his timing was off. His face was a bloody smear. Mike's fist smashed into his jaw again . . . into his stomach . . . back to his face . . . back to the jaw—it was more violent than anything she had ever imagined. And she stood watching it in a stupor as if it wasn't quite real. It was all happening so fast. Tom flailing out . . . beginning to falter under Mike's merciless onslaught . . . Mike pulling Tom to his feet . . . his fist crashing against Tom's face again and again. The blood was pouring from Tom's mouth. His eye was cut. She saw him stand groggily against the wall and spit teeth. She rushed to her father. "Let him alone . . . stop it! STOP IT!" She screamed.

Mike let go and Tom slipped against the wall to the floor. January knelt beside him. She looked up at her father. "Do something . . . help him . . . oh God, you've knocked out all of his front teeth."

Mike walked over and pulled her to her feet. "They're caps. They've probably been knocked out before." Then suddenly for the first time he seemed to realize she was naked. His face went dark with embarrassment. He turned away. "Put your clothes on. I'll wait in the next room."

"Just like that!" she shouted. "You come in here and half kill the man I love . . . and then give orders. Why? Are you jealous?" She jumped in front of him. "Is that it? Well, I never burst into your bedroom and beat up Dee. I come to Palm Beach and smile like a good little girl."

"He's a bum!"

Tears were running down her face. "I love him. Don't you understand? I love him . . . and he loves me."

He pushed past her and looked at his watch. "Get dressed. I've got the plane waiting."

"Why did you come here?" she sobbed.

"Because when I talked to you on the phone yesterday you sounded spaced out. I was afraid you were in some drug scene. I couldn't get here fast enough. Now I wish I hadn't come. But I'm here. So let's cut out. We'll forget any of this happened. Come back to Palm Beach with me."

"No way," she said.

He looked at his watch. "I'll sit in the Polo Lounge for half an hour. If you don't come by then, I'll leave. But if you have any brains at all, you'll pack your things and tell him to call his wife to come and get him. I'll be waiting in the Polo Lounge —for exactly one half hour." He slammed the door of the bungalow.

For a moment she stared after him. Tom had made it to the bathroom. She rushed after him and got a wet towel and held it to his face. He put on a robe and with her help made it back to the bedroom.

"Tom . . . your teeth . . ."

He tried to smile and winced. "Like the man said . . . caps. I can get them fixed. It's my jaw . . . I think it's broken . . ."

"Oh, Tom!"

"Don't worry . . . it's been broken before. Your father's got a good punch."

"I'm sorry."

"I hate the bastard," he said. "But I guess I would have done the same thing if it had been my daughter."

"You're not mad?"

He shook his head. "No. He's just brought things to a head. I've always had a hunch that maybe I was just a replacement. Now I know. So you better get dressed and go to him."

"Tom . . . I love you. I told him I loved you."

"That line you pulled about his wife was the clincher, honey."

"What line?"

"Skip it." He turned away.

She got into her slacks and shirt. He looked at her and nodded. "So long."

"I'll be back," she said.

"Back?"

"Yes. I just want to see him . . . to tell him I'm staying."

"If you don't show in half an hour he'll know that."

"But I've got to tell him."

He grabbed her hand. "Listen, baby. This is it. This is the moment when you make the big choice. It's me or Daddy . . . not both. Because if you go out there, you've made your choice."

"I'm just going to tell him . . . I mean, I can't let him go off like this. I can't let him just sit and wait."

"If you walk out, there's no coming back," he said slowly.

"But Tom, I have to talk to him. Can't you understand?"

"You love me, right?" She nodded anxiously. "Okay," he went on. "Someone just came in here and beat the shit out of me because you loved me. Now, if you walk out on me—even for ten minutes—to make peace with that guy—then you make a bum out of me."

"But he's not just a guy . . . he's my father."

"Right now he's the guy who smashed me up . . . and you're my girl. Mike knows the rules. You walk out there for any goddam reason and it's like another clout at my jaw." He looked at the clock. "You've got twenty minutes left."

She hesitated. She thought of Mike sitting in the bar waiting. Then she looked at the bruised man on the bed. She nodded and walked slowly back to him. He held her in his arms and they both lay very still listening to the minutes tick by. . . .

When he left Bungalow Five, Mike went to the men's room and let cold water run over his hand. It was beginning to swell . . the knuckles were split in several places. His hand felt like it was busted. He hated to think how Tom Colt's jaw must feel.

He went to the Polo Lounge and ordered a Scotch. He looked at his watch. Ten minutes had passed. She'd come. She was probably seeing to it that Tom Colt was fixed up. He hadn't meant to mangle the guy. But he had seen Tom Colt in fights before. No one had a chance against him. So he knew he had to keep hitting. All along he had expected Colt to let one fly that would demolish him. He kept expecting it—and it was that expectation that had driven him on. If he had thought about it, he might have hesitated in tangling with Colt. But the sight of him on top of his daughter . . . something had just snapped and he hadn't been able to *stop* hitting him.

He was amazed that he had come out of it with nothing more than a busted hand. But then, when a guy has just shot a load he's not exactly in fighting form. He felt sick in the stomach thinking of him with January. Her body was so slim and beautiful . . . too clean and nice for a man like Colt to handle.

He looked at his watch. Fifteen minutes. She was probably packing now. He ordered another drink. Was the captain looking at him with sympathy? No . . . it was all in his mind. They probably didn't even know she was his daughter. A guy sitting alone in the Polo Lounge always looks like he's been stood up. But he wouldn't be stood up. Any second now she'd come dashing in . . . and he would smile and not even discuss it. Hell, he had made plenty of mistakes in his time. He certainly couldn't lecture her.

Twenty minutes. Why was she cutting it this thin? Well, all that mattered was getting her back. And it was going to be different from now on. He'd take her to Cannes in May. They'd talk about that on the trip back to Palm Beach. He'd tell her about his luck, the way it was coming back.

Twenty-five minutes! Jesus, it couldn't be that she *wasn't* going to show! No . . . She'd come. She was his daughter . . . she belonged to him. But what was that crack she had made about Dee? Was she jealous of Dee? She had no reason to be . . . she knew damn well he didn't love Dee. He wasn't jealous of Tom Colt . . . he was just sick about her being with a man like him. He was too old . . he had a wife . . . he was a drunk . . . and he had shacked up with every kind of broad around. He wasn't fit to touch his daughter.

The half hour was gone. He stared at his watch as if he couldn't quite believe it. He looked toward the door. He'd give her five more minutes. He ordered a third drink. Christ, he never drank three drinks in half an hour. His hand was throbbing, but the pain in his gut was worse. Because he knew she wasn't going to show. But he'd have the drink . . . it would give him an excuse to hang on an extra ten minutes.

He nursed it for fifteen minutes and ordered another. He was giving her an hour. Bullshit . . . he was giving himself time. He was too stunned to move. He had to think this thing out. His little January . . . turning him down for Tom Colt. He had always felt she'd walk out on the world for him. And he'd do the same for her. It had always been that way . . . it *had* been that way! But now Tom Colt had the corner suite at the Plaza. Tom Colt had Bungalow Five. Tom Colt's book was number one on the list. Yes, Tom Colt was a winner . . . and Mike Wayne was just Dee Milford Granger's husband.

Okay. She wasn't coming out. She belonged to Tom Colt for now. But when the romance phased itself out—as it had to in time—how would he go about reestablishing their old relationship? Would she ever forgive him for breaking in like that? Would she ever respect him like she did that drunken bum in there? To stay with a guy who's had his teeth knocked out . . . she had to care for him. Or feel pity. No. January wouldn't stay out of pity. She was *his* daughter, and he had never stuck with anyone out of pity. She was with Tom Colt because she respected the sonofabitch. Well, why not? He was number one. And he was probably also a great cocksman. He winced as he thought about it in relationship to his daughter. But he forced himself to face the facts. Tom Colt always charmed the broads. No doubt about it . . . he was great in that department. And January . . . well . . she was his daughter. So she probably dug sex, too. He clenched the glass so hard it broke. Now his bad hand was cut on the inside as well. The waiter rushed to him . . . Mike brushed it off . . . it was just an accident. He wrapped his handkerchief around his hand, dropped a twenty-dollar bill on the table, and left the hotel. He had waited one hour and fifteen minutes.

He thought about it as he drove to the airport. How did he go about getting her back? No woman had ever walked out on him before. And he'd never forget the way she looked at him. As if she was seeing a stranger.

He lit a cigarette and tried to think it out. To start with, he'd have to win back her respect. He could do it. His luck had changed. So far he had won over one hundred and thirty-five thousand dollars gambling on golf, gin, and even backgammon. If he kept this up . . . He ground out his cigarette. If he kept this up he'd be nowhere! If your luck was hot you had to push it. In the old days he'd have pushed this streak and run it into a couple of million. What was he doing sitting around like a dame . . . hoarding his winnings . . . putting them into a safe deposit box in his daughter's name? What good was the money if she despised him? And if he kept up this penny ante stuff, he'd never win back her respect.

He got to the airport and walked across the field to his plane.

"Back to Palm Beach?" his pilot asked.

"No," Mike snapped. "Get clearance for Las Vegas. We're going there for a few days."

He sat in the plane as it made the turbulent flight. He remembered when he used to fly to Vegas from the Coast every weekend. One thing—being married to Dee, his markers would be good. He was going to shoot the whole works. He'd build up a big bankroll for Cannes. He was playing for big stakes again . . . perhaps the biggest in his life. He was rolling the dice for his daughter.

Twenty-two

January awoke when she heard the rain. Oh, God . . . not again. There was nothing worse than California in the rain. The light on the clock radio said seven-thirteen. She closed her eyes and tried to go back to sleep. It had been raining for three days. The monotonous clatter it made on the roof of the bungalow was now something she accepted as part of her day —the way she accepted the eternal clicking of Tom's typewriter. She had been in California one month and it seemed like forever. Perhaps it was the sameness of each day. When the sun shone . . . it seemed eternal. And when it rained . . . the rain seemed eternal.

But with the rain, she became a captive of Bungalow Five. Tom was still asleep. She looked at him in the shadowy morning light. He still had a small bruise under his left eye. His recuperative powers had amazed her. His face had healed in less than two weeks. And his teeth were back in three days. He explained his dentist always kept an extra set of his caps on hand. Oddly enough it was the broken ribs that gave him the most pain . . . but he took it all philosophically. He had been in too many barroom fights to let a few cracked ribs get him down. "When your nose is broken and your jaw is wired, then you can complain." He laughed. "And those were fights that I won." Besides, as he put it, he needed the rest and it gave him a chance to be on hand when his agent finalized the picture sale of his book. When the deal was set, they'd go off to New York and celebrate.

He made the deal and they celebrated. And it was her fault they were still in Bungalow Five.

Tom had been exuberant the day he had signed the contract. He had spun her around the room. "Five hundred thousand against twenty-five percent of the net profit. Do you realize what that means! They want to bring the picture in for two million. So after it grosses five million, everything is gravy. If it's a big one and goes through the roof, I could make a million."

"It will if they do the book," she said. "But I've seen so many hit books changed . . . and ruined."

"Well, let's hope they get a good writer and a hot director. But meanwhile, we'll go to Matteo's tonight and celebrate. Tomorrow I'll visit my son. And the next day we take off for New York and I'll sign the lease on the apartment."

"Tom, why don't you do the script?"

"I told you. I don't do scenarios."

"Why?"

He shrugged. "It's not prestigious."

"That's a hang-up from your early days. Plenty of novelists are writing their own screenplays. Look at Neil Simon . . . he always does his own adaptations. Besides, if I had twenty-five percent of the profits, I'd want to be damn sure that my money was protected with a good script."

He looked at her for a moment. "Know something? You've given me something to think about. I never had a share of the profits before."

And then he was on the phone with his agent and for the next few days the phone calls went back and forth. And finally, at the end of the week, they sat in the Polo Lounge with Max Chase, his agent, and toasted the deal. Tom was to get fifty thousand for the treatment. And after that was approved, he'd get another hundred and fifty thousand to write the screenplay itself.

"That'll buy the apartment in New York," he said. "Here's to you, Max . . . the deal is great. And here's to January for making me do it."

"What apartment in New York?" Max Chase asked.

"I'm buying one. My lawyer is still checking out a few points in the deal they sent us. Mortgages and stuff. But it's practically set. The way I figure it, we can get in by June, January can furnish it, and I'll knock out the treatment. Then I guess I'll have to come back here to talk about the actual screenplay."

Max Chase smiled. "I'm way ahead of you. I managed to get a few more goodies put in the contract for you. I got Century to pick up the tab on the bungalow, plus supply you with a car while you're working on both the treatment and the screenplay. So forget about New York for the time. Besides, it's best for you to write it out here. You stay in touch with things that way. You'll be able to see who they pick for a director, the actors . . . When you're right here, you get a chance to argue about it—not read about it after the fact."

Tom turned to January with a grin. "Think you can rough it out here in Bungalow Five for a few more months?"

She nodded. "I'll tell Linda I'm quitting the magazine."

"Don't be ridiculous," he said. "She can give you some assignments to do out here. Keep you busy."

And Linda had been enthusiastic. "Sure. Get me a story on Doris Day . . . and George C. Scott . . . Dean Martin . . . and get one on Barbara Stanwyck, find out how she feels about TV, the new Hollywood as opposed to the old one . . . I hear Melina Mercouri is out there—try for her. And do something on the elegant Malibu colony where your man has a house. . . ."

But it wasn't that easy. She had tried to contact the press agents of the stars and learned that most of them were on vacation. After a few calls, she stopped trying. A strange kind of lethargy had come over her. When the stimulant from the shot had worn off she had gone through two tortuous days of headaches and nausea. But Tom had been with her and forced her to sit it out. She was all right now, but she felt oddly disoriented. As if an arm or leg had been amputated. She knew that in some way it had to do with Mike. She knew her complete disinterest in *Gloss* also related to him. She realized her job had been just a means of attracting his attention . . . seeking his approval. And now she could never win his approval. She would never forget the way he had looked at her when he walked out. And now she had nothing to live for except Tom . . . Mike had walked out on her. It was Tom who cared.

In the beginning she sat at the pool and read all the current novels. Tom was still number one. He was caught up in his writing now, and she forced herself to stay away from the bungalow until late afternoon and tried to ignore the gnawing realization that nothing was happening with them at night. Of course he had been too battered the first two weeks, and he said ribs took a long time to heal. But she felt it was his writing that was coming between them. When she came in, he would often motion her to go into the other room. He didn't want to break his rhythm by even saying hello. Occasionally he would tell her the television set was on too loud. At night they'd have room service and he'd read her the stuff he had written during the day.

Now as she lay listening to the rain, she wondered why she felt so despondent. This was the way it should be. In a way she was working with him, just by being there and listening. But something was missing. She reached out and touched his shoulder. He mumbled in his sleep and turned away. She felt the tears come to her eyes. Even in his sleep he was rejecting her. What was this ego trip she was on . . . about helping him? It was all in her mind. She wasn't helping him! She wasn't even necessary in his life! She slipped out of bed and dressed quietly.

She sat at the counter of the coffee shop and had a corn muffin and coffee. Every seat was taken. And everyone in Los Angeles seemed alert and alive at eight in the morning. Some were reading the trades. She heard snatches of conversation—distribution costs . . . foreign distribution . . . the Eady plan . . . no tennis during lunch hour because of the damn rain. She paid her check and went upstairs to the lobby and ordered Tom's car. The rain was still slicing down. Cars were arriving in one lane and leaving in the other. There were cracks about the glorious California sunshine; the inevitable reply: "This is just heavy dew." She saw Dr. Preston Alpert get into a car with a recording star who had arrived from London to do a Special. Good Lord! Was he on the shots too? Finally her car arrived and she drove down Sunset and out to Santa Monica. Then she sat and watched the rain pelt down on the desolate beach.

Perhaps Tom sensed her mood, because when she returned he stopped writing and insisted they have a drink together. He had stopped drinking while he was writing, but now he poured himself a double, insisted she have one also, and took her to The Bistro for dinner.

His entrance caused a rush of conversation. It seemed he knew everyone in the restaurant. Before the meal was over several actors and directors were sitting at their table talking shop—exchanging stories, making suggestions on who should play certain roles. She sat there feeling more shut out than ever.

He was in great spirits when they got back to the bungalow. And when they were in bed he made the attempt . . . but nothing happened. He finally made love to her and after she was satisfied and he thought she was asleep he got out of bed and went into the living room. She waited a few minutes and then peeked inside. He was rereading the pages he had done that day. She went back to bed. Hadn't he originally said he'd work four hours a day and spend the rest of the time with her? In the beginning he had often come to the pool for a brief swim. But it was always the typewriter he rushed back to. Where had she gone wrong? What had happened to the excitement in their relationship?

On Monday it rained again. She tried to watch the soap operas. On Tuesday it was still raining and she tried to read. On Wednesday she tried to write an article called "The Heavy Dew"; but it didn't work. On Thursday, when the sun finally broke through, she threw her arms over Tom's shoulders as he sat at the typewriter. "Come on to the pool with me . . . let's take a walk . . . let's do something."

"Why don't you take tennis lessons?" He was staring at the sheet in the typewriter.

"Tom, I play tennis real well. I don't need lessons."

"Fine. Then I'll ask Max Chase to find you some players."

"Tom, I stayed in California to be with you . . . not to play tennis."

"You are with me."

"Yes, but you aren't with me."

"I'm a writer." He kept staring at the paper in the typewriter.

"For God's sake, it's only a movie treatment. It isn't *War and Peace*."

"Writing is my work. You should understand that."

"Producing was my father's work, but he certainly took time out for someone he cared about."

"January, for God's sake, go out and amuse yourself. Buy some clothes at the shop in the hotel. Charge it to the bungalow."

"I don't want clothes. Tom, it's only eleven in the morning. I'm lonely . . . I feel lost . . . tell me what to do."

"I don't give a damn what you do just as long as you get off my back."

"I'm going back to New York," she said quietly.

He turned and his face grew hard. "Why? To crawl back to him?"

"No . . . to save what we have. I'll go back to my job. At least I'll be able to walk in New York . . . see people on the street . . . talk to a blind man with pencils and a big dog . . . go to the park and get mugged—anything. But at least I'll be off your back!"

He grabbed her in his arms. "I didn't mean it. Please, baby. I need you. I want you here. Look, you've never lived with a writer before. Our relationship is great. I've never been happier. I've never written better. If you walk out on me I'd feel I had failed you. Don't do this to me now . . . not when the end is so close. Look, this will all be over soon. And we've learned something from it. We've learned we can't live in Los Angeles when I write my next book. And that's what living together is all about—you find out what works and what doesn't. But one thing we do know that works is us. Right?"

"I don't know, Tom. I really don't. I feel . . . lost."

He turned away. "I see. It's Mike, isn't it?"

"Tom, I'd be a liar if I said I didn't think about him . . . subconsciously that is. I mean . . . well . . . I loved him . . . I still love him. I've loved him all my life. I wish that night had never happened. But I made the decision. I stayed with you . . . and I lost him."

"What makes you think you've lost him?"

"Tom, if I left for New York tomorrow . . . would I lose you?"

"Yes," he said quietly. "Because I'd know why you left."

"And don't you think Mike knows why I've stayed?"

He nodded slowly. "I guess I've been selfish. Look, let me just get this draft done. Then I'll hand it in and we'll get into a car and go to San Francisco for ten days. I have a lot of friends there. You'll like them. We'll have a ball. And I promise from this moment on, I'll only write four hours a day."

"Then I'll wait and we can go swimming at two. It's only eleven now."

"I don't feel like swimming. But you go. Maybe I'll come down later."

He didn't come down. And he spent the following day at the typewriter working straight through until eight o'clock.

On Saturday it rained again. He left in the morning to go to Malibu to see his son. He promised to be back by five. They'd go somewhere for dinner. Maybe even a movie. He called at nine. She could hear music and the sound of people laughing and talking. His voice was blurred and she knew he had been drinking. "Look, baby, it's coming down real hard out here. I think I'd better stay for the night. Order some room service. I'll see you tomorrow." He clicked the phone.

She sat very still for a few seconds. He was having a marvelous time at his wife's house. And he was in no rush to get back to her. Why should he be? All she had done was complain. Where had all the excitement gone? Where was her vitality, her high spirits? She was the girl who had once made him function like a man. Now he never even tried anymore. Just satisfied her when he felt she needed it. A mercy dive. Yes, that's what Linda would call it. And now he was staying overnight at Malibu. He'd come back tomorrow. But if she kept this up, there'd be a time when he wouldn't come back. Suddenly everything seemed so desolate . . . so hopeless. She couldn't lose Tom . . . she couldn't! He was all she had. She had to make it all shining and wonderful, as it had been before.

She sat very quietly for a few minutes. Then she picked up the phone and called Dr. Preston Alpert.

Twenty-three

David stood at the bar at "21," waiting for his father. The old man was ten minutes late. This was unusual. He glanced at the empty table being held for him at the banquette against the wall. The restaurant was filling up. Peter was checking his list as some V.I.P.'s arrived without reservations. Walter had just put up a table in the archway that divided the first and second sections. Mario was giving white carnations to three attractive women. David finished his drink and decided it would be better to wait at his table. Too many people at the door were eyeing it.

He was on his second martini when his father came in. He apologized profusely as he ordered a drink. "My God, but women can be impossible." He sighed.

David laughed. "Don't tell me you've got a romance going again?"

His father colored slightly. "David, I've always had great respect for your mother. But she— Well, she isn't what you'd call a physical person. However I've never had, as you put it, a romance going. Naturally I've had an occasional discreet foray. But never any real relationship."

"Well, who is the new impossible discreet foray?" David asked.

"Nothing like that. It's your mother who is impossible. That's why I'm late. We're going to Europe in three weeks. Our first time in six years and our passports have to be renewed. Would you believe we've been at the passport office since eleven this morning, and your mother is *still* there?"

"Was it that crowded?"

His father shrugged. "Not very. This is off-season for tourists. But she's on her third photographic session. She refuses to have an unflattering picture on her passport. Now who in the world is going to see that picture other than customs officials and some foreign hotel clerks?"

David laughed. "Well, if it matters that much to her, maybe she should have her face lifted. She'd look marvelous then."

"Good God, whatever for?"

"Her own ego. It *is* being done, you know."

"Not your mother. She goes into a panic when she has to go to the dentist. It's not for her. Besides—" He paused as a murmur went through the restaurant. Everyone was staring at the woman making an entrance.

"It's Heidi Lanz!" George Milford exclaimed. "Now speaking of face-lifts—she must have had about ten. Good Lord, the woman is close to sixty and still looks thirty."

David stared at the Viennese actress who was accepting the embraces of the owners of the restaurant and shaking hands with the captains. She was with two young men and greeted everyone as she made her way to her table. She was magnificent-looking and, unlike Karla, Heidi Lanz had *never* retired. When her luck in pictures ran out, she came to Broadway and appeared in a musical. She did a yearly Special on television and played Vegas every year.

"Don't know how she manages to keep that figure," George Milford went on. "Did you happen to see her on television last month in that clinging dress? She has the body of a twenty-year-old."

David nodded. "I saw it with Karla. She said she was positive Heidi wore a body stocking—to get that firm look."

"Well, Karla should know," George Milford said.

"Why?" David's voice bristled. "Karla's figure is sensational. But she works at it, she—"

"Calm down, son. I just meant that Karla should know about this Heidi woman's figure. They were lovers, you know."

David colored and took a long sip of his martini. "Those were just Hollywood rumors."

"Perhaps. But I recall reading stories about them in the gossip columns. In the forties there were pictures in the newspapers of the two of them dashing around in pants—that was quite daring then. Your Karla, of course, was not ducking photographers as she does today. She was just beginning to make it here, and Heidi was the big star then—"

"Karla also almost eloped with one of her leading men," David reminded him.

"True." George Milford's eyes were still on Heidi. "But let's not forget that Heidi is married and has grandchildren now. But they say she still has her little girlfriends on the side."

"Karla cares only for men," David said.

"Still going on?" George Milford asked.

David nodded. "I see her almost every night."

"January still on the Coast?"

David nodded. "Don't worry. I keep my hand in. We correspond."

"Isn't it about time you came to some decision?"

David stared at his drink and nodded. "I'm afraid it is. Especially now that Dee is back. When January returns we'll announce our engagement. Oh, don't worry. I'll make a concerted effort to get her to really care. I don't think I can stall any longer. This California trip of hers was a bonanza for me. I suppose I know the end is in sight. That's why I can't seem to get enough of Karla."

"Marriage isn't always the end of the line," his father said.

"I think it would be with Karla and me. After all, to get January to agree to marriage will mean really devoting myself to romancing her. And Karla isn't the kind of woman you can just put on ice and say, 'I'll see you every odd Thursday.'" David's sigh was heavy.

"Marriage always means sacrifice of some sort," his father said. "Come now. Let's have another drink. I've always found that brightens any horizon."

When David left his father he stopped off at the men's shop at Bonwit's and bought the Cardin sport shirt he had admired all week. Sixty dollars. But it was just right with his gray slacks. He'd wear it tonight. There was a "Movie of the Week" on television that Karla had underlined in her *TV Guide*. She was cooking steaks, and it was one of those rare occasions when she had promised he could spend the night. "It is a long movie. We will watch it in bed. Then we will make love. And since it will be so very late, I shall let you stay over."

He didn't really need it, but he shaved again when he got home. Then he sat under the sunlamp for ten minutes. It helped to hold his Palm Beach tan. He tried the new shirt with the gray slacks; then he tried it with the navy. He went back to the gray. He tied a scarf inside the collar. Then he mixed himself a martini. Karla drank only wine. And he still needed that first martini to bolster his courage with her.

He thought about it as he sipped his drink. It was insane. In a few days it would be a year that they had been together. Yet at the start of each evening with her, he still had to deal with a case of schoolboy nerves.

Damn it! He was her lover! Right now she was making salad . . . for *him*! With her own hands! For *him*! And later when he held her in his arms she would moan and cling . . . to *him*!

When would the time ever come that he could feel casual about it, take her for granted? God, if he still felt this way after a year, how would he ever be able to break it off and start really romancing January?

He couldn't! But he wouldn't think about that now. Besides, January's letter gave no hint of any imminent arrival. She had even said she might do some other stories while she was out there. He looked at his watch. He still had half an hour. Time for one more quick drink. Straight vodka this time. He was really off the beam. Just the thought of giving up Karla had thrown him into a tailspin.

He sipped the drink slowly. The vodka felt warm. He knew he was getting slightly high. But it didn't matter. He liked to be a little high when he saw her—it made him feel more relaxed. He felt better when he finished the drink. Maybe his father was right. Perhaps marriage to January wasn't the end of the line. Maybe he could explain the entire setup to Karla, even the ten million dollars. No, she'd despise him. Then how could he explain it and ask her to wait? *No* way! He felt a heavy wave of depression. But this was ridiculous. January was three thousand miles away. She might stay away another month, maybe longer. Meanwhile he had all this time with Karla. He would not think of next month . . . or even next week. He would enjoy each day as it happened. And tonight he was going to see Karla.

The phone startled him. He jumped up and caught it on the second ring. "David, I'm so glad I caught you." Karla's low voice sounded breathless.

"I was just leaving," he said cheerfully.

"You can't come tonight."

"Why?"

"A . . . a friend has arrived unexpectedly."

"I don't understand." It was the first time he had not accepted one of her cancellations in good grace. "Karla, we have a date."

"David—" Her voice was warm and almost pleading. "I also am very sad to cancel this evening. But this is a very old friend. From Europe . . . my manager . . . he came in unexpectedly . . . And it is about business. I must be with him."

"Oh, you mean Jeremy Haskins. The man you told me about?"

"Yes, my old friend."

"Well, it certainly won't last all evening, will it? Maybe I could come by later."

"I think not. I shall be tired."

"Maybe you won't be. Let me call. Give me your phone number, Karla."

"David, I must hang up."

"Damn it, Karla! Give me your number!"

The phone clicked in his ear. For a moment he panicked. He had gone too far. She was angry. She might not call tomorrow. She might not ever call again! He tried to get hold of himself. There was no reason to feel this way. She'd call him tomorrow and they'd laugh about this. He poured himself a big slug of vodka and added a few drops of vermouth. One more drink and he'd be drunk. But why not! Why not get good and sloshed! His face was beginning to sting from the sunlamp treatment. He looked at himself in the mirror. The shirt looked great, the sunlamp had added a reddish glow to his tan. He had never looked better. Stood up for an old man!

He finished his drink and made another. Maybe he should call Kim. It was only six-thirty. But he didn't feel like being with Kim. He was drunk and he knew it. He poured himself another drink—straight vodka now. He sat in the dark and drank it slowly and methodically. He was in his new shirt and his face stung and he had no place to go. No place he wanted to go. Except to Karla's. . . .

Well, there'd be tomorrow. . . . Maybe he should take off the shirt and save it for then. But somehow he knew he'd never wear it again. It was a bad luck shirt.

He lit a cigarette and tried to sort things out. Nothing drastic had happened. Okay, so he had asked for her phone number, demanded it. And she had hung up on him. Big deal. But they hadn't really had a fight. Tomorrow everything would be fine. After all, this Jeremy character was an old man. She had told him how he had become her agent. How he had found her in an air raid shelter. In fact it was one of the few things she had told him about her life. And Jeremy had been a middleaged man then. He was her oldest friend. He remembered her telling him that. "Jeremy is so good, so kind . . . You two must meet one day."

He put his glass down very slowly. "You two must meet one day." Then why hadn't she brought it about tonight? Why hadn't the three of them had dinner together in her kitchen? She didn't have to cancel him out. She and this Jeremy could talk business tomorrow . . .

Unless it wasn't Jeremy who was with her. The thought made his stomach feel tight. But there was no other man in her life! She saw him almost every night. And the nights she didn't see him, it was always because she was tired. In fact she often called him and told him what television show she was watching. No. There was no other man.

Suddenly the vision of Heidi Lanz entering "21" flashed before him. Beautiful Heidi! Heidi the dyke! She had just arrived in town too!

It couldn't be! He poured himself another drink. Then he toasted himself. David Milford. Prize jock. Prize idiot! In love with a fifty-two-year-old woman with a face-lift . . . who wouldn't even give him her phone number.

Only she wasn't just a woman. She was Karla! And right now she was with Jeremy Haskins, and he was drunk and imagining crazy things . . .

Goddammit! Why did he have to see Heidi Lanz at "21" today? And why did the old man have to put that idea in his head? Sure, he had heard rumors about Karla. But then he always figured most European women had had that kind of a fling in their past just as he was sure all English men had tried it with boys. But Karla couldn't really love a woman. Not the way she reacted in his arms, the way she clung to him . . . No. She was with Jeremy now.

He felt he couldn't stay in the apartment another moment. He dashed out and walked down Park Avenue. The air cleared his head. He cut over to Lexington. And kept walking. He knew he was heading toward Karla's apartment building. Well, why not . . . why *not*! He could just walk in. The doorman would think he was expected. So would the elevator man. He'd ring her bell. If it was Jeremy and she was angry, he'd beg forgiveness, he'd–he'd tell her it was his birthday. Yes, that was a good excuse. He'd tell her he had to see her, even if it was for a moment. And then even if she said he could stay, he'd leave. Yes, that was it. Even if she was warm and felt guilty, he'd refuse to stay–just one birthday drink–and then leave. But at least when he went home, he'd be able to sleep.

When he reached her block his courage evaporated. He cut over to First Avenue and went to a bar. He had a double vodka. He felt better. There was nothing to be nervous about. He was building it all up in his own mind. She'd probably laugh, think he was charming, young and impetuous. He walked down the street. When the doorman nodded he felt reassured. He felt even better as the elevator man discussed the Yankees' winning streak as he took him up to the fifteenth floor.

He walked down the hall. He waited until the elevator door closed. The he stood in front of her door for a moment. There was no sound inside. No television. He hesitated. It still wasn't too late. He could turn around and leave and she would never know. He started back for the elevator. But what would the elevator operator think? And the doorman? They knew she was in.

He went back to her door and quickly rang the buzzer. He could actually feel his heart pounding in his throat. He rang again. Then he heard footsteps. She opened the door cautiously–and kept the safety chain on. When she saw him the large gray eyes went dark with anger.

"What do you want?" her voice was cold.

He couldn't believe this was happening. Karla, who always flung the door open for him—Karla peering through the small chained opening, staring at him like an intruder.

"It's my birthday." His voice sounded thick. Not light and easy as he had planned.

"Go away," she said.

He wedged his foot in the door. "It's my birthday. I just want one birthday drink with you . . . and Jeremy."

"I told you to go away!"

"I won't leave." He tried to smile, but he was frightened. The whole thing was out of hand. She was really angry. There was no gracious way out now. He had to get inside, he had to explain how much he loved her . . . How he couldn't live like this, not being able to call.

"If you don't leave, I'll have to call for help," she said.

Oh God, he had ruined everything. "Karla, forgive me. I'm sorry . . ." He backed away and in that split second she slammed the door in his face.

He stood there unable to believe it. Karla. Doing this to him! The bitch! Of course there was no Jeremy inside. She was probably with Heidi Lanz. He rang her bell again. He banged against the door. "Open the door," he shouted. "Open it and prove you have your old business manager in there. Open it and I'll leave. Just prove to me you're telling the truth!"

He waited a few seconds. He was aware someone down the hall had opened the door and peered out. He felt his face burning. The door down the hall finally closed. He rang Karla's buzzer again. "Let me in, damn you . . . let me in!" He kicked at the door. Then he took out a match and stuck it in the buzzer. "I'm going to stand here and wait," he shouted. "I'll wait if I have to wait all night. To see who comes out of that apartment." He gave the door another violent kick. He knew he had lost all control but was powerless to stop. He heard several doors opening in the hall.

Then he heard the elevator door open. And he felt two pairs of strong arms grasp him. He fought and lashed out. The doorman and the elevator man were trying to get him away from Karla's door. His old smiling friends—the doorman who had taken all the dollar tips, the elevator man who had discussed the Yankees with him. They were trying to drag him down the hall.

"Take your hands off me," he shouted. "Miss Karla just doesn't hear the bell. She's expecting me!"

"Take it easy, son," the doorman said. "She called down and asked us to come and get you. Said you were making a disturbance."

He couldn't believe it. Karla was having him thrown out! He stared at them. And then at the door. He gave it a final kick. "You bull dyke," he shouted. "You double-crossing bull dyke. I know who you've got in there. Heidi. *Heidi Lanz*! *Heidi*. Not Jeremy . . . *Heidi Lanz*!"

Doors opened. The other tenants on the floor stared in amazement. Tenants, who in the past had looked at him with envy because he had access to their glamorous neighbor, were watching him being dragged down the hall by the doorman and elevator man. He was kicking and yelling. He heard a rip and knew it was his new shirt. She was having him thrown out! Thrown out! This couldn't be happening. It was all a nightmare.

Then he was in the elevator, and the doorman relaxed his grip. "Now listen, son. Looks like you've had a little too much to drink tonight. Let me put you in a cab and you be on your way. Tomorrow's another day. You send her a few flowers and everything will be as good as new."

He wrenched himself away from the man's hold. He walked outside and tried to stand erect. "There won't be any tomorrow. And I'll never send flowers to that lesbian cunt again! And don't worry about getting me a cab. I don't want anything from any of you. I'll never set foot near this building again." Then he stared up at the windows on the fifteenth floor. "I hate you, you bitch . . ." he muttered. Then he staggered down the street.

Karla stood by the window and watched him until he was out of sight. Then she walked to the bathroom and tapped on the door. Her face was drawn and white. "It's all right, Dee. You can come out now. I don't think David will bother us anymore."

Twenty-four

DEE STRETCHED OUT in the foamy bathtub. WPAT was playing some old Sinatra songs. They were beautiful. The whole world was beautiful. May was such a beautiful month in New York. April had been a beautiful month too. Any month was beautiful when Karla was around. This past winter in Palm Beach had marked their longest separation. Five long months. It had been murderous. There were times when she had to summon every ounce of will power to keep from picking up the phone and pleading with Karla to come down. Maybe it had worked, because on her return she found Karla actually eager to see her.

Of course there had been that dreadful night when David had hammered at the door like a bull in heat. She would never have believed David could lose control like that. But he had been drinking. She hadn't heard too much of the racket—she had been so terrified when the commotion had begun that she had dashed into the bathroom. But it obviously finished David with Karla. He was no longer one of her "nice little" men who took her to the ballet or an art movie.

Oddly enough, David didn't seem to be suffering any loss. According to the columns, he was seeing that Dutch model occasionally, and he talked about January constantly.

He had been heartbroken when she had been unable to come to Palm Beach over Easter. Of course it was an important assignment writing a story on a man like Tom Colt. She had been in California for some time now. She wondered if there was something going on between them. Ridiculous!

Tom Colt was married and much too old-fashioned for January. Mike had been oddly unenthusiastic about the importance of January's assignment. He had insisted on flying out to see her. He had stayed almost a week and when he returned everything seemed fine. Well, she'd have to get around to changing her will. Now that David posed no threat as far as Karla was concerned there was no reason to care whether or not he married January.

When she got out of the tub, she put in a call to George Milford. He came on the phone immediately. "Dee . . . I was just leaving. How nice to hear from you."

"George, I want to change my will."

"Fine. Is it urgent?"

"No, but let's meet tomorrow afternoon."

"Well, that's why I asked if it was urgent. Margaret and I are leaving tomorrow for Paris. Her sister's daughter is getting married, and we haven't had a holiday abroad for some time. So we're doing it right . . . going by boat . . . taking a whole month off. We're sailing tomorrow."

"Oh—" Dee bit her lip thoughtfully.

"But if it's urgent, I can wait in my office now. It's five-thirty. We can draw up the changes. I don't mind staying here for a few hours tonight . . . that is, if you are free. We can go over things together and I'll make notes. Then tomorrow morning I'll have it typed up and if you can come around, say, at ten, we can have it witnessed and notarized and—"

Karla was expecting her at six-thirty. This would take too much time. "No, George, it's not that urgent. It can hold until you return. Have a nice trip, and give Margaret my best."

She hung up and began to dress. Mike was at the Friars Club. She had told him she was going to a Class Reunion. And she insisted he stay there for dinner and play cards. "I've *got* to go. It's something I do every year. There's just twenty of us, and we sit around for hours discussing our days at Miss Briarly's. And if you get home before me, don't wait up."

The marriage was crowding her. With Karla so available, it tortured her to be with Mike. Ever since her return from Palm Beach, Karla was always exuberant whenever Dee said she was free. And lately there had been none of the old excuses. ("Oh, Dee. I've invited the Maestro over for a steak. He hasn't worked for so long and he's going to the motion picture home soon.") Karla's reasons had always been valid . . . but they had come just often enough to keep Dee off balance. Yet there hadn't been one excuse since her return. Each time she called and said, "I can get out tonight," Karla sounded joyous. "I am so glad!" . . . "I await eagerly . . ." or "I have been invited to a dinner at Boris's, but I will cancel."

Of course she could see Karla during the day if she wanted to tag along and do things Karla's way. But somehow she felt a loss of dignity in trailing along after Karla, sitting in some dreary studio and watching her do bar exercises. She had done that the first few years when just seeing Karla—being allowed to be with her—was a privilege. Oddly enough, after all these years, she still felt a sense of giddiness each time she saw Karla. But once their relationship had become firmly established, she felt it was demeaning for her to sit around like a stupefied fan. She also wouldn't go walking in the snow and rain. She wasn't like Karla, who looked fantastic with snow on her hair or rain on her face. Dee's nose and eyes ran when it got cold. Karla could stand under a shower and come out and towel-dry her hair and look magnificent. Dee would be lost without a hairdresser to fix her hair each day.

No, the only way to see Karla and keep their relationship on an equal basis was to have Karla as a houseguest in one of her homes . . . or to see her in New York at night. No woman over forty looked glamorous in daylight. Dee had tried everything. Whatever makeup base she used looked too pink, too orange or too pasty. But at night she looked marvelous. Especially in front of a fire, or sitting with Karla and having dinner by candlelight. She had taken a firm stand against eating in the kitchen. There was no romance to it. Besides, she looked dreadful in that light. Karla always looked slightly tanned, she never needed a makeup base. Karla was Karla—there was no one like her. Even after eight years it still seemed unbelievable that Karla belonged to her. No . . . not belonged. Karla would never belong to anyone. Not even to Jeremy Haskins, who she said had been her manager and great friend. She openly admitted they had made an attempt at being lovers but it hadn't worked. Dee had met Jeremy when he came to the States in 1966, and when she saw his white hair and bent shoulders, she had been so relieved she had even given a dinner party in his honor. And each year she sent him a Christmas gift.

On an impulse she took out her checkbook and wrote a check for ten thousand dollars. She had stopped trying to surprise Karla with gifts. Karla never wore jewelry. And the sable coat she had given her was used like a trench coat. She walked in the snow in it, and to the rehearsal hall and back. Karla only really came alive when she was given money. It was a phenomenon Dee couldn't understand. After all, Karla had plenty of money. My God . . . all those years when she made those pictures. And she spent nothing now . . . just the maintenance on the apartment. It was a fabulous apartment as far as the physical layout went. A decorator could turn it into a showplace. But Dee doubted if there was even five thousand dollars' worth of furniture in the apartment. Of course, it was kept immaculate. Karla thought nothing of scrubbing floors and windows herself. And there were the paintings—a Monet, two Raoul Dufys, a Vlaminck, and the Daumier sketches. But they had all been gifts. And in answer to Dee's "Why do you need a ten-room duplex when you use only three rooms?" Karla had shrugged and said, "It was a gift . . . and it is now worth twice the original price." She had given up trying to rationalize Karla's eccentricities. Eccentricities hell! Karla was downright penurious. Even her Christmas presents to Dee were what Karla called "gag" presents. A beer mug saying "Souvenir of New York" . . . a red flannel nightgown . . . a Polish ornament for the Christmas tree. Dee chalked it up as a wartime neurosis. All refugees were slightly peculiar.

Dee left the house at six-fifteen. She had let the chauffeur go. She took a cab that rocked and wheezed its way across town; but nothing could disturb her high spirits. It was spring and the night was beautiful and in a few minutes she was going to see Karla. Oh God, if only she could hold time still. Make tonight last forever. She played a game with the traffic lights. When the cab came to a red light, she'd count. One . .

then spell it . . . O-N-E. Two . . . T-W-O. For as many numbers as she could say and spell before the light changed . . . that's how many more months she and Karla would have together. She got to sixteen on one light . . . but by the time she got to Second Avenue, she had developed some expertise and was up to thirty-five. She frowned. That was just three more years. No, she wouldn't settle for that. They'd be together forever. Oh God, if she could only believe that. If she could really believe that Karla would never leave her . . . she'd never have married Mike. But even during their most intimate moments, Dee was aware that Karla could never be really possessed by anyone. And if Karla ever thought she was Dee's whole life, Karla might disappear . . . perhaps forever. No, Mike was her safety valve, her crutch of sanity. But Mike was also a problem . . . the devious lies she had to tell him to get her "free nights." In July, she'd insist that Karla come to Marbella. But right now it was only the beginning of May. That meant six weeks in New York to worry about. She thought she had been very clever about her enthusiasm for Cannes with Mike. There was no backgammon tournament in Monte Carlo, and she never had the slightest intention of going there in the first place. But it had to be planned carefully, and so far everything was going according to schedule. The suite at the Carleton was booked for May 14. She planned to wait until the day before and then tell him that the tournament was canceled. But she would insist that he go—the suite was reserved and he deserved two marvelous weeks with all his movie friends. She'd just rest in New York and attend to getting her wardrobe together for the summer. She had the speech all rehearsed. He had to go without her. Then she would have two fantastic weeks with Karla . . . they could be together every night!

Karla was waiting for her when she arrived. Her face was scrubbed and the heavy hair was pulled back with a barrette. She threw her arms around Dee and led her to the table near the window. It was set for dinner, and Karla pointed to the candles. "Look. I bought them today. They do not need the stick to sit in . . . they melt into themselves. Oh, it was wonderful! This marvelous little shop and the little man didn't recognize me. He liked me just for myself. And he took such pains letting me smell all the different smells. Tonight we have gardenia. Dee, do you like gardenia? I love it . . . I hope you do. . . ."

"Of course I do." In the candlelight, with the dusk just beginning to settle on the East River, Karla looked like one of her most perfect movie stills. The shadows falling across her face, the hollow under her cheekbones. Suddenly Dee realized she was staring. She reached into her bag. "Karla, I brought you a little gift."

Karla didn't even look at the check. She smiled and slipped it into her desk drawer. "Thank you, Dee. Now come, sit down. I have prepared a big salad of shrimp and lobster. And look . . . a pitcher of sangria. We shall have a feast."

And that night when they made love, Karla was joyously demonstrative. In fact her whole mood was lighter than usual. Later as they lay together she sang some Polish song she had known as a girl. Then, as if embarrassed because she had revealed some hidden facet of herself, she jumped out of bed and switched on the television set. "There's a good late movie, but I know you prefer the news. I am going to take a shower. Tell me if anything important happens to our sad little world."

Dee watched the news. She heard Karla singing in the shower. Karla was happy. And she was happy. Yet along with her own happiness there was a sense of despair. Because in a short time she would have to leave and go back to Mike. She reached over to the night table and decided to try one of Karla's strong English cigarettes. As she picked up the pack, an envelope fell to the floor. It was Karla's telephone bill. She was suddenly curious. The amount had to be minuscule. Karla rarely called anyone, and if she did, she merely stated her business or request. There was no such thing as a telephone conversation with Karla. Dee took the bill out of the envelope. Her eyebrows lifted when she glanced at the total. Four hundred and thirty-one dollars! She looked at it again. How could Karla run up a bill like that? She examined it carefully. Karla had not exceeded the maximum in local calls. But there was a long list of overseas calls to England—Bostwick 3322. Sixteen calls to that number! And all of the calls lasted longer than three minutes. There were three to another number with a Lowick exchange and two to a Belgravia exchange. But sixteen to Bostwick 3322. She wrote the numbers down on a slip of paper, shoved it into her bag, and replaced the phone bill under Karla's cigarettes. But when Karla came out of the shower and made love to her again, the entire incident went out of her thoughts. She didn't think of it again until she went home and found the slip of paper in her bag. She put it in her jewel case. Karla probably had some business in London. Maybe she was in constant touch with Jeremy. Perhaps her phone bill was high every month. People who were known to be penurious often had one crazy extravagance. Perhaps with Karla it was transatlantic phone calls.

The next day was one of those rare days, when Dee had been unable to connect with Karla. There was no point calling in the morning; Karla would be out walking. And at one, when Karla would be just getting home, Dee was trapped at a luncheon at the Plaza for Baby Town, U.S.A., a rehabilitation home for pregnant girls who were on narcotics. Dee wasn't terribly interested in the whole thing, but it was a good way to get proper newspaper exposure. All the right people were on the committee, and this would be good for her image.

She had called Karla at five, but Karla wasn't in. Then just as she was about to try again, Ernest had arrived to do her hair. She and Mike had to go to a ghastly sit-down dinner at Princess Marina's Park Avenue apartment to honor some Senator, which meant they'd have to sit and listen to his witticisms on Washington. But the Princess gave great parties in Marbella, and if the Princess had this thing about being *au courant* about politics . . . well, she'd just have to sit through one of those nights.

The following morning she lay in bed with her breakfast tray, waiting until twelve-thirty when Karla would be home from her walk. She was also trying to think of an excuse to get away from Mike for the night. The rest of the week was filled, but tonight was free. Mike had said something about seeing two movies in one night. He actually liked sitting in those filthy theaters, and even ate popcorn. In fact he was trying to talk her into building a projection room at the Winter Palace so they could run their own movies. Movies bored Dee. She adored watching all of Karla's reruns, but today's pictures held little interest for her. She hated those dreary motorcycle pictures with young people where everyone wore blue jeans and smoked pot. She could remember when you went to a movie and looked forward to seeing the fashions. But movies were ugly and dirty now. Her own life was much more exciting and beautiful.

She glanced through the newspapers. She had made *Women's Wear* with yesterday's luncheon. Good picture—she would show it to Karla. But right now she had to think of a plan to get out of being with Mike tonight. Backgammon was no longer an excuse. He *liked* backgammon. Dear Lord, why had she ever taught him? She looked at the clock. Maybe she should tell him to go to the club and play golf, that she wanted to—she wanted to *what*? It infuriated her that she had to lie here and think of an excuse. She was Dee Milford Granger. She was supporting this man. Why couldn't she just say, "I want out tonight," as she had with all the others. Because deep down she knew she just couldn't say that to Mike. He might just say, "Okay. You can have out for good." Especially since he didn't seem as concerned about that daughter of his. He never seemed to mention her lately. Maybe that ten million she had left in trust had relaxed him. Well, when he got back, he'd learn that it wasn't an irrevocable trust. She'd change all that. Put David back as an executor. Oh, she'd let the ten million stand for January, but there would be a codicil . . . the ten million would go to January only if Mike Wayne was the husband of Dee Milford Granger. She began to smile. Of course . . . then she'd be able to walk out any night she chose. But meanwhile she had to think of something for tonight. She couldn't invent a fictitious girlfriend for backgammon anymore. He knew all of her friends. This was ridiculous! All of her life she had always done just as she pleased, and now, for the most important person in her life, she had to scheme like a criminal to get a free night.

Maybe Karla might have an idea. Not that she was ever inventive. Dee loved her insanely, but she was still a dumb Polack. It was only ten of twelve; but she tried Karla. Sometimes she got home early. She dialed, but there was no answer.

Of course . . . this was Thursday. The maid wasn't in. Imagine running that place with a maid who only came in three times a week!

She picked up the *Daily News* and leafed through it. The Princess had gotten only half a column. She and Mike were mentioned. But it was the Senator who had gotten all the publicity. She tossed the paper on the floor. It fell with the centerfold open. She stared for a moment. Then she jumped out of bed and grabbed the paper. There was Karla . . . hiding her face from the camera, arriving at Heathrow Airport.

Karla was in London!

She rolled the paper into a ball and tossed it across the room. All the while she had been lying there planning—wondering how to be with her—that bitch was in London.

London!

She got out of bed and rushed to her jewel case and found the piece of paper with the three numbers. Then she went to the telephone. Noon. That meant it was five in the afternoon in London. She placed a person-to-person call to Anthony Pierson. The firm of Pierson and Maitland handled all of her business in London. In less than five minutes, they rang back and Anthony Pierson was on. He was delighted to hear from her. They talked about the wonderful spell of good weather London was having, about some of her holdings . . . Then, trying to sound casual, she said, "Tony, I know this isn't in your line at all . . . but . . . well . . . you see, I have to find out about three phone numbers in London. Oh, it's not for me. It's—it's my stepdaughter. Yes, you see . . . she lives with us and I just happened to come across my phone bill and there are three London numbers that she's been calling. And she's only twenty-one. And naturally I worry. You know how it is . . . some of your rock artists come over here and girls of her age fancy themselves in love—" She laughed. "Yes . . . that's exactly it . . . I wouldn't want her to make a nuisance of herself or get involved with the wrong kind of people. So if you could check out those numbers . . . Oh, Tony, I do appreciate it." She gave him the numbers, then she said, "How long will this take? . . . Only an hour? Oh Tony, you are divine."

She took a bath and kept her eye riveted to the light on the phone on the dressing table. She watched it as she made up. And precisely at one the light came on, and Anthony Pierson was on the line.

"I do have the information," he said. "But it baffles me a bit, I must say. The Bostwick number belongs to a private home near Ascot. The Lowick number belongs to Jeremy Haskins, a retired gentleman who has a bit of fame because he is often seen with Karla when she is here . . . incidentally you do know her, do you not? She's here now, staying at the Dorchester. And the Belgravia number belongs to a well-known psychiatrist. It does seem a bit confusing, because none of the numbers seem to add up to anyone a twenty-one-year-old girl would care to phone."

"Who lives in the house in Ascot?"

"A couple named Harrington. They have a daughter. I pretended I was the postal clerk and needed information on them for rezoning. I thought it was dreadfully clever of me . . . don't you think?"

"How old is the daughter?"

"I didn't ask, but the Harringtons sounded as though they were well up in their fifties or sixties."

"Tony, I have to find out more about them all. Especially the psychiatrist."

"Well, this is all a bit out of my line . . . but I do know a chap . . . a Donald Whyte . . . sort of a private investigator . . . he's quite trustworthy . . ."

"Yes . . . please . . . find out everything you can. Don't worry about Jeremy Haskins. My husband was a producer, so it's quite possible my stepdaughter would know him. But find out about the Harringtons and their daughter."

She hung up and tried to control the panic she felt. Maybe the Harringtons were old friends of Karla's . . . maybe they were people she had met through Jeremy . . . or old friends she had made when she first came to London . . .

Sixteen calls in one month!

No friend was worth sixteen calls to Karla. Unless she was in love. Maybe the girl was rich and was calling Karla sixteen times a month as well. Maybe they talked every night . . . or twice a day. That bitch probably had a double life going.

Ascot was lovely countryside. The girl *had* to be rich. Maybe that was why she was always taking off so secretly.

Maybe the girl had broken up with her . . . yes, that could have been it. That would explain the sixteen calls. Karla begging to come back . . . it would also explain why Karla had suddenly been so nice and warm to her . . . No, she couldn't picture Karla begging anyone for anything. But *sixteen calls in one month!*

When Mike came home that evening, Dee had already made her plans. She was going to learn what Karla was up to and face her with it! But she had to play it carefully with Mike.

She went to the two movies with him . . . and later when they were at Sardi's, she made her first move. She stared into space and sighed heavily.

They had ordered steak. He was almost finished with his. He looked over at her untouched plate. "Aren't you hungry?"

"No . . . I . . . Oh, Mike . . . I feel like an idiot."

"What about?" He helped himself to some of her steak.

"I made a stupid error."

"What kind of an error? It can't be the end of the world."

"Mike, the backgammon tournament is in London."

"When?"

"Oh . . . I think the fifteenth, sixteenth, and seventeenth."

"Well, no big deal! We'll get to Cannes a few days later. Are you going to eat the rest of your steak?"

She pushed the plate toward him. "Mike, I was thinking . . . Look, I'm not that wild about Cannes . . . and it is *your* town. I mean, you'll know everyone . . . and you'll want to be with your old friends . . . and there is the Casino. I'm not a real gambler, not at the tables anyway, and—"

He looked at her closely. "Stop with the build-up. What are you trying to tell me?"

"Mike . . . I'd love to go to London and—"

"I said we'll go."

"But I'll feel so guilty each day I keep you from your film festival. I have friends in London. I'd like to stay there a week. Then go to Paris and buy some clothes. And then join you in Cannes for the end."

"Fine."

"What did you say?"

"I said fine. We'll leave on the fourteenth, drop you in London, and then I'll take the plane on to Nice. I'll send it back for you and you can join me whenever you like."

"Oh, Mike . . . you're an angel."

"Look, babe, it's a two-way street. No one says you have to like a film festival. I think you'll have a great time in London."

"It won't be great," she said. "But it will be interesting."

Twenty-five

DEE SAT in Anthony Pierson's office and stared at the pictures. She was still off balance from the time change. She had arrived in London at ten the night before; but it had only been five in the afternoon, New York time. She had called Tony Pierson at home. He said he had a full report, but he hardly thought it would be relevant to her stepdaughter. She told him she'd be in his office the following morning at eleven. Then she drugged herself to sleep with three Seconals. She couldn't bear a sleepless night alone in London. There was no all-night television, and she couldn't concentrate on reading. She had checked into the Grosvenor House because Karla was staying at the Dorchester. She didn't want to run into Karla. Not yet.

She felt the beginnings of a migraine headache as she sat in Anthony Pierson's quiet conservative office, but she managed to appear calm.

She leafed through the pictures he had given her. "They're excellent," she said tonelessly.

Anthony Pierson nodded. "This chap, Donald Whyte, the one who did the–shall we say research? He covered that house with a telescopic lens for days. The poor chap actually sat in a tree. The psychiatrist is on holiday . . . left two days ago . . . so we didn't fare too well there. But the shots of Karla and the girl are quite fantastic, don't you think? Of course, I got the negatives . . . that was part of the arrangement. Whyte is a top man and quite reliable, but what with Karla still being very much of a public figure, I think it's quite fortunate I took this precaution."

"For God's sake," Dee said testily. "It's not as if he found them in bed together!"

Anthony Pierson nodded. "Quite right. But that one picture

. . . with the girl's arms around Karla's neck . . . and the other where they are kissing . . . and look here . . . walking with their arms entwined. No, they've not been caught in bed . . . but it would make for jolly good speculation in one of those scandal magazines."

Dee stared at the pictures. Her head was beginning to throb. How could she compete with anyone as young and lovely as this girl?

"She's very beautiful," Dee said slowly.

"Quite fabulous, isn't she? Whyte learned that the Harringtons are not her parents. They obviously work for her. Because the girl's name is Zinaida Jones. The house is rented; it's a lovely house. Not too large, but secluded—nice piece of land and all that. Karla has been there every day. On three occasions she stayed overnight."

Dee's hand shook as she fumbled for a cigarette. She stared at the girl. The picture was fuzzy from enlargement. She inhaled her cigarette deeply. "Have you got any aspirins, Tony? I'm afraid I've a bit of jet lag."

"Of course." He went to a chest in the bathroom. When he came out, Dee was still studying the pictures.

"It does look rather peculiar, doesn't it?" he said. "Looks like the great Karla has found herself a bit of new young love life. But then . . . there's always been that rumor about the lady, hasn't there?"

"I've heard it," Dee said. "But I know Karla. She's been to my home, and I never saw anything that would give it any credence."

"Except these pictures, I'd say," Anthony Pierson said. "Pretty damning. Why can't these people confine their amorous inclinations to the bedroom? Why would she walk around the grounds with her arms around that girl?"

"Perhaps because she didn't know Mr. Donald Whyte was sitting up in a tree with a telescopic camera. You say it is a secluded place?"

"Has about an acre of its own ground. But my dear Mrs. Wayne, how can any of this affect your stepdaughter?"

Dee shook her head. "Well . . . perhaps . . . perhaps she knows this Zinaida."

"Oh." For a moment Anthony Pierson colored slightly. "Well

. . . oh . . . I see. All the calls . . . you are thinking that perhaps your stepdaughter was, ah . . . friendly with this Zinaida Jones?"

Dee shrugged. "Why not? She went to school in Switzerland. She was raised in girls' schools." She stood up. "Do you have the exact address of the house?"

"Yes. Right here. It's about an hour's drive from town."

"Thank you. And will you take care of Mr. Whyte's services and send the entire bill to me? Send it around tomorrow to the Grosvenor. For obvious reasons, I wouldn't want this to go to New York."

She tried to think of a plan of action as she drove to the country. The chauffeur knew the way, and now they were out of London, coming into lush green scenery, approaching Ascot. . . . But then what? She couldn't just ring the bell and say to this Zinaida Jones: "Look . . . she's mine!" Perhaps if she got off outside of the house and tried to catch sight of them. The whole thing was so distasteful that she shrank back in the seat. But she was determined to go through with it. All the years of devotion she had given Karla . . . all the "gifts." Had Karla used that last ten-thousand-dollar check to dash off to be with her young new love? For the first time she knew how a man felt to be cuckolded. Cuckolded! Now how did she ever come up with an expression like that? But that's exactly how she felt. Cuckolded! It was a great word. She couldn't say she was being cheated on . . . no doubt Karla had done that off and on all the time. She had never really asked her, just as Karla never asked about her sex life with Mike. She had tried to tell Karla about it once . . . how she really just put up with Mike . . . how relieved she was when the sex part was over . . . because that meant he wouldn't bother her for at least two or three days. She thought about it now. Funny . . . in the last few months, weeks had gone by without Mike coming near her. She hadn't even noticed. The thought disturbed her. Not that she wanted him to touch her . . . but was she that unattractive? She knew there was a certain softness to her body . . . her thighs . . . her stomach. She was aware of it when she was lying close to Karla, because Karla didn't have an ounce of spare flesh. But she hadn't minded her own soft body . . . somehow it had made her feel more feminine with Karla. But why had Mike stayed away? Was it too much golf? He was always gambling lately. She wondered how much he had won.

But that wasn't her concern. Right now her concern was Karla . . . and the new girl. But maybe she wasn't a new girl. Maybe they had been together for some time. Maybe Karla was going through a "young" period. There had been David for a time . . . now this girl. . . .

The driver pulled up along a huge row of hedges. "This is the house, madam. The entrance is down the road a bit. But you said you wanted to stop here."

"Yes. I want to surprise some old friends. If the car comes in the driveway, well . . . there wouldn't be any surprise, would there?"

"No, madam."

She wondered if he believed her. The English could be so damned expressionless when they wanted to be. He probably thought she was surprising a lover. Well, she was!

The small iron gate had no lock. She opened it and walked up the driveway. It was beginning to rain. She was wearing a raincoat and she put her scarf over her head. It was a very modest driveway; but the grounds were well tended. The house was Tudor in style. There was a small English car parked out front.

Dee approached slowly. She wondered if this Zinaida owned a dog. It would be horrible if some English mastiff lunged at her throat. She could see the headline: DEE MILFORD GRANGER ATTACKED BY DOG FOR TRESPASSING. God, how would she ever explain that? There were lights inside the house. Zinaida was probably home . . . or was she off walking the countryside with her arm around Karla's waist like in the pictures? Karla liked to walk in any kind of weather. And she could just bet that Zinaida pretended to adore it too.

She tiptoed over to the window. It was a cozy living room, nothing pretentious; and no one was there. Perhaps if she went around to the back . . . Karla always loved kitchens . . .

"Why don't you come in . . . it's very wet outside."

She gasped when she heard the voice. She turned . . . Karla

was standing behind her. The rain was on her face and she was wearing a bandana and a trenchcoat.

"Karla . . . I . . ."

"Let's go inside. It is damp and cold."

Karla opened the door. Dee noticed she had a key. She wanted to run. This was the end. . . . She never should have come. Karla's face was a mask. She was obviously cold with anger and she would probably tell her that everything was over between them. Oh God, why had she done this? She had once seen a play where the mistress had done her best to have the wife find out . . . because once the wife confronted her husband with the evidence, there was nothing for him to do but admit it. And if Karla admitted it, Dee would have to walk away. Even though she would die inside . . . she'd have to walk away with pride. Because without pride . . . there could be no relationship. Yet at the same time she longed to fall on her knees and tell Karla to forget she was there . . . to forget this whole horrible incident.

Karla hung up her coat on a rack near the door. She was wearing gabardine slacks and a man's shirt. Her hair was long and straight. She looked weary but as beautiful as ever.

Dee stood very still. Karla turned and pointed to the rack. "Take off your coat. It is wet."

Dee took it off and knew that her hair was squashed down by the scarf. She probably never looked worse. And somewhere in this house—waiting for Karla—was this gorgeous young creature.

"Sit down," Karla said. "I will get some brandy." She disappeared into another room.

Dee looked around. There was a picture of Karla in a large frame. Then there was a picture of a German shepherd dog, obviously long deceased, because the girl with it was a child. Probably one of Zinaida's childhood pets. Where was she? Probably upstairs, respecting Karla's desire for privacy like everyone else, giving in to Karla's moods.

Karla returned with a bottle of brandy and poured two glasses. Dee watched with surprise the way Karla tossed down the drink in one gulp. Then she sat down. "All right, Dee. . . . I'm not going to ask how you found me. I'll save you that embarrassment."

Tears came to Dee's eyes. She got up and walked toward the charred fireplace. "I'd give ten years of my life if I could take back this afternoon."

"Do I mean that much to you?" Karla's voice was almost gentle.

Dee turned toward her, forcing back her tears. "Do you mean that much to me? Oh, God . . ." She walked across the room and went to her bag for a cigarette. She lit it and turned to Karla. "No . . . you don't mean very much. Just enough to make me sick every time you take off . . . enough to make me become a devious liar and a sneak with my husband . . . sending him off to Cannes alone while I . . . I . . . called a friend . . . and learned of your whereabouts . . . and found out about Zinaida. And I must be some kind of masochist. Instead of just putting you out of my life, I come out here . . . wanting to see her for myself . . . wanting– Oh, God knows what. Why should I torture myself like this? I know she's years younger than I . . . and very beautiful . . . and I wish to God I hadn't come . . . because if I hadn't . . . we'd still be together."

"Where did you see her?" Karla asked.

Dee opened her bag and dropped the pictures in Karla's lap.

Karla studied them. She looked at Dee in amazement. "This is the work of a paparazzi."

Dee shook her head helplessly. "No . . . it's an Englishman named Donald Whyte. Don't worry . . . I have the negatives. Look, Karla . . . I have my car outside . . . I'd better go." She started for the door. She reached for her raincoat and turned to Karla. "Just tell me one thing . . . how long has this affair been going on?"

Karla looked down at the pictures . . . then at Dee. Then with a sad smile she shook her head. "Yes . . . I see . . . the pictures . . . What else do you know?"

"I know that you've been spending several nights here."

"Ah, your man is thorough. But not thorough enough . . . right?"

"Do you enjoy this game?" Dee snatched her coat from the wooden rack.

"No . . . I am suffering inside more than you would believe. But since you have come such a long way . . . and gone to so much trouble . . . I think that before you leave, you should meet Zinaida."

"No." Dee struggled to get into her coat. With a sudden movement, Karla sprang to the center of the room and pushed her into a chair.

"You have snooped . . . and you now wish to walk away. Well, a snoop deserves to see the finish. Perhaps it will teach you some kind of lesson in the future." Karla walked to the staircase and shouted, "Mrs. Harrington."

A small gray-haired lady peered over the balustrade. "Tell Zinaida to tear herself away from the TV set and come downstairs. I want her to meet a friend of mine."

Karla poured herself another glass of brandy. She pointed to Dee's untouched glass. "Drink yours. You'll need it."

Dee kept her eyes fastened on the stairs. Then she saw the girl. She was more beautiful than the photographs. She was tall, almost as tall as Karla. Her hair was blonde and it fell to her shoulders. She looked much younger than her pictures. Dee guessed her to be about January's age.

Karla's smile was gentle. "Come in, Zinaida. We have a guest. This is Mrs. Wayne."

The girl smiled at Dee. Then she turned to Karla. "Could I have some chocolate cake? Mrs. Harrington just made it this afternoon and she said I can't have it until dinner."

"We do what Mrs. Harrington says," Karla said slowly. "Perhaps she wanted the cake to be a surprise."

"But now you know about it, so it's no surprise. So can I have it? Just one piece? Please? I'm so dreadfully sick of those oatmeal cookies she always makes."

"Go back to your telly," Karla said.

The girl sighed in disgust. Then she pointed at Dee. "Is she staying for dinner?"

"Shall we ask her?"

Zinaida smiled. "Sure, as long as you tell me the Red Shoes story before I go to bed." She ran out of the room.

For a moment Dee stared after her. Then she looked at Karla. "She's very beautiful . . . but what was all that? Some kind of a private joke? I thought she acted like a twelve-year-old."

"Actually, she's ten."
"What are you talking about?"
"Her mentality. It is that of a ten-year-old."
"And she's your great love?"
"She's my daughter."
For a moment, Dee couldn't speak. "Drink your brandy," Karla said. This time Dee swallowed it in one gulp. Then Karla poured them each another. "Take off your coat and stay for dinner. That is, if you like chocolate cake."
"Karla, when did you have this child?"
"Thirty-one years ago."
"But . . . she looks so young."
Karla shrugged. "They always look young. Perhaps because they do not have grown-up worries."
"Do you . . . want to tell me about it?"
"After dinner. But first—I suggest you dismiss your car. I will drive you back into town."
It had been an easy dinner. Dee was so relieved at the change of events that she was filled with affection for the beautiful child-woman who tore into the food and chattered incessantly throughout the meal. Mr. and Mrs. Harrington were obviously the couple who took care of Zinaida. Dee noticed Zinaida addressed Karla as "Godmother." When dinner was finished she jumped up and said, "And now Godmother is going to tell me 'Red Shoes.' "
Dee sat spellbound as Karla half talked, half danced, and half acted out the story. She had never seen Karla give this much of herself. But her warmth toward Zinaida was fluid and easy. At nine o'clock, Mrs. Harrington appeared. "Come, Zinaida . . . Godmother has company, and it is time for a bath and bed."
"Will you come up later and hear my prayers?"
"Of course," Karla said as she kissed the girl.
Karla added more wood to the fire. She sat and stared at it morosely. "She is very lovely, isn't she?"
"She's fantastic-looking," Dee said. "I see a lot of you in the bone structure of her face . . . but her eyes are dark. Her father must have been very handsome."
"I don't know who he was."

Dee didn't answer. She sat motionless . . . afraid to break the mood. Karla spoke hesitantly. "You see, I was raped by almost a dozen Russian soldiers in one night. Any one of them could have fathered her." Then she sat down and stared into the fire. She spoke slowly . . . never moving her eyes from the flame. Her voice was low and unemotional as she told Dee about her girlhood in Wilno . . . Sister Thérèse . . . the ballet . . . the war . . . the Russian occupation . . . and the violence and rape. She also told how it had been impossible for her to leave Wilno until after the baby was born. She talked about Gregory Sokoyen—how he had stayed with her the night she was in labor . . . how she could not cry out because of the other children sleeping in the convent . . . the nineteen hours of unbearable pain . . . Gregory always there . . . even in the final moment when they had realized something was wrong . . . a breech birth . . . it had been Gregory who fought his own panic and reached up, straightened the baby, and literally pulled it out. She could still see him, standing under the awful little overhead light . . . smacking the bottom of the bloody child . . . until the first pitiful wail emerged.

Karla looked over at Dee. "In pictures, and even in hospitals, one always sees the mother being given a sweet-smelling little bundle in an immaculate blanket. But my cubicle of a bedroom looked liked a slaughterhouse that night. The baby was covered with my blood . . . the long umbilical cord hung down . . . Gregory attended to everything while I went into another violent spasm of pain delivering the afterbirth."

She shuddered slightly. "I'll never forget that night . . . getting the baby cleaned first . . . then destroying bloody sheets . . . putting the baby to my breast for the first time. I had never dreamed I would have a golden little girl. Somehow, I guess I had always thought it would come out looking like a little miniature Russian soldier with a bulbous nose and whiskey on its breath. And when I held her in my arms, I knew I could never leave her."

She talked on in a quiet voice, telling of the hazardous trip with the A.K. Twenty of them, hiding in barns during the day . . . crossing rooftops and underground tunnels at night . . .

carrying the baby strapped against her stomach . . . stifling the baby's cries with a few drops of vodka when the Russians were close.

"And that is how it all happened. Zinaida was about three months old . . . a beautiful normal baby girl. We were close to the Corridor . . . the Nazis were all around us now . . . and the baby began to cry. We did everything—the vodka didn't work . . . nothing worked . . . even the chocolate candy which we hoarded like gold. Her cries grew piercing. I put her to my breast . . . but I had so little milk. I couldn't quiet her. Suddenly one of the men grabbed her from my arms and placed a pillow over her face while another held my mouth so I couldn't scream. And when the Germans were gone . . . Zinaida was dead. Oh God! I'll never forget that moment . . . when we are stared at that lifeless little body. I was sobbing silently . . . And the man who had held the pillow had tears running down his face. Suddenly he grabbed her and started breathing into her mouth. We all stood so still. Twenty cold dirty people who had traveled together, slept huddled against one another for warmth, picked lice off one another—lived together for three long weeks with just two thoughts. Survival and escape. And everyone had tears in their eyes as the man worked on Zinaida. Even the small children with their pinched faces—some were perhaps only five or six, but they knew what was happening. And when Zinaida let out that first hint of a wail, everyone fell to their knees and thanked God. Zinaida had been brought back to life. I suppose she was dead for a few minutes . . . maybe five . . . maybe ten—just long enough to lose the oxygen that damaged her brain. But I didn't know it at the time. And when we got to Sweden she seemed just like any other baby, only far more beautiful. I left her with a family named Oleson. They thought she was an infant who had been abandoned at the convent that I had 'adopted.' I was going to London and I promised to send money for her care . . . and send for her as soon as the war ended. You see, I was to stay at Uncle Otto's. I could not saddle them with a child, and I hoped to get into the ballet. Then I would be able to support her.

"You know the rest. Jeremy found me in a bomb shelter and

I went into pictures. It sounds pat and very easy, but it was such a strange world to me, with a new language to learn . . . I was so shy and thought everyone was laughing at my English, and I had so little confidence in my acting. Dancing was the only thing I knew. But I was able to send Mrs. Oleson good money every week, and she was very kind and sent me pictures of little Zina constantly. Zinaida was about three when the first rumblings of trouble began. Mrs. Oleson's letters became less enthusiastic. Zinaida was a slow walker . . . she still babbled rather than talked . . . all the other children were ahead of her. At first I tried to tell myself many children were slow—you know how it is. Everyone tells you Einstein didn't talk until he was five . . . and you push it from your mind. The child would catch up. And then finally Mrs. Oleson sent another letter, asking for permission to institutionalize the child. As she put it, 'After all, it is not yours, it is an orphan. Why should you waste any more money on it?' "

Karla began to pace the room. "Can you imagine how I felt? I insisted on having the child brought to London . . . to raise it as my own. But Jeremy was the practical one. By then I was quite well known in London, and Jeremy explained that divulging the existence of an illegitimate child—a retarded one at that—would destroy any career I might have. You must remember, this was not 1971, when that sort of thing is now accepted. This was 1946, and an actress with a bastard child would be thrown out of the business. It was Jeremy who went over and got Zinaida. He also arranged for an English birth certificate and selected the names Jones. We put Zinaida in a psychiatric hospital while the neurologists made every possible test. The reports were all the same. Brain damage. She would be teachable. . . . But what mentality she would have, one could not definitely say." Karla walked across the room and poured herself another brandy. "Well, I suppose we are fortunate in a way—she is ten years old mentally and about six emotionally."

"But a ten-year-old is capable of doing many things," Dee said.

Karla nodded. "Unfortunately, you are right. She is pregnant." Karla walked to the stairs. "And now I must go up and hear her prayers."

When she came down, Dee was standing by the stairs waiting.

"Karla . . . what are we going to do?"

"We?"

There were tears in Dee's eyes. "Yes . . . *we*. Oh, God, Karla . . . now I understand so much . . . all the times you disappeared . . . why you're so . . . so—"

"So cheap?"

"Not cheap . . . but . . ."

"Cheap," Karla said with a sad smile. "Dee, I do not have the money people think I have. I retired with a quarter of a million dollars. That is invested. I live off the interest and whatever gifts I receive." She looked at Dee with a faint smile. "Jeremy is getting old. He cannot always call me when things go wrong . . . like now. So I have come here and found a companion for Zinaida. Actually, she is a nurse. But she will not dress as one. She will live with Zinaida and be in constant touch with me. The Harringtons are marvelous people . . . they run the house . . . and do their best . . . But they cannot be with her every second. When Miss Roberts arrives, she will be with Zina constantly. She will ride horses with Zina, play checkers, read to her . . . She will cost me three hundred dollars a week, but I will rest easier. I cannot stay and take care of her . . . the child worships me. When I stay too long she becomes attached. She . . . she tried to make love to me one night." Karla stood up and threw her hands to the ceiling. "Well, why not? Good God, she has a woman's body! It craves sex . . . it craves sex wherever it can find it. We have her on tranquilizers now. But it is best I do not stay too long. The psychiatrist we saw . . . he is arranging for a legal abortion."

"Who was the man?"

"A delivery man, we assume. Who knows? The Harringtons suddenly noticed the morning sickness, the thickening of her waist . . . and they questioned her. She was quite candid. She said a man told her if he put his number-one thing into her number-one thing it would feel good. But she didn't like it, she said it hurt. We have told her never to do that again, and she says she will not . . . But I shall feel better when Miss Roberts arrives next week."

"Karla, I want to help."

Karla smiled and took Dee's hand. "You have helped. Your checks have helped so very much."

"No . . . more than that. Look, most people with my kind of money leave it to foundations and charities. I have my foundations and trusts. But I'm also going to do some good while I'm alive. When I go back . . . I'm changing my will immediately. I'll put ten million into an irrevocable trust for you and Zinaida. I'll have it worked out so that it can go to you and Zinaida now. The interest alone will be over half a million a year. And when we get back to the States we'll start the Zinaida Foundation . . . we'll build a school in her name . . . to help people like Zinaida. We'll work on it together. And maybe later on we can bring Zinaida back to the States. She and the nurse can live at a guest cottage on the grounds of the Winter Palace. I'll build a projection room so she can see movies . . . Mike wants one anyway . . . and perhaps we'll have a big benefit . . . and even teach Zinaida a little speech. Let them see how beautiful a retarded child can be. And you can come out of retirement and tell them she is an adopted godchild of yours . . . use your time and *my* time for something worthwhile. I can stop all those needless luncheons and you can stop those goddamn bar exercises. You've got some real work to fill your days now. And so have I. And Karla . . . we'll work together." She took Karla into her arms because she suddenly realized that Karla was sobbing.

And that night as they lay in bed together, Karla whispered, "I love you, Dee. I will never leave you. I will never go off again. Now I can breathe easier. You see, Zinaida has no one but me. I always worried—what if I got ill? Perhaps that is why I tried to stay so physically fit. The money I have—I could live fine. But old age or a prolonged illness could wipe it out; and then where would Zinaida be? I couldn't bear the idea of a state hospital. Also, I will die before Zinaida—the estate I would leave after taxes might not be enough to take care of her for the rest of her life. But now, because of you, for the first time I can live without fear of the future."

Dee commuted between Grosvenor House and the cottage near Ascot. She waited until Zinaida had the abortion, then she left for Cannes. Karla would stay with Zinaida for another week, and then they planned to meet back in New York.

Dee sat in her plane and wondered if anyone had ever known the kind of happiness she felt. She would even pretend to like Cannes. She would give Mike a pleasant week. She could afford to be generous. Because when she came back to New York her life was really going to begin . . .

Twenty-six

Mike threw the third seven in a row. He was having the same kind of hot run he had had that week in Vegas. A large crowd had gathered behind him at the Casino in Monte Carlo. He let the money ride and threw the dice again. His point was eight. He covered the four, five, nine and ten. Then he rolled again. A four came up. He pressed the bet. "Numbers!" he shouted as he rolled the dice. He made a nine. He pressed it . . . then rolled two sixes, a four, three nines, a ten, and another four before making his point. He rolled again. Eleven! He was hot now. His next point was six. He kept rolling, calling for numbers. He made hard eights, fours, tens . . . he pressed as far as the limit would allow. He made eight straight passes, and when he cashed in his francs, he had won close to twenty-five thousand dollars. He kept ten thousand francs in chips and roamed around the Casino.

It had been a good night. But he felt it wasn't over. He walked past the Chemin de Fer table and yelled Banco. He got the bank and lost. He waited for the next deal and yelled Banco again. He got half the bank and won. Then he waited his turn and took the bank. An hour later he walked away with over a hundred thousand francs. He wandered over to the roulette table where Dee was playing. She played a chip on number thirty-six. He reached out and surrounded it. Number thirty-five won. She stared in amazement as the croupier pushed all the stacks of chips toward him. He took them off the table and walked away. He went to the cashier. All together he had won close to fifty thousand dollars. Time to quit for the night.

Time to quit. Period. He had spent a week at the Casino without having a losing night. He had found the picture he was looking for. A seamy story about a girl pushing thirty who made her living entering beauty contests. She never won any titles, but she was always up there in the finals. Always in the money. Always on a bus . . . going to another town . . . another contest. He had seen the picture three times before he made his decision.

It had been shot on location in Texas by two young independent producers. They had run short on money and borrowed three hundred thousand from a bank to finish it. Then they came to Cannes, looking for a distribution deal. Mike got 60 percent of the picture by paying off their bank loan and guaranteeing the advertising costs. He ran into Cyril Bean of Century Pictures and talked him into taking a look at the film. Before the film was over, they shook hands. Century would get 35 percent for distribution and share in the costs of advertising. Mike Wayne was back in action again.

He planned to open it at an art house and back it with a big advertising campaign. The girl who played the tired beauty contestant was an Off Broadway actress, unknown to the public. Several of the critics who saw it in Cannes were giving it raves. He couldn't lose. Even if it wasn't an all-time box-office winner, it would make a hell of a splash, he'd get his money back. But more important it would put him back in action. The girl was a cinch for an Academy Award nomination. Everything was set. He had the signed contract in his vault at the hotel. He had paid off the bank, and he still had over a half-million dollars in cash . . . and a few more nights at the Casino. Then back to New York. . . .

And *then* he'd call January. He had rehearsed the call in his mind, night after night. He knew exactly how to handle it. He wouldn't even mention Tom Colt. He'd tell her he was back in action again and ask her if she wanted to work with him. He'd open his own office. She could help him in the overall campaign—travel to all the cities with him to open the picture. If she refused . . . he'd take a different attack. He'd play it cool . . . accept her decision. Then a few days later he'd call back, and ask a favor. He'd tell her he needed publicity on the picture. Would she do a story for that magazine of hers? Cover the opening . . . take some pictures of him in his office, on the road . . . (The story in *Gloss* was the last thing he needed. He had hired a top publicity firm to do a tremendous job, but he wouldn't let her know. He'd act like he *needed* her help. She couldn't turn him down.) He was confident that once they saw one another, spent some time together, everything would fall into place. It would be like old times. The old razzle-dazzle . . . the old excitement. Because from now on he was going to generate plenty of excitement and action. He had also done some clever wheeling and dealing in the lobby of the Carlton Hotel in Cannes. He had practically stolen the American distribution rights of a great Italian picture by a new director. He also had 50 percent of the American rights of a Czech picture that wasn't going to make any money but would win prizes at every festival. And his name would be on it. In 1972, Mike Wayne would be right up there again.

He was also going to leave Dee. He'd let her divorce him. He'd thank her for giving it a try and explain it just hadn't worked out. Of course that would mean she'd change her will and January would blow ten million bucks. But the year with Dee had brought a lot of things into focus. He had married Dee to get security for January. And where was she? Shacked up with an overaged married stud in a bungalow at the Beverly Hills Hotel. What security did she have with Tom Colt? She had to know his work would come first . . . and that his wife and kid would also eventually take precedence over her. But she had gone into it knowing she had to finish a poor third. She had taken the gamble. She didn't want life to be gift-wrapped or dropped into her lap. And neither did he. He couldn't face another winter in Palm Beach . . . a summer at Marbella . . . the small talk at dinner parties . . . the bland empty serenity of Dee . . . No wonder she had no lines in her face—she felt nothing. She lived in a world of "small talk," backgammon, shopping . . . A life of trivia. She probably wouldn't even go into any real scene over their split-up. Oh, it might upset some of her plans for Marbella—especially the seating arrangements at her dinner parties—but she wouldn't feel any great loss. And January wouldn't really lose anything in not becoming an heiress. As soon as they got back he'd take out a healthy life insurance policy, and no matter what happened, he'd never borrow on it. He'd get his old suite back at the Plaza . . . with two bedrooms. He'd ask her to move back. No, he'd tell her the room was there—would always be there —if she wanted it.

Several times he had almost placed a call to her at the Beverly Hills Hotel. But he always caught himself in time. He saw to it that his acquisition of the picture got a big story in *Variety*. He had cut it out and mailed it to her with no comment.

They planned to leave for New York on Friday. Two days before, he made a quick trip to Switzerland and deposited half a million in cash in a numbered bank account. Then he cabled the Plaza to reserve his old suite for Saturday, May 28. He would wait until they got to the Pierre . . . then break it to Dee, and check into the Plaza.

On Thursday afternoon, Dee ran around the Rue Antibes buying perfume and little gifts for her friends. Mike ran into a producer he had never liked. He invited Mike to his suite for a game of gin. Mike hesitated. The producer was notoriously lucky. Then he nodded. Why not! This would be a final test of his luck.

He left the suite late that afternoon, thirty thousand dollars richer, and went to Cartier's and bought Dee a thin platinum cigarette case. He managed to get a rush job done on the engraving. The following day as they drove to the airport, he tossed it in her lap. The inscription said TO DEE. THE LADY WHO BROUGHT ME BACK MY LUCK. IN GRATITUDE. MIKE. She leaned over and kissed his cheek. Maybe he should tell her now and get it over with . . . But then he thought better of it. It'd be murder to be trapped in a plane for six hours with nothing to do but rehash a "nothing" marriage. Besides, it wasn't her fault. She had bought herself a legal escort. And now it was time for her to find another. This one was returning to the human race.

They left Cannes and boarded their plane at Nice. He sat across the aisle from Dee. He had brought caviar and champagne aboard. Paid for it himself. He had hesitated at first, because this was a ritual he reserved for January. But then, this *was* for January. He was on his way back to her and freedom.

They opened the champagne and caviar after they were airborne. The new attendant served them. He was a young French boy who had driven for them while they were in Cannes. His dream was to see America. Mike had offered him a ride, and Dee had told him there was always room for a gardener or driver at the Winter Palace. His name was Jean Paul Vallon, and he had lived all of his nineteen years in Cannes. He had never even been to Paris. His mother, and aunt, three cousins, and his sister and brother-in-law had come to see him off. None of them had ever been in a plane before—and the opulence of Dee's private jet overwhelmed them.

Dee held up her glass and smiled at Mike. "To Cannes . . . and your friends."

He held up his glass. "To Marbella . . . and your life and friends."

She smiled and sipped her drink. Mike put his glass to his lips . . . but couldn't bring himself to drink it. Suddenly it seemed wrong to drink Dom Perignon with anyone but January. He held the glass and stared out the window. It wasn't going to be easy breaking this to Dee. After all, she hadn't done anything . . . except be herself. Only it just wasn't for him.

Dee opened the cigarette case and took out a cigarette. She stared out the window at the clouds below. The inscription on the case was beautiful. Mike was so kind . . . so sweet . . . he really cared about her. But she just couldn't go on like this. She had no intention of lying awake night after night trying to plan excuses to be with Karla. No, after she changed the will, she would have to tell him. And then announce that she intended to lead her own life—and that he could do the same —as long as he got into no scandal and was always available when she needed him. If he accepted those terms, then January's inheritance would be safe.

She looked over at his strong profile. She would be castrating him. Yet there was no other way. She stared at the cigarette case. It was the first expensive gift she had ever received from any man. She fingered it gently. He had spent a lot of money on it. Probably all of his gambling winnings. Her eyes blurred. Oh God, why was there always someone who had to get hurt? She took a deep drag of her cigarette. Then she jabbed it out in the small ashtray. She had given him a good year . . . done the best she could for his daughter . . . and the daughter would wind up being a very rich woman if Mike played along. But her conscience still bothered her. She looked at the case again. A man had to be in love to write an inscription like that: THE LADY WHO BROUGHT ME BACK MY LUCK. But there was no reason for her to have a guilt complex like this. If a man were in her spot, would he be as generous toward the woman? Of course not! And he'd feel no guilt either. Karla had left London for New York three days ago . . . they had talked on the phone for close to an hour. Zinaida had taken to Miss Roberts and Karla was eager to return to New York and see Dee.

Karla's voice had been low. "Dee . . . please hurry back."

Just thinking about it now made her feel weak with happiness. She closed her eyes and leaned back, trying to cement the vision of Karla in her mind. Karla belonged to her now. Really belonged to her!

The plane lurched, but Dee kept her eyes closed. Mike's drink had spilled, and Jean Paul came rushing over to mop it up. Mike wiped off the attaché case he was holding. The contract for the picture was inside. Along with one hundred and fifty thousand American dollars in cash. Enough to get him started in an office and get the publicity rolling.

Jean Paul refilled Mike's glass even though he motioned that he didn't want any. He took the bottle from the boy and refilled Dee's glass. "Here's some for you too, Jean Paul. This is a big occasion . . . your first trip to America. And from now on, anytime anything special happens in your life . . . buy yourself a bottle and make this a ritual. A ritual of luck."

The boy watched carefully as Mike filled his glass. The plane lurched again, and some of the wine spilled on to his new dark trousers. Mike laughed. "That means good luck, Jean Paul." The plane lurched again and dropped fifty feet . . . then it seemed to rock. The boy's eyes went glassy with fright. Mike smiled. "Strap yourself in, kid. Looks like we're probably hitting some weather."

Mike leaned back and closed his eyes. The plane jolted . . .

then leveled out. He was thinking about January when he heard an uneven sound in the jet's engine—like the revving of a motorcycle. He sat up and listened carefully. Dee looked at him questioningly. He unstrapped his seatbelt and went inside the cabin. Both pilots were working furiously at the controls. Smoke was pouring out of one of the jet's motors. The plane began to weave crazily.

"Release the motor. Drop it," Mike said hoarsely.

"I can't," the pilot shouted. "It's jammed. Wire Mayday," he told his partner. "Go back and sit down, Mr. Wayne. Looks like we'll have to go for a crash landing."

Mike returned to his seat. Dee was staring at him apprehensively. The young French boy had taken out a rosary. His face was ashen. He looked at Mike, his eyes pleading for some reassurance.

Mike managed a smile. "Everything's fine . . . we've sprung a little engine trouble. We're gonna put down and get it fixed. Just relax."

Then the pilot's voice came through. "Mr. and Mrs. Wayne, we're going for a crash landing. Will you please unstrap your seat belts. Take off your shoes and get into a kneeling position on the floor. If you are wearing glasses, take them off, and put your head in your hands."

Jean Paul began to sob. "I will never see America. We are all going to die . . ."

Dee was silent. Her face was strained and white. Oh God! This was something you read about that happened to other people. It couldn't be happening to her . . . not now . . . not when she really had something to live for . . . Oh, please not now!

Mike knelt down and held the attaché case firmly. Then he leaned over and picked up the champagne bottle that was on the floor. He put it to his mouth and took a long swallow. It was an occasion now . . . one hell of an occasion. And just before the plane exploded in mid-air, he thought of January. He would never have the chance to apologize and tell her how much he loved her. And when the explosion came, the last thing that occurred to him was the numbered bank account in Switzerland and that this certainly was one hell of a place for his luck to run out. . . .

Twenty-seven

January closed her eyes as the 747 began its descent to Kennedy Airport. She couldn't face the sight of New York knowing Mike wouldn't be at the airport to meet her. Knowing he'd never be at any airport to meet her.

Less than an hour after his plane had exploded into the Atlantic the news had flashed on television in New York, cutting into all regular programming. Fortunately, George Milford reached January at the Beverly Hills Hotel before she heard it on the air.

It had all seemed completely unreal. When she hung up, the sunlight was still streaming into the room. Tom was still banging away on the typewriter in the next room. Mike was dead . . . and the world was still going on.

She had listened quietly while George Milford told her the details. She was silent when David offered condolences on the extension phone. Should they come and get her? Should they make arrangements for the services? Should they? . . . Somewhere in the middle of one of the "Should they's" she had hung up. She had sat quietly at first, wondering why the birds were still singing . . . wondering why she was still breathing.

She didn't remember when she began to scream. She just knew she was screaming and couldn't stop . . . and Tom was holding her in his arms and pleading for an explanation. And then suddenly the phones were ringing in every room and Tom finally told the operator to stop all calls, and she could tell by his face that he knew . . . and all the while the goddamn sun kept shining and the birds called out to each other and the operator paged people at the pool.

She remembered a kind man named Dr. Cutler who arrived

and gave her a shot. A different kind of shot from Dr. Alpert's. This was a soft easy shot . . . it made her stop screaming. It made everything sound very quiet . . . even the sunlight grew dim . . . and she felt as if she were floating and the birds sounded as if they were far away. And then she slept.

When she awoke, she thought perhaps it had all been a dream, a crazy nightmare. But Tom wasn't at the typewriter. He was sitting beside the bed, and when she asked him if it had been a dream he turned away.

He had held her close all night. She didn't cry. She was afraid to cry because she might never stop. . . .

Keeping it locked in was almost like refusing to admit that it had really happened.

Tom had finally turned off all the phones. Linda had gotten through; she had offered to come out and bring January back. Both George and David Milford had made the same offer. But January didn't want anyone to come out for her. Tom took charge and booked her on TWA's noon flight the following day. He wired David and George her flight number and arrival time. He drove her to the airport and got permission to take her on the plane before the other passengers boarded. She sat in the front seat of the huge empty plane and suddenly panicked.

"Come back with me, Tom. I can't face it alone."

"You won't be facing it alone," he said quietly. "I'm always with you. Just remember that—hold that thought all the time. And George and David Milford will be waiting at the airport."

"Oh, Tom, I don't want it this way."

He managed a smile. "It's not what we *want* . . . but what has to be. Let's face it, honey . . . I *am* a married man. David and his father actually believe you're here doing a story on me. Not that I care what they think, but it's you I'm worrying about. After all, there will be reporters waiting at Kennedy."

"Reporters?" She looked dazed.

"Well . . . your father was a hell of a colorful guy in his time, and Dee Milford Granger was one of the richest women in the world. It is news, and the public is morbid—"

"Tom." She reached out and gripped his hands. "Please come with me."

"I want to, baby. But there's nothing I could do to help. I'd have to hide out in a hotel while you made the arrangements. Because that's all the press would need—you coming to make funeral arrangements with a married lover in tow. Besides, I'm way behind with my work. The studio is on my neck. Seems like I've been too much of a lover and not enough of a writer."

She clung to him and he assured her he'd be there . . . waiting. "You get things settled . . . and call me . . . any time . . . all the time . . . whenever you need me . . . I'll be here."

The plane was circling Kennedy waiting for ground clearance. She opened her bag and took out the *Variety* clipping and reread it again. And once again she asked herself—Why had he sent it without a note? Was it because he was still angry? But then, he wouldn't have sent it at all. It was his way of saying everything was okay. It had to mean that! Oh God . . . it had to.

The plane touched the runway. It was a smooth landing. Everyone released their seat belts . . . the Muzak came on . . . people stood up even though the stewardess kept pleading for everyone to remain seated until the plane stopped taxiing. People reached for hand luggage . . . a baby cried in the back section . . . the ramp stairway was wheeled to the plane . . . the stewardesses were standing at the open door now . . . smiling . . . saying goodbye to everyone with sincere-looking smiles . . . thanking everyone for flying TWA . . . She was walking to the door like all the other passengers. It was crazy how the world could come to an end and you still functioned and did all of the ordinary things. Like sitting through a four-and-a-half-hour flight . . . even picking at some food . . . and now walking down the ramp like everyone else. She saw the photographers, but it never occurred to her that they were waiting for her until the lights were flashing in her face. They were crowding in on her, and then David and his father broke through and led her into a private room at the airport while a chauffeur took her baggage stubs.

Then there was the ride back to New York, the same ride she had taken with Mike. The same road, the same leftovers from the World's Fair. They were still there . . . but Mike was gone.

". . . and that's why we think it's best . . ." George Milford was saying.

"Best. Best what?" She looked at the two men.

David's voice was gentle. "Best for you to stay at the Pierre. It will take some time for the estate to be probated. Eventually the Winter Palace, the place in Marbella, and the apartment at the Pierre will be sold, and the money will go into the foundation. But until then you are welcome to live anywhere. And you'll be comfortable at the Pierre."

"No . . . I have my own place."

"But you'll have your privacy guaranteed at the Pierre."

"Privacy?"

"The newspapers will blow this up for days, I'm afraid," George Milford explained. "You see, when the news broke, the press called me to ask about Dee's estate. And I'm afraid that I inadvertently let it slip that you would come into ten million."

"Ten million?" She looked at them both. "Dee left me ten million dollars? Why? I hardly knew her."

George Milford smiled. "She loved your father very much. I'm sure she did it to please him. She told me how much he loved you . . . and that's why you should live at the Pierre. After all, your father wanted it that way."

"How do you know what he wanted?" she asked. "You didn't really know him."

"January, I knew him . . . quite well, toward the end," David said quietly. "We talked a lot at Palm Beach that Easter weekend when you didn't come. He told me he had hoped we would eventually get married . . . I told him how I felt about you and he said to wait, not to push it. Those were his words. He never wanted to push you into anything. He hated the idea of your living in that tacky apartment. But he said he would never let you know, just as he never told you how disappointed he was when you left the Pierre."

She felt the tears slide down her cheeks. She nodded in the darkness. "All right, David. . . . Of course I'll stay at the Pierre."

During the next four days, with the help of Librium and sleeping pills, January functioned in a mechanized manner.

She had just gotten a shot from Dr. Alpert the day before the plane crash. It wore off while she was in New York, but her mental anguish outweighed any physical reaction. She almost welcomed the headaches, the tightness in her throat, the aches in her bones—this kind of pain she understood and knew would pass. The unbelievable emptiness of a world without Mike was something she could not accept.

Sadie hovered over her like a devoted nurse. She was a lost soul without Dee. She seemed to be constantly listening, as if any second she would hear one of Dee's crisp orders. Sadie had been with Dee for thirty years. She *needed* someone to "tend to," and she transferred this need to January, bringing trays of food that January barely touched, answering phones, keeping everyone away except the Milfords, standing guard like a gaunt sentry, silent . . . sad . . . waiting.

David sat beside January at the memorial service for Dee and Mike. Her face was expressionless, almost as if she were asleep with her eyes open. His father sat on the other side of her. And his mother sat next to her husband, tense, clutching her handkerchief, and looking properly distraught. The church was mobbed and the presence of all the socialites and celebrities had brought out the entire news media. The International Set was represented by bona fide royalty. Some of Dee's friends from Europe had chartered a private plane to attend. And many show business celebrities, sensing the television cameramen would be on hand, had suddenly found it necessary to pay their last respects to Mike. But it was Karla's appearance that caused the biggest sensation. The crowd of curious onlookers had almost broken through the cordon of police when she arrived.

David hadn't seen her. But he had heard the screams go up outside, fans calling out her name. He knew she was sitting in the back somewhere and he prayed he wouldn't see her. After that traumatic night he had forced all thoughts of her from his mind. He had actually used a form of self-hypnosis to exorcise her from his thoughts. He thought "hate" whenever her name came to mind. Then he would think of things the word hate conjured—Hitler, child molesting, poverty. And somewhere along the line, his mind would latch onto some other subject. He also took on new accounts and extra work. And he made sure he was never alone at night. He alternated between Kim and Valerie, a gorgeous Eurasian girl. And when word of the plane crash occurred, he dropped everything and plunged into the immediate urgency of the "care and consideration" of January.

And from now on it was going to be January all the way. His slim, pale, beautiful little heiress. The news cameras had given her a hard time when she arrived at the church. She had clung to him in bewilderment. She really was a beautiful girl, a beautiful little lost girl—a beautiful little lost girl with ten million dollars. He reached out and touched her gloved hand. She looked up, and he hoped his slight smile conveyed sympathy and reassurance.

The memorial service droned on. He knew the church was jammed. People were standing three-deep in the back. Someone had said the governor was there. Where was Karla sitting? He realized with a certain amazement that today—this minute—was the first time he had "allowed" himself to think of her. He pushed her from his mind. But it didn't work. Somehow, in the crowded church, he felt her presence. It was ridiculous. But he actually *felt* it. And now, suddenly, even the self-hypnosis didn't work. He sat helplessly and allowed his thoughts to take over his mind. Had she come alone? Or had she been accompanied by Boris or one of her trusted escorts? Or was there someone new? He had to stop this! Think of January, he told himself. Think of Dee. Think of family. He was here as "next of kin." "Next of kin," but cut out of the will. God, why did that plane have to crash! Couldn't it have crashed *after* Dee changed her will? She had wanted to change it. Why had she waited to call his father till the day before the old man was leaving for Europe? And she had also cabled from the South of France that she wanted extensive changes when she returned. Why?

Would he have been reinstated? Would January have been out? But all the speculation in the world didn't matter now. The will was airtight. And January was the new rich girl in town.

Then he heard the organ and the muffled sounds of everyone murmuring the Lord's Prayer. He bowed his head and rose automatically with the others. He held January's arm as his father and mother started out of the pew. He kept his head bowed as he led January up the aisle away from the serene twilight of the church, toward the gaping hole of daylight where the curious public and television cameras waited.

And as he passed the third row from the back, he saw her. She was wearing a black chiffon scarf around her head and was preparing to make her own dash toward an exit. But in that one moment, before she shoved on the perpetual dark glasses, their eyes had met. And then she was gone, ducking her way across an aisle, hoping to make her escape through a side entrance. He held January's arm and continued the solemn pace toward the limousine. And he managed to look properly somber as the TV cameras photographed them for the six o'clock news.

He took January back to the Pierre. And for the next three hours the drawing room housed an avalanche of celebrities, café society, and clinking glasses. Security men stood on guard as the paying of respects turned into a gala cocktail reception. He stood by January's side until she showed visible signs of fatigue. Sadie led her off into the bedroom, but the party continued. New arrivals continued to flow through the door. He watched his mother play hostess. Even the old man seemed to be having a marvelous time. There was something barbaric about the whole thing. He glanced at the shining silver frames on the piano. Most of the famous faces were represented in person in the huge drawing room at the Pierre. All but one. His eyes rested on Karla's picture. He walked over and stared at it. The eyes were distant, with a hint of loneliness, just as they had been today.

He saw Sadie come out of the bedroom. She tiptoed over and told him January was resting. She had taken a sedative. And when he was sure no one noticed, he slipped out of the apartment.

He knew where he was going. He had thought he could never go there again, that he could never face that doorman, or the elevator man. But suddenly it didn't matter. After looking into her eyes today, he knew he could face them all—an army of them. He had to see her!

Nevertheless his relief was enormous when a strange doorman stood in front of her building. Of course—he had never come around at noon. The doorman stopped him with a perfunctory, "All guests must be announced." For a moment he hesitated. If Karla sent back word that she wouldn't receive him he would have the embarrassment of facing this strange doorman.

But now all that seemed so unimportant. He gave his name and waited while the man lumbered inside to the house phone. This hulk of a stranger in the braided uniform would have the privilege of talking to her . . . and perhaps *he* might not. He lit a cigarette while he waited. It seemed forever. Maybe she hadn't come home. If the doorman said she was out, it might be the truth. But he'd never know.

The doorman walked back slowly, as if his arches pained him. David ground out his cigarette and waited.

"Apartment Fifteen A," the doorman said. "Front elevator."

For a moment David stood very still. Then he strode through the lobby quickly. This was no time to allow himself to feel any nerves. He was grateful that the elevator was waiting. And when he got off, she was standing at the door of her apartment.

"Come in," she said quietly.

He followed her inside. The sunlight turned the murky East River into shades of yellow gray. He saw a tugboat inching its way, causing miniature waves in the water as it passed. "I had no idea you had such a view," he said.

"Perhaps because you have only seen it at night," she said quietly.

"Or perhaps I never really looked," he said.

For a moment neither of them spoke. Then he said, "Karla . . . I can't live without you."

She sat down and lit one of her English cigarettes. Then, almost as an afterthought, she extended the pack to him. He shook his head. Then he sat beside her. "You don't believe me, do you?"

She nodded slowly. "I believe that you mean it . . . now."

"Karla, I'm sorry about that night," he said stiffly. Suddenly it all rushed out. "Oh, God, I must have been insane. I can't even blame it on being drunk, because I got drunk intentionally. To give me the nerve to come over, to make that scene." He looked down at his hands. "It's just that the whole scene was closing in on me. The constant worry of time, of how long we would have, when would you suddenly take off again. But today when I looked at you I got my head together and I knew what it was all about. I love you. I want to be with you . . . openly. I want to marry you—if you'll have me. Or I'll stick around as your consort if that's the way you want it. I've lived all my life worrying about inheriting Dee's money, and now it looks like I'm supposed to spend my life trying to get at January's money. And I was willing to go along that way until I saw you at church. Because until that moment I had nothing better to do. But when I saw you again—"

She put her hand to his lips. "David, it is good to see you. And I am sorry about that night."

He grabbed her hands and kissed them. "No. I'm the one who is sorry. I didn't really mean any of those things I said. I—" He knew his face was burning. "I didn't believe what I was saying about Heidi Lanz. I didn't really think she was in here."

"None of that is important," she said. "Heidi—" She smiled. "I knew her so very long ago, when I first came to America. I haven't seen her in years, except reruns of her old pictures on television."

"Of course. And I had seen her that day at "21" and she just came to my mind and—"

She put her fingers across his lips and smiled. "Please, David. None of that is important. Heidi, or—"

"You're right," he said. "Nothing is important. Except us."

She stood up and crossed the room. She smiled at him, yet there was a sadness in her eyes. "No, David, we are not all that important. I have lived a very selfish life. I have always meant to do so many things, but always felt there was so much time. Dee's death taught me differently. We never know just how much time there is. Jeremy Haskins, my old friend, is close to eighty. Every time I hear from London I hold my breath. Yet who would have thought Jeremy would outlive Dee?"

He came to her and tried to take her in his arms, but she broke his embrace. He held her by the shoulders and looked into her eyes. "Karla, that's why I'm here. For just that reason. We've talked about the age difference between us. But now it all seems so stupid. All that matters is being together, having one another."

"No, David, that is not all that matters." She turned away. Then she pointed to the couch. "Sit down. I want you to listen to me. Yes, we have had our wonderful times. But that is past. Now I will tell you about what does matter. I will tell you about a girl called Zinaida. . . ."

David crumpled his empty package of cigarettes. He stared at Karla as she stood against the mantel. Several times he had felt tears come to his eyes as she recounted her struggle to raise her child. Her quiet composure as she told him about the rape of the nuns at the convent only added to the horror of the scene. When she had finished, she said, "So you see how unimportant anything between us really is. Until now I had coasted, letting others take care of Zinaida. But now it is all different."

"Did Dee know about your child?" he asked.

Karla hesitated. Then she managed a smile. "Of course not. Why would Dee know? Actually we weren't that close. I was just one of the silver frames on her piano."

"If she knew, she might have left something in her will."

Karla shrugged. "I have enough money. But only if I change my life style. I have put this apartment up for sale. That should bring me a good sum of money. And there is a marvelous little Greek island called Patmos. Not many tourists go there. It is quiet, and I am going to buy a house there and live with Zinaida and the Harringtons."

"Bring her here," David begged. "We can all live together."

"Oh, David, you do not understand. She is very beautiful. But she is a child. She would think nothing of skipping along the streets. Or bursting into tears at Schwarz's because you would not buy her all the toys she wanted. She is a child. A thirty-one-year-old child! I am a very private person. And you know how I have to fight for whatever privacy I get. It would not be fair to Zinaida to expose her to the photographers who would chase her. Her life would become a mockery. But on Patmos . . . we can swim together, walk together, play together. No one will know me there. We will have complete privacy. Jeremy has sent a man to arrange things. I leave tomorrow to select the house."

"Karla . . . marry me! Please! You have enough money to support Zinaida. I make enough so that we can live and . . ."

She stroked his face gently. "Yes, I am sure you do. And we would have a wonderful year together."

"Years," he corrected her.

"No, David. A year at the most. Then you would see your lovely little January marry. You would think about the ten million dollars, you would think about the life style you could have had . . . No, David, it would never last. My place is with Zinaida. I must teach her so many things. Especially that I am her mother. She is so very lost. And your place is with January. I saw her today. She is also lost. She needs you very much."

"I need you," he said.

She opened her arms and for a moment he held her close. He covered her face with kisses. Then she broke away from him. "No, David . . ."

"Karla . . ." he pleaded. "If you are sending me away, then please, let me be with you for the last time . . ."

She shook her head. "It would only be harder for both of us. Goodbye, David."

"Are you sending me away again?" he asked.

She nodded. "But this time I am sending you away with love."

He walked to the door. And suddenly she rushed to him and held him close. "Oh, David. Be happy. Please. For my sake . . . be happy." And he felt the tears running down her face, but he did not turn and look back as he walked out of the door, because he knew his own eyes were filled with tears . . .

Twenty-eight

JANUARY HAD BEEN TOO SEDATED even to remember the memorial service. She knew David had been at her side. But the whole thing seemed like a newsreel without sound. Dr. Clifford, Mrs. Milford's internist, had given her some tranquilizers, and she had taken triple the amount prescribed. She knew the church had been crowded, and she recalled thinking, "Mike would have liked the idea of playing to a full house." But she felt oddly removed from the news cameras that flashed when she left the church, or the curious onlookers who called out her name.

She had been amazed at the people who crowded into the apartment at the Pierre, stunned by the fact that she was supposed to greet them as if they were invited guests. And when it had gotten too much for her, she had slipped into the bedroom and taken some more tranquilizers.

And the days that followed were just as dreamlike. Days of serious meetings and signing of documents at George Milford's office—with David always at her side. Dee had left her ten million dollars! The enormity of the amount failed to arouse any distinct emotion. Could it bring Mike back? Could it take back that evening at Bungalow Five?

Somehow the days dragged by. David took her to his parents' home for dinner each night. She managed to make some kind of conversation with Margaret Milford, who nervously tried to anticipate every wish. Through it all, she was duly grateful for David. Sometimes she felt as if she were drowning when she was surrounded by all the new strange faces and the battery of press that seemed to pop up everywhere. That was when she would cling to David . . . find relief in seeing the familiar face. And there was always Sadie . . . waiting when she returned to the Pierre. She slept in the master bedroom now, on the side of the bed that Sadie said Mike used. And Sadie would know, because she had brought Dee's coffee to her every morning.

Sadie also doled out Dr. Clifford's sleeping pills each night. Two Seconals and some warm milk. At the end of the week, January found that lacing the milk with Jack Daniels brought instant sleep. And through it all, she called Tom constantly. She was never quite aware when she called him . . . or how many times. She called him when she woke up . . . whether it was in the morning or the middle of the night. Whenever she found herself alone, she reached for a phone and called him. He always consoled her, even though he sometimes sounded harassed or sleepy. A few times he gently accused her of being drunk.

But most of all, she liked to sleep. Because of the dream. It came every night. The shadowy vision of a beautiful man with aquamarine-colored eyes. She had dreamed of him once long ago, when she had first met Tom. It had been a disconcerting dream then, because somehow the man had reminded her of Mike. But once she and Tom became lovers, she had forgotten the dream. And when she was on Dr. Alpert's shots she never dreamed because she never really fell into a deep sleep. But the dream had come again the first night she took the Seconals and the milk with the Jack Daniels. It had been an odd dream. She was in Mike's arms and he was telling her he was still alive . . . that it had all been a mistake . . . another plane had crashed . . . he was fine. And then suddenly he fell from her arms and she saw him slip into the ocean . . . down . . . down . . . down . . . and just as she tried to go after him, she was caught by a pair of strong arms. It was Tom . . . holding her and telling her he would never leave her. And when she clung to him and told him how much she needed him . . . she saw that it wasn't really Tom. He was like Tom . . . and he was like Mike . . . except for the eyes. The most beautiful eyes she had ever seen. And when she woke up she could still see the eyes. . . .

She asked Dr. Clifford for more sleeping pills, and he suggested that she start trying to sleep without them. "If you were a widow or an older woman, who was alone in the world, I might give sleeping pills for a longer time to help you through the loneliness. But you are a young beautiful girl with a fiancé who adores you, and you must start trying to function."

She spent a sleepless night, and then in desperation, when her head ached and her throat felt thick, she went to Dee's medicine chest for an aspirin and stumbled into the Comstock Lode. Bottle after bottle of sleeping pills. None of them had Dr. Clifford's name on the label. Evidently Dee had a "pill doctor" all her own. There were dieting pills (she recognized them because Linda occasionally used them), two bottles of yellow sleeping pills, three bottles of Seconal, a bottle of Tuinals, and several boxes of the French suppositories. She quickly took them all from the cabinet and hid them.

The dream came every night now. Sometimes it was just the eyes. They seemed to be trying to comfort her, trying to give her hope, telling her there was a wonderful world waiting for her. . . . But when she woke up there was just the loneliness of the dark room and the empty bed. Then she would call Tom . . . and talk to him until her speech grew thick and she fell back to sleep.

It was in the middle of the third week that the pills stopped working. She would fall asleep immediately . . . and wake up a few hours later. And then one night she woke up and realized she hadn't had the dream. Sleep had just been a few dark hours of nothingness. She went to the closet where she kept the pills and took another Seconal and tried a yellow one with it. She felt groggy but she couldn't sleep. She called Tom. It took several rings before he answered. He sounded groggy.

"January, for God's sake . . . it's two in the morning."

"Well, at least I didn't get you in the middle of your writing."

"No, but you woke me. Honey, I'm way behind. The studio is on my back. I've got to finish this thing."

"Tom . . . I'll be finished with everything in a few days. Then I'll be back."

There was a slight pause. Then he said. "Look, I think it's best if you wait."

"Wait for what?"

"Wait until I finish the treatment. If you come out here, you can't move in with me now . . ."

"Why not?"

"For God's sake, haven't you been reading the newspapers?"

"No."

"You've been plastered all over them. That ten million bucks turned you into an instant celebrity."

"You sound like Linda. She . . . she . . . she keeps saying . . . I'm—" She stopped. Her tongue was getting thick and she couldn't remember what she was trying to say.

"January, have you taken anything?"

"Sleeping pills."

"How many?"

"Just two."

"Well, go to sleep. Look, I'll be through with the script soon. Then we'll talk it over."

She fell asleep with the phone in her hand. And when Sadie woke her the next day at noon, she couldn't remember any of the conversation. But she had the feeling that something hadn't gone quite right.

A few days later, she invited Linda up for dinner. The room service was excellent. Sadie had chilled a bottle of Dee's best wine. But something in their old relationship was missing. Linda had let her hair grow past her shoulders, picked at her food, and was wearing a body stocking that made her look thinner than usual. "I want to be bone thin," she said. "That's my new image. How do you like my glasses?"

"They're great. But I didn't know you needed them."

"I always wore contact lenses. But I like this look better. I'm dating Benjamin James now." She waited for January's reaction. When there was none, she said, "Look, darling. He's not exactly Tom Colt. But he's won a lot of minor prizes. Actually, he's considered too literary to ever really make it. His last book of poems only sold nine hundred copies. But there's a real 'In' group that consider him to be a genius. Besides, he's very good for me right now."

"Linda, don't you ever want a permanent man?"

"Not anymore. When I saw your pictures in the papers—" She paused and looked around the room. "When I look at this layout, it only proves my point. There's only two ways to make it. With money . . . or fame. If you've got either of those things, then you can have any man you want. And when I'm famous I won't really need a permanent man."

"Why not?"

"Because when I make it, there's going to be room for only one superstar in my setup . . . *me*. Until then, there has to be the Benjamins who can help. But once I get there, then I'll take no more shit from any man. That's the way I want to live—not being part of a man, but being *the* Linda Riggs. And that's why I wash Benjamin's socks and cook for him—because he's bright and he's in with a lot of cerebral people. I need him for now. Until the convention. In fact I'll start working for my candidate in September. Then I'll go all out."

"For whom?"

"Muskie. Benjamin says he can't lose." Then, almost as an afterthought, Linda said, "Now, what's happening with you and Tom?"

"He's finishing his screen treatment."

"You're going back then, I take it."

"No."

"Don't tell me it's over. But then you don't really need him now."

"It's not over. And I need him more than ever," January said. "But with all the publicity I've gotten . . . well, Tom feels I'm too well known to . . . well . . . to just arrive and move in with him."

"Well, go out there and rent a big house. A mansion. Good Lord, you can do anything you want now. Hire a press agent, get yourself invited to all the 'A' parties. Give a few yourself. Now that you've got ten million dollars maybe he'll be a little more flexible about divorce."

"Divorce?"

"Look, January, let's face it. You're a born pussycat. You need a man, and what's more, deep down you want it to be all nice and legal. You've been trying to go along with this living together stuff. But I can tell, it isn't sitting right. You told me way back that he was writing this screen treatment to protect his percentage deal, to pay for the co-op. In other words, just for the money. Well, he doesn't have to worry about that now. *You* can buy the apartment for him. And if you want to really be the generous lady of all time, you can pay his wife such a big settlement that she'll hand him *and* the child over to you on a silver platter. And if he's really freaky about playing Daddy, you can offer to have your own baby with him. I mean, you're the type who wants all that, aren't you?"

"I want to be married. *Yes*, I really do. And I could give Tom a baby. I could . . . why not? Linda, you're right. I'm going to talk to him about it tonight."

Linda picked up her bag and stared at the pictures on the piano. "Did Dee really know all of these people?"

"Yes."

"See. It's just as I said. With money or fame, you can own the world."

January smiled. "I don't want the world. I just want to feel there's a reason to get up each day."

She thought about it when Linda had gone. She hadn't slept well the night before. She had waited for the dream. But it hadn't come. She had awakened feeling desolate, almost as if she had suffered some personal rejection. Lately the dreams were more real than the thoughts she had when she was awake. The beautiful stranger with the blue eyes was tender and compassionate. She could never remember whether they ever spoke . . . or touched . . . she just knew he was there when she went to sleep. Lately she had found herself lying down in the afternoon and trying to drift off. But Dr. Clifford was right. She had to face reality. Tom was real. Tom was working in Bungalow Five, working on that screen treatment just to buy their apartment. She could be furnishing it now, doing something. She'd have that reason to get up each day!

She picked up the phone and started to dial. Then she remembered the time difference. It was eleven o'clock—eight o'clock in Los Angeles. Tom would just be settling down for his evening's work. He always worked from eight until eleven. That meant three hours to wait. . . .

She tried to watch television. She switched from Johnny to Merv to Dick. To a late movie. But nothing held her attention. She undressed and took a bath. That took time. Then she stretched out on the bed. She knew she had fallen asleep, because she was aware that she was dreaming. But it wasn't "the dream." It was a nightmare. There was water and moonlight. And then she saw a plane going down. Mike's plane. It was spinning. Down . . . down . . . down . . . until it disappeared into the silvery path the moon spread on the ocean. She felt panic, as if she were falling too. And then she felt some force lift her and she was safe. Then she saw the blue eyes. He was walking to her from a distance. She tried desperately to see his face. It was in the shadows, but somehow she knew it was a beautiful face. . . .

"Do you really want to come to me?" he whispered. And before she could answer, he disappeared, and she woke up.

The dream had been too real. She looked around the bedroom, half expecting to find him standing there. Whoever he was—he was the most beautiful man in the world. And yet she had never seen his face. It was something she just sensed. But this was ridiculous. He didn't exist. He was a man she had created in her dreams. Maybe she was losing her mind. Wasn't this the way it happened? People started seeing visions, hearing sounds that weren't there. She was really frightened. Because she could still hear his voice . . . and there was a jangling noise in the darkness.

It took her a moment to realize the jangling noise was the phone. A very real sound. And she had awakened because it was ringing. In the darkness, the luminous dial of the radio clock said one fifty-five. Who would be calling her at that hour! Except . . . *Tom!*

She grabbed the phone, and when she heard his voice she wasn't at all surprised. Just elated. She needed him more than ever right now. She needed the reassurance of a real man, not a fantasy man.

"Oh, Tom, I'm so glad you called. I was going to call you . . . as soon as you finished writing for the night."

He laughed. "How come this new burst of consideration?"

She groped for her cigarettes in the darkness. "I don't understand."

"January, for the past three weeks you've called me at the rate of twenty times a day, at hours ranging from nine A.M. my time straight through till five A.M.—and now this sudden curfew."

"Oh, Tom, I'm sorry, I hadn't realized. . . . It's just that whenever I'm unhappy or lost I reach out for you. Tom, I can't stand it. I'm coming out. Tomorrow."

"Don't bother, January. All you have to do is cross the street."

"I don't understand."

"I'm at the Plaza. I just got in."

"*Tom!*" She sat up in bed and switched on the light. "Oh, Tom, I'll throw on some slacks and come right over."

"Baby, hold it! I'm beat. Besides, I have a nine o'clock meeting tomorrow morning at my publisher's."

"Well, when do I see you? I can't wait!"

"Lunch."

"Lunch? Oh, Tom! Who needs lunch? I want to be alone with you. I want—"

"Honey, my lawyer is meeting me at the publisher's. We'll be working out details on the contract for the next book. After that I'll need to relax and have a few drinks. So let's make it at Toots Shor's. Say . . . twelve-thirty?"

"Tom . . ." Her voice was low. "I want to see you now. I can't bear the idea that you're just across the street. Please. Let me come over."

He sighed. "Baby, do you realize you are talking to a fifty-eight-year-old man who feels the jet lag and needs his sleep?"

"Fifty-seven," she said.

"Fifty-eight. I had a birthday while you were gone."

"Oh, Tom . . . You should have told me."

He laughed. "That's hardly the thing I feel like advertising. See you tomorrow, baby. Twelve-thirty. And, January . . . For God's sake, don't bring a birthday cake . . ."

He was standing wedged in at the bar when she walked into Toots Shor's. He had already met a few old friends and was buying them drinks. He held out his arms when he saw her, and she snuggled into them as he forced a space for her at the crowded bar. He made the introductions all around, then grinned as he looked at her. "Okay, boys. I'm out of circulation from here on." He kissed her gently on the cheek. "White wine?"

"No. Whatever you're having."

"Jack Daniels for the lady. Heavy on the soda."

"Tom, you look wonderful. All tanned and–"

"I finally finished the script. That is, the treatment. And spent the last few days at my producer's pool learning that the ending has to be changed."

"Tom! You can't change the end–"

"If I don't, they'll assign someone else who will."

"You mean you have no control?"

"None. Once I take their money for the book, the book belongs to them. And once I take their money to write a screenplay, that means I agree to write a screenplay that will please them."

"What would happen if you refused?"

"Well, for one thing, they wouldn't pay me. And then they'd put on a guy who would do exactly what they wanted." He swallowed the rest of his drink and said, "But don't look so sad. That's par for the course. I knew what I was getting into when I signed to do it. The only thing I didn't know . . . was that it would hurt so much." Then he signaled the waiter and motioned he was ready to sit down.

She waited until they were at their table and he had ordered another drink. Then she said, "Walk away from it, Tom. Let someone else do it. It's not worth all the pain."

He shook his head. "I can't now. At least this way I'll have some control. And parts of it are great. And if I have to compromise, at least I want to be there to make sure that the compromise works."

"But you only did the screen treatment because it would pay for the apartment in New York and–"

"I did it because I have a piece of the profits. Remember? And I'm there to protect my book."

"But you also said it would pay for the apartment. And now you don't have to worry about that or . . . I mean . . . Well . . ."

He reached out and took her hand. "January, I canceled the apartment."

"What!"

"Look, I've done a lot of thinking while we've been apart. I've also gotten a lot of work done while you've been gone. And I realize I can never really write if I live with you."

"Tom . . . don't say that!"

The waiter placed the menus in front of them. Tom studied his. She wanted to scream! How could he look at food? Or think of anything when their life together was at stake?

"Try the scallops," he told her. "They're real tiny—the kind you like."

"I don't want anything."

"Two hamburgers," he told the waiter. "And bring some hot sauce. Make mine rare. How do you want yours, January?"

"I don't care."

"Make the lady's rare too."

The moment the waiter left, she turned on him. "Tom, what do you mean? Of course you can write if I'm living with you. Maybe you can't when we're in the bungalow. But if we have a large apartment in New York, I'll never be in your way. I'll stay in the background. I won't interfere. I promise."

He sighed. "Unfortunately, you do, baby. Look. I've had a hell of a lot of love in my time. And I always thought I'd go on loving and drinking forever. But each year the work gets harder and the love seems less important. I've already faced the fact that I'm fifty-eight and I haven't written half the books I promised myself I'd write. I don't think I can allow myself the luxury of love anymore."

She was trying not to let the tears come to her eyes. But they made her voice hoarse. "Tom . . . don't you love me?"

"Oh, Jesus, January. . . . I'm so damned grateful to you. You gave me something pretty wonderful. And I'll never forget it. Look, what we had was great. But it would have ended anyhow. Maybe a few months later . . . But maybe it is best to wash it up now—"

"Tom, once you said you could never be without me. Were they just words?"

"You know damn well I meant them at the time."

"At the time?"

The busboy came by to fill their water glasses. They were both silent until he left. Then Tom reached out and took both her hands. "Now listen . . . What I said . . . I meant. At the time. And they weren't lying-on-top-of-a-dame words. I meant them. But things change . . ."

"Nothing's changed," she said tensely.

"Okay. Let's say I've changed. Let's say just the one more year changed things. Honey, at your age, you've got the world ahead, you've got time. God, that's a great word–time. And you've got it. Time for love, time for dreams, time for crazy escapades . . . And I've just been one of them."

"No!"

"Maybe I'll be an important one when you're old enough to do some looking back. Maybe the most important. But baby . . . just think–in thirty-seven years–that's the year two thousand eight–you'll just be my age." He paused and smiled. "Seems inconceivable to you, right? And I'll lay a few more inconceivable facts before you. In two thousand eight, *if* I am still around, I'll be ninety-five!"

The waiter arrived with the hamburgers. January forced a smile as he served them. The moment he left, Tom plunged into his. January touched his arm. Her voice was low and urgent. "Tom, you said if we had a year, two years . . . whatever we could grab–it would be worth it."

He nodded. "That's exactly what I said."

"Well, let's take it. Don't cancel me out before it's run its course."

"But damn it, January, it has run its course. It can't work any longer. Don't you see? I've got to go back to that bungalow and work. Then I've got to write some more books. I've got–"

"Tom." She was swallowing hard and keeping her voice down, because she was positive the people at the banquette beside them were trying to listen. "Tom, please, I'll do anything you say–just don't end it now. I can't live without you. You're all I've got. All I care for."

He looked at her and smiled sadly. "Twenty-one, worth all that money, loaded with beauty and health–and I'm all you've got?"

"All I want." The tears were brimming in her eyes now.

He was silent for a moment. Then he nodded. "Okay. We'll try it. It's not going to be easy. But we'll try. I once promised you that I'd never leave you, that as long as you wanted us to be together, we'd make it. And I'll keep that promise."

"Oh, Tom . . ."

"Now eat your hamburger. Because you've got to get home and start packing. I've got to be back in L.A. tomorrow."

She nibbled at the meat and tried to push it around her plate. As the restaurant filled, people he knew stopped at the table to compliment him on his book, to congratulate him because it was still holding the number-one spot. Some asked about the movie, about casting . . . And through it all, she managed to smile as he made introductions. Some of the men gave Tom playful insults, asked her what she saw in an ugly old man like him. But she knew their jokes sprang from genuine admiration and affection for him.

They were finally alone as they had espresso. He spoke first. "Well, if you think you can face it, it's back to Bungalow Five."

She tucked her arm in his. "Is it still raining out there?"

"No. At least it wasn't when I left." Once again he sighed.

"You don't really want me to come," she said.

"It's not that. It's the fucking script."

"Don't do it, Tom."

"Maybe you weren't listening to me earlier when I explained . . ."

"I heard every word. I also remember you saying that you're fifty-eight, that you want to write all the books you promised yourself to write. Then why bury yourself for another six months hacking away and butchering your own work? Start doing the things you really want to do."

"There's also a little thing like seventy-five thousand bucks involved."

"Tom, I've been doing a lot of thinking while we've been apart. Look. I've got ten million dollars. I'll give your wife a million if she'll divorce you. I'll leave another million in trust for your child. That frees you from all guilts and responsibilities. We can be together, get married, have a child of our own, as many as you want . . . And you can still write."

He looked at her curiously. "This is the first time you've made noises like a millionaire."

"What do you mean?"

"Everything and everyone is on an auction block. Right? Everyone has a price. One million, two million. It doesn't matter what the poor bastard you're buying wants. As long as you pay the price, he's yours."

"Tom, that's not true! I want you to be my husband. I want us to be together all the time. I've got enough money so that you don't have to shut yourself up with that typewriter and do what the producer or director tells you to do. I want you to be able to write the way you want to write. And above all, I want us to be together. To love one another and be happy."

He shook his head sadly. "January, can't you see? It's not going to work. There isn't room for what we once had anymore. You came along when I was floundering. I needed you. God, how I needed you. And you gave a middle-aged man his last pretense at being a stud. For that, I'll always be grateful. We found something special together at the right time. You gave me warmth and a sense of pride while I was prostituting myself on the tour circuit. And in return I replaced Daddy for you. So we're even. I'll go back to my writing and you go back to the money Daddy got for you. Go back to a young girl's life. It's all out there, waiting for you."

"No! Tom, you don't really mean this. You're just depressed. I don't want any other kind of life. I just want to be with you and—"

"But my life is writing! Can't you understand that? Writing comes first. It always will."

"Fine. Okay. You can write. You can write all you want. I want you to write. I'll buy us a house in the South of France, away from everyone. You'll never have to write screen treatments. You'll never have to write anything you don't want to write. I'll be very quiet. I'll have servants to attend to everything you want. If you like writing in New York I'll buy you the biggest apartment you ever saw. I'll—"

"Cut it, January! You're talking to Tom Colt. Not Mike Wayne."

She was silent for a moment. When she spoke she stared at

the table and her voice was strained. "What did you mean by that?"

"Just what it sounded like. I'm not your father. I'm not going to be kept by a rich woman."

She pushed the table away and stood up. She knew the espresso had spilled, but she never looked back as she walked out of the restaurant.

Twenty-nine

January slept off and on for three days. Sadie diligently arrived with trays and tried to coax her to eat. Sometimes she would wave her off or mumble incoherently that she wasn't feeling well. When Sadie threatened to call Dr. Clifford, January made an attempt to eat something and explained she was just having a bad siege with the curse. This relieved Sadie, who in turn told David, "Miss January is just going through a bad time of the month."

She had reached a point where the pills no longer sent her off into a soft empty sleep. By the fourth day she lay half awake, too drowsy to read, too oversedated to sleep. She was also aware that tomorrow night she would have to go to the Milfords' for dinner with David. Because no one could have a "bad time of the month" longer than five days.

Whenever she reached for a pill, seeking the fuzzy unconsciousness it brought, she told herself that it was just for "now" —to help her get over the hurt Tom had inflicted. It wasn't that she wanted to die. It was just that she couldn't face the heavy depression that hit her the moment she realized where she was and what had happened. Mike and Tom were both gone . . . and now even "the dream" had deserted her.

She found herself reliving those last weeks with Tom. Where had she gone wrong? What had she done? She kept remembering the sincerity in his voice, the tenderness of his eyes when he had said, "I can never be without you again." How could he say that in February and tell her they were through in June? But she had to try to go on. She thought back to the days when she had fought so hard just to walk—and here she was lying in bed, trying to buy a little bit of death each day with sleeping pills. She told herself God would punish her. Then she buried her head in the pillow because it seemed to her that God had punished her enough in twenty-one years . . .

She had her health . . . and she had money. But right now, to her, they were just words. She heard the house phone ring and waited for Sadie to pick it up, but it kept on ringing. She picked up the extension just as Sadie came on. She heard Sadie state that she wasn't taking any calls. Suddenly she recognized the voice and cut in. "It's all right, Sadie. I'll take it. Hugh! Where are you?"

"I'm lying on a sand dune with my private phone plugged in to a star."

She managed a laugh. He sounded so alive . . . so good. "You nut . . . Where are you?"

"Down in your lobby. I was just passing by and I thought you might like to go out for a bite."

"No . . . I'm in bed . . . but come on up."

Hugh sat in a chair near the bed. His vitality made the room seem cramped and oppressive. "Do you want something?" she asked. "I can have Sadie get you a drink, or even a quick steak if you like. She always keeps the freezer loaded."

"No. But why don't you throw on something and we'll find a hamburger joint."

She shook her head and reached for a cigarette. "I'm not feeling great. Nothing serious. Just that time of the month."

"Bullshit."

"I mean it, Hugh."

"You never took to your bed any time during the months you went with Tom unless it was to ball him." He saw her flinch, but he went on. "I had a drink with him before he left for the Coast. He told me about the Toots Shor's episode." She studied the ash of her cigarette without answering. "It had to end, January," he said quietly. "It never could have worked out. You've got to realize that Tom's writing does come first. It always has. Personally I don't think he's capable of ever really loving any woman."

"He loved me," she said stubbornly. "He . . . he even made me split with my father."

Hugh nodded. "He told me about that. Said it was the worst move he had ever made. He regretted it as soon as he thought it all out. Because he realized from that moment on he had a commitment to you. And Tom doesn't want any commitments except to his work. He said you were the one who finally cut it. You walked out on him."

"I had no choice."

"Okay. But he feels in the clear. You gave him back his head when you walked out of that restaurant."

"But Hugh . . . Tom does love me! I know he does. He told me he could never be without me."

"I'm sure he said that. And he probably meant it at the time. I've said the same thing to women. And I've meant it too—at the time. Men always mean what they say *when* they're saying it. If women could only realize that, and not hold them to it as a lifetime contract. Look, Tom's a writer . . . and a boozer. You made him your whole life. He couldn't take it."

"Why are you telling me all this?"

"Because I care about you. I figured you might take it hard." He looked around the room. "But I didn't expect to see you laid out like a corpse. Christ, with those flowers—all we need is soft organ music."

"Tom will come back," she said stubbornly.

"It's over, January. Over. Finished! *Done!* Sure, Tom might come back if you went down on your knees and forced him back out of guilt. If you want him back that way . . . then go ahead. But if you do, then you're not the girl I thought you were. Now snap out of it. You've got everything any girl could ever want."

"I've got ten million dollars," she said. "I live in this gorgeous place and I have a closet full of clothes." The tears spilled down her face. "But I can't go to bed with ten million dollars. I can't put my arms around this apartment."

"No. But you can start in proving that you really loved your father."

"Prove I loved him?"

"That's right." He leaned close to her. "Look, this Dee Milford Granger was a nice lady. But from what I hear, Mike Wayne always shacked up with the most beautiful girls around. He made Tom Colt look like an amateur. But suddenly he marries this rich lady and now you've inherited ten million bucks. Okay . . . you tell me. Do you think she left it to you because she loved those big brown eyes of yours?"

She shook her head. "No . . . I still don't know why she left it to me."

"Holy Jesus! You're so busy lying around feeling sorry for yourself that you haven't even bothered to think things out. Look, sweet lady. Your father *earned* that ten million for you. Maybe he worked at it for only a year, but I'll guarantee you it was the hardest money he ever earned." He stared at her as the tears ran down her face. "Now stop crying," he snapped. "It won't bring him back. Get out of that bed and go out and have some fun. If you don't, it means Mike Wayne threw away the last year of his life for nothing. And he's probably feeling worse than you, knowing you're lying around crying for a man who doesn't want you."

She reached out and hugged him. "Hugh, it's too late tonight . . . I took two sleeping pills before you came in. But how about tomorrow . . . will you take me to dinner?"

"No."

She looked at him in surprise. "I only asked you out tonight to speak my mind," he said. "I've said it all now."

"But that doesn't mean we can't be friends—"

"Friends . . . yes. I am your friend. But don't try to turn me into another substitute for your father and Tom."

She smiled and her voice was teasing. "Why? I think you're a very attractive man."

"I'm fit and in my prime. And I've met a very nice widow who is forty-one and attractive and who cooks dinner for me about three times a week, and sometimes I take her into New York to see a show, and I consider myself a lucky man."

"Why are you telling me all this?"

"Because I know you're still in deep water and you'll latch on to whatever log floats by . . . and that's all wrong. If you ever tried to be anything more than a friend to me, I just might weaken, and that would kill your old man all over again. After all, he didn't go through all this to have you wind up with an overaged ex-astronaut."

"I think he wanted me to wind up with David."

"David?"

"The flowers." She looked over at the roses.

"Do you care for him?"

"I don't know . . . I never really gave myself a chance. In the beginning I thought I did. Then, well, then I met Tom and—"

"Give yourself another chance. Give yourself a lot of chances. Whether it's David or Peter or Joe or whatever . . . go out . . . meet them all . . . the world is your oyster now. Your old man saw to that. Go out and take it so he can sleep in peace."

She began to go out with David every night. His mother had insisted that neither Dee nor her father would want her to go into any extended period of mourning. So she forced herself to sit through the blasting music at Le Club . . . smiled through the noise at Maxwell's Plum and the Unicorn . . . went to Gino's on Sunday nights . . . met new people—girls who invited her to lunch, young men who were friends of David, who pressed too close when they held her on the dance floor. Through it all she smiled, made conversation, accepted luncheon invitations. . . . And all the while she knew she was waiting only for the evening to pass so she could take two red pills and go to sleep.

One day dissolved into another. Some of the beautiful young women she met called and invited her to lunch and she forced herself to accept. She sat at "21," Orsini's, La Grenouille . . . listened to gossip about new romances . . . the latest 'In' boutiques . . . the latest 'In' resort. She received invitations for weekends at Southampton, a cruise of the Greek islands (three couples were going to charter a boat; David said he was positive he could get the four weeks off if she wanted to go). And then, of course, there was always Marbella—Dee's house was fully staffed, available to her at any time.

Yes, there was a bright world out there. A whole brilliant summer waiting.

It was the middle of June, and she knew she had to make

some plans. Everyone told her she couldn't just sit in the hot city. No one who was civilized stayed in town. She listened and agreed and knew that David was waiting . . . patient and kind . . . holding his plans in abeyance . . . waiting for her to come to some decision . . . any decision—yet he never complained. He called her every day and saw her every night.

There were others who called every day. A Prince, a good-looking movie star, a young Italian whose family was very social, a broker who worked in a rival firm of David's.

They called . . . they sent flowers. She wrote thank-you notes for the flowers but felt the same lethargy toward them all. She read that Tom had handed in his treatment for the screenplay and had gone to Big Sur for ten days. Had he taken his wife or was there someone else?

Even Linda was going away. She had rented a house in Quogue for the month of July. She and Benjamin would spend long weekends together; Benjamin would spend the entire month . . . writing.

Everyone was going somewhere. She had read that Karla had bought a house on a Greek island called Patmos. Yes, everyone had survived, the world was going on without Mike, without Dee and all her money. The same sun was shining. And all the people in the silver frames on Dee's piano were still smiling, still functioning and feeling. . . .

She *wanted* to feel something. She wanted to wake up one morning and feel eager to start the day. Sometimes when she opened her eyes . . . those first few seconds before full consciousness took over, she felt good. Then everything rushed back to her, and she felt the weight of depression take over. Mike was gone . . . Tom was gone . . . even the dream was gone. The man with the beautiful eyes had disappeared along with her father and Tom . . .

Hugh called several times. He gave her pep talks. Told her it was a beautiful day, that she must go out and try to be happy. It was one thing to try . . . but another to make it work.

Her closet was filled with clothes for Marbella and St. Tropez. Each day she had shopped with her new friends and made identical purchases with them. She wore a figa around her neck . . . Gucci shoes . . . Cartier gold loop earrings . . . a

Louis Vuitton shoulder bag. She knew she was beginning to look and dress like Vera and Patty and Debbie because one day Vera showed her their picture in *Women's Wear,* and she had to look for her name to distinguish herself from the others.

She stretched across the bed. She had told Sadie she would rest for half an hour. But she hadn't been able to sleep. She wondered where David would want to go for dinner. She hadn't worn any of the new clothes; maybe she'd wear something special tonight.

She saw the light flash on her phone. She always forgot to turn the sound on. She picked it up just as David was telling Sadie not to bother her if she was resting. "Tell her I have to cancel tonight. There's been a minor crisis at the office. Tell her I'll call her tomorrow."

She walked into the bathroom. It was five o'clock. Might as well take a bath and have a tray. She let the water run and dropped some bubble powder into the tub. Did David really have a crisis . . . or was he just not up to another monotonous evening with her?

She stood very still. Another monotonous evening with her . . . *She* had said it! Until now it had always been another monotonous evening with David . . . but suddenly it was as if she had penetrated into his thought process. . . .

Of course she was monotonous and dull. All she did was try to get through an evening without yawning. Why should he want to spend every evening with her? Come to think of it, Patty hadn't called in two days, and Vera had said something just today about not having time for lunch anymore—she was too busy buying last-minute things for her trip. She *was* a drag. A king-sized drag . . . And soon everyone would leave her.

She walked back to the bedroom and stared down at the park. The whole world was out there. A world Mike had given her on a platter and she couldn't rouse herself to take it. What had happened to all that boundless energy she had with the magazine . . . with Linda . . . with Tom?

She stood very still. Of course! Why hadn't she thought of it before! Instead of taking sleeping pills, she needed a shot! Tom had said they were bad for her. Well, they couldn't be worse than sleeping pills and this zonked-out feeling of inertia.

She looked at the clock . . . five-thirty. Dr. Alpert would still be in his office. She let the bath water go down the drain and dug into the back of the closet for a pair of blue jeans Sadie had tried to throw out. She got into them, pulled on a T-shirt, grabbed some dark glasses, a bag and dashed out.

She wouldn't chance calling Dr. Alpert and being told to come the next day. They *had* to take her now.

At first she thought she was in the wrong office. It looked like a motorcycle club convention. Boys and girls sat slouched in jeans and sleeveless T-shirts. The smell of pot hung heavy in the room. The receptionist stared at January in amazement. Then she flashed a bright smile and held out her hand. "Congratulations. I mean . . . I'm sorry about your father, but congratulations on your fortune. I keep reading about you."

"About me?"

"Of course. You're in the columns everyday. Are you really going to Marbella or is it St. Tropez? I read you were practically engaged to David Milford."

January couldn't answer. She hadn't read a newspaper since California. She knew there had been a lot in the paper about the funeral. But why were the columnists writing about her? Did having ten million dollars cause the world to suddenly be interested in where she went to lunch or where she planned to vacation?

She looked at the crowded waiting room. "I have no appointment," she said.

"Oh, I'm sure we can work you in," the receptionist said. "It's always hectic at this hour. You see we have the cast of a big Broadway show here now. They come in every night at this hour." She nodded toward the actors sitting around the waiting room. "But we'll make an opening for you. Dr. Preston is back from the Coast. So we have both our doctors here now."

"What happened to all his big clients out there?"

"Oh, he actually has no office out there. He just went because Freddie Dillson couldn't sing unless Dr. Preston was backstage."

"But last week . . . on the news on television . . . I saw Freddie being carried out to an ambulance."

The receptionist nodded sadly. "He had a complete breakdown . . . right in the middle of the show. And after Dr. Preston worked so hard—he stayed out there close to seven weeks trying to get him into shape, but Freddie's voice is shot."

"But he was so great," January said. "I played his records all the time in Switzerland."

"You should have seen him when he came here two years ago. His wife had walked out on him—he's a big gambler you know—and he was broke. Dr. Preston took him in hand, and he opened at the Waldorf and made a spectacular comeback. Then he played Vegas and fell apart. Dr. Preston went out there to try and get him in shape for the Los Angeles opening . . . and he did. But he couldn't stay with him forever. Dr. Preston isn't a nursemaid, you know."

"But if he needed the shots?"

The receptionist shugged. "My dear, Dr. Preston has taught two of our biggest senators to give themselves I.V. shots, but Freddie just couldn't make that scene with the needle. I mean . . . after all . . . suppose one has diabetes . . . We must not be afraid of the needle."

"I'd rather have Dr. Simon if I can," January said.

"Well, he has the cast . . . but let's see what we can do. I'll tell you what . . . follow me and I'll sneak you into an inside waiting room. That's where we always put our V.I.P.'s."

She followed the receptionist down a hall just as a young man walked out of a cubicle rolling down his sleeve. He stopped when he saw her. For a moment they both stared at each other. Then he threw his arms around her.

"Hey, heiress . . . What are you doing here?"

"Keith!" She hugged him eagerly. He was thinner and his hair was longer. She suddenly was so glad to see him. "Keith, what are *you* doing here?"

"I come here every night. I'm in *Caterpillar.* You've seen it, of course."

"No . . . I've been away."

"I've read about you. Wow, have you got it made! What do you need happy shots for?"

She shrugged. "No blood, I guess."

"Well, anytime you want to see the show—" He stopped. "Say—" Then he shook his head. "Nah . . . forget it."

"Forget what?"

"There's a big party tonight. At Christina Spencer's town house. She'd flip out if you'd come . . . But I guess you're all booked up."

"No . . . I'm free."

"All evening?"

"As soon as I get my shot."

"Want to see the show?"

"I'd love it."

"Great! I'll wait. I'll put you out front, only this time I can't sit with you."

"And this time I won't run out," she said.

"There's some nudity in it," he said warningly.

"I'm a big girl now, Keith."

"Okay. Get your happy shot. I'll wait out there."

Thirty

SHE SAT mesmerized by the frantic activity of the show. Keith had one song, which he "talked." To her surprise he wasn't very good. Somehow she had expected him to be more exciting on stage. But the vitality of his own personality never came across. There was one scene with frontal nudity. Keith was in that along with most of the cast. She was suddenly aware that everyone's penis was the same size. About the size of David's. Maybe that was standard. It looked as though most men came off the assembly line like that. Except Tom. Poor Tom! Wow, she could really feel sorry for him. Was it the shot? Or was she finally able to see things in their right perspective? She began to giggle. Imagine seeing a bunch of penises floating around on the stage, and here she was, philosophizing about life.

She thought of Mike. She knew he was gone . . . but suddenly she could accept it. For the first time she could think of Mike without feeling dead inside. Mike had lived a full life. As he would have put it—he went out in style. Mike had lived a bigtime life and he had enjoyed every minute of it . . . except, perhaps, the last year. And as Hugh had said, he had lived that year for her . . . so she could have many many good years.

Thank God for Hugh. And thank God for Dr. Alpert. Maybe the shots were bad for you; Tom had said they were. But it couldn't be worse than all that Jack Daniels he consumed. He was fifty-eight, but even with all that bourbon, he could still write and be what Linda called a "superstar." And with that small penis of his, he could still afford the luxury of letting her walk out of his life. Suddenly it struck her as being amusing. How had she ever felt so desolate because it was over? She felt alive and eager sitting in the audience. She was snapping her fingers to the beat. She could think clearly. She was sitting in the third row watching *Caterpillar* and enjoying herself. She wasn't lying in bed at the Pierre taking sleeping pills. There *was* a world out here, a world where people were leaping about on the stage, girls baring their breasts in a frenzied rock dance . . . and it all seemed just fine.

They decided to walk to the party after the show. Christina Spencer's town house was in the East Sixties, and the night was warm and clear. January clung to Keith's arm. She wanted to skip, to run . . . She stared at the dark sky. "Oh, Keith, isn't it great to really feel good?"

He nodded. "Dr. Alpert probably gave you the full dose. He was so high himself tonight, he probably thought you were a member of the cast."

She giggled. "Is that why he didn't even talk to me? You know I felt bad that he didn't even give me a 'Welcome Home' or a 'Glad to see you.' "

Keith smiled and looked down at her. "Feel great, huh?"

"I feel like I can hear the trees grow, smell the summer coming . . . I *can* see the leaves growing. Keith, look at that tree—can't you *see* that leaf getting bigger?"

He smiled. "You bet. And it's important to see and feel all these things. There will only be this Thursday in June just once. Tomorrow will be Friday and this Thursday will never come back."

"Why did you leave Linda?" she asked suddenly.

"Linda wanted too much of me."

She nodded. No one could have all of anyone. That was why Tom had put her out of his life. She stopped and stared at the sky. This one minute, she felt on the brink of something . . . as if she could look into the future . . . understand everything . . . She turned to him. "Keith, can you get hooked on these shots?"

"No, but no matter how out of sight everything's been, it's a bad scene when it wears off. Because you drop to the bottom . . . and the colors are gone. You look up and realize there's dust on the sun and brown on the leaves and shit in the street. Well, if you want to live in a dirty tired world, you can stop taking the shots. Everyone has the right to live the way they want—the Jesus Freaks have their bag, the nature freaks have their thing . . . I'm a speed freak, and as long as it makes everything green and orange . . . fine. And one day, maybe I won't want it all to be technicolor, and on that day, maybe I'll quit. But why should I right now?"

They had stopped in front of a brownstone on a tree-lined street. There were several limousines in front. Keith led January inside. She saw a well-known rock singer standing in the hall. They pushed into the living room. It was packed solid with familiar faces. Pop artists, underground movie stars, recording artists, several young screen actresses. There were blue jeans, velvet pants suits, see-through blouses, striped jackets, and a sprinkling of Indian outfits.

And there was Christina Spencer. She floated toward them, her much photographed face a bit toothier in person. Her figure even more fantastic than the photographs showed. She had to be in her late fifties. Her face was taut from several lifts. She wore a midriff outfit of flowered silk. Her full breasts peeked above the low-cut neckline. She had the body of a twenty-year-old.

She welcomed January warmly. "I knew your father, my dear. We had a few gorgeous nights together once in Acapulco. That was right before I met dear Geoffrey."

Keith steered January away. "Personally, I think she killed Geoffrey," he whispered. "She's married three times and each husband died and left her more money. And with her luck she backs *Caterpillar* with her own money and it's a smash."

"I thought you were her lover," January said.

"Oh, I balled her. But she spreads herself around. She needs a new young lover every week to prove to herself that the doctor from Brazil who tightened everything did a good job. But she's not bad. And what the hell . . . she lets everyone do their own number. Maybe I am top boy, but tonight she thinks I'm balling you . . . and she's not mad . . ."

A girl walked over to Keith. "Baby . . . the sangria is out of sight, it's in the den upstairs."

Keith led January upstairs into a dark sitting room. Everyone was sitting on cushions. He pulled January to the floor and reached into his pocket and took out a skinny cigarette. He lit it and passed it to her. She inhaled deeply and let the smoke out in a thin stream. "Jesus, baby . . . you're smoking it like it was a Chesterfield."

"I inhaled it," she said.

"But with grass you're not supposed to let the smoke out. You got to take air in with it." He held it between his middle fingers and illustrated the technique. She tried . . . but couldn't keep the smoke down. Suddenly he said, "Hold still. I'll give you a shotgun." Then he leaned over to kiss her, only he blew the smoke into her mouth and held her nose. "Now swallow it." She gagged, but kept most of it down. He did it twice again and she began to feel giddy and light-headed. Then he lit another and this time she inhaled properly. A beautiful young girl came over carrying a pitcher of sangria. "Here's some paper cups. Want some great stuff?"

Keith nodded and took the cups she handed them. "This is Arlene, January."

"Drink the wine . . . you'll blow your mind . . . Anita is strung out in the other room."

January sipped the wine. "It's great," she said.

"Sip it slowly," Keith said. "It's laced heavy."

"What?" She put down the cup.

"Relax. There's just enough acid in it for a good trip. Trust me. Look, we all have the show to do tomorrow. I'm drinking it . . . Just sip it slowly."

She looked around. The sweet smell of pot was everywhere. Music was piped into all the rooms. Everyone was sipping the sangria. She shrugged . . . why not? Everyone here had done it before . . . and they seemed eager to do it again. The sensation had to be great. Besides, as Keith had said, there would only be this Thursday in June, once in her life!

She finished the wine. Then she handed him the empty cup. She leaned against his shoulder. She felt no great reaction . . .

just totally relaxed. She had been taut from the shot, taut and high . . . overactive . . . Now everything seemed calm and tranquil. That was a funny word . . . tranquil . . . but the whole world seemed tranquil . . . she felt warm and saw the sun . . . then a rainbow of color flashed by and hung over water. She saw waves and the ocean . . . and it seemed soft and blue and she suddenly knew with a strange clarity that Mike had felt no fear when the plane went down . . . he had almost welcomed slipping into that soft blue sea . . . he would rest . . . just as she was resting her head against Keith's shoulder . . . and Mike hadn't died . . . nothing ever died . . . life existed always . . . and people were good . . . Keith's lips were warm . . . Keith was kissing her . . . he was unbuttoning her shirt and she had no bra on . . . but it didn't matter . . . everything seemed to be going in slow motion now . . . maybe it wasn't right for her to kiss Keith . . . because Linda had loved him . . . *had* . . . *had* . . . everything was so long ago and nothing was forever.

She leaned back on the cushions. Keith's lips were on her breasts. She saw a girl completely naked dancing alone . . . a boy was naked and he held another boy close to him and they danced. Arlene floated through the room and turned a switch . . . psychedelic lights floated against the walls. January rolled over and put her head in Keith's lap. He sat there gazing into space stroking her breasts. She stared up into his face, but she knew he didn't see her . . . he was listening to sounds of his own. It seemed as if she could actually see his hair getting darker . . . and everything was so still that even through the music she could hear her own heart beating, and suddenly she felt she could see the past and the future. The future without Mike. It was as if God was opening the heavens for a moment. And then she saw him . . . his blue eyes. He had come back. She stretched out her arms. He had been away so long . . . and now he had come back and she wasn't asleep. His eyes were so blue . . . maybe it was God. Did God have blue eyes . . .

She heard voices . . . they seemed so far away. One of the voices came from a young man standing near Keith. Norton . . . yes . . . he had done a big number in the show. Norton was smiling down at her . . . but she stared past him . . . where had God gone . . . Norton's eyes were brown . . . amber brown . . . golden brown.

"Man, her tits are small but beautiful . . . such tiny pink nipples . . . I dig pink nipples. Man . . . can I have them?"

And then Norton was stroking one breast and Keith had knelt down and was stroking the other. They each kissed one . . . and it was sweet and friendly and she held both their heads. Everyone loved one another . . . everything was so peaceful . . . and Christina came over . . . she had taken off the top of her dress . . . her breasts were hanging. Why were they hanging? They had been so nice and round sticking out of her dress. Christina reached down and pulled Norton's arm. "Norton, come with Arlene and me . . ." She pulled Norton to his feet. Another boy walked over. He smiled at Keith. "Hi, man. She's outta sight . . ." He knelt down and looked into January's eyes. "I'm Ricky. . . ."

She smiled and touched his legs. "You did the dance . . ." Ricky had no clothes on . . . he had worn very little in the show . . . but now he had no clothes on . . . he started moving his body . . . doing the dance from the show . . . he held out his hands . . . he wanted her to do the dance with him. She got up slowly . . . she felt she could do anything . . . even fly across the room . . . float over everyone's head.

"You can't dance with clothes on," he said.

She smiled as she dropped the jeans to the floor. Then she stepped out of her pants. He slid his hands down her body and she smiled. She felt free . . . she moved sensuously . . . in rhythm to his movements . . . following all of Ricky's gyrations. They were a foot apart with their eyes locked together. He moved closer. Everyone began to clap in a far-away rhythm to their movements. She raised her hands over her head and joined in. Clap . . . Clap . . . Clap . . . Ricky snapped his fingers to the same beat. Keith came behind her and lifted her . . . she felt lighter than air. Someone was spreading her legs . . . Everyone was clapping . . . slowly . . . in rhythm . . . Clap . . . Clap . . . Clap . . . She was clapping . . . She saw the strong young penis coming toward her . . . Clap . . . Clap . . . Clap . . . Ricky's penis . . . Clap . . . Clap . . . Clap . . . it was a chant . . . the penis moved into her. Everyone chanted . . . Fuck . . . Fuck . . . Fuck . . . Keith was moving her body back and forth . . . a group was holding Ricky too. . . . Fuck . . . Fuck . . . Fuck. . . . Nothing wrong with it . . . The young penis entered . . . in and out . . . in and out . . . in and out . . . Clap . . . Clap . . . Clap . . . Fuck . . . Fuck . . . Fuck . . . everyone is a friend . . . Fuck . . . Fuck . . . Fuck . . . Lights going . . . Christina kissing her breasts . . . nice friendly gesture . . . poor Christina with long hanging breasts . . . across the room she saw several girls take off their clothes . . . all in a slow rhythmic movement . . . Another boy came by and kissed her breasts . . . Everyone loved everyone . . . it was nice and good . . . Clap . . . Clap . . . Clap . . . ritualistic clap . . . clap . . . clap . . . fuck . . . fuck . . . fuck . . . suck . . . suck . . . suck . . . everyone was loving her. Oh God, it was wonderful . . . She was floating . . . she had never felt anything like this before . . . Ricky's penis . . . someone's lips on her and on Ricky's penis at the same time . . Christina at her breast . . . She felt the orgasm coming . . . she saw Keith hold something under her nose . . . Fuck . . . Fuck . . . Fuck. . . . "Sniff hard, January . . . it's a popper." She breathed deeply . . . her head felt like it was coming off . . . and the orgasm was lasting forever and ever. She wanted it to go on and on . . . on and on. . . . . "Oh, Mike, I love you," she shouted. Then she passed out.

When she opened her eyes she was curled up on a fur rug clinging to Keith. Her blouse and jeans were on the floor beside her. She sat up. Her head felt clear and she thought about the bizarre dream. Then she looked at her body. She was naked! Ricky was sprawled across the floor . . . also naked and asleep. She stood up and slid into her jeans. It hadn't been a dream. She had been part of something insane . . . ritualistic. She carried her blouse and walked among the sleeping people. She had to find her shoes. A clock struck in the hall . . . she wandered out there . . . two girls were nude . . . locked in an embrace. They stopped when they saw her and smiled. She smiled and they came over to her and each one kissed her lightly on the cheek. She smiled at the gesture of friendship and love . . . a rush of wonderful lightness streaked before her eyes . . . she saw flashing colors . . . she felt warm all over . . . but she felt she should go home. There were sandals lying all over the place . . . she must find a pair that fit. She found her bag and slid it on her shoulder.

Keith came over to her. "Where are you going?"

She smiled as she put on her shirt. "Home . . ."

He handed her a cube of sugar. "Eat it . . . it's great." Then he shoved an envelope inside the bag she had slid on her shoulder.

She sucked the sugar cube. "What did you put in my bag?"

"A gift," he said as he began to unbutton her shirt. She felt like she was floating again . . . there was a whirring noise inside her head. But she broke away with a smile. "No . . . you belong to Linda."

As she walked back to the foyer, the two girls who were still embracing each other looked up. They each reached out and pulled her toward them. They kissed her. They opened her shirt. One slipped her lips on one of January's breasts. Both began fondling her. It was beautiful . . . these two girls she had never seen before . . . wanting to make her happy . . . wanting to be friendly . . . she felt them unzip her jeans . . . she felt one of the soft hands touching her . . . no . . . that was wrong . . . only a penis should do that . . . or a man . . . She pulled away . . . she smiled and shook her head. The girls smiled. One buttoned her blouse. The other helped her with her zipper. Each waved and went back to making love to one another. She watched them . . . it was like a ballet . . .beautiful . . . she walked to the door.

She went outside. The summer night felt cool and clean. If possible, she felt more light-headed than before. She could see beyond time and space . . . through buildings . . . through that brownstone house she had just left, where people were making love—happy beautiful people.

It was a wonderful marvelous world, and tomorrow she'd tell Mike all about it. No, Mike was gone. Well, when she saw him again. . . . because she would see him again . . . everyone existed forever . . . and he would know she loved him. Because everyone should love everyone . . . everyone should love everything . . . even a tree—a tree could love back. She stopped at a tree and threw her arms around it. "You're just a young skinny tree . . . but don't be afraid . . . because one day you'll be a big tree. And I love you!" She clung to the tree. "Such a weak little tree . . . this whole street has such young weak little trees . . . But know what, little trees? You'll all be here long after we are gone. And maybe someone else will tell you how much they love you. Don't you hope so? Tell me, tree—if that tree next to you told you it wanted to belong to you forever . . . intertwine its branches with yours . . . become one . . . wouldn't you like that? Wouldn't the two of you together make a real big strong happy tree?" She sighed. "But no, you've got to stand here all alone, skinny and lonely . . . and maybe some of your leaves will blow against his . . . and with the wind you both can whisper and speak . . . and be together . . . yet apart. Is that the way nature wants it to be? Then maybe that's the way we're supposed to be too. But oh, tree . . . it's so nice to belong to someone . . ."

She left the tree and began to walk in a zigzag pattern. She was aware of the way she walked, just as a child is aware when it is consciously trying not to step on the cracks of the pavement. She looked up at the sky. The stars were separated too. Were they lonely? Then she saw one shoot across the heavens. She shut her eyes and made a wish. Maybe right now her father was watching the same star from the ocean. Or maybe he was on one of those stars, beginning a whole new life.

"Twinkle, twinkle, little star." She laughed. That was silly, because a star wasn't little. A star was a big sun. . . . "How I wonder what you are!" She knew what a star was. She fastened her attention on one that seemed to be blinking at her. It was so bright, but she was aware that the velvet sky was starting to fade . . . morning would begin soon . . . that very special Thursday in June was over. Never to be gotten back. Only now it was a very special Friday. She got up and began to walk . . . sometimes she zigzagged . . . sometimes she skipped. The red light on Madison Avenue looked so red . . . and the green light so green. And those lights told people and cars what to do . . . when to go . . . when to stop. It was a world of stop and go lights. But who needed them? People wouldn't hurt anyone. What was everyone trying to protect her from? Why did people try to instill fear? People were taught to fear and obey. Fear strangers . . . fear cars . . . obey lights! Who needed lights! The world would be much better without stop lights. People would stop and go quite properly without those lights. Because people cared. She stood in the middle of the street and threw her head back and stared at the sky. There were no stop signals in the sky . . . and with that whóle big sky . . . Mike's plane had gone down . . . from that soft sky into the soft water . . . and now Mike was looking at the sky too . . . and nothing could ever hurt him again . . . just like right now . . . nothing could hurt her . . . no one would hit her . . . because at this moment she was part of infinity. Nothing bad could ever happen . . . even death wasn't the end . . . it was just part of another existence. She was sure of that now. She stared at the sky and waited for an answer . . . she heard the screech of brakes . . . a cab pulled to a stop inches in front of her. The driver got out . . . "You dumb drunken broad!"

"Don't say that." She smiled. She slipped her arms around his neck. "Don't be angry because I love you."

He pulled away and stared at her. "You coulda been killed. Oh, Christ . . . you're one of them. You're stoned out of your mind."

"I love you," she said and put her head against his cheek. "Everyone should love everyone."

He sighed. "I got two daughters your age. I work nights so they can study. One goes to teacher's college . . . the other is studying to be a nurse. And you . . . flower child . . . what the hell are you studying?"

"To love . . . to know . . . to feel. . . ."

"Get into the cab. I'll take you home."

"No . . . I want to walk . . . to float . . . to feel."

"Get in . . . no charge."

She smiled. "See, you do love me."

He dragged her by the arm and put her in the seat beside him. "I don't trust you in the back. Now . . . where's home?"

"Where the heart is."

"Look, I finished work at four, but I had an airport call. It's quarter to five in the morning. I live in the Bronx. Right now my wife is sitting, waiting with the coffee, picturing me being held up with a knife at my throat. So let's get with it. Where do you want to go?"

"To the Plaza. My daddy lives there."

He headed for the Plaza. After a few blocks she touched his arm. "No . . . not the Plaza . . . he's not there now. The man I loved was at the Plaza . . . now's he at the Beverly Hills Hotel."

"Look . . . where do you want to go?"

"The Pierre."

"What are you? Some kind of a hotel freak? C'mon . . . where shall I take you?"

She looked at his registration card. "Mr. Isadore Cohen, you are a beautiful man. Take me to the Pierre."

He started down Fifth Avenue. "And what's your name, flower child?"

"January."

"Naturally," he said.

It was beginning to rain when Isadore Cohen walked her to the entrance of the Pierre. She looked up at the heavy gray sky. "Where are the stars? Where did my beautiful night go?" she asked.

"It's turned into morning," Isadore Cohen grumbled. "An ugly wet morning. . . . Now go back to wherever you belong."

She turned and waved as he walked back to his cab. He had refused to take any money, but she had left a twenty-dollar bill on the seat. She tiptoed into her bedroom and closed the drapes. Sadie was still asleep. The whole world was asleep except dear sweet Mr. Cohen who was on his way home to the Bronx. He was a wonderful man. Everyone was wonderful if you took time out to understand them. Like Keith, now that she knew him—he was wonderful too. She undressed slowly and tossed her bag on the chair. It slipped to the floor. She leaned over and picked it up gently. "You, Mr. Bag, are a Louis Vuitton, and I happen to think you are ugly. But they say you are very 'in.'" She studied the bag. Vera had made her buy it at Saks. ("But I don't wear much brown," January had said. "A Louis Vuitton bag isn't just brown," Vera insisted. "It goes with everything.")

Well, for one hundred and thirty dollars she damn well intended to wear it with everything. Then she laughed. What was a hundred and thirty dollars if she had ten million? But the idea of ten million dollars belonging to her was impossible to grasp. Any more than she could feel that this apartment belonged to her. It was still Dee's. She wondered if Mike ever felt it belonged to him. But the Louis Vuitton bag that cost one hundred and thirty dollars belonged to her. That kind of money she could understand. She sat on the edge of the bed and stroked the bag. She put the bag on the pillow and crawled into bed.

She wasn't sleepy. She thought about taking a sleeping pill. She reached for the bottle in the drawer of the night table . . . then put it away. Why should she? She felt too marvelous . . . And as Keith had said, "There will never be this Thursday again"—only now it was Friday and there'd never be *this* Friday again. She lay very quietly and savored the wonderful feeling of weightlessness that flowed through her body. She knew she wouldn't fall asleep . . . she couldn't . . . yet she realized she had because the dream came again. First the eyes . . . so clear and blue. The face was vague . . . it was always vague, but she knew it was beautiful. He was a stranger, and yet instinctively she felt he was someone she wanted to be with. He held out his arms . . . and she knew she had to go to him. She felt she was getting out of bed and going into his arms . . . yet she knew she had to be *in* her bed dreaming the whole scene. That was it . . . a scene . . . because she saw herself getting out of bed . . . she watched herself follow the outstretched arms. Yet each time she reached him it was as if she hadn't come quite close enough. He kept waiting. She followed him into the living room . . . to the window. But now he was outside the window! She opened it . . . the sky was dark . . . filled with stars. Now she knew it was all a dream because it had been dawn just a few minutes ago when she fell asleep . . . a gray sticky dawn . . . so that meant she was still in bed and not standing at the window, staring out at the stars and this mystical man. But this time, she was determined to see his face. She leaned out the windowsill. "Do you want me?" she called out.

He held out his arms. "If I come to you, you have to really love me," she told him. "I can't bear to fall in love with you and have you disappear, even if you are only a dream."

He didn't speak. But the eyes told her he would never hurt her. And suddenly she knew that all she had to do was jump out of that window and float up into his arms. She put one leg over the sill. And then she felt someone dragging her back. Keeping her from him . . . She struggled . . . And then she woke because Sadie was pulling at her and screaming . . . pulling her inside. She looked at the street below . . . she had been halfway out of the window!

"Miss January! Oh, Miss January! Why? . . . Why!" Sadie was sobbing from fright.

She clung to Sadie for a moment. Then she managed a weak smile. "It's all right, Sadie. It was just a dream."

"A dream! You were going to jump out of that window. Thank God I was in the kitchen when I heard the window open."

January stared out the window. It was dark and there were stars. "What time is it?"

"Ten o'clock. I was just fixing myself some tea and going to watch the news. I tried to wake you at noon and you mumbled something about having been up all night. Mr. Milford called at seven and I told him you were still asleep. He was very concerned. He's been calling every hour."

"Don't worry, Sadie. I . . . I took some sleeping pills this morning. I couldn't sleep last night. I guess I just slept round the clock."

"Well . . . will you call Mr. Milford? He's very concerned."

She nodded and went to her room. "Can I bring you anything, Miss January?"

"No . . . I'm not hungry."

She picked up the phone and started to dial David. Suddenly the room went dark. Then bright lights shot through her eyes and she saw him again . . . just for a flash . . . the blue eyes . . . almost mocking her . . . as if she had been a coward. "You would have killed me!" she shouted. "Killed me! Is that what you wanted?"

Sadie came rushing in. January stared down at the phone, which was now buzzing with the phone-off-the-hook-too-long signal. "Miss January, you were screaming!"

"No. I'm . . . I . . . I shouted at the operator because I got a wrong number twice. Don't worry, Sadie . . . please. I'm going to call Mr. Milford. You go to sleep."

Then she dialed the number. Sadie hovered by and waited until she heard January say, "Hi, David!" Then she discreetly left the room.

David sounded genuinely concerned. She tried to make her voice light. But the room was growing dark again and the splashing array of colors had returned. "I went to a party," she said as she blinked hard to make the colors disappear.

"It must have been a late one," he said. "You slept all day."

She closed her eyes to block out the flashing lights. "It was late. Some . . . some friends of my father's . . . actors . . . directors . . ." The colors were gone and she was all right now. Her voice was strong again. "It was a late party . . . it didn't start until midnight. And then when I got home for some strange reason I wasn't sleepy. So I read . . . until morning. And then I took two sleeping pills . . . and . . . well . . . you know the rest."

"How are you going to be able to sleep now?"

"Easy. I'll read a dull book and take some pills. By tomorrow my time schedule will be straightened out."

"January, I don't like this sleeping pill business. I'm against all pills. I never even take an aspirin."

"Well, after tonight I won't take any again."

"It's my fault. I left you alone. And you shouldn't be alone now . . . ever. January, let's not wait out the summer. Let's do it now."

"Do what now?"

"Get married."

She was silent. He had never asked her to go to bed with him since that first time. But his whole attitude since the accident had been different. He was gentle . . . considerate . . . and always concerned.

"January, are you there?"

"Yes . . ."

"Well . . . will you marry me?"

"David . . . I—" She hesitated. But what was she hesitating about? What *was* she waiting for? Another Tom to come along to destroy her? A relationship with Keith . . . and his friends? The full impact of it was just beginning to hit her. And even the dream was dangerous. She had almost jumped out of a window. She was suddenly frightened. What was happening to her? Where was the girl she had once been . . . still was. But that girl had allowed a stranger to make love to her in the midst of a room filled with strangers. Yet it had all seemed perfectly proper at the time. She began to tremble . . . she felt unclean . . . violated.

"January, are you still on?"

"Yes, David. I'm . . . I'm just thinking . . ."

"Please, January. I love you . . . I want to take care of you."

"David—" She clung to the phone. "I do need you. Yes . . . Yes. I do!"

"Oh, January! I promise you'll never regret it. Look, we'll celebrate tomorrow night at dinner. I'll invite a few friends. Vera and Ted . . . Harriett and Paul . . . Muriel and Burt . . . Bonnie and—" He stopped. "Where shall we do it? The Lafayette? Sign of the Dove?"

"No. Let's go to Raffles. That was the scene of our first date, wasn't it?"

"January, you're sentimental! I never would have thought it."

"There's a lot of things we'll both have to find out about each other," she said. "David, do you realize . . . we really hardly know one another."

"That's not my fault," he said. "I . . . well . . . I haven't invited you back to my place or asked to stay with you because I thought you were too upset and—"

"Oh, David, that's not what I mean. Strangers can go to bed together."

"I guess I'm not very demonstrative," he said. "I mean . . . when I care for someone . . . maybe I don't know how to show it. But January . . . you don't either. Know what all my friends call you? 'Her Coolness.' Even the newspapers picked it up . . . they called you that in a column yesterday."

"Do I seem cool?"

"Detached at times," he said. "But good God, why shouldn't you? After all that's happened to you in less than a year."

"Yes, you're right. A lot has happened . . ." She suddenly remembered that first night at Raffles. It all seemed unreal. Could she really spend the rest of her life with David . . . live with him . . . sleep in the same bed with him? . . . She began to panic.

"David, I can't! It isn't fair to you."

"What's not fair to me?"

"To marry you. I . . . I'm not really in love with you."

He was silent for a moment. Then he said, "January, have you really ever loved anyone?"

"Yes."

"Besides your father?"

"Yes . . ."

He hesitated. "Is it over?"

"Yes." Her voice was very low.

"Then don't tell me about it."

"But David . . . if I know I can love someone in a certain way and I don't feel that way about you, then is it fair to you? I mean . . . oh, I don't know how to put it–"

"I understand. Because I've loved someone too. And not in the same way I love you. But no two loves are the same. If you keep searching for the same kind of love each time, then you never really love again, because each new affair merely becomes a continuation of that first love."

"How do you know that?" she asked.

"I was talking to a big shrink at a party of my mother's. Dr. Arthur Addison. My mother went to him when she began having her changes and got a little depressed. I don't believe in psychiatry–unless someone is really batty–but I have to admit he helped my mother, and since then he has become a big friend of the family. But, January, the kind of love we're both talking about only happens to a person once. And since we've both had it . . . what we have now is something new for both of us. And we can build it into a new life and forget all the old memories."

"Do you think we can do it?"

"Of course. Only a neurotic person clings to something that's gone. And you strike me as a very levelheaded girl. Now go to sleep and try to dream of me."

She hung up and thought about their conversation. David was right. She couldn't bring Mike back or regain what she once had with Tom. That part of her life was over. But how could she shut out the memories? Maybe it was easier for a man. God, if she could just shut out last night. All the feeling of love for everyone was gone. She felt nothing but loathing and disgust. For Keith, his friends . . . but most of all, herself. And then to top it all she had tried to jump out of the window. If Sadie hadn't come in time, she would be dead. Or would she? Was there something out there? Something calling to her? She looked out the window . . . at the stars . . . then she ran to her closet and found another pair of jeans. She put on a shirt, took a sweater, and grabbed her bag. It was only ten-thirty . . . she would drive to the beach and talk it all out with Hugh. Tell him everything. The happy shots . . . the party . . . the orgy scene . . . and the man with the blue eyes. She would also tell him about almost jumping out of the window.

She crept out of the apartment so as not to awaken Sadie. She knew Dee kept her cars at a garage on West Fifty-sixth Street. She walked over.

There were several garages on Fifty-sixth Street. She hit the correct one on the first try and took it as an omen of good luck. The night manager recognized her and gave her the Jaguar. She left the garage and headed downtown. She recalled Tom's driver had taken the Midtown Tunnel to the Long Island Expressway. The car handled beautifully.

There was no traffic. She'd make Westhampton by one. Perhaps she should have phoned Hugh . . . But then he might have asked her to wait until tomorrow, and she had to talk it out now. She cut off the Expressway and pulled into a garage. The attendant filled the gas tank and gave her directions for Westhampton. The gas took all of her money, and she gave the attendant her last quarter as a tip. But the tank was filled, the road was good, and soon she'd see Hugh. Somehow she felt talking it out with him would make everything come out right.

It was one-fifteen when she pulled up to the house. She rang the bell . . . it had a hollow sound . . . an empty sound. Oh, Lord . . . was this one of his nights with his widow? She got into her car. She would sit and wait. She stared out at the dunes. They seemed so far away and so high and unfriendly tonight. But that was silly . . . they were just globs of sand. Hugh often slept out there. Of course! Maybe he was out there now! She got out of the car and started for the beach.

It was hard going. Wild grass grew in crazy patches. Several times she tripped over pieces of driftwood. Sand filled her sandals, but she ploughed on. She was physically exhausted by the time she reached the dunes. She stood on the top of the highest hill and looked down the stretch of beach. No sign of life anywhere. Even the ocean seemed abnormally calm. The waves seemed to whisper a hushed apology as they lapped against the sand. Perhaps Hugh was on another dune, farther down the beach. . . .

She stood and shouted his name. There was no answer . . . just the empty sound of her voice. Not even a gull called out. Where were all the gulls at night? They were always swooping around and screeching at one another during the day. She flopped on the ground and let some of the cool sand sift through her fingers. Where *did* sea gulls go at night? She looked back toward the house. It was dark and lonely-looking. The calm night, the bright stars, and the sighs of the waves seemed much friendlier than the empty house.

She rolled her sweater into a ball and cushioned it under her head. Then she lay back and stared at the sky. It seemed to come closer and blanket her. Suddenly she felt as if *it* was the world and earth was merely the floor. What *was* up there? Other planets? Other worlds? She looked back toward the house. Maybe Hugh was spending the night at the lady's place.

She could go back to her car, and sleep there until he came back. But she wasn't sleepy and it was so peaceful on the dune. All those stars. The Wise Men had looked at these same stars the night Jesus was born. Galileo had looked at them . . . and when Columbus was looking for his new route to India he had also relied on them. How many people had made love under them? How many children had made wishes on them and prayed to the God they imagined sitting above them as she had when she was a child. God's lights. Her mother had told her that! It suddenly came to her—God's lights. Her mother! Until this second her mother had always been just a misty memory. A quiet lady always "resting." Always beautiful when she was up and about . . . great brown eyes staring adoringly at her father . . . never at her. In fact she couldn't recall ever looking into those eyes herself . . . *Yes! Once!* . . . It came to her now. The memory of snuggling in her mother's arms and seeing those great brown eyes looking tenderly at her. She had had a bad dream and cried out. The nurse came immediately. But this time her mother had come too. And it was one of the rare times that her mother rather than the nurse comforted her. And when she had shown fear of being alone in the darkness because the bad dream might return . . . her mother had held her close and told her nothing bad could happen in the night. That sometimes the light made things look bad, but the night was soft and comforting. They had sat before the window and looked at the stars together and her mother had said, "They are God's little beacon lights . . . to remind you that He is always watching you . . . always there to help you . . . to love you."

She thought about it now as she watched the stars. That was really a beautiful story to tell to a frightened little girl. What had her mother been like? Suddenly she wished she had been older and could have comforted her. Her mother loved Mike . . . but he had other girls. God, how she must have suffered. She remembered how she had felt that day Tom stayed at the beach with his wife. Tears came to her eyes. Her poor, poor mother. In love with Mike . . . left alone with a little girl while he was in California. Probably in Bungalow Five with a girl of his own. Suddenly, lying there, it was as if she saw herself split into two beings. She was Mike's girl in Bungalow Five . . . and she was her young helpless mother . . . alone too much . . . sobbing too much . . . She called out, "Mother . . . you shouldn't have done it. The girl with him suffered too. At least you knew he would always come back to you. And you had me. Why did you leave me? Didn't you love me?" Her voice rang out in the night . . . and the stars stared back. But suddenly they no longer seemed warm and friendly. They looked hard and cold . . . as if they resented this intrusion into their privacy. They were aloof and secure . . . so sure they would always be there. Laughing at this little speck of humanity on the beach. And they weren't God's beacon lights . . . they were worlds and suns and meteorites. And now there was even space junk floating around in that velvety darkness. She saw a star streak across . . . then another . . . the moon looked so low. Like a mother dominating the heavens with the stars as her children. It was sad to know that the moon wasn't silver and bright. That it was just a wasteland . . . scarred . . . pitted . . . smaller than earth . . . an ash in the sky. Man had landed on it and revealed its mystery and taken away all of the romance.

She still felt alert and colors were still strong. The sky was black but she saw shades of blue and purple in its blackness.

She glanced toward Hugh's house. The moon hung over it, its brilliant light illuminating the dark windows. Maybe he had taken the widow to New York tonight.

She opened her bag and groped for her cigarettes. Her hand came across an envelope. She took it out. A plain white crumpled bulky envelope. The envelope Keith had stuck into her bag just as she was leaving. She ripped it open. It contained a small plastic pill bottle with two sugar cubes. There was also a note. She flicked on her cigarette lighter. "DEAR HEIRESS: I LOVE YOU. I CAN'T TAKE YOU TO MARBELLA OR THE SOUTH OF FRANCE. BUT IF YOU'LL BE MY GIRL I CAN TAKE YOU ON TRIPS OUT OF THIS WORLD. FOR STARTERS—HERE'S TWO ON ME. LOVE, KEITH."

She opened the bottle and held the sugar cubes in her hand. She started to toss them away, but something held her back. Why not take one? If she did, all of her depression would evaporate. She'd be able to reach up and touch the stars. She put the cubes back into the bottle and dropped it back into her bag. No, taking acid wasn't going to solve things. The problem would still be there when the "trip" was over. But what was the solution? Try to conform? Try to learn to love David? Learn backgammon? Have lunch every day? Buy clothes? *No!* She didn't want a life that had no highs. Even the lows were worthwhile if you knew there would be highs.

And not an acid high. A real high. Like seeing Mike stride toward her that day in the airport at Rome, hearing Tom say he could never be without her. . . .

But they were both gone. Tom and Mike. . . .

She took out the bottle again. What would happen if she took *both* of them? Maybe she'd go on a trip that would last forever. Maybe she'd never come back.

She shivered. A wind had come up from nowhere. For some reason it chilled her. Sand began to spray against her face. She stood up and brushed the sand from her clothes. The wind was really blowing now. She put on her sweater. And then as suddenly as it had come, the wind stopped. And there was a curious silence—like the silence she had once heard in California right before a minor earth tremor. When the crickets had stopped and even the leaves made no sound. She looked toward the ocean. It was like glass, and the moon hung over it casting a bright path over the dark water. But that was impossible! Just a moment ago the moon had been behind her, hanging over Hugh's house. She turned and looked back. Of course. There it was . . . A pale friendly light over the dark strip of beach-front houses. Then she looked back at the ocean . . . and there *it* was! Clear and bright . . . another moon!

She was hallucinating! It was that sugar cube Keith had given her at the party. She jumped up and turned her back on the "new moon." She began to run, but it was like one of those dreadful nightmares where you ran but remained in one spot. It was happening to her. Her feet were moving, her breath was coming fast, but she remained on top of that dune . . . trapped between two moons.

She turned and looked back. The new moon had disappeared. The ocean was black and lonely. The stars seemed more distant than ever. She was frightened now. She started running. This time her feet moved. She stumbled and slipped in the darkness. Oh, God, acid was really dangerous. It had almost made her jump out of a window. Now it had made her see another moon. This must be what they call re-hallucinating. Or had she taken another sugar cube? Or both of them! Oh, God . . . had she? She looked back. She could see her bag on the dune where she had dropped it. She could see it because it was illuminated by moonlight. Moonlight from the *other* moon! It was back!

Maybe she *had* taken the sugar cubes. But she was positive she had put them back. Or had she? It didn't matter. She was hallucinating, seeing two moons . . . Anything could happen. It might drag her out to the ocean. If she could think she could jump out of a window and float upward, then there was no telling what would happen. Oh, God, she'd never take anything again. She'd marry David and have children. A child of her own to love. Maybe she'd never feel for David what she felt for Mike. No . . . what she felt for Tom. But at least she'd be marrying someone Mike approved of. And she would have a little boy who would look just like Mike. And a girl too. And she'd love them and be a good mother. She would! Only, please, God. Just let her make it back to that house.

Why did the house seem so far away? She was off the dune now. In a valley, climbing another. . . .

It was still there. She turned and saw it hover over the ocean. Suddenly it streaked across the sky, returned and spun around, pirouetting—as if it were doing an eerie ballet just for her. It shot into the heavens until it looked no larger than a star, until she was positive it was a star. Then it returned to its normal size, throwing its glow into a perfect lane across the water.

She stared at it for a moment. This was no hallucination. This was real! Because when you hallucinate you don't know it. Like going out of the window. She had thought she was dreaming. But maybe *this* was a dream too. Maybe she wasn't on the beach. Maybe she was home in bed. Maybe she wasn't at the Pierre. Maybe that had all been part of a dream too. Maybe she was still with Tom, and Mike wasn't dead. Maybe the happy shots caused all this to be one long horrible nightmare. And when she woke up she'd be at Bungalow Five and Tom would be there and she would leave him and rush to meet Mike and make things up. Or maybe they hadn't had the fight, maybe the fight was part of the nightmare—then she wouldn't have to leave Tom. But maybe she had never met Tom. Maybe she was still in Switzerland, and she was getting well, and she was coming home to Mike and he hadn't met Dee, and none of this had happened . . . But then maybe there never was a Franco, and there had never been a motorcycle accident. Maybe she had never been born—because she couldn't tell just when the nightmare began.

But it hadn't all been a nightmare. Some of it had been marvelous. Going to Miss Haddon's had even been all right because there had been wonderful weekends to look forward to, the Saturdays when she'd rush into his arms. And even the Clinique hadn't been all bad because there were his visits, and most of all the expectation and the dream of getting well, especially the month before she came home, when she knew she would be with him. . . .

At least there had been that month of dreams, and sometimes dreams were better than reality. You couldn't call a month of wonderful dreams a nightmare. And the month had culminated in a moment of fantastic reality that afternoon when she found him at the airport waiting. She didn't know about Dee then. So for a few hours he belonged to her, as he had in Rome until Melba came on the scene. There had been happy moments once. Just as her mother had probably been happy—once—and then had to face it, accept the fact that everything was gone, a special kind of happiness comes only once . . .

"No!" she cried out. "Once is not enough! Oh, Mother, how did you ever live through it as long as you did!"

She stood very still. She had shouted at the ghostly light. And all the while she stood rooted in one spot. She stared at it as it hung over the ocean. It looked exactly like the other moon. Only this one didn't have any dark areas.

And then a new thought struck her. Maybe there was a logical explanation for all this. Maybe this was one of those UFO's that occasionally crop up in the news. Well, if it was, she certainly couldn't be the only person in Westhampton who was seeing it. She looked toward all the dark houses. Wasn't anyone in town awake? Wherever Hugh was, couldn't he see it? All those nights he spent on the dunes, nothing like this had ever happened to him. She had to come along *one* night . . . And look at the mess she was in!

She stood there bathed in that strange light, alone on the

beach. Somehow she felt that if she stood very still it wouldn't see her. But that was ridiculous. Whatever it was, it couldn't possibly see her—it was thousands of miles away.

Maybe she should try to remember everything. How large it was, how many miles away it seemed, what direction it was traveling. Maybe she should report it. Oh, sure—that's all she'd need!

But it was there, hanging in front of her. She began to shout. "WAKE UP, SOMEONE! DOESN'T ANYONE IN WESTHAMPTON KNOW YOU'VE SUDDENLY GOT TWO MOONS!"

There was nothing but silence. There was no use in running, because she felt locked in that one spot. She dropped to the sand. It felt cool and soft. She felt the glow of the new moon upon her. It almost felt like sunlight—warm, comforting. And then she saw him walking toward her. He was coming from the shoreline. And when he walked directly into the path of the moonlight his face was in shadow. But she wasn't the least surprised that he had those startling blue eyes she had seen so many times before.

And as she watched him approach, she felt no fear. She suddenly remembered a verse from a poem by John Burroughs called "Waiting." Long ago she had memorized it in Switzerland and . . .

> Serene, I fold my hands and wait,
> Nor care for wind, nor tide, nor sea;
> I rave no more 'gainst time or fate,
> For lo! my own shall come to me.

And now for the first time, she felt all the waiting was over. He came closer and suddenly she couldn't breathe. It was Mike!

But it wasn't Mike. His smile was like Mike's, he looked like Mike . . . yet he wasn't Mike. He stood before her and held out his arms. She scrambled to her feet and went to him. He held her close. "I'm glad to see you, January."

"Mike," she whispered.

He stroked her hair. "I'm not Mike."

"But you look like Mike."

"Only because you want me to."

She clung to him. "Look. This is my hallucination. So it's going to go my way. Whoever you are—I've wanted you all my life. Maybe I always knew you would come. Maybe I loved Mike because he looked like you. Maybe I love you because you look like him. Maybe you both are one. It doesn't matter . . ."

She dropped to the sand, and he took her in his arms. When their lips met it was everything she knew it would be. And when he took her, she knew it had been the moment she had waited for all her life. His caress was gentle yet firm. She reached out for him and held him close . . . closer . . . until they were united like the sand that joins the wave that draws it back into the sea.

"Please don't ever leave me," she whispered.

And he held her close and promised he would never let her go again.

JUNE 29, 1972

NEW YORK (AP)

TODAY MARKS ONE YEAR SINCE THE DISAPPEARANCE OF JANUARY WAYNE, HEIRESS TO THE GRANGER MILLIONS. HER FIANCE, DAVID MILFORD, WAS UNAVAILABLE FOR COMMENT, AS HE IS VACATIONING SOMEWHERE ON THE GREEK ISLAND OF PATMOS. BUT FRIENDS STATE THAT HE STILL CLINGS TO THE HOPE THAT SHE IS ALIVE.
DR. GERSON CLIFFORD, MISS WAYNE'S PERSONAL PHYSICIAN, SAID MISS WAYNE HAD BEEN IN A DEEP DEPRESSION OVER THE DEATH OF HER FATHER AND STEPMOTHER. IT IS DR. CLIFFORD'S THEORY THAT MISS WAYNE MAY HAVE WALKED INTO THE OCEAN AND DROWNED, SINCE HER CAR WAS FOUND PARKED NEAR A BEACH ENTRANCE THE MORNING AFTER HER DISAPPEARANCE.
LATER THAT SAME MORNING, TWO YOUNG BOYS, EDWARD STEVENS, 9, AND TOMMY KAROL, 8, FOUND A HANDBAG ON THE BEACH WHICH WAS IDENTIFIED AS BELONGING TO MISS WAYNE. THERE WAS NOTHING IN THE BAG EXCEPT AN EMPTY WALLET WITH CREDIT CARDS AND A PLASTIC BOTTLE CONTAINING TWO SUGAR CUBES . . .